"I'm sorry, Colt. So

He didn't make a sound but his body shook under Jen's touch and he slid his face down to bury it against her belly. Her shirt grew damp under his cheek, her heart squeezing harder with every silent heave of his shoulders. She paused every few minutes to wipe away a tear of her own, swallowing the lump in her throat and holding back as many as she could.

His hold loosened and he raised his head. The weak expression crossing his striking features stabbed her chest. She leaned in and drifted soft kisses over his forehead, lean cheeks and bearded jaw. Hoping to lessen the heavy shadows hanging over him.

He looked at her then, his blue eyes welling, tears coating the thick lashes and clinging to the ends. She pressed gentle kisses there, too. The taste of salt touched her tongue as his eyelids fluttered shut.

His strong hand slid into her hair, palm cupping the back of her head and fingers kneading her nape. "Jen?"

The husky whisper had barely escaped when he touched his mouth to hers.

Dear Reader,

Like a lot of girls, I met the first man I'd ever love on the day I was born. My dad.

But I was lucky. Because there was a second man there that day, too. My brother.

Of course, he was a boy then and I'm sure my squalling face was the least welcome sight in his universe. Only, you'd never know it after looking at pictures of us as kids.

My mother was a photographer and took more photos of us than we could count. In some, he kissed my cheek. In others, he held my hand. But in all of them, he was right by my side. Just as he was the day we lost our mother.

I was sixteen and he was the first person to hold me that day. As much as he was hurting, he didn't let go and say it'd be okay like others did. Because he knew what we'd lost...and how much I needed him.

That's the kind of love a girl never forgets.

In *The Bull Rider's Cowgirl*, Colt Mead is appointed guardian of his little sister, Meg. Being responsible for a child isn't something he's used to. He makes mistakes (as we all do) but he loves hard. And Meg is very lucky to have him.

Thank you for reading Colt's story.

April

THE BULL RIDER'S COWGIRL

—

APRIL ARRINGTON

HARLEQUIN® WESTERN ROMANCE

Recycling programs
for this product may
not exist in your area.

ISBN-13: 978-0-373-75743-5

The Bull Rider's Cowgirl

Copyright © 2017 by April Standard

All rights reserved. Except for use in any review, the reproduction or utilization of this work in whole or in part in any form by any electronic, mechanical or other means, now known or hereinafter invented, including xerography, photocopying and recording, or in any information storage or retrieval system, is forbidden without the written permission of the publisher, Harlequin Enterprises Limited, 225 Duncan Mill Road, Don Mills, Ontario M3B 3K9, Canada.

This is a work of fiction. Names, characters, places and incidents are either the product of the author's imagination or are used fictitiously, and any resemblance to actual persons, living or dead, business establishments, events or locales is entirely coincidental.

This edition published by arrangement with Harlequin Books S.A.

For questions and comments about the quality of this book, please contact us at CustomerService@Harlequin.com.

® and TM are trademarks of Harlequin Enterprises Limited or its corporate affiliates. Trademarks indicated with ® are registered in the United States Patent and Trademark Office, the Canadian Intellectual Property Office and in other countries.

Printed in U.S.A.

www.Harlequin.com

April Arrington grew up in a small Southern town and developed a love for movies and books at an early age. Emotionally moving stories have always held a special place in her heart. During the day, she enjoys sharing classic literature and popular fiction with students. At night, she spends her time writing stories of her own. April enjoys collecting pottery and soaking up the Georgia sun on her front porch. You can follow her on Twitter, @april_arrington.

Books by April Arrington

Harlequin Western Romance

Men of Raintree Ranch

Twins for the Bull Rider
The Rancher's Wife

Visit the Author Profile page
at Harlequin.com for more titles.

Dedicated to my big brother, Steve.

I love you to the moon and back. Always.

Chapter One

15.32. Left, right, right. Go for great.

Only a fraction of a second separated a good barrel racer from a great one. The faster the run, the higher a name moved up the scoreboard. Tonight, Jen Taylor was determined her name would be at the top of the list.

"We can do this, Diamond."

Jen nudged her quarter horse into a jog across the grassy warm-up area. His white mane rippled over the edge of the saddle and fluttered against the reins. The crowd, inside Kissimmee's Silver Spurs Arena several feet away, burst into applause, signaling the end of another barrel racer's run.

"Easy." Jen dropped her weight in the saddle, took hold of the saddle horn and executed a sharp left turn.

She drew Diamond to a halt in front of the arena's alley entrance, sucked in a lungful of warm Florida air and tried to still the frantic flutters in her stomach. One more run and she'd be up. The clear April evening was a perfect night for racing. If she could just get a handle on her nerves...

"That was Autumn Langley of Texas," the announcer blared over the PA system.

Jen cringed, her face heating. Autumn Langley was

one of the best in the arena. And a reminder of one of Jen's biggest humiliations outside it.

She craned her neck, focused on the illuminated board and tried to make out Autumn's score. The numbers and letters shifted. A few broke. Others floated. It was impossible to focus on them from this angle and her attention was too shot to concentrate.

Gut churning, she tore her eyes away. Diamond jerked his head and stomped his foot.

"It's okay, boy," she whispered, patting his neck.

Thankfully, the announcer spoke again. "Give it up. Autumn just cranked out a 17.12…"

Jen released a slow breath. The time to beat was still 15.32.

Ignoring the tremble in her hands, Jen raked her gaze over the cluster of cowboys leaning on the fence inside the arena and focused on their relaxed expressions. In less than an hour, several of them would be battling to hang on to the back of a massive, bucking bull. But not a hint of anxiety showed on their faces.

"It's just another run," she said softly, weaving her fingers through Diamond's mane and drawing strength from the men's carefree features. "We're as strong on the dirt as any of those cowboys."

The man closest to the alley gate glanced up. His tan Stetson cast a shadow over his chiseled features and blond, close-cut beard beneath the floodlights. He straightened, his blue eyes finding her, and issued a tight smile.

Jen's belly warmed. Colt Mead's sexy grin and muscled form had always had that effect on her. As well as other parts of her anatomy. It never mattered where she was or what she was doing. All it took was one crooked grin from Colt and her blood rushed. Her mind shot straight to imagining what it would be like to be kissed by him. To have his strong hands running over her bod—

Her mouth twisted. It'd been that way since they'd first met, four years ago. Twenty years old, Jen had been touring the rodeo circuit alone for over a year. Colt, twenty-one at the time, rode bulls professionally. Jen had immediately pegged Colt for the player he was, but she'd still gotten a kick out of his flirtatious banter and it hadn't taken long for them to form a strong bond.

Only, there'd always been a sexual undercurrent to their friendship. One she'd been foolish enough to act on two weeks ago.

Colt leaned farther over the rail, his muscular bulk stretching his blue shirt and snug jeans. His smile vanished as he studied her expression.

Jen's breath caught at the hot effects of his sensual eyes traveling to her chest. An aggravating inconvenience, since he'd insisted they remain friends.

She dropped her gaze and squirmed. *Get it together, girl.*

Here she was, about to start a run, and her focus was on Colt. He was becoming a distraction. A threat to what she'd worked so hard to achieve. She had to perform well to get to the finals in Vegas. And she would. No matter how hard she had to work. That board at the Thomas & Mack arena was going to light up with her name at the top of the list.

There was no room in her life for a womanizer. Especially one who had already shot her down, then taken off with another woman. Autumn Langley, to be exact.

The gate clanged open. Autumn trotted out on her beige mare, her dark gaze narrowing on Jen's face.

Great. Just great. Of all the people to catch her salivating over Colt. And why the heck was Jen even concerned with either of them, anyway? She had a race to win.

Jen firmed her grip on Diamond's reins and looked away from them. Both of them...*together*. Her stomach roiled at the images flashing through her mind.

"Colt's looking fine these days." Autumn smirked and led her mare in a circle around Diamond. The rhinestones and elegant embroidery on her shirt glinted under the light spilling from the arena, drawing attention to her shapely figure. "Tell him to swing by my RV if he gets bored later." She laughed throatily. "That man knows how to give a woman a good time."

Ignore her. A bad run could make anyone angry. *Focus on winning.*

Jen lifted her chin and smiled. "I'll be sure to let him know."

"Good." Autumn's mouth flattened into a thin line, her voice curt. "He'll be grateful to you."

Jen dismissed the furious heat sparking through her veins and repositioned herself in the saddle. It wasn't any of her business who Colt spent time with. She knew he partied hard. Had watched firsthand as he'd sweet-talked women in the arena over the years. That was the very reason she'd initially refused to give in to her attraction to him.

One she should've remembered when she'd had too many beers, pulled a boneheaded move and kissed him. Instead, she'd suggested they act on their attraction, get it out of their system and consider being friends with benefits—behaving more like a buckle bunny than a seasoned, focused athlete.

She swallowed hard past the lump in her throat, finding it difficult to drag in air.

Autumn shook her head and tossed her black hair over her shoulder. "Dirt's bad in there." Her tone softened. "Makes for a tough run. Sure sucks being last."

Last. Jen winced. She'd always been last. The last student in her class to learn to read. A skill she'd struggled to master due to a learning disability. And the lowest ranked student in her graduating class. Her grades were the worst of all and far below the acceptable level of universities.

She hadn't let that stop her from pursuing success, though. No way was she going to end up just another small-town nothing. She'd gotten that high school diploma, found work on a local ranch and earned enough money to strike out on her own. Chasing a dream of making a name for herself in the one thing she'd always excelled at.

Racing. Jen flashed a brighter smile and met Autumn's stare head-on. "I don't mind bringing up the rear. Being last just makes you hungrier to be first."

That she knew from experience.

Autumn sighed, eyeing Diamond. "Seriously, girl. Take care out there. That roughed-up dirt can trip up any horse."

"Don't you have some cooling down to do, Autumn?" Tammy Jenkins, Colt's cousin and Jen's traveling partner, squeezed between the horses, her elbow bumping Jen's leg. "This is the warm-up ring."

"Warm-up ring?" Autumn scoffed, surveying the grassy patch surrounding them. "More like someone's backyard. No wonder everyone's time is off tonight, with no decent place to prepare."

"You're the only one whose time is off," Tammy said. "There's plenty of space to prepare and practice for those that put in the effort. You're just used to having things handed to you."

Jen's face heated. "Tammy—"

"No problem." Autumn held up a hand. "I know when I'm not wanted." She raised a brow and grinned. "Also know when I am. Don't forget to pass my message on to Colt." She tugged on her reins and walked her horse away, chiming over her shoulder, "It's always *so* nice talking to you, Tammy."

Tammy clucked her tongue. "That no good, trash-talking—"

"Calm down, Tammy." Jen stifled a laugh and reached down to squeeze her shoulder. "She was being decent for a change."

"Decent, my butt." Tammy crossed her arms, her green eyes flashing. "You cut people way too much slack. Autumn only speaks to you when she's up to something. She's trying to get in your head and trip you up. And no matter what she says, I don't believe Colt would ever be dumb enough to carouse with her."

Jen sighed. She could. Autumn wasn't just a talented racer. She was smart and attractive, too. And Colt had left the bar with her two weekends ago, his brawny arm around her waist and broad hand at her hip. Just a half hour after he'd slipped from Jen's drunken embrace on the bar stools.

"Doesn't matter." Jen ran shaky fingers through Diamond's mane. "Colt's fun to flirt with but I'm not interested in him in that way."

"Right..." Tammy's lips twitched. "I oughta kick you in the behind."

"For what?"

"For lying to your best friend. I've known for a while now that you have the hots for Colt. Anyone can see it on your face." Her lip curled in distaste as she glanced over her shoulder. "Even someone as self-absorbed as Autumn."

Jen's cheeks burned. Had it been that obvious?

"I'm just proud of you for staying focused and steering clear." Tammy gave a wry smile. "And proud of him for respecting you enough to do the same. I love Colt, but he's trouble when it comes to women. He knows that." She frowned. "I don't know what's happened between the two of you lately, but I wish you'd straighten it out. It was bad enough listening to y'all flirt all the time, but it's worse with you not speaking to each other."

Jen's stomach flipped. If Tammy only knew what a fool she'd made of herself. And how much Colt's rejection had hurt...

No matter. She wasn't a schoolgirl anymore and knew the rules of the game. Colt was just another sexy bull rider on the circuit who wasn't looking for a relationship. Even a casual one. At least he'd been a good friend and had been honest with her up front.

"Hey." Tammy touched her arm. "The higher you are, the harder people try to pull you down. That's all Autumn was doing. Trying to pull you down." She patted Diamond's rump. "You and Diamond are the greatest pair tearing out of the alley. He hugs those barrels like they're his mama, and you rate him right on the money every time. Your skill surpassed mine and most other racers' a long time ago."

Jen doubted that. Other than Autumn, Tammy was the best racer on the circuit. Tammy had taken Jen's breath away the night they'd met, blasting down the alley and breaking a barrel racing record. Several hours of practice together, thousands of laughs and a mutual love for the sport had led to a solid friendship.

A scattered round of groans sounded from inside the arena. The gate clanged open and a downbeat racer trudged out.

"Show the gal some love." The announcer's voice blared. "Knocking over barrels beats eating dirt, and she gave it her best. Time with penalties is 28.17, putting her in last position."

Jen renewed her grip on the reins, blood rushing and panic welling inside her again. She offered a sympathetic nod to the tearful brunette passing by on her mare.

"Where's your head, Jen?"

Jen glanced back down, her spirit lifting at Tammy's encouraging expression and gentle smile. There was no Autumn. No Colt. Just barrels and a run. Tammy was the best dang friend a girl could ask for.

"On tight," Jen said, tapping her hat down more firmly on her brow. "Can you remind me what the time to beat is?"

"15.32."

Turn and burn. Jen led Diamond to the alley. Rough dirt or not, that was exactly what she was gonna do.

JEN WAS STILL PISSED. And he couldn't blame her.

Colt ducked his head and eased back from the fence as the most recent racer exited the arena. The speakers blared overhead on a stream of heavy metal as Jen made her way to the gate.

Colt tried to catch her eye again. Tried to get one more look at her face to reassure himself she'd shaken off the angry glare she'd shot him earlier and regained her focus. But her head was down, her hat making it impossible for him to get a clear view.

A fresh wave of tension assaulted his muscles. He uncurled his fists from the rail, flinching as his fingers cramped. Such a foolish state he'd worked himself into. He'd never gotten this tense over tangling with an angry bull. So why the hell would he get so terrified of watching a horse run around metal buckets?

"Arlene and I were together for seven weeks. *Seven damn weeks.* That's the longest I've stayed hooked up with any woman." His friend Judd Marsh, another bull rider, smacked the rail with his palm and vented at Colt's side. "She called it quits last night. Right after I got thrown off that nut job of a bull."

Colt winced. "Sorry, man."

"That ain't the worst of it, though. You know what she said to me?"

Colt shook his head.

"She said I don't pay her enough attention." He propped one hand on his hip, waved the other in the air and adopted a high-pitched voice. "'*Judd, you're just not sensitive to my needs.*'" He slapped his leg and scowled. "Shit, man. I'm sensitive."

Colt bit back a laugh.

"Don't you think I'm sensitive?"

"Yep," Colt said. "Sensitive enough."

Colt's smile slipped. That was what he was becoming. What Jen was turning him into. Too damned sensitive. Which was exactly why he was standing here hyperventilating over the risk of Jen getting thrown off her horse despite the fact that she was a strong rider and it'd been months since her last fall.

Though it'd probably help if he didn't know how hard that dirt hurt when you slammed into it at high speed. Or how difficult it was to roll outta the way, get back on your feet and avoid a thousand-pound animal crushing the air out of your lungs.

Yeah. He might deal with it better if he hadn't experienced that himself.

"Hell. Whatever." Judd scanned the stands, gaze lingering over one section. "There's always another one out there."

Colt nodded. Judd was right on that count. There was always another woman. Plenty of them. And Colt had spent more nights than he cared to remember over the past four years trying to enjoy them. Only problem was, he no longer wanted them. Hadn't wanted anyone but Jen since the second he'd laid eyes on her.

He glanced to his left, managing to catch a quick glimpse of her face as she looked up before facing the barrels. Her long, red curls slipped over her shoulder, obscuring the curves of her cheek and mouth.

His body tightened. That mouth. That beautiful, soft mouth she'd used two weeks ago to whisper a sweet plea in his ear. That she'd trailed temptingly across the stubble on his cheek before kissing him.

What would those lush lips of hers have felt like if he'd given in and kissed her back? Kissed her the way he'd wanted to for years? Deeply and passionately. How would she have responded? With slow, coaxing movements? Or hot, hungry—?

Colt jerked his head to the side. *Shut it down.* He had no right wondering. No right even contemplating it. Jen was too good a woman for a sexy, meaningless fling. And that'd never be enough for him, anyway. Not with her. Jen wasn't like the women he played with on the circuit. She was a competitive, focused athlete. One who wasn't impressed by smooth talk or skilled touches. She was above that. Deserved better.

A woman like Jen deserved a ring, a picket fence and a baby. The whole shebang. The kind of woman he wasn't interested in and wouldn't be any good with.

So he'd turned her down. He'd torn himself away before he had a chance to screw up and give in. Had arranged for a mutual friend he trusted to get her back to the motel safely, then had hauled ass with the first woman who threw herself in his path.

Colt's face tingled, his neck burning. He'd known just the sight of him leaving with another woman would tick Jen off enough to sober her up a bit and take her mind in another direction. She didn't need to know the farthest he'd gone with Autumn Langley was to the parking lot to help her into her truck. That he'd pulled a 180 right there on the cracked pavement and politely refused the rest of Autumn's advances.

He winced and rubbed his fingers over his cheek. Or that Autumn had smacked him a good one and accused him of leading her on. Using her to make Jen jealous. Which, no matter how good his intentions had been, was exactly what he'd done.

Yep. It was better he just be that guy. The one not worth crying over. That was the kind he'd been for years, anyway. The kind he'd always be.

"Next up, folks, is Jen Taylor." Cheers broke out

around the arena at the announcement. "She hails from Hollow Rock, Georgia."

Colt straightened, hands grabbing the rail again.

Jen took her place at the top of the alley. She sat tall in the saddle, her red hair shining against her turquoise blouse, providing a fiery contrast to Diamond's white hide.

A shot of heat streaked through Colt. Damn, she was beautiful.

"Jen's partner is Diamond," the announcer shouted over the crowd, "though you probably know them as Fire and Ice."

The fans in the bleachers above Colt jumped to their feet, yelping as handfuls of their popcorn bounced off his hat. Colt's smile returned. Jen was good. Better than good. And everyone knew it. He'd seen her work her way up through grueling hours of practice, endless tours on the circuit and dogged determination.

The same determination that scared the hell out of him when she rode. She didn't hold back during a run. Wouldn't let Diamond, either. She burned across the dirt like a flame and Diamond curved around those barrels like a slick coating of frost.

"Jen looks ready," Judd said, nudging him with an elbow. "Think she can pull it off?"

"Hell, yeah."

A 15.32? Jen could crack that in her sleep. So long as she kept her focus.

Colt trained his gaze on Jen's face. Her brown eyes remained pinned to the pocket by the left barrel, lush lips moving slowly in a silent mantra. Diamond shuffled his feet in anticipation as he waited for her permission.

A nod, a swift kick and they were off, blasting down the alley and heading for the first barrel at full speed.

The first turn was flawless. Jen checked him with two hands at just the right moment, gripped the saddle horn and led him around clean and easy. Diamond tore out of the turn and dashed to the next. The second rotation carried off without a hitch.

The pair blazed over to the last barrel but Diamond stumbled. His front hoof slipped on the uneven dirt, jerking Jen forward. The rail rattled under Colt's grip and his boot shot to the lower fence rung. His stomach heaved as the audience gasped.

"Hold on, Red," he bit out.

She did. Diamond regained his footing and darted around the last turn. Jen loosened the reins, giving Diamond control, and they blasted across the finish line to the applause of the crowd.

Colt relaxed and released his death grip on the fence.

"Damned shame," Judd said. "That trip's gonna cost her."

"Don't care." Colt pushed off the rail and headed for the exit. "She's still in one piece."

Though her pride had probably taken a hit at not earning the best time.

"Hey, where you going?" Judd called. "We're up soon."

"I know." Colt waved him off. "Be back in a minute."

With swift strides, he dodged whooping spectators under the blaring voice on the PA system.

"Beautiful ride by Jen Taylor. Time is 15.37, placing her second. Let's give that gal a hand…"

Nope. No way would Jen be happy with that. She'd said on more than one occasion that getting second only meant you were the first loser. Something he had a sudden desire to help her see differently.

Colt continued forcing his way through the chaotic mass of people. He'd made it several feet when a cry cut through the air at his side. A pink bundle banged into his left knee and he grabbed it before it tumbled to the floor.

A young girl—three, maybe four?—tossed her blond curls off her cute face and steadied herself with a small hand on his leg. She had brown eyes and freckles, just like his younger half sister, Meg. At least that was what he remembered. He'd last seen her when he left home seven years ago.

An uncomfortable ache formed in his gut. One that appeared every time he remembered leaving Meg behind. "Whoa, there. You all right?"

The girl looked up at him, blinked, then spun back to scowl at the man chasing after her.

"But I want it!" Her outraged shriek almost took the roof off the arena.

"No, Annabelle." The man took her arm and tugged her back to his side. "You've already had one cotton candy and that's enough for tonight." He nodded at Colt, dragging a hand through his disheveled hair. "Sorry about that."

"No problem, man."

Colt glanced at the girl straining against her dad's hold. Her cheeks turned cherry red and her eyes squinted.

Here it comes. Colt did his best to navigate around the group in front of him and gain some distance.

"But Ty got two," she screeched. "I want two."

"Your brother only had one. The same as you. I said no and that's that."

She jerked away and hit the floor, her pink skirt flopping around her flailing legs. Her screaming sobs prompted everyone within a mile radius to frown in her dad's direction. He bent, hissed admonishments and tried to gather up her writhing form, with no success.

Colt cringed. Poor bastard. Kids might be cute but most of 'em turned out to be little devils disguised in pink ribbons or baseball caps. A man had to be crazy to saddle himself with one on a permanent basis.

The girl's cries strengthened, piercing Colt's ears and provoking a pained laugh from him. He shook his head and forged through the crowd, making his way outside. The fresh air enveloped him and the girl's shrieks faded.

"Hey." Tammy bumped him with her shoulder and fell in step beside him. Her lopsided smile didn't hold its usual sparkle. "Come to console our partner?"

Colt shrugged. "No need for consoling. Jen had a good run."

"Yeah. I know." Tammy nodded toward the outskirts of the warm-up area. "But try telling her that."

Jen was cooling Diamond down, apart from everyone at the edge of the grass. She walked him in slow lines, chin lifted. If Colt hadn't spent years studying every sweet curve of her body and how she moved it, he might've missed the overly stiff set of her shoulders and hard clench of her thighs around the saddle. But he didn't.

Colt cut his eyes away and watched the other racers mingling around the cooldown area. "I'm gonna touch base with her before I ride. You mind giving us a minute?"

"Sure." Tammy's brows raised, her green eyes encouraging as she walked away. "Take your time."

Colt walked over to Jen, stopping as she maneuvered Diamond into a turn and faced him. Her eyes flashed.

He squared his shoulders then nodded up at her. "That was a damn good run, Red."

Jen stilled and the hard glint in her eyes softened. She smiled. The action small and beautiful. But hesitant.

"Thanks." She patted Diamond's thick shoulder. "I've got a talented partner."

"It wasn't all him," Colt said. "You had a part in that, too. The hardest part." His hand lifted, reaching toward her. He brought it back to his side and shifted his stance. "Second place is fantastic considering the tough competition you had. You really were great."

Jen looked away, brushing light touches over Diamond's mane. Her smile fell. "Wasn't quite enough, though," she whispered.

Colt's throat closed. She was so hard on herself. More critical of her performances than anyone else was. Almost to the point of erasing all the joy from a competition. Her face had stopped lighting up at the start of a run like it used to. And at the moment he wanted to see that glow in her smile again. *Needed* to see it.

"It'll be more than enough next time," he said, freezing at the husky note in his voice.

Something soft heated his palm. He blinked and looked down, stiffening at the sight of his hand curled around her thigh, easing its way up toward her hip. Just as it had with so many other women.

Her rich, brown eyes narrowed their focus on his hand, then shot to his face. "Feeling sorry for me, Colt? Trying to help me feel better by throwing me a little attention?" Her face flushed and her voice shook. "I don't need soothing. But Autumn might. She said you're welcome to pay her a visit later." She eased Diamond back a few steps, sliding away from his touch. "Seems you're good at a lot more than just sweet-talking women."

Ah, hell. That was called for. But it stung. It squeezed his chest so tight, his lungs threatened to collapse.

Still, Jen's anger was an improvement over the defeated expression she'd had moments ago and a lot easier to deal with than her adoration. Especially since he knew that in the long run, he'd only disappoint.

"Yeah." He choked back his pride, knuckled his hat farther up his forehead and conjured a sly grin. "I am. You just haven't seen me at my best yet, baby." He widened his smile, easing back into the safe, familiar role. "Stick around and watch me ride."

Colt spun on his heel and ambled away. Jen's hard stare burned a bigger hole in his back with each step. He took the long way around to the bull pens, avoiding every buckle bunny and child within sight.

Women. He understood them only in the bedroom. And kids? He didn't understand them at all. Bulls, however, he got. And the massive, black-and-white-speckled monster glaring at him through the gate was about to get to know him, too.

Chapter Two

"Careful. That son o' a bitch can spring."

Colt handed the end of his rope to Judd and studied the restless bull being prepared in the chute below them. "I hope so."

A bull that jumped, kicked and spun right out of the chute guaranteed a shot at a high score. The kind of score Judd had failed at grabbing several rides ago when he'd drawn a flat bull that took a Sunday stroll out of the chute instead of blasting out of it. Hopefully, Sonic, the burly beast Colt had drawn, would be feistier.

As if on cue, the angry animal slammed his thick horns into the metal rails, then sprang up, hooking his hooves over the top of the eight-feet-high gate. The cheers filling the Silver Spurs Arena strengthened as the cowboys surrounding the chute yanked on the ropes draped over the bull's back, pulling him off the gate.

Colt smiled. Hell, yeah. This one was a damn deal feistier.

He glanced around the arena, taking steady breaths and visualizing a successful scenario on the dirt. But his eyes snagged on a cream-colored hat and red hair in the stands.

In the front row, Jen no longer sat, but had shot to her

feet, eyes on the bull banging around in the chute below him, and face creased with apprehension. Tammy and another woman he recognized as a barrel racer—Karla, was it?—stood at her side, looking equally dismayed.

Colt turned away, started wrapping tape around the glove on his left hand and did his best to ignore the warm satisfaction rippling through him. Pissed though she was, Jen had not only stuck around for over an hour to watch his ride, she was worried about him.

"Told you this joker could spring," Judd shouted over the hard rock music. "You ready to get slung?"

"Yep." Colt bit the tape off, handed the roll to one of the spotters at his side and jerked his chin. "So long as it's after eight seconds."

A buzzing in Colt's back pocket rattled through the denim of his jeans. He yanked his cell phone out, glancing at the lit screen. Mead Enterprises.

Colt shook his head. Friday night. Approaching 10:00 p.m. No doubt his father, John W. Mead, would still be holed up in his high-rise Atlanta office closing another deal. It was always about business with John W. Mead. Never personal. And never about actually building a relationship with his son. That had become especially true after Colt's mother died.

Nope. His old man probably wanted the same thing he'd been hassling him about for the last year.

Time to get your ass home, Colt. You've played long enough and there's work to be done.

Colt rejected the call with a rough swipe of his thumb and shoved his cell toward Judd. "Mind hanging on to that till I'm through?"

"Sure." Judd shoved it in his pocket, then firmed his grip on the rope.

Colt scrutinized Sonic's movements and regained his focus. He shoved in his mouth guard, grabbed the opposite rail and climbed into the chute, placing a boot in the center of the bull's back. He waited a couple seconds as Sonic shifted and stomped, then slid his legs down around the bull's muscular sides and sat.

The rich scent of musky hide filled his nostrils and the tang of dirt drifting on the air touched his tongue with each breath he took. He grabbed hold of the rope Judd stretched up, and yanked his gloved hand over it briskly, tapping it with his fist when he finished to cue Judd to hand it over. Hooking his gloved fingers through the handle laying over the bull's back, he set the rope, then wrapped the long end of it around his palm. He closed his fist, opened it, then curled it again.

Satisfied with his grip, Colt secured his position, then nodded.

The gate clanged open and Sonic catapulted into the arena, his back end twisting and lifting vertically several feet into the air on a vicious kick. Colt stretched his right arm high above his head as they rose up. He leaned back and the muscles in his left forearm seized with his strained grip on the rope.

Sonic's hard haunches slammed against Colt's shoulder blades. The bull's long tail whipped over Colt's head and smacked across his face, the coarse hairs stinging his eyes and knocking his hat off his head.

Gravity snatched them back down and Sonic's front hooves hit the dirt, yanking Colt forward. Colt jerked his head to the side, his cheek missing the sharp point of a horn by inches.

Sonic lurched again, lifting them both so high so

fast that Colt's gut swirled on an intense wave of panicked excitement. A shout exploded from deep within his chest and blasted through the smile stretching across his mouth guard.

Hot damn! This beast could fly.

Clenching his thighs to counteract each of Sonic's moves, Colt held on with his left fist, but let go of the world around him. The spectators' cheers dimmed to barely discernable echoes and the violent thrashings of the bull rattled away every care or concern he'd ever had.

They soared, spun, then thudded hard against the earth. Over and over. Each of their grunts and harsh breaths flooded Colt's senses as he pitted his will against Sonic's.

A buzzer sounded and reality struck, ripping his attention away from the battle and back to survival. He wrestled his hand free of the rope and leaned to the side as Sonic writhed in the air, allowing the momentum to sling him from the bull's back and tumble him across the dirt.

He sprang to his feet and ran. Sonic followed, charging twice before the bullfighters distracted him and directed him back toward the pen.

Colt spotted his Stetson in the dirt. He scooped it up, settled it back on his head, then tipped the brim at Sonic. The bull snorted, kicking the metal gate one more time as he bulldozed his way into the pen.

Colt pulled his mouth guard out, shoved it in his pocket and laughed. "Nice meetin' you, too, you big bastard."

He waved at the cheering crowd, then made his way out of the ring, rubbing a hand over the sore muscles of his lower back and grimacing at the sharp ache in his left ankle.

Judd met him at the gate, handed him his phone, then slapped his shoulder. "I think you just locked this one down, man. No one's going to pull off a better ride than that tonight."

"Let's hope not," Colt said, breathing hard. "That bull made me earn it."

Judd laughed. "I gotta get back and spot another rider." He jerked his thumb over his shoulder as he left. "Your fan club's calling."

Colt glanced toward the stands. Tammy stood on the floor beside the front row, laughing and waving her hat wildly. Karla was at her side, whistling through two fingers and making catcalls. Jen stood nearby with a blank expression, clutching a beer.

Colt made his way over but slowed when Jen's dark eyes ran over him, hovering on the slight limp of his left leg. His grin widened and that tingle of satisfaction returned.

"That was fantastic," Karla yelled over the noise in the arena.

"Fantastic?" Tammy threw her arms around his shoulders and squeezed. "It was phenomenal!"

A chuckle escaped him despite the painful twinge Tammy's snug hold caused. "Glad you thought so."

"Are you all right?"

Jen scrutinized his left leg. Her eyes lifted and locked with his, the gentle concern shining there sparking an unwelcome yearning in his chest. It made his palms itch with the need to reach out and tug her to him. Made him miss the friendly banter they used to share.

"Why?" Colt slipped out of Tammy's embrace and

flashed a cocky grin, teasing her like he used to. "Worried about me, baby?"

Jen didn't respond in kind as he'd hoped. Just scoffed, her mouth flattening as she cut her eyes away.

He wasn't sure what got under her skin more. The suggestive tone he'd used or the arrogant smile he'd adopted. Though it could've been the wink he'd thrown in, too.

What he did know for sure was that the damage he'd done that night in the bar caused all three actions to fall flat and made him feel like more of a heel than ever.

Tammy's small fist punched his chest. "Watch it, Colt."

Duly chastised, he ducked his head and ignored the heat singeing his cheeks.

"After you collect your check, we need to pack up and head out," Tammy said. "That big money pot is still up for grabs at the Davie Pro Rodeo tomorrow night and I could use the extra time to prepare. I really need that win if I'm going to make it to the finals this year."

"You've got nothing to worry about," Colt said, squeezing her shoulder.

Tammy's brows rose. "Oh yeah, I do. You think Jen felt bad about placing second tonight? I'd have killed for that spot. I was fifth, Colt. *Fifth*."

"I know, but— "

"And I was eighth," Karla added, tucking a short strand of black hair behind her ear. "Tammy and I have already crunched some numbers. Jen can get by without another win this weekend, but if Tammy and I don't place in the top three at Davie, we'll be so far behind we'll never qualify for Vegas."

"You'll make it," Colt said, meeting Tammy's uncertain expression with a determined one. "I know you will."

"Not if I don't place at Davie tomorrow night." Tammy shook her head. "Without that win, I'm out."

Colt nodded. A trip to Davie was just in time. Maybe he'd have more luck finding a woman there who stirred his interest. One who would help him shake off this lust he had for Jen. Then maybe he'd have a decent shot at rebuilding their friendship.

"So we'll head to Davie." He grinned and patted his front pocket. "Right after I collect my check."

Yep. That was the way he liked it. No baggage. No responsibilities. Just an endless string of nights filled with fun and freedom. All provided by the bulk of bills lining his pockets. Money he'd earned himself on the back of a bull. Free and clear of his corporate raider father.

The phone in Colt's hand went off, jerking with rhythmic pulses. He glanced at the screen. Mead Enterprises again.

He groaned. John W. Mead wasn't giving up tonight. Might as well get it over with.

"Gotta take this." Colt nodded in apology to the ladies, exited the arena and accepted the call, striving for a nonchalant tone. "Before you ask, I'm headed south. In the opposite direction."

Silence hung heavy on the line. There was no sharp reprimand from his father. No cynical comeback. Just empty air.

Colt huffed out a breath and kicked the ground. The old man was trying a new tactic. "Go ahead. Lay that guilt on thick 'cause it doesn't matter. I'm not interested in joining up with the company. I have business of my own to take care of." Bulls. Beaches. And beauties. Not necessarily in that order. "You hear me, Dad?"

"Mr. Mead? Colt Wyatt Mead?"

He stilled. The voice on the other end of the line was feminine. Hesitant but businesslike.

"You got him. Who's this?"

"This is Angela Reed. Your father's secretary."

Colt's fingers squeezed the phone, his laugh hesitant. "You're working late tonight. He ask you to pass along new marching orders to me?"

"Sir." A swift intake of air sounded across the line. "I'm sorry to deliver news this way but…" An odd tapping started, as if a phone cord was being jiggled. "There was—" Her voice cracked. "Your father's partner, Jack Evans, has been trying to reach you. He asked me to call and tell you…"

He froze. "Tell me what?"

"There's been an accident." Her words were short and swift. "Your father's jet crashed this morning. I'm sorry to say he didn't make it."

Colt's stomach heaved, a wave of nausea surging over him. "What?"

"I'm very sorry, Mr. Mead," she whispered. "But Mr. Evans wanted you to know in time to return home for the funerals if you desired to do so. Services have been arranged for Sunday afternoon."

"Funerals?" Dear God. *Meg.* "My sister. Was she—"

"No, sir," she said hastily. "Your sister wasn't on board. Just your father and Mrs. Mead."

A strange tingling spread over him, buzzing through his blood and clouding his vision. The ground warped beneath his feet. He moved closer to the paddock fence in front of him and grabbed at the top rail.

His father. His stepmother. *Dead.*

"Mr. Mead?" The secretary's voice softened. "Your sister is the other reason for my call. There are several matters that require your attention. May I tell Mr. Evans that you'll be returning?"

Colt squeezed his eyes shut. His throat thickened, strangling his words. "Y-yes. I'm returning."

The trembling in his limbs turned violent. Colt cut the call and clenched both hands into fists. He continued standing there as winners were announced over the PA system. Stayed still as the throng of spectators left the arena and made their way to the parking lot, leaving only rodeo participants behind.

Colt waited until his stomach hardened and the feeling in his limbs vanished. Until there was no feeling left anywhere. Numb was a damned sight better than breaking down right now. He had to stay in control to make the long drive home. And he was a world away from Atlanta's Tuxedo Park.

"Colt?"

Jen took a few hesitant steps forward, her boots whispering over the grass as she approached him. He didn't answer. Just stood there, motionless as he stared straight ahead at the paddock, fists at his sides.

The crowd outside the Silver Spurs Arena had dwindled to a few rodeo riders, every one of them eager to find the next party and unwind. All except Colt. One phone call had extinguished his flirtatious demeanor.

Jen's skin prickled at the unusually tight set of his broad shoulders. She stopped, fiddled with the soggy label on her beer and tried again.

"Colt. What's wrong?"

A crack of laughter rang out. Jen glanced over her shoulder to find Tammy and Karla sauntering through the exit and sharing a joke.

Tammy's eyes brightened as they landed on Colt. "Well, finally. We've been waiting for you for forever. You won. They've got your check…"

Her steps faltered at his lack of response and she shot a look at Jen.

Jen shook her head.

"Who was on the phone, Colt?" Tammy moved to his side and placed a hand on the small of his back, releasing a small laugh. "Come on. You're scaring us. Who was it?"

A muscle in his jaw ticked. "My father's secretary."

"Bad news?" Tammy asked.

He nodded.

"Well, wha—"

"My father's dead."

Tammy gasped and wrapped her hand around his upper arm. "Oh, no."

Jen froze, her fingers clutching the beer bottle hard. Karla made a sound of dismay at her side.

"He and my stepmom." His brow furrowed. "Their jet crashed."

The words were flat. Emotionless. His blue eyes were empty and his expression remained stoic.

Jen's vision blurred. "I'm so sorry, Colt," she whispered, unsure what else to say.

They rarely spoke of family. His, Tammy's or hers. Just made vague comments when necessary. He and Tammy were close and that was about as much as she knew.

Colt's features hardened and he shrugged away from

Tammy's touch. "They always flew on a private jet." A muscle ticked in his jaw. "It's faster and my father says it's safer. At least that's what he used to say." A sneer crossed his face. "Truth was, he thought he was too good to fly commercial with common people. Both of them did." His voice weakened. "Death doesn't discriminate, though, does it?"

Jen's heart squeezed at the shadows in his eyes. She glanced at Tammy, her throat closing at the tears streaming down her friend's cheeks. Jen crossed to her side and squeezed her hand.

Colt planted his back to them, saying, "My sister's alone."

"You have a sister?" Jen asked.

Colt nodded and thrust his hands in his pockets. "Meg. My half sister. She's around nine now. I haven't seen her since she was two."

Jen hesitated. "Surely a family member's with her—"

"What family?" Scorn tinged his words. He spun around to face her. "My father's work was his family. It's not surprising that his secretary was the one to give me the news." He hesitated, his sculpted mouth opening, then closing as he eyed his cousin. "Tammy, I need to go home. Just for the weekend. For the funeral and to see Meg."

"Of course." Tammy pulled her hand free from Jen's and wiped her cheeks. "I'll go with you. We can have the horses loaded in no time."

"No." Colt held up a hand. "I'm going alone. You have a race to win."

Tammy's jaw fell. "Screw the race, Colt. I'm not—"

"You *are*." He shook his head, jaw clenching. "You know what it's like back there. And I'm not staying for any longer than the…" He stopped, looking away before continuing. "I'm not staying any longer than necessary."

Jen ached at the bleak tone in his voice. She longed to wrap her arms around Colt and comfort him but knew he wouldn't accept it.

"Colt." Tammy's tone turned hard. "There's no way I'm letting you go alo—"

"You don't have to let me do anything. This is how I want it." Colt's chest lifted on a rough breath. "You knew what he was like. He never gave a shit about me. Or you. Or anyone for that matter. I'm not letting you blow your chance at success for that—"

His voice cracked. He spun on his heel to leave.

Tammy grabbed his arm and jerked him to a stop. "Colt. This is ridiculous." She stepped close, her face pleading. "You can't expect me to waltz off to a race while you're dealing with this."

"You think I'd want you going back there? Ever?" Colt took her shoulders and peered down at her. "Do you *want* to go back, Tammy?"

Jen studied her friend. Tammy looked down, hands twisting and face paling.

Colt's chin trembled. He dragged his teeth over his bottom lip. "You weren't welcome there before he died. You think you'll be more welcome now? Take my word for it that whoever he left in charge of that place will be just as cold and hateful as he was. I'm not letting you go through that again."

"Colt, please. You can't…" A sob broke from Tammy.

Colt tugged her close and tucked her head under his chin, his voice strained. "You'll go to Davie and you'll win. And I'll be back before you know it."

Jen closed her eyes, her heart still clenching at the mixture of pain and tenderness in Colt's face.

"Then let Jen go with you."

Jen's eyes sprang open at Tammy's words. "What? Tammy—"

Tammy spun to face her, expression fierce. "I can't let him go alone, Jen. And you'll be fine without competing at Davie."

"No," Colt stated, stepping back.

Tammy followed and grabbed Colt's vest. "Let her go with you. If for no other reason than to make sure you get there and back safely. There's no way I'll be able to focus tomorrow night knowing you're dealing with this on your own." She jerked her chin at Karla. "You traveling to Davie alone?"

Karla nodded.

"You mind me and Razz catching a ride with you? That way Jen can take Diamond with Colt. I'll pitch in for gas and expenses."

"Of course," Karla said. "I'd be happy to help."

Jen shook her head. "Tammy, this is not a good idea."

"Jen's right. I'll be fine on my own." Colt pulled free of Tammy and walked back into the arena.

Tammy hesitated, staring after Colt for a moment. Then she rushed to Jen, taking her forearms, hard and desperate. "You've got to do this for me, Jen. I'll talk to him. He'll be fine with it."

"I know you're worried," she said gently. "But you heard him. He wants to go alone."

"Colt wants to do a lot of things that aren't good for him. And he usually does." Tammy's small smile died quickly. "But this is one time that I can't let him. Please, Jen. I know him. He needs someone right now no matter what he says. Too much has happened for him to let me go back—" She bit her lip and waved a hand in the air. "There's no way he'll bend on letting me go, but he will for you." She stepped forward, hugged Jen and whispered, "No matter what went down between you two, I know you care about him as much as I do. Colt and I are lucky we found you. You're not just a friend to us. You've become family. I know you'll take care of Colt and I know he needs you. It's only for the weekend. So, please, do this for me."

Something wet tickled Jen's cheek. She rubbed it off on Tammy's shoulder and huffed out a breath.

Tammy laughed and released her, brushing a new flood of tears from her face, too. "I may love you like a sister but that doesn't mean you can use my shirt as a hanky."

"That's what you get for being so sappy." Jen smiled, blinking hard to clear her vision. "I'll go. But only if he agrees to it."

"He will." Tammy headed after Colt, calling over her shoulder, "I'll be back in a few minutes to help load up, Karla."

Jen watched Tammy leave and felt the weight of Karla's stare, her cheeks heating under her scrutiny. Jen glanced away and stood still as fellow racers laughed and climbed into their vehicles. Engines turned over and trucks began lining up on the paved road leading to the exit. No doubt once the night's fun was had, they'd rise early tomorrow morning, hook up their trailers and head to the next event. Davie, most likely.

Jen looked down at the soggy beer label and picked at the corners. If she went with Colt, she'd miss the Davie Pro Rodeo. Lose an opportunity to gain a better advantage over her competitors. And she'd have to work that much harder to earn a ticket to Vegas when she returned.

Only, seeing Colt in pain had tied a knot in her chest that she didn't think would disappear when she hit the alley at Davie.

"Tammy's right." Karla dragged the toe of her boot over the grass and shoved her hands in her pockets. "I've never seen Colt clam up like that before. It's good you're going with him."

"Yeah," Jen whispered. "It's a good thing."

She hoped it was. A couple days. That was all. She'd help Colt through this, then she'd plan a new schedule, get back on the road and hit the circuit again.

Aside from their recent falling out, Colt had always been a good friend to her. It was time for her to be a good friend to him. Just as long as she remembered being friends was all he wanted. And all she could afford to be.

Chapter Three

Colt rubbed a hand over his gritty eyes and sat up straight in the driver's seat. The entrance was close, about three blocks ahead. He'd know it as soon as he saw it. There'd be a broad metal gate, security checkpoint and endless paved driveway.

He glanced in the rearview mirror, cocking his head and straining for any abnormal sounds from the white trailer hitched to his truck. Diamond was quiet. Just as he had been the entire eight-hour drive from Kissimmee to Atlanta. It seemed he'd taken full advantage of the quiet night drive to sleep and wasn't ready to start his Saturday morning yet.

"Where are we?"

Jen pushed up from her slumped position in the passenger's seat, blinking slowly. The soft glow of the dashboard instruments was the only light in the dark stillness of the truck's cab.

Colt managed a small smile before looking away. Jen had been quiet, too. She'd stopped her gentle attempts at conversation and gone to sleep six hours ago, after he'd refused her offer to drive. Desperate for a distraction, he'd held on to his position behind the wheel, focusing on the road instead of the burning ache in his throat.

He'd fought against Jen coming. Had argued with Tammy for a good ten minutes and made it clear that he preferred to make the trip alone. The fear of breaking down in front of Jen was as unsettling as the challenge he already faced. But Tammy had refused to budge, and he had to admit that traveling the dark stretch of the interstate had been less grueling with someone at his side.

Even if that someone had every right to be angry with him and every reason not to offer her support.

"Colt?" Jen thumbed her hat higher on her forehead, her brown eyes searching his face. "Where are we?"

His smile fell. "Tuxedo Park."

Colt looked out the window at the streetlights underscoring the lush greenery lining the road. The urge to hit the brakes, swing the truck in the opposite direction and drive for days was strong. He wanted nothing more than to forget. To pretend last night hadn't happened and return to the status quo. Imagine that he'd never gotten the call and learned—

He clutched the steering wheel tighter. That was one thing he couldn't do. No amount of distractions could change the fact that his father and stepmother were gone. Or that Meg was now the only remaining member of his immediate family.

The entrance appeared. Tall trees and shrubs lined each side of it.

Colt slowed the truck, maneuvered the sharp turn and stopped at the gate. A guard leaned out of the security office's entrance and waited for Colt to let down the window.

"Good morning, sir." He swept a flashlight briefly through the interior of the cab, then over the trailer. "May I ask who you're visiting?"

Colt didn't recognize him. Not that he would recognize any of the staff after a seven-year absence. His father had consumed them like water, always finding fault with even the best employees and promptly trading them out for new ones.

Colt leaned to the side and dug in his back pocket for his wallet. "Meg Mead."

"Is she expecting you?"

He winced. "Probably not."

"May I see your identifi—" The guard stopped as Colt pressed his ID into his hand, then flicked his flashlight over it. "Thank you, Mr...." He glanced up, eyes widening. "Mr. Mead?"

"Yeah."

"I'm sorry for your loss, sir."

Colt nodded.

"I apologize, Mr. Mead, but..." The guard motioned toward the inside of the cab. "I'll need to see—"

"Of course." Colt glanced at Jen. "He needs your license, Red."

Her brows raised but she murmured an assent, bending over to the floorboard and fishing her ID out of her purse. Colt took it and handed it over, watching as the man examined it, then flashed his light into the cab.

"Could you remove the hat, please, miss?"

Colt's jaw tightened. *Procedures*. His father had insisted on them being followed to the letter. So much so that his expectations were still met despite the fact that he was as good as in the ground.

Jen removed the leather cowgirl hat, tucking it between her knees and brushing her red bangs back. The guard tipped the flashlight up, flooding Jen's face. She squinted and shrank back against the door.

Colt hissed in a breath and threw up a hand to block the glare. "It's fine. Open the gate."

"Yes, sir."

The guard handed him the license, stepped back and buzzed the gates open, which swung out in wide arcs. Colt shifted gears, accelerating through them and heading down the winding, paved path ahead. They drove in silence for a few minutes, the headlights illuminating clusters of trees and healthy plants with bright, bountiful blooms on either side of the wide driveway.

Jen tossed her hat in the back of the extended cab and rubbed her palms over her jean-clad thighs. "Pretty intense security for a subdivision."

"This isn't a subdivision." Colt pressed his foot harder on the pedal, plowing up the steep incline in front of them. "It's my father's house."

She laughed, the sound short and nervous as she took in the thick foliage surrounding them. "There's a house? Where?"

When they cleared the top of the hill, the sun broke over the surrounding trees, flooding the sprawling grounds with light.

Colt tipped his head toward the massive structure in front of them. "There."

Jen stilled, lips parting. He followed her gaze and gritted his teeth as he surveyed the familiar estate. A French provincial–style mansion consisting of thirty-five thousand square feet of space, stables, theater, pool, tennis court and caretaker's suite sat center stage on a manicured twenty-acre lot.

"That's not a house," she whispered.

Colt sighed. "I know."

He guided the truck around the circular drive,

rounded a large churning fountain and brought them to a halt. After cutting the engine, he glanced up to find Jen studying him.

Her eyes narrowed, scrutinizing his features as though she didn't recognize him. She turned her back to him and stared up at the massive flight of stairs that led to the double door entrance. "I wish Tammy were here."

Her words were so soft he barely caught them. But he did.

He squeezed his eyes shut, wishing circumstances were different and that Tammy could be here, too. She kept him grounded. Reminded him of who he really was and, most importantly, who he didn't want to become.

His gut roiled. The kind of person his father had been. The kind of person Jen had just searched for when she'd inspected his face. A pompous, entitled man who put his own desires above the needs of others.

"Why wouldn't you let her come?" Jen asked, turning to him. "I mean, besides the race. I know that can't be your only reason."

Colt looked away and placed his hands on the steering wheel. "Tammy's mom was my dad's sister. My dad had basically disowned her. She'd blown all her money, lived hard and apparently wasn't worth knowing anymore. Tammy's dad and mine were both cruel. But where my dad just used his words, Tammy's liked to use his fists. And her mom did nothing to stop it."

The air grew thick and heavy in the cab. His throat closed and he swallowed, waiting for Jen to speak. When she didn't, he forced himself to continue.

"Things got so bad, Tammy finally called me and asked for help. I was seventeen. A dumb kid, thinking if I brought Tammy here, my dad might actually man up and do something." Colt tightened his grip on the wheel, his nails cutting into his palms. "Suffice it to say, he made it clear Tammy didn't belong here. And I already knew I didn't, either. So when I turned eighteen, I left and took Tammy with me."

"How did you end up on the circuit?"

Hearing Jen's shaky voice, Colt glanced over. The tear slipping from her dark lashes sent a stabbing pain through his chest.

"Riding bulls was a quick way to make money and I found out I was pretty good at it. Tammy knew horses and I made enough to set her up to race." A bitter laugh burst from his lips. "We were both angry at the world in general. Riding bulls let me fight back and racing horses let Tammy run. Tammy wasn't born tough. She was made that way. And there's no way in hell I'd ever let her revisit what got her there."

A soft sound escaped Jen. She leaned over and wrapped him in a hug.

A wave of soothing heat swept over him, causing his hands to dig into the silky fall of her hair and his body to hum. He longed to tug her closer, drive away and leave it all behind. But Meg needed him and his focus should be on her. Not Jen.

Colt held on for a few moments, then forced himself to let go, pull away and jerk his chin toward the main house.

"I might as well get this over with."

Jen ducked her head, her cheeks flooding with color. She grabbed her purse and whispered, "I need to take care of Diamond before we go in."

He nodded and opened his door, forcing himself to

ignore the sudden desire to ease back into her comforting hold and explore her inviting mouth.

It took a few minutes to unload Diamond. By the time they'd managed it, a groundskeeper approached, offering assistance, and Jen reluctantly handed Diamond's care over to a stable hand. Colt retrieved their overnight bags and they made their way up the steep flight of stairs to the front entrance, pausing two-thirds of the way to catch their breath.

"This is ridiculous," Jen muttered, glancing below them at the truck.

Colt relieved her of her bag. "*Too* ridiculous."

Her eyes locked with his and they both laughed, his rigid muscles relaxing and his pain easing. Thank God she was here.

A click sounded as a door swung open. Jen's laughter died on her lips. Colt's chuckle trailed away, too, and he turned to find a tall, slim woman standing in the open doorway. She stood motionless in a stiff-collared shirt and dark slacks, her only greeting a stern expression.

"Hey," Colt called, shielding his eyes from the glare of the sun. "I'm here to see Meg Mead."

"It's a bit early for visitors," the woman replied, tucking a stray gray hair back into her updo. "I'm Ms. Parks, Margaret's nanny. May I have your name, please?"

Colt bit back a retort. His father's strict protocols were always followed and it was routine for guests to be announced once they passed the outer gates. She'd known who he was long before his boots ever hit the driveway.

Forcing a polite smile, he climbed the last few stairs to the front door. "I'm Colt Mea—"

He jerked to a halt when they reached the landing.

The sharp glare of the sun's rays shifted and he could just make out a young girl's face peeking around the woman's hip. Blond hair, brown eyes.

Colt's chest burned. "Meg?" His voice emerged in a rasp and he set the bags down, clearing his throat.

"Margaret, I asked you to wait inside." The woman reached behind her and tapped the child's shoulder. "Since you're here, you may as well come out and introduce yourself properly."

The girl blinked, her guarded eyes moving from Colt to Jen and back, but made no move to step forward.

Colt dragged his clammy palms over his thighs. "Do you know who I am, Meg?"

She stepped around the woman and straightened, the top of her head barely reaching his waist. "No one calls me that."

He let out a slow breath, his smile tentative. "I used to."

Her small mouth tightened. "I don't remember."

Colt's gut churned. Her frown was overly fierce and the tilt of her chin too pronounced. She kept cutting looks at Jen, brows drawing farther down.

"That's okay," he said gently. "I remember. I'm Colt. Your brother."

His tongue clung to the roof of his mouth, the last word foreign and strange.

The woman at Meg's side twisted her hands together and her nose wrinkled slightly.

"My name is Margaret." Her fingers picked at the hem of her khaki skirt, which brushed the tops of her knees. "That's what everyone calls me."

Colt examined her as she shifted from foot to foot. Her shoes were a shocking hot pink, but she had on navy blue knee-highs and a matching collared shirt with an emblem.

His throat ached. "Are you on the way to school, Margaret?"

"No. I just got back. The driver doesn't pick me up for weekends until six on Saturday mornings. I stay Friday night to take music lessons. We pay extra for private ones. Mr. Evans told me yesterday on the phone that Dad always said…" Her chin wobbled. "Mr. Evans said you can never get too far ahead. And that I shouldn't miss a lesson, no matter what."

Mr. Evans. Colt scoffed. Jack Evans. His father's business partner.

Jen shifted at his side and touched her fingertips to her lips, features strained. Ms. Parks's face flushed and she smoothed a hand over Meg's blond curls.

A spark of anger lit in Colt's gut. Ten years older than Colt, Jack had been a hanger-on from the moment he'd entered their lives, clawing his way into the family business and endearing himself as a second son. Enough so that he'd taken it upon himself to deliver the devastating news to Margaret. By phone, no less. Then hadn't even bothered to bring her home early.

Colt shook his head. "Margar—"

"Who's she?" Margaret stared at Jen, eyes flashing over her from head to toe.

"This is Jen Taylor. A friend of mine."

Jen smiled, bent and offered her hand. "Hi, Margaret."

"Hello." Margaret kept her arms at her sides, looking down at her pink shoes for a moment before glancing back up. She surveyed Jen's outstretched hand, then the other one, and squinted up at her. "What should I call you? Miss Taylor? Or Miss Jen?"

Jen shrugged, hand and smile dropping. "Whatever you want. Jen is fine."

"Was that your horse they took to the stables?"

"Yes. His name's Diamond." Jen slipped her hands in her back pockets, her tone nervous. "You saw us pull up?"

Margaret nodded. "They always announce guests. I watched from the window." She examined Jen again, her brown eyes narrowing on Jen's jeans and clinging to the shiny rhinestones ringing the front pockets. "Those are some tight pants."

"Margaret," Ms. Parks admonished. "Your manners."

Colt tensed. *Nice effort.* But the nanny's disapproving glance at Jen proved she agreed with Margaret's declaration.

"I'm sorry," Margaret muttered. "But they *are* some tight pants."

Jen's mouth twitched and she gestured to Margaret's feet, smile returning. "Those are some bright shoes." She winked, adding softly, "I like them. A lot."

Margaret nibbled on her bottom lip, digging the toe of her right sneaker into the doormat and dodging Jen's gaze.

Colt lowered himself to his knees and nudged her chin up with a knuckle. "I'm sorry, Margaret."

"For what?" she mumbled, still looking down.

He grimaced. "For Dad and Rach—"

"Why?" Her eyes shot to his face, narrowing to slits. "She wasn't your mother. She was mine."

His breath caught at the reminder. Rachel had been

his third stepmother. And hadn't cared for him any more than the other two. "I know."

"She was *mine*," she repeated, rosebud mouth trembling.

Her lashes spilled over and a large tear slipped down each cheek, dripping off her chin and plopping onto her shirt. Colt's body felt heavy. But he lifted his arms, drawing Margaret close and enfolding her in a loose embrace.

"I'm sorry," he whispered, leaning down and brushing a kiss across her cheek.

She jumped and shoved him back, scrubbing her hands across her face. "That hurts."

Colt held up shaky hands. "What?"

"That." She jabbed a finger at his chin.

He blinked and touched his jaw, the stubble of his beard rough against his fingertips.

"You came for the house, didn't you? That's why you're here." Margaret jerked her chin at Jen. "That's why she's here. Mr. Evans said Dad left it to us and that you'd come for it."

Margaret had composed herself again. There were no more tears. No chin wobble. Just a defiant, judgmental expression. So like their father's. The pain in Colt's chest flooded his veins, coursing in hot streaks through his body.

"Where is Jack, Ms. Parks?"

"Mr. Mead," the nanny said, stepping between them. "Perhaps it's best if—"

"Where—" Colt gritted his teeth "—is he?"

"In Dad's study." Margaret nodded. "He said you'd come."

"Wait here, Red." Colt stood and eased around Margaret, taking long strides across the foyer.

"Colt?" Jen's voice shook.

He paused, glancing over his shoulder. A worried shadow lurked in Jen's eyes as they swept over his frame.

"I'll just be a minute." He softened his tone. "Promise."

She didn't look convinced. Colt spun and made his way down the long corridor, finding the marble floor and walls as cold and hard as he remembered them. He gripped the thick handles of the wide double doors leading to his father's study and shoved them open.

Jack Evans sat behind a massive, ornate desk. His dark head was bent over a pile of scattered files and folders, and the shiny pen he held flashed under the lamplight with each movement of his hand.

"Making yourself at home?"

Jack stilled. He clicked the pen, placed it on the desk and rose. "Colt."

He looked the same. Lean. Polished. Professional. And as bland as the slate-gray suit and tie he wore.

"It's good to see you," Jack said, sliding his hands in his pockets and rocking back on his heels. "Though I wish it were under different circumstances."

Slick bastard. Words were the cheapest thing in this high-priced mansion.

Jack hesitated at the silence, dipping his head and saying, "It's a difficult time for all of us."

"Yeah." Colt sneered. "I can see you're all torn up about it."

Jack jerked his hands from his pockets. "Really? This is where we're going to start?" He straightened his tie, tucking it beneath the edge of his jacket. "Picking right back up where you left off, aren't you?"

"What? By being honest? That's the only way I operate." A hard smile stretched Colt's cheeks. "I'm sure the concept's alien to you."

"Cut the shit, Colt." Jack shook his head. "You haven't come by anything honestly. Don't have a clue what it's like to work to the bone for something. You were born into all of this."

"Not everything's about money," Colt bit out.

Jack's laugh grated across the room. "It sure as hell isn't to those who haven't earned it." He leaned forward, his palms on the desk. "Those of us that sweat blood for it have a greater respect for its value. You think this place materialized overnight? It took generations to build this estate and it'll take several more to ensure its survival."

"And you're the man to see to it, right?"

"I'm the only one that *can*." His brows rose. "What? You want to do it? Think you can waltz in here after seven years, step into Daddy's shoes and make it happen?" He shoved himself off the desk. "It doesn't work like that, Colt. You might own the place now but you're no one out there—where it counts."

Colt balled his fists. "And Margaret? She counts as no one, too? That's why you didn't even bother to deliver the news of her parents' death in person?"

Jack brushed a hand over his upper lip. "She was at school. The headmistress was with her. What else could I have done? There were important business matters that had to be tended to. Things your father worked hard for. You know as well as I do how much he would've wanted me to finish them. Remember his mantra?" His jaw hardened. *"No matter what."*

Colt's gut roiled, the taste of bile rising at the back

of his throat. He eyed Jack, uncurled his fists and shook his head. "How lucky Margaret is to have you."

Jack hissed in a breath and rounded the desk. "You sanctimonious, condescending little prick." His voice rose. "Where the hell were you, huh? Cruising through every Podunk spot on the map? Riding bulls and women? You couldn't even be bothered to answer your damned phone last night when I called."

Colt flinched. Heat singed his face and chest.

"She's *your* sister." Jack scoffed. "Not mine. But I was the one left to deal with it. Hell, I couldn't get a single soul with her blood running through their veins to respond to my calls. Your grandmother's the only one I managed to reach and she's on a European tour. It took me an hour and a hefty support check to convince her to collect Margaret when she returns next month."

"Next month? Who's looking after her till then?"

A snide expression crossed Jack's face. "Should be you. Your father designated you as her legal guardian in his will."

Colt's stomach dropped. "What?"

Legal guardian? The old man must've overlooked that detail when he signed off on the document. There was no way Colt was fit to be any kid's guardian. Especially Meg's.

"That's got to be a mistake." He held up a hand. "There's no way... I can't—"

"I figured as much." Jack straightened. "I've already made arrangements with the school. She stays there during the week. Your father and Rachel had her picked up on weekends, though they didn't always hang around to greet her when she arrived. People are paid to do that, and God knows, it costs enough. The headmistress has agreed to board her full-time at the end of next week. Right after spring break. There's a nanny and enough staff here to meet her needs until then." He gestured to the stack of papers on the desk. "Once you sign these documents, your grandmother will take over responsibility for her. Thank God money matters to most people. Otherwise, Margaret would end up being a worthless aggravation. As it is, money's the only thing that's going to ensure a solid future for her."

Colt's legs grew weak and his shoulders sagged.

Jack smiled, flashing bright white teeth. "Aw, buck up, boy. You'll be back to groping bulls and beauties in no time."

"That's enough."

Jen's voice, quiet but firm, sounded at Colt's back. She stood in the entrance, pulling the doors closed and fixing her eyes on Jack.

"Margaret's right down the hall," she said. "This place echoes like a museum and your voice carries."

Jack's smile morphed into a slow grin as his gaze drifted over Jen. "You must've changed course, Colt. Don't think you picked this one up in Podunk. Though I doubt you found her in Tuxedo Park, either."

Colt stiffened, his skin prickling.

Jack held out a hand. "Charmed."

Jen made no move to take it. "I'm not."

Jack's eyes flared and he cut a look at Colt. "Fiery piece of ass, is she?"

The crack as his fist met Jack's face was enough to sharpen Colt's focus. Jen yanked at his biceps, attempting to dislodge his grip from around Jack's neck.

"Let him go, Colt." Jen's low words barely overcame the roaring in his ears.

His gut heaved on a renewed surge of pain and disgust. For his dead father. For the ambitious fool stretched across the desk beneath him. And for himself.

"Colt." Jen sobbed, her mouth moving against the skin of his neck. "*Please*. Margaret could come in. You want her to see this?"

A wave of remorse flooded him. Colt let Jack go, hanging his head.

"I might be no one out there." Colt struggled to suck in air, lungs stinging just as they did every time he conquered a bull in the arena. "But in here, I own you." His eyes burned as he glared at Jack's crumpled form. "Now get the hell out."

Jack turned over, braced his palms on the desk and struggled to a standing position. He cupped a hand over his nose. Blood seeped between his fingers, trickling over his smile and onto his tie.

"You might not have a taste for money, Colt, but you sure as hell have one for power." Jack laughed, wincing as the sound left his lips. "You're more like your father than you think."

Colt froze.

The doors closed behind Jack with a sharp click.

Jen touched his back. "Colt—"

He jerked away, moving on weak legs to the window and almost choking on the words tearing from his throat. "Margaret heard? Everything?"

"No," she said, "But more than you would've wanted her to."

And more than he'd have wanted Jen to hear, too.

Colt cringed, looking away from her faint reflection in the glass and down at the extensive grounds below him. The pristine gardens, sparkling pool and spacious tennis court were all beautiful. But barren and lifeless. Just like John W. Mead.

You're more like your father than you think.

Colt sucked his teeth. To hell with Jack Evans and his arrogant declarations. Colt was nothing like his father. And never would be.

"We're leaving," he growled. "Right after the funerals tomorrow."

The words were easy. They rolled off his tongue with finality. But they left a hollow in his gut. One that made him wonder if he could actually follow through.

What kind of man would leave a little girl behind? Allow her to fade into empty surroundings, forgotten and unseen?

Colt frowned, stilling his thoughts and avoiding the answer. But it whispered through his mind just the same.

Men like Jack Evans. Men like John W. Mead.

Chapter Four

Jen had never seen so much green in her life. It covered everything.

"Perfect." Mac, an older stable hand with a kind face and friendly voice, propped his hands on his hips. "Absolutely perfect."

"Yeah," Jen breathed.

She glanced around, taking in the sprawling acres of lush grass and the thick lines of trees forming a boundary on both sides of the wide pasture. If there was ever a paradise for horses, the riding grounds on the Mead estate were it.

"He fast?"

Jen glanced at Mac, squinting through the sharp rays of late afternoon sunlight. "What?"

"Your horse." He jerked his chin toward the field where Diamond had been frolicking for the past hour, pearl hide flashing through a sea of green. "He's a fine specimen. But is he fast?"

She cocked a brow and grinned. "What do you think?"

Mac chuckled, his leathery cheeks lifting and white teeth gleaming. "I think if we let those pampered ponies out of the stable, he'd trample 'em just on principle."

Jen laughed with him, dropping her head back and soaking up the fading warmth of the day. It'd been nice to get out of that marbled mansion for a few hours. Colt's father's estate was void of any true warmth. Only cold corners and empty hallways could be found in that monster of a house.

After that arrogant jerk Jack Evans had left, Colt had gathered up their luggage and led her up another massive staircase to the third floor, where the guest rooms were located. They'd stowed their bags in their bedrooms and Colt had immediately left to seek out Margaret. But Margaret hadn't responded to any of his attempts at conversation. She'd just looked him over with narrowed eyes, then retreated to her room.

Colt, more stoic than ever, had excused himself and holed up in his father's study. Jen had tried to persuade him to join her outside, but he'd continued to pore over the guardianship papers Jack Evans had prepared, lingering over each page before moving grimly to the next.

Jen glanced back at the long path up to the mansion. Neither Colt nor Margaret had come outside all day. Ms. Parks had insisted Margaret not be disturbed, and the door to the girl's bedroom had remained shut for hours. Which was a shame. Fresh air and warm sunshine were the best antidotes for pain.

"Mr. and Mrs. Mead never really cared for riding," Mac said, a note of disgust in his tone. "Or the horses, for that matter. They just liked the idea of owning them."

"What about Margaret?" Jen asked. "She never rides?"

"Not since—"

"Never."

Jen spun to find Margaret standing behind them. She'd traded her school uniform for a white skirt and blue blouse, but still wore her hot-pink shoes. Her long hair fell in loose waves around her face, but her expression remained blank.

"You should come in now," Margaret said. "Dinner is being served."

Jen's stomach growled at the mention of food. She'd stayed outside so long she'd missed lunch. "Sounds good." She smiled. "Thank you for telling me, Margaret."

"Ms. Parks said it's important to personally invite guests to the dinner table." She shrugged. "Even if you weren't expecting them. It's the polite thing to do and it's never polite to be late."

Margaret hesitated for a moment, her chestnut eyes lingering on Diamond, then turned and left.

Jen released a bitter laugh. "Ms. Parks sounds like a pretty tough customer."

"I don't know," Mac said. "She's a lot better than the last four nannies that little girl's had."

"Four?" Jen shook her head. "Why so many?"

"Mrs. Mead was real particular about who she kept around. She always found something she didn't like about them." Mac grimaced. "Usually right after they'd suggest she pay more attention to her daughter."

He squinted, staring at Diamond in the distance. "Imogene Holden was the child's first nanny. Was with her from birth. She was Margaret's favorite. Took Margaret out for her first ride." He dragged a hand across the back of his neck. "They weren't out long before the horse spooked. Took off so fast Imogene couldn't catch hold of it. Margaret was thrown. Got hurt pretty bad."

"And now she doesn't trust them," Jen murmured.

Mac nodded. "Imogene was fired right after. That kid loved Imogene something fierce. She cried for days after she left. Shed a lot more tears over that nanny than she has for her own parents, that's for sure." His features fell and his voice deepened. "Not that anyone can blame her for that."

Mac's hunched shoulders and defeated expression proved the loss of Imogene had been a cruel blow to others besides Margaret. So strange that a place equipped with every material comfort imaginable would be filled with an equal amount of pain. Was no one happy here?

"Well," Jen whispered, clearing her throat. "I guess it's time for me to go in. Would you mind tucking Diamond in for the night? I'd really appreciate it."

"No problem," he said, straightening with a smile. "Any time."

Jen made her way up the winding stone path to the main entrance. A housekeeper met her at the door, ushering her inside with rapid waves of her hands and leading her quickly down several hallways to a formal dining room.

"Good evening, Ms. Taylor." Ms. Parks sat on one side of a long cherry table, Margaret seated at her side. "We were beginning to wonder if you'd make it."

Colt rose from his position at the head of the table and tugged out the high-backed chair to his left. "We weren't aware there was a schedule," he said in a firm voice.

Jen winced. The circles under Colt's eyes had darkened and new lines of strain were etched in his expression. His formal gesture only added to his distant demeanor.

"I'm sorry I kept everyone waiting," she said, unable to stop herself from squeezing his hand before taking her seat. "When we're on the road, Colt and I don't have time to stand on ceremony. We just grab and go. Right?"

The corners of his mouth tipped up slightly as he sat. "Yeah."

Jen's chest constricted. Grief was taking a toll on him and this place was only intensifying it. Fine friend she was being. Nothing she'd done so far had helped ease his pain.

She glanced around the room and shifted uncomfortably in her chair. A large, crystal chandelier hung above from the center of a ceiling mural. Ornate floral arrangements and elegant place settings were strategically arranged on the polished cherry table.

Jen flexed her fingers to shake off a fresh surge of anxiety, then tugged the napkin ring from the cloth in the center of her plate. "So," she said, settling the napkin in her lap, "what's on the menu?"

Ms. Parks and Margaret exchanged glances, and after an encouraging nod from her nanny, Margaret recited, "Chilled scallops with saffron mayonnaise, asparagus and buttered leeks and radishes."

Jen suppressed a shudder. "That sounds…different."

It smelled different, too. And judging from the curl of Colt's upper lip, he was just as impressed with the sparsely covered plate that appeared in front of him as she was. The housekeeper filled their crystal glasses with water and left to retrieve sliced lemon at Ms. Parks's request.

"Please eat, Margaret." The nanny speared a scallop with her fork and dipped it in the yellow sauce.

Margaret wasn't as adept. Her scallop fell off the

fork and plopped into the sauce bowl, splattering yellow drops onto the white place setting. She fished around for a few seconds with her fork, but when Ms. Parks turned her head, she retrieved it with her fingers and slipped it in her mouth quickly.

One grimace and hard swallow later, Margaret placed her fork on the table and sat back. Colt followed suit, pushing his plate away with the tip of his finger and casting tired eyes over his sister.

Ms. Parks sighed, forehead creasing. "Margaret, you need to eat."

Jen frowned. Colt needed to eat, too. But the meal in front of them was about as appetizing as baked rubber.

The housekeeper returned, placing a small plate of lemon wedges on the table near Ms. Parks. "May I bring you anything, Mr. Mead?"

Colt shook his head. "No, thanks."

Jen leaned forward, halting the housekeeper's exit with a raised hand. "I could use something, please." She smiled. "I'm sorry—what's your name?"

The woman hesitated, darting glances at Ms. Parks and licking her lips. "Nancy."

"Do you happen to have any peanut butter, Nancy?"

She tilted her head. "Yes, ma'am, we do."

"Could you bring it, please? And honey. Do you have honey?"

"Yes, ma'am. How would you like it?"

Jen shrugged. "Just a jar of both would be fine. And some bread. I'd like to fix it up myself."

The housekeeper nodded, then left, the fading swish of her slacks filling the silent room.

Margaret sat up, confusion clouding her features. "Aren't you supposed to eat jelly with peanut butter?"

Jen's smile widened. "That's the go-to for most people. But I found something better growing up."

She picked up her plate of scallops and unappealing vegetables, then dumped them on top of Colt's.

Ms. Parks's eyes widened. "There's no point in making a mess. If you need another plate, we'll happily provide one for you."

"Nah." Jen met Colt's eyes, her belly fluttering at the amusement brightening his dark expression. "Wouldn't want to dirty up more dishes than necessary."

The housekeeper returned, placing the requested items on the table. Jen dipped out a hefty portion of peanut butter and honey, plopped them onto her plate and stirred them together.

"When I was in elementary school," Jen said, "the lunchroom lady, Mrs. Shirley, would sneak me a special sandwich every Wednesday. It was always white bread with this thick, sweet stuff in the middle that I loved. I knew peanut butter was in it, but it took me a while to figure out what the sweet stuff was." She picked up a clean spoon and scooped up a dollop of the mixture. "Turned out it was honey. But you have to combine just the right amounts to get the same taste."

Ms. Parks's left eyebrow lifted almost to her hairline. "This was in public school, I imagine?"

"Yep." Jen held the loaded spoon out to Meg. "There's a lot more to learn in public school than just academics." She waited as Meg took the spoon and placed it gingerly in her mouth. "I learned that lunchroom ladies are moms, sisters and daughters, too. That most teachers care about other people's children as if they were their own. And that some kids you'd never thought you'd like can end up being the best friends you ever had."

Margaret's mouth curved up and she said, "Wis is uh beft swuff evah."

"Margaret," Ms. Parks gasped. "Don't speak with your mouth full."

"Buh i' is," Margaret said, lifting the spoon in an obvious request for more.

Colt laughed, picked up his spoon and held it out, as well. The deep rumble tingled over Jen's skin, dancing in her chest and bringing a wet sheen to her eyes. She blinked rapidly, filled both their spoons, then her own, and even offered one to Ms. Parks.

"No, thank you."

"Oh, come on," Jen teased. "Just try it."

Surprisingly, she did. The sound of pleasure that followed indicated she approved.

The next few minutes passed in companionable silence as they assembled sandwiches and filled their bellies. Colt ate three, and when Margaret asked for a second one, he put his half-eaten fourth sandwich aside to make her another.

"Thank you," she murmured, taking the sandwich from him with a gooey, crumb-laden smile.

"You're welcome." Colt's grin couldn't get any wider.

Jen sneaked her napkin to her cheek and wiped her eyes before anyone noticed. Such a foolish thing to do— tearing up like a baby when Colt and Margaret were the ones who needed a good cry.

"All right, Margaret," Ms. Parks said, standing. "It's time for homework then bed."

"But I want another—"

"You've had two and that's quite enough for a little girl." She ushered Margaret from her chair.

"If she wants to stay and have another sandwich, she can." Colt's tone hardened as he watched Margaret trudge slowly across the room.

"It's up to you, of course," Ms. Parks said. "But considering the long day she'll have tomorrow, I think it's best that she get a good night's rest. Don't you?"

Colt's expression fell at the reminder of the funerals. He nodded.

Ms. Parks waited until Margaret was out of earshot, then said, "I understand what you're both trying to do and no one appreciates it more than me. That's the first genuine smile Margaret's had in ages." She bit her lip and lowered her voice. "I'm paid to supervise and advise Margaret. Not love her. But I do. And I can't, in any good conscience, step aside and allow you to fill her heart with hopes of things that will never happen."

"I have every right to visit Margaret," Colt said. "I'm her brother."

"In name only." Ms. Parks fidgeted. "Forgive me, but I wasn't under the impression that you planned to stay."

Colt released a ragged breath, his eyes dropping.

"Please understand," Ms. Parks continued. "None of what you're teaching Margaret right now will do her any good in the life she'll soon lead. It will only be a disservice to her. As I'm sure you already know." She hesitated, then whispered on her departure, "I'm sorry, Mr. Mead. I truly am."

Colt dragged his hand over his face then slid his palm around to knead the back of his neck. "I think it's time to call it a day."

His voice sounded strange. Heavy and unfamiliar, as though it belonged to a different man.

"Colt." Jen wrapped her fingers gently around his forearm. "I'm here if you want to talk. It might help if—"

"I'm tired." He pulled away and stood, tossing his napkin on the table. "Good night."

He ambled out, his steps slow and defeated.

Wet heat streaked down Jen's cheeks. She didn't bother to wipe her face. Just let the steady stream continue. She'd cried more in the past twenty-four hours than she had in three years put together. And Colt had yet to shed a tear.

Jen pushed her chair back and stood, taking in the empty room around her. It was impossible to imagine Colt or Margaret having a good childhood here. The loneliness of the place hung on them like a thick shroud, and it was beginning to fall over her, as well.

This wasn't a home. And no matter how much her heart bled for him, Colt wasn't hers. The sooner she put this weekend behind her and returned to the circuit, the better.

THERE WASN'T A wet eye in the church. Not a single tear was shed during the funeral, and Colt wasn't surprised. That was the way John W. Mead wanted things done in his world.

"John Mead will be missed as much for his philanthropy as for his strength of spirit." The preacher paused, shifting behind the pulpit and sweeping his gentle eyes over the first pew. "Those who knew him best can be proud of his generosity to others. So many have benefited from John's charity and goodwill."

Colt bit back a scoff. His father's checks were easy to cut, always signed by secretaries. They allowed for greater tax write-offs. And no one, including his family, had ever really known John W. Mead. He never let anyone close enough.

But there was no need to split hairs at this point. They'd already sat through an hour of services for Rachel, and were on the second one for his father. Besides himself and Margaret, Jen and Ms. Parks were the only people seated in the family pew. And the strain of the day was beginning to take its toll.

He dropped his head and gripped the edge of his seat, the rough upholstery of the pew abrading his fingertips. Margaret's pale hand, one-third the size of his, lay flat on the seat beside his thigh and shook slightly.

A heavy weight pressed on Colt's chest. He ached to reach out, place his palm over the back of her small one and squeeze. To still her nerves with solid strength and help her feel less alone.

Because that was exactly what she was. Alone. With no knowledge of how much her gurgling toddler laugh had comforted him all those years ago. Or how relieved he'd always been as a teenager to see her at the end of each school day. Her rambunctious demeanor had been the only bright spot in that dark mansion.

I don't remember.

Meg's—*Margaret's*—words returned, dropping like a stone into his gut. She didn't remember him and he wouldn't be around long enough to remind her. He'd packed his bags first thing this morning, loaded the truck and mapped out the fastest route back to the circuit. His plan hinged on driving away the moment the funerals ended.

Only he hadn't counted on the news he'd received from Tammy when she'd called to check on him.

"Colt." Jen's soft lips brushed his ear as she tugged gently at his wrist.

He glanced up, taking in her worried expression, then noticed everyone was standing. Clearing his throat, he released his hold on the pew and stood. Jen took his hand in hers, then wrapped her free one around his biceps, squeezing firmly.

The gesture was calm and kind. An act of one friend supporting another. But it reignited all sorts of emotions within him, ones he'd only ever felt with Jen. The kind he couldn't define or understand.

It'd be so easy to lean into her. To pass this pressing weight to her and absorb every bit of supportive comfort she offered. But he couldn't. Not when Margaret stood silent at his side, expression empty and posture aloof. An exact replica of his father's demeanor, void of any traces of the affectionate girl Colt once knew.

The pallbearers gathered around the caskets and the procession began. Another hour passed at the cemetery. By the time Colt's small group exited the limo and climbed the steep front steps of the Mead estate, his sister had lost her last bit of color. She fiddled with the black bow at her waist as she followed Ms. Parks across the foyer toward the hall.

"Margaret." Colt struggled to force her name past his constricted throat, the syllables echoing off the marble walls. "Would you like to sit with me for a while?" He shrugged, his tense shoulders screaming in protest. "Or we could take a walk?"

She stopped, then glanced over her shoulder, blond

curls and thick lashes drooping. "Ms. Parks said you're probably leaving soon. Are you?"

Colt hesitated, glancing at Jen, who stood by the closed doors of the front entrance. She looked at him sadly but pointedly.

His body sagged and he moved to the window, staring out at the long driveway and trying to still the trembling in his limbs. "Yeah."

"Then we won't have time to, will we?" Margaret's quiet voice barely reached him.

Time. That's what it all amounted to. The hours it took to make the drive here. The days he'd sacrificed to attend the funerals. And the years of obligation that would pile up if the papers sitting on his father's desk remained unsigned.

Colt dug his fingertips into the windowsill, pressing hard against the wood until his nail beds turned red. Taking responsibility for Margaret on a permanent basis was out of the question. There was no room in his life for a kid and he didn't have the first clue how to raise one.

But how could he walk away again with no attempt at reconciliation? Remain as much a stranger to his sister as John W. Mead had been to him? A relative in name only?

Each one of Margaret's fading footsteps ripped another hole in Colt's chest. A familiar ache began to seep from the pit of his gut, the kind he'd felt ever since he'd left her behind seven years ago. It coursed through his veins, stealing his breath.

"I can make the time." He froze, unable to believe the declaration had left his mouth.

"She's gone, Colt." Jen stepped to his side and rubbed

his arm. "It may be for the best, anyway. It's a long drive to the next competition, and if we don't leave soon, we won't make it."

"I need to stay with Margaret. Just for a little while longer." He reached up, stilling Jen's hand and peering down at her. "What if you sat the next race out? Or two or three, for that matter?"

Her dark eyes clouded with confusion. "What are you talking about?"

He drew in a deep breath and took her hands in his. "I spoke to Tammy this morning. Checked the stats. You're ranking eighth."

Jen's brows rose, pink lips curving slightly. "Eighth?"

He nodded. "Right now, you're qualifying for Finals. You and Tammy both. She won last night and is ranking ninth, right behind you and well above the top fifteen cut for Vegas."

"Vegas?" Jen whispered.

"Vegas, Red." He licked his lips. "You can afford to take a break." Her expression dimmed and he held up a palm. "Margaret's school is on spring vacation and she'll be alone until classes start back up if I don't stay with her. It'd just be for a week."

"One week?" Jen frowned. "This trip was only supposed to be for a couple of days, Colt. That's all Tammy asked me for and that's all I promised."

"I know. But I'm the one doing the asking now." He put his shoulders back and forged ahead. "I might've taken care of Tammy when I got out of here seven years ago, but by doing that, I left Margaret behind. That guilt has followed me for a long time. I don't want that feeling hanging on me again. I need to get rid of it."

Jen sighed, her expression gentle. "But how would

a week help? Don't you think it'll be harder for you to leave her after another week than it would now?"

A strange feeling of unease moved over him. Colt dismissed it, shaking his head and firming his features.

"No," he said. "It won't. I know I'm not fit to take care of her full-time. Would never want to. But I can be here for her now. I can help her through all of this and show her another way to live."

"Colt—"

"I can give her better memories. Ones she can carry with her when she moves on. That way when she comes of age, she can choose for herself which life she wants to lead. Like I did seven years ago." He stepped closer, trying to lighten the pleading note in his voice. "I can't do it on my own, though. I need your help."

"I don't know how I'd be of any help. I barely know her."

"That doesn't matter. You've made more headway with her in one day than a nanny who's been with her for months. You proved it last night, pulling that smile from her. Hell, Ms. Parks said so herself."

Jen drew back, shaking her head. "One smile doesn't make me an expert on kids. And this place isn't good for anyone. I can't stay here any longer, Colt."

"You won't." He firmed his tone. "We'll leave here today just as planned."

"And go where?" She splayed her hands. "You can't wander from motel to motel like you normally do, not with a nine-year-old in tow."

"I'll take care of that. I'll call in a favor."

"This is… I'm sorry, but I can't. I've got to get back to the circuit. A weekend was one thing, but a whole week—"

"You're ranking so high right now, you've got plenty of cushion. It'll take the rest of 'em that long just to catch up with you."

Jen laughed, the sound abrupt and derisive. "I doubt that."

"Seven days, tops," he insisted. "Diamond will get a well-deserved break. You'll have extra time to train. And Margaret and I will be able to get to know each other again. That way she'll feel comfortable coming to me in the future if she ever needs me." He moved close, cradling Jen's face with his palms. "This is me asking. Not Tammy. I need your help and I could really use a friend right now."

The curves of her cheeks blushed beneath his thumbs and her lush lips parted on a shaky inhalation. Her eyes met his and softened.

His throat burned. Damn, he was begging. But it didn't prevent him from whispering, "Please, Red."

Her full lashes fluttered shut as she blew out a heavy breath. "Only for one week. If my ranking drops before then, you have to promise you'll get me and Diamond back to the circuit—no matter what." She opened her eyes, expression determined. "That's a nonnegotiable."

"You got it." He pressed a kiss to her forehead then stepped back quickly, ignoring the pleasurable sensation in his belly and the sudden desire to hold on to her.

Jen looked away. Her drawn expression indicated regret had already set in.

Colt flexed his fingers to ease the ache running down his arms and choked down the words fighting their way up his throat. The ones urging him to take it back. To pack up and get out while he could. Instead, he dragged his phone from his pocket and dialed. It rang twice before someone answered.

"Well, hell," a deep voice said with a chuckle. "Must be my lucky day, hearing from you."

Colt managed a smile. "Dom." Dominic Slade. A former bull rider. Known as champion to the world, though Colt knew him as best friend. A good man. One Colt trusted above any other. "Got time for an old friend?"

"Of course." Dominic's laughter faded. "You all right, man?"

"Yeah." Colt dragged in a breath and steadied his voice. "I need a favor."

Dominic responded immediately. "You name it."

Chapter Five

"Are you sure you want to do this?"

Jen winced, pressed the cell phone closer to her ear and sneaked a glance at Colt in the driver's seat. He cut his eyes her way briefly, then refocused on the road. A quick peek in the rearview mirror revealed Margaret sleeping soundly in the back of the extended cab, just as she had since leaving the Mead estate hours earlier. Thank goodness.

Tammy's voice was pitched higher as it came across the line. "You're ranking eighth. That's not a given for Finals this early," she stressed. "There's still months to go before we officially make the cut, and you can't sit on the sidelines and expect to hold your position."

Jen rubbed her forehead, feeling as though it was midnight rather than four in the afternoon. "I know. But it's only for seven days."

"Seven days?" Tammy's voice was still strained. "Might as well be seven years. Things move so fast out here, you'll fall behind before you know it." Her tone lowered. "This is my fault. I should never have talked you into going in the first place. That's why you feel like you have to do this."

"That's not true," Jen whispered, turning to look out the passenger window.

The landscape passed by in a blur of green, wide fields separated by thick woods stretching endlessly. Each mile took them deeper into Georgia country and away from the circuit.

Why *had* she agreed to Colt's request?

Tammy sighed. "How's Colt doing?"

Jen stole a glance at him. His knuckles turned white around the steering wheel and he blinked slowly, his eyes heavy.

Jen's chest ached. Now she remembered why she'd given in.

"Okay, I guess," she murmured. "It's going to take some time."

"I'm glad you're there for him," Tammy said. "And for Margaret. I really am. I just worry that if you don't get back soon, you won't make the cut. You've worked so hard for so long, Jen. I'd hate for you to…"

Jen closed her eyes briefly, her own fears finishing Tammy's sentence.

I'd hate for you to lose it all. End up a small-town nothing like everyone predicted, mopping the floor of The Greasy Spoon every day and surviving off a few dollars' worth of tips. Living in a cramped house filled with more hungry mouths than working hands. Exactly like Jen's mother, Nora, had.

Nora Taylor, a widow and overworked waitress, had dismissed her daughter's ambition to become a world champion barrel racer despite Jen's repeated success at rodeos near their hometown. Her outlook on life was as weary and bleak as the abandoned house rotting next to theirs.

It's dangerous, Jen. Not to mention improper. Prancing around an arena, rubbing shoulders with sweaty cowboys. Since you're not going to college, the best thing for you is to find a good man and settle down. Start a family.

Jen scoffed. *Hogwash.* "I'm coming back in one week." She smiled. "You better stay on your toes if you plan to keep up. Diamond and I always burn brighter after a good rest."

Tammy laughed, but the joyful sound faded quickly. "Take care of them."

"I will." Jen disconnected the call and tucked her cell phone back in her pocket.

"Tammy meeting us later?" Colt asked.

Jen shook her head. "She's already lined up more runs with Karla. Says they've paid entry fees for three competitions, started the drive yesterday and are halfway there. She can't afford to dip out now. It'd put Karla in a bad position."

She cringed. The kind of position she'd left Tammy in when she'd decided to stay behind with Colt.

Colt's big hand settled over hers and squeezed, his blue eyes weary. "We'll be back before you know it, Red."

"We're not going to worry about that at the moment," Jen said, covering his hand with her free one. "Right now, we're taking a break. One you and Margaret desperately need."

His big body shifted and he tugged his hand away, reaching up and squeezing her shoulder. He returned his attention to the road, easing across a bumpy set of railroad tracks, then accelerating down the highway.

Jen inhaled, relishing the spicy scent of his aftershave and the warmth his touch had left on her skin. It was easier to travel with him when Tammy was around. Tammy's cheerful chatter helped take the focus off Colt's charisma. But Jen didn't have that luxury on this trip.

Colt's biceps brushed her arm as he maneuvered another turn, causing her belly to flip over. She placed her hands in her lap and tamped down the urge to scoot closer and press against him.

It was ridiculous, really. Indulging this attraction she had to him. She tried to convince herself that any man with Colt's good looks and muscular frame would stir the same desire. They were friends. That was all he wanted. Nothing more.

A sleepy sigh emerged from the back of the cab. Jen glanced over her shoulder. Margaret had sat upright in her seat during the first half of the journey, but exhaustion had finally taken over. She was now slumped against the window, her shiny hair falling forward, hiding her face. A few strands lifted and fell as she breathed.

A lump formed in Jen's throat at the sight. After arranging a place for them to stay, Colt had gently explained to his little sister that he needed a break, a vacation of sorts, and that he'd like her to come with him.

Ms. Parks had disapproved and Margaret hadn't responded much one way or the other. But after a half hour of coaxing from Colt, they'd given in to his declaration that he wasn't leaving without Margaret, and gone upstairs to pack a bag. Jen had offered to help, but Margaret declined in a formal manner that was much too mature for any nine-year-old. Especially one who had to be hurting as much as she was.

Jen bit her lip now and tried her best to make out

Margaret's face through the fall of her curls. The girl shared the same blond shade of hair as Colt. The brief glimpse Jen had had of her smile last night proved that was another similarity the siblings shared. Jen just wasn't sure she'd ever see her smile again.

Her arms ached to wrap around Margaret and hug her. To offer comfort in some small way. But she knew the attempt would be refused. Margaret might have been provided for in every other way, but she'd been neglected in the most important respect. Being loved. And noticed.

Jen's heart squeezed. Margaret was such a sad, beautiful girl—

Vibrating snorts rang out. Margaret's head shifted against the foggy window, her hair slipping back and her small mouth falling open on a massive snore. A raucous chorus began, thundering against the roof and filling the cab. For the sixth time in the last hour.

Jen cringed, sharing a pained glance with Colt. Three hours ago, Margaret's snores had been cute and endearing. Two hours ago, they'd become aggravating. Now they were excruciating.

Jen's head pounded. Good grief, she couldn't wait to get out of this stuffy truck, collapse onto a bed and savor some silence. Alone.

Ten snore-filled minutes later, Colt turned onto a long dirt drive, and a familiar wooden sign appeared ahead. Jen would recognize the rustic corners and rich brown of it anywhere. She'd driven past it with Colt several times over the past couple of years, to visit friends from the rodeo circuit.

Raintree Ranch. They'd finally made it. Privacy, silence and sleep were just up ahead inside the white, multistoried main house.

Margaret's rhythmic snorts stopped as the truck bounced over a rough patch of road. Jen swiveled, to find her sweeping her hair back from her face and blinking sleepy eyes at the view outside her window.

"A ranch?" Margaret asked as the truck eased past the sign. "You said we were taking a vacation."

Colt glanced in the rearview mirror, his smile strained. "We are. Raintree's the best guest ranch in Georgia. There are lots of fun things to do. There's a pool, game room and a pond with paddleboats. And there are a couple boys here around your age to play with. I'll take you fishing one day this week. You'll love it, Meg."

Her expression fell. "It's Margaret," she whispered.

"I'm sorry." Colt shifted uncomfortably, cheeks reddening. "Margaret."

Margaret turned away and stared at the line of white fencing sweeping by. The air grew thick and heavy inside the cab.

Jen hit a button on the passenger door and the window slid down with a whisper, letting in a warm breeze. She stuck her head out, inhaled and pulled in a lungful of sweet spring air. The chirp of crickets and low notes of bullfrogs rushed into the cab; the late afternoon hour and misty fog coaxed songs from the ranch wildlife.

She soaked it up. The tension between her shoulder blades eased and the throbbing at her temples lessened. Just the wide green fields speckled with grazing horses were enough to lift her spirits.

The trailer squeaked as the truck dipped into a pothole. Jen lowered her cheek to the silver windowsill trim and looked back, catching a glimpse of Diamond's white mane through the slats of the trailer.

She hadn't ridden him in two days. Neither one of them had felt the whip of wind striking their face in ages. Or smelled the rich, earthy aroma of dirt kicking up from beneath them. And she was surprised by how eager she was to ride outside an arena rather than in one.

"Not long now, boy," she whispered. "We can both stretch our legs soon. I'll have you back in shape in no time."

"What?"

Jen pushed herself off the door and straightened, glancing at Colt. His brow was furrowed.

"Just telling Diamond I'm gonna let him out soon. We're anxious to stretch a bit. Maybe hit up some training in the morning."

Colt nodded. She turned back to the window, an excited buzz spreading through her veins. Training. One benefit to taking a break was the opportunity to hone her racing skills. She and Diamond would be better than ever when they returned to competition.

Jen closed her eyes and savored the thrills chasing through her blood. Eighth overall. The Thomas & Mack. *Vegas.*

"There's Dom." Colt perked up, a pleased note entering his voice.

A tall, broad-shouldered man stood at the end of the driveway, a black Stetson on his head and dimpled smile on his face.

Colt cut the engine, jumped out and started toward him. The man met him halfway, tugging him forward for a brief hug and strong clap on the back. When they broke apart, Jen she could see that they were talking.

Before long, Colt nodded and motioned toward the truck.

"Who's he?"

Jen swiveled, glancing back at Margaret. "Dominic Slade. He used to ride bulls with your brother. He co-owns this ranch with his father, Pop, and his brother, Logan." She smiled. "They're good people. And they're all anxious to meet you."

Margaret's brown eyes drifted over Jen's shoulder and she leaned forward, squinting up at the main house. "It looks small."

Jen reassessed the building. The wide front porch, large double door entrance and multileveled structure was anything but small. It'd grown over the last two years with renovations and the addition of more guest wings. But she supposed it paled in comparison to what Margaret was used to.

"There's plenty of room." Jen stretched her legs and grinned. *Rooms.* One, in particular. With a large bed, en suite bathroom and plenty of sleep-inducing silence. All for her. *Hallelujah!* "Come on. I'll help you get your bag."

Jen had just hefted Margaret's bag from the bed of the truck when the front door slammed and feet pounded down the front steps. Two blond boys loped across the lawn, shouting greetings to "Mr. Colt" and high-fiving him.

Jen smiled and set the bag on the ground. "That's Kayden and Jayden, Dominic's twin nephews. The boys Colt told you about. They oughta be fun to hang out with, don't you think?"

Margaret tucked a curl behind her ear and ran a hand

over her plaid skirt. "They live here all the time? With their mom and dad?"

Jen's smile slipped. "The boys live here, yes. With Dominic and his wife, Cissy."

She hesitated, unsure of how much to share. Kayden and Jayden had lost their mother several years ago to cancer. Their father planned on giving them up for adoption, but their aunt Cissy had taken them in. After finding Cissy and the boys stranded in a broken-down car, Dominic had brought the trio to Raintree and they'd eventually become a family.

Jen shrugged, thinking it best to keep the darker details of the boys' journey to herself. It might help soothe Margaret's grief to know she wasn't alone in her pain, but it could backfire just as easily. Jen didn't want to add more negativity to Margaret's world at such a difficult time. Besides, they were here to help her heal. The brighter the thoughts, the better.

"The boys have baby sisters, too. They'd be about, oh…" Jen squinted, counting the months "…almost two years old now." She waved at Dominic. "Hey, Dom. It's good to see you."

He flashed a dimpled grin and called out, "Back atcha, Red. It's great to have you here."

Jen eased to the front of the truck and motioned for Margaret to follow. "Come on. I'll introduce you."

The little girl stepped forward, but her hot-pink tennis shoe halted in midair over the dirt.

Jen followed Margaret's stare. The boys had left Colt and now stood stock-still, side by side, a few feet away, big blue eyes fixed on Margaret. Their hushed voices carried.

"Another girl?" Kayden shared a frown with his brother. "Ain't we got enough of those around here?"

Jayden harrumphed, crossing his arms over his chest. "I know. Thought it was gonna be a boy." He shook his head. "That messes up all our plans."

Great. Preadolescent disdain for the opposite sex. A fantastic first impression.

Jen smiled. "Aw, now. Y'all cut that out, boys. I'm a girl, too. Aren't you happy to see me?" She laughed at their eager nods, dropped to her knees and spread her arms. "Then get your cute tails over here and show Miss Jen some love."

They flashed crooked grins and sprinted over, barreling into her and wrapping their arms around her neck. They'd grown since she last saw them, Kayden a good three inches and Jayden at least two. They'd be almost nine now.

"You bring Diamond, Miss Jen?" Kayden asked, pecking a kiss to her cheek.

"I sure did." She jerked her chin toward the trailer behind them. "Go tell him hi. He's been cooped up a long time and would appreciate the company."

Kayden released her and headed for the trailer, his step slowing as he passed Margaret. Their eyes met and then drifted down the length of each other. Kayden's attention returned to her blond curls, and he blushed.

Jen stifled a laugh and stood. "You know, it's usually routine to at least say hello when you meet someone new."

Kayden shrugged a shoulder. "Hey."

"Hello." Margaret held out a hand. "I'm Margaret Mead."

Kayden's nose wrinkled. He studied her outstretched

hand for a moment before shaking it awkwardly. "I'm Kayden." He nodded toward his brother. "That's Jayden."

"It's nice to meet you," Margaret said.

Kayden eyed her flashy sneakers. "Me and Jayden race a lot. He's fast but I'm faster." His head tilted. "You ever race?"

"No."

"You build forts?"

"Uh-uh."

"Shoot BB guns?"

Margaret shook her head, her expression appalled.

Kayden sighed. "Then what do you do?"

Jayden snorted. "She paints her toes and stuff." He walked over, shoving his brother toward the trailer. "Come on. Let's pet Diamond."

Attention diverted, Kayden sauntered over to the trailer with his twin. They climbed up on the tires, slipped their hands through the open window and patted Diamond, praising him. Margaret took a hesitant step toward them, but froze when Diamond shifted, hooves clanking on the bed of the trailer. She looked at the boys' T-shirts, jeans and boots, then lowered her head and picked at her silk blouse.

Jen stepped close and placed a hand on her shoulder. "You're welcome to pet Diamond, too, if you'd like."

Her head shot up, face pale and tone tense. "I don't want to."

The boys' hands stilled and they glanced over their shoulders, examining Margaret, who flushed and tilted her chin higher.

"No, thank you." She glanced at the twins out of the

corner of her eyes. "I'd prefer to go inside and recuperate. It was a long trip."

Kayden hopped off the trailer and settled his hands on his hips. "She talks funny."

Margaret's brown eyes flashed.

"Dresses funny, too," Jayden said, climbing down.

"That's enough, boys." Jen stepped between them when she saw Margaret's chin begin to wobble. "I think your aunt Cissy would expect you to be more polite to a guest."

They both dropped their heads, studying the scuffed toes of their boots.

Margaret's eyes filled to the brim and she spun away, snatching at the handle of one of her bags. She couldn't manage to lift it so she dragged it through the dirt behind her instead.

"What's going on here?" Dominic rounded the truck and cast a stern eye on the boys.

They squirmed and Kayden peeked up from beneath his lashes. "Sorry, Uncle Dominic."

"Yeah. Me, too," Jayden added.

"Wait, Margaret." Colt bent and reached for her bag. "Let me get that."

"No, thank you." His sister scrubbed the back of her hand over her cheeks and stomped off, dragging the case behind her. "I can do it myself."

Colt frowned as she struggled across the lawn to the porch steps, her bulky bag flattening the lush blades of grass along the way. His shoulders sagged and the shadows darkening his expression deepened.

Jen cringed. Colt wanted so badly for this to work. For this visit to restore his relationship with Margaret.

But the outlook was grim and she didn't have the heart to tell him.

She glanced up at the large house and sighed. Margaret had a point, though. It was past time for some private recuperation. She and Colt both needed it.

"After I unload Diamond, why don't we go in, too?" Jen asked, nodding at Colt. "Get settled in our rooms and turn in early? I think we could use some rest."

"Yeah." Dominic cleared his throat and shifted his stance. "About that."

Jen's eyes shot to his face. His grin widened.

"We had a bigger crowd than I expected. There's only one guest room available." Dominic held up a hand. "But I don't consider y'all guests, anyway. You're both family. Colt's chosen to take the smaller guest room and I'm setting you up in a larger family room in the main house."

"That sounds great. Thanks." Jen shrugged and smiled. "Where's Margaret staying? Family floor, too?"

Dominic nodded. "Yep. With you."

Jen's smile froze, a nervous tick forming in the corner of her eye. "Great."

NOTHING WAS GOING according to Colt's plan. Barely twenty-four hours after arriving at Raintree, he was beginning to believe he'd made a grave mistake.

He knuckled his hat higher on his forehead and wiped the sweat from his brow. At his side stood Margaret, squinting against the sun's glare and wringing her skirt with both hands. They watched as Jen rode Diamond across the grassy field in front of them.

Though he tried to avoid it, Colt found himself focusing on the graceful way Jen moved with the horse.

Each tap of her heel drew his eyes to the curves of her legs and every lift of her wavy hair in the breeze made him long to run his fingers through the fiery strands.

He shoved his hands in his pockets, stilling the desire stirring within him. His attention should be on Margaret right now. Not on Jen.

"Diamond's big but he's gentle," Jen called, nudging the quarter horse with her heels and walking him farther out. "See, Margaret? He'll do anything I ask."

Colt's sister looked down and edged closer to the fence. Wisps of hair stuck to her sweaty cheeks and her fair skin had turned red. The short-sleeved blouse and knee-length skirt she wore did little to block the strong afternoon rays.

From what Colt had gathered at the mansion, she spent a lot of time indoors. And she'd remained outside for the majority of her first day at Raintree. He hadn't even thought about a hat or sunscreen. He'd been too busy thinking about Jen.

Colt frowned. *Strike one for big brother.*

"You don't have to ride if you don't want to," he said. "It was just an idea."

One of many he'd had that failed. And one Jen had tried to talk him out of. He glanced at Jen and shook his head.

No need to drag this out. Margaret had made it clear all day that she wasn't interested in anything other than holing up in the guest room. She'd rejected every suggestion he'd made for entertainment, offering either a polite excuse or silent refusal.

"It's okay, Margaret." Jen threw her leg over Diamond's back and hopped down, her boots sloshing on the muddy ground as she led the horse toward them.

It had rained hard last night after they'd retired. Rained for three hours. Colt had counted. Unable to sleep, he'd slumped in a chair by the window and listened to it pound the roof. Had even been grateful for it at the time. The sharp cracks of thunder and blinding flashes of lightning had silenced his thoughts. Ones that involved fears of failing Margaret and guilt over keeping Jen from the circuit.

Jen trudged closer, her eyes heavy. A knot of unease formed in Colt's chest. It looked as though she'd got as little sleep as he had. If he had to guess, he'd say Margaret's snoring had probably been just as loud in the guest room as it had been in the truck during the journey here.

He longed to reach out and tug Jen close. Slide his hands over her back and press his lips to her silky hair. But that would only increase his desire to do more, which would threaten the fragile rebuilding of their friendship and steal his focus from Margaret.

"How about we just walk him around a bit?" Jen suggested, drawing Diamond to a halt in front of Margaret. "Let him explore the ranch?" She smiled. "You could help hold his lead."

Margaret watched the big animal for a moment, then bent over and brushed a speck of mud off the toe of her shoe. Just as she had several times throughout the day when she'd declined an offer with silence.

Muffled groans broke out behind them.

"We got other horses," Kayden said, trailing a hand slowly along the top rung of the fence he and Jayden sat on. "Some of 'em ain't as big as Diamond. And they're slower."

Jayden puffed a gnat out of the corner of his mouth.

"Yeah. We got ponies, too." He looked down, frowning and swinging his feet. "They're a lot slower."

Colt smiled at the world-weary note in Jayden's tone. It was clear Dominic had persuaded the boys to spend the day showing Margaret around. They'd issued the invitation first thing that morning, before gobbling down their breakfast. Then they had bounced their knees impatiently as they'd waited for Margaret to finish picking at her food so they could get started.

Unfortunately, that was how the boys had spent the entire day—issuing invitations in hopes that Margaret would respond favorably. But she never did. She'd just hung back and stepped carefully along the winding paths of the ranch as they'd toured.

"I don't mean to be a bad sport or nothin', Mr. Colt," Jayden said, squinting up at him. "But today's almost gone and we ain't really done nothing yet. We don't got long, you know? Spring break won't last for forever."

"Yeah." Kayden untucked his feet from the lower fence rail and jumped to the ground. "School starts back up next week and we had every day planned out. We were gonna build a fort today, shoot the BB guns tomorrow, go to a pool party on Wednesday..."

Colt stilled as Kayden rambled on. One week. That's all he had. And he'd wasted a whole day with no progress to show for it, feeling even more removed from his little sister than before they arrived.

He closed his eyes, frustration making his muscles seize. *Strike two for lousy big brother.*

"We already got a bunch of wood for the fort," Kayden said, jumping over a deep mud hole behind Margaret and stepping to her side. "It's stacked up by the shed and Uncle Dominic said we could use as much as we wanted." His expression turned hopeful. "Wanna help us build the fort instead, Margaret? You ain't got to ride a horse if you're too scared."

Her head shot up. "I'm not scared."

Kayden smirked. "Yeah, right."

Colt cast his eyes heavenward. Perfect. The last thing they needed today was a mini showdown.

"All right, that's enough," he said. "Margaret's not scared. She just doesn't feel like riding a horse right now. That's all."

Kayden shrugged. "If you say so. But being scared ain't no big deal. She's a girl."

Margaret scowled. "So?"

"So—" Kayden splayed his hands "—girls are always scared of somethin'."

"No, we're not," she snapped.

"Let's forget about riding for now," Jen said, leading her horse forward a few steps. "Why don't I untack Diamond and then we can go in for a while and get a soda or something?"

"Go in?" Jayden cried. He climbed down from the fence and darted over. "You mean we don't get to do nothing fun today?"

An ache formed behind Colt's eyes. He rubbed his temple and glanced at Jen's dismayed expression. Her thoughts were clear in the lines of strain on her face—the same thoughts he was sifting through at that exact moment.

How in the world did someone go about appeasing three disagreeable kids? And why had he put Jen and himself in the position of having to do it?

"Yep," Kayden grumbled. "We gotta go in because Margaret's too scared to do anything."

"I'm not scared," she retorted.

"Yeah, you are. 'Cause you're a girl. All girls are scared."

Colt held up a hand. "Kids—"

"That's not true." Margaret balled her hands into fists. "You're just ignorant."

"No, I ain't." Kayden flushed, glancing at his brother and whispering, "What's ignorant mean?"

Jayden shrugged. "I don't know."

"No one's scared *or* ignorant." Colt blew out a breath and headed for the gate. "And we're going in."

"I'll ride him."

Colt stopped and glanced over his shoulder. Margaret dragged her hands over her skirt and took an unsteady step toward Diamond.

Unease trickled down Colt's spine as he eyed her awkward posture. "I don't think it's a good idea right now, Margaret. You don't have to ride if you don't feel like it. We can always try again tomorrow."

"No," she said. "I want to ride today."

Her voice shook, but she took another hesitant step. Sensing her movement, Diamond tilted his ears in her direction and jerked his broad head toward her.

The girl started, then stumbled backward over the uneven ground and plopped into the mud behind her with a splash.

"Oh, no," Jen gasped, releasing Diamond's reins and rushing over.

Colt reached the girl first, crouched at her side and helped her sit up with a hand on her elbow.

Margaret looked down at her soaked clothes and submerged feet. Her shoulders jerked as she broke into loud sobs, and she covered her face with muddy hands.

Colt patted her shoulder awkwardly, eyeing her small frame and asking, "Are you hurt?"

Her sobs grew louder. He glanced up, meeting Jen's worried gaze. She looked as lost as he felt.

"Hey," Kayden said, kneeling at Margaret's side and touching her shoulder. "I didn't mean what I said. And we ain't got to ride the horses. We can go in if you want."

Margaret bent over farther and pulled her knees to her chest, her breathing turning hoarse.

"It's all right, now," Colt soothed, rubbing a hand over her back. "Everything's okay. Everyone has a bad spill now and then. We'll go inside and get you cleaned up."

She curled into a tighter ball, rocking slightly.

Colt's chest ached. "Everything's okay—"

"N-no, it's n-not," she cried, struggling for air. "N-nothing's okay."

Margaret raised her head and shoved hard at Colt's shoulders. He rocked back on his heels, bracing himself on the ground as she scrambled to her feet.

The girl's hair tumbled in slimy clumps around her red face, and her muddied skirt clung to her legs. She bent over and rubbed furiously at the sludge covering her shoes. The formerly pink sneakers were covered in thick brown mud. Not a speck of the bright color remained.

Her face crumpled. "They're r-ruined."

"I'll get you new ones," Colt said hastily, standing. "First thing tomorrow."

She shook her head and squeezed her eyes shut. "My m-mother gave me these."

Colt winced, his throat closing. He reached for her. "I'm sorry, Marg—"

"No." She sidestepped him, shaking violently and backing away. "I don't want you. I want…I want…"

Her gaze flicked from him and Jen to the boys, tears coursing down her cheeks. Another sob escaped her and she spun away, ducking between the fence rails and running toward the house.

"I didn't mean to make her cry again," Kayden said quietly, studying the ground. "I'm sorry, Mr. Colt. I really am."

Colt swallowed the lump in his throat and lowered his head, avoiding Jen's eyes. He was sorry, too. Sorry he'd left the circuit and put Jen in this position. Sorry he was arrogant enough to believe he could ever play at being a decent brother. And sorry as hell he'd dragged Margaret away from the only home she'd ever known, to surround her with strangers. Because that was exactly what he was to her. A stranger.

I don't want you.

Colt walked away, taking swift strides toward the bunkhouse. *Strike three.* This was the biggest mistake he'd ever made.

Chapter Six

Jen hesitated, shifting from one foot to the other in the hallway, then raised her fist and knocked on the bedroom door.

"Margaret?"

No response. Not that she'd expected one. Jen pressed her ear to the wood and strained to catch any sounds from the other side. Margaret's cries had finally subsided and only a few sniffs were audible now.

After the unpleasant scene a few minutes earlier, Colt and Margaret had taken off in opposite directions. It'd been difficult to choose which one to pursue first. The defeated slump of Colt's shoulders had intensified the ache in Jen's chest just as much as Margaret's stumbling steps had. And she'd longed to comfort Colt.

But Margaret's choked sobs had won out, leading Jen to leave Diamond with a ranch hand so she could make her way up to the main house. Hopefully, easing Margaret's pain would help relieve Colt's, too.

"Margaret? I'm coming in, okay?"

Jen turned the door handle and entered quietly. She blinked as her eyes adjusted to the darkness of the room, then focused on the small lump in the center of one of the twin beds. Margaret rolled to the side and hugged her knees to her chest, the sheet wrinkling beneath her muddy legs.

"Do you mind if I open the window?" Jen asked, crossing the room. "It's a bit stuffy in here."

Margaret flopped over and buried her face in the pillow.

Jen frowned. Seemed like every Mead she met was intent upon turning their back to her. The action was yet another similarity Margaret shared with Colt. They both pushed people away.

Jen swept the curtain back and lifted the window, inhaling the surge of fresh air. She stood in the stream of sunlight, lingering over the scent of honeysuckle and pine, and searching for the right approach.

What could she possibly say to a child who'd just lost both parents? And was there any use for words at all under these circumstances?

She couldn't remember how she'd been soothed as a child after losing her father. He'd died when she was five, but she'd been too young to really understand what she'd lost. Or remember him now.

His name had disappeared over the years, Jen's mother the only one remembering or saying it. Apparently, a small-town mechanic with greasy hands and few customers didn't stick in folks' memories too well.

Jen walked over and hovered by the bed. "May I sit down for a minute?"

Margaret's grubby fingers pulled the edges of the pillow tighter over her face.

Grimacing at the muddy footprints on the hardwood floor, Jen sat. "I've made a mess." She lifted her right leg and tugged at her wet boot. "If there's dirt in a ten-mile radius, my boots will attract it." She shrugged. "Well, in this case, mud."

Still no response.

"Good thing I've had lots of experience with it," she continued, pulling her foot free and laughing. "I'm a pretty messy girl, you know? So I always pack an extra pair and I've learned exactly what to do to get them looking good as new again."

The bed shifted. Jen looked over her shoulder to find Margaret's brown eyes peeking above the white pillow.

"Goo'...a'...'ew?" Margaret asked, her words muffled by the pillow.

"Yep." Jen proceeded to remove her other boot. "A day as warm and sunny as this, all you have to do is set them out on the front porch and let them bake until they dry. Then bang 'em until all the dried clumps fall off."

Margaret lifted her face, her muddy hair plastered to her flushed cheeks. "Does it work with sneakers?"

Jen pursed her lips. "Mostly. Sometimes they look a bit worse for wear, but that just gives them character."

Margaret glanced down and picked at a dried glob of mud on her knee. "Could you do mine, too?"

"Sure," Jen said, inspecting the girl's damaged shoes. "Might need to scrub them with a toothbrush afterward, but I think there's a good chance I'll get most of that pretty pink back."

Margaret sat up and wiped her eyes. "I could help."

"I'd appreciate that," Jen said. "Sometimes I have trouble getting the laces good and clean, but I expect if we worked together, we could handle it. And I got to thinking..." She hesitated, then reached out and rubbed a smudge of mud from Margaret's cheek with her thumb. "There's a lot more dirt, bugs and horse patties out here than you're used to. So it might be a good idea for us to go shopping tomorrow. Get you a pair of jeans and some boots, maybe?"

"Okay." Margaret sniffed, her brow wrinkling. "But what's a horse patty?"

"The same thing as a cow patty except it comes from horses." Jen grinned. "Poop."

The girl laughed. A real honest-to-goodness giggle that brightened her face. The gleam in her eyes and tilt of her mouth were so similar to Colt's.

Jen caught her breath at the sight, an affection she always felt looking at Colt welling inside her.

Margaret began untying the laces on one shoe and Jen tackled the other, trying not to show the sappy feelings coursing through her. Jen would be leaving soon and the less attached Margaret became to her, the better.

"Hi, guys," a voice called from the doorway. "Hope we're not interrupting."

A short, blonde woman stood in the doorway with a pair of black-haired twin toddlers at her side.

"No, not at all," Jen said, smiling. "Margaret, this is Cissy, Dominic's wife. You turned in so early last night, I don't think you had a chance to meet her."

"Hello," Margaret said, eyes lingering on the little girls.

"It's nice to meet you, Margaret. I'm sorry we didn't get to talk at breakfast this morning." Cissy gestured at the twin girls as they waddled toward the bed. "These two were cranky and didn't want to cooperate, so we didn't make it down in time." She laughed and glanced at Jen. "Can I still blame it on the terrible twos if they're not quite two yet?"

"Aw, they get a free pass for being so cute," Jen

teased, bending down to kiss one twin's smooth cheek as the toddler hugged her leg. The girls' raven hair and blue eyes were identical, making it impossible to tell them apart. "Who do I have here?"

"Gwen," Cissy said with pride, before pointing to the other toddler. "That's Grace."

Grace grabbed the sheet and pulled, scrambling onto the bed. She stood by Margaret, examined her bedraggled hair, then touched it.

"Ew," Grace said, shifting her attention to Margaret's face.

Margaret squeezed her eyes shut as the child's grasping fingers traveled over her nose and mouth. Grace gurgled, patted Margaret's cheeks, then plopped onto her lap, evoking another laugh from Margaret.

"I think Grace has claimed you as a new friend, Margaret," Cissy said, smiling. "Kayden has, too. He asked me to check on you. Tell you he was sorry for what happened."

Margaret shook her head, watching as Grace's small fingers picked at her muddy skirt. "It wasn't Kayden's fault." She glanced at Jen. "I…guess I was afraid of Diamond."

Jen squeezed the girl's knee. "A lot of people are nervous around horses. I can help you get to know him better, if you'd like."

Margaret nodded and reached down to steady Grace, who bounced excitedly in her lap.

"I was just about to take the girls down to the creek," Cissy said. "We have about an hour to explore before it gets dark. Would you like to join us, Margaret? We could help you wash that mud off, and then come in, grab a bite to eat and watch a movie afterward."

Margaret flashed an excited smile at Jen. "May I go with them?"

"Sure," Jen said. "Have fun. I'll put our shoes out in the sun, then tomorrow morning we can get started cleaning them."

A quick thank-you and Margaret left with Cissy, giggling again as a twin grabbed each of her hands and wobbled along at her sides.

Jen's shoulders relaxed on a rush of warmth. A child's laugh had never sounded so sweet.

After setting the muddy footwear on the porch steps, Jen put on a clean pair of boots and made her way around to the nearest guest wing. She heard the thump and creak of a truck bed being loaded as she rounded the corner. Colt's pickup was parked in front of the open door, tailgate down.

Moments later, Colt appeared, hauling a covered bucket. He halted at the sight of her, then ducked his head and eased past her, sliding the bucket onto the truck bed between two others with more focus than necessary.

Jen tensed. "What are you doing?"

"Storing water for Diamond." He spun and walked away, saying over his shoulder as he entered the guest room, "He didn't take to the taste in Longview last year."

Longview? Jen stilled. Texas. He was packing for Texas.

She followed him inside and closed the door.

Colt stood in front of the dresser, pulling out drawers, scooping up the contents and dumping them into his overnight bag.

"If we leave first thing tomorrow, we can both make

the next competition without having to break our necks to get there." He emptied another drawer. "I called Tammy. She's booking us some rooms at that same motel we stayed in last year. Cheap but decent."

Jen eyed the set of his shoulders and his jerky movements. She was so tempted to agree. To throw her own things in a bag and spend the next hour planning out the fastest route to Longview.

But Margaret's mud-slicked sneakers were busy baking under the sun. And Margaret was probably at the creek right now, splashing in the water with Cissy's girls, laughing and soothing herself with the knowledge that her shoes might regain some life tomorrow with Jen's help.

The wave of guilt sweeping through Jen overpowered her longing to abandon the plan and return to the circuit immediately. She couldn't break her word to Margaret or encourage Colt to do the same.

"Have you thought this through, Colt?" she asked.

His T-shirt strained over the thick muscles of his back as he lifted his overnight bag, then dropped it on top of the dresser. "We have to leave soon if we want to make the first round."

"What about Margaret?"

He slammed the middle drawer shut with his knee. "We swing through Atlanta, drop her off, then take a shortcut to the interstate. Won't lose but a few hours."

"Is that all?" Jen asked softly. "I think you stand to lose a lot more than that."

His broad hands stilled over the bag.

"I know I was against this," she said. "No one hates leaving the circuit more than I do, and if this is really what you want then I'm all for it. But I think you were right about Margaret needing a break."

"This was a mistake," he said. "It's not working."

"We've barely started and we've never been quitters. If we were to give up now, I'd think you'd regret it before we crossed the state line."

Colt shook his head. "I was foolish to think I could pull this off. She's doing worse here than she was there. You saw her earlier."

"Yeah. I did. I saw her have a healthy cry. One I suspect was long overdue. You're not alone in this, Colt. I'm with you. Dom and Cissy are with you. We're all ready and willing to help. But this won't work if you don't open up." Jen moved close, placing a hand on his back. "I think it'd be good for you to take some time for yourself, too. Take time to grieve—"

"I don't know what you want from me, Jen," he bit out, yanking the zipper shut on the bag.

"Just talk to me," she said. "Tell me what you're feeling."

"I don't feel anything." He shrugged off her touch, strode across the room and slumped on the edge of the bed.

"You just lost your father," she whispered. "I know you feel something—"

"I don't feel a damn thing, because I barely knew him. Is that what you want to hear?" He balled his fists on his knees, the knuckles turning white. "He was never around and the times he did show up, all he did was criticize or judge. Margaret and I were no more than possessions to him. Something to show off at parties. A way to pass himself off as a family man." Colt refused to look at her, staring over her left shoulder. "He was a cold, heartless bastard and I hated hi—"

His voice broke, a ragged breath lifting his chest. He dropped his head into his hands and his shoulders jerked.

Jen sat at his side and pulled him close. She smoothed her fingers through his blond hair and tugged gently at the back of his neck, bringing his face to her chest and cradling him. His strong arms slipped around her waist, squeezing so hard the painful grip stole the air from her lungs. But she held on.

"I'm sorry, Colt," she whispered, rocking him gently back and forth. "So sorry."

He didn't make a sound, but his body shook and he slid his face down, burying it against her belly. Her shirt grew damp under his cheek, her heart beating harder with every silent heave of his shoulders and renewed bout of moist warmth soaking into her middle. She paused every few minutes to wipe away tears of her own and held back as many as she could.

Finally, his hold on her loosened and he raised his head. He opened his mouth but hesitated, no sound emerging.

The bereft expression crossing his striking features stabbed her chest. She leaned in, dropping soft kisses over his forehead, cheeks and bearded jaw, hoping to lessen the heavy shadows hanging over him.

He looked at her then, his blue eyes welling, tears clinging to the ends of his thick lashes. She pressed gentle kisses there, too. The taste of salt touched her tongue as his eyelids fluttered shut.

His strong hand slid into her hair, palm cupping the back of her head and fingers kneading her nape. "Jen?"

The husky whisper had barely escaped when he touched his mouth to hers.

Her belly fluttered at the light, coaxing movements of his lips. A gentle throb began in her belly, then moved through her blood, clouding her thoughts but heightening her senses. His masculine scent enveloped her, and each stroke of his callused fingers against her skin sent more thrills through her body.

Colt drew back with heavy breaths, his gaze lingering on her mouth and a plea lighting his eyes. Grief hung thickly around them, removing logic and obscuring good intentions.

Trembling, Jen rested her palms against the hard wall of his chest. She should say no and sidestep regret before it had a chance to edge between them. Let him go; stand up and leave him to grieve in private.

But her body ached to comfort him. And her heart strained to absorb his pain.

She moved closer, sliding her arms around his back and parting his lips with hers. "Yes."

COLT OPENED HIS eyes and blinked, adjusting to the darkness surrounding him. A weak ray of light pierced the dark interior of the room. Gentle air whispered over his bare chest and he glanced down, breath catching at the fiery spill of red hair across his skin.

Jen. He closed his eyes. God forgive him.

His hands tightened around her, the graceful curves of her shoulder and hip filling his palms. The tips of his fingers tingled from the silky feel of her skin. Just as they had hours earlier when he'd unhooked her bra, then smoothed gentle circles over her back. When he'd unbuttoned her jeans and slid them down her legs, his mouth tracing her toned thighs.

He gritted his teeth, attempting to tamp down the enticing thoughts. Even now, his tongue drifted over his bottom lip, seeking one more sweet taste of her kiss. Wanting to hold on to her as long as possible.

His heart tripped in his chest, the jolt sending a chill through him. He shouldn't have done it. Shouldn't have kissed her or taken comfort in her sweet warmth. But her gentle touch had filled the dark hollow in his gut and brightened his gloom. And when her body had wrapped as tightly around him as her soothing whisper, he'd surrendered completely. He'd focused solely on the pleasurable throb in his blood and her welcoming embrace.

Colt held his breath and moved carefully, easing Jen onto the pillow as he slid from beneath her. A quiet murmur escaped her and she shifted into a more comfortable position, settling back to sleep.

Colt sat up on the thick mattress and dropped his bare feet to the hardwood floor. He rubbed his palms over his thighs, savoring the last hum of sleep pulsing through him, reluctant to leave Jen's side. But he forced himself to pad over to the window.

He pushed the curtains back and cracked opened the window to discover a chorus of croaks and chirps drifting on the warm breeze. The sun had almost set and dusk was falling. He and Jen had spent a little over an hour in bed.

He hooked his fingers on top of the window frame, dropped his head and leaned forward, stretching the muscles of his shoulders and neck. Sighing, he raised back up and surveyed the moonlit ranch outside.

Raintree's grounds were peaceful, the riding trails,

pond and wide, grassy fields empty. He could just make out the low lights escaping from the stables down the hill. The hands' silhouettes moved in and out of it, performing the evening duties, their laughter ringing in the night air.

He smiled. Raintree was more beautiful than he remembered. Every corner of it was full of laughter and comforts, the kind of supportive and rejuvenating surroundings he'd hoped would help Meg…

Margaret. He squeezed his eyes shut, gut churning.

At the quiet rustle of sheets, he glanced over his shoulder. Jen's knees drew up toward her chest, her red curls dancing over her back with the push of the breeze.

Colt crossed the room and reached for the blanket, tugging it up from the foot of the bed and drawing it over her. His eyes followed the trail of beard-burn marks scattered over her pale thighs, hips and breasts, her bare limbs shivering as he covered them.

That hurts.

Margaret's words from days ago returned. Colt shook his head and rubbed a hand over his face, his palm rasping against his beard. Margaret had refused his offer of comfort so abruptly that he wondered if she'd ever been hugged.

He cringed. Knowing his cold father, she probably hadn't. But their father had taught Margaret other things. She'd learned to remain detached and unfeeling to the point of not being able to stand anyone's touch. Least of all Colt's. Because in her eyes, he was an absent and uncaring son of a bitch like their father. And up to this point, he had been.

Still was, in fact. He should never have considered leaving Raintree after the first setback. And he should've been with Margaret for the past hour instead of lying in bed seeking comfort with Jen.

Colt sat beside Jen and brushed a strand of hair from her face. His hand stilled, a realization hitting him hard in the gut.

He'd never returned to the same bed after leaving a woman in it. Had always grabbed his things and left, never looking back or seeking anything permanent. But none of those women had been Jen, and he found himself wanting to stay. Wanting to sink right back into the mattress, gather her against his chest and cling to the comforting warmth he'd discovered in her arms a few hours ago.

Only, that would mean putting his own interests before Margaret's. An act that would make him no better than his father—a man who had chosen his career and a succession of wives over his children.

Careful not to wake her, he brushed a kiss across Jen's brow, then tucked the cover more securely around her shoulders. He grabbed his bag and edged into the small bathroom.

Flicking on the fluorescent light above the sink, he winced at the bright glare and studied his face in the mirror. It was so similar to John W. Mead's. The same eyes and nose. A Mead man through and through. The kind of man who never stuck around and always took the easy way out. One who would ship Margaret off to boarding school for most of her life. One who would pack his bags, load his truck and take off, leaving Margaret behind without a second thought.

You're more like your father than you think.

Colt raked his nails through his beard, the phrase cutting through him. He'd done everything possible to rebel against his father. Had left home for the circuit, refused to take part in his father's business and grown a beard to hide the features that looked so similar to a man he no longer respected. And by doing so, he'd become no better than his father.

Colt straightened. It was time to stop running. He may look like John W. Mead but he was a different man. A better one. A man who would live up to his responsibilities and put his family first.

He dug his shaving kit out, retrieved a razor and got started.

Ten minutes later, he tossed the dull blade in the trash and unstopped the sink, running a hand over his clean-shaven jaw as the dirty water gurgled away.

"Colt?"

He heard the bed creak, then shuffling movements and the light click on.

Heart stalling, he dressed quickly then stepped out of the bathroom.

"Colt—" Jen jerked to a stop in the middle of the room, her hesitant smile slowly melting away as she paused in the act of buttoning her jeans.

His face heated and he swept a hand over his cheek. "You don't like it."

She blinked and shook her head, her shiny hair spilling over her shoulders. "No. I mean, yeah. I do." She adjusted the collar of her T-shirt and cleared her throat. "I like it. It's just…different."

Different. Colt blew out a rough breath. Different like the strength of the feelings coursing through him. Feelings he'd always had for Jen but one's which had intensified.

"I'm sorry, Jen." Colt cringed at the strained sound

of his voice, his hands spreading helplessly in front of him. "I didn't mean for things to go as far as they did."

"It's okay," she said quietly. "I wanted to. It was…" Her face flushed and a small smile emerged. "I enjoyed it."

So had he. And if circumstances were different, her tender grin would be a welcome relief.

The hopeful expression on Jen's face made his chest clench painfully at what he had to do. Colt looked away, focusing on the flutter of the curtains over the window and digging deep for the right words.

"I think you were right about staying," he said. "I'd like to give things with Margaret another try and I could still use your help." He sucked in a strong breath. "I want you, Jen. But I need to concentrate on rebuilding a relationship with Margaret and I think it's best if my attention is on her right now. What we just did doesn't have to change anything between us," he stressed, trying to convince himself as much as her. "We can pretend it didn't happen. Forget…"

Forget the sweet taste of her skin against his tongue. Like warm honey. The soft press of her breasts against his chest. Like—

"We can forget it happened," he choked out, facing her. "Go back to the way things were."

Jen's expression dimmed and her smile vanished. "Yeah." She ducked her head and moved toward the door, her long hair obscuring her face and muffling her words. "That's probably for the best."

"Red?" Colt forced himself to root his boots to the floor and ball his hands into fists to prevent himself from reaching for her. He could endure her disappointment in him but not the thought of her feeling betrayed by him. "Nothing happened between me and Autumn. I left that bar with her, but that's as far as it went. And that's the God's honest truth."

Jen's hand stilled on the doorknob and her back stiffened. She stayed silent for a few moments, then asked, "Why tell me this now?"

"Because I know what you're thinking." His throat tightened and it hurt to speak. "And I won't be that guy anymore, you know? Not with you."

She looked over her shoulder, her features clouded with confusion.

"Your friendship means more to me than any fling ever could." He shook his head. "I won't risk losing that. I won't treat you the way I treated other women."

Her features cleared and her eyes turned sad. "But despite all of your good intentions, isn't that exactly what you're doing now? Pushing me away? Reminding me of my place?"

His lungs constricted, making it hard to drag in a breath. "No. That's not—"

"Let's forget about it, Colt. Just like you said." She sighed heavily. "It's getting late. Margaret's probably looking for us. I told her I'd take her shopping tomorrow, and you've got enough to deal with right now." Her face flushed, her tone hardening. "Besides, it's my fault. I knew the score going in."

Colt stood still after she left, listening as the spring chorus of night life filled the room, and waited for the familiar relief to set in. The kind he'd felt after every other sexual encounter had ended. The one he experienced when he was alone again. Free of obligation to a woman.

But it never came. And the hours he spent tossing and turning that night proved the emptiness on the other side of the bed had crept its way into his heart.

Chapter Seven

Jen bent, slipped the jeans under the dressing room door and wiggled them. "These are the last two styles in your size, Margaret. How are the shirts working out? Do you need me to grab you a few more?"

"No, thank you." A small hand shot out and tugged the jeans into the dressing room. "I think I found some I like."

Jen's shoulders sagged and she smiled. *Thank goodness.*

It'd taken an hour to make the drive from Raintree to Trudy's Treasures, which, according to Cissy, was the best clothing store near the ranch. It'd taken another hour for Margaret to browse the entire clothing section and the past hour for her to try on every garment within her size range. And this had all begun at nine o'clock this morning, after they'd spent the first two hours of daylight banging the mud off Margaret's sneakers and scrubbing them with a toothbrush until they were pink again.

Jen straightened and puffed a strand of hair out of her face, trying to keep the relief in her voice to a minimum. "Good. Come out and show me whenever you're ready, okay?"

"Okay," Margaret said.

The clang of hangers and rustle of clothing resumed on the other side of the door. Jen started for the chairs in the waiting area, a restless sensation buzzing down her legs. The nagging thought that she needed to get back to the ranch and spend some time with Diamond returned. It had been four days now since she'd left the circuit. She hadn't checked her stats or squeezed in a lick of training yet.

But Jen was surprised to discover the anxiety she usually felt about not practicing had diminished. That each hour she'd spent with Margaret—though exhausting—had relaxed her nerves.

"Just look at what I found!" Trudy, a pretty brunette with teased hair and big earrings, held up two cowgirl hats. "They'd go perfect with that beautiful blond hair of hers."

Jen shook her head. Hats? That'd add another hour to their shopping visit and delay her training even more. "Oh no, please—"

"Don't worry," Trudy said with a laugh. "Given the pile of clothes she's already put by the register, I can stand to throw in a couple hats for free." She looked over her shoulder and grinned, voice lowering to a whisper. "I think your husband's getting a bit restless."

Jen leaned to the side and peered past her. Colt shifted in his chair across the room, closing his eyes and leaning his head back against the window. Jen's fingers tingled, wanting to rove over the strong line of his freshly shaved jaw and trace the contours of his muscular chest. She wanted to wrap her arms around him just as she had last night.

Only, she knew exactly where that would lead.

Jen ignored the heat scorching her cheeks. "He's not my husband."

"Oh?" Trudy's pink mouth stayed suspended in a perfect oval for a moment, her perfectly manicured eyebrows lifting. "Boyfriend, then?"

Jen shook her head. "We're just friends."

Just friends, she repeated silently. That was all. Last night was a onetime thing. A moment of weakness for them both that would never happen again.

I want you, Jen. But I need to concentrate on rebuilding a relationship with Margaret...

She looked down and shoved her hands in her pockets, the pain in her chest strengthening. Colt had chosen to do the honorable thing and focus on supporting his sister. Something she'd promised to do as well.

Jen repeated her words with conviction. "We're friends. That's all."

Trudy giggled and leaned in, whispering, "Well, he sure is a handsome devil."

"Yeah." She forced a grin. That was something she couldn't argue with.

The shopkeeper's smile widened. "I'll just slip these to our VIP and see how she's doing."

Trudy swept off toward the dressing room, the aroma of hair spray and floral perfume trailing in her wake.

Jen rubbed her brow and headed for an empty chair, avoiding Colt's narrowed eyes as she sat next to him. He'd studied her with the same expression almost a dozen times across the breakfast table this morning and at least once every mile during the drive into town.

"You all right?" he asked, leaning forward and propping his elbows on his knees.

He'd rolled his sleeves up and the defined muscles

of his forearms were on full display as he dangled his hands between his legs. Hands that had caressed every part of her last night. Skilled fingers that had—

"Yeah." Jen cleared her throat, trying not to savor his spicy, male scent. "I'm fine."

He dipped his blond head in the direction of the dressing room. "Margaret getting close to finishing up?"

Jen nodded. "I think she's on the last round. We should be able to head out soon."

"Thank God for that." Colt chuckled. "I've never spent this much time shopping in my entire life."

A fresh surge of longing coursed through Jen at the deep tone of his laugh and wide smile.

She stifled a groan of frustration. He'd shaved. So what? The look wasn't *that* different. His eyes were still the same crystal blue she'd admired countless times in the past— without this strong a reaction. His features were still as handsome as they'd always been—no surprise there.

"I told you this morning that you didn't need to drive us," she said. "Cissy gave me good directions and I'd have found the place okay."

"I know." His mouth wobbled slightly, the smile slipping from the sensual curves. "I wanted to come. Wanted to spend time with Margaret." His voice lowered, his lips barely moving as he continued, "And with you."

Jen stilled. That was what it was. She'd never had a clear view of his lips before. And now she knew exactly how they felt when he—

She tore her eyes from his face and focused on the

floor, hoping he didn't notice the heat snaking down her neck at the last three words he'd said.

"Jen." Colt shifted, his tanned hand landing gently on her thigh. "I…"

The heat of his palm seeped through the denim of her jeans and trailed up her leg to pool in her belly. She tensed then pulled away, fighting the urge to lean into him.

He muttered a curse, withdrawing his hand and shuffling his boots awkwardly across the floor.

Jen gritted her teeth and stared at the dressing room door. Colt had touched her out of habit, just as he had a thousand times over the past several years. She was sure of it. And she wouldn't look for something more. Something a friend wouldn't notice or anticipate. And something she was ashamed to admit she still craved despite their agreement to forget.

Jen closed her eyes and blew out a breath. What a great friend she was. Lusting after a grieving man. Wanting things he would never have agreed to last night had she not pushed.

It was time to set this longing for Colt down. Put it behind her and get back to the business of racing—the one thing she should be focused on above all others. The success she'd worked so hard for was too precious to let slip away because of one night of weakness.

"We need to talk," he said in a low rasp. "I know I said we should put last night behind us but—"

"How's this look?"

The dressing room door squeaked on its hinges as Margaret emerged, strutting to a stop in front of them.

Grateful for the distraction, Jen scooted to the edge

of her chair and waved a hand. "Turn around so I can get the full effect."

Margaret did, then propped her hands on her hips and tipped her head back, her blond curls bouncing under her tan cowgirl hat. The blue button-down shirt she wore matched her eyes and the jeans fit perfectly with the aid of a wide belt.

"Ms. Trudy said it's authentic Western wear and that it's just right for staying on a ranch," Margaret said. She touched her jeans pocket. "There are rhinestones just like yours, Ms. Jen." She pointed a toe and turned her foot from side to side. "And the boots have pink stitching, too."

Jen laughed, unexpected pleasure bubbling in her belly and easing her discomfort. "They certainly do."

She had to hand it to Trudy. The brown boots with pink accents suited Margaret perfectly. As did the rest of the ensemble. And the proud tilt of Margaret's chin made every hour of scrubbing shoes and scouring Trudy's clothing aisles worth it.

"I love it," Jen added.

Margaret bit her lip and sneaked a glance at her brother from beneath the brim of her hat. "What do you think?"

Colt stood, his gaze moving from Margaret to Jen and then back as he said, "I think you look beautiful. Like a real cowgirl."

Margaret's smile almost blinded them both.

It took an additional twenty minutes to pay for the mountain of clothes and haul them to Colt's truck.

"I'm hungry," Margaret said, skipping to the tailgate and pointing at a diner across the road. "Can we eat there before we go back to the ranch? Ms. Trudy said they have the best hash browns on the planet."

"Well, Ms. Trudy hasn't been wrong yet, has she?" Colt asked, taking his sister's elbow and halting her eager steps as a truck swept past them. He held out his other hand. "How 'bout it, Red?"

He sure is a handsome devil. Jen's belly warmed.

Margaret smiled and threw out her hand, too. "Come on, Ms. Jen."

Jen hesitated for a moment, eyes roving over the two siblings. They were a striking pair. Colt, tall and muscular, holding his sister's arm protectively. And Margaret, her eyes bright and welcoming.

The sight of them stirred a strong rush of feeling in Jen's chest, but she tamped it down, forcing herself to focus on the training that needed to be undertaken when she returned to the ranch. And it wouldn't hurt to eat a good lunch before she started.

She edged past Colt's outstretched arm and slipped her hand around Margaret's. She felt the weight of Colt's scrutiny more than once as they crossed the street, the girl bouncing between them excitedly. They made their way into the diner and settled in a corner booth.

"There's so much to choose from," Margaret said, eyes flicking over the menu and knees bouncing under the table.

"Order whatever you'd like. If you're in the mood for a peanut butter and honey sandwich, we can ask if they'll make you one." Colt stretched his brawny arm across the top of the seat above his sister's head. "Though I'm sure it won't be as good as Jen's."

His gaze settled on her, his gentle expression warming Jen's cheeks. She grabbed her water and shuddered at how cold it was.

"I'd like to try the hash browns," Margaret said. "But they have grilled cheese sandwiches, too." She leaned forward, brow furrowing as she read the menu. "And they've got a chee-paht-el…"

"Chipotle," Colt corrected, grinning.

"Chipotle," Margaret repeated. "A chipotle burger. That sounds good, too."

"Chipotles are kind of hot," Jen said. "It might be a little too spicy for you."

The excited gleam in Margaret's eyes dulled slightly.

"I tell you what," Colt said, collecting the menus and tapping them into a stack on the table. "How about we order all three and share? That way you can get a taste of everything."

Margaret perked up. "Can we get chocolate milk shakes, too?"

Colt laughed. "Chocolate milk shakes, too."

The diner was a bit run-down but the service was top-notch. An older woman with graying hair and a wrinkled smile waited on them and took an instant liking to Margaret. She returned to the booth several times to top Margaret's milk shake off with a fresh squirt of whipped cream and regale them with more anecdotes about her grandchildren.

The waitress had just left them laughing over her most recent tale of Budd Jr. when the timer on Colt's wristwatch beeped.

"Switch," he said.

Jen dropped her fork, shoved her plate of hash browns toward Colt, then caught the grilled cheese platter spinning across the table from Margaret's direction.

Margaret laughed. "You almost weren't fast enough that time, Ms. Jen."

"Oh, I'm always fast," she said, winking. "But I'll be faster once I get back to training. Which is something I need to start on as soon as we get back to Raintree."

"For the rodeo, right?" Margaret asked. "Mrs. Cissy told me you and Diamond barrel race."

"Yep. And it won't be long before I compete again."

Jen's hands began to shake. She eyed them closely and tried to still the tremors.

Catching Colt's gaze on her, she gestured toward the ketchup on her fingers. "Will you hand me a napkin, please?"

Colt tugged one from the dispenser and pressed it into her palm. He frowned as he examined her face, and his fingertips hovered against her skin longer than necessary.

"Bet you can't be in the races if you're not fast," Margaret said, popping a fry into her mouth.

"Sure you can." Jen took a bite of the grilled cheese sandwich and ignored the churn in her stomach. "Everyone has to start somewhere. Other than training, competing is the best way to learn. You just have to be brave enough to try."

Margaret pondered that as she stared at the chipotle burger.

"Jen might be right about that burger," Colt said, reaching for his sister's plate. "Chipotle peppers are kinda hot. You wanna skip this one?"

"No." Margaret brushed his hand away. "I'd like to try it, please."

Margaret picked up the half-eaten burger and took a small bite, chewing slowly. She made a face and reached for her milk shake. Her throat moved with several hard swallows and a tear escaped her eye.

Colt leaned close, an anxious expression crossing his features.

"It's spicy," Margaret said at last, sitting back and smiling. "But I like it."

He chuckled and dug into his hash browns.

"Colt?" Margaret bit her lip, casting hesitant looks at her brother. "If I promise to try harder, would you help me ride one of the horses?"

Colt stilled. "I'd love to."

They shared a smile and Jen's heart turned over in her chest. She looked away and took another bite of her sandwich.

"Will you help, too, Ms. Jen?" Margaret asked, brows lifting. "Please?"

Jen finished chewing and swallowed, thinking of how much she needed to resume training and how little time she had to prepare for the next race. Both great reasons why she should refuse. But they dissipated at the hopeful expression on Margaret's face.

She nodded slowly and conjured up a smile. "Of course."

The pleasure lighting Colt's blue eyes stole Jen's breath and threatened to melt her into a puddle right there in the booth.

The timer went off again and he dropped his fork, shouting, "Switch."

They slid their plates counterclockwise around the table, laughing. Jen took a bite of the chipotle burger and stole a quick glance at Colt. The lines of strain on his face had eased and the sadness that had fallen over him seemed to be lifting.

Her gaze clung to his chiseled jaw as he drank. She followed his broad hand as he lowered the glass to the table, his blunt fingertips drifting lazily through the condensation. The slow movements were so similar to the gentle touches he'd swept across her skin last night.

Colt glanced up and caught her stare, his blue eyes peering into hers, then lowering to her mouth and lingering.

The heat in his expression intensified Jen's craving to touch him again. The need to feel his mouth trailing down her neck and over her breasts. To welcome the sculpted weight of his body edging between her thighs, pressing her hips into the mattress.

Jen took another bite of the burger and avoided Colt's gaze, the heat of the chipotles nothing compared to the blaze of desire spiraling through her. It was best to put last night behind her. To forget. But Jen was beginning to wonder if she could. Or—even worse—if she really wanted to.

"HORSES CAN SMELL FEAR, you know."

Colt tightened the cinch on the saddle, then straightened and glanced over his shoulder. Jayden sat astride a small mare, holding the reins with one hand and fanning away gnats with his hat. The late afternoon sun blazed overhead and sweat and humidity attracted every mosquito and fly within an eighty-mile radius.

"Yep." Kayden nudged his own horse with his heels, walked him across the field to his brother's side and said, "They got a sick sense."

Colt stifled a laugh. "You mean they have a *sixth* sense."

Kayden shrugged. "Whatever." He leaned forward

in his saddle, expression solemn. "Now, I ain't trying to start nothing, Mr. Colt. I done learned my lesson. But Jayden's right. You might wanna tell Margaret about that fear thing. You don't want her climbin' up on Destiny and freakin' her out, do you? Destiny's gettin' kinda old. Maybe she can't take a shock like that."

"Nah." Colt smiled and patted the brown mare behind him. "She'll be fine. Dominic said Destiny has seen her share of nervous guests."

"Maybe," Kayden said, eyebrows rising. "But she ain't seen Margaret."

"Hey, Kayden. Look!" Jayden stood up in his stirrups, waving a hand and pointing.

Margaret and Jen ducked between the fence rails and made their way across the pasture. Margaret walked a foot ahead of Jen, chin lifted and shoulders back, her boots stomping with purpose through the grass.

Colt smiled. Seemed like scouting out new clothes and conquering a chipotle burger had improved Margaret's confidence. Well, that and the oohing and aahing Cissy and her twin girls had done when they'd seen Margaret. He'd barely brought the truck to a halt when his sister had hopped out and scrambled up to the front porch to show off her new look. Colt had left to saddle up Destiny before Margaret changed her mind about riding, stumbling upon the roaming boys in the process.

"She's got a hat," Jayden said.

"And boots," Kayden added, narrowing his eyes as she drew closer. "You said she got some jeans, Mr. Colt. You didn't say nothing 'bout her going straight-up cowgirl."

"Easy, boys," Colt said. "I invited you out here to encourage Margaret and give her moral support, not rattle her. You remember how things ended up yesterday."

"Yes, sir," the twins chimed.

Margaret arrived with Jen close behind, slowing as she neared Destiny and the boys. She drew to a halt and the confidence in her expression faded as she examined the horse.

"Hey, Margaret," Kayden said, straightening in his saddle. "I like your gear."

Her brow furrowed as she squinted up at him. "My gear?"

"He means your hat and boots," Jayden said, jerking his chin. "They're cool lookin'."

Margaret's smile reappeared and she hooked her thumbs in the pockets of her jeans. "Thanks."

"We're glad you're gonna ride with us," Kayden said. "But what about you, Ms. Jen? Where's Diamond?"

"He's out roaming in the pasture with his buddies," she said, placing a palm on Margaret's shoulder. "I'm just going to watch today and be on hand to help if Margaret needs me."

Today. No mention of tomorrow.

Colt froze at the unease invading his gut. It was the same feeling that had taken hold of him in the diner earlier, when Jen had mentioned needing to train and return to competition soon. The nervous tension in her expression had unsettled him. And the possibility of her leaving Raintree earlier than they'd planned had made him reach out and touch her, with the urge to keep her at his side.

Jen had been right last night. He'd treated her exactly as he had other women by suggesting they return to the status quo and avoid a more serious relationship.

But how could he make a commitment to Jen without sacrificing time that should be devoted to Margaret?

The sun broke free of a stray cloud, lighting up the field with a golden glow. Colt squinted against the glare and traced the graceful fall of Jen's red hair with his eyes, remembering the pleasant glide of it across his chest and the feel of it between his fingertips.

He didn't want to forget last night. Was damned foolish to think he could. He wanted another night. Needed more of her. More of the intense connection they'd shared. More of her soothing touch and tone. And, though he knew he shouldn't, he wanted her to need him, too.

Jen tapped the brim of Margaret's hat, held up a pink helmet and smiled. "Ready to swap out?"

Margaret nodded. They made swift work of removing the cowboy hat and securing the helmet, Margaret inching closer to Jen's side and casting nervous glances at Destiny every few seconds.

"How 'bout we get you two introduced first?" Colt asked.

He took hold of Destiny's reins and led her toward Margaret, stopping a few feet away. Flies followed them and buzzed around the mare's back end, causing her to flick her tail in a wide arc.

Margaret jumped and moved closer to Jen.

Colt released the reins and walked over, lowering to his haunches in front of Margaret. "You sure you want to do this? There are a lot of other things we can do instead."

Margaret glanced over his shoulder at the boys, then back at Destiny. "I—" Her voice broke, a thread of fear straining it, but she continued, "I want to try."

Jen gathered Margaret's long curls in her hands, sweeping them over the girl's shoulders and bending to whisper in her ear, "We'll be right here with you. Colt and I both. We won't let anything happen to you."

A gentle heat lit in Colt's chest as he listened. The word *we* had never sounded so sweet.

"But what if…" Margaret's voice faded and her face paled. "What if Destiny gets scared or something? She might…"

"Destiny's done this a lot," Jen said. "She's calm. And she's trained to be patient."

"But what if I mess up?" Margaret's eyes widened. "What if I can't hold on?"

"Colt will be right there the whole time," Jen said. "He won't let you fall."

"Have you ever fallen?" Margaret blinked up at Jen, breathing quickly.

"Twice." A smile flitted across her lips. "But I was riding recklessly both times and lost my focus. Colt helped keep me safe." She brushed Margaret's bangs back, tucking them under the helmet. "It doesn't happen as often as you might think. And I promise Colt won't let that happen to you."

Colt glanced up at Jen, chest swelling at the patient look in her brown eyes and the gentle reassurance in her touch. She had to be itching to put out barrels, saddle up Diamond and hit the dirt by now. But she'd put her needs on hold for Margaret. And for him.

He tore his gaze away from the sweet freckles sprinkling her cheeks and the cute dimple in her chin, focusing on Margaret's wary frown as it dissolved.

"You ready to give it a try?" he asked.

The girl took a deep breath and nodded.

Colt stood and led the way over to Destiny, keeping track of Margaret's hesitant steps behind him. When they reached the horse, he took the lead and rubbed the mare's muscular neck.

"Destiny's real friendly and loves attention." Colt swept his hand over the horse's back. "It always helps to introduce yourself before you ride. Wanna come over and let her get a good look at you?"

Margaret crept closer and Colt waited as her eyes roved over Destiny, starting with the horse's broad nose, then trailing down her thick midsection to her slowly flicking tail.

"She's big," she mumbled.

"Yeah. But she's safe." Colt nodded toward Destiny's muzzle. "Hold your hand up and let her get acquainted with your scent."

His sister raised her hand, stepping closer hesitantly. Destiny dipped her head and nudged Margaret's palm with her nose, nostrils working.

Margaret pulled back, cradled her hand to her chest and laughed. "That tickles."

Colt smiled. "Come closer and pet her."

She did, barely brushing her fingers against the horse's hide. After a few minutes, Margaret grew bolder, touching Destiny with her whole palm and applying long strokes along her shoulder. Destiny made a sound of pleasure and nuzzled her nose against Margaret's hair.

"She likes you, Margaret," Kayden said, walking his horse in a wide circle around them.

"Does she?" Margaret asked, looking up at Colt.

He nodded and gestured toward the saddle. "Ready to mount?"

Margaret glanced over her shoulder at Jen.

"Go ahead." Jen smiled and nodded. "We're right here with you, Margaret."

The girl inhaled and squared her shoulders. "Okay."

Colt helped hook her left foot in the stirrup, gripped her waist and boosted her up. He kept his hands at her sides as she straightened.

"All right?" he asked.

Margaret nodded jerkily, her small hands grappling for the saddle horn and holding it tightly.

"We'll just stand still a minute and let you get used to her," he added, slowly removing his hands and reaching for Destiny's lead.

His stomach churned as Margaret shifted slightly in the saddle. Her torso bent forward, her fingers scrambling for a death grip on the saddle horn. She looked so small up there on Destiny. So light and frail.

Colt shot a worried glance at Jen, his hands clenching on the reins. Dominic had assured him Destiny was the best choice for Margaret. But maybe he should've started with one of the small ponies no matter how big a blow to Margaret's newfound pride that might've been. Or maybe he should never have agreed to this at all.

"You look great up there," Jen said, issuing an encouraging smile. "Like a real cowgirl. Don't you think so, Colt?"

"Yeah." He cleared his throat. "You look great."

Colt licked his lips, his mouth suddenly dry. A familiar anxiety ran through him. The same one he experienced every time Jen positioned Diamond in the alley, preparing to tear around barrels at top speed. It was an irrational fear but he couldn't shake it.

"Wanna walk around with us, Margaret?" Kayden

asked, continuing his slow circle around Destiny. "We'll go slow."

"Yeah," Jayden said, joining his brother. "There ain't nothing to it."

"Wait, boys—"

Before Colt could finish, Destiny took a few steps across the grass, following in line with the other horses as she did routinely during her daily trail rides with guests.

Margaret gasped, a panicked cry escaping her. "C-Colt?"

Heart lurching to his throat, he tugged on the reins and brought Destiny to a halt. He reached up and wrapped one hand around both of Margaret's on the saddle horn.

"Hey," he said gently. "You just say the word and I'll get you down. You've done a lot today already."

Margaret's wide, brown eyes moved over his face, then settled on his hand. Her breathing slowed and she tugged one hand free of the saddle horn to clutch his. Her small fingers twined with his larger ones and squeezed.

"Will you stay right here?" she asked.

"Of course."

She sat up straighter and nodded, the sunlight gleaming off her pink helmet and golden strands of hair rippling over her back. "Then I'm okay. We can keep going."

Colt's chest swelled, a surge of pride rising in him at the brave light in his sister's eyes. He nodded and tugged Destiny's reins, guiding her forward slowly. The first few steps were rocky, but after a few minutes, the anxious set of Margaret's mouth eased.

"Wonderful job, Margaret," Jen called out as they moved farther out across the field.

They continued in silence for a while, listening to the birds chirp overhead and the ranch guests laugh softly as they strolled the grounds nearby. Margaret sat taller in the saddle with each of Destiny's steps, causing Colt's smile to widen.

"See, it ain't so bad," Kayden said. "You like it?"

"Yeah." Margaret laughed. "We're doing good, aren't we, Colt?"

We. That word again. And just as sweet.

The rush of pleasure sweeping through Colt caught him by surprise. It bloomed in his chest and pooled in his eyes. He blinked rapidly, clearing his vision to absorb Margaret's bright, adoring smile.

"We sure are," he said.

Colt concentrated on the warm press of Margaret's palm, the strong surge of peace enveloping him suddenly giving the word new meaning. One he had let go of long ago. Something he'd finally stopped begging for from his father seven years ago, when he'd left home.

Family.

His hand tightened around his sister's, the rhythmic pulse in her wrist fluttering against his thumb.

Other than Tammy, Colt couldn't remember the last time he'd touched someone with his blood running through their veins. And it'd been years since he'd laid eyes on a face with as strong a resemblance to his own. He'd never experienced a moment of solidarity as powerful and unconditional as this before with anyone...

Except Jen. For a brief while last night in that guest room bed. When he'd joined his body to hers and settled into her comforting embrace, her tender touch dissolving his grief and infusing him with strength.

Margaret's head swiveled to the side, her shiny helmet flashing in the sunlight as she called out, "Colt and I are doing good, aren't we, Ms. Jen?"

"Fantastic," she shouted back, waving from the other side of the pasture.

Colt craned his neck, peering past Margaret. Jen had turned away to lean against the fence, her curvy profile highlighted by the low-hanging sun and her gaze focused on an adjacent field, where Diamond frolicked with the other horses.

Jen's name hovered on Colt's tongue, the need to bring her attention back to him strong. He wanted to call her over to share the moment. Ask her to join him. Take her hand in his and tug her close to his side.

But he couldn't. Both his hands were already full. One gripped Destiny's reins and the other still clasped Margaret's hand tightly, supporting and urging her on. And at the moment, his sister's needs were more important than his own.

Chapter Eight

Eight seconds of being thrown around by an angry bull had always taken a toll on Colt. But it was nothing compared to the four hours he'd spent waiting for Margaret to return safely from a neighbor's mid-morning pool party.

"They're late getting back," Colt said, hopping off the lowered tailgate of his truck.

He walked to the middle of Raintree's dirt driveway and peered down the winding lane, hoping to catch a glimpse of a truck emerging over the hill. A strong breeze swept across the grounds, spiraling up dust, then blowing through the long blades of grass in the fields.

"Kayden and Jayden have the ability to make anyone late," Dominic said, leaning against the side of the truck. "They've perfected it into an art form." He crunched into a large apple, chewed then swallowed before adding, "The Grangers may be our closest neighbors, but they're miles from here and they've got five kids of their own, plus however many children they invited to this party. That's enough to throw anyone's time off. Logan would've called if anything serious had happened. The kids are fine."

Colt nodded. Dominic's brother, Logan, was the most

responsible man on the planet and he'd offered to pick the kids up on the way back from town. Logically, Colt should have nothing to worry about. Emotionally, however, well…that was a different story.

After a full afternoon of riding Destiny yesterday, Margaret had played cards with the boys, then stayed up late to watch a movie. She'd settled in between Colt and Jen on the couch and laughed often. But the long day had caught up with her, causing her blond head to tip onto Colt's chest and her snores to overpower the TV.

Colt rubbed a palm over the base of his throat, recalling the soft press of Margaret's hair as she'd slept. "Even if you know they're okay, don't you still worry about the boys when you're not with them?"

"Hell, yeah. Every day. Why else did you think Cissy and I took up residence out here a half hour ago?" Dominic asked, taking another bite of the apple. "Worrying is just part of being a parent. Part of wanting to keep your family safe. But wearing a hole in the driveway isn't gonna get 'em here any faster. Work's about the only thing that helps ease the stress while I'm waiting." His smile was only half-joking. "You given any more thought to my offer? 'Cause that'd keep your mind busy."

Colt ducked his head and looked away, focusing on the driveway again. It was nothing unusual for Dominic to reference his proposal that Colt partner up with him and Logan and invest in bulls. He'd mentioned it every time Colt visited over the past two years, and again when he'd arrived at Raintree with Margaret and Jen.

Dominic had given up bull riding years ago for Cissy and the boys, and had never looked back. But Colt knew Dominic still harbored a love for the sport. And Logan, shrewd businessman that he was, saw an investment in bulls and riding clinics as another opportunity for Raintree to grow.

"I've thought about it," Colt murmured.

He *had* thought about it. Much more often during this visit than he had before.

He'd thought about what it'd be like to slow down. Take more than one week off from touring the circuit. Give his body time to rest and heal from all the damage he'd done grappling with bulls over the years.

He'd also thought about Margaret. How staying longer would give him more time with her. Delay their separation and strengthen the new connection he'd begun to establish with her.

"It feels good walking across the dirt instead of slamming into it," Dominic said. "We'd be advising more than anything. Guiding newbies through the tricks of the trade. There's nothing wrong with slowing down. It's a hell of a lot more peaceful than dragging everything you own from one state to another every week."

The thundering of hooves erupted from an adjacent field. Diamond's white mane rippled along his back as Jen drove him around barrels.

Colt's mouth twisted. Jen hadn't slowed down. Despite their long day yesterday, she had saddled Diamond up at dawn and spent the entire day conditioning and bonding. Every time Colt sought her out she'd been either in the fields or in the stable with Diamond. And the only time she'd offered more than a one-word response to him was when Margaret had come to hug her goodbye before leaving for the pool party.

Colt looked down and dragged his boot over the dirt. He'd hoped after Margaret left for the party that he'd have an opportunity to talk to Jen. To try to discuss the night they'd shared and explain that even though he knew he should focus on Margaret, he was finding it difficult to ignore how he felt about her. He needed to know if Jen felt as strongly for him.

But would he just be causing Jen more pain by restarting something he wasn't sure he could finish?

Delighted babbles rang out, interrupting Colt's thoughts. Dominic's twin girls stood outside the fence with Cissy, watching Jen and Diamond. Gwen's squeals of excitement cut across the peaceful spring air each time Diamond executed a turn, but Grace was oblivious to it. She was busy doing her best to climb the fence rails.

"No, Grace," Cissy said, catching the toddler as she lost her grip on the second rail and toppled toward the ground. "You'll fall and hurt yourself."

Grace let loose a plaintive shriek, threw her arms up and writhed in Cissy's hold, her ruffled shirt rising above her protruding belly as she slithered free to the ground.

Diamond balked at the piercing sound, jerking his head and skittering out of the barrel pattern to trot in the opposite direction.

"Whatcha giving your mama such a hard time for?" Dominic asked, tossing his apple core away and ambling over to scoop Grace up in his arms.

Cissy smiled, mouthing *thank you* as Dominic bent to kiss her cheek before returning to Colt's truck with Grace in tow.

"All that hollerin' isn't going to get you anywhere." Dominic gently tickled the tips of Grace's toes, peeking out of her sandals.

The little girl's screams ceased and a grin broke across her face. She kicked at Dominic's fingers and laughed.

"There's my good girl." Dominic kissed her forehead and hugged her to his chest.

Grace laid her cheek on his shoulder as he rocked her from side to side, her blue eyes blinking up at Colt.

Colt shifted uncomfortably and looked away, but when he glanced back, the child's attention was still planted on him. She bounced in her dad's hold and yelped.

Dominic leaned back and smiled. "You want to visit with Colt a minute?"

Aw, hell. Colt didn't know the first thing about holding a baby. He froze as Grace's tiny hand stretched toward him, her fingers grasping for his arm.

"How 'bout it, Colt?" Dominic asked, leaning with Grace as she reached for him.

Colt held up a hand and shook his head. "Nah. I don't want—"

Grace cut him off, yelping in frustration and straining harder to grab his arm. Her face contorted.

Colt cringed. He knew that look. Temper tantrum time.

"Come on, man," Dominic said, laughing. "She just wants to get to know you, that's all."

Grace held her breath, her cheeks almost turning purple.

"All right," Colt grunted. "But just for a minute."

Dominic transferred Grace to Colt's arms, the toddler's bottom settling in the crook of his elbow, her hands grabbing hunks of his shirt.

She stared at him again. Silently. Her rapid breaths puffing in and out of her rosebud mouth.

"Hey," Colt whispered.

Grace smiled, baby teeth on full display.

"Say hi to Mr. Colt," Dominic directed, grinning.

"Hi, Col'," Grace said.

Colt's mouth twitched as Grace released his shirt then patted his cheeks. She leaned in and hugged his neck, the light scent of baby shampoo releasing with her movements.

A wave of warmth flooded Colt's chest and he squeezed her gently in return.

Grace lifted her head and chortled up at him, her bright eyes shining.

"She's got a beautiful laugh," Colt said.

A hand clapped his back. "Just one of those makes all the struggles of being a parent worth it," Dominic said. "As soon as you hear it, you forget whatever frustrations came before. That's another benefit to hanging around here. You're able to spend quality time with people you care about. Time that's not squeezed in between eight-second intervals and weeks of driving."

Grace bounced and babbled, jostling Colt's arms and pointing.

Colt smiled as he wound a finger in one of her raven curls, the softness of it reminding him so much of Margaret's. "What is it?"

"I think she wants me," Jen said, her long legs carrying her gracefully to his side.

Colt swallowed hard. *I can understand that.* He tore his eyes from Jen's shapely figure and caught a glimpse of Diamond being led off by a stable hand. "You finished for the day?" he asked, his hopes resurfacing.

Maybe there'd still be a chance for him to coax her into a talk, after all.

She shrugged and drew closer, rubbing a hand over Grace's back. "I had a lot more planned, but *someone*," she teased, tapping the little girl's nose, "broke our concentration."

Grace babbled in a high-pitched voice and threw her arms out, grabbing for Jen.

Jen tugged her gently from Colt's arms, then settled the baby on her hip. "Just what are we gonna do with you, gorgeous?" She shook her head. "You're a handful and a half."

"Tell me about it," Dominic said, his voice tinged with amusement.

Jen lifted Grace in the air and blew raspberries against her belly, causing the baby's laughter to escalate into breathless squeals.

"Oh, I forgive you," Jen said, settling her back on her hip and kissing her rosy cheeks.

Colt's smile slipped. It was a breathtaking sight, Jen cradling Grace in her arms, pressing light kisses to her face, the spring breeze billowing her hair out in fiery waves around them.

A tingle started in Colt's middle and traveled upward, heating his chest and making his eyes heavy.

He'd never imagined it before. What a child would look like in Jen's arms.

Oh, he'd known it'd be a given one day. Jen was a keeper. The kind of woman you married and stayed committed to for a lifetime. And a man would be a fool if he didn't want her carrying his baby at some point along the way.

But the thought of Jen having another man's child

hit Colt hard in the gut, causing him to suck in a breath between clenched teeth. For some reason, the possibility no longer sat right with him, and it sure as hell didn't fit the images he had in his mind. The ones that had formed the moment Jen bent to cuddle Grace.

The vision of a little boy with red hair just as bright and vibrant as Jen's, his personality as charming and feisty as hers, and blue eyes the same shade as—

Colt stilled, the realization fully forming. Blue eyes the same shade as his own. The child's entire makeup a perfect blend of his and Jen's best attributes, inside and out.

"Ah, here come the rest of the rascals now," Dominic said, tipping his chin toward the driveway. "Told you everything was fine."

Colt tore his eyes away from Jen, grateful for the distraction.

A large truck traveled slowly up the driveway, the rotating tires kicking up dust until it pulled to a stop in front of them. The passenger door opened and Kayden and Jayden sprang out of the backseat of the crew cab. Margaret exited next and her eyes were as bright as her smile.

"Guess what, Mr. Colt?" Kayden asked, bounding to his side. "The Grangers had a basketball hoop so it was a pool *and* basketball party." He paused, rubbing at his eyes as the dusty wind pushed him back on his heels for a moment. "We did one of those scrummage things."

"You mean *scrimmage*?" Colt asked, biting back a laugh.

"Yeah, that." Kayden waved away the correction, then punctuated the air with his hand. "But the thing is, it was mostly boys, right? 'Cause—"

"'Cause the girls didn't want to play," Jayden said, moving to his brother's side.

"Yeah, the girls didn't want to play," Kayden added. "None of 'em except—"

"Margaret," Jayden said. "Margaret was the only girl at the pool party that played—"

"Oh, hush up, Jayden." Kayden stamped his foot. "I'm telling it, okay?"

"All right, all right." His twin made a face, then bounded off toward the front of the truck.

Kayden smirked, shaking his head. "Anyways, Margaret was the only girl that played. And guess what?" He paused for emphasis, brows raising and mouth widening. "She made every shot she took and whopped every one of the boys." He hesitated, frowning, then straightened. "'Cept for me and Jayden. She didn't beat us."

"Yes, I did," Margaret said, her smile stretching from ear to ear. "I scored seventeen more points than both of you."

Kayden rolled his eyes and shrugged. "All right. She made more baskets than us. But she wasn't as fast as we were. *And* she didn't steal the ball as much as we did."

Margaret cocked her head to the side. "That's true."

Colt laughed and squeezed his sister's shoulder. "That's fantastic, Margaret. I'm proud of you."

"Thanks." She blushed, then skipped past him to greet Jen and coo up at Grace.

A door slammed on the truck and Logan ambled around to the other side, Jayden following close at his heels.

"So can we, Uncle Logan?" the boy pleaded. "It's windy enough today."

"Well, I suppose one early birthday gift wouldn't hurt," Logan said, grinning.

A tall, raven-haired woman slid out from the front passenger seat and ruffled Jayden's blond hair. "The kites were supposed to be a surprise. I bought them in town for the boys' birthday before we went to pick them up, and thought I'd hidden them pretty well." She laughed, glancing at Colt. "But I guess I didn't do as good a job as I thought."

"We'll pretend we didn't see 'em if you want us to, Aunt Amy," Jayden said, his expression dimming. "But it sure is a perfect day to fly a kite."

"Their birthday's tomorrow, babe," Logan said, kissing his wife's neck as he eased around her to reach into the cab. "And today's as good a day as any."

"Oh, all right." Amy's expression warmed as Logan emerged from the cab with a dark-haired baby in his arms.

Colt smiled. Dominic had told him that Logan and Amy had reconciled some time ago after a prolonged separation, and had had a child. Judging from the warm glances they exchanged over the smiling boy in Logan's arms, and the closeness they'd displayed since Colt's arrival, he could tell they were happy and very much in love.

They'd created the same kind of strong family Dominic and Cissy had made. The kind Colt found himself admiring more with each passing day at Raintree.

"Well," Logan said, cupping a broad palm against the baby's cheek to block the wind. "If we're gonna do this, we better get this show on the road while the breeze is still blowing."

Margaret, Kayden and Jayden squealed. They huddled together and pointed to various areas of a nearby field, each laying claim to a corner. Colt lowered the tailgate of the truck and he and Dominic unpacked the kites.

The women chatted and laughed, Cissy and Gwen having joined the group, and it wasn't long before Jen held baby Ethan on her hip with one arm and wrapped the other one around Grace, who clung to her leg. The babies giggled and bounced in Jen's embrace, basking in her attention.

Colt's eyes hovered on Jen, that warm buzz returning to his middle and heating his face. The feeling, though pleasant, unsettled him. He'd never imagined being this at ease surrounded by babies and kids. But the comforting family atmosphere made him long for children of his own and led him to imagine new possibilities. Ones that would allow him to provide the support Margaret needed but also enable him to build a real relationship with Jen.

The notion made him reconsider Dominic's offer. And it also spurred thoughts of a different kind of partnership.

One that had nothing to do with Dominic's business venture but everything to do with Jen.

"Don't let it get away!"

A laugh burst from Jen's chest, her lungs aching as she gasped for air and kept her eyes glued to the white string flicking through the lush blades of grass. She pumped her legs harder, running faster across the field and casting occasional looks at the colorful parafoil kite whisking higher into the blue sky. Colt's and Margaret's boots made swishing sounds through the grass behind her as they struggled to catch the runaway toy.

"We can't let it get away," Margaret squealed again.

Her voice faded more with each of Jen's sprinting steps. Jen pried her attention away from the string long enough to glance back at Colt. He nipped at her heels, but his breath wasn't coming half as fast as hers. And his grin had a smug tilt to it.

She faced forward again and sped up, ignoring the desire pooling in her belly, and focusing on the burning sensation in her thighs instead.

"Watch out, Jen!"

Colt's concerned tone swept across her neck, raising goose bumps that chased each other down her spine. She swung her arms faster, quickened her pace and kept tabs on the escaping kite.

"Jen."

"Wha—"

Her heel hit a gopher hole, twisting her ankle and stealing her balance.

Colt's caught her upper arm and pulled her, keeping her from slamming to the ground. But his feet tangled with hers and they fell, anyway, Colt landing on his back with her clutched to his side.

Jen lay winded for a moment, gasping for breath. The thin string snaked away with a whisper and the kite soared above the tree line. Each flap of its tie-dyed wings beat in time with the pounding of Colt's heart beneath her palm, and the hard length of his thigh against hers sent a wave of heat through her.

A round of cheers echoed across the field and Jen shifted her head to the side, her cheek pressing against the grass. The Slade family waved from their position on the far side, where the boys were trying to outrun each other, their kites flapping behind them, and the adults were helping the younger ones hold on to their strings. They were all smiles and good-natured teasing.

Laughter escaped Jen. She looked back at Colt, his sexy smile shooting a delicious thrill through her. "Seems we're the entertainment for the afternoon. And all because you were too slow."

Colt's broad chest shook with deep chuckles. "Now, don't blame it on me. You're the one that caused the wreck." His laughter dissolved and his blue eyes darkened as they dropped to her mouth. "Jen. I wanted to—"

A strong *oof* erupted from Colt's lips as a small body landed on his middle.

Margaret giggled breathlessly as she lay on him, blinking up at both of them with laughing eyes before she stated the obvious. "It got away."

Jen's breath stuck in her lungs at the surprised happiness on Colt's face.

He lifted his big hands and swept his sister's hair away from her fluttering lashes and laughing mouth. "It sure did."

Margaret propped her chin on Colt's chest and smiled. "Guess what? Mrs. Cissy said I can help cook supper tonight if I want to. They're making biscuits from scratch and she said they put honey butter on them after they come out of the oven." She glanced at Jen excitely. "You'd like those, wouldn't you, Ms. Jen?"

Jen nodded and avoided Colt's eyes, the diversion coming at just the right time. "They sound delicious."

"Will you come help make them, too?"

"Sure." Jen held up a hand and wiggled it. "But you're gonna have to help me up first."

Margaret sprang to her feet and tugged at Jen until she stood. "Will you come, too, Colt?"

He sat up and brushed at the grass on his jeans. "Yep. Just as soon as I help pack up the kites."

Margaret hesitated. "Want us to wait for you?"

"Nah." Colt waved a hand. "Go ahead, Margaret. I'll catch up."

"Meg's okay," Margaret said.

Colt's hand stilled over his pant leg as he glanced up. "What?"

"You know." His sister bit her lip, her cheeks flushing. The breeze shifted a wispy curl across her face and she pushed it back. "If you still want to call me Meg, that'd be okay."

The warmth in Colt's blue eyes and Margaret's shy grin caused Jen's heart to turn over in her chest. And for a moment, she didn't want to go inside. Or anywhere else.

She had a strong desire to remain standing in the green field between Colt and Margaret, skin heating beneath the glow of the sun and chest humming with the sweetness of the moment they shared.

Colt's chest rose on a deep breath. "I'd like that very much, Meg," he murmured.

Margaret's smile returned full blast and she grabbed Jen's hand and pulled. "Come on, Ms. Jen. Let's go make some biscuits."

It took about twenty minutes to gather the ingredients and mix the dough, and an additional half hour to cook them. But the frequent laughter and comforting warmth of the kitchen had Jen and Margaret staying for a lot longer. They dived into the preparations for the other dinner dishes, following the head chef's directions to the letter. Betty, Amy's mother, was the best cook in a ten-state radius and ran an organized kitchen. She was also a jubilant lady who gave snug hugs and kind praise for all their efforts.

It wasn't long before Cissy, Amy and Amy's younger sister, Traci, joined them. In two hours, they'd whipped up a spread worthy of a banquet. And by the time everyone was seated, the dining room was packed. The clink of ice in glasses and silverware against plates was steady. And so were the smiles.

The kids chatted nonstop about the boys' birthday and Logan told them he'd planned an outdoor movie night to celebrate the occasion. The kids approved, releasing delighted cheers and immediately talking about preparations.

The moment was welcoming and warm, but the family atmosphere settling over the table stirred an ache in Jen's chest. An ache that throbbed long after dinner was over and must've shown on her face, causing Colt's eyes to find her several times.

After helping Betty clear the table, Jen excused herself and headed for the door. The warm night air cradled her bare arms as she made her way down the steps, the crickets' and cicadas' rhythmic chirps pulsing around her. She hesitated, slipping her hand in her pocket and running her thumb over the edge of her cell phone.

"Taking a walk?"

Jen glanced over her shoulder. Colt stood on the front porch, brow creasing with concern.

"Yeah," she said, rubbing her palms over her jeans. "Thought I'd check out the old barn on the back lot. Cissy said there's a good view from the hayloft."

His features relaxed and he rocked back on his heels.

"That sounds like a plan. Mind if I join you?" He nodded toward the house. "I'm gonna check on Meg and make sure she's settled. Then I could grab us a beer on the way out."

Jen smiled slightly at the way his voice lingered over Margaret's nickname. He'd repeated it all night when he'd spoken to her, as though holding the syllable on his tongue to savor it.

"It'd give us a chance to talk." He hesitated, voice lowering. "I was wrong about the way I left things between us and I want to hear what you think. See if we can work out a way to move forward together. I'd really like to talk, Jen."

Jen bit her lip hard, but nodded. "Okay." Her voice caught and she cleared her throat. "I'm gonna go ahead."

The worried glint returned to his blue eyes, but he turned, heading back into the house and saying over his shoulder, "I'll be right behind you."

Jen took her time navigating the winding trail to the old barn. The moon was full and its white glow lit up the wide fields and spilled over the dirt path.

She spotted the large barn at the end of the trail, its angular shape outlined against the backdrop of stars. The spring sun had set, but the bright night sky highlighted the building and surrounding grounds with soft light.

Weathered wood squeaked on its hinges as she pushed the barn door open. Jen inhaled the sweet scent of hay and musty aroma of age hanging in the air. She climbed the rickety ladder, hitching her legs carefully over gaps left by missing rungs, then settled onto a pile of loose hay at the edge of the loft.

She tugged her cell phone from her pocket and dialed, holding her breath until the long succession of rings stopped.

"Hello?"

The voice droning over the line was hoarse with sleep and tinged with irritation.

Jen sat up straighter. "Hi, Mom."

A beat of silence was followed by a rustling sound. "Jen? What's happened? Are you all right?"

"I'm fine, Mom. Nothing's happened."

Jen swung her legs nervously, bumping the back of her calves against the loft's ledge. A fresh wave of shame swept through her. She couldn't blame her mom for the anxious reaction. It'd been over three years since she'd last called her. And calling, then almost immediately saying goodbye each time, had eventually become too painful to continue. So she'd stopped phoning altogether.

"I just…" Jen pulled in a shaky breath. "I just wanted to hear your voice."

Nora's sigh drifted over the phone. "I'm glad to hear your voice, too. But you scare me to death calling this time of night, Jen."

Jen clutched the phone tighter, her stomach churning. It'd been late the night the call had come years ago, notifying Jen's mother that her husband had been in a car accident. Jen couldn't remember much from that night, she'd been so young. But she did recall how hard her mother's fingers had trembled when she'd buttoned Jen's coat and hustled her outside to make the trip to the hospital.

"I know," Jen said, guilt gnawing at her insides. "I'm sorry. I just thought I'd check in. See how you're doing."

"I'm fine," Nora said, her tone hard and heavy with the grit of tough living. "Always am. Where are you?"

"Back in Georgia." Jen hesitated. "I'm taking a break from the circuit."

"A permanent break?" Her mom's tone lifted. "Are you coming home?"

"No." Jen forced out the words. "I'm just helping out a—" she swallowed hard "—a friend for a few days. Then I'm going back. So I won't have time to visit, but I promise I will once this tour is over."

Nora was silent for a moment before saying, "You've been roaming the road for a long time now, Jen. Whatever it is you're looking for, you're not going to find it out there. Thought you'd have learned that by now."

Jen stilled, reminding herself of the rewards all the hard work would eventually bring.

"I'm an athlete, Mom. If I want to be successful, I have to make sacrifices. Traveling is just part of the life."

"I suppose. But I still think you do too much of it," Nora said softly. "The girls asked about you the other day. They look for you on the box from time to time."

The girls. Jen smiled. The women that bused tables with her mother had always gotten a kick out of her rodeo tales during her rare visits home. And "the box" was an old, beat-up TV barely clinging to the wall above the bar at The Greasy Spoon.

"Tell them to keep watching," Jen said. "Because they're going to see me win a title soon."

"Jen, how long are you going to do this?" Her mom's voice gentled. "I know I'm hard on you, but I keep at you because I love you. You've wasted years already, and if you're not careful you're going to use up the best ones you've got left chasing something that will never happen—"

"It *will* happen," Jen said. "I'm good at what I do and I'm going to win big soon."

"There's an opening at the diner. I could put in a good word for you."

"I'm not coming back to Hollow Rock to break my back wiping scraps off dirty tables and trying to live off crumpled dollar bills like—"

Jen clamped her mouth shut and closed her eyes, dismay heating her face.

"Like me, you mean?"

Her shoulders slumped. "I'm so sorry, Mom. I didn't mean it that way," she whispered. "But please try to understand. It's just…you know nothing's ever come easy for me. Except racing. It's the only thing I've ever been any good at." Her throat tightened. "I'm a joke in Hollow Rock. But on the circuit, Diamond and I shine, Mom. We stand out. I'm someone important that people notice and remember. Someone you can be proud of. And when I win, I'll be able to take care of both of us. I'll be able to get you out of Hollow Rock."

"I've been proud of you every day of your life, Jen. And I'm doing fine here. I've never needed anything more than what I got right now. Except for maybe seeing my daughter more often." Her voice turned brusque. "I gotta go. I'm working the graveyard shift tonight and a double tomorrow. I need to snag sleep when I can. Be careful out there."

"Mom?" Jen clutched the phone harder, straining to hear something other than silence, her vision blurring. "You and the girls keep watching the box, okay? You're going to see me soon."

Nora's voice broke on her next words. "I'd rather see you in person, Jen."

The phone clicked and the line went dead.

Jen looked up at the sparkling sky, the stars winking and the moon bigger than she'd ever seen it. Transfixed, she reminded herself how much more there was outside Hollow Rock and Raintree Ranch. How much more to experience and how much easier she'd be able to make her mother's life after earning a good reputation and enough money to support them both. And how hard she'd worked to become someone that mattered.

"You okay?"

Jen jumped and glanced over her shoulder, blinking rapidly to clear the tears from her eyes and shoving the phone back in her pocket.

Colt stood a few feet away.

"Yeah." Jen faced forward, swallowing the lump in her throat. "Just touching base with home."

"Everything all right there?" Colt asked, sitting beside her.

"Same as always," she said drily.

"I can be a good listener." He nudged her with his shoulder. "Want to talk about it?" He pressed something cold into her hand.

"Not particularly." Jen narrowed her eyes. "What's this?"

"A juice box."

She glanced at him and raised a brow.

He shrugged, mouth twitching. "They were out of beer and it was the easiest thing to grab. It's grape."

They unwrapped their straws and drank their juice in silence. "Not as refreshing as a beer, but pretty good, huh?" He laughed at her nod and shook his head slowly, saying, "How things have changed."

Jen stilled, a trickle of dread creeping through her at his thoughtful expression. Things *had* begun to change. No matter how much she tried to forget.

Jen longed to lay her head on his chest again. To feel the warm swell of emotion when he touched her. And she longed for the feeling of family she'd experienced this afternoon. The carefree sound of Margaret's laughter earlier had her palms itching to grab another kite and chase it across the field again. To feel that surge of affection when Margaret smiled, and savor the comforting squeeze of her small hand inside Jen's own.

Jen frowned. It was Raintree's doing. The family atmosphere had stirred an ache of homesickness through her blood, prompting her to call home for the first time in ages. And the strengthening attraction she shared with Colt, plus the new connection she'd formed with Margaret, threatened to steal her focus from racing and make her forget…

Vegas. Tammy. All the years Jen had spent apart from her mother. Everything she'd sacrificed so far. How ridiculous she'd look if she failed now, all the hard work in vain if she quit.

She froze, realizing that Colt and Margaret had become more important than checking stats and training. More important than winning and earning a name for herself. And every day she spent at Raintree threatened to derail her resolve to return to the circuit.

"I need to compete," Jen said, dropping the juice box. "I checked the stats last night and I'm twelfth now."

Colt's smile melted away. "Twelfth's not bad, Jen."

"It's only four ranks away from not making the cut

for Vegas and it'll keep dropping the longer I sit out."
She straightened. "There's a competition in Springfield
Saturday. There's a big pot and winning would really
help me climb again."

Colt frowned and propped his elbows on his knees.
"The boys' birthday is tomorrow." He rotated the juice
box slowly between his strong hands, watching it turn.
"Meg's looking forward to the party and we'd planned
to stay until at least noon on Sunday."

"She won't miss the party. Springfield is only a
three-hour drive from here, so I can wait until Saturday morning to leave." Jen hesitated, dragging her
teeth over her bottom lip and wincing at the guilt rising within her. "I'll come back to Raintree Saturday
night and stay Sunday if you want. But after that, I've
got to get back on the road. I'm losing my position and
I need the wins." She touched his forearm, resisting
the urge to wrap her fingers around it, and whispered,
"You promised, Colt."

He glanced up, his troubled eyes roving slowly over
her face. "I did promise, didn't I?" A tight smile appeared and he reached out, tucking a strand of hair behind her ear and brushing his knuckles gently over her
cheek. "Okay, Red. We'll go to Springfield Saturday."

Jen pulled away and looked at the sky, trying to
ignore the warm press of Colt's arm against her own
and the pleasant sensations fluttering in her chest. She
avoided any further conversation, concentrating on the
race and the fact that Colt had agreed to make the trip
with her. And tried not to linger over the painful thought
of leaving Margaret the day after.

Chapter Nine

Flirty Fuchsia or Romantic Rose?

Jen stood in the middle of the bedroom, reading the label on a tube of lipstick in each hand. Flirty Fuchsia was more a light shade of pink than purple, so it was always a good fit with her warm skin tone. But the red in Romantic Rose matched her hair exactly and really made her lips pop—

Wait. Jen clenched her fists around the lipstick tubes. *This is a children's birthday party.* An outdoor movie night with mosquitoes, gnats and squealing toddlers running all over the place. It was *not* a flirty or romantic occasion. And it certainly wasn't an opportunity to tempt Colt into touching her again…

I was wrong about the way I left things between us and I want to hear what you think. See if we can work out a way to move forward together.

She sighed as she recalled Colt's words, her cheek tingling from the remembered feel of his fingers brushing against her skin. It'd been almost a day since they'd sat in the hayloft, sipping from juice boxes and watching the stars, but she still couldn't shake the effect he had on her. Which made it harder than ever to forget the night they'd spent together, and even more difficult to keep her distance from him.

On more than one occasion this morning, she'd found herself inching closer to Colt's side as they'd watched Margaret ride Destiny across the field, his sister's trust in the horse having increased tremendously.

And Jen's pulse had tripped every time she'd caught Colt's eyes lingering on her mouth as they'd blown up balloons for the boys' birthday party.

Which, she reluctantly acknowledged, might account for why she was so dang fixated on which shade of color would dress up her lips more, when she should be focused on prepping for the race in Springfield tomorrow night. The one that could make or break her ability to hold on to her spot in the top fifteen.

"Vegas," she whispered, shaking her head.

That was where her attention needed to be. Not on Colt. No matter how tempted she was to give in to his suggestion to reconsider their relationship.

"Wow! You look really pretty, Ms. Jen."

Margaret flicked the light off in the en suite bathroom and walked over, her eyes widening as they drifted over Jen.

A familiar affection stirred within Jen. She and Margaret had had a rough start sharing the guest room. The girl's snores and Jen's fondness for long soaks in the tub had caused irritation for both of them. But a pair of earplugs and a daily bathroom schedule had solved those problems the second day, and Jen had enjoyed Margaret's company the rest of the week.

No. More than that. Whispers and giggles with Margaret each evening had become endearing, and sneaking a glimpse of Margaret peacefully sleeping first thing in the morning had become a pleasant start to each day.

Margaret reached out, touching Jen's sleeveless turquoise blouse, then rubbed the silky material between her thumb and forefinger. "I like this," she said.

"Thank you." Jen smiled, admiring Margaret's ruffled tank top and dressy jeans. The pink butterflies sewn below the pockets matched her designer boots. "You look nice, too. I like what you've put together."

Margaret grinned, stuck her arms out and spun in a circle, her long hair swinging in a wide arc. "Ms. Trudy said it's authentic—"

"Western wear," Jen finished for her, laughing. "Indeed, it is."

Margaret stopped spinning and eyed Jen's hands. "What's that?"

Jen showed her. "Lipstick." She shook her head. "Not that there's any real need for it."

Margaret sprang forward and plucked the tubes from her hands, then uncapped each one. "Oh, I like this one better," she gushed, thrusting out the Romantic Rose and eyeing Jen's mouth.

Jen hesitated. Romance should not be on the agenda tonight. But the thought of sharing a few more precious moments with Colt was tempting. And the excited gleam in Margaret's eyes won out.

Jen faced the dresser mirror and swept the color over her lips, trying not to smile as the little girl poked her head in close, her face appearing in the reflection.

Margaret's brown eyes tilted upward, clinging to the movements of Jen's hand.

Jen finished applying the lipstick, rubbed her lips together a few times, then glanced at Margaret. "There. How does it look? Is it even?"

She nodded, smiling. "Can I wear some?"

Jen shook her head. "I think this color is a bit too dark for you."

Margaret's features fell. "Okay," she whispered.

"But," Jen said, digging out a slim tube from her makeup bag on the dresser, "I have a lip gloss that I think would suit you perfectly."

Margaret's face brightened and she took it eagerly, taking off the cap and smiling at the tinted stick. "It's pink."

"Yep. Give it a try."

Margaret stepped close to the mirror, parted her mouth and made careful sweeps across her lips, mimicking Jen's movements exactly.

When finished, she put the top back on and looked up at Jen. "How's that?"

Jen smiled. "Perfect."

"Can I have some blush, too?" Margaret's hands shot out for the makeup bag. "And eye shadow and mascara?"

"Oh, no." Jen laughed, squatting in front of her and stilling her hands. "Let's not get carried away." She squeezed the girl's fingers. "You're naturally beautiful. Besides, you've got a lot of years to wear all that stuff and it can become a real aggravation after a while. So let's not rush it, okay?"

"Does it aggravate you? Putting on makeup?"

"Yep," Jen said. "So does tweezing and waxing and conditioning…" She shrugged. "And all the other ten thousand things a woman does to look nice. Men have it easy and most of them don't even appreciate it." She wrinkled her nose. "The stinkers."

Margaret giggled and fiddled with a ruffle on her shirt. "Do boys like makeup on a girl?"

Jen smothered a grin at the pink flush blooming on Margaret's cheeks. Though she and the boys had played together as a trio over the past week, Margaret had begun to stick slightly closer to Kayden's side than Jayden's.

"Are you asking about a certain boy in particular?"

She shook her head rapidly, her hair spilling over her shoulders. "N-no. I was just wondering, you know?"

"I see." Jen tapped a finger under Margaret's chin and met her eyes. "A girl shouldn't make decisions based on what a boy wants. It's not important whether a boy likes a girl wearing makeup or not. What's important is whether or not *she* likes to wear it. Sometimes I like to put it on and sometimes I don't."

Margaret's eyebrows rose. "But you wanted to wear it tonight, right?"

Jen's face heated, her belly flipping at the thought of Colt's gaze lingering on her lips. She was suddenly overwhelmed with the desire to feel his mouth touching hers again, regardless of what regrets tomorrow might hold. "Yeah," she whispered. "I guess I did."

Margaret's smile returned. "I did, too."

"Well, that's all that matters then." Jen stood, ducked her head to hide her burning cheeks and zipped the makeup bag.

"Colt said he's taking you to a race tomorrow," Margaret said, leaning against the dresser and examining her boots.

"Yep." Jen put on a pair of stud earrings, then grabbed

a comb and made adjustments to a few wayward strands of Margaret's hair. "In Springfield."

"Is that far away?"

Jen's hand paused over a blond curl. Margaret's question was so faint she barely caught it.

"Not too far," she said, putting the comb down and ignoring the uneasiness in her middle. "Colt has already talked to Mrs. Cissy about taking care of you while we're gone tomorrow afternoon, and we'll be back after you go to bed."

"Can I go, too?" Margaret pushed off the dresser and straightened. "I won't get in the way, I promise. And I don't get tired very easily, so you don't have to worry about getting me back in time for bed."

Jen hesitated. "Well, that's really up to Colt. He'll know what's best."

"But if it were up to you, would you let me go?"

Pleasure swept through Jen at the thought of seeking out Margaret's affectionate smile—so similar to Colt's—at the start of the race. And the thought of disappointing Margaret made it impossible for Jen to refuse.

"If it were up to me, I think I would." She held out a hand, avoiding Margaret's eyes and flinching at how much pain she'd cause the little girl when she had to leave for good. "Now, are you ready to head to the party?"

Margaret took her hand and hopped to her side. "Yep."

They each grabbed a brightly wrapped present from the bed and made their way outside, following the luminarias lining the winding path to the old barn. It was an ideal evening for an outdoor movie. A warm breeze whispered across Raintree's grounds, carrying the cheerful songs of frogs and crickets. The moon and stars were out in full force and even if the luminarias hadn't been in place, the two of them could've easily found their way by following the laughter hanging in the air.

"Wow."

Jen's heart tripped in her chest at the low comment, and she glanced up to find Colt standing at the end of the path, his eyes traveling slowly over her, his expression lifting with masculine approval.

Vegas. Remember Vegas. Jen held her breath and mentally ran through the barrel pattern.

"Doesn't she look great?" Margaret asked, skipping up to his side. "I picked out the lipstick."

Colt blinked, glanced down at his sister, then cupped his palm to her cheek. "You did a good job. You both look beautiful."

"You clean up pretty well yourself," Jen said then cringed at the flirtatious, almost seductive note in her voice. She'd strived for flippancy but had failed miserably.

"Clean up" was an extreme understatement. She couldn't tear her eyes away from Colt. They clung to his broad shoulders and chest stretching a blue button-down shirt. They traveled over his slim-fitting jeans, the faded material hugging his hips and muscled thighs and creasing in the most enticing places.

"Thanks."

Her eyes shot back up to his face, and his sexy, lop-sided grin made her cheeks heat right along with her blood.

His grin widened.

"Ms. Jen said I could go with y'all tomorrow if it's okay with you," Margaret said, tugging at her brother's arm.

"Oh, she did, did she?" Colt asked, surprised eyes darting back to Jen.

"Yep." His sister pulled at him harder. "So can I go, Colt? I've never been to a race before."

He nodded, a pleased smile appearing as he examined Jen's face. "Yeah. It'd be nice to have you with us." He took Margaret's free hand, then turned to the side, bending his arm and gesturing with his elbow to Jen. "May I?"

Jen hesitated, the gentlemanly move one she'd never seen Colt make. One that matched his clean-shaven look and suited him far more than it should. She tried her best to refuse, but the tingling in her blood made her limbs move forward, anyway.

"You may," she whispered, shifting the birthday present to her other hand and slipping her arm through his.

His spicy male scent enveloped her and she pressed closer to his side as he escorted them across the open field toward the old barn. With each step, his strong leg brushed against her and his biceps flexed beneath her palm.

That tingling in her blood morphed into searing heat. It rushed through her veins and danced beneath her skin, making her long to slide her arms around him and press as close as possible. It tempted her to forget the race, stay at Raintree tomorrow and take him up on his offer to talk.

Jen pried her attention away from Colt and focused on the field ahead, admiring the setup. The doors of the old barn were shut and a large white sheet was tacked to it. A popular kids' cartoon projected onto the sheet from a machine propped on the lowered tailgate of a truck, and large speakers amplified the sound. Several hay bales were stacked into makeshift seating, draped with plaid blankets and arranged in a big semicircle in front of the barn. The balloons she and Colt had blown up were tied to each one and danced in the night breeze.

Guests had spread out blankets several feet in front of the hay bales and were propped up on pillows or seated on lawn chairs. A row of pickup trucks were parked at the back, tailgates down and pointed at the screen. Blankets and pillows were stacked in each and a red-and-white popcorn machine stood nearby, a steady stream of puffed kernels bouncing out of the silver cooking pot and piling high.

"Hey, Margaret."

Jen smiled as Kayden and Jayden bounded over, their blond hair tousled and lips stained punch red. They skipped to a breathless stop and gestured over their shoulders.

"Ain't it cool?" Kayden asked. "Uncle Logan set up the movie and Uncle Dominic fixed all the hay bales and—"

"Aunt Amy did the popcorn," Jayden added.

"And there's punch and cake and—"

"All right, boys." Colt laughed. "Slow down or your motor is gonna run down halfway through the movie."

"Thanks for fixing up the trucks with the pillows, Mr. Colt," Jayden said.

"Yeah, thanks," Kayden added. "Can we sit in your truck, Mr. Colt? Aunt Cissy said we could as long as it was all right with you."

Colt smiled and nodded. "Sure. There should be enough room."

"Oh, we'll fit," Jayden said. "Hey…" His blue eyes drifted over the gifts in Jen's and Margaret's hands. "Are those for us, Ms. Jen?"

She laughed and nodded. "Sure are," she said, handing hers over. "Happy birthday, boys."

Margaret smiled, blushing as she placed her gift in Kayden's hands. "Happy birthday."

The boys said thanks and shook the boxes before putting them on a nearby table stacked high with presents.

"So, how old are you two now?" Colt asked when they returned, squinting and tilting his head. "About six or seven?"

Kayden pursed his lips, amusement lighting his eyes as he clucked his tongue. "We ain't been six or seven for years, Mr. Colt."

Jayden shared a glance with his brother. They stuck out their chests, adopted deep voices and stated in unison, "We're nine."

They all laughed, then weaved their way through the scattered guests to Colt's truck, stopping along the way for popcorn and punch.

"All right," Colt said, setting all the snacks safely in the truck bed. "Ms. Jen and I'll hop up first and y'all can have the tailgate."

Colt climbed into the truck bed then leaned over, extending a strong hand. She slipped her hand in his, her palm tingling in his warm hold, and stepped up. She bit her lip as he grabbed her waist to steady her, his fingers tightening around her for a moment.

"You good?" he asked, trailing his hands away slowly.

"Yeah," she said, trying to ignore the flutters in her belly and taking a seat against the pillows at the back.

He nodded, then reached down and assisted Margaret up. The boys clambered onto the tailgate beside her. Once they were settled, Colt made sure the kids had their snacks before easing down beside Jen with a grunt.

"It's a chore keeping up with them, isn't it?" Jen teased, studying the three children's backs, their blond hair ruffling in the breeze.

Colt laughed. "I guess, but—"

Kids groaned and booed all over the field, drowning out the cheerful chatter of the adults, as the cartoon was cut off and the feature film was loaded. Children on the hay bales threw popcorn at the sheet until a new image flashed and the movie started, the booing quickly transforming into excited cheers as the opening music swelled.

Margaret and the boys joined in, whooping with the others. Kayden and Jayden tucked their popcorn bags at their sides and pumped the air with a fist. They whistled around their fingers, attention fixed on the movie and backs jerking with each of their movements.

"It might be a chore," Colt answered, raising his voice above the happy cries of the children and easing closer, "but it sure is a fun one."

A delicious shiver swept through Jen at the boyish tilt of his smile. No matter how much she tried to fight it, the magic of the moment slipped beneath her skin and lit her up inside. She closed her eyes, listening to the happy sounds of the children, and inhaled the rich scent of popcorn and butter lingering in the spring air.

"It is fun," she agreed, hugging her knees to her chest. "Kind of makes you feel like a kid again." She smiled and glanced at Colt, stilling as his blue eyes darkened.

"I wish I'd known you back then," he whispered.

Her breath caught and she cleared her throat before asking, "Why? So we could've raced our bikes? Or so you could've seen my skinned knees and buckteeth?"

Colt smiled. His hand lifted, halted in the air briefly, then drifted through her hair. "So I could've been the first boy to kiss you."

Something shifted in Jen's chest and settled firmly inside her heart. The phrase was softer and sweeter than any she'd ever imagined Colt would say to her. And she realized she finally knew the real Colt. An honest, honorable man she understood, had forgiven and trusted more than ever.

She melted beneath his touch, closing her eyes again and savoring the intoxicating feel of his presence surrounding her.

His lips brushed her ear and his gentle breaths tickled her skin. "May I?"

She tilted up her face and whispered back, "You may."

Her lips trembled, anticipating his kiss, but the soft heat of his mouth touched her neck instead, drifting slowly upward and brushing gently over her chin and the curves of each cheek.

His palms cradled her face, his thumbs gliding over her temples. "Jen."

The low syllable was coaxing and tinged with wonder. She opened her eyes to find him looking down at her, something new and different moving through his expression.

His mouth parted on a swift breath and he lowered

his forehead to hers, eyes clinging to hers, his broad chest pressing warmly against her. "I—"

"Mr. Colt and Ms. Jen sitting in a tree…" Kayden's singsong voice faltered. "No, not a tree…"

Jen glanced to the side to find Margaret and the boys watching them. The twins sported goofy expressions and Margaret's smile was dreamy.

Kayden tried again, keeping time with his fist on the tailgate. "Sitting in a…"

Jen faced Colt again, her cheeks heating as she watched his eyes slide shut in dismay.

"Truck," Jayden hollered.

A smack sounded. "No, Jayden. That don't rhyme with *g*."

"Well, you can't say *tree* because they're not in one," Margaret said, giggling.

Colt shook his head and groaned, his chest vibrating against Jen's.

"I got it," Kayden declared, scrambling to his feet. He propped his hands on his hips and shouted, "Mr. Colt and Ms. Jen sitting at a moo-*vee*. *K-i-s-s-i-n-g!*"

Margaret and Jayden cackled and applauded. Kayden took a bow, then doubled over with laughter, attracting amused looks from the adults nearby.

"Oh, Lord," Jen murmured, covering her face.

Colt chuckled and tugged gently at her hands, removing them from her face and threading his fingers through hers. "Well," he said, "that certainly ruined the mood."

Thank goodness. One more moment and she would no longer have cared if she returned to the circuit. Her palms grew clammy, her fingers shaking between his.

She tugged them free and shifted away, staring at the movie and avoiding Colt's eyes.

It wouldn't do to linger over the way he'd slipped into her blood, his gentle words and warm touch streaming through her veins and nourishing new feelings within her. Feelings that fought to dive deep inside her heart and take root, planting her feet and slowing her down. She needed every bit of speed she had to make her way to Vegas, and she'd worked too hard to throw it all away. But just for tonight, maybe she could enjoy these moments with Margaret and Colt.

COLT COULDN'T FIND the words for it. There was no phrase that fit the way Jen's arm had nestled so perfectly in the crook of his elbow or the way Margaret's hand settled so sweetly inside his own. But he felt it. It'd hummed within him the entire time they'd sat in the back of his truck, Meg giggling at the movie and Jen pretending to watch it. And that feeling stayed with him now as he escorted them back to the main house for the night.

Colt maneuvered them around a deep dip in the path, adjusting his grip around Margaret's hand and tugging Jen closer to his side. It was almost eleven, and the farther they walked from the brightly lit field, the darker and more silent it became.

He glanced at Jen, his chest aching at the sight of her furrowed brow and solemn expression. No doubt she was replaying the moment they'd shared hours earlier. When he'd asked to kiss her and had every intention of doing it properly. And thoroughly.

Only, he'd been too overcome by the surge of emotion welling inside him to continue. Had become focused on her eyes instead, peering deep and trying his damnedest to see if what he'd felt was reflected there. The need to know had overtaken him and the questions still hovered on the tip of his tongue.

Jen glanced up, locking eyes with him briefly before looking away.

Colt took a deep breath. He might not know which word fit these unfamiliar emotions coursing through him, but he knew for a fact which one didn't. *Friend* was no longer an accurate representation of his feelings toward Jen.

Hearing Margaret yawn, Colt looked down, smiling gently as his sister scrubbed the back of her free hand over her eyes. She'd argued hard against leaving the party.

"Yep," he said. "That's exactly why I suggested we call it a night."

Margaret blinked up at him and grinned. "All right," she grumbled good-naturedly. "I might be a little bit tired, but I'm not too tired to go to the race tomorrow."

He slowed as they reached the front porch, reluctantly releasing Margaret's hand and nudging her toward the door. "You will be if you don't get a good night's sleep, which is why you're gonna go straight to your room, brush your teeth and crawl in the bed."

"Okay." She bounded up the steps, but stopped at the door and turned. "Will you come up and say goodnight?"

Colt nodded, relaxing at the thought of his new nightly routine. Tucking Margaret safely in bed and whispering good-night had become the highlight of the last two evenings. "Of course."

"G'night, Ms. Jen," Margaret called out, spinning around and opening the door.

"Good night, Meg."

Jen's gentle tone sent a fresh wave of longing through Colt, but he waited until Margaret made it inside before facing her.

"We need to talk, Jen." He tensed as she slid her arm from his and took a step back.

"About earlier?" she asked, shoving her hands in her pockets and studying the ground.

"Yeah. That and—" he glanced over his shoulder at the soft light emanating from inside the house, where Margaret was preparing for bed "—other things."

Jen rocked on her heels and lifted her head. Her brown eyes lingered on his mouth and sparked a sense of urgency within him.

"I still want to kiss you," he rasped. "And more than that. I want to—"

"Please don't," she said, rushing the words out, her fingers fumbling over his lips, stilling them. Her whisper was strained with the same desperation that filled her eyes. "Whatever it is you're about to say, once you say it, it'll always be there. It could change everything between us."

He took her hands in his and kissed her fingertips. "Things have already changed. They changed that night in that bed, and I was a fool to think we could just forget it." His gut roiled as a new possibility formed, and he pressed closer. "Have *you* been able to forget?"

She shook her head, then turned her hands over in his, squeezing his palms. "No. But I just… I can't do this right now, Colt." Her chest lifted on a deep inhalalation and she gestured over her shoulder toward the stables. "There's so much riding on tomorrow's race. I need to focus. And Margaret's looking forward to the trip." She bit her lip, eyes pleading with his. "Please. Can we put this on hold for now? I've got to keep my head in the game."

Dread surged through him at the thought of her losing focus in the alley or while tearing around the dirt at top speed. "Okay." He forced himself to release her and move back. "It can wait."

Jen straightened, a heavy breath leaving her. "Thank you." Her slight smile vanished as soon as it appeared. "I'm going to spend some time with Diamond before turning in. We're still pulling out at seven tomorrow morning, aren't we?"

"Yeah. That'll give you plenty of time to check the place out and prepare." The tense lines beside her mouth reminded him how anxious she always became the night before a competition. "Take your time with Diamond. I'll get all the gear loaded early so you can squeeze in some extra sleep."

She nodded, eyes moving slowly over Raintree's grounds for a few moments. "It's nice here. But it's time for me to get back into the routine again." She stared ahead blankly, chin trembling. "I need this win tomorrow, Colt. It could make or break me."

His throat ached at the fear in her expression. "You're gonna do great, Red," he whispered.

Jen nodded and strolled down the winding path toward the stables. Colt watched until she disappeared from sight. He forced himself to turn on his heel and make his way inside to knock on Margaret's door.

"Meg?"

"Come in," she called.

Colt opened the door, a chuckle escaping him as Margaret, clad in pink pajamas, dashed out of the bathroom. She raced across the hardwood floor, then jumped onto the bed and snuggled under the blankets.

"All set?"

"Yep," she said, smiling widely and clutching the sheet beneath her chin.

Colt walked over and reached down, tucking the blankets around her as she giggled. "There. Snug as—"

"A bug in a rug," Margaret finished for him, laughing. She stopped giggling and blinked up at him, a shy look crossing her features. "Colt? Can I ask you something?"

He nodded. "Shoot."

"How do you know when it's the right time to kiss someone?"

Ah, hell. He winced, his face heating at the eager curiosity in her eyes. And it was his own fault, putting the moves on Jen like he had in front of her.

He rubbed his hands awkwardly over his jeans, then sat down on the bed, carefully collecting his thoughts. "Well. It depends."

She wiggled, pushing her way up from the blankets to a seated position. "On what?"

"On...lots of things, really." He gripped the back of his neck, kneading the knot forming there. "Like how well you know a person. Or the circumstances."

"What kind of circumstances?"

"Well..." His breath left him in a helpless exhalation. "You don't want to just jump into something like that. When you do it, it should mean something."

Colt looked down, the guilty heat in his cheeks snaking down his neck as he recalled all the random, meaningless nights he'd shared with women in the past. All the hearts he'd broken on the circuit. And all the kisses he'd wasted that, had he waited, he could've saved for Jen.

He shifted, facing Margaret. "Wait, Meg. For as long as it takes. Just wait until you meet the right person. Until you know for sure it's something you really want to do and that you're ready."

Her brow furrowed, confused frustration clouding her expression. "How will I know I'm ready?"

Colt stilled. His arms tingled as he remembered holding Jen, and his chest warmed at the thought of holding her forever.

"You'll know because it'll feel right."

He pictured Margaret years from now. Attending high school. Going to football games and parties with friends. Dealing with peer pressure. Dating. Making her first life-changing decisions.

A heavy fear lodged in his gut at the thought of his sister being alone. Without him to guide and protect her.

Colt slid his hands down her arms and squeezed. "I want you to listen hard and remember this. Don't ever let any boy talk you into kissing—or anything else— before you're ready. No boy who truly loves you will push you into anything. He'll wait, too. Because if he loves you, what he really wants to touch is your heart."

Her small teeth nibbled on her lower lip and she looked down, whispering, "But what if a boy never loves me?"

Colt sighed and smoothed a hand over her blond curls. "The right one will, Meg. Just wait till you find him."

"Do…" She glanced up, cheeks flushing. "Do you love me?"

Colt's heart stopped beating. It halted painfully right there in his chest, waiting for Margaret to smile again and give it a reason to start back up.

His throat closed and he swallowed hard before saying, "More than anything, baby girl."

Margaret smiled. "I love you, too, Colt." She threw her arms around his neck and squeezed, kissing his cheek and whispering in his ear, "I like it here. I wish we never had to leave."

That feeling returned, swelling so much in his chest he thought he'd burst. He wrapped his arms around Margaret and hugged her tight, wondering if he could manage to let her go. Questioning if he could load up, drive back to the circuit and leave Margaret behind.

If Jen won tomorrow, she'd begin mapping out the best route to hit the most competitions. She'd ask him to help her find the best opportunities to earn the highest rank in the smallest amount of time. And she'd expect him to leave first thing with her and Tammy. Just as he always had.

Unless he took Dominic up on his offer and decided to stay at Raintree.

Colt froze, unable to imagine standing still while Jen moved on without him. And even more disconcerted by the thought of her traveling on her own. Preparing for races without his encouragement and hitting the dirt without his support.

An uneasiness trickled through him. He could name it now. What he felt for Jen. It was the same thing he felt for Margaret.

Love. He loved Jen. As much as he loved his sister. And he was suddenly terrified that circumstances might not allow him to love and support them both.

Chapter Ten

Jen adjusted Diamond's girth strap for the fifth time, her fingers shaking so badly she could barely maintain her hold on it. She balled her hands into fists and tried to force the shaking to stop. Just as she had a thousand times since her boots had hit the dirt of the Springfield fairgrounds several hours earlier.

The hard rock blaring from the PA system increased in volume and the sounds of the crowd gathered in the outdoor arena at her back grew in tandem, scrambling her thoughts and blurring her focus. After a series of loud clicks, floodlights brightened the grounds, signaling the race would start soon.

Jen glanced to her left at the warm-up ring. Several racers were already walking or jogging their horses, performing turns and circles wherever space allowed. She should have Diamond in there already, but her nerves were too shot to start yet. And the last thing she needed was for her anxiety to pass on to Diamond.

Flashes went off by the alley gate, startling her. A line of reporters and photographers were setting up equipment and testing camera angles in order to capture just the right shots during the race. The Springfield rodeo was much bigger than Jen had anticipated. Despite being one of the smaller venues, Springfield's 1D race had enticed a high number of the best competitors, which in turn had brought out the largest crowd of spectators Jen had seen in months.

"You all right, boy?" she asked, moving a clammy palm over Diamond's broad shoulder.

He shuffled his feet and settled into a solid stance, attention on the other horses.

"You're always ready, aren't you?" She pressed her forehead to his thick neck and whispered, "We can do this."

But even to her ears the phrase sounded weak and ineffective. Her heart pounded painfully fast, making it hard to breathe. She'd gotten used to a bad case of nerves before the start of a race, but she'd never been this anxious before. And after Colt's attempt to discuss the change in their relationship last night, sitting so closely to him during the drive to Springfield had only increased her anxiety.

Colt's muscular form and handsome smile had always captured her attention. But now, something more pulled her to him. The rich tone of his voice had her longing to press her cheek to his chest. To hear his strong heartbeat and feel his words vibrate beneath his warm skin. To lie still within the safe circle of his arms and never leave.

All of which were the very last kind of thoughts she should be entertaining at the moment.

Lord, she wished Tammy could've made it to Springfield in time to compete. Or just to meet her. But her friend had texted last night to say she and Karla had already begun driving in the opposite direction for another competition. Jen had called more than once this morning just to hear Tammy's voice, but voice mail kicked in each time, which meant they were already busy preparing for a race, too.

Just relax. Jen inhaled, trying to calm the trembling in her fingers. *Focus.*

"Hey, Jen."

She straightened quickly, composing her features, and looked over her shoulder.

Laice Clements stood with her paint horse at her side, smiling.

Jen relaxed slightly at the sight of her friendly eyes. Laice had always been a joy to compete with. She was supportive of everyone around her, no matter how tough the competition.

"It's good to see you again," Laice said. "I got worried when I didn't come across you in Davie last weekend. I can usually count on bumping in to you there."

Jen nodded. "I couldn't make it this year. I took a week off to help Colt out."

Her friend's smile faded. "Word travels fast on the circuit. I was sorry to hear about Colt's parents. How's he doing?"

"Better." Jen gestured toward the stands surrounding the dirt arena. "He's here with his sister."

Laice's green eyes brightened. "Colt has a sister?"

"Yeah." Jen smiled, a pleasant sensation moving through her. "Her name's Margaret. She's nine."

Jen craned her neck, straining for a glimpse of Margaret's blond hair or Colt's wide shoulders in the stands. Her stomach dropped when she couldn't pinpoint them. Where were they?

She cleared her throat, scanning the crowd and adding, "Margaret's never been to a race before."

Laice laughed. "Oh, she'll love it. Once she sees you ride, she'll be begging for her own horse." Her laughter faded. "I'm really glad I ran into you. You probably don't remember, but I was competing in my first race when I met you. I was so nervous I could barely see straight, and you stood right at my side and gave me a pep talk before I hit the alley. I suppose it's fate that I'd see you again at my last one."

Jen spun back to her. "Your last one?"

"Yeah. I'm going to hang up my saddle after tonight." Laice's smile was wistful. "I've been at this for a few years now and I just don't have what it takes."

Jen started to speak, but Laice held up a hand.

"It's okay," she said, shaking her head. "I'm not above admitting it. There's only a few spots at the top, and so many of us, you know? Besides, I'm getting tired. It took me a while to realize that if you run at top speed all the time, it's just a fact that your motor's bound to break down at some point." She shrugged. "This isn't something you can do forever." Her smile returned. "I'm starting college in the fall. I've put it on hold long enough and it's time to get serious about the future."

Jen's mouth ran dry. She pried her tongue from the roof of it and asked, "What are you going to major in?"

Excitement flitted across Laice's features. "I've been thinking about medicine." She laughed. "I've had more success on the circuit helping racers with injuries than I have actually winning. So that's something I'm going to explore. But the possibilities are endless, really."

Jen forced her voice to remain steady. "Congratulations."

"Thanks." Laice dipped her head toward Diamond. "Have a safe run today. I'm pulling for you, Jen." She gathered up her horse's lead and clucked her tongue, walking toward the warm-up area.

A wave of nausea swept through Jen. She spun back to Diamond, placing her hands flat on the saddle and closing her eyes.

I just don't have what it takes.

She sucked in a sharp breath, recalling Laice's words and thinking about her conversation with her mom.

You've wasted years already, and if you're not careful, you're going to use up the best ones you've got left chasing something that will never happen.

Her mother's words cut deep, causing the violent shaking in Jen's hands to travel down her torso and invade her legs.

What would she do if she failed to come in first again? If she continued losing and didn't make it to Vegas?

Go back to Hollow Rock? Accept a dead-end job with no hope of improving her or her mother's future? Prove she was just another nobody from nowhere?

Her shoulders dropped. She'd be a bigger joke than ever in Hollow Rock. A ridiculous dreamer who had the audacity to think she could make it big. It'd prove to everyone how foolish she'd been to believe she could hold her own against talented athletes. And all the years of hard work would be exactly what her mother had predicted.

Wasted. She stifled a groan and hung her head, her chest aching.

"Red." Big palms settled over her hands and warm, solid strength pressed against her back.

Jen almost sagged against Colt in relief.

"You all right?" His low murmur tickled her ear.

"We waited for you by the warm-up ring for over half an hour. You should be out there by now."

She lifted her head and turned, squirming beneath the weight of his stare. "I'm about to. I just…"

Her throat closed and she looked away, her eyes scanning the competitors milling around the warm-up ring. She studied the reporters and photographers lined up along the alley and the spectators laughing in the stands.

"Jen." Colt cupped a hand to her cheek. "You can do this."

The pressure in her chest eased. She nodded and pulled her shoulders back.

A sharp whistle cracked the air and they jumped, Diamond jerking his head with a snort.

Margaret skipped over, pulling two pink-stained fingers from her mouth and pumping the air with a fist. Her other hand clutched the white stick of a massive cloud of cotton candy.

"Go, Ms. Jen," she shouted.

"Hey," Colt said hastily, placing a hand on Margaret's shoulder and frowning. "Let's save that for the stands, okay? You're gonna rattle Diamond."

Jen smiled, the sight of Margaret in her pink cowboy boots and tan hat too adorable to resist. The knot between her shoulder blades untied at the excited gleam in Margaret's eyes.

"Oh, she's all right," Jen said, squatting down to brush one of Margaret's curls away from the cotton candy. "Are you having fun so far?"

"Yep." The girl nodded, her eyes darting over the arena and the warm-up ring before returning to Jen. "Colt let me watch the other racers warm up. There's lots of big horses over there and they're fast. So fast I bet I'd fly right off if I were on 'em. But you wouldn't, Ms. Jen." Her expression grew serious. "You're faster than all of them and you're going to whoop the stew out of 'em."

Jen laughed, though her stomach still churned. "That's nice of you to say. But I have my work cut out for me."

"Uh-uh." Margaret shook her head and looked up, her expression full of admiration. "You're gonna be the best one out there." She pointed to a wrinkled poster tacked to a wooden light pole. "There's a band playing after the race. Colt said we could wait for you and dance after you cool Diamond down, if you want. And they have all kinds of stuff to eat if you get hungry later. Like boiled peanuts and popcorn and corn dogs and—"

"Cotton candy?" Jen asked, tapping the stick. "Exactly how many of these have you had tonight, hmm?"

"One." Colt eyed Margaret's furrowed brow and added, "And that's plenty."

She wrinkled her nose but grinned.

"I think that's for the best," Jen said, wiping a bit of pink fluff from the corner of Margaret's mouth. "If you eat much more of this you're gonna turn pink all over."

Margaret smiled and stuck her tongue out. "Mah tongue ith alweady pink."

Jen laughed, then caught her breath as the girl hurled herself forward, wrapping her arms around Jen's back.

"Colt said he always stays up front so you can see him when you come out," Margaret whispered, her lips warm and sticky. "We already got a place saved for us by the gate. So look for me, too, when it's your turn, okay?"

Jen hugged her back, a sweet peace settling inside

her and stilling her nerves. "You'll be the first one I look for," she whispered.

"All right, Meg," Colt said, touching her shoulder. "We need to head back so Jen can warm up."

Jen stood, smiling as Margaret bit off a hunk of cotton candy and took Colt's hand.

He hesitated, his blue eyes moving over Diamond, then hovering on Jen's face. "You're gonna be great. Just stay focused and be careful out there."

"I will," she said.

Jen watched them leave. Colt moved with purposeful steps, tall and strong, while Margaret swung his hand in hers, strolling along at his side. The crowd swallowed them up.

Jen flexed her hands, turned back to Diamond and gathered up his lead. "Ready, boy?"

They spent twenty minutes warming up in the ring before moving into place at the back of the line, walking every few minutes to keep Diamond's legs supple. She shook her head as they walked past the other waiting riders. Ironic that she'd end up running last two competitions in a row. Seemed last was the only position she'd ever been guaranteed in her life.

Night had set in and the bright lights hummed overhead as she and Diamond waited their turn in the rear. A familiar rhythm took over the arena. An announcer shouted names over a continuous stream of music. The alley gate clanged open repeatedly with each racer's entrance and exit. And the shouts of the crowd rose as the line grew shorter.

"Bring her home, folks! Bring her home," the announcer yelled.

The crowd cheered the most recent racer in and the horse drew up at the gate, breathing hard as the rider slowed him to a stop, then circled back around toward the alley. A flash of light exploded as the cameras snapped and whirred.

"That's a 15.27 for Karen Thompson, which puts her in second place. Time to beat is still 14.43 and we have one more cowgirl up. Put your hands together for Jen Taylor."

Jen closed her eyes as the voice continued to blare over the speakers, her palms tightening around the reins. *14.43.* She'd never earned above a 15.12 in competitions. And that was on her best day.

The gate clanged open and she glanced up, scouring the crowd for Colt. There were so many strange faces and unfamiliar voices, the constant camera flashes and heavy beat of music only adding to the chaos.

Beads of sweat broke out on her forehead, slipping from beneath the brim of her hat and streaming down her cheeks. Diamond jerked his head and stumbled back.

A 14.43. There was no way—

A sharp whistle rang out to the right. Jen's eyes shot to the stands, then moved to the fence, landing on Margaret's smiling face. She stood beside Colt, holding her cotton candy with one hand and waving her hat wildly in the air with the other.

You're gonna be the best one out there.

Jen's hands steadied and she released a slow breath as Colt nodded. His blue eyes were warm and supportive.

She pushed her hat more firmly on her head and

faced forward, eyes planted on the first pocket. "Go for great," she whispered.

Jen gave Diamond a swift kick and they blasted down the alley.

COLT TENSED AS Diamond tore into the arena at top speed. The horse's white mane and tail, a sharp contrast to the dirt, rippled in wild arcs as he and Jen shot toward the first barrel.

"Fire and Ice are running hot right out of the gate," the announcer blared over the PA. "Let's see how they take this first turn…"

Margaret grabbed the top fence rail and pulled, hoisting herself up on the bottom rung.

Colt put one hand around her arm to help her balance and his other hand grabbed the top fence rail. He held his breath, his lungs burning, as Jen arrived at the first barrel, gripped the saddle horn and anchored down.

Dirt flew from beneath Diamond's hooves as the horse dug deep, carving a close curve and hugging the barrel. They rounded the turn smoothly and Jen immediately rose higher in the saddle, lifting the reins and urging Diamond on to the next.

Margaret whistled. The high-pitched sound rang in Colt's ears as she bounced against his side in excitement. "Look at her go!"

Diamond and Jen streaked across the dirt and angled in toward the next turn. A bright flash exploded just as they began curving around the second barrel, the photographer crouching on the ground aiming for the perfect shot.

"Focus, Red," Colt whispered, lifting his foot and

pressing it on the lowest rung of the fence. "Stay focused."

She did, executing the second turn as flawlessly as the first. Excited cries spilled into the arena.

"Two down and on to the third," the voice blared from the PA, shouting over the stadium noise and music. "Help her out, folks. She comes out of this clean and she might have a huge check waiting for her on the other side."

"Faster, Ms. Jen," Margaret yelled, pumping her cotton candy in the air.

Colt's heart stalled as Jen and Diamond shot toward the third barrel. The fence rattled beneath the relieved jerks of his hand as she hit the mark perfectly, then sprinted toward the finish. "Go, baby," he urged.

"This could be a record setter, folks." The speakers distorted the shouted words, mixing the announcer's fast chatter with the fans' shouts. "Help this gal home!"

Jen and Diamond were a blur as they whipped across the finish line, before cutting to the side and slowing to a trot along the fence.

"Put your hands together. We might have ourselves a winner here." The speakers crackled over the noise filling the fairgrounds. "The final scores will be up in just a moment."

"She was fantastic," Margaret shouted. Her cotton candy fell from her hand onto the grass as she clambered higher on the fence.

"Careful." Colt chuckled, steadying her.

Margaret thrust her arm out, palm in the air, as Jen and Diamond approached. "Way to go, Ms. Jen!"

Jen laughed, breathing hard. She leaned over in the saddle and high-fived Margaret. Several fans followed suit, lining up on the fence and waiting for their high fives as Jen and Diamond walked by, then circled back.

"And the score is up," the announcer bellowed, his voice pitching higher. "It's a 14.38. One of the highest scores we've had here in Springfield. Jen Taylor is your winner for the night. Keep your eye on this gal, folks. Come December, she may be leading the pack in Vegas."

The cheers grew deafening. Colt's chest swelled as Jen made her way back, her gaze locking with his. He'd never been prouder or happier for her.

She smiled, her flushed cheeks lifting and brown eyes sparkling. "Not too bad, huh?" she called out breathlessly.

"Not too bad," he shouted back.

The gate swept open, clinking and groaning on its hinges. Rapid flashes and whirring clicks erupted on both sides of the exit.

Jen glanced down, her red hair bouncing over her back. "See you in a bit."

She winked, nudged Diamond with her heels and headed toward the alley, smiling even wider as reporters called out questions and requests for interviews.

"Can I go help Ms. Jen cool Diamond down?" Margaret asked, hopping off the fence.

"Not right now, Meg." He grabbed her elbow. "Jen's going to be busy for a while doing interviews and packing up. We'll have to wait until things die down and she's able to get away."

Margaret's face fell.

"We can stand outside the cooldown area and watch, though," Colt added, taking her hand and tugging her out of the moving throng of spectators.

He reached down, scooped up the cotton candy and threw it in a nearby trash can. They paused by the alley gate, waiting for the crowd to thin out, then made their way over to Jen.

She was walking Diamond in slow lines. A group of reporters stood close by the racers, snapping pictures and shouting questions. The number of bystanders surrounding the small space made it impossible for Colt and Margaret to get through.

"I can't see," she said, rising to her tiptoes.

"There's not much to see, Meg," Colt replied.

Almost half an hour passed before Jen finished cooling Diamond down. Then the interviews started, each new round of questions lasting longer than the one before it. And photographs followed. A few with Jen posing on her own, some of her standing with fellow racers and the majority with her astride Diamond.

They waited through all of it, Margaret leaning more heavily against Colt's leg with each passing minute. She perked up a bit when the music from the band started.

"Wanna go back to the arena?" Colt asked, glancing over his shoulder at the brightly lit stage. "We could dance a time or two."

Margaret shook her head. "Not without Ms. Jen," she said quietly, wrapping her arms around his waist and pressing her cheek to his side.

Colt hugged Margaret, suddenly having no desire to return to the arena, either. Not to dance, ride a bull or for any other reason.

He watched as Jen moved farther away with Diamond for another round of pictures. Several photographers followed, scrambling with their gear and calling out Jen's name.

Colt's stomach sank deeper with each step they took, the separation becoming more acute when Jen didn't look back or search him out in the crowd like she usually did.

He tensed, the elation he felt from Jen's win at odds with the painful knowledge that she was moving in another direction. And he found himself wishing Jen was by his side again, looking up at the stars, enjoying a cool drink and sharing a few laughs.

He'd enjoyed doing that so much at Raintree Ranch. Where time moved at a slower pace and every day was just that much sweeter. Where Margaret knew she was loved and every one of her days began and ended with him at her side. It was a place he'd never thought he'd find.

Home. A fullness entered Colt's chest, expanding his heart and bringing him peace. That was what Raintree had become. For him and for Margaret. What he'd helped to create for her. And he knew he could never take Margaret away from it. Or ever leave her again.

"When's she coming back?" his sister asked. She blinked up at him, her eyes and voice heavy.

He rubbed a shaky hand over her back and decided right then that he'd do everything in his power to make sure Margaret never felt forgotten. That she would always know, without a doubt, that she was loved. And that with him, she would always come first. Whatever it might cost him.

Colt pulled her closer, drawing comfort from the press of her small frame, and tried to accept the fact that he and Jen might have to go their separate ways.

Chapter Eleven

Colt palmed the steering wheel and turned slowly onto Raintree's dirt driveway. The truck bounced and swayed over several familiar dips and bumps, the trailer squeaking rhythmically as they drew closer to the main house.

His muscles relaxed and his pulse steadied, the knowledge that his feet would be on the solid ground of the ranch again soothing him.

The drive back from Springfield hadn't taken that long, because there'd been little traffic on the road. But they hadn't left the fairgrounds until hours after the race ended, and it was now after midnight. They'd waited for Jen's interviews and photo sessions to finish before loading up Diamond and packing away their gear.

"According to that reporter, I should rank fourth when the standings come out next week," Jen whispered at his side. She shifted in the passenger seat, her cell phone lighting up the truck's cab as her fingers moved over the screen.

Colt frowned and focused on navigating the winding driveway. Jen had looked up from her phone only once the entire trip back. Her attention had remained focused on her texts with Tammy and her nervous search for the results of other races in neighboring districts.

"I think he might know what he's talking about," she said, pointing a finger at the glowing screen. "I added everything up, and I've cleared forty thousand dollars this season, with tonight's winnings included in the count." She hesitated, dragging her teeth over her bottom lip. "I don't know if that's right, though. I've never been real good with numbers." Her voice lifted. "But it could be right. By the time we get back to the circuit, I might actually be ranked fourth with the pot I just won."

Unease settled in Colt's gut. He propped his elbow on the windowsill and rubbed a hand over his jaw.

"Colt? That could be right, couldn't it?"

He glanced at her. The hope raising her dark brows and lighting her face made his chest ache. "Yeah," he whispered, managing a small smile. "That could be right."

A low rattle sounded from the back of the cab. Colt looked in the rearview mirror, catching a glimpse of Margaret huddled against the window. Her small mouth fell open and a louder round of snores began.

He smiled, turning back and meeting Jen's amused eyes before facing forward.

"She's knocked out," Jen said. She laughed softly and reached back to sweep a strand of hair away from Margaret's face. "It'll be a shame to wake her."

His smile slipped, drawing his spirits down with it.

They reached the end of the driveway and he eased the truck to a stop, then cut the engine. "I'm gonna get her in bed. Then we've got to talk, Jen."

Her smile disappeared, too. But she nodded, unbuckling her seat belt and lifting her hip to slide her phone into her pocket. "Okay. I'll get Diamond settled, then wait for you in your room."

Colt took his time getting Margaret tucked in for the night, walking her into the house and standing by her side as she brushed her teeth, her eyes drowsy.

"In you get," he said, helping her into bed and tucking the covers around her shoulders.

"G'night, Colt," she murmured.

A sleepy smile crossed her face as he kissed her forehead, her eyelids fluttering shut.

"Good night, Meg," he whispered.

He stayed there for a while, closing his eyes and leaning against the doorjamb, before making his way to the guest wing. His legs grew heavier with each step.

Jen was waiting inside for him. She stood at the window, her back to him as she stared out into the dark night.

"You're not returning to the circuit with me, are you?"

Colt drew to a halt in the middle of the room, his heart tripping painfully at the sadness in her low voice.

He pried his tongue from the roof of his dry mouth and answered, "No."

Her shoulders slumped and she lowered her head, her red hair rippling across her back.

He forced himself to continue. "I've decided to take Dominic up on his offer. It'll give me a chance to slow down. Put down roots." He inhaled, his lungs stalling. "I'm going to buy some land from him and build a house on one of the back lots."

"For you and Meg?" Jen pushed her hands into her front pockets, drawing further into herself. "You're going to keep her?"

Colt nodded, knowing she couldn't see him, but aware she didn't need to. "I'm calling Jack first thing in the morning. I'm gonna tell him to send me the guardianship papers and let my grandmother know I'm keeping Meg." His chest tightened at Jen's silence. "I won't leave her. She's my sister. My family." He held the word on his tongue, savoring the soothing feel of it and weighing it against the knot in his gut. "You've got to understand—"

"I do," she choked out. She spun to face him, her smile weak and chin trembling. "I do understand. I just wish…" Her brave expression collapsed and she turned her head to the side, a tear streaking down her cheek.

He strode swiftly across the room and wrapped his arms around her. She shook in his embrace, the entire length of her body trembling against his own. He held her silently for several minutes, sliding his hands over her back and lowering his lips to kiss the top of her head.

"There's something else I need to say." Colt breathed her in, closing his eyes at the sweet scent of her hair and relishing the rapid pounding of her heart against his own. "I love you, Jen." He clutched her closer and raised his head, meeting her eyes as she looked up at him. "I love everything about you."

Her mouth parted on a swift breath and he slowly traced the outline of her lips with a fingertip.

"I love how brave you are, regardless of what you're up against. I love how gentle and patient you are with Meg. How generous, kind and forgiving you are with everyone, including me." A low laugh escaped him. "I even love the way you brushed me off when we first met." He sobered, his hands moving to cradle her face. "How you've expected more of me. And how you've made me into a better man."

Her breasts lifted against him as she took a deep breath, her hands leaving her pockets and curling against his chest.

He touched his mouth to hers, parting her lips with his and whispering again, "I love you and I don't want you to leave."

With a soft cry, she slid her hands up his chest and wrapped them around the nape of his neck, kissing him back.

The sweet taste of her touched his tongue and the gentle press of her body against his heated his blood, urging him to delve deeper into the kiss and move his hands over her curves with greater purpose.

He lifted his head and nudged her chin up with a knuckle until she met his gaze again. "Do you love me?"

"Yes," she whispered.

His chest warmed at her words but his heart tripped at the dismay in her expression. "Then stay with me, Red. Marry me."

She squeezed her eyes shut and tugged his mouth back down to hers, her kiss almost desperate as it silenced him.

He let her take over for a few moments, relishing the passionate movements of her body and hands as she explored him. And he became more anxious than ever to hear the words he hoped for spilling from her lips.

"Stay," he urged, lowering himself to his knees and tugging her shirt from her jeans. "Be my wife. We'll build a home of our own. Start a family."

Her belly rippled, quivers chasing across the flat expanse of her creamy skin and he gave in to the overwhelming urge to nuzzle his face against it. Imagining the possibility of a child nestled safely there one day. His and Jen's. Protected and loved.

He pressed his lips to the smooth skin above her belly button and hugged her legs, his callused palms moving over the denim covering the toned muscles of her thighs.

"Colt." She looked down at him with dark eyes, her fiery curls spilling over her shoulders. Her fingers cradled his head gently, her mouth moving, but no sound emerging.

He was afraid to let go of her. Because if he did, he knew he may never be able to hold her again.

He flexed his arms around her, getting a solid grip on her hips and hoisting her up. He carried her over to the bed, laid her down gently, then lowered his body onto hers. "You want me to stop?" he asked, smoothing her hair from her face and waiting.

She shook her head and rose to kiss him again.

Logic left him, the strength of emotion that blazed in his chest drove his hands to remove her clothing. To caress and cherish every inch of her. He lingered over her breasts and the curves of her hips, pausing briefly to help her remove his own clothing, then moved to his back and savored her gentle advances.

At the sight of her flushed cheeks, kiss-reddened lips and yearning eyes, he rolled over her to seek her warmth.

Her arms and legs parted, her fingertips sweeping over his back and her heels hooking around his thighs. She opened to him completely, welcoming him. Urging him on as he entered her slowly, moving with the rhythm of their shared breaths.

Colt held her gaze as soft cries escaped her and the increasing intensity of pleasure swept over her face.

She came apart in his arms and he followed, holding himself still above her. He knew what the answer would be. Had known all along. But he had to ask one more time. "Stay with me."

Jen squeezed her eyes shut and tears seeped from the corners, gliding slowly across her temples and disappearing into her hair.

Colt flinched, an unbearable pain piercing through the pleasure that still throbbed so strongly in his veins. Her mouth barely moved, but he heard the fractured words just the same.

"I can't."

JEN SHIVERED AS Colt disentangled himself from her and left the bed. Her skin, which had flamed under his touch minutes ago, turned ice-cold, and the chill cut through her all the way to her bones. She'd tried so hard not to hurt him. Had tried to say goodbye the best way she could. But she'd failed at both.

She dragged the sheet over her breasts and sat up, her stomach churning as he jerked his jeans on. "I'm sorry, Colt."

He didn't answer. The rasp of his zipper closing and the clang of his belt buckling filled the room.

"Colt?" Jen wrapped the sheet around her and stood, pressing her palm to the warm skin of his broad back.

He turned, capturing her hand and squeezing it in his, his eyes peering down at her. "Do you want to marry me?"

Yes. Jen bit back the word, stilling her tongue. She ached to say it. To tell him. But if she did, she wouldn't have the strength to walk away.

"Because if you do, I'll wait," he said. "I'll figure

out a way to keep Margaret with us until you win at Vegas. Then afterward, we can all come back and settle at Raintree."

She shook her head, forcing sound from her constricted throat. "It's not that simple, Colt. I can't just quit after Vegas. There are so many other things to consider."

He stilled. "What things?"

She slid her hand from his, holding the sheet at her chest to keep from reaching for him. "Tammy, for one. I can't leave her on her own out there. She—"

"Tammy's a grown woman. And a strong one at that," Colt said. "She knows the road and has plenty of connections. She'd be fine without either one of us. Has been since we left the circuit."

"Maybe. But I promised her I'd come back."

"What else?" he asked quietly. "Tell me what else there is to consider, Jen."

She moved closer, wincing at the pain in his expression. "I'm so close to winning. Closer than I've ever been. And even if I do win, I can't just hang up my saddle and walk away. It's part of me. It's what I do. The only thing I've ever been good at. I've worked too hard for too long to give it all up. I've sacrificed so much…" She straightened, steadying her voice. "I can't throw it all away. I have to keep going. No matter what."

"No matter what?" Colt stepped back, his face paling. "I used to know someone who lived by that mantra."

A wave of nausea swept over Jen. "I'm not like your father, Colt. And neither are you."

"I used to think I wasn't," he said. "But I did exactly what he would've done, initially, had he been in my position. I decided right off that I wasn't going to take Meg. That I was just going to leave her in the care of strangers and go on my way. Leave her like I did every other female that crossed my path." He grimaced. "Like I tried to leave you a couple of weeks ago in that bar."

"But you changed your mind. You've chosen to be honest with me." Jen's voice broke. "And you're staying with Margaret now."

"Yeah. I am." He tilted his head, his eyes thoughtful as they roved over her face. "Who did you call that night in the hayloft? When you said you were touching base with home?"

She ducked her head, her cheeks flaming.

"Who was it?" he prompted. "Jen?"

"My mom."

Colt nodded slowly. "You've never talked about her. Not in all the time we've known each other. I only recall two times over the years that you left to go home, and both times, you were back on the circuit within three days." He looked away. "I can't really fault you for that, since I did the same thing. But now I know what it feels like to be on the other end of it."

Jen's eyes blurred and she blinked rapidly in an attempt to clear them. "You and I both know what has to be sacrificed in order to make it out there. There's too much at stake for me to walk away. This is my chance. My shot at making something of myself. A shot at being someone who matters."

"You matter to me," Colt said softly. "And Meg."

"I know. I love you and Margaret. But I need more than that."

"Can you understand that Meg and I need more, too?" His eyes turned sad. "I'm proud of you, Jen. I know what's waiting for you out there and there's no limit to how high you could climb. But I don't think racing makes you happy anymore. Not really. No matter how much you win, the fans will stop cheering when the fun ends and they'll leave when the competition is over like always. My father valued his career more than anything else. He made enough money to build a mansion that could hold ten families but it's remained empty in every way that matters." He shook his head. "Meg has been unseen, unheard and unloved for the majority of her childhood. I know how much that hurts. And I won't ever let that happen again. With me, Meg will always know she's loved." He stepped closer. "And so would you."

Jen looked down and curled her toes underneath the fall of the sheet, unable to face him. "I know it sounds selfish and I know I'm hurting you. And that I'll hurt Margaret…" She choked back a sob, ignoring the hot wetness coursing down her cheeks. "That's the very last thing I'd ever want to do. But I can't give up racing. I need it. I need to prove that I can make it and that I can stay on top."

The warmth of his palms cupped her jaw and his thumbs drifted over her cheeks. "Who are you trying to prove this to?" he whispered.

She looked up then. "Everyone. People back home. The ones on the circuit."

Colt frowned, sweeping a blunt fingertip beneath her eyes and wiping away a fresh stream of tears. "I don't think that's what you're looking for, Red. But if it really is, is what all those other people think that important?" He paused, tipping up her chin. "More important than what I think? Or Meg? Because to us, the woman who rides into that arena is the same one riding out of it. And win or lose, we still love you just as much as we did before."

A choked cry escaped her and she hid her face against his broad chest, laying her cheek against his warm skin and absorbing the scent of him. The feel of him.

"I have to do this," she whispered.

He exhaled, his heavy breath ruffling her hair. His arms wrapped around her, holding her loosely, his callused palms moving over the bare skin of her back above the sheet.

She pressed closer, her chest squeezing to the point of pain. "I can come back and stay for a while. Once this season's over."

His chest vibrated beneath her cheek. "And what happens when the next one starts? When the next opportunity arrives?"

She closed her eyes and didn't answer.

Colt released her and moved away. He collected his shirt and boots from the floor, then paused at the door. "It's not just me anymore. I have to consider what's best for Meg. Time is the most valuable asset I have and I'm not wasting any more of it. I'm staying here with Meg and I'm going to make sure she knows that my family is what's most important in my life. Meg deserves to be remembered and loved all the time. Not just when it's convenient." His voice firmed. "And so do I."

"Colt, please—"

"I assume you and Tammy have already lined up another competition."

Jen nodded, tremors tearing through her. "Texas."

"I'll check the truck and trailer over. Pack some fresh

supplies." He turned to leave. "It'll be ready for you by tomorrow morning."

Jen followed, stumbling over the sheet trailing across the floor. "I can't take your truck."

"Why not? I'll just get a new one." He stopped and looked over his shoulder, his tone resigned. "Money's not what I'm short on."

Jen stood there long after he left, staring at the empty doorway.

Eventually, she headed to the room she shared with Margaret and hesitated by the girl's bed. A couple strands of blond hair had fallen forward and settled over her mouth. They lifted gently with each soft snore.

Heart clenching, Jen reached down and carefully pushed the hair back from Meg's face, then kissed her temple.

A fresh surge of tears streamed down her cheeks and she stepped away quickly, crawled into bed and closed her eyes. Sleep eluded her, though, and she gave up as the first tendrils of morning light crept between the closed blinds. Getting up, she began packing quietly.

Afterward, Jen loaded Diamond in the trailer. She said her goodbyes to the Slade family, hugged both sets of twins and baby Ethan, then stood outside by the truck, watching as Colt made one last inspection of the vehicle.

"Everything looks good," he said, rounding the back and stopping at the driver's side door. His eyes were heavy and the shadows beneath them had darkened. "I filled the tank so you'll have plenty of gas. And I double-checked the air pressure on the tires, so they're full, too."

Jen's breath caught at the gruff sound of his voice and she managed a strained whisper. "Thank you."

"Ms. Jen?"

She turned to find Margaret standing beside the trailer. The girl wore her hat and one of her new outfits, her pink boots dusty and well broken in. She smiled, but her eyes were red-rimmed and her cheeks flushed.

A streak of pain traveled through Jen. "Hey." She knelt and held her arms out, her palms aching to pull Margaret close.

Margaret ran across the dirt and hurled herself into Jen's embrace.

Jen held her and kissed the top of her head, focusing on the green field. The image blurred in front of her. "I'm going to miss you, Meg."

"I'll miss you, too." Her thin voice shook and her shoulders jerked. "Colt said we're staying here, you know? For good."

Jen nodded, biting her lip. "I know. I bet you were glad to hear that."

"Yeah. I like it here." Margaret stepped back and dragged her hand over her tear-streaked cheeks. "So that's where we'll be," she said, her expression earnest. "If you want to come see us. We'll be here. You are going to visit soon, aren't you?"

"Of course," Jen whispered.

"Meg." Colt's big hand squeezed his sister's shoulder and he gestured toward the trailer. "Go say goodbye to Diamond. Jen has to hit the road."

Margaret nodded and left, walking back to the trailer and climbing up on the wheel to pet Diamond through the slats.

Colt cupped Jen's elbow and pulled her to her feet.

"Don't make her promises you have no intention of keeping."

"I do plan to visit," she said, wrapping her hands around his biceps. "As soon as I finish the season. And I'll call—"

"Let's not do this. You have a long drive ahead of you and…" Colt's voice trailed away. His throat moved with a hard swallow and he pulled her close, wrapping his arms around her and squeezing.

Jen slid her arms up and gripped his nape, kissing his neck and breathing in the scent of his skin, memorizing as many details as she could.

"You're breaking my heart, Red," he said in a choked whisper. "But, damned if I don't still love you."

A chill swept over her and she rose on her toes, grabbing on to him and holding tight. "Colt—"

"Go." He tugged her arms from him and spun on his heel, pausing to help Margaret down from the trailer, then taking her hand and leading her away.

Jen watched them leave, forcing a smile as Margaret glanced back at her several times. It faltered, though, once they climbed the porch steps and disappeared inside the house. And she needed every bit of strength she had left to climb into the truck, crank the engine and drive away.

Chapter Twelve

"Next up, we've got a gal from Spokane, Washington. Let's give her a strong, Southern welcome, folks."

Jen centered her seat and ran her fingers through Diamond's mane, watching as the alley gate opened and the next competitor took her position under the bright lights.

The noise inside the arena increased as the brunette kicked her horse's flanks and charged across the dirt. The Priceville, Alabama, crowd was smaller than most, but what they lacked in numbers they made up for in enthusiasm. And in winnings. An additional six thousand dollars had just been added to the pot over the last few days and the resulting payout was big by anyone's standards.

"Only six more and you're up."

Jen glanced down to her left, smiling at Tammy's excited expression. They'd both performed well over the two weeks since Jen had left Raintree, placing in all three of the competitions they'd entered. Tammy had clocked one of her best runs yet, scoring well enough to secure a position in tonight's top five. And Karla had joined up with them at each competition, holding her own with the more experienced riders.

"A 15.12 is the highest so far," Tammy continued, patting Diamond's shoulder and smiling. "Don't think you'll have a problem cracking that."

Jen shrugged. "Maybe. But only one person can get that top spot."

Tammy shook her head, stepping closer and rubbing Diamond's neck. "I don't mind coming in second as long as first goes to you," she said. "And even if you don't get first, you won't be far behind. You certainly won't be last."

Jen's smile slipped as she turned the word over in her mind, surprised to find it had lost its sting. "I don't mind being last," she said.

And for the first time, she really meant it.

She turned back to the gate, searching the stands and scanning the fence by the alley. Her stomach dropped at the sight of so many strangers' faces and the absence of two people in particular. Just as it had at each competition over the past two weeks.

Jen moved her hand across her front pocket, tracing the outline of her cell phone. "You mind watching Diamond for a minute?" she asked, swinging her leg over and hopping down.

"Sure," Tammy said, wariness crossing her features as she took the reins. "But what're you doing? You'll be up soon."

"I know," she said over her shoulder, tugging her phone from her pocket and walking away. "I just need to make a quick call."

"Don't be long," Tammy called out. "You'll miss your spot."

Jen nodded, waving away the concern and dialing. She stood outside the warm-up area, watching racers turning and loping from one end to the other. The warm night air caressed her cheeks and whispered across the phone. Her heart fluttered as she counted the rings.

"Hello?"

Jen blinked and cleared her throat, expecting the deep tone of Colt's voice, but hearing the high-pitched lilt of Margaret's.

"Hey, Meg." Her chest warmed at the sound of Margaret's excited gasp.

"Hey, Ms. Jen," she said, almost breathlessly. "Are you in Alabama already?"

Jen smiled. She'd called Colt almost every night since leaving Raintree. He'd answered every time, asking how she was doing and filling her in on Margaret's activities at school, before handing the phone to his sister.

Jen's smile slipped at the thought of the last couple calls. Colt's voice had sounded heavier each time he'd answered, his responses growing shorter with each conversation.

"Yeah." Jen forced a bright note into her tone. "We made it to Priceville last night and scoped out the arena this morning."

"Are there lots of racers at this one?"

"Quite a few." Jen watched the movements of the horses nearby, an ache blooming in her chest. "How are things your way? Did you and the boys play basketball at school again today?"

"Yep. And I beat 'em."

"All of them?" Jen teased.

"Every one of 'em. Kayden and Jayden made almost as many baskets as I did, but not enough to win. I whopped 'em good." Margaret laughed, the joyful sound ringing clear over the line. "Colt said he's gonna get us our own basketball hoop and put it up this weekend so we can practice. He said he'd show me some moves so that I'll be ready to try out for the basketball team when I get to middle school if I want to. Do you think I could make the team if I practice real hard?"

"You can do anything you put your mind to, Meg," Jen said, stilling as the phrase echoed over the line. "Anything at all."

"We all had good grades on our report cards and Mr. Logan said we can have another movie night to celebrate. I can let you know when it is ahead of time. Then maybe you could come back for that?" Margaret hesitated. "Are…" Her voice stalled, the bright cheer in it dimming. "Are you going to visit soon? 'Cause I miss you."

Jen winced at the sadness in Margaret's tone. "I—"

The sound of muffled movements came across the line and she heard Colt's voice in the background. There was silence for several moments, then the line was clear again.

"Jen."

Jen closed her eyes, wishing she could see his face. "Hey." She dragged her teeth over her bottom lip. "How…how are you?"

"Fine." His tone was short, the word clipped. "You and Tammy make it to Priceville okay?"

"Yeah. We're at the race now. My run's almost up."

A heavy sigh sounded and Colt's voice lowered. "You can't keep doing this, Jen."

"Doing what?"

"Calling like this. Talking to Meg every night and promising to visit. She does okay until she hears your voice. Then she cries when she gets off the phone."

"I'm sorry," Jen said, heat engulfing her face and her limbs turning heavy. "I never meant to upset her. I just miss her. And you. I miss you, too, Colt." Her voice grew weak and she whispered, "So much."

He remained silent for a while, then said, "I can't do this anymore. I can't be here for Meg one hundred percent and worry about you out there at the same time. Every damned morning I wake up wondering where you're headed next and if you made it there okay. I wonder if you had a safe run or if you—" His voice broke and there was a scuffling sound before he said heavily, "You've got to let me let you go, Red."

Jen fought to draw a breath, clutching the phone closer to her ear. "If that's really what you want." She had to force out the words.

"It's not what I want," he said. "But it's what I have to do."

The announcer's voice crackled over the speakers, calling up the next competitor.

"Sounds like you need to go," Colt said. "Red?"

She stifled a sob, biting her lip until the metallic taste of blood touched her tongue. "Yeah?"

"Good luck. And be careful out there."

"I always am," she whispered.

But the line had been cut and her answer hovered on dead air.

"Jen?"

She lowered the phone to her side and looked over her shoulder. Tammy stood near the gate, holding Diamond's reins in one hand and beckoning frantically with the other.

Jen made her way over slowly, avoiding her friend's eyes as she took the reins from her.

"It's almost time," Tammy said, glancing anxiously at the line of racers surrounding them. "You're about to lose your spot."

Jen hooked her heel in the stirrup and lifted herself up, straddling Diamond and settling in. The shouts from the arena grew louder as a racer exited through the alley gate and the rider in front of Jen lined up.

"How are Colt and Margaret?"

Jen glanced at Tammy. "Okay, I guess," she said.

She turned away and gripped the saddle horn to still the shaking in her hand, recalling the strained tones of Colt's voice and the sadness underlying Margaret's.

A tremor tore through her and she flexed her fingers, realizing this was the first time she'd had a case of nerves since leaving Raintree.

"Jen?" Tammy tugged at her pant leg and peered up at her, asking softly, "Where's your head at, girl?"

Jen stilled, but didn't give her usual reply. She couldn't. Her head wasn't in the game. She wasn't focused on the winning time or the barrel pattern. And she'd given no thought to the outcome of the race.

Because it didn't matter...

Jen sagged in the saddle, the tension leaving her limbs in a peaceful rush and the trembling in her hands subsiding. It no longer mattered whether she won or lost. It didn't matter if her name was on the board or if the crowd applauded for her. Or if everyone saw her come in first.

You can do anything you put your mind to...

She no longer felt the need to prove anything to anyone. Including herself. She knew she could do it. She knew Diamond could, too. Heck, they'd already done it. More times than not lately. And she finally believed it deep inside. Believed it to the point that coming in first in the arena no longer mattered.

What mattered most was putting Colt and Margaret first. That they knew her, flaws and all, and still loved her. Just as she was. With or without a title. Because who she was what was important to them, not what she could do.

I've been proud of you every day of your life.

Her mother's words returned, filling her heart to the point it overflowed, escaping from her eyes and trickling down her cheeks.

She'd spent so much time trying to earn approval from strangers instead of spending it with those she loved. And no amount of money or success could replace the joy she'd felt when loving and supporting Colt and Margaret.

"Where's your head, Jen?" Tammy repeated, reaching up to squeeze her knee.

Jen wiped away a tear and whispered, "Don't you mean where's my heart?"

Her friend smiled. "With Colt and Margaret?"

Jen nodded and tilted her head back, looking up at the night sky. The stars here were drowned out by the floodlights. She recalled how bright the moon was at Raintree. How green the fields were and how the fun continued well past the last ray of sunshine each day.

She smiled at the thought of juice boxes and kites. Children, outdoor movies and kisses in pickup trucks. So many beautiful babies and happy kids safely at play. The ranch is a perfect place to make a home and start a family. A family with Colt and Margaret. Something worth more than any number of gold buckles. And something she wanted more than anything.

Her heart skipped a beat and she straightened, tugging on Diamond's reins and stepping out of line. "I want to go back to Raintree."

Tammy nodded. "I kind of expected that. You haven't been the same since you came back. I guess I was being selfish trying to keep you to myself."

"Come with me," Jen urged, swinging her leg over the saddle and hopping down.

Tammy shook her head, glancing toward the arena as the announcer called the next contestant. "My ride's not done here. I want a title and Karla needs a buddy for the road, so it'll work out well." She smiled through the sadness in her eyes, stepping forward and hugging her. "I want you to be happy. Don't worry about me. Just be careful going back." Her laugh ruffled Jen's hair. "Make an honest man of my cousin and don't forget that you've already got a maid of honor lined up. I'll be expecting a call once you set the date."

Jen squeezed her close once more and stepped back, wiping away a tear. "You got it. And I'll be calling you before then. A lot."

They said one last goodbye, then Jen led Diamond through his cooldown, removed his tack and loaded him in the trailer. She paused on the way to the driver's seat, walked back to the trailer and reached through the slats to give Diamond one more pat.

"Can you handle a few extra miles, boy?" Jen smiled, mentally plotting the fastest route from Alabama to Georgia. "Because there's one more stop I'd like to make before we head to Raintree."

Colt shielded his eyes against the Sunday afternoon sun and called out, "Good job, Meg. Stay centered and slow it down a bit."

"Like this?"

"That's right," Colt said, watching as she realigned herself in the saddle and tapped Destiny's flanks, urging her farther out into one of Raintree's fields.

The slow gait lasted all of thirty seconds before Margaret tapped Destiny again and quickened the pace, catching up with Kayden and Jayden, who rode their horses several feet ahead of her.

"She's getting good," Dominic said at his side.

"Yeah." Colt shoved his hands into his front pockets and leaned back against the fence. "Too good. She's been begging for barrel racing lessons a lot lately."

"Yep. She's asked me, too." Dominic propped his elbows on the top fence rail and looked to his left, studying the bulls roaming in a pasture on the far side of the grounds. "Of course, I wouldn't know where to start with something like that. Bulls are more my thing."

Colt nodded, glancing at the animals he and Dominic had purchased and doing his best to keep his thoughts from straying to Jen. Just as they had every day since she'd left Raintree.

In actuality, he shouldn't have had time to think about her over the past two weeks. He'd been so busy helping Margaret with homework, riding lessons and settling in permanently at the ranch that his afternoons and evenings were full. And during the day, while Margaret attended school, he spent whatever free time he had planning and implementing the first stages of his and Dominic's new business venture, and pitching in with the daily chores.

He'd thrown himself into work purposefully, hoping the long hours and tedious tasks would keep him from thinking about Jen. Keep him from picturing her bright smile and sexy laugh. Help him avoid remembering how her gentle touch had made his skin tingle and his body hum. Maybe put an end to the way his heart bled every time he faced getting through another day without her.

Only, none of it had worked. He still missed her like hell. Still woke every morning thinking of her. Dreamed about her every night when he closed his eyes. And saying a final goodbye to her last night over the phone had been the hardest thing he'd ever had to do.

He flinched at the pain lashing through him. He'd lost so much more than a friend.

"...could hire someone."

Colt blinked, forcing his thoughts to subside and turning back to Dominic. "What?"

"I said we could hire someone. To give Meg lessons."

Colt nodded absently, a small smile fighting its way to his lips at the sight of Margaret nudging Destiny into a trot behind the boys, following them to the other end of the field. Her blond curls bounced against her back and she sat taller in the saddle than she ever had before. Her confidence had grown so much over the past weeks at Raintree and he had no doubt that he'd made the right decision to keep her here permanently.

He hadn't completely cut off Margaret's access to their father's estate, though. He'd retained ownership and would sign over his share in John W. Mead's company to Margaret in a few years. That way, she could choose which path to take when she came of age. And he'd support her decision.

Colt sighed. He just wished the path he'd chosen for himself was the one Jen wanted, too.

"Who knows?" Dominic shrugged. "If whoever we hire to give Meg racing lessons does a good job, we could consider keeping them on permanently. Maybe even make them a partner. Expand the riding clinics to include barrel racing lessons, too."

Something in Dominic's tone was off. Colt looked at him, studying the amused lift of his brow and knowing gleam in his eye.

"What's going on?" Colt asked, frowning.

Dominic adopted a bland expression. "What do you mean?"

"Don't ask me that like you don't know what I'm talking about." Colt pulled his hands from his pockets and shoved himself off the fence. "Something's up. I can tell."

Dominic's mouth twitched and he waved a hand in the air, turning away. "Just tossing ideas around, that's all."

"The hell you say—"

"Hey, Mr. Colt," Jayden shouted, galloping up the center of the field and pointing behind him. "Ms. Jen and Diamond are coming!"

Colt's eyes snapped to the driveway, scanning the empty dirt road. There was no familiar growl from his truck and no white trailer clearing the hill.

He jerked back to face Dominic, looking for some sign that what Jayden said was true.

A broad smile spread slowly across Dominic's face. "Well, hell," he drawled. "Guess we won't have to look too far to find the right person for the job."

A distant thundering of hooves erupted. Colt spun

back around, his heart stumbling in his chest as a flash of red and white emerged over the hill.

Diamond galloped along the narrow strip of grass between the fence and the dirt road. Jen sat high on his back, leaning forward and moving rhythmically with each of his powerful strides. Her hair arced behind her in a fiery wave.

Excited cries erupted from the field. Kayden and Margaret trotted along the fence, doing their best to keep time with Jen. They couldn't keep up and fell farther and farther behind, but it did nothing to dampen their spirits. If anything, their whoops and cheers grew louder.

"Go, Ms. Jen," Margaret hollered, her jubilant cry echoing across the grounds.

Colt moved quickly, striding to the pasture gate and tugging it open as Jen slowed to a halt in front of it. He looked up at her, his breath catching at the rosy flush of her cheeks and the flirtatious spark in her brown eyes. Her full breasts rose and fell with her rapid breaths and her lush mouth parted enticingly as she stared down at him, almost causing his knees to buckle.

He forced himself to speak and picked out the only coherent words he could manage, stringing them into a gruff question. "Where's my truck?"

Her smile widened and she nodded toward the hill just as the pickup came barreling into view. The engine's racy roar and the clang of the trailer bouncing over potholes filled the air. Dust flew up from the tires as it sped down the drive, then screeched to an awkward halt.

"Diamond got restless a mile or so back and wanted

to stretch his legs," Jen said, swinging herself to the ground. "So I saddled him up and rode him in."

Colt rubbed his hands over his jeans, gripping the denim to keep from crushing her to him. He glanced back at the dust cloud settling around his truck. "Yeah, but who…"

The driver's door creaked open and a tall woman with red hair jumped out. She slammed it shut and crossed to the front of the truck, patting the hood and chuckling.

"Woo," she gasped. "I've never driven a rig as racy as this. It's a nice ride, Jen."

Jen laughed, her warm eyes returning to his. "My mom. She likes to ride fast, too." She flushed a deeper shade of red and released Diamond's reins, allowing him to amble into the field. "I stopped by to see her on the way back and talked her into coming with me for a vacation. I thought I'd let her check out the ranch. See the sights. I called ahead and asked Dominic to reserve a room for her."

"You did?"

Now it made sense. Colt glanced over his shoulder at his friend, his own mouth quirking when Dominic ducked his head and walked over to the kids, helping them down from their saddles. The boys ran up, hugged Jen quickly, then shot over to the truck, cornering her mother and firing off questions.

Jen knelt as Margaret rushed toward her, catching her in her arms and pressing kisses to her cheeks.

Colt's chest warmed at the happiness in Jen's eyes and smile.

"You came back," Margaret said, bouncing in Jen's arms. "I'm so glad you came back."

"Me, too," she murmured, sitting back on her heels. "That's my mom over there. Ms. Nora. Why don't you go over and say hi with the boys? I've told her a lot about you and she's anxious to meet you."

Margaret smiled and nodded, then darted over to join the twins. Kayden stood on one side of Nora and Jayden on the other. Both boys had their hands propped on their hips.

Kayden's authoritative voice carried over to the field. "So how good are you at fort building?"

"Oh, Lord," Dominic rumbled, easing past Colt and Jen and striding across the driveway toward the boys. "Better head this off at the pass."

Colt and Jen shared a laugh.

Jen's laughter faded and she sobered, her shoulders lifting briefly. "My mom and I haven't always had the best relationship. A lot of that was my fault. I've been judging us both too harshly. I thought spending some time together at Raintree might help us grow closer. I was hoping, maybe, after my mom saw the place, she might decide to relocate."

Colt studied the hesitant movements of her mouth and the slight shake in her hand as she tucked a strand of hair behind her ear. His belly flipped over at her shy expression and he tried to tone down the hopeful note in his voice as he asked, "And why would she want to do that?"

Jen stepped closer, placing a palm on his chest. "Because I plan to stay."

He pulled in a deep breath and placed his hand over hers, squeezing it.

"It's simple, you see?" Jen hooked her thumb over the back of his hand, rubbing his knuckles. "There's this man I can't stop thinking about." Her voice lowered to a whisper. "He's patient and kind. He's a good listener and very considerate. And he's the best friend anyone could ask for." She paused and cleared her throat. "Only, there's this one problem."

Colt bit his lip. "What kind of problem?"

Jen smiled and placed her other hand on his chest. "I fell in love with him. He makes me happier than I've ever been. And now I want to be more than just a friend. I want to be his wife. I want to share my life with him. Every second of it. I want to wake up with him every morning and lie down beside him every night. And I want to start a family with him." Her gaze dropped to his mouth. "That is, if the offer still stands?"

Colt pulled his free hand from his pocket and cupped her face with his palm. "It does."

A shaky breath escaped her and he tugged her closer, lowering his head and covering her mouth with his. Her lips parted, her sweet taste and her light scent heating his blood.

Conspiratorial whispers turned into a chorus of children's voices. "Mr. Colt and Ms. Jen sitting in a tree. *K-i-s-s-i—*"

Colt groaned, lifted his head and spun around, chasing them with playful smacks to their backsides as they scattered. "Get your little tails outta here."

The boys guffawed. Margaret blushed. And Dominic and Nora chuckled as they rounded the children up and herded them toward the house in the distance.

Colt laughed and shook his head, returning to Jen and rubbing his hands up and down her bare arms. "Now, where were we?"

"You were about to tell me you love me," she said.

He pulled her close again, wrapping his arms around her and pressing her against him. "I love you, Red."

"I love you, too. Now kiss me like you mean it," she teased.

Colt laughed and kissed her properly this time, his tongue slipping between her lips and his hands kneading her back. He angled deeper, savoring her soft moans of pleasure.

He raised his head briefly, his skin tingling under the desperate caress of her hands as they moved over his shoulders, and his chest warmed at her dazed expression. *Beautiful.*

"We better set the wedding date early." She smiled up at him. "Because I'm already eager to start the honeymoon."

Colt chuckled, his whole body humming with happiness. "You haven't seen me at my best yet, baby."

Jen's smile gentled. She glanced over her shoulder at the main house, which Margaret had entered, then looked back, running her eyes over his face and whispering, "Yes, I have."

Colt kissed her again and knew, without a doubt, that he'd finally come home.

* * * * *

Western Romance

Available February 7, 2017

#1629 THE TEXAS VALENTINE TWINS
Texas Legacies: The Lockharts
by Cathy Gillen Thacker
Estranged lovers Wyatt Lockhart and Adelaide Smyth have a one-night stand resulting in twin babies. While figuring out how to coparent they discover they are already married!

#1630 HER COWBOY LAWMAN
Cowboys in Uniform • by Pamela Britton
Sheriff Brennan Connelly, champion former bull rider, reluctantly agrees to help Lauren Danners's son learn to ride bulls. But his attraction to the much younger single mom is a distraction he doesn't need!

#1631 THE COWBOY'S VALENTINE BRIDE
Hope, Montana • by Patricia Johns
An IED sent Brody Mason home from Afghanistan, but he's determined to go back. There's nothing for him in Hope, Montana...except maybe Kaitlyn Harpe, the nurse who's helping him to walk again, ride again and maybe even love again.

#1632 A COWBOY IN HER ARMS
by Mary Leo
Callie Grant is stunned—the daughter of her ex and former best friend is in her kindergarten class! Widower Joel Darwood thinks what might be best for him and his child is Callie, if only he can convince her he's changed...

HWESTCNM0117

REQUEST YOUR FREE BOOKS!
2 FREE NOVELS PLUS 2 FREE GIFTS!

HARLEQUIN®

Western Romance

ROMANCE THE ALL-AMERICAN WAY!

YES! Please send me 2 FREE Harlequin® Western Romance novels and my 2 FREE gifts (gifts are worth about $10). After receiving them, if I don't wish to receive any more books, I can return the shipping statement marked "cancel." If I don't cancel, I will receive 4 brand-new novels every month and be billed just $4.74 per book in the U.S. or $5.49 per book in Canada. That's a savings of at least 12% off the cover price! It's quite a bargain! Shipping and handling is just 50¢ per book in the U.S. and 75¢ per book in Canada.* I understand that accepting the 2 free books and gifts places me under no obligation to buy anything. I can always return a shipment and cancel at any time. Even if I never buy another book, the two free books and gifts are mine to keep forever.

154/354 HDN GJ5V

Name	(PLEASE PRINT)	
Address		Apt. #
City	State/Prov.	Zip/Postal Code

Signature (if under 18, a parent or guardian must sign)

Mail to the **Reader Service**:
IN U.S.A.: P.O. Box 1867, Buffalo, NY 14240-1867
IN CANADA: P.O. Box 609, Fort Erie, Ontario L2A 5X3

Want to try two free books from another line?
Call 1-800-873-8635 or visit www.ReaderService.com.

* Terms and prices subject to change without notice. Prices do not include applicable taxes. Sales tax applicable in N.Y. Canadian residents will be charged applicable taxes. Offer not valid in Quebec. This offer is limited to one order per household. Not valid for current subscribers to Harlequin Western Romance books. All orders subject to credit approval. Credit or debit balances in a customer's account(s) may be offset by any other outstanding balance owed by or to the customer. Please allow 4 to 6 weeks for delivery. Offer available while quantities last.

Your Privacy—The Reader Service is committed to protecting your privacy. Our Privacy Policy is available online at www.ReaderService.com or upon request from the Reader Service.

We make a portion of our mailing list available to reputable third parties that offer products we believe may interest you. If you prefer that we not exchange your name with third parties, or if you wish to clarify or modify your communication preferences, please visit us at www.ReaderService.com/consumerschoice or write to us at Reader Service Preference Service, P.O. Box 9062, Buffalo, NY 14240-9062. Include your complete name and address.

HWR16

SPECIAL EXCERPT FROM

Western Romance

*After their spontaneous reunion results in twin babies,
rancher Wyatt Lockhart insists on staying close to
Adelaide Smythe...even if the proximity makes it hard to
remember why he should stay far away...*

Read on for a sneak preview of
THE TEXAS VALENTINE TWINS,
the latest book in Cathy Gillen Thacker's series
TEXAS LEGACIES: THE LOCKHARTS.

"When were you going to tell me?" Wyatt Lockhart
demanded, furious.

Adelaide Smythe looked at the ruggedly handsome
rancher standing on the front stoop of her Laramie, Texas,
cottage, and tried not to react. An impossible task, given
the way her heart sped up and her knees went all wobbly
any time he was within sight.

Ignoring him, she picked up both duffel bags of baby
clothes, blankets and burp cloths, and carried them to her
waiting SUV.

"I wasn't."

Wyatt moved so she had no choice but to look up at
him.

He looked good, but then he always looked good.
Radiating an impressive amount of testosterone and kick-
butt attitude, he stood, brawny arms folded in front of
him, legs braced apart. Backed against the rear corner of
her vehicle.

His gaze drifted over her as if he were appraising one

of the impeccably trained cutting horses that he bred and sold on his ranch. "You didn't think I would find out?"

She lifted her chin defiantly. "I knew your mother might mention it."

Wyatt stepped back. "My mom knows?"

It was her ranch. Of course Lucille Lockhart knew Adelaide and her six-week-old twins were moving temporarily into the Circle H bunkhouse!

Adelaide marched back to the porch. She picked up the large monogrammed designer suitcase that held her own clothing. The one that, unfortunately, had accompanied her on another, fortuitously ill-begotten, trip.

The way Wyatt was eyeing it said he remembered, too.

Ignoring the heat and strength radiating from his tall body, Adelaide stepped around him and headed for the porch. Unable to help the defeated slump of her slender shoulders, she asked, "When are you going to let our last mistake go?"

He joined her on the porch. "I never said making love with you bothered me."

"Then that makes two of us," she drawled, refusing to admit how small his six-foot-three frame made the portico feel.

Wyatt's gaze roamed her postpregnancy frame, dwelling on the voluptuousness of her curves. "Enough to go again?" he taunted softly.

Adelaide stiffened. "Not if we were the last two people on earth," she vowed.

Don't miss
THE TEXAS VALENTINE TWINS
by Cathy Gillen Thacker, available February 2017
wherever Harlequin® Western Romance®
books and ebooks are sold.

www.Harlequin.com

HWREXP0117

HARLEQUIN®
A Romance FOR EVERY MOOD™

Love the Harlequin book you just read?

Your opinion matters.

Review this book on your favorite
book site, review site, blog or your own
social media properties and share
your opinion with other readers!

HARLEQUIN®

A *Romance* FOR EVERY MOOD™

JUST CAN'T GET ENOUGH?

Join our social communities
and talk to us online.

You will have access to the latest
news on upcoming titles and special
promotions, but most importantly,
you can talk to other fans about your
favorite Harlequin reads.

Harlequin.com/Community

 Facebook.com/HarlequinBooks

 Twitter.com/HarlequinBooks

Pinterest.com/HarlequinBooks

HSOCIAL

HARLEQUIN®

A *Romance* FOR EVERY MOOD™

Stay up-to-date on all your
romance-reading news with the
Harlequin Shopping Guide,
featuring bestselling authors, exciting new
miniseries, books to watch and more!

The newest issue will be delivered right to you
with our compliments! There are 4 each year.

Signing up is easy.

EMAIL

ShoppingGuide@Harlequin.ca

WRITE TO US

HARLEQUIN BOOKS
Attention: Customer Service Department
P.O. Box 9057, Buffalo, NY 14269-9057

OR PHONE

1-800-873-8635 in the United States
1-888-343-9777 in Canada

Please allow 4-6 weeks for delivery of the first issue by mail.

Interactive Storytelling:
Techniques for 21st Century Fiction

Andrew Glassner

A K Peters
Natick, Massachusetts

Editorial, Sales, and Customer Service Office

A K Peters, Ltd.
63 South Avenue
Natick, MA 01760
www.akpeters.com

Library of Congress Cataloging-in-Publication Data

Glassner, Andrew S.
   Interactive Storytelling : techniques for 21st century fiction /
Andrew Glassner
      p. cm.
   Includes bibliographical references and index.
   ISBN 1-56881-221-3
      1. Interactive multimedia. 2. Virtual reality. I. Title.

QA76.76.I59G55 2004
006.7--dc22

                                                              2003062324

Set in 11pt Garamond by Adobe using TeX
Printed on 60lb. acid free paper
Printed & manufactured: Friesens, Altona, Manitoba
Cover design: Karin Hansen
Production editor: Jonathan Peters

Printed in Canada
08 07 06 05   10 9 8 7 6 5 4 3 2

Ad astra per aspera
(Through difficulties, to the stars)

To Steven Drucker

Contents

Preface

E verybody loves a great story, and everybody loves a great game. It seems natural to bring these two very human activities together to create something new that is different from either, but artistically engaging and a lot of fun.

The Quest

History has shown us that finding this new art form is surprisingly difficult. A few plays and staged entertainments involve the audience to some degree, and there are games in which players take on character roles and act them out. But these are niche activities, and haven't caught on in the mainstream to anywhere near the same degree as movies, books, or professional or amateur sports.

The quest to find a way to combine storytelling and gaming has all the qualities of a great story or game: there's a noble goal to be acheived, difficulties to be overcome through understanding and insight, and success to be won by the careful use of skill, planning, and execution.

This quest took on new life in the last years of the 20th century, when video games moved beyond bouncing a white square back and forth, and started to incorporate realistic environments, and then well-written stories and characters [39]. As computers and consoles improved technically, video games became more visually interesting, their sound and music improved dramatically, and new interaction techniques appeared. As designers sought to make their games deeper and more engaging, they naturally started to incorporate stories and characters into their work.

I wrote this book because I want to play really great games that are blended with really great stories. I hope that this book will help hasten the day of their arrival.

Who This Book Is For

This book is for everyone who's involved in creating and developing games that have story qualities. Everyone from the lead designer to a software engineer, from the person who lays out the instruction manual to the composer creating the soundtrack, has a hand in shaping the final product. The more they all share common ideas and vocabulary, the easier it is for them all to share the same vision of the product, and work together towards that vision.

This isn't a theory book. I don't review or critique various theories of narrative, or abstract principles of human competition. Rather, this is the nuts-and-bolts material that I think needs to be a part of the creative toolkits of everyone working on projects that combine both games and stories.

For example, suppose that we're creating a new space exploration game, and the art director asks you, as one of the staff artists, to create a "scary alien." Sure, you could draw something that could scare the shoes off a zombie, but it might or might not fit in with the rest of the game. As a wise and thoughtful artist, you'd come back to the team planning the game and ask them questions about the purpose of this alien, what feelings it should evoke, how the main character is going to react to it and why, how it moves the story forward, and so on. If our hero is afraid of slimy things, then we might make the first few aliens smooth and dry on the outside, so we can hit him with a sudden blast of slim-iness later on for emotional impact. Is the hero smart? If so, this alien might be scary indeed, yet have a subtle but fatal weakness that the hero only uncovers by using his brains. So although we can design an alien that simply accomplishes the task of looking scary, but how much better if that alien, and the hero's response to it, tells us something about the hero and his world.

If you're the software engineer writing the artificial intelligence for how this alien behaves, this all applies to you as well. The same goes for the composer, the 3D modeler, the lighting designer, the engineer designing the motion of the camera, and everyone else on the project.

If you work on any aspect of games that have stories and characters, or you plan to work on them, this book is for you.

The Big Picture

This book is organized into four parts.

In Part I, I discuss the classical structure of stories. The goal is to lay down a solid groundwork of the basic ideas and vocabulary that form the core of the storyteller's craft.

In Part II, I talk about the varieties of games, and those qualities of an experience that make it feel more like a game than like something else.

In Part III, I compare the structures discussed in the first two parts. One of the interesting things that will emerge from this discussion is that the qualities that make good stories and games are fundamentally contradictory in several important ways. Each of those contradictions is a potential problem, which we need to consciously address in our designs.

In Part IV, I bring these pieces together, and introduce the idea of Story Environments. These are places where players come together in a shared social experience created by game builders and storytellers. Some other directions for bringing together stories and games are sketched out in a series of experiments, so that we can discover what people will enjoy the most in this new medium.

Stories and Games

I play a lot of games. I've played most of the video games mentioned in this book, usually to completion. As much as I enjoy playing, I've been frustrated by seeing many bad designs appear time and again.

Game designers are in a bind today. If they design a game that uses storytelling ideas in a new and creative way, odds are that the game will fail commercially, artistically, or both. Relying on today's clumsy and clunky techniques results in a poor storytelling experience. To make matters worse, there's rarely enough time or budget available to develop something new.

Designers can turn to ideas from theoreticians who have published papers and books on new forms of storytelling, based on everything from literary deconstruction to post-modern analysis. But although many of these ideas are intellectually fascinating, they're abstract and theoretical: they talk about interesting possibilities, but they don't describe stories that people actually want.

We know what kinds of stories people want, and they don't require a new theory of story. Billions of people have been telling each other stories for millennia, and millions have done it professionally. Every possible form of story structure and storytelling technique has been explored, probably many times over, by people who were passionate, creative, and skilled. The result has been the type of stories that we are familiar with today. In the Western tradition, modern readers can read Ovid (either in the original Latin or in translation), and although the language may be challenging, the structure of his stories is familiar and easy to follow. From fairy tales to Beowulf, from the Bible to the plays of Shakespeare, most of the stories we know and remember have similar structures and forms.

There's a simple reason for this consistency: the dominant, time-honored form of story structure works. If some other form worked better, or other forms worked as well, we'd see them around in profusion today. But the marketplace of stories, from television to film, from novels to magazines, is almost entirely populated by structures that are familiar to us: one or more engaging characters is engaged in a struggle to achieve a goal, and works towards that goal. Even simple character studies are propelled by this structure, though the goals can be internal, and psychologically subtle.

Games, on the other hand, have much less unifying structure. The solitaire card game of Klondike has little in common with chess or tennis except that they are bound by a series of rules. A backgammon player and a soccer player are engaged in radically different activities. Of course, there are unifying ideas (and I'll discuss them in this book), but the diversity of game structures is broad and constantly expanding.

Most games have no story qualities in them. We can relate last night's poker game in story form, but the game itself isn't a narrative. In fact, very few games incorporate much in the way of story, and there's no reason they should. From soccer to *Scrabble*, we play for the pleasure of the game, spending social time with friends, and refining and demonstrating our skills and abilities. This is all true of video games as well, and games from *Tetris* to *TextTwist* are great fun with no story.

But clearly many designers are reaching out to put more story and characterization into their games. Characters are becoming financially important to game studios; Lara Croft has made the transition from *Tomb Raider* video games to the movie screen. We can see characters develop from one game to the next. For example, the character of Jak in *Jak and Daxster: The Precursor Legacy* reveals a new aspect to his personality in the sequel *Jak II*, and the bond between the title characters in *Ratchet and Clank* matures in the sequel *Ratchet and Clank 2: Going Commando*.

My interest in this book will be in the types of games that further this trend of including story into active gameplay experiences. I have nothing against games that don't have stories; in this direction; I play lots of them and enjoy them. But they won't get much of our attention here, except as examples.

The goal of melding the two very different experiences of storytelling and gaming will be our companion throughout this book. We'll start with the basics of both fields, and then talk about how we can bring them together.

A Couple of Notes on Style

As everyone who has tried to write in a gender-neutral way has realized, English is a very inconvenient language for avoiding gender bias. Omitting any gender makes for awkward sentences, and constantly using phrases like "he or she" and "his or her" quickly becomes repetitive. I also find that switching between "he" and "she," and using new constructions like "s/he," are both jarring. So in this book I will use, without prejudice, the historical convention of the masculine pronoun.

I've broken the bibliography into several sections, grouped by the type of entry. The only reference numbers that appear in the body of the book are those in the first section of the bibliography, which covers mostly works of non-fiction. Games, novels, television shows, and movies are identified in the text with italics, and they have corresponding entries in the bibliography, arranged alphabetically by medium.

Acknowledgements

Throughout the writing of this book, I've relied on friends, family, and colleagues for encouragement, feedback, and focus. It gives me great pleasure to thank Eric Braun and Wendy Siegel, Steven Drucker, Glenn Entis, Bruce Glassner and Lisa DeGisi, Eric Haines, Christopher Rosenfelder and Becky Brendlin, Sterling Van Wagenen, and Curtis Wong for discussions, encouragement, and support. Thank you to Klaus and Alice Peters and the entire staff at A K Peters for their help and support.

Part I
Introduction

People, Stories, and Games

Stories are an important part of our lives. Our media tell us stories every day, in movies, the nightly news, and even advertisements. Some of our stories are very personal: "the story of our life" isn't just a metaphor, but something we actually tell to ourselves and other people to give shape and meaning to who we are.

Every one of us tells stories every day. These aren't of the formally scripted and produced variety, but the kind that we make up as we go: we tell what we've done, and how other people responded. We're all natural storytellers and story audiences.

Authors who study the craft are able to raise storytelling from this informality to a more universal level, where their stories have meaning to large numbers of people. Stories as old as *Hamlet* and as recent as *Star Wars* have captured the imaginations of millions of people all over the world.

For many of us, there's something appealing about the idea of being able to not just watch great stories, but to actually be *in* them: to step into their world and become participants. We'd love to be there with Sam Spade as he searches for the black bird in *The Maltese Falcon*, help Indiana Jones save the day in *Raiders of the Lost Ark*, or just float down the river with Huck and Jim in *The Adventures of Huckleberry Finn*.

3

Probably the best-known example of this idea is the *holodeck*, introduced in 1990 on the TV show *Star Trek: The Next Generation*. The holodeck is an imaginary room that is capable of simulating any environment and everything inside it, including other people. You can run or walk anywhere to your heart's content, eat and drink, and even get into fistfights, all with perfect simulated reality, without ever leaving the room. The idea of such technology has been around since at least 1950, when Ray Bradbury wrote a short story called "The Veldt"[305]. In this story children played in their "nursery," which could envelop them in any environment.

But neither *Star Trek* nor "The Veldt" told us how such environments would actually support stories. Instead, we watched (or read) authored stories that showed authored characters participating in their simulated worlds. What if these characters were removed, and we took their place? Would our adventures be as interesting as theirs?

Suppose that someday we are able to develop such a device and use it to become fully immersed in a story. Will our time spent there be enjoyable? Will it be rewarding? And, of course, there's the big question:

Will it be *fun*?

In this chapter I'll discuss some of the big issues that come up when we think about becoming part of a story. I'll return to many of these topics later in the book.

It's All About People

People have told one another an untold number of stories, and there are an untold number yet to come. Yet throughout all cultures and eras, there is something in common to them all.

Great stories are about people.

Sometimes the people look like bugs (*Antz*), savannah animals (*The Lion King*), or even old cartoons (*Who Framed Roger Rabbit?*), but behind their appearances the characters are always people. The main character in the children's book *The Missing Piece* is a simple line drawing of a circle with a dot for an eye and a missing pie wedge for a mouth, but that circle is still recognizably a person "inside." Science-fiction and monster stories like *Alien* or *Jurassic Park* are usually more about the people who must deal with the bizarre and dangerous creatures than about the creatures themselves.

When we enter into the world of a story, we may find ourselves in a world where teleportation is an everyday activity, dogs have colonized

Mars, and politicians tell the truth, among other improbabilities. Exploring unusual worlds will be a lot of fun, but it won't be unlike exploring an unfamiliar city or taking a hike in a new park. Just as with those activities, most people will find it more fun to explore interactive story worlds with friends than do it alone. And though the spaceships in those worlds may be fun to fly, the monsters exhilarating to battle, and the mysteries a challenge to unravel, it will ultimately be the other people we share it with who will make our experience meaningful.

It will be a long time before any computer simulation of a person will be anywhere nearly as interesting as a real person. Computers today simply don't have much range of expression, knowledge, or common sense, nor the command of language and the mix of unpredictability and coherency that we recognize in other living people. So as we think about the imaginary worlds we might enter, we should keep our eye on the fact that it's the other real people we'll meet there who will make us want to go back again.

Foundations

The central theme of this book is that we'll find a way to combine participation and storytelling by looking at stories and games and learning from the history of both subjects. I'll also refer to some commercial and artistic works that have tried to merge stories and games, and see what we can learn from them. The goal is to find out both what has worked and what has not. That way we can continue to try new things, exploring the best ideas and not repeating mistakes.

We'll also look at what people like about these activities. Historically, people have enjoyed professionally-written stories as audience members, rather than as participants. In contrast to this quiet absorption and imaginative engagement, we usually play games actively with friends or watch professionals play them in tournaments. The difference between these passive and active roles will prove to be a significant challenge when looking at how to bring stories and games together, but it's not insurmountable.

Looking at Stories

As I said earlier, we're all fine informal storytellers. But casual stories are different from those created by professionals who have studied the craft.

There's an old anecdote that goes like this:

> Suppose you're talking to a group of 8-year-old children. If you ask them, "Who here is an artist?" you'll probably find that they all raise their hands. If you ask, "Who can play piano?" or "Who is a dancer?" again most of them will raise their hands.
>
> Now ask the same questions of a group of 15-year-olds, and you'll get a very different result. When you ask them, "Who here is an artist?" you'll find that almost none of the teenagers raise their hands; maybe only one or two brave souls will dare.

The typical interpretation of this story is that we drain creativity and spirit out of our children as they grow, replacing their youthful enthusiasm with disillusion and self-limiting boundaries. I'm sure that some children are indeed belittled and made to feel uncreative as they grow up, but I don't think that's the norm.

Rather, I think what this anecdote tells us is that as we grow up we develop an appreciation for skill and ability. Most of us have probably picked up a guitar at some point, or sat in front of a piano and tried to noodle around a bit. We compared the results with the music we hear every day, and we realized that those who have studied and practiced have indeed developed a specialized ability. If an 8-year-old says he's a piano player, he probably means he can sit down and amuse himself at the piano for a while. When a 15-year-old who's never played piano seriously says he's not a piano player, it's because he's heard professional jazz and rock pianists and has discovered for himself that he doesn't have their skills. With study and practice, he could learn to be a piano player. But until then, he willingly reserves the title "pianist" for those who have developed the skills.

Similarly, most of the casual stories we tell to each other work well as part of informal conversations with people we know, but they probably wouldn't work as well if they were transcribed and turned directly into a novel, television show, or movie, and had to compete for attention with professionally authored stories. In Part I we'll look at the structure of stories and see some of the tools used by authors to create stories that have a wide and lasting appeal.

Looking at Games

Regardless of how we finally do it, when we "enter a story" we'll be voluntarily entering a shared, structured environment. We already share structured environments all the time, from the roads we drive on to the restaurants we eat in. The rules and conventions of these environments help us get along with other people, and for the most part the structure of our society enables us to make our own decisions and choices without interfering with the lives of other people.

But if we're inside a story, then getting enmeshed in other people's lives is going to be pretty important. And these interactions themselves are key, because they're the elements that make up the story.

What we seek is some kind of structured environment where people know the rules and understand not just what their options are (and what options are disallowed), but also what they're trying to achieve.

Happily, we have thousands of years of experience with precisely this kind of thing: games. Games are as much a part of human life as stories. Every culture and every era has had its games, some played in private by one or more people, and some played in public before crowds of spectators. Some games are fads that catch fire and then fade away, and some last for centuries or millennia.

One of the most appealing things about games is that they are incredibly diverse: there are word games, physical games, mental games, action games, and an endless array of other types. In Part II we'll look at the structure of games, and what most games have in common with each other.

Economics

Designing entertainment of any kind is hard, but when we start designing interactive activities involving computers and networks, things get very complicated very fast. A lot of companies and a lot of people lost their way in the first half of the 1800s trying to find the Northwest Passage, and the same thing is happening in the pursuit of a mixture of online interaction and storytelling.

I think that, despite the lack of results, this idea is still appealing to people for a few different reasons. First, there's simply the gut feeling that it could be *fun*. For some of us, the idea of getting "inside" a story just has an innate appeal. Second, it feels like something that's just too natural not to happen. After all, the technology we use for entertainment (e.g., television and the Internet) and the technology we use for communicating (e.g., telephones and mail) are quickly moving towards each other. Today, you can play video games on your cell phone, listen to the radio on your computer, and send email from your time organizer. With all of these hardware and software mergers happening, it seems inevitable that the activities they support should gracefully merge as well. Third, there's a lot of money to be made.

In fact, there is a *lot* of money to be made. It seems very likely that any form of participatory storytelling will draw at least partly on the techniques developed for video games. The economic impact of these games has grown rapidly in the last few years. Let's look at just a few typical pieces of information to get a feeling for the big picture.

In 2001, the video game industry made $9.4 billion in revenue. Compare this revenue to the movie industry, whose U.S. box office ticket sales were $8.5 billion (this box-office figure doesn't include related income from sales of merchandise, sales and rentals of videos and DVDs, television broadcast rights, and other income streams). The risks are pretty high as well: many contemporary video games now require an investment of around $8 to $10 million to produce [8].

It's no secret that professional sports have a lot of emotional and financial appeal to a lot of people. But the number of video and electronic games sold in 2001 dwarfs the number of tickets sold to professional sporting events [65]. In 2001, about 225 million computer and video games were sold. This is 11 times the number of NHL tickets sold, 11 times the number of NBA tickets sold, and 14 times the number of NFL tickets sold. And there are a lot of consoles, too: over 38 million dedicated game machines had been sold by May 2002 [133]. The audience is skewed heavily towards adults: 70 percent of PlayStation 2 gamers are over 18 [73].

Individual games can demonstrate amazing sales figures. The console game *The Legend of Zelda: Ocarina of Time* was released in late 1998 for the Christmas holiday season. It sold nearly 2.5 million copies at a price of about $60 each, which comes to about $150 million. During the last six weeks of 1998, that one game made more money than any feature film playing in that time (its nearest competitor was the film *A Bug's Life*, which made about $114 million) [86].

Games are changing the business models of even some of the largest companies. In 2001, the Sony Corporation, a huge company that designs and manufactures consumer and professional high-technology equipment and owns record labels and film studios, made 62 percent of its operating income from games [96] (more information on the finances of the field can be found at the Interactive Digital Software Association [66], and at NPD, Inc. [129]).

So game designers have a lot of financial as well as creative incentive for developing products that people are going to want to buy and enjoy.

Right now it's still very hard to predict which games will be commercial or artistic successes and which will be failures. A big part of the problem is that video games are signnifcantly shaped by their underlying technology. When the game hardware changes (such as from the PlayStation to the PlayStation 2, or from the Nintendo 64 to the GameCube), the games themselves change radically. And players' expectations change right along with them. *Myst* was a big hit on PCs when it came out in 1994, but it probably wouldn't sell very well if it was released today. With each new advance in the hardware, everything about the games changes: sound and graphics improve, the worlds get larger, more people can get involved (and from increasingly remote locations), and generally everything gets bigger and more complex. Games that sell fast and are great fun one year often appear technically primitive and full of clichés just a few years later.

Perhaps the safest approach to making a new game is simply to copy a hit, changing just enough so that it feels like a new experience. That keeps the risks down if you believe that what sold well yesterday will also sell well tomorrow, but it also limits the opportunities for innovation. Being too innovative has its own risks as well, since a game that is too different from its peers may confuse or not even find its audience. So most of the time we find that if a game is a hit, we can count on seeing an official sequel before too long, as well as plenty of copycats.

One problem with tinkering with a winning formula is that you can accidentally dilute or even eliminate a vital element. And changing one thing in a complex system is almost always going to affect one or more other things, often in surprising and unexpected ways.

For example, most of us are not airplane designers, but we ride in airplanes, and we like some types of planes more than others. So if we had the chance to take an existing plane and improve it, we might space the rows farther apart to give everyone more leg room and widen the aisles so it's easier to get baggage on and off the plane. But moving the seats (and the people inside them) might affect the balance of the plane, and thus its aerodynamics, creating a choppier ride. It could also result in fewer seats, raising the price per seat, which could result in reductions in the quality and quantity of the service we originally set out to improve.

Suppose an opera set designer decides that a balcony would look better a few steps higher up than originally planned. That change might require just enough extra exertion from the singers to make them slightly out of breath when they reach the top, resulting in a little less control when they sing, and thus a diminished musical quality in their performance. The lesson is that as we try to make one part of a complex system better, we can accidentally make another important part worse.

The right way to improve a complex system like an airplane, an opera, a video game, or any kind of participatory story experience, is to first understand how and why it works. Then we can make informed changes that won't cause other parts of the system to be accidentally damaged or upset the overall balance of the parts.

Where We Are

The quest to "enter the story" has been around for many years. We can see discussions of this idea directly and indirectly in recent books, such as *Hamlet on the Holodeck: The Future of Narrative in Cyberspace* [98], *Computers as Theatre* [81], *The Art of Computer Game Design* [31], *Cybertext*[1], *The New Media Reader*[137], and *Digital Illusion: Entertaining the Future with High Technology* [42]. Despite these books, and many independent and commercial projects, the structure of participatory stories remains unknown.

Let's take a brief look at where we are now.

When fictional characters resonate with us, we often find ourselves caring deeply about them as we watch them move in their world. Soap opera fans are famous for becoming emotionally attached to their most loved (and despised) characters. People often talk about television shows, comparing notes on what the characters did, or should have done, or shouldn't have done.

Audience involvement in TV is at one end of a one-way pipe from the people producing the show to their audience. The fans of a TV show usually have little or nothing to do with the production of the show itself. They may get so wrapped up in it that they spin their own stories that take place in the world of the show or book (a phenomenon known as fan fiction), but that's different from actually entering that story and talking to the characters.

Even if one were to visit a television or movie set, there are no "characters" to be found, only actors reading lines provided by the writers and following the blocking provided by their directors. The physical world of the show exists no further than the edges of the sets. Unless one or more actors want to improvise in-character, our visitor will find that there is no story to enter, no world to inhabit, and no characters to engage.

When we look at pieces of contemporary "interactive theater," such as *Tony and Tina's Wedding*, and Renaissance Fairs, and games like *Dungeons & Dragons*, we can see examples of stories where people are truly able to join in and deal with each other as characters. You can do or say almost anything in such environments, and the other people will do their best to see it in the context of the event and keep the shared imaginative experience going.

A lot of people play participatory games on a regular basis: in 1999, about 2.8 million people people played a paper-based tabletop role-playing game (such as *Dungeons & Dragons*) at least once a month [114]. This group is skewed heavily towards younger players: 79% of those players are 18 or under [37] (this is almost exactly the opposite of the PlayStation 2 demographic). That's still a lot of people and an important audience. But it's nowhere near the number of people who read books, watch television, and go to movies. For example, the season finale of the TV show *Seinfeld* drew about 50 million viewers in the U.S., and the ice-skating finals at the 2002 Winter Olympics were watched by about 52 million people in the U.S. [4]. These are exceptional numbers, but popular shows still draw huge audiences. In 2002 the average U.S. audience for an episode of the TV show *Friends* was over 30 million people [54].

Technology has a large role to play in all storytelling. Whether it's a flickering campfire and the sound of a lone voice, words on a page, the electronics of radio, or the latest virtual-reality gear, the medium is an essential part of any story. Technology is also vital to gaming. Dice and cards are used for many games, and tennis racquets, baseball gloves, and paintball guns are all essential to their respective games.

Technology is changing at a furious rate: today many people rely on devices from personal computers to cell phones that simply didn't exist even 20 years ago. Though we can't be certain how technology will develop, we can anticipate changes in broad terms and design for systems we believe will be available in the next few years.

Talking About Participation

The language of stories, games, and participation is far from settled. There are a lot of terms floating around right now in everything from ads for the latest video games to theoretical academic papers. With everyone using the same few words to cover a wide variety of different ideas, there's a lot of misunderstanding.

When we talk about people becoming part of ongoing stories, we often hear words like "interactive" and "nonlinear" cropping up. These words have wildly different meanings to different people, and in my experience they usually cause more confusion than clarity.

Let's look at a couple of examples of how ambiguous these words can be.

Reading a book is often described as a "passive" experience: we sit comfortably, read words, and turn pages. There's not much physical activity going on. Now, when we picture a novel's main character in our head, how shall we describe that? Have we become "active"? In some ways, we have: we're doing creative work (the character isn't imagining himself). But the words on the page don't change in response to what goes on in our heads. If the book describes a character as a short man in a red coat, and because we didn't read it closely, or don't like that image, we instead see in our mind's eye a tall man in a blue coat, the character isn't going to start bumping his head on low doorways. So although we're doing work to create the story in our own heads, we're not actually affecting the story.

Should we describe this then as an "interactive" experience? In some ways that seems reasonable: the book needs us to create the imaginary world it describes, and we need the book to describe that world so that we can imagine it. This mutually dependent relationship might be described as "interactive," but that doesn't seem to capture the inability of both the reader and the author to modify the work as it's being read.

How about if the book periodically stops the narrative and literally asks us to make a decision and then turn to a particular page based on that choice? The children's book series *Choose Your Own Adventure* [26] lets readers do exactly that. For example, in the book *A New Hope* readers move through sections in a sequence that's determined by their choices. Is this "interactive?" It seems more active than just reading, because our choices affect the story we read, but they still don't change the words on the page (just which ones we read and in what order).

These issues crop up in media other than books and don't require any kind of special production techniques. Suppose we're watching a mystery movie at home on a DVD, and halfway through we get really anxious to know who committed the murder. So we jump to the last few minutes and watch the detective spell out the crime and arrest the bad guy. Now that we're more relaxed, we can go back to the place where we stopped and watch the rest of the movie.

What happened here? When we jumped to the end, we made a conscious decision to alter the flow of the story from how it was designed to be seen, and instead we watched it in the order we wanted. Unlike *A New Hope* nobody prompted us to make a decision and offered specific choices; we just did what we wanted. Was this an "interactive" movie experience?

There's no general agreement on what "interactivity" means when it comes to stories. You can make a good argument both for and against calling any of these examples "interactive."

The words "active" and "passive," "interactive," "participatory," "linear" and "non-linear," "co-creative," and a dozen more are floating around with ambiguous and contradictory meanings. The result is that when someone speaks of "interactive fiction," it's like speaking about "morality" or "God": you need to stop the conversation and have a separate discussion to make sure you know what the speaker means by that word, and even then there's a lot of ambiguity.

Larger phrases like "interactive hypertext," "non-linear story," "interactive fiction," and "participatory narrative" (and many others) have the same problems. The result is that all of these terms are now pretty ambiguous except in a context where everything has first been very carefully defined.

In this book I'll use the term "interactive storytelling" to refer to the most general ideas, or to the idea of story participation as a concept. I'll use the new phrase "story environments" to refer to the new ideas I'll be introducing later on.

One-Way and Two-Way Stories

Earlier I talked about the trouble of describing even the common act of reading as "interactive." To avoid another linguistic whirlpool, I'll call this a *one-way* experience. The information flows from the book to your head, but not the other way around. Both you and the book are essential to the reading experience, and you can do whatever you want with the words you read, but nothing you choose to do in your mind will alter the words on the page. The flow of information is in one direction only: from the book to you.

Now let's suppose that we make this a *two-way* experience. This is really the distinction that most people are trying to make when they speak of "interactive fiction," or "participatory story," or similar phrases. The idea is that you, the audience member, actually affect the story itself.

You can certainly do that now: the next time a friend is telling you a story, you could interrupt frequently and ask for more information about some detail, or tell him to skip over a section of the story, or ask him to hurry up here and slow down there. Of course, you'd drive him crazy. And if someone did this to us, it would drive us crazy as well, and we might finally ask him just to be quiet and let us tell the story the way we think it's best told. Authors of stories intended for general audiences would similarly ask to be allowed to tell their stories their way.

Suppose that to avoid this problem, we deliberately build in opportunities for an audience to make decisions in a story as it's being told. Let's take as an example the movie *Blade Runner*. During the film, government agent Rick Deckard interviews a woman named Rachael, who works as a secretary for the powerful Dr. Eldon Tyrell. Deckard is trying to determine whether Rachael's a human being or a replicant (or android) manufactured by Tyrell. The interview takes far longer than usual, but he eventually determines that Rachael is, indeed, a replicant, although she seems to be unaware of this. Tyrell later confirms Deckard's conclusion. When Deckard returns home that night, he finds Rachael in his apartment, waiting for him. She wants to convince him she's not a replicant.

And now, we place Deckard's response in the hands of the audience. Should he:

1. Apologize and say he was wrong?

2. Prove to her that she's a replicant?

3. Tell her a story from his past?

4. Offer her a glass of wine?

14

There's no need to stop with this set of questions. We can ask the audience to help out in other ways, too. Should we:

1. Introduce a sub-plot involving a stolen tree?

2. Score the scene with happy music?

3. Give Deckard an itch on his right forearm?

4. Foreshadow something about fish scales?

The first set of four questions may seem reasonable (they're not, as I'll argue later), but the questions in the second set are clearly ridiculous to ask of an audience. The last one in the list doesn't even make sense, since the audience doesn't know that fish scales are going to appear later in the story. So there's a continuum here. The audience might be asked some things about the story and how it's presented, but not others.

If you've seen the movie, then you know that Deckard's choices in this encounter with Rachael are crucial to the rest of the story. They're not cosmetic choices, such as whether he should wear brown or black shoes, but fundamental decisions that tell us a lot about both Deckard and Rachael and give a heightened emotional meaning to later events.

One of the issues here is the internal coherency of the narrative. A great story is like a thread in a tapestry: it's held in place by many other threads, and it has its own rhythm for weaving through them. Although we see only one thread, by virtue of resonant detail and consistency we perceive the larger fabric that surrounds it, and that helps to give it an internal coherency. These details appear in everything from a character's wardrobe to his vocabulary.

Great stories aren't just sequences of events: everything is there for a reason, and often that reason isn't apparent until much later in the story.

Suppose that when Deckard finds Rachael in his apartment, we are given control of the situation, and we decide that he should shoot her on sight. So he does. Now what do we have? I don't know, but it's certainly not *Blade Runner* any more. Could it be a good story? Maybe. It's a whole new ball game at this point. But who's writing it? Where's the consistency and coherency going to come from? It's not likely that we, the audience, are going to be able to supply it, because we don't know what's coming up. There's no way for us to shape the story in a general way. Rather, we'd be like drivers in heavy fog, steering our car on unmarked streets in an unfamiliar city: we can see only a few feet ahead of us, we have no idea where we're going, and we feel fortunate if we can just avoid causing a wreck.

Let's focus for a moment on a single, but important, aspect of the scene: the music. Should we score their meeting with tension-building music? Sure, if there's a chase just around the corner. But if Deckard's going to go to bed and get a good night's sleep, then we probably want more contemplative music. We, the audience, don't know what's coming, so we can't pick the music. And until we make our decisions, *nobody* knows what's coming, so picking the right music is impossible. We'd end up either with no music or with something so bland and generic that the scene could go either way later on. That means we've lost all the emotional power that music could have brought to this scene.

Finding a form of two-way participation in a story that doesn't drive the storyteller crazy, and doesn't interfere with the story itself, has proven to be very hard. Most of the obvious approaches have been tried and haven't gained a lot of popularity.

If the goal is to simply provide an experience that has elements of both games and stories, that's easily accomplished. For example, the action-based game *Star Wars: The Clone Wars* offers you a series of missions, each of which is basically a small game that requires fighting and shooting your way through an environment filled with enemies. Between each mission there's a movie-like scene that presents another little segment in an ongoing story. You can view this overall experience as a story that's moved along by playing the games or as a set of games that are given some context by the story. But neither of these elements actually affects the other: if you removed the story sequences, it wouldn't change the games at all (you'd still do exactly the same things to win each mission); and if you removed the games, you could still watch the story segments in order (though you'd need a little bit of connective material to explain that the objectives of the game segments had been achieved).

This genre of alternating game-and-story can be a lot of fun. But there is no communication between the story and game elements: each lives in its own world. The story pieces are like books: they're one-way communication from the game to you. The game elements are two-way while you're playing, but then the story returns, and you're back to one-way communication. Not all games work this way, but it's a common approach.

When I talk of developing a new entertainment form in which we are able to participate in a story, I'm thinking of activities that are inherently two-way all the way through, where each piece fundamentally affects the others, and our participation in the experience doesn't switch between one-way and two-way.

Control and Conflict

An important difference between reading a book and being a part of a story is that in the latter case you can make a difference in what happens. That's the whole appeal of participating. When we're able to make a difference, we're able to exert *control*. But fiction has traditionally gotten a lot of mileage out of frustrating the audience's desire for control.

In the horror movie *The Shining*, Jack Torrance, his wife Wendy, and their son Danny move into the remote and isolated Overlook Hotel as the winter caretakers. As time goes by, Jack starts to hallucinate and to become increasingly disturbed and violent. Eventually Wendy realizes that her family is in danger and decides to use the CB radio, which is their one and only link to the outside world, to call for help to get them out of there. Jack promptly sabotages the radio (and the snow tractor as well, for good measure).

Now, when we discover that Jack has prevented his family from either calling for help or getting away, thereby trapping them in the hotel with his growing murderous insanity, I doubt that very many people in the theater are cheering him on. In fact most of us are probably cringing in our seats, hoping he'll snap out of it, or wishing that Wendy could find a way to fix the radio or tractor, squirming as we picture terrible fates for Wendy and Danny.

If we were able to exert some control over Jack in this moment, we probably wouldn't let him disable the radio. Some people would encourage him to do it, and perhaps even goad him on further, out of a sense of mischief or curiosity. But most people who were wrapped up in the story and cared for Wendy and Danny would want to stop Jack.

Now if Jack were in fact to be stopped, we'd have a different story. If the Fire Service were to fly out and rescue the family before they came to any more harm, that would be the end of *The Shining*. Things might then develop into an interesting story, or they might not. But in any case, it would be a different story.

The problem with giving the audience control of a story is that they will often, quite reasonably, act to reduce tension and avoid conflict. But tension and conflict are at the heart of great stories. Without these qualities a story has no dramatic pressure. Things may happen, but they have no emotional force.

This problem gets even harder when our heroes are not likable (such people are often called *anti-heroes*). In the film *Taxi Driver*, the lead character, Travis Bickle, is violent, angry, and anti-social. In the TV show *Lexx*, the ship's captain, Stanley Tweedle, is petulant, selfish, and thoughtless. In the TV show *The Sopranos*, the lead character, Tony Soprano, is a caring family man, but also a mean-spirited, brutally vengeful mobster and murderer. If we had some control in these stories, what would we do? For starters, most of us probably wouldn't let these people continue to abuse and hurt the people around them. But if we did that, the stories themselves would immediately collapse and we'd have nothing left. Children enjoy watching the happy television world of *The Teletubbies*, where any problems are minuscule (and are quickly resolved anyway), but as adults we quickly tire of stories where everything is just peachy all the time.

So we have a problem: our natural inclinations are to stop people from doing hurtful things, or things that cause conflict and tension, but those are the essence of drama.

In some forms of participatory theater (such as *Tony and Tina's Wedding*), and some games (such as *Dungeons & Dragons*), people in the story have a lot of freedom to control what goes on. But they are kept from eliminating all conflict and breaking the narrative by the active participation of talented human beings who are dedicated to keeping the tension alive in as natural a way as possible. These very skilled people are not in abundant supply. We're not going to get very far in developing a new form of storytelling if we require such experts to be around to support us every time we want to enter a story.

So control is a very tricky problem. No control means no way to affect the story, and that puts an end to our dream of being "part" of the unfolding tale. But too much control, or the wrong kind of control, and we can easily eliminate conflict, perhaps even accidentally, and thus cut the story off at the knees and end it.

Finding a solution to this problem requires recognizing and balancing the responsibilities, freedoms, and desires of both the creators of stories and the audiences that can inhabit them. I'll return to these issues in later chapters as we discuss stories and games.

Hardware

Movies have come a long way since the Lumière brothers showed their first film at the Grand Café in Paris on December 28, 1895 [214]. The movie started with a scene they shot on their father's lawn. As Auguste pointed his camera, his brother Louis stepped on the lawn hose. When the family gardener came out to water the lawn, he picked up the hose as usual, but no water came out. When he looked down into the hose to see if it was blocked, Louis stepped off. The gardener got a faceful of water, and the slapstick film was born. Technical improvements such as sound, color, and widescreen followed, and so did artistic ones.

Not all technical advances have been widely embraced. In 1952, 3D movies made their debut [100]. The first theatrically released 3D movie, *Bwana Devil*, required the audience to wear special glasses in order to see people and objects in the film jump out of the screen and into their laps. Although more 3D movies have been made, nobody's found a way to show them to a theater full of people without the need for special glasses. The inconvenience and discomfort of the glasses has prevented 3D movies from becoming much more than a novelty.

The completely realistic virtual environments described in "The Veldt" [305] and shown on the holodeck are not around the corner. Of all the senses that are stimulated by computers, vision is probably the one that's most satisfied right now. With enough time and money, feature films like *Star Wars: Episode II–Attack of the Clones* can populate their cast with entirely digital characters that appear as realistic as anything else in the movie [44]. These characters can even take on major roles in the film, as Gollum does in *Lord of the Rings II: The Two Towers* [49]. Sound is the next most advanced stimulated sense, but it's far behind graphics. Although certain musical instruments can be simulated very well, I've yet to hear a synthesized human voice that sounds like a real person. Although many people are working on the science of touch (called haptics), that field is far behind even sound. There are many other types of sensory stimuli that people have yet to simulate well, such as taste and smell, balance, pressure, and hot and cold. All of these will be vital to any fully realistic simulated environment.

Although a complete holodeck is nowhere on the horizon for any amount of money, smaller pieces of specialized equipment are being manufactured for specific activities. Home flight-simulator pilots can buy a yoke and console like that in a real plane, and enthusiasts of driving games can buy steering wheels with force feedback mechanisms that let them feel the potholes in the road and the vibration of the engine.

There's little doubt that game consoles and home computers will continue to improve, offering increasingly complex and believable images and sounds. But the most important hardware advance on the horizon will not come from an ability to render larger numbers of polygons, more textures, or more channels of sound. Rather, it will be the increasing ease with which computers of all types (including those inside game consoles and television sets) will be able to connect to each other and to centralized computers.

But even then it's not really the networks between computers that are the interesting thing here; it's that the connections bring together the people using those computers.

The future is just as it's always been: people.

As our computers get better at bringing people into shared experiences, we will find that we have game and story opportunities that simply don't exist today.

Many of today's computer games are solitaire or solo experiences. That's fine when you want to be alone. When you want to be with other people, there are many different ways to be social while gaming today. When nobody else is around, you can play against computer-controlled characters who act as your competitors and teammates in *Battlefield 1942*, your helpers in service of another character in *Final Fantasy X*, your underlings in *Pikmin*, or a mix of all of these in *Grand Theft Auto: Vice City*. If other people are in the same room with you, you can play head-to-head in a sports simulation in *Madden NFL 2003*, all-out combat in *Unreal Tournament 2003*, or just good-natured competition in *Mario Party 4*. If you want to play with other people but they're not right there with you, you can play one-on-one at the *Internet Gaming Zone* [128], or in large groups in *Everquest*.

The latest generation of game consoles have some ability to connect to the outside world, either right out of the box or with the purchase of an additional piece of equipment. This connection lets people begin to play with other people, both in cooperation and competition, no matter where they are. Connected consoles are important, because that's where the people are. In 2001, the console gaming market was larger than the computer-gaming market both in sales (by a factor of about 2.6) and in the number of games sold (by a factor of about 1.7) [64]. In the first week of Microsoft's Xbox Live online gaming service, over 200,000 people subscribed worldwide and together played over 5 million games, totalling over 1 million hours of gameplay [102].

As of October 2003, about a million people had subscribed to an massive multiplayer online game. *Everquest* had 460,000 subscribers, and *Star Wars Galaxies* and *Dark Age of Camelot* each had about 300,000 [74].

As more games emerge that let players connect to one another, shared environments will start to become more popular and interesting.

Reactive Environments

Traditional games and stories will continue to entertain us in the future, just as they have in the past. They're both very human activities, and neither one is going away.

The most obvious difference between traditional media and one we'll be able to join into is that the latter will change in response to what you do. I call this a *reactive* environment.

Let's take a look at the continuum of reactivity, starting with those experiences that don't change at all.

Static: A traditional novel doesn't respond to you in any way. The words on the page are the same whether the book is brand new or you're reading it for the tenth time. A great book can change us, but we can't do much to change it.

Novels, whether classically structured like *Riven Rock*, or more modern like *Room Temperature*, present the same words in the same order to everyone who reads them.

Self adjusting: Some authors have experimented with stories that give their readers explicit opportunities to make choices, and then present them with different pieces of the story based on those choices.

The branching narrative *A New Hope* periodically offers the reader a chance to choose from several options for how the story should advance. You pick one and then skip to the page corresponding to that choice. The hypertext novel *afternoon, a story* provides similar opportunities for choices, though they're not presented as explicit questions about the plot.

Rail ride: A common theme park ride is a car that rides on a curved rail set into the ground. Typically the car drives itself at a fixed speed. The person sitting behind the wheel can steer the car to a small extent, but a mechanism at the bottom prevents the car from going off the rail.

The video games *Eternal Darkness: Sanity's Requiem* and *Star Wars: Rogue Squadron II* work this way: with few exceptions, you go through the game experiences in the order that was determined by the game's designers. Most of the time you can go as fast or slow as you please, but except for relatively minor choices, the sequence of events that you encounter while playing the game is fixed.

Riding the current: Some theme park rides offer a little more freedom than a rail, but not a whole lot. Bumper cars generally go around an oval track either clockwise or counter-clockwise. You can fight the flow of the traffic, but usually not for long. River canoeing also provides some opportunity for steering, but if the current is swift you'll find it very difficult to go upstream for long periods of time. In each of these activities, you have some flexibility, but the general shape of your path is predetermined.

The snowboarding game *SSX* is like this. You're restricted to one of several predetermined courses (and the shortcuts built into them), but as you plummet down the mountain, you can choose whether or not to bump other racers, whether or not to take particular jumps or shortcuts, and which tricks you want to perform while airborne, if any. The adventure game *Final Fantasy X* keeps you on a fixed path, usually forcing the movements and options of your characters and those of the computer-controlled characters in your party. As characters accumulate experience, they are able to learn new abilities. As the player, you get to determine who learns what, and that affects how your party will fare as they fight their way through packs of monsters.

Some theme parks are introducing rides that allow some of this flexibility. The DisneyQuest installation *Pirates of the Caribbean* lets

22

guests steer a pirate ship and shoot cannonballs at enemies. The players in the room have a lot of freedom in their actions, and though the game has a built-in sequence of events, there's still enough flexibility that you feel like you have a lot of control and that the environment is responding to you.

Stage sets: Some experiences are mostly about environment and the physical space, and not much about story or characters. People who come to these experiences are invited to step up on stage, perhaps take some clothes from the wardrobe, and join into an ongoing activity.

The online experience *Everquest* is basically a stage set. The game includes some computer-controlled characters to make the set seem more alive, and there are plenty of monsters to kill. The game also offers some assignments and errands (called quests) for players to carry out in the game's world, and it rewards people who complete those tasks. But in general there's no ongoing, authored narrative in the *Everquest* world. Players make up their own stories all the time, but the creators of the world haven't provided one. The fun in this type of game is showing up on the set in costume, with your own personal powers and clothing, and then spending time talking and playing with your friends as you walk around the scenery and whomp the monsters.

Guided group: In some experiences we participate as a member of a group. Our individual actions are important, but no one person can turn the tide. This is like voting in an election: everyone has the same opportunity to influence the result to a small degree, with a result that comes from the sum of everyone's contributions.

A modern version of this experience is the *Cinematrix Interactive Entertainment System* [27]. Everyone in a large, darkened theater is given a paddle with red reflective tape on one side and green tape on the other. A camera watches the room, and when people hold up their paddles, the computer determines which color is facing forward (or back) on an individual basis. This red-and-green map of the audience is fed to a program which uses it to control some simulation or game. As the audience watches a projected video image at the front of the room (and listens to computer-generated sound and music), they find themselves controlling experiences as diverse as flying a plane, piloting a submarine, or playing a video game. Typically a guide walks the audience through a variety of these activities. Each person gets a single vote, as important as every other, and participants can see the ongoing experience respond to their aggregate influence.

Audience participation: In some entertainments the audience isn't required to participate actively, but they get more out of it if they do. These activities typically combine elements of a stage play with an evening's socializing with friends.

Taking a ride on a typical *Murder Train* [115] usually means several hours of evening rail travel, often including dinner. Sometime during the evening, one of the passengers on the train is "murdered," and then everyone tries to figure out who did it and why. The train is populated by actors schooled in improvisation, who know their roles and also the complete story behind the murder. Sometimes these actors are easily recognized by their flamboyant costumes and over-the-top personalities, and sometimes they blend in with the paying passengers, so that the audience can't really be sure who's an actor and who isn't. Audience members can simply sit back and watch the evening's proceedings, or they can talk to the actors, search the train cars, and otherwise enter the world of the story. They can even make up roles for themselves, and stay in character the entire evening.

A similar event is the play *Tony and Tina's Wedding.* Typically held in a large reception hall, the audience gets to be part of a big Italian wedding, with all the people, music, and food that goes along with it. Improvisational actors mingle with the audience, who again can sit back and watch, or join into the festivities, talk with the actors, and get involved in their lives.

Guided improvisation: Some people enjoy getting together as a group to spend time together and share in the creation of an ongoing story and game experience. Because this is such an open-ended activity, there is usually some agreed-on structure that provides a theme to the gathering, and the players improvise around that theme.

The *How to Host a Murder* series of games gives everyone a role to play in a murder mystery. The game is typically played over the course of an afternoon or evening, and over time each player is given new information (in a series of sealed envelopes that come with the game) that slowly deepens and elaborates the plot. Players share their information with each other, usually acting in character with roles and settings as varied as 18th-century medical doctors, coal miners trapped in a cave-in, or business tycoons trying to corner a market. In the role-playing fantasy game *Dungeons & Dragons*, players take on the identities of fantasy creatures as they explore an imaginary world, encountering the citizens of that world and defeating dangerous monsters.

In each of these games, there's a governor built into the system to keep the story on track. In the murder-mystery games, it's the information that's revealed to the players over time. In *Dungeons & Dragons*, a person called the Dungeon Master is responsible for maintaining the world and keeping the players from heading too far off course.

As we move from one-way media like books to two-way media like role-playing games, the popularity of the experience generally decreases. A lot of people read books and watch television and movies; somewhat fewer play video games, and fewer still play role-playing games. Traditional one-way media are firmly embedded in today's mainstream, while two-way media are still picking up speed.

I think that this is partly due to the fact that participatory experiences demand more of the player. I'll talk about this more in Part III, but in general if we're going to ask people to put effort and energy into an activity, we have to make that effort worthwhile. As technology makes these activities easier to create and participate in, there will be more varieties produced and enjoyed, and more people will find that they're getting back enough pleasure that they'll want to return to the experience again.

As we move to increasingly reactive environments, the other human participants become more and more important. Computers are getting better at playing chess, but they still can't hold a decent conversation.

Looking Forward

The idea of entering the world of a great story and becoming an active part of what's going on is an appealing dream to many people. No matter what label we give it, creating a mainstream form of this kind of activity is proving to be a difficult but fascinating challenge.

The Lay of the Land

I believe that the way forward begins by acknowledging a few realities.

First of all, there may be many successful forms of participatory story experiences to be found, or there may be none. Nobody knows what mainstream success will look like. The best we can do now is try to learn as much as we can from every bit of information we can get our hands on and design with that knowledge in mind.

Second, just as mature high-tech media such as novels and films, video games, and television have done during their own development, we need to embrace and respect the knowledge learned from many fields. Developing ways to enter a narrative that will appeal to a wide audience will require a kaleidoscopic understanding and integration of characterization, plot, participation, social play, gaming, user interfaces, production, synthetic graphics and sound, psychology, speech and gesture recognition, and many other fields.

Third, this is a hard problem. Despite a lot of serious effort by a lot of creative and intelligent people, and lots of books and lots of products, we're still looking for the genre-defining work that will help us all see what this medium can become.

Works that help open up a new medium exert a huge influence on what follows. People argue over when the modern novel was born, but whether it was in 1615 with the publication of the conclusion of *Don Quixote*, 1719 with *Robinson Crusoe*, or 1726 with *Gulliver's Travels*, it was clear that by the mid-1700s, this artistic medium was capable of as much emotional depth as any other and that the novel was here to stay. Films came into their own in 1915 with *The Birth of a Nation* and were fully mature by 1941's *Citizen Kane*. The CD-ROM medium was shaped in 1995 by *A Passion for Art* [144]. Video gaming is still rooted in the very recent *Tetris*, *Doom*, and *Myst*. These examples were all immediately followed by many other works, building on the basic form and exploring variations. Creators found, in these models, a framework around which to shape their own creative visions. We don't yet have such breakthrough works for pieces that allow the audience to become active and influential participants in an ongoing story.

26

The Plan

I think that the best way to make progress in advancing the state of our work in this field is to take it in three steps, which form the basic outline of this book.

1. **Study the basics:** Storytelling and gaming are going to be the dominant influences on our new medium. To use the techniques of these fields wisely, we need to understand them.

   Stories and games have both been an important part of every human culture, and we know a lot about why people like them. They've also both been the target of endless experimentation and variation, and the forms that have survived have a lot to teach us about what people want from their stories and games and what they don't. In many important ways, we can explicitly articulate the features of stories and games that "work" or have widespread appeal.

   Once we have a solid foundation in storytelling and gaming in their traditional forms, we can experiment with them from an informed point of view, guided by knowledge and intuition.

2. **Learn from the present:** There's a lot we can learn from recent attempts to actively involve an audience in the telling of a story. The majority of these products are video games, though live theater and festivals provide some examples as well.

   For each experience that's out there, we can ask ourselves what is and isn't working. This is a subjective decision, since one person's fun is another's tedium. We can try to temper our own personal judgments with information from the marketplace. Is a particular approach broadly popular? Do people return to it? Are they clamoring for more? If the answers to these questions are yes, then it's probably doing something right.

   If we think we know why something is working well, we can test our theory with a working prototype. We can try out new ideas that way, before we commit the resources to build a fully-fledged version.

   But when we test an idea in a prototype, we need to give it a fair chance. Poor or incomplete prototyping can actually give us not just useless answers, but, worse, wrong answers. Suppose you're a soft-drink manufacturer, and you're toying with the idea of adding

27

raspberry flavor to your line of cola drinks. So you go to the lab and have the chemists make a few batches and take them out to shopping malls to see what people think. Now, the raspberry flavor is going to change the balance of other flavors that go into your product. And there might be other changes: the raspberry juice might lower the carbonation of the soda so that it's less fizzy, and it might give it a slightly thicker consistency. Now suppose that someone samples your new flatter, goopier, raspberry-tasting concoction and that he doesn't like it. It's pointless to tell him that it's just a prototype, and the final version will taste a bit better, and it will be more fizzy, and the consistency will be smoother. The best that someone can do with that is nod, try to guess what this drink might taste like in the future, and give you his imagined response. But that's asking a lot. A raspberry-flavored cola might be a great idea, but if your prototypes don't reflect the reality of the experience, the responses will be of little value.

3. Build with balance: When we have knowledge of the principles we'll be building upon, and we understand recent experiments well enough to distinguish what works and what doesn't, and we can articulate the reasons why, then we can start using that insight to create new pieces that will be both appealing and original and will help us move the field forward.

Since the medium that combines stories, games, and people is still being born, everyone involved is simultaneously both inventing new technology and finding ways to use it.

It's therefore important that we try lots of ideas, in lots of combinations. Each well-designed technique will add to our knowledge. If we think it moves us closer to our goal, we'll probably call it a success and rejoice. The next step will be to try variations on the method to learn more about it. If it doesn't move us forward, or even sends us backwards, we'll probably call it a failure, and once again we'll rejoice. Understanding why it didn't work will increase our understanding of the field. The failures are as important as the successes.

Getting Started

The rest of this book will be directed to helping us understand the principles of stories and games and then interpreting what we've learned in recent years in terms of those principles.

Creating technology for art is a tricky problem, because when it doesn't seem to work well we can have a hard time knowing if it's because the technology isn't the right tool for the job, or if we just haven't learned the right way to express ourselves with it.

We aren't the first to walk down this road. We can take inspiration from the story of Theobald Boehm (1794–1881), the inventor of the modern flute. Boehm combined his expertise as a silversmith with his sensibilities as a professional musician to solve problems that nobody else even saw. Boehm is a model for how one person, armed with technical and creative skills, can revolutionize a field.

Developing the Flute

Born in Munich in 1794, Theobald Boehm was trained from an early age to be a goldsmith, silversmith, and jeweller like his father. He took to that work rapidly, showing a natural aptitude for working with metal and designing complex settings. His parents encouraged him to learn music by studying the flute, and here again he demonstrated a natural flair and talent. By his 20's, Boehm was giving recitals on a regular basis, as well as working as a goldsmith and flutemaker. In 1818 he was appointed as a flautist to the Royal Bavarian Court in Munich, and he gradually shifted his energies towards performance, developing a reputation as a virtuoso.

Boehm enjoyed travelling in Europe, giving concerts of famous music as well as his own compositions. While in London in 1831, Boehm heard a performer named Charles Nicholson play on a flute that had tone holes slightly larger than the norm. Boehm liked the resulting sound so much that he resolved to duplicate the instrument.

Thus began many years of experimentation and development. Boehm discovered while reproducing Nicholson's flute that when he enlarged the tone holes, he improved the tone in some ways, but also interfered with the air flow for some other notes, making them sound harsh. He realized that the proper solution would be to keep the large holes but move them to new locations where they would interact better with the flow of air through the instrument. The only problem was that if he moved the holes to where he wanted them to go, most people (including himself) would have to strain to reach them, and some players might not be able to reach them at all. Boehm wanted the technical advance of larger and correctly-spaced holes, but he was unwilling to compromise the convenience and flexibility that made the flute such a versatile instrument for himself and other performers.

So Boehm invented a new kind of mechanism that used tiny levers and pivots, allowing a player to close a hole at one part of the flute by pushing on a lever somewhere else. By positioning the levers comfortably, where a musician's fingers would naturally hold the instrument, he not only got the kind of tone he wanted, but allowed performers to play quickly when they wanted to. He built these mechanisms on a conically-shaped flute, which was standard those days, and started to perform with his instrument professionally. Because of its beautiful tone, other professionals started placing orders for copies of Boehm's flute from his workshop.

Boehm's training and ability as a flautist, combined with his skills as a silversmith and machinist, continued to lead him in directions that nobody had gone before. Over time, Boehm changed the basic shape of the flute to a cylinder with a conical bore at the end, and then he invented ring keys which let a musician cover multiple holes with a single finger.

Boehm continued his professional performance career and also continued refining his instrument. He studied acoustics at the University of Munich with Professor Carl von Schafhäutl, who gave him insight into how the shape of an instrument affects the flow of air within it and the tone it produces. Armed with this engineering knowledge, in 1847 Boehm essentially re-designed the flute from the ground up. He settled on silver as the base material, and broke with tradition by using a cylinder rather than a cone for the basic shape. He gave his flute a parabolically-shaped headpiece, a foot joint, large holes placed where they sounded the best, a system of levers and ring keys to cover remote holes, and padded cups to cover those holes when they should stay shut. His new flute was a worldwide hit with players and audiences alike.

Boehm continued to play and develop his instrument, and his 1878 design became the flute of choice for professionals all over the world. The standard professional flute used by classical musicians today is essentially unchanged from that design, now over 120 years old.

His book on the design and construction of his instrument, *The Flute and Flute Playing* [12], is still widely read today.

Boehm's development of the modern flute is a great example of how creative artistic ability and creative technical ability can serve each other to mutual benefit. Boehm's desire to space the tone holes wider apart came from his musician's ear for beautiful sound, and his ring-key mechanism that made it possible came from his silversmith's skill for inventing and building new problem-solving mechanisms.

By mastering both the artistic and technical aspects of his craft, Boehm created the design for a musical instrument that has served the highest aspirations of art for over a century.

An important part of this story for us is that Boehm didn't throw out centuries of hard-won knowledge about musical instruments. To the contrary, he studied music, mechanics, and physics. Once he was fully grounded in the principles of his craft, he started experimenting, exploring variations on all the design principles underlying the flute, and inventing new mechanisms to let him try out new things. Many of these mechanisms were not successful, but he discovered the good ones from the bad ones by building them all and trying them out. It was his seemingly endless flow of prototypes that taught him, through trial and error, to see new principles, which he then used as a guide to radically re-invent the professional flute.

The field of participatory storytelling is ripe for an approach like Boehm's. People following in his footsteps will be deeply grounded in both the artistic and engineering principles discovered by the generations of artists, storytellers, computer scientists, and others that have come before.

The Authorial Voice

In our quest to develop a new medium, I believe we should aspire to something that is capable of deep human expression. Films, plays, novels, and even television are all capable of telling stories that are profound and deeply moving. These media also can be trivial, offensive, or just bland. But without the range to include the lows, these media couldn't reach the highs. I am excited by the idea that we can develop a new form of expression that is capable of not just entertainment, but depth.

I believe strongly that art is created by individuals, not committees. Great books, sculptures, paintings, poems, and other classical creations are largely the work of inspired individuals.

31

But individuals don't always do all the work. Some media are inherently collaborative because of the sheer scope of the enterprise.

For example, television and feature films, in addition to their need for actors, usually require large crews of specialists and generalists, but there's always someone at the helm. Usually this leader is the director, who makes sure that everyone's creative contributions combine in the right way. For example, the writer creates a very personal work, but the director can hire new writers to revise the script until it satisfies his own desires. Similarly, the director guides the production designer, cinematographer, costumers, and all the other people who bring their special skills to the project. The director can't do it all himself but instead orchestrates the efforts of the people who work for him.

Whether it's one person writing with a blunt pencil in an attic, or a multi-million dollar film or game, great stories result from a strong authorial voice, resulting from thousands of small and large decisions, many of which the author himself might not be able to articulate or explain.

A solo artist can work solely by intuition and feel. A collaborative leader like a film director or game designer usually tries to explain his vision to the crew, but there's no way to completely communicate intangibles like the "feel" of the work, or whether the pacing is just a bit off, or if a character seems just a little more likeable (or unlikeable) than he wants. His vision can only come out through his guidance and feedback.

No committee shares the kind of intuition that a committed and skilled artist holds inside himself. Art is the result of such intuition, and that means a unified and coherent authorial voice.

A great designer will have some understanding of each of the many different fields I've mentioned in this chapter and a feeling for how they all interact. Forging new creations in this new medium will be like building up a complex mobile: adding a little bit of weight here means adding a longer arm there, which might mean adding another piece way over on the other side to keep everything in balance, and so on. This requires an intuitive feel for how everything interacts and contributes to the overall experience, and that only comes from study and experience in these diverse disciplines. A team may be able to get a mobile to balance, but to make a beautiful piece of kinetic art that also has grace in its design and motion requires a single motivated person with passion, vision, and the competence to either create the work himself or guide others as they help him.

As we look towards creating our new medium, it's important that we try to find, nurture, and develop such broadly-based, creative individuals, and give them the freedom that Boehm had to experiment frequently and fail often, so that we can discover the principles that will guide our success.

Part II

Story Structure

In order to deviate successfully, one has to have at least a passing acquaintance with whatever norm one expects to deviate from.

—Frank Zappa, from *The Real Frank Zappa Book*
by Frank Zappa with Peter Occhiogrosso, 1989

The Nature of Stories

There are countless varieties of stories in the world, told in every style imaginable and with a seemingly infinite variety of techniques.

But stories are more than just a reporting of events. Mark Twain defined life as "one damn thing after another" [93]. That's a pretty good description of daily life, but not of the stories that have moved and affected us. What are the qualities that transform a simple series of events into a story?

This part of the book answers that question by focusing on the nature of stories. My intention is not to try to replace, or even summarize, the vast literature on story structure that already exists (primarily for the education and development of writers). Instead, my goal is to highlight and summarize those ideas that will be of the most relevance to us as we develop participatory story environments. Though I'll mention a few literary classics, I will generally illustrate my points with examples from contemporary mainstream media. Recent popular examples demonstrate that these ideas are not artifacts of the past but are very much alive in contemporary stories.

There are probably as many definitions of story as there are people to define it. A precise definition may not be possible, and may not even be desirable, because it might close off some doors we haven't even imagined yet. But a good working definition will help us shape our discussion and understand the ideas. So here's a definition that gets us going without getting too burdened in details:

A story follows an interesting protagonist seeking a clear goal by addressing an ever-escalating set of difficulties.

This definition embraces three criteria: a protagonist, his goal, and his challenges in obtaining it. In this chapter we'll examine each of those criteria so that we can explicitly discuss the *structure* of stories.

Like a building, a story has both an internal and external structure. When looking at a building, it's easy to see its visible external structure of walls and windows. What is not so obvious is the equally essential but internal structure of its foundation, bracing, and supports. And completely invisible are the calculations, engineering tests, land surveys, and even the aesthetic reviews that went into the design of the building before construction was even begun.

Certainly nobody would start construction on a large building by walking into a site with a truck full of beams and rebar and then start planting them in the ground directed by nothing but whimsy. That's a great way to build a tower when playing with blocks, but it's not a viable strategy for constructing a safe building for habitation.

Stories also have structure, both seen and unseen. Their obvious external structure is formed by the words, sounds, and images of the final work. Acts, scenes, and chapters are also structural elements. Often invisible are the writer's outlines and notes, maps, and character biographies; these are the equivalent of blueprints and engineering reviews. Most films and novels are *designed* before they are written.

This analogy is not perfect, because art is not engineering. Building designers cannot afford to work on intuition and a gut feeling: if their design is not reliable, people's lives may be lost. So building engineers usually have a mostly finished, verified design before they begin construction.

The costs of failure for writers and storytellers aren't usually so dire, so they can afford a more informal creation process. Many writers do begin by working out the shape of their story in detail and using that outline as a guide. On the other hand, some storytellers trust their intuitions for important decisions and generally make things up as they go. But even in these cases, authors are aware of the evolving structure of their pieces and strive to add new material coherently, to make works that are recognizable as stories. Most authors are aware of the principles of the writing craft, having learned them formally or informally.

On the other hand, some "naturals" work strictly from their passions and are not explicitly thinking about the structure of their work.

Naturals in any field are a fascinating phenomenon. It is a mystery that some children appear to be born with an innate ability to compose music, play an instrument, paint, act, or otherwise express themselves in creatively sophisticated ways. Similarly, some adults (whether they were prodigies as children or not) are able to produce deeply expressive works without any apparent attention to the craft and technique that most other artists work to learn and refine. The dual mystery of prodigies and naturals is how they seem to intuitively understand the structure of works in their field, and how they find and develop their abilities. Natural writers who produce successful stories have a built-in sense of story structure that guides them even without their explicit attention; we can see that this is true simply by observing the strength of the structures in their completed works.

Choosing and Arranging

Structure results from two separate but important activities: *choosing* and *arranging*.

Both of these activities take place at a range of abstractions or levels. For example, a composer who's planning a symphony may start out thinking about movements and overall themes. As the piece is developed, he'll choose specific rhythms, harmonies, and arrangements, and ultimately choose and arrange particular notes. A painter often starts with a sketch and a rough color scheme, finally choosing the color and location of each brush stroke.

Without choice and arrangement, there is no structure, only chaos.

Some artists have experimented with moving some or all of the responsibility for creating structure from the creator of the work to the performer or the audience. A composer may specify that the performance of a musical piece must include the live sounds of ocean surf or a busy highway [22]. In these instances the audience becomes part of the process of finding and creating meaning in the work.

Some visual artists write computer programs to modify or even wholly create images [89]. And some writers take the output of computer programs that have been programmed with some rules of style and offer them to audiences as poetry or stories [77]. I'll have more to say about these techniques in Chapter 11. For now, I'll stick to the much more common situation where an artist has something in mind and is trying to communicate it to the audience.

Character

We all have our favorite fictional characters. They're the ones that create a lasting impact and stay with us. Cultures often share common characters as a reference for everyone in the society: Hamlet is familiar to contemporary English-speaking cultures, and Coyote appears in many North American legends.

Why do some characters stand out from the rest and endure, becoming known to entire cultures and generations? Many of the most famous and popular characters share one or more unusual qualities. This doesn't mean that every character shares all of these traits, but they are important enough to merit our attention in the next few sections.

Exaggerated Traits

Great characters are recognizable as human beings, but they are extraordinary in some way. Sometimes it's their situation that makes them different (this is the classic "fish-out-of-water" scenario).

For example, in *Shogun*, an Englishman shipwrecks in 16th-century Japan and must find a way to survive in a culture that is totally unknown to him. In the movie *Dave*, Dave Kovic is an ordinary guy who runs a job-placement agency. But he just happens to look exactly like the president of the United States, who has fallen into a coma. Dave is recruited by the president's advisors to stand in for the president in public appearances, thrusting Dave into the world of national politics. In *Rain Man*, Charlie Babbitt finds himself spending time with his autistic brother Raymond. He kidnaps Raymond from the facility he's living in, and takes him on a cross-country trip. Charlie finds himself in a psychological world he's never been in before, where he actually starts to care for his brother. Raymond is literally in a world that's new to him: the society outside of his institution.

Frequently a character is special because of something that is within him. Great characters usually possess some trait in their makeup that is present in all of us but is developed or exposed to a degree that makes it stand out.

We all have some degree of tenacity, but in *Moby-Dick*, Captain Ahab elevates it into an all-consuming obsession. Everyone possesses the ability to be sneaky, but Iago in *Othello* is such a great villain because he plans and executes schemes craftier than that most of us would ever contemplate. In *A Christmas Carol*, Scrooge takes penny-pinching to a new level. More recently, Darth Vader of *Star Wars: Episode IV–A New Hope* isn't just a little bit evil, but is so vicious that he is calm as he orders the total destruction of a planet of innocent people. Major Charles Winchester of television's *M*A*S*H* takes self-importance and snobbery way beyond what most of us encounter in everyday life.

Most classic heroes have one or more exaggerated, admirable traits. In *The Odyssey*, Odysseus is braver and stronger than most men; the princess Aïda in the opera *Aïda* is loyal to her people to the point of painful self-sacrifice; and Tom Sawyer takes a pleasure in mischief so extreme in *The Adventures of Tom Sawyer* that he allows his family to hold a funeral for him, which he attends. We have all felt at our wit's end, but in *Dog Day Afternoon*, Sonny is under such intense pressure that he initiates a bank robbery and then sticks with it even when the situation turns hopeless. In *Terminator 2*, the Terminator is stronger and more stubborn than any ten normal people, and Sister Helen Prejean in *Dead Man Walking* is a model of compassion.

Great characters tend to have many of the traits of normal people, but they also have something more. Often this extra something is overt and obvious: the character is richer, sexier, smarter, stronger, more influential, more famous, more fanatical, or more generous. Villains too are like us, but their dark side is stronger: they are angrier, tougher, more insecure, more arrogant, more aggressive, more vengeful, or more unbalanced.

Generally, if you think of a character that has moved you or has stuck with you, you'll find that the character has one or more things going on inside him that are recognizable as human, but are exaggerated to extreme proportions, or are demanded in unusual quantity and quality.

This exaggeration may seem surprising, because it seems natural to think that we would usually be interested in stories about people like ourselves. Even in science fiction, friendly aliens tend to be mostly human-like in their behavior (if not their appearance), and certainly almost all animated characters (human, animal, or otherwise) are basically people inside. This is true even of inanimate objects like the silverware in the animated *Beauty and the Beast* or the children's toys in *Toy Story*. So why is it the case that the stories that have lasting impact on a culture, and on many of us as individuals, are those that feature heroes and villains who emphasize one or more traits beyond their normal limits?

Basically it's because these characters are simply *more interesting* because of their exaggerated traits. They are still recognizable as people, but their personalities are more starkly drawn and the issues in their lives are easier to grasp because of the artful emphasis of some aspects of their character. If Ebeneezer Scrooge were just a hurtful miser, we could dismiss him as nothing but a cold-hearted monster, but the very depths of his indifference leave the door open for us to gradually feel sorry for this lonely, bitter old man.

All great characters are motivated by passion: their intense need for something important. Their exaggerated traits make this passion easier to see and to recognize within ourselves. The villain of a story is typically acting out of negative passions, such as greed, fear, or revenge. The hero typically acts out of positive passions, such as love or justice. Really interesting characters are not ruled by such black-and-white distinctions but are driven onward by more complex passions.

Inner and Outer Lives

Great characters lead two fascinating lives at the same time. The *outer life* is their presence in the world and is described by what they do and say. Usually this outer life is not difficult to identify, since all we have to do is watch. A character's *inner life* is his self-awareness, composed of feelings, beliefs, self-image, self-doubts, hunches, intuitions, and the millions of other mysterious and often ill-defined and contradictory forces that work within him. It's typically much harder to get a handle on most people's inner world simply from observation. Some people are very composed and let little of their inner life show, while others disguise or filter it.

The difficulty that most people have in accessing and dealing with their inner world is one of the most powerful tools in the creation of great characters. Heroes may need to overcome their greatest fears and prejudices to rise to an occasion. Villains may have to actively crush positive impulses when they appear and remind themselves repeatedly of the need to hang on to their anger so they can continue their assault.

When a story has some time to grow and develop its characters, it often starts with a hero who has found some kind of stable compromise between his inner and outer lives. There is a balance, often delicate, between those things in the character's inner heart that are being expressed and those that are suppressed, and even those that are simply acknowledged and those that are denied.

At the start of *The Insider*, Jeffrey Wigand is working for a major cigarette manufacturer. Though he knows that his employers have lied about the safety of their products for years, he has managed to hold his tongue and is living in a delicate balance. Soon after the start of the film, external forces press on him, and he decides to go public with the truth, creating serious problems for himself and his family.

Some stories begin with characters who have long ago suppressed or ignored their dreams or ideals and compromised themselves in ways that they don't even recall. Another common starting point is a character whose inner drives and abilities have never had a chance for expression. Such a character possesses internal resources that nobody has guessed at, perhaps including the character himself.

In *Bound*, Violet is a woman who is very different inside from her outward appearance. She appears to be heterosexual, soft, compliant, and little more than a passive ornament for her gangster husband. In reality, she is tough and resourceful and at least as interested sexually in women as she is in men. When the opportunity presents itself, Violet demonstrates that she has the power within herself to take control of her life.

To summarize, interesting characters often find themselves in situations where their external and internal worlds are in conflict. This stress forces them to ultimately resolve the conflict by confronting their own nature.

Figure 1.   The Four Nested Masks.

It is important to introduce this conflict between the inner and outer worlds early in the story and then intensify it. When skillfully executed, the deepening contradictions can draw the audience's sympathy, so they will come to feel that they understand the character's dilemma better and better as the story unfolds. This is important for all major characters, but it's most important for the hero and the villain. We obviously want to know and care about our hero, but the more deeply we know and understand the villain, the more we understand the magnitude of the challenge the hero faces, and the more we are drawn into the hero's plight.

Nested Masks

Human nature is complex and diverse, and the sciences are a long way from giving us much practical guidance in designing the internal forces that drive a great character. But there are some general, abstract concepts that are now a widely-accepted part of mainstream thinking about contemporary human nature, and we can use these structural tools as a starting point.

Figure 1 shows the way I like to think about this. I call it the Nested Masks diagram, in reference to the famous Russian nesting dolls, or matryoshka. Though it's obviously not any kind of a deep psychological theory, I'll describe this hierarchy here because I have found it useful shorthand for summarizing what's going on inside a character's head. As we'll see, it's also a useful tool for keeping a character growing and developing through a story.

The true self: At the very core of the character is his *true self.* It is the character's soul, essence, or that which is discovered at the end of a spiritual path of self-discovery. It is the bedrock source of his most basic impulses and desires, which are the engines that power his actions in the world. The true self's primal energies are diffuse and general.

Conscience: The true self's impulses are filtered by the forces and conventions that enable us to live with other people in social groups. These are the essential rules of culture and society that we are taught explicitly and by example from the moment we are born. These principles govern our basic ideas of society, family, and belief in the structure of the world. Because they are taught so early and forcefully, these concepts permeate our being and shape and color everything we do. In other words, they take the impulses and desires of the true self and give them a social interpretation in the form of *values.* I'm using the term here in a very general sense, referring to broad concepts like respect for truth, fairness, revenge, family, or honor. These values determine how we believe the world works or should work. They are the source of our most fundamental views of society and culture. I call this stage the character's *conscience.*

Self-image: A character's notion of himself as an individual shapes the conscience's values into *desires.* Desires are the result of channelling values through a personal belief system or *self-image.* Someone's self-image describes how he sees himself when he is at his most honest with himself (though the depths of this introspection, as well as the results, change over time). It is shaped by all the things that go into a character's self-perception, such as his hopes and fears, guilts and responsibilities, expectations, insecurities, and confidences. Some of these concepts are nothing more than statements that he has been told and has accepted as true. Others will be conclusions he has drawn from his own experience. Some may be objectively true (e.g., a tall man's belief that "I am taller than most people"). Some concepts of self-image may be objectively false (e.g., an anorexic's belief that "I am too fat") yet are believed with utter certainty. But most of these truths are subjective and are true for that person simply because

44

he believes them to be so (e.g., "I am attractive" or "I am unattractive"), regardless of whether most other people in the world would agree with the statements.

World mask: From these inner truths come impulses to act in order to change the world. These acts may be small and personal, like taking a drink of water, or large and very public, like building a new sports arena or declaring war on another country. In most cases a character's actions are somewhere between these extremes. Characters don't always act on their intentions. We live in a world where there are implicit and explicit laws, and breaking these can mean social censure, ranging from disappointing one's friends to serving a jail sentence. When someone is unexpectedly but deeply offended, his first response may be fury, but most people don't act on this and immediately lash out physically. Rather, we take a moment and try to steer our emotions and impulses into directions that are as satisfying as possible while still socially acceptable. This final stage of filtering I describe as *appearance* or the *world mask*. This is where we explicitly take into account the world around us before acting.

At this step characters apply deliberate changes to their actions so that they present an image to the world that represents how they wish to be perceived. A person who is working on being more assertive, for example, may push himself to be more aggressive than he actually feels. The result of the world mask is *action*. These actions, we will see, are what make up the external reality of the character.

To recap briefly, a primal force, by definition true to the core being of the person, is first transformed by the person's beliefs to conform with the values of his society, which are typically taught and reinforced from birth. This modified impulse then passes through the person's own self-image, where it is adjusted to prevent actions that the character doesn't see as being appropriate for the person he wishes to be, regardless of how the world reacts. Finally, the people and laws of the external world, and the influence of their perceptions, are taken into account, shaping the final action.

In many people, the three outer layers (conscience, self image, and appearance) are inconsistent, and unraveling them can lead to a fascinating revelation of character.

There are many other models for personality, each leading to their own ways of creating conflict and memorable characters. The book *Maps of the Mind* [61] surveys several dozen different approaches, each of which could serve as a model for developing interesting characters and finding points of tension between them.

The conflict among the different impulses inside the same person is fertile ground for creating great characters. They are able to act in unexpected ways which are still consistent, because their choices spring from a coherent though contradictory personality. Like the internal supports that hold up a building, this structure is invisible to most observers, but it is critical.

Change

As we will see later, most great characters change over the course of the story. Scrooge in *A Christmas Carol* transforms from a stingy loner to a generous and friendly visitor, Lear in *King Lear* declines from a powerful ruler to a pitiful madman, and in the *The Godfather* trilogy, Michael Corleone changes from a young man insulated from his family's business to its new leader.

Although characters usually change, sometimes characters instead act as *catalysts*, changing the world around them through their mere presence. Notable examples of this kind of character include the title character in *Forrest Gump* and Chauncey Gardener in *Being There*. But despite these exceptions, it's generally true that great characters undergo great changes.

Characters don't change randomly. The strongest changes are those that bring forth what has been inside the character all along, either undiscovered or suppressed. For example, a villain might discover a thirst for revenge he never suspected before, or a hero might find that he is capable of sacrifices he would have never thought possible.

In a great story, the challenges of the world force the character to examine his assumptions from the outside in, starting first with his world mask, and then self-image, and then conscience, until he finally discovers, and must act from, his core personality. This is hard and challenging work because it means examining assumptions and beliefs that have been held for a lifetime and that the character may closely associate with his identity.

The events that happen in a great story are chosen and sequenced by the author to put the character into a position where he is unable to avoid this inward journey. It is literally forced on him, and the pressure continues to mount until his journey is complete. We use the term *growth* to refer to this stripping-away of layers of belief and behavior until the character's core is revealed.

A character grows when he is forced by story events to question and resolve identity-defining inconsistencies in ever-deeper layers of belief and behavior.

In other words, a great character evolves when plot events force him to journey inward and discover himself.

Note that even when a person is forced to change, he will almost always change as little as possible. When confronted with any challenge, most people take the smallest amount of action they think will address the issue. Characters must be forced to take big steps through the pressure of big forces.

If the plot events force the character to grow, then they have fulfilled a large part of their mission in the story. But we can make the connection between these two elements even tighter and crank up the pressure on the character. The key is to *create and sequence plot events that contradict the character's inner journey.*

This makes life even tougher for the character and increases our feelings of connection to him.

In *Antz*, the lead character, named Z, has bumped into the Princess in a once-in-a-lifetime encounter. Desperate to find a way to see her again, he proposes a clever little subterfuge to his friend in the army: they'll switch places for a day, and by being part of the upcoming military parade, Z will have a chance to see the Princess again. They make the switch, but it turns out that parade is marching right into battle. Suddenly the passive and intellectual Z finds that instead of finding love, he is in the midst of violent, deadly conflict.

In *Jaws*, Chief of Police Brody is afraid of the water, but he has to head out on a boat to catch the shark that's terrorizing his community.

A great plot forces a character to reveal himself by directly contradicting the currently outermost levels of his personality. He must be forced to choose either to examine his beliefs and move closer to his core, or to reject the challenge and become harder and more brittle.

The journey to depth is a discovery of authenticity and self-honesty. It is a process of incrementally stripping away layers of habit and artifice. Some of these layers are difficult to question because they are shared by, and held in esteem by, almost all other members of the society. Some layers are difficult to shed because they are a legacy from parents and loved ones, and losing them can feel like a betrayal of those people. And some protective habits are strong because we associate ourselves with them closely; we see ourselves as a person who moves through the world in a particular way, and by changing those behaviors we risk changing how we perceive ourselves and how others perceive us.

For example, some people see themselves as flirts, or founts of knowledge, or wise men, or curious children, or mature adults. Changing the way we deal with other people and the rest of the world can risk changing these internal and external images, which many people expend a great deal of effort creating, maintaining, and advertising. A journey to authenticity does not mean that one has to abandon these images, but they must be questioned, tested, and retained only if they pass the test of being in harmony with deeper, more soulful impulses.

In *The Lion King*, Simba runs away from home as a young prince and grows up far from home. He doesn't want to be the king and in fact doesn't want to know about his family or old friends at all. But his past catches up with him, and he is given no choice: he must reconnect with his past and grow into his role as King.

The Structure of Great Fictional Characters

Great fictional characters are fascinating. Such characters need not be likable. Jake LaMotta in *Raging Bull* is a misogynistic, angry, violent man, but he's a great character. Some great characters are villains: the Wicked Witch in *Snow White and the Seven Dwarfs* is a memorable villain. Good or evil, great characters simply need to be people that somehow matter to us and that we want to know more about. Most great characters are flawed in at least one important way, and dealing with that inherent shortcoming is often key to solving the very problems that they face.

There are many different theories about what makes a great character, and as with any attempt to describe human nature, many of them conflict with each other other. In this section, I'll describe the ideas that will be the most useful to us.

Great characters are almost always complex. And they are contradictory. As we have seen, this contrary behavior is not random, but springs from the internal contradictions that the author builds into the character's psyche.

This is why a character appears to be a sane human being, rather than a puppet, robot, or madman.

A great character is not a perfect copy of a real person, but an artful representation of a person. Because most stories don't unfold in front of us over many years, we don't have the luxury of gradually dissolving the many conflicting layers of the hero's personality Some television shows run for many years, and some books appear in serialized form or over multiple volumes. But few authors know at the start that this extended run is ahead of them.

Because the time we spend with fictional characters is so constrained, it's important that they are comprehensible and interesting soon after they are introduced. If they aren't, the audience may become bored or confused and tune out. But great characters grab our attention right away. So what's the thing that's common to all great characters?

Great characters are driven by irresistible passions.

Many powerful passions are positive. Some characters want to get something: more money, or the man or woman of their dreams. Others want to achieve something: opening their own business or rescuing a loved one from danger. Others want to become something they are not: a better father or husband, or a world-known violinist.

Other passions are negative, pushing the character to avoid or resist something: a character might be trying to avoid corruption when offered a lot of money to betray his friends.

These driving passions are often known to the character, but not always: sometimes a person is propelled by internal forces that he is barely aware of, or knows about but suppresses and denies. These passions may be obvious to an outside observer, such as the character's friends, or the audience, while the character himself is blind to them. In the film *Best In Show*, Cookie is driven by a need for constant sexual attention from men, and that shapes everything from her clothing to how she chooses to wear her name tag at a party.

All of the forces acting on a character influence his actions. This also leads to a rich source of motivations, since in a well-balanced character some actions may be simultaneously helpful and destructive, and the character must find a way to accept those tradeoffs, or find another solution that is free of them.

The tension between known and unknown passions can lead to great and memorable characters. One of the most powerful dilemmas a person can face is when his internal and external passions come into conflict. People will typically do everything they can to avoid this conflict, but a dramatist can shape the plot and actions of the other characters to keep the heat on and the pressure inescapable.

In *An Enemy of the People*, Dr. Stockmann is a civic-minded doctor who only wants to do what's best for his community, a tourist town whose economy depends on its therapeutic baths. When he discovers that the water supply is contaminated, he finds that his professional and personal desires to publicize the truth and act on it are met with anger from the townspeople, who want to keep the information secret. Dr. Stockmann is torn between his responsibility as a physician and what he's told is his responsibility as a citizen.

A terrific story will often place a person into situations where the conflict between these forces is increasingly intolerable, building up the inner emotional tension. I'll talk about that in some more detail below.

Conscious vs. Unconscious Desires

Great characters often experience conflict between their inner and outer needs, and they are affected by them in different ways. The active or conscious goal is the major influence on short-term or immediate actions. If a character wants to become married, for example, he may start dating and placing personal ads. On the other hand, the dormant, or subconscious goal, controls longer-term actions. If our dating man had been psychologically hurt in his last relationship and is actually afraid of starting a new one, he might concurrently move to a remote town where the chances of meeting women are slim, justifying his action with rational arguments.

The important point to notice here is that the inner and outer (or conscious and unconscious) desires contradict each other. This contradiction gives the character some problems to address, and helps keep him under pressure.

The ultimate conflict of a great story often occurs when the hero must face up to the fact that his external actions have created a fundamental conflict with his internal beliefs, and he must make a decision that will alter his life forever.

Real people aren't so simply broken up into conscious and unconscious needs. But as we saw earlier, fictional characters tend to be more concentrated versions of their real-life counterparts, so these traits are often easier to spot in the world of fiction than in the world of real life.

At the start of the film *American Beauty*, Lester Burnham appears to be living a perfect life: he has a lovely house which he shares with his wife and daughter, and a job that keeps them all living comfortably. But the reality of his life is very different: his marriage is loveless, his daughter is depressed, and Lester hates his job. Lester's image to the outside world, which also reflects his own aspirations for himself, is in conflict with his desperate and unhappy inner life. The pain of this contradiction gives Lester the strength to make huge changes to his life.

Great fictional characters are also worthy of our attention and time. One way they earn this respect is by acting in ways that match their needs. In general, when faced with a problem, people will choose to address that problem with the smallest and least-demanding action that is likely to improve the situation. But unless our hero is deeply troubled, he will never deliberately behave in a stupid or self-destructive way. Bad plots are often moved along by characters acting stupidly. But it's worth keeping in mind that a great character will always work as hard as he can to achieve his goals and will never willingly jeopardize his pursuit by getting into dangerous situations that he could otherwise avoid.

Although principles can help guide the creation and development of a character, great characters are still created by a combination of skill, imagination, and an innate understanding of human nature.

Plot

A story is a sequence of events. Usually we refer to these events as the *plot*. There are many different kinds of plot structures used in modern fiction. The most common structure is called the *three-act form*.

The Three-Act Form

This form is used in virtually all contemporary television dramas and feature films lasting a half hour or more. The three acts may be described by the terms *complication*, *development*, and *resolution*.

Act I: Complication

Typically the story begins with a character who is in a state of balance in his life. This doesn't mean that he is happy, or even that his life is in any way attractive or desirable to us or to him. But the character has some form of stability. In other words, left to his own devices, his life would likely continue on for a while just as it is.

Then a complication comes along that upsets that balance: Rose Sayer's religious mission is attacked in *The African Queen*, Clarice Starling needs the help of a murderer in *The Silence of the Lambs,* or Sam Spade's business partner is murdered in *The Maltese Falcon.* Often it's hard to tell whether the complication represents good news or bad news. That judgment call can even change over time.

The following apocryphal story illustrates the complexity of characterizing events as they occur.

> Long ago, a wise Chinese farmer named Wu lived on a small farm with his wife and teen-aged son Mei. The farm made just enough money for Wu and his family to live. An essential part of the farm was a beautiful and beloved horse named Lei-chen, who did everything from plowing the ground to carrying water. One morning, just before planting season, Wu awoke to find that Lei-chen had left the corral and run away in the middle of the night. His neighbors were very concerned. "Wu," they said, "How will you and Mei manage to plow the fields without your horse? This is terrible for you. How unfortunate!" Wu nodded and replied, "Perhaps."
>
> A few days later Wu awoke to find that Lei-chen had returned, with four strong young stallions following behind her. Wu closed the corral gates as his neighbors gathered around. "Wu," they said, "What a wonderful thing that your horse had run away. Now she has returned, and with four beautiful young stallions besides! How fortunate!" Wu nodded and replied, "Perhaps."
>
> Several days later Wu and his son decided to break the stallions so that they could sell them. Mei selected the sleekest and most beautiful horse to train. The animal was wild and strong, though, and he threw Mei, who fell badly and broke his leg. The doctor set Mei's leg in a splint and declared him unable to work on the farm for at least two weeks. Wu's neighbors were very concerned. "Wu," they said, "What a tragedy! Getting those horses was terrible luck. Without your son, you will have to work from dawn to dusk just to get in basic planting for the next season. It's a terrible thing for your son to break his leg, how unfortunate!" Wu nodded and replied, "Perhaps."
>
> Several days later the king's heralds passed through the village with news of the latest wars going on far away. The king

needed more warriors and pressed all able-bodied young men into his service. Because he was lame, Mei was allowed to stay home with his father. But all the other boys in town were taken away that night, and the people knew they would probably never see their sons again. Wu's neighbors complimented Wu on his good fortune. "How lucky for you that Mei had broken his leg! That was truly fortunate." Wu, of course, only nodded and replied as usual.

The informal *Law of Unexpected Consequences* says that we never really know what's going to happen in the long run. Winning a million dollars in the lottery may sound like great news, but not if it leads to someone trying to kill the winner in order to steal the money. If a man loses his job, the loss could cause great distress, but it could lead to much better opportunities that he'd never have had at his old job. Both of these events could turn out the other way as well, with the lottery winner living a happy life and the laid-off man falling into destitution. In a great story you never know just how things are going to develop, but you feel confident that they will indeed develop in some interesting or surprising way.

On the other hand, consider the opening of the movie *Jaws*. A young girl leaves a beach party, pulls off her clothing, and jumps into the ocean for some nighttime skinny-dipping. Suddenly she is violently attacked by a hungry great white shark, and is quickly, though not instantly, killed. As her blood spreads out on the water, it's hard to see this event as anything but . . . well, bad.

Once a character's life has been thrown out of balance, he will do what's necessary to correct it. If his car is essential to him and it has broken down, he will try to fix it. Whatever has gone wrong will receive his best efforts until it's made right again.

The event that disrupts the character's life ideally will present two related but ultimately contradictory challenges: one overt, and one subtle. The overt challenge is the action that our hero must take in the world, such as going to another state to find his runaway daughter. The subtle challenge is the one that addresses his inner beliefs, such as what it means to be a good father.

Act I may build slowly, as the hero deals with a series of smaller problems before the biggest obstacle confronting him comes into clear focus. The course of Act I typically shows the character slowly coming to grips with the major problem facing him and trying a number of minimal solutions to address it. Finally, the hero understands the existence and magnitude of his most important problem and knows that some major work will be required to correct it. The act typically ends when the character makes his first significant effort to address his problem.

Suppose our hero's daughter is kidnapped. He may first think his daughter is just staying out late with friends. Then he may think she's gone on a trip without telling him, and then after several days go by, he believes that she's run away. He would address each of these interpretations as they come up until, finally, he is forced to conclude, because of circumstances or other realizations, that in fact she has been kidnapped. He may find that the police are of no help and decide to take matters into his own hands. Believing that his daughter is being held in another country, he gets his passport and traveller's checks and boards an international flight to go looking for her. His escalating actions match his escalating perception of the problem: he didn't hop on a plane the first time his daughter was late for dinner.

Act II: Development

In Act I, our hero comes to understand his biggest problem and takes significant action to correct it. In Act II, the hero finds that the problem is different or worse than he thought, and he faces a series of developments that steadily raise the stakes. Sometimes the fundamental problem itself proves to be deeper or more complex than the hero thought, and sometimes he finds that the problem was only a small piece of a larger problem.

Act II plunges the hero into a new situation. He may be there because he helped cover up the killing of an organized crime untouchable (*Goodfellas*), or was taken aboard an alien spacecraft (*Galaxy Quest*), or decided to enter a world of cartoons (*Who Framed Roger Rabbit?*).

At the start of Act II, our hero has begun to fully engage in solving his problem. But each time he commits to an action, he finds that instead of solving everything, even greater acts and risks are required of him. This can be because the villain keeps increasing the difficulty of the problem, or because the hero learns more about the magnitude of the situation, or even because the situation itself is becoming increasingly difficult, often as a result of the hero's own actions.

Think of Act II as a mountain-climbing expedition. At the end of Act I our hero has decided that he must reach the top of the mountain. It might look like a strenuous one-day hike, so he loads up with high-quality gear, waits for good weather, hires a guide, and heads up. Within a few hours our hero and his guide are caught in a snowstorm. Seeking shelter, they stagger around on the mountain's face and lose one of their packs. Finally they settle into a cave, emerging the next day to find that their route back down has been cut off. They continue the climb, but the guide slips into a crevasse and plummets to his death. Alone, with only a few of his original supplies, our hero moves on. But the climb gets harder and harder, and he suffers one setback after another: his coat tears, his goggles break and fall off, his camp stove runs out of fuel, and his gloves fall to pieces. When the clouds part, our hero discovers that what he thought was the peak was only the first plateau. By the time he's near the summit, three days after starting out, our hero is scrambling up loose rocks and dirt with bleeding fingers and worn-out boots, bereft of food and water. His descent is blocked: his choice is to die or continue climbing.

These increasing challenges, and the hero's need to respond to them, form a sequence of *developments*.

That's the essence of Act II: the hero strives and does everything in his power to solve his problem, but it just gets harder and harder. Sometimes the problems are of his own making, sometimes they are deliberately put in his way by other characters, and sometimes they're simply there because of the nature of the situation. In *The Perfect Storm* a terrible storm bears down relentlessly on the heroes, gathering in fury with every passing moment.

As I mentioned before when discussing character, this struggle is at its most engaging and profound when it simultaneously taxes our hero's inner and outer worlds: his physical struggle is matched by an internal struggle with his own emotions or beliefs. And in great stories, these struggles are increasingly at odds with one another, so that the character cannot simultaneously satisfy both the inner and outer pressures.

Finally, at the end of Act II, the hero faces a critical decision. At the end of Act I the hero entered into the struggle, while at the end of Act II he must re-confirm his intention by utterly committing to it.

Suppose that our hero who has travelled to a foreign land to retrieve his daughter discovers that she has been kidnapped by a small, self-contained group of revolutionaries within that country's government. To get his daughter back, our hero must create a false identity for himself in order to infiltrate that group and join their closed community. Once he's in, there is no way out: this paranoid group lives together, eats together, and watches each other constantly for signs of betrayal. The risk that he will be unmasked is huge and would mean instant death for himself and his daughter.

This is a point of no return: if he enters the compound, everything in his life will be different. His seemingly monumental decision at the end of Act I, which involved flying to a new country, now looks like nothing compared to this risk. Just as Act I ends with a commitment to action, so does Act II, but with even greater stakes.

Act III: Resolution

When Act III begins, our hero is in a situation where there is no turning back. He must commit all of his resources to achieving his goal. Act III continues to build on the pressure and problems from Act II, until it reaches the *climax*, or the point of ultimate conflict.

At this point the character must risk everything to achieve his goal, or perish in the trying. The meaning of "perish" can be literal, as in physical death, or it can be an intimate spiritual or emotional loss. Abandoning an important quest at a key moment can be a kind of moral failure that results in a spiritual death.

In *A Bug's Life*, Flik tries to save the colony from the domineering grasshoppers by recruiting a gang of warriors, but then he and the colony discover that these warriors are only circus performers. Ashamed, Flik and the circus bugs leave the colony. Princess Dot follows them, and she convinces Flik and the others to return. They do so, putting their reputations and everything else on the line to turn themselves into the leaders that the colony needs.

At its most powerful, this pressure will put the hero's inner and outer worlds at their greatest peril and conflict. Somehow the hero must choose an action in this, the most terrible of moments, and in doing so, he discovers who he truly is. The hero may find he is strong and brave, or weak and afraid. He may be resourceful, or he may escape into madness. Whatever he does, he will display his truest essence in the choice.

In *The Graduate*, Benjamin defies Mrs. Robinson in the end and dashes for the church, where he interrupts Elaine's wedding and takes her away with him. Ben doesn't really know what's going to come next, but he's definitely committed to his decision.

In this final, ultimate action the hero will act at the very upper limits of his abilities to bring about a *resolution* to his problem.

The resolution may cleanly end the problem, leading to a happy or sad ending. The resolution might also be ambiguous, so that the hero has both won and lost in the process.

Returning to our example of the father searching for his kidnapped daughter, he may rescue her, but only after killing several men. He may have gained his daughter back, but he's lost his innocence and soul in the process. Is that a happy ending? Mixed endings such as these are more rare in popular culture than clearly-cut happy and sad endings.

The Hero's Journey

The folklorist and historian Joseph Campbell studied myths and stories from many different cultures and eras and discovered that many of them shared a similar structure. He called this 12-step structure *The Hero's Journey* (also sometimes called the *monomyth*) [23]. The steps of the hero's journey are clearly present in many of today's stories, including popular feature films [134].

Although the Hero's Journey is only one of several general story architectures, it's perhaps the most common and versatile one used today. Unfortunately, Campbell's original presentation is academically formal and can be a challenging read. Because I think it's such a useful tool, I'll review the Hero's Journey here, with a focus on its general principles. I'll phrase the basic ideas so that they will be most directly useful for our purposes.

The Hero's Journey is applicable not only to big adventures, but also to personal and intimate stories that take place largely in a world of emotions and private feelings. In this case, the many external characters and objects in the Hero's Journey are encountered metaphorically and symbolically, rather than literally.

In many stories only some of the elements of the Hero's Journey appear, and sometimes they occur out of Campbell's 12-step sequence, repeat, or go backwards. The Hero's Journey is not a rigid prescription to be obeyed, but a general-purpose tool for analyzing the structure of many stories.

To illustrate the Hero's Journey I'll use two recent, well-known feature films that are worlds apart in their style, pace, and substance. *The Matrix* combines science-fiction with action to create a complex and fast-paced story. *Sling Blade* is a mostly quiet and contemplative character study of a man and some people he comes to know. I'll also show how this structure also underlies the classic video game *The Legend of Zelda: Ocarina of Time* (simply *Zelda* for this discussion).

Step 1: The Ordinary World. The story begins with the hero in his every-day, *ordinary world*. This setting gives the audience the opportunity to either recognize this world as their own or to be quickly introduced to its qualities. The character's life is typically in balance: without some kind of external pressure, things will continue on as they are, at least for a while.

Starting in this ordinary world gives the audience a chance to become familiar with the world of the story before any emotional demands are made on them.

The ordinary world of *The Matrix* is Neo's apartment and the office building in which he works. The ordinary world of *Sling Blade* is the state mental hospital in which Karl Childers has been institutionalized for the last 25 years. The ordinary world of *Zelda* is the Kokiri Forest where Link has lived his entire life.

Step 2: The Call to Adventure. Now that we've been introduced to the balance of forces in the hero's world, something happens to upset that balance. Sometimes a herald delivers shocking news: a doctor reports bad test results, a knight announces the arrival of a dragon in a nearby town, or a soldier staggers home with a story of a surprise attack and imminent invasion. Sometimes the hero discovers the problem by himself, often by accident. This is the *Call to Adventure*, when the hero learns that his world his been changed and he must respond.

In *The Matrix*, the call to adventure is literally a phone call that Neo receives on his cell phone from the mysterious Morpheus. In *Sling Blade*, the call comes when Karl is finally released from the mental hospital and is free to re-enter the real world via the local town of Millsburg. In *Zelda*, the call comes from the fairy Navi who wakes Link and tells him that he needs to go to the Deku Tree.

Step 3: Refusal of the Call. Once the hero has accepted the reality of his problem, and the necessity of taking action to address it, he will often try to avoid it. Campbell refers to this denial as the *Refusal of the Call*.

In *The Matrix*, Neo refuses the call by rejecting help from Morpheus as he stands on the outside of the office building, which leads to his detention and interrogation by the agents. In *Sling Blade*, Karl returns to the mental hospital and asks to be allowed to live there. The game *Zelda* skips this step; our hero Link goes to the Deku Tree as quickly as we can get him there.

Step 4: Meeting with the Mentor. At this point the character often finds himself at a roadblock: he feels the need to take action, but he cannot or will not because someone or something stands in his way.

The roadblock is broken when the hero *meets his mentor*. The mentor may be someone the hero has known all his life, or it may be someone who has suddenly appeared, usually in a way related to the onset of the problem. The mentor is there to give our hero the push he needs to accept the call to adventure. Usually this is a gentle push, but sometimes it can be violent.

In *The Matrix*, Neo meets with Morpheus at the hotel. Morpheus's experience, resources, and information make him a powerful mentor. In *Sling Blade*, Jerry Woolridge is in charge of the hospital. He takes Karl under his wing and offers to let him sleep at his house for an evening and then promises to set him up with a job. In *Zelda*, Link is befriended by the owl Kaepora Gaebora, who guides him on his adventure, offering advice and help.

Step 5: Crossing the Threshold. Now that our hero has has decided to act, he must start somewhere. This often means that the hero travels into a different world, which Campbell calls the *special world*. The special world may be another physical place like a different city or country. The hero may instead enter the special world by staying in the same place, but becoming part of a different social stratum or culture. He may simply enter a new world of perceptions and ideas entirely within himself, created in response to his decision to act.

In *The Matrix*, Neo crosses the threshold when he swallows the red pill, initiating a transformation from which there is no turning back.

In *Sling Blade*, Karl enters the new world when he gets a job at Bill Cox's fix-it shop and starts his new life outside the institution. In *Zelda*, Link enters the new world when he passes through the tunnel out of the Kokiri forest and enters the greater world of Hyrule.

Step 6: Tests, Allies, Enemies. Upon arrival in the special world, our hero is immediately confronted with the need to understand how the world works, what is expected of him here, and how to not only survive but be effective. Often he is alone in this special world, which can make him easy prey for bad characters. As our hero meets new people, some will become friends and allies, and others will become enemies.

In *The Matrix*, Neo finds powerful allies in Morpheus, Trinity, and the rest of the crew of the ship, and discovers that the agents are his enemies. He goes through several tests, including an attempt to jump between buildings. In *Sling Blade*, Karl is befriended by Frank Wheatley and his mother Linda, and their friend Vaughn. Karl immediately recognizes the abusive Doyle as his enemy, as well as the enemy of his friends. He is tested constantly as Doyle makes fun of him in front of others. In *Zelda*, Link makes friends with Malon at the ranch with Zelda's guardian Impa, and with the Princess Zelda herself. He also witnesses the evil Ganon kidnapping Zelda.

Step 6b: Meeting With the Goddess. At this point the hero sometimes encounters a character that Campbell calls the "goddess," representing a mother figure. Like all archetypes, the goddess has both positive and negative aspects. She can help our hero through gifts and insight and help him access his own intuition, emotions, and spirit. But she can also encourage acts and beliefs that are unwisely irrational, overdependent on sentimentality, or driven by emotions like guilt or fear.

In *The Matrix*, Neo meets the goddess when Morpheus brings him to talk to the Oracle. In *Sling Blade*, the goddess is represented by the kind and warm Linda, who welcomes Karl into her home and family. In *Zelda*, Link meets the goddess in Princess Zelda, who gives him the Ocarina of Time.

Step 6c: Atonement with the Father. The hero often also finds himself facing a character who represents the archetypical father. While the mother typically provides support and encouragement, the father typically tests and judges the hero and then offers a reward if the hero proves worthy.

In *The Matrix*, Neo's world is turned upside-down when Cypher betrays the crew. He and the others are forced into extraordinary action by this test, and Neo proves himself worthy by his response. In *Sling Blade*, Vaughn explains to Karl how much he cares for Linda and Frank. Vaughn, playing the father, tests Karl to make sure that he's not dangerous by explicitly asking him if he could possibly hurt them and carefully watching him answer. In *Zelda*, the father figure is represented by Impa, Princess Zelda's guardian.

Step 7: Approaching the Cave. As the hero proceeds through the special world, he builds up increasing skill and confidence to deal with his ever-increasing challenges. As these challenges become more difficult, the risk of failure becomes more likely and the cost of failure more extreme.

Eventually the hero realizes, perhaps with the prompting of his allies or mentor, that he must face a specific and difficult peril. A common mythological embodiment of this step occurs when the hero enters the cave of monster that he must defeat, so Campbell calls this stage the *approach to the cave*. Often this step requires the hero to either symbolically or literally confront his own darkest nature.

In *The Matrix*, Neo approaches the cave when he works in the imaginary world of the Matrix to save Morpheus. In *Sling Blade*, Karl sits through an evening of abuse by the very drunk Doyle, taking the full force of Doyle's abuse without fighting back. In *Zelda*, Link literally enters many caves as he journeys into a variety of dungeons.

Step 8: The Ordeal. When the hero enters the cave, he must face the *ordeal* that awaits him. The ordeal is the final obstacle before the attainment of his goal. This is the big fight before the hero can claim his reward. But this is not the ultimate climax of the story: that comes a little later. Rather, this is the confrontation that sets up the final climax.

In *The Matrix*, Neo fights the agents to save Morpheus. In *Sling Blade*, Karl goes to talk to his abusive and distant father. In *Zelda*, Link confronts and defeats the boss of each dungeon.

Step 9: The Reward. When the ordeal is complete, the hero can finally claim his *reward*. Referring to the magical potion or weapon that appears in many myths, Campbell calls this stage *stealing the elixir* or *seizing the sword*. It is the moment when the hero attains the overt goal of his quest.

In *The Matrix*, Neo saves Morpheus from the agents. His reward is his understanding of his true power in the Matrix and the knowledge that he doesn't have to obey the rules that simply appear to be real. In *Sling Blade*, Karl confronts his father. He stands up for himself and tells his father that he shouldn't have treated him so badly. This act of independence rewards Karl with a new inner strength and peace. In *Zelda*, Link gains important new pieces of adventuring equipment in the dungeons he visits.

Step 10: The Road Back. In the classical hero's journey, the story is not over when the hero has obtained the object of his desire. He is still in the special world and must return to the world of his normal life, bringing the fruits of his quest to the ordinary world. In the process, he will find a way to internally integrate what he knows of both the ordinary and special worlds. Sometimes the hero doesn't want to return to his ordinary world. That's usually not too hard to understand: he's spent significant time and effort learning about the special world and mastering its rules, and now he is truly a hero there. Although he may recognize the need to return home, he may refuse to step foot on *the road back*.

In *The Matrix*, this integration is part of the final battle between Neo and the agents, where he finds that he is the master of both their world and his own. In *Sling Blade*, Karl decides that he wants to give his friend Frank the childhood he never had and methodically murders Doyle. In *Zelda*, the road back begins when Link defeats Ganon and the villain's tower crumbles, forcing Link and Zelda to run for their lives.

Step 11: Resurrection. The return home holds challenges of its own. It is at this point that the hero confronts the villain in his most elaborate and dangerous form. Even more than the ordeal, this final encounter is a brutal, life-and-death situation. The only way forward is to destroy the opponent, whether it is inside or outside, psychological or physical.

But brute force will not be enough. To defeat the villain, the hero must take the ultimate step of facing that which he himself is most afraid of, whether it's a physical monster or an internal demon. In the most powerful of stories, he must face both of these at once, as the demands on his inner and outer worlds pull at him in contradictory directions.

In *The Matrix*, Neo's eyes open in the ship. He has survived the battle and is reborn, more powerful than ever before. In *Sling Blade*, Karl calls the police, tells them that he's killed Doyle, and then calmly sits down to eat one of Linda's biscuits, finally sure of having done a good thing. In *Zelda*, Link must defeat the final version of the evil Ganondorf without his Master Sword.

Step 12: Returning with the Elixir. The final stage in the hero's journey is when he returns to his home with the physical and spiritual knowledge he gained on his quest. Campbell refers to this as *returning with the elixir*. This triumphant return is sometimes met with mixed reactions.

On the one hand, he is indeed a hero. If he originally journeyed off to defeat an army or dragon that was threatening his village, then he obviously deserves gratitude and cheers.

But sometimes there is a darker side to the return home. Some people may not believe his stories of the special world; they may think them to be exaggerations, or even outright fabrications and lies, leading to resentment and anger.

But even more threatening than his stories is the mere presence of the hero in his newly enlightened state. As part of his journey, the hero has examined and questioned many of the beliefs that he was raised with and that are shared by his contemporaries. Based on his experiences far from home and what he has learned on his quest, the hero often finds that his prior beliefs were limiting, or even wrong or misguided.

This is dangerous knowledge. Societies do not appreciate people who challenge their fundamental assumptions, even if they are heroes. In *Contact*, Dr. Arroway is ridiculed and discredited when she tells her story of meeting with another species.

If the hero's truths are not too radical or threatening, or he doesn't feel the need to express them, then the culmination of his journey need not end in such conflict. He has found peace in himself and a place in his world and can move forward on an optimistic and positive note.

In *The Matrix*, Neo places a phone call into the Matrix and tells it directly that he plans to make some changes. He has brought back from his experience the secret of the Matrix. In *Sling Blade*, Karl is again in the mental hospital. But he is stronger than he was before. When another inmate named Charles starts talking to him and implies that Karl was sexually involved with Frank, Karl stands up for himself and tells Charles never to speak to him again. Karl has brought back a sense of strength and self he never had before. In *Zelda*, Ganondorf is sealed away, and Link is returned to his original time, where he resumes his childhood from where he left it when he started the quest.

Summary

The Hero's Journey is a general structure shared by many stories around the world. It is not a formula, in the sense that following it does not guarantee a great story, and deviating from it does not guarantee a bad story.

Pieces of the Hero's Journey can be found in many popular contemporary stories. The steps don't always appear in this sequence, some steps can be visited more than once, and others can be omitted altogether. The three-act form can be thought of as a compressed version of the Hero's Journey.

It is not uncommon in contemporary stories for the tale to end soon after the climax. The steps of returning home and sharing the fruits of the quest with the hero's peers are often omitted or only briefly suggested.

Other Plot Considerations

Whatever structure the plot follows, certain elements are always present. There is an *inciting incident* that starts the events off. The hero must then take action to restore the balance of forces, passing through a series of struggles, each one more difficult and with higher risks than the one before.

As the issues become more complex, the character's understanding of his inner and outer worlds deepens. He often develops in several ways at once: physically, intellectually, emotionally, and spiritually.

An exception to this type of structure may seem to exist in documentaries and "reality TV." In fact, those are both very structured forms, though sometimes this structure can be a little harder to see.

Works in each of these genres are typically created by first obtaining a wealth of source material and then carefully selecting and editing that material to create a narrative.

In the case of episodic reality television shows such as *Survivor*, an entire season's worth of episodes are usually filmed before the first broadcast. Once the entire production is concluded and the producers know everything that happens along the way, up to and including the final outcome, they use that as raw material to build a structured narrative. This shaping of the events is particularly important in shows where people are eliminated over time, because the audience needs to care about the last few people left (otherwise, viewers will tune out when their favorites leave the show). Thus the last couple of people that remain at the end are presented as interesting people right from the start. This is a delicate balancing act, because the producers need to make the audience care about the people who will end up as the last few members of the cast without giving away who they are from the start and ruining the suspense.

As with all heroes, the last few people remaining don't necessarily have to be pleasant or even likable; they just need to be fascinating and get the audience to tune back in week after week.

Plot and Character

In the *Poetics* [3], Aristotle presented a list of what he considered the six elements of tragedy, in descending order of importance: plot, character, thought, spectacle, diction, and music. He stated, "But the most important of these is the arrangement of incidents of the plot; for tragedy is not the portrayal of men [as such], but of action, of life." In other words, the single most important aspect of any story is the plot.

Some people have taken issue with this assertion. The most popular opposing view has been that character should be elevated to the highest position, with the plot subservient to it. A lucid example of this argument is presented by Egri [45].

But this is a pointless argument without a resolution, akin to asking whether a magnet's north pole or south pole is more important. Neither one can exist without the other. Even in a movie as character-driven as

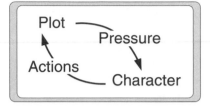

Figure 2. Plot puts pressure on characters, which causes them to act, resulting in changes to the plot, causing new pressures, and so on throughout a story.

Geri's Game, there is a thread of plot, and even in in a movie as plot-driven as *Jurassic Park*, there is evidence of character.

In its most basic form, plot describes what people do in the world: it is the result of their actions. The essence of character is revealed by the actions they choose to take.

From each character's point of view, plot is what happens to him, and character is what he does in response. To the hero, the villain's actions serve to propel the plot, while his own actions reveal his character. To the villain, the situation is reversed.

Plot and character are even more closely bound than two sides of the same coin: they are the risers and treads of a flight of stairs. Both are essential and mutually dependent, and to assert one is somehow more important than the other is to miss how neither one can last very long without the other.

We can think of plot and character as two interlocking mechanisms. The plot forces the hero to act, the nature of his character determines his action, the world's response to that action is another step in the deepening plot, the hero's next response springs from his developing and changing character in response to those forces, around and around, plot and character leading into each other and growing ever-more entwined.

Figure 2 shows this cyclic relationship.

As we've seen, the increasing demands of the plot compel increasing changes in the hero's character, forcing him to grow. The plot is carefully constructed to create this relentless pressure on the hero and to bring about the slow exposure of his innermost self. If the pressures are too small, they will fail to make him change; if they are too great, his response may be impossible, or it may damage him, in the way that a person can lift an automobile to free a trapped loved one but still damages his body in the process of that extraordinary effort. The plot must gradually, but relentlessly, push the hero into deeper and deeper growth.

Finally, when the hero's core being is revealed, he can act directly from his heart. Even this innermost layer, when exposed, may be different from what it was at the start, in response to what the hero has learned during his journey.

Obviously what a man says is important, and the act of speaking is itself an action. But what any of us thinks or says we are capable of may not match reality.

For example, a man may say that he loves all children and would do anything for them, including sacrifice his life. He may believe this with all his heart. And in everyday situations where he is called upon to sacrifice in some small way for a child, he may gladly do so. It's easy to be charitable and generous when it's convenient and the costs are low.

Imagine that one day he's walking down the road and sees a bus barrelling down the street at high speed towards a little girl who is chasing her ball. He has no time to consider his actions; the bus is approaching fast. He has only two choices: to stand and watch the girl be hit and certainly killed, or to jump out into the street, push her away, and be killed himself. Regardless of what he has said before and what he believes of himself, his true character will be revealed by what he actually does in that moment.

To capture this idea briefly, *character is action under pressure of plot*, and *plot is what happens when characters act*.

Premise

Regardless of their different structures, all stories exist for some purpose. That purpose may be simply to amuse and entertain, but often there is something more at work as well: the author has some idea or thought that he wants to communicate. Sharing that idea is one of the author's reasons for writing the work.

By analogy, a suspension bridge may be built in many different styles and serve many purposes. Yet it always has a single ultimate purpose: to create an easier way to get things from one side of a chasm to the other. If there are elements of the bridge that do not further that specific, utilitarian goal, they are superfluous to the mechanism of the bridge. A bridge may have other purposes, both functional and aesthetic. Many elements are included in bridge designs to enhance or adorn them, such as ornamentation on the towers and the color of the paint. These elements add to the overall spirit of the work without diminishing the bridge's basic function.

Anything that does not contribute to the bridge's purpose must be examined to be sure that it does not detract from or compromise that basic purpose. Suppose that the designer of an otherwise conventional suspension bridge considered replacing the middle of the span with a pair of large matched ramps like those used by motorcycle daredevils to jump over a tank of sharks. Cars on this bridge could get across only by revving up to high speeds, launching off the first ramp, flying through the air, and then landing on the far side. Would this be interesting? You bet. Would it add to the bridge's aesthetics? It's very likely: a pair of separated, matched ramps offers all kinds of nice design possibilities. Would it add to the bridge's popularity and perhaps even serve as a tourist attraction? Undoubtedly.

But obviously this idea would be scrapped by any serious designer. There are all sorts of problems with it, though many of the problems, from safety to crowd control, could theoretically be addressed. The essential problem with this idea is that it violates the central purpose of the bridge, which is to help people and vehicles travel from one side to the other. The bridge's towers support this purpose, and the ornamentation is neutral to it, but a car-jump ramp is antagonistic to it, and thus it would be rejected from the design.

Every story has its own purpose, its own reason for being. Franklin calls that reason its *premise* [50]. The word "premise" is used by Franklin in a way that is both similar to and different from its everyday meaning, so let's define it a little more carefully. It will be a useful exercise, because knowing a story's premise is one of the strongest tools a storyteller has for creating and editing a great story.

The premise is the truth that is learned by the character as a result of his experiences. Note that this is a very personal truth. It's not a universal lesson for all people, nor a "message" for the audience to take home. Rather, it's the personal conclusion that the character comes to as a result of his actions.

Let's see a couple of different premises rising from similar starting situations. Imagine that David, an unhappy and badly-adjusted high-school student, has been in a lot of trouble both at school and at home for years; his parents and most of his teachers are at the end of their ropes with him. Now suppose that he has cheated on his final exam in Geography class. His teacher, Mr. Lowell, discovers the evidence as he's grading the tests. Mr. Lowell asks David to stay after class one day, and he asks David point-blank if he cheated.

David decides to lie and denies cheating. If Mr. Lowell has proof that David cheated, this incident could be disastrous for the young man. He could be thrown out of school, which would be the last straw for his parents. They ship him off to a boarding school for "troubled" kids, where he becomes even more alienated and unhappy. The lesson, or premise, that David learns from this experience is that lying leads to misery.

Now suppose instead that Mr. Lowell doesn't have firm proof that David cheated, so the young man gets away with it. He's just careful enough in the future to not get caught again, and he manages to get through school and find a job he likes. He's learned that though the risks are high, lying leads to happiness.

Rewind again to Mr. Lowell's question, but suppose this time that David tells the truth and admits to cheating. Mr. Lowell might be so impressed with David's honesty that he takes the young man under his wing, and David flourishes as a student and as a person. He's learned that telling the truth can make his world a much better place.

On the other hand, Mr. Lowell might only have been suspicious that David had cheated and was secretly recording this conversation. Armed with David's confession, Mr. Lowell has David expelled, and once again David's life spirals downwards. He's learned that telling the truth is a sure way to ruin his life.

It would be silly to try to identify which of these conclusions is the "right" one. These different moral lessons are all reasonable conclusions, given their corresponding events.

Each of these conclusions is a *premise*, or the lesson that the character learns as a result of his experience. The more simple and direct the premise, the stronger it is.

The value of the premise is that it provides a test for the inclusion or exclusion of every element in the story. If some action, dialog, scene, chapter, or other element contributes to the premise, then it is a contribution to the story and should be retained. In other words, we can ask ourselves whether some given piece of the story helps propel it in the direction of the lesson that the character learns.

Because of its value as a test, the more sharp and succinct we can make the premise, the more valuable it will be. "Peace is good" is a premise, but it's vague: there are lots of forms of peace. "Refusing to fight leads to personal strength" is better.

A strong story tests a premise all the way through, showing each side of each choice. If the premise is "Honesty leads to harmony," then its opposite might be "Honesty leads to conflict." The main character should see in every choice that he makes just how honesty could lead to either outcome, usually in their most extreme forms. Then when the climax arrives, he will have seen both sides of the question and will truly understand the nature of his choice.

Franklin notes at least four useful ways to frame a premise. In the following, X and Y refer to events, forces, situations, or feelings. Z also refers to those elements, as well as change.

chain reaction: X leads to Z: sorrow leads to compassion, or duplicity leads to ruin.

opposing forces: X defeats Y: love vanquishes evil, or brutality defeats integrity.

conflict: Pitting X against Y leads to Z: a righteous plaintiff and a great lawyer bring victory, or selfish corporations and an uncaring government lead to the destruction of a country.

situational: Being X, or having X done to you, leads to Z: fighting injustice leads to honor, or being sent to jail leads to a life of crime.

Each character in a story has his own premise, resulting from his own experiences.

The best premises are those that flow sensibly and logically from the experiences that lead to them. They feel not only reasonable, but inevitable.

Social Tools

Stories are social glue. They allow us to share our experiences with each other and to see how different cultures and people respond to different situations.

Stories are an important tool for helping children internalize the values and conventions of their culture. The stories of Aesop, the Brothers

Grimm, and Hans Christian Andersen continue to be told to children in many Western societies. Those stories survive and prosper because they are first and foremost great stories; if they were simply blunt delivery vehicles for moralistic preaching, they would have been forgotten long ago.

Stories can help us develop an understanding of situations we will never have the chance to experience personally.

Nobody reading these words now can personally know what it was like to travel on the Lewis and Clark Expedition in the early 1800s. Yet through well-researched and vividly described stories, we can get some idea of what was going on in the minds of those explorers [2]. Few people will physically travel to every country on the globe, but we can read stories from every one, if we care to, and learn something of each culture in the process.

Stories can also serve a much more active and personal role. We each face important decisions in our lives: Should I marry this person? Should we have children? Should I take this job? By reading stories of other people's responses to these questions and the results of their choices, we can find inspiration for our own choices. Stories can expose us to possible futures that we might otherwise not imagine. A midwestern farmer's son might find himself captured by the idea of a life at sea, or a girl growing up in Texas might resonate strongly with the way business is practiced in Japan. When we try to imagine the results of life-changing choices, such as getting married and raising children, we rely on the real and imagined stories of our friends and our culture to help us get a feeling for what we're getting into. Someone contemplating a one-night stand might reconsider after seeing *Fatal Attraction*.

Stories give us windows into options that we might otherwise not consider, because we never even knew about them. A man might be living a comfortable life and then read a story about the life of a marine biologist and become intrigued. This man might have always had an interest in living things, a love of travel and an analytical, organized mind, but simply never realized that he could put these pieces together into a single occupation. He could learn of such a job simply by reading a description of it, but a story also helps give us an active and emotional understanding of not just the particulars of the job, but the life and the other people who find it attractive.

Conflict

The essence of drama is *conflict*. Conflict is born of thwarted desire and grows in proportion to the obstacles in its way and the effort already expended towards overcoming them.

Conflict is abundant. Anyone who has any unfulfilled desires in his life experiences some conflict. This is one source of the famous Buddhist teaching that "life is pain." Some Buddhists believe that part of the work of becoming enlightened is giving up all desires and thereby break free of the painful conflict that we feel when reality doesn't conform to what we imagine it should be. This is a difficult attitude to cultivate and pursue, particularly in contemporary Western consumer cultures where entire industries exist to manufacture new desires and then sell products and services to satisfy them.

Important conflicts are more interesting and pack more emotional and intellectual power than trivial conflicts. If our hero desires a more expensive car simply because he believes it will raise his status in his neighbor's eyes, that is not likely to gather much sympathy from an impartial audience that knows little else about him. If the hero needs a more expensive car because it will allow him to start a limousine service to raise money for his daughter's life-saving operation, we're more likely to care about his success or failure.

Conflict comes about because some force stands between the hero and his desire. Aristotle identified three distinct forms of conflict [3]:

Man Versus Man: In this form of conflict, the opposing force is another person, whom we usually call the *villain*. The villain may be a group of people, but usually there's a single individual we can identify as the driving force. In *Die Hard*, Hans Gruber is the criminal mastermind, and John McClane is the hero out to defeat him.

Man Versus Nature: In this conflict, the hero struggles against the impartial forces of the universe. He may be trapped on a desert or an alien planet or lost in a dark forest. In *A Perfect Storm*, the physical power of a storm at sea creates trouble for the sailors.

Man Versus Self: In this form of conflict, the hero's biggest problem is himself. The main barrier that prevents him from achieving his heart's desire lies within his own heart. For example, our hero's goal may be to rebuild a failing marriage, but he is insecure and has a violent temper, both of which cause each attempt at conciliation to end in a bitter fight. In *Raging Bull*, it's Jake LaMotta's own failings that are the source of his problems.

Some limitations are not in our power to change. If a hero's goal is to be a professional basketball player, but his biggest problem is that he is unusually short, his problem is partly man versus nature and partly man versus himself.

In a really good conflict, the hero faces a really good challenge. If it's easy to get past the obstacles in his way, the hero won't gather much of our sympathy. In fact, if his problem appears to the audience to be one that he should reasonably be expected to solve without too much trouble, the audience may decide he is stupid or not really motivated and thus turn against him.

In general, *the villain should appear to be stronger than the hero*. This strength could be physical, mental, moral, financial, or come from any other source. The greater the disparity between the resources of the hero and the resources of the villain, the greater the hero's predicament and the greater the tension. An able-bodied man in a hotel room who is thirsty would reasonably be expected to pour himself a glass of water; if he complained of his thirst we'd probably find him simply annoying. Place this man in the desert, without a canteen, far from an oasis, and his thirst becomes a serious problem. The dry desert is the villain here, and in almost every way it is more powerful than a single man struggling without water.

The more that the villain dwarfs the hero, the harder the hero must struggle. If we believe in the hero's quest, then we empathically hope with him, and we feel something of the challenge he faces. This is one reason some stories pack such an emotional punch: when the hero succeeds, we feel in some ways that we've been along on the journey, and the joyous victory is partly ours as well.

The key to keeping the protagonist growing and pushing forward on his quest is *pressure*. This is what makes him act and forces him to continue to grow. Under sufficient pressure, the hero must confront his greatest internal and external challenges and slowly grow.

Protagonist

The hero, or protagonist, is the person who is at the focus of the story. Usually heroes are attractive in some way, though some stories feature "anti-heroes" who are unpleasant yet fascinating.

The hero is the person who is striving to restore balance to his world. Usually he is prodded into action by some external event, which may range from the normal working of the world or the deliberate action of a villain.

Heros act not because they want to, but because they *must*. Like most people, heroes prefer to avoid struggle and conflict when they can. But they are forced into action: their life has been upset and they need to bring it back into balance.

The most important issue at the center of any hero's quest is what he wants. In any great story, the audience can easily state explicitly and clearly what the hero wants, and the more focused that answer is, the better. So "he wants world peace" is clear enough, but "he wants to rescue his kidnapped daughter" is better.

In 1943 Abraham Maslow developed a now-famous characterization of human motivation. He suggested a *hierarchy of needs* shared by every person. Maslow's hierarchy has eight levels, which are often clustered into three groups in a pyramid, as in Figure 3 [87].

The first group addresses the basic physical and emotional needs of every person:

1. Physiology: The needs of the body, such as food, warmth, sex, cleanliness, and health.

2. Safety and security: The need for shelter from harm and a safe place to relax and sleep.

3. Belonging and love: The need for acceptance by a social group, and one or more intimate relationships.

4. Esteem: The need for social approval and self-worth.

These first four needs are basic to every person's physical and psychological well-being, and most people will focus their energies on these issues until they've been satisfied. Many of the stories that Aristotle characterized as man-versus-nature are fundamentally survival stories, which come about when these needs are disrupted or interfered with.

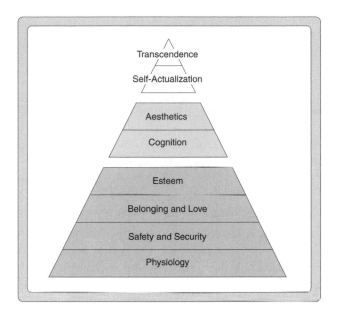

Figure 3. Maslow's hierarchy of needs.

When the four basic needs are in place, and our survival is addressed, then our attention can turn to the second group of needs, which are more abstract:

5. Cognition: The need to know and understand one's self and the world.

6. Aesthetics: The need to know and appreciate beauty.

These needs address the human desire to understand the world and make it a beautiful place. For example, shelter appears in the first group of needs. But once a place has been found that is safe and dry, then we can turn our attention to making it attractive by furnishing it with comfortable and pleasing objects and art. Finding a cave to live in is a survival need; painting pictures on the wall is aesthetic. When we're dry and our bellies are full, we can begin to study our world and try to find ways to improve it for ourselves and each other (as Macheath, London's most powerful criminal, puts it in a song from *The Threepenny Opera*), "Food is the first thing, morals follow on.").

Many of the stories Aristotle characterized as man-versus-man take place when these cognitive and aesthetic needs are thwarted. Man-versus-man stories can also involve direct confrontation on more basic emotional and physical levels.

When our basic animal needs are satisfied, and we have found a comfortable intellectual and emotional balance with the world, then we begin to look inwards again, to consider other states of consciousness and what is possible for us, rather than what is only comfortable:

7. Self-actualization: The need to discover internal peace and harmony, and a sense of connection with the world.

8. Transcendence: The need to help others on their journeys to their own self-actualization.

These last two levels are sometimes described as religious or spiritual enlightenment: they represent a desire to find a deeper connection between ourselves and other living things. Many of the stories Aristotle described as man-versus-self take place when these needs are not satisfied. When a man is his own worst enemy, he is the one standing in the way of his own self-development and progress in the hierarchy of needs. When he finds peace and a resolution in his own heart, he moves closer to self-actualization. Figure 4 shows the relationship between Maslow's hierarchy and Aristotle's three types of drama.

The Hero's Growth

When a hero finishes his quest as a fundamentally better person than he was at the start, the audience cheers his positive growth. A great hero not only overcomes obstacles to achieve his goal, but he becomes a better person in the process. In Campbell's terms, he learns to master two worlds. In Maslow's terms, he moves closer to self-actualization. And in everyday terms, he simply becomes a better person.

Thus we often think of characters as growing from one extreme to its opposite. The meaning of "opposite" is itself very flexible.

Contradiction is the most directly contrasting state. For example, a sad person becomes a happy one. In *A Christmas Carol*, Scrooge starts out as the most miserly of misers, and ends up freely giving gifts to the Cratchetts.

Rejection is stronger, where the fundamental principle is not only contradicted, but the entire subject is rejected. For example, suppose that our hero desperately wants a woman he knows to become his lover. He starts

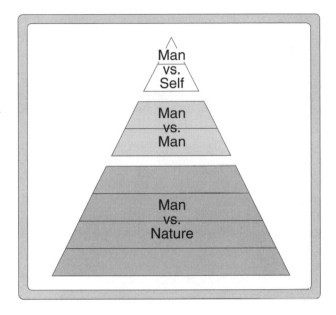

Figure 4. The relationship between Maslow's hierarchy of needs and Aristotle's three types of drama.

out infatuated, filled with positive emotions. He may over time travel to the contradictory state, where he decides that the object of his affection is worthless and undeserving and his feelings turn to hate. But there can be yet one more twist, where he loses all emotional connection to the woman and ends up lonely and empty. McKee calls this the *negation of the negation* [90].

Rejection is a powerful psychological event, and a character may react in a positive or negative way. In our example of thwarted love, our loving hero first becomes angry (that's the contradiction part), and then loses all feelings, good and bad, for the woman he used to desire (that's the rejection part). Here's another example: our hero is a scientist, largely motivated by a strong curiosity. In the course of the story he moves to contradiction and loses interest in new ideas, ultimately becoming indifferent to the suggestions of his colleagues. If he moves on to rejection, he may decide that new ideas are dangerous and mounts a campaign to shut down his department and end that entire line of research.

To see rejection used in a positive way, imagine a hero who starts the story as a high-powered business executive. He has little time for people, except for those that are useful to him. Thus he has many professional acquaintances, but no friends. Over the course of the story he comes to feel badly about these shallow relationships based on what people can do for him. This shift in understanding causes him to move into a contradictory state: he quits his job, retires to a small house far out in the country, and becomes a hermit. But this isolation proves to be no more pleasant than his job. So he rejects the whole way that he's been thinking of other people, either as creatures of use to him, or as creatures of no use at all, and realizes that other people are inherently interesting in themselves. He sells his house and embarks on a trip around the world, with the express purpose of simply meeting and talking to as many different kinds of people as he can. By rejecting the basic assumption behind his original attitude, he is able to move to a situation that is not just a contradiction, but a re-interpretation of the entire situation.

Characters rarely jump from one extreme to another. Rather, they take many small steps along the way. I think of this as something like Lewis Carroll's game of word transformation called Doublets (it's also known as Word Chains and Word Ladders). As he described it in an 1879 issue of *Vanity Fair* [24], the idea is to take two words of equal length and turn one into the other by changing only one letter at each step, always creating valid words along the way. For example, here's one way to turn "hero" into "tale":

```
HERO
HERD
HELD
HOLD
HOLE
MOLE
MALE
TALE
```

The analogy here is that at each step along a person's journey, he is always in a believable emotional and intellectual state and moves from it to the next one in small steps. This helps the audience stay interested in the character's gradual unfolding and allows him to be surprising without radical shifts in behavior that could cause the audience to feel they've lost the sense of the character.

Depth of Immersion

In a great story, the audience vicariously joins the hero in his journey. They don't literally travel with him or meet the people he meets, but they can be a fly on the wall and become engrossed in his story. We often say that the audience *identifies* with the main character, though as we'll see in a moment, identification is just one of the ways that audiences bond with a character.

The more deeply the audience identifies with the hero, the more they will be affected by the story. It's useful to consider the different degrees to which an audience can be engaged.

I see several levels of *engagement* or *immersion*, which are characterized by the depth of the bond between the audience member and the character. To say that the audience is "engaged" or "immersed" is simply to say that they're in some way involved. It's useful to have a finer scale in which to measure the degree of this involvement. I see this a continuum, the *depth of immersion*, which contains some common terms that we use to describe different levels of audience involvement.

Curiosity is the weakest, most distant form of connection. Though we sometimes speak of an intense or burning curiosity, the term usually refers to a casual desire to know more without expending too much effort. This is about the level of interest we have when we're sitting on a couch at a party and notice a clump of people nearby having an animated conversation. We might casually listen in without bothering to get up.

Sympathy arises when we start to see the world through the character's eyes. We aren't personally moved by anything that happens to the character, but we're paying attention. In our party above, sympathy would be listening to a stranger tell a good story: we'll tag along, but only while we're actively drawn in.

Identification is the first of the strong forms of connection to the character. We begin to see elements of ourselves in him, and elements of him in ourselves. In this state we wonder what we would do in his situation and begin to feel some of what the character is feeling. This is like actively listening to an acquaintance at a party or a casual story told by a good friend.

Empathy is a strong sense of emotional bonding with the character. We remain aware of ourselves, but we become engrossed in the character's struggles. We feel for the character and allow ourselves to share in his emotions and problems. This is the highest form of emotional engagement that we typically enter in everyday life. It's how we attend to good friends and loved ones when they are speaking of important matters.

Transportation is the state when we actually lose the boundary between our self and the character. Rather than reaching out to the character, as in empathy, when we are transported, we feel that we actually are the character. Hypnotists call this the *plenary state*, referring to that condition in which we feel as though we're no longer ourselves, but are someone else. This dream-like condition creates the deepest bond with a character, but it's difficult to achieve and fragile to maintain. It's a peronally vulnerable state, because our emotions are completely exposed and available. We can also enter this state in private, intimate moments with loved ones.

This is also the state that filmmakers, novelists, playwrights, and other storytellers hope to coax us into when they tell their stories.

To summarize, there are many levels of immersion, from a casual curiosity to a state of transportation. Most fiction tends to achieve results somewhere between the extremes.

Action

Most people resist taking actions that are risky, dangerous, or carry other large personal or professional costs, unless there's a compelling reason. Usually, that reason is to meet a need that is being frustrated.

Action is not simply motion. Great stories are structured so that each action has a purpose.

There are three principle reasons why any action is included in a story: it *advances the plot*, it *reveals character*, or it's inherently *exciting or funny*. The most economical actions will do several of these things at once.

There are many ways that an action can move the plot forward. The most obvious are those that create significant stress on the hero: e.g., he loses his job, his daughter refuses to speak to him, or he wins the lottery.

Each of these stresses requires action on the part of the hero in order to order to put the situation right again. If he's shipwrecked on a desert island without food, he must find something to eat or die: the plot propels the character into action. If he finds fruit on the island, but after eating it he finds that it's poisonous, his problem now becomes finding the antidote. So the character's actions are directly in response to the stresses put upon him by the plot. Anything contributing to his survival is relevant to the story of his rescue. Actions that don't contribute to his mental and physical health and safety don't move his plot forward.

Actions that do nothing for the plot may instead reveal a hero's character. Suppose that the hero's problem is that his daughter suddenly refuses to speak to him. In response, he might refuse to speak to her, revealing his own tendencies towards petulance and spite. Or instead, he might try to force her to speak to him, or talk to her friends to find out what is bothering her, or examine his own behavior to find the cause of the problem. Each of these responses tells us something about his character.

On the desert island, our hero might name the trees for his family members and spend his time talking to them more honestly than he had ever had the courage to speak to the real people. This would certainly help us learn more about him. Much of the film *Cast Away* is about the psychological development of its marooned hero, Chuck Noland.

Finally, actions that neither advance the plot nor reveal character may be included because they are simply exciting or funny. The sequence at the start of *Raiders of the Lost Ark* in which Indiana Jones escapes a temple full of booby traps is thrilling for its own sake. The opening cartoon in *Who Framed Roger Rabbit?* is simply silly and funny. Although both of these sequences also reveal character, they would be perfectly at home in the movie anyway; they are simply their own reason for being. Humor doesn't need to serve any purpose beyond its own: we all love a good joke and are happy to enjoy it for its own sake. And action need be nothing more than an exciting thrill ride.

Actions can combine two or more of these functions. When Alvy is picked up by his friend Rob in *Annie Hall*, Rob puts on an elaborate radiation suit. He says that it keeps out the alpha rays, so that he won't age. The visual gag is funny, but combined with Rob's vanity it's even better. In *Ghostbusters*, we meet Dr. Peter Venkman as he administers an ESP test to several students. To a nerdy young man Venkman delivers negative reinforcement through a series of electric shocks, but to an attractive woman he offers praise and encouragement, even when she's consistently wrong. The scene is funny, and tells us a lot about Venkman.

Action and humor can be combined to advance the plot with simultaneous fear and comedy. In *Toy Story 2*, Buzz Lightyear and several other toys need to cross a busy street and choose to manage it by using traffic cones for cover. They're in danger, but the scene is still funny.

In a similar way, scary action and character can be developed together. In *The Silence of the Lambs*, Hannibal Lecter manages to break free of his high-security cell through an audacious attack and an equally clever escape. His actions are horrifying, yet they serve to remind us just how intelligent and resourceful Lecter is.

In addition to developing character, moving the plot along, and providing humor and suspense, actions can also be used for many secondary purposes, such as to control timing and pacing, to create a transition from one time or place to another, or simply to give the audience a more well-rounded view of the story's world and characters.

Pacing is an important use of small actions: the audience needs time to catch its breath after an action sequence or to absorb new information after a big revelation. A relatively simple or inconsequential action can give the audience a chance to digest what's just happened and prepare for the next development.

Actions are also useful as a technical device to bridge from one sequence to another. For example, one scene may end with a college football star throwing a pass during a big game, the camera zooming in on the ball to follow it as it flies through the air. The next scene begins with a player catching the ball, and as the camera pulls back, we discover that our high-school star is now playing professionally.

An action can also serve as exposition of the world, particularly if it's a time or place that's foreign to the audience. Science-fiction stories often have actions that are meant only to help the audience understand what technology is present in that world and what people routinely do with it.

Scenes

The *scene* is the basic unit of plot. A scene is usually a group of actions and sequences (including physical activity, dialog, or even just mental reflections) that occur in the same place at around in the same time.

Generally we think of one character or another as *owning* a scene. This refers to that one character who is pushing the action along. A character can own the scene simply by being the most forceful presence, exerting his dominance through action, dialog, or emotional intensity.

Suppose that our hero is in a one-on-one confrontation with the kidnapper of his wife. The hero is angry and a hair's breadth from attacking the kidnapper but is holding back because he needs to learn where his wife is being held. The kidnapper, on the other hand, is dispassionate and almost calm, toying with our hero.

Who owns this scene? It depends on who is in control of the conversation. In the game of Go, the term *sente* (pronounced SEN-tay) refers to the situation when one player has freedom to make many moves, but the other player is being forced to respond. In chess, this ocrresponds to being in check. the checked player cannot go on the offensive because he must always respond to the immediate threat.

In a scene, only one character at a time can have *sente* and thus have control of the conversation or events. A man shooting a gun forces his target to jump from the bullets. A man with a secret to tell can extract promises from someone desperate to hear it.

Scenes frequently have one dominant person throughout, who, by virtue of holding *sente*, owns the scene from beginning to end. Often, it's the person who initiated the confrontation and is trying to steer it in a specific direction. Characters can also turn the tables and take control. If this happens just once or twice in the scene, we may think of the scene as broken up into smaller chunks, each owned by one character or the other. The reversals can also come fast and furious, like a well-played ping-pong match.

In *The Maltese Falcon*, the mysterious Joel Cairo comes to visit the offices of our hero, the private eye Sam Spade. Cairo is in search of a black statue of a falcon, and after Spade denies that he has it, Cairo pulls a gun on the detective. Cairo seems to have the upper hand, but then Spade disarms Cairo and knocks him out cold. Spade is in charge now and after searching Cairo, has a short conversation with him. When Spade gives Cairo back his gun, Cairo immediately points it at Spade again and resumes his search for the statue. Although Cairo holds Spade at gunpoint twice during this single scene, Spade really owns it all the way through by virtue of sheer force of character and confidence.

Another central issue in every scene is what is being risked by each character and what is at stake. Almost every human contact involves some form of risk. It may be simply the risk of rejection if the other person doesn't want to engage. But in stories, scenes typically carry a larger payload of risk. Often the risk is emotional: the character reveals something private or is willing to enter a vulnerable state of mind. Even something as commonplace as asking another person for a date often carries a significant amount of emotional risk. Many risks are overtly physical, like jumping into the street to rescue a child from an approaching car.

There are many kinds of risks, from political and spiritual to professional and and personal. Much of the power of a well-written scene comes from the balance of forces between the risks taken by the person who owns the scene and those taken by the others. For example, when our hero from the kidnapping story confronts the kidnapper, the kidnapper is clearly in charge: he has the hero's wife as a hostage. When facing the object of his enmity, the kidnapper risks overplaying his hand and losing his hostage, and thus all his leverage. The hero's risks range from simply losing track of his wife again to seeing her get killed. Though the kidnapper is in charge, the hero may have more at stake and thus may be willing to take greater chances.

In a great scene, the characters change bit by bit. Just as we earlier saw how a character changes gradually over the course of a story, bit by bit, so too do characters change over the course of a scene. The unit of emotional change in a scene is called a *beat*. Often a character leaves a scene in a mood or emotion that is far from where he entered it. The other characters in the scene go through their own changes as well, each one moving one beat at a time.

Suppose a man and wife are out at dinner in an expensive restaurant. The man is happy and content with everything, while the wife has been working up the courage to tell him of an affair she'd had, but has now broken off because she's realized she truly loves her husband. Nervously, almost dispassionately, she tells him the details. As she does, she can see him growing angry. Her tone becomes more intimate, as she tries to explain to him how much she loves him. But his first reaction of surprise turns to anger and then jealousy. When he learns that the man is someone he works with, he explodes in fury, disturbing the entire restaurant. She tries to soothe him, but he responds by screaming at her and then storms out, leaving her mortified and in tears.

Let's break this scene down.

Ownership: Who owned this scene? Initially it was the wife, because she started the development of conflict where none existed before. But power shifted to the husband as his anger dominated the conversation and eventually took over.

Risk: What was at risk? The wife risked her marriage and her emotional connection with her husband, as well as the simple pleasure of a good meal. She took the chance that telling him would work out for the best. When he learned of the affair, the husband risked appearing in his own eyes to be a cuckold and a fool. He chose to instead risk public humiliation and emotional harm to his wife by making a public scene.

Change: How did they each change? The wife started out nervously, became calm, then afraid, tried to quiet the situation with intimacy, and finally ended up ashamed and broken-hearted. The husband went from happy and relaxed to shocked, disappointed, angry, jealous, and then furious. Through dialog and action, we would see each of these characters explicitly move through each of these beats, so that every step along the way made sense, and the final results, so far from the starting conditions, were more than just believable, they felt inevitable.

Every character enters a scene with an *intent*, that may be simple or complex, small and personal or large and public. When a well-written scene is over, each character usually has a new purpose: the character's world has turned as a result of the scene.

The changes in a scene can turn entire stories around. Partway through the film *Chinatown*, Evelyn Mulwray comes to the office of Jake Gittes. She reveals to Gittes that he has been working as an investigator for a woman who used her name but was an imposter and that she is very angry. She threatens Gittes with action from her lawyers. Gittes realizes that he's been set up by someone and could be discredited, broke, or even jailed.

Suddenly Gittes's problems have changed from his original investigation to a new and urgent need to understand who conned him and why.

This example was overt and explicit in its threats and changes. Things can be much more personal and subtle. The change in a character's emotions can simply shade from one type of feeling to another, and the change in action may be very small. Perhaps the change is simply that the character decides not to stop for lunch at this town, but instead at the next. If that's a meaningful change for that character, then it still counts as a dramatic shift for him from the beginning of the scene to its end. Such small, subtle differences in attitude shape many of the scenes in the novel *Remains of the Day*.

Villain

The villain, or antagonist, is the character that is most responsible for obstructing the hero's progress towards his goal. Villains take on many forms, from a person to a political or religious system, to a force of nature.

One characteristic of almost all great villains is that they are stronger and more resourceful than the hero. After all, if the hero could easily defeat the villain, then he would do so immediately and the story would be over.

In mystery and action stories, the bad guy is usually smarter or more clever than the hero, or just has many more resources. James Bond is but a single man, yet he often goes out alone to confront villains with huge physical installations and hundreds of henchmen. The murderer in most thriller mysteries is more clever and intelligent than the hero and toys with him through the story. In action movies, the hero is often up against a clever villain (*Speed*), or well-funded and well-trained groups (*Die Hard*), or even entire armies (*The Great Escape*). In stories where heroes battle the elements, the forces of nature can be as extreme as limitless deserts, icy tundras, or once-in-a-lifetime storms (*The Perfect Storm*).

People rarely think of themselves as evil. Even people who commit the most terrible injustices tend to think of themselves as justified or even morally compelled to act as they do. A murderer may believe that his killing is defensible because it's appropriate revenge for real or perceived injustices. Many villains see themselves as having been wronged in the past, and their present actions are only designed to even the score.

Hardly anyone wakes up in the morning and says to himself, "Today I will do unjustified evil in the world." Even when someone recognizes that he is doing a terrible thing, he rationalizes it somehow: perhaps it's for the greater good, or it will bring about a better world.

The Wicked Witch of the West in *The Wizard of Oz* is out to get Dorothy because Dorothy killed her sister. Her anger is fuelled by what she sees as a need for justifiable revenge.

Like all characters, villains see themselves as the heroes of their own stories. They believe that they possess special insight or knowledge that compels them to act as they do in order to ultimately help other people. Sometimes villains even see themselves as martyrs, actually doing good even though nobody else yet recognizes it as such.

In *Mutiny on the Bounty*, Captain Bligh thinks he's a good guy, motivated by his desire to make money for himself and the crew. If the *Bounty* is able to complete its mission, he's promised promotions and bonuses all around. Bligh punishes his men brutally for any transgression, because he believes that when his men are fearful they will be obedient, and such blind obedience is their best guarantee of survival and success. When Bligh finds that his intended shortcut around Cape Horn is blocked by utterly impassable weather, he becomes furious with the crew, claiming that they could have made it through if not for their incompetence, and so he punishes them accordingly. The men know that his brutal retribution is fundamentally unfair, but there's nothing they can do about it. Bligh doesn't think of himself as evil: he thinks he's doing what's best for himself, the ship, and even the crew themselves.

There are several common motivators for villains who consciously set out to create trouble for the hero. Fear, greed, power, jealousy, and revenge are frequently behind the acts of the villain. Though he may try to cover these emotions with layers of rationalization and justification, usually there is emotional pain at work anytime someone deliberately hurts another person. The closer the audience can see that pain and the reasons behind it, the more complete and believable the villain appears to be and, often, the more menacing his actions appear.

The conflict between the hero and the villain can be made more powerful when they are matched in an interesting way.

For example, the villain may be driven to act because he sees in the hero something that exists in himself which causes him pain, such as fear or loneliness. Rather than address his own problem, he externalizes it, with the hope that by killing the hero (either literally or symbolically), he will simultaneously eliminate that part of himself that the hero represents. Alternatively, the hero can embody a trait such as honesty or happiness that the villain lacks. By getting rid of the hero, the villain hopes to also be rid of the unpleasant reminder of his own limitation.

By the same token, the hero can see in the villain traits that he also possesses but doesn't like, such as anger or violence. Thus the hero's desire to thwart or stop the villain coincides with the villain's desire to eliminate that quality within himself.

When the Queen in *Snow White and the Seven Dwarfs* goes after Snow White, it's because her magic mirror tells her that the younger woman is prettier. The Queen sees Snow White as her rival in several ways, but perhaps most important is that the Queen wants to remain "the fairest of them all." In *Sling Blade*, the malevolent Doyle sees his girlfriend and her son respond warmly to Karl's gentleness, a quality he knows he himself lacks, and he resents Karl for it.

Ensemble Casts

In stories with many major characters, one way to keep the characters distinct is to give them complementary attributes.

Just as the villain can embody a repressed or unknown quality of the hero, so can the other characters embody explicit aspects of the hero.

It's not unusual for heroes to be surrounded by people who give them contradictory advice, appealing to different elements of their nature. In the original *Star Trek* television show, Captain Kirk's two main advisors were Mister Spock and Doctor McCoy. Spock's observations and advice were based on logic and reason, while McCoy operated from emotion and passion. Together they were like the proverbial angel and devil perched on one's shoulders. These two characters represented two parts of Kirk's own nature and gave voice to his conflict when his mind and his heart were pulled in different directions. The characters made his internal conflicts explicit for the audience by articulating the pros and cons of each approach he contemplated.

When there are many characters, there are more opportunities to expose additional points of view that reside in the hero. As the hero debates with these other characters, we can develop a more complete understanding of the chorus of different voices in his own head and how he weighs their different attitudes, integrates or resists new ideas, and responds to challenges to his existing attitudes and point of view.

Climax

Over the course of a story the hero must often make important decisions. But the most important and critical decision of all comes at the very end, in the *climax*.

The climax is the point of ultimate tension in the story. In plot-driven stories, the climax is often a high-stakes action sequence. In a character-driven story, the hero typically must make a decision of huge proportions. The stakes of that decision vary widely, involving physical, emotional, and spiritual risks, or anything else of great importance to the hero.

This climactic decision arrives in such a way that the hero cannot avoid it. He must decide and act, knowing that not deciding is also a decision. The hero is fully aware of everything involved in this decision, so that his choice is completely informed and thus reveals his deepest inner character. Earlier I referred to the layers of character being stripped away over the course of the story until the innermost core of the hero is revealed. The climax is the moment of final revelation: the essential nature of the character is brought to the fore, bringing together all he has learned and become. Everything in his history, including his recent transformative past, comes together in this moment when he says, "*This* is who I am and what I believe in," and then acts.

In some stories, this choice is clear: a weak man must find the strength to defeat the giant and save the town, or the man afraid of water must swim into a raging storm to save someone who's drowning.

But often the choices are more complex, and the results ambiguous. Let's return to our hero confronting his wife's kidnapper. Suppose that he has spent his life as a pacifist. He left his home country to avoid the draft, unwilling to become a soldier and possibly kill people. He has gone to extremes to not kill any living creature in his world; his habit of catching and releasing spiders and other household animals was one of many quirks that led his first wife to divorce him. He quit his job at a manufacturing plant because some of the products were tested on animals. And he's gone to jail twice for civil protests against university labs using animals for experiments. He has suffered greatly because of his core belief that he has no right to kill any other living creature.

91

But now he's in the locked basement of the man who is holding his wife. She is before him, gagged and tied to a chair. The kidnapper, enraged, is rushing towards her with a huge knife to cut her throat. Our hero is too far away to run and tackle him. But on the table next to our hero is a loaded gun. He has two choices: pick up the gun and shoot the kidnapper before he reaches his wife, or let the gun sit and watch her die.

This is his choice: shoot and kill, or don't. If he shoots, he will have negated the core principle which he has defined himself by, and for which he has suffered greatly all his life. He will be a murderer. If he doesn't shoot, then his wife will die.

There is no "right" choice here: either decision can end in success or tragedy. His choice is what he values more: his wife's life, or the principle of pacifism. One of these must be lost, and he must choose which.

This final, ultimate climax appears at the end of the story. But it is so powerful that it can drive the story even if it happened in the past. For example, in the novel *Sophie's Choice* the emotional power of the critical decision of the title informs the entire narrative, though it is not revealed until the end.

This final crisis need not be external: it can be intimate and private. In *Casablanca*, Rick must decide whether to take up again with Ilsa or let her go with her husband, Victor Laszlo. His choice is intensely personal and internal, and his decision reveals the kind of man he really is once the layers of bitterness and self-pity have been burned away.

⤜ 4 ⤛

Story Technique

K ey to any successful story is the bond between the storyteller and the audience. When we as audience members give another person our time and attention, we expect that our investment will be rewarded. The essence of the bond between creator and audience is trust. The creator relies on the audience to willfully enter the world of the story and make themselves open to the characters and the plot. The audience in turn trusts the artist to respect that investment and provide a rewarding experience.

Audiences enter a storytelling experience in many different states of mind. Going to a movie or a play often involves expense, preparation, and travel. We use this ritual to put us in a receptive frame of mind. Many people go through a similar procedure when starting a new novel: we'll get into a comfortable chair when we have a good chunk of time and give ourselves over to the author. At the other extreme, television is a much more casual event. People turn on the television for all sorts of reasons, ranging from the eager anticipation of a favorite show to simple boredom. People watch television in just about every possible mood. Other forms of storytelling, from radio drama to travel lectures, carry with them their own range of expectations and investments.

Audiences usually enter the storytelling experience with a hopeful attitude, so the storyteller starts off with the audience on his side. It's the author's job at that point to build on that good will and create a perception of trust on the audience's part: each audience member needs to be assured that his investment of time will be rewarded.

The author wins trust by making a series of promises, implicit or explicit or both, and then keeping those promises.

One promise is the emotional tone of the work, which is often communicated to the audience through the work's genre. If a movie is titled *On Golden Pond II*, then audiences will expect a personal, character-based film like the original *On Golden Pond*. If suddenly armies of phaser-wielding space aliens emerge and the film becomes bloody and violent, audiences will feel betrayed. Similarly, if a film is marketed as "*Jurassic Park* meets *E.T.*," audiences will expect to see dinosaurs and space aliens. If the film turns out to be a romantic comedy set in Texas during the 1800s, they will resent the broken promises made to bring them into the theater. The same expectations and payoffs hold true in every medium.

We can classify most books, movies, plays, and other stories into genres, such as comedy, science fiction, action, or road-trip. Many stories combine two or more genres. For example, three recent films take the science-fiction genre and add another genre: *Star Wars: Episode IV–A New Hope* combines science fiction and action, *Galaxy Quest* combines science fiction and humor, and *Alien* combines science fiction and horror. The movie *When Harry Met Sally* combines features of romantic comedy and documentarys. Combining genres helps old stories find fresh expression. Stories can also turn a genre on its head, reversing the normal roles. In the film *Dog Day Afternoon*, the lead character Sonny is not at all the hard-nosed bank robber we are used to from classic robbery films. We feel for him and his plight and find ourselves hoping for him rather than for the police who are trying to capture him.

When a genre is turned upside-down, it is generally made clear to the audience sometime in advance. It is very rare for a successful story to switch genres completely and unexpectedly. Westerns do not suddenly become horrors, and romantic comedies don't turn into children's cartoons. Audiences choose stories the way they choose a meal at a restaurant: from the available choices, they make an informed decision based on their mood. If someone orders a mild eggplant lasagna and halfway through it finds that it has been filled with layers of jalapeño chutney sauce, he probably won't be pleased by the unexpected change. Any good story will have surprises, just like any good meal, but those surprises can't violate the agreement of trust between the author and the audience. When the author promises a certain type of story, it's his responsibility to stay true to the type of experience he's promised the audience.

To build a relationship of trust with the audience, the storyteller often begins by revealing the emotional tone of the piece from the very start, confirming the audience's expectations. This is like the flight check made by the captain of an airplane when he announces where the flight is headed before departing the gate. Thus a scary story may begin with a horrifying decapitation or even just a tangible air of spookiness. If the author is well-known and has already established a trust relationship with his audience, he can play with this immediate confirmation, for example by starting off a scary story in the most mundane and ordinary of circumstances. The audience will stick with him because they know from past experience that things will eventually get scary. But when that bond doesn't already exist, it must be built. Filmmakers use music, cutting patterns, lighting, and other techniques to let audiences know right from the start that they are indeed about to watch a romantic comedy, or a serious Elizabethan drama, or a violent war film.

Storytellers build trust with a series of small promises that are almost immediately paid off. These promises can take a wide variety of forms, but they are designed to demonstrate the author's reliability and credibility.

A common way to demonstrate these qualities is through the use of specific, carefully-chosen detail. Suppose a character is introduced as a classical guitar player. During an intense lovemaking scene he clutches at his lover's back with both hands and draws blood, but only with his right hand. This bit of detail is consistent: classical guitarists grow their right fingernails long but trim those on their left. As these sorts of details accumulate and lock into place, the audience feels a growing sense that the author is in control of the material and thus able to create a rewarding experience.

A storyteller creates and maintains this important sense of authority through consistent and judicious use of detail and tone. Sometimes less is more: a flood of overwhelming detail is less effective than a few carefully-chosen observations. For example, we may be introduced in a novel to Lord David Battenworth, a man who is destined to play an important political and diplomatic role in a story set in the British Empire in the late 1800s.

He was once an influential diplomat, but his fortunes have dwindled in recent years, and at the story's start he is forgotten and desperately poor. How can we establish his history and situation?

This is a basic problem of exposition: how does one get across important background information?

The author could simply present our hero's life story like an encyclopedia entry, but that could hardly be more dull. Only slightly better would be if one of his few remaining friends stopped by to cheer him up by reminding him of his many accomplishments and loaning him some money. A better solution would show our hero at a used bookstore, selling a copy of a book titled "Great Moments in British History." The book carries a hand-written dedication on the first page reading "To Lord Battenworth, Our Finest Royal Negotiator, with Deepest Thanks for Exemplary Service, Queen Victoria." When the bookseller offers him an absurdly low price, Battenworth balks, but eventually gives in and takes the money. In that exchange, we've learned a lot about the man, his past, and his present situation, but we've done it in a way that uses an economy of detail. We've also managed to get that expository information across in the midst of conflict which reveals his character, rather than simply a recitation of his situation.

As the bond between the author and the audience grows, the author's promises can become larger and deeper in scope, duration, and specificity; and buoyed by their experience, the audience will continue to tag along.

Engaging the Audience

There are as many kinds of stories as there are ways to tell them. Although stories for young children are usually direct and people say just what they mean, stories for adults tend to be more sophisticated and complex. Stories can be told in a poetic way in which almost nothing is stated explicitly.

In general, the oblique reference is stronger than the direct statement. It provides more room for nuance and deeper levels of meaning, as well as richness of expression. If someone asks, "How's my new haircut?" another person could answer, "I like it very much." Though true, it's not very revealing. A better response would be, "It makes you look respectable," or "You look five years younger," or even just, "Well. Finally." These responses each carry a wealth of interpretations that help the audience build a more interesting interpretation of both characters.

The reason the audience becomes engaged this way is because people naturally want to fill in holes in their knowledge. If we have a partial understanding of something we care about, we tend to try to fill in what's missing. There are two benefits when an audience willingly fills in missing pieces of a character or plot.

First, the mere act of *imaginative involvement* causes us to become more engaged in a story. Because we as the audience have invested creative energy, we have taken a step into the story ourselves, rather than simply observing it. We often then wonder if our guesses were correct, and so we attend even closer to the story as it unfolds, looking for clues that will help us confirm or revise the holes we've filled in.

Second, when we fill in missing information, we're building personal connections from the fiction of the story into our own idiosyncratic experiences and realities. For example, a turn of phrase used by a character may remind us of someone we know, so we may internally draw some parallels between them. We often draw on our own personal histories to flesh out the characters and plots that we see. These connections serve to bind the fictional experience to our own mental worlds. This bond makes them more interesting to us, because we're choosing to incorporate events and traits that we found interesting enough to remember and retrieve.

An important personal contribution is the interpretation of *subtext*, or the thoughts behind our words. Particularly in emotionally ambiguous situations, subtext is enormously important. Suppose that a man comes home from work in an irritable mood. His spouse asks him why he's upset, and his response is, "I don't want to talk about it." Does this mean he doesn't want to talk about anything at all? Or that he doesn't want to talk about his job, or about the particular provocation that upset him? Perhaps he doesn't want to talk about being upset. Or perhaps he really does want to talk about it but doesn't know how to start, and is hoping his wife will ask a more specific question so he can find a way to describe his troubles to her.

This is one place where performance can carry much more immediate information than is obvious from printed dialog. An actor's vocal inflection or body language can take an ambiguous line like this and make it very clear what the subtext is. The actor can also choose to keep it unclear, or even deliver the line in such a way that it eliminates some possibilities while keeping others open.

The act of *imaginative elaboration* can bond an audience with a character very quickly. This is the value of ambiguity: it gives each of us the chance to fill in the missing pieces with personal information that the author could never have guessed at. Each of those filled-in pieces acts like a tether, or personal link, to the rest of our psyche, giving us a connection to the character or story.

Sometimes this is described as the value of abstraction over specificity. McCloud talks about the difference in cartooning between a simple stick figure and a highly-detailed, realistic rendering of a person [88]. The stick figure of a man is just "*a* man," in the sense that all we know about him is that he is some man. A realistic drawing of Charlie Chaplin is very specifically "*the* man," in the sense that it is that one specific man. It's much harder to feel comfortable filling in details for a real person than for an abstract figure.

Handled carefully, giving audiences the chance to fill in holes in a character and plot with informed imaginations can help get them quickly connected to, and interested in, the characters and story. The author should be careful not to invite the audience to fill in information that will later be provided. Otherwise when the information does come out, the audience may feel that they were misled or tricked. For example, if the author shows a man running in fear from snakes, mice, and spiders, the audience can reasonably assume that he is afraid of those kinds of creepy-crawly things. If later in the story he saves the day because he is eager to eat a plate full of worms, the audience will feel deceived. Characters frequently surprise audiences, but those surprises must be organic in that they make sense with the rest of what we know. If our hero is suddenly going to eat worms, the revelation is organic if we can connect it to something that came earlier that lets us accept the fact that to him, worms are in fact a delicacy. Without that precedent, the author is essentially changing the rules of the game in mid-stream, breaking an implicit promise to the audience that they have been given an accurate presentation of the character.

The general guide is that a character should not be so vague that we cannot comprehend him, nor so complete that we cannot imaginatively engage by filling in some holes from our own experience.

The development of storytelling technologies has generally been to provide increasingly detailed and complete presentations of characters. In the oral tradition, one person acted out the story and all the characters using just his or her voice. The written story, because of its permanence, could take a much more leisurely approach to the story and spend significant time describing detailed nuances of characters, clothing, places, and events.   Radio gave each character his or her own personal voice, as well as realistic sound effects to place the action.   Cartoons added a moving visual aspect to each character, though it was very stylized. Television and film present a literal interpretation of people and places: everything from what they wear to how they move is provided in complete detail.   3D computer graphics has followed a similar path of development, primarily focused on photorealistic renderings of the real world.

Narrative Devices

Authors make use of a wide variety of narrative devices to get audiences involved and then keep their attention. Some books on writing are entirely devoted to discussing these mechanisms. In particular, Howard and Mabley [63] provide excellent presentations of many tools.

Here are several writer's devices that I think are important to our purposes in this book, either because we will be able to find ways to incorporate them, or because they will prove to be difficult to adapt.

Accordion time: In performed stories, such as plays and movies, events often take more or less time to occur than they do in real life. We might say that time is handled like an expanding and contracting accordion. At one extreme, the stage play *Same Time, Next Year* covers decades of time in an evening. At the other extreme, in any number of boxing films the climactic fight is shown in ultra slow-motion, taking far longer than real time.

Advertising the future: An author can tell the audience about something that is yet to come, in order to whet their appetite. "I'm taking Sally out to dinner tomorrow night," David tells his best friend, "and then over dessert I'm going to ask her to marry me." Anticipating this moment, the events that lead up to it are infused with an extra meaning. If David and Sally have a big fight during dinner, it has more impact because of his intended proposal. In the film *All About Eve*, Margo advertises the future when she begins her party by telling her friends, "Fasten your seatbelts, it's going to be a bumpy night."

Coincidence: The world is full of coincidences. Something reminds us of an old friend, and we hear from him the next day. Or we're searching for a hard-to-find part and call the last store on our list just as their shipment of that part comes in the door.

A coincidence kicks off the main plot of *North by Northwest*. While our hero Roger Thornhill is eating in a restaurant, he decides that he wants to send his mother a wire. He signals to a bellboy at just the moment that a man named George Kaplan is paged. Two men in the lobby interpret his gesture as a response to the page, infer that he is Kaplan, and then kidnap him, kicking off the story.

Another name-based coincidence gets the plot of *Brazil* off the ground. A machine is typing out a list of people to be detained for interrogation. It's working through last names beginning with T when a beetle lands in the machinery, causing it to mistakenly type the name "Buttle" instead of "Tuttle." Soon after this, security troops crash into the Buttle apartment, where Mr. Buttle is captured, stuffed in a bag, and taken away. Our hero Sam Lowry discovers the mistake. He later meets up with the Archibald Tuttle that the system had originally sought, and the plot gets into full swing.

Coincidences are a great way to get a story going, but they're dangerous if they appear too long after the start. Although coincidences abound in the real world, we tend to be suspicious of them in fiction, because it seems like a too-easy way to make improbable events occur.

As with so many guidelines of structure, one can break the rules for comic effect. In the film *Sweet and Lowdown*, Emmet Ray is a jazz guitarist whose expenses so far exceed his income that his manager has decided to intercept his paychecks and put his client on a budget. This arrangement is almost impossible for Ray to tolerate, but it's made worse when Ray finds a car he desperately wants to buy. A few days later, Ray is climbing on a rooftop when he slips and crashes through into the apartment below, which just happens to be occupied by a gang of counterfeiters. As the crooks run, Ray looks around and is amazed to find himself sitting in the middle of a big pile of cash, with more heaps of money all around him. In the next scene he's driving his beautiful new car.

Crucible: Sometimes conflict happens because people who don't get along are forced to deal with each other. They are in a *crucible*, a small confined space they cannot exit. The film *Lifeboat* forces nine people together in a small boat as they await rescue. *Twelve Angry Men* locks together a dozen jurists who cannot leave the deliberation room until they come to a verdict. In *Key Largo* everyone has to stay inside a small hotel while a storm is raging outside.

Dramatic irony: When the audience knows something the hero doesn't, we say the author is exploiting *dramatic irony*. The Wicked Witch in *Snow White and the Seven Dwarfs* prepares a poison apple and takes it to Snow White in disguise. We know the apple is poison, but Snow White doesn't, so as we watch the scene unfold, our tension is heightened because we know what's at stake.

The second half of the movie *La Vita è Bella (Life is Beautiful)* is about a family struggling to survive in a World War II concentration camp. To protect his son from the reality around them, Guido Orefice finds a way to carry on the pretense that their time there is nothing but an enormous, convoluted game. Much of the power of the movie comes from watching how Guido builds and maintains this illusion for his son, while we the audience understand exactly where they are and what is really happening.

Note that dramatic irony is different than literary irony, verbal irony, and other forms of ironic expression. It refers only to when the audience knows something that the character in the story does not.

Foreshadowing: The process of foreshadowing is like advertising the future or dramatic irony, but it's not as explicit. Foreshadowing suggests what is to come but usually without an explicit description of just what is on its way or what it will mean. This is often called "waiting for the other shoe to drop": if a man is in his apartment and hears one shoe hit the ceiling as a man upstairs undresses, then he and the audience are pretty sure that the second shoe is on its way. Another expression of this idea is called *Chekhov's Rule*, attributed to the playwright Anton Chekhov, which states that if a gun is introduced at the start of a drama, it must be fired by the end.

Hope vs. fear: A great story can make us aware of the possibilities that lie ahead. Knowing what's around the corner, we simultaneously hope for a positive outcome and fear a negative one.

The dark comedy *Dr. Strangelove or: How I Learned to Stop Worrying and Love the Bomb* is all about hope versus fear. Planes have been dispatched to drop atomic bombs on Russia during the height of the Cold War. Should one of them go off, it will trigger the automatic detonation of a Doomsday Machine that will kill all living things on Earth. Throughout the film we are kept on the edge of our seats hoping that the planes can be recalled. While we hold this hope alive, we also fear for what will happen should any of the bombs explode.

When we are aware of both positive and negative futures, an author can play our hopes and fears against each other to heighten tension.

Planting and paying off: These techniques are related to foreshadowing. A plant is something that is done at one point in the story that is later revealed to have special significance or a deeper meaning.

In *One Flew Over the Cuckoo's Nest*, McMurphy tries to win a bet by lifting a massive marble tub from the sanitorium washroom floor. He is unable to budge it, but he exults in the glory of having at least tried. At the end of the story, Chief Bromden honors McMurphy's spirit by heaving the tub through a window and escaping to freedom. The significance of the act is heightened because of McMurphy's earlier, failed attempt. If Bromden instead threw a random chair through the window, the act would make less of a statement and pack less emotional power.

Propelling transitions: When an author knows where the next scene or sequence of the story is going to occur, he can set it up with a transition that drives us headlong into it.

The action film *Speed* uses this device repeatedly. Each time the hero Jack Traven figures out a way to reduce the tension of the situation, it only gets worse. Each solution turns out to be nothing more than a setup for the next challenge.

Plot twists: A plot twist occurs when a story turns in an unexpected or unusual direction. Generally, the audience is unprepared for these twists, so they come as a surprise.

The short stories of O. Henry are famous for their climactic plot twists. Many of the original *Twilight Zone* television programs end with some extra bit of information that re-frames the entire story.

In the film *Bullets Over Broadway*, playwright David Shane turns to a gangster for money to support his new play. The gangster assigns one of his partners, Cheech, to supervise the rehearsals. To Shane's surprise, Cheech starts to make rewrite suggestions which turn out to be quite good, and soon Shane and Cheech form a partnership. The audience couldn't be expected to anticipate this surprising twist, but it is believable because Cheech is revealed to be a sensitive and literate man.

Many *film noir* style movies use a plot twist at the end to change the interpretation of the whole story. Films like *Body Heat* and *The Usual Suspects* both deliver a twist of surprise at the end.

Rewind: Audiences recognize that they are usually seeing a story from a single point of view. A book is told by a character or a narrator. A film is captured by the camera, and the director, cinematographer, and editor decide what will be visible at a given time.

One way to try to show other points of view is to present the same events repeatedly. Because time is backed up before each presentation, I call this technique *rewind*. It's a surprisingly flexible technique.

In the film *Rashomon*, a man is found dead deep in the forest. Over the course of the movie, we see the crime from four different points of view: a thief who intercepted the man and his wife, the dead man's wife, the dead man himself (through a medium), and an eyewitness. They all tell very different stories, and the characters emerge as very different people in each one. The film leaves the story on an ambiguous note: we never know who (if anyone) was reporting the events "correctly."

The comedy *Groundhog Day* also uses rewind as its central mechanism. The hero, Phil Conners, is an arrogant and sarcastic television weatherman. Through some unexplained phenomenon, he re-lives one day of his life over and over. Everything in that day starts just the same, but he is free to act as he wishes, and his choices affect the people around him. Over the course of the film, he gets to try out many different ways to live his life. Over time, he changes and grows into a more compassionate man.

In an episode of *Star Trek: The Next Generation*, titled "A Matter of Perspective," a laboratory blows up, killing an important scientist. One of the starship's crew, Commander Riker, is charged with murder, and a trial is held. The computer is loaded with the testimony of several witnesses, and during the trial a complete re-creation of the days leading up to the explosion is presented on the holodeck from the point of view of each witness. Each person remembers things differently, so the court (and the audience) gets to see several similar but different versions of the events that resulted in the scientist's death.

In an episode of *The Simpsons* titled "Trilogy of Error," the same period of time is covered from the point of view of three different sets of characters. The first time through, we see a series of improbable events that occur to Homer as he stumbles through his day. After the commercial, we see the same opening moments, but now we're following Lisa and her mother. We see how their actions caused some of Homer's problems in the first segment and how his actions affect Lisa. The third segment begins the same way as the first two, but this time we follow Bart and his friend Milhouse. Their actions explain some of the events that seemed improbable in the first two stories, and we get to see how Homer's and Lisa's actions indirectly and directly affect Bart. When then third segment is done, we are left with a set of interlocking events told from three different points of view. This technique requires very careful planning so that each sequence is rewarding in its own right, and meshes with and illuminates the other sequences.

A different approach to rewind appears in the drama *Run Lola Run*. Lola is called by her boyfriend Manni from across town: he was supposed to deliver a bag of money to a drug dealer, but he accidentally forgot the bag on the subway. He needs Lola to somehow raise the sum and then get the cash to him before the handoff, which will occur in only 20 minutes. The film follows Lola in her quest to both get the money and then get it to Manni. After the 20 minutes have passed, the movie stops and re-starts again just moments after the initial phone call. The events unfold in a very slightly different way, but the aftershocks of that slight difference turn out to have dramatic effects on the outcome of the story, as well as on the lives of some of the people that Lola encounters. The film repeats this several times, running through to the climax and then backing up to explore the results of each minor change.

A technique related to the rewind is the *simultaneous presentation*, where multiple images of the same events are presented simultaneously with a split-screen effect, such as in the movie *Timecode*.

Fractured or *shattered* time is like rewind, but events are presented in much less coherent pieces. The short story *The Babysitter* describes an evening from several different, fragmented points of view, many of them contradictory. The film *Urbania* frequently switches between the present, past, and future as it tells the story of a man coming to grips with an event that changed his life.

Timebombs: A ticking clock on the top of an explosive is a timebomb. Many action movies literally use a timebomb to create excitement: the hero is in a race against time and, naturally, our tension goes up. If it's repeated too often, or goes on too long at too high a pace, the audience can burn out. But used judiciously, timebombs are useful tools for adding peril to a scene.

A timebomb can be anything that will cause terrible harm in a fixed, relatively near moment. In *Apollo 13*, three astronauts are in a spacecraft headed for the moon when there's an accident, and they lose most of their oxygen. Working with the crew on the ground, they need to find a way to return safely to Earth before they run out of air or freeze to death. The timebombs here are the dwindling resources of the spacecraft: if they don't get back home before they run out of air and electricity, they will die.

In *The Adventures of Robin Hood*, Sir Guy of Gisbourne sets a trap for his enemy Robin Hood, captures him, and sentences him to hang in the public square on the next day. The timebomb is ticking for Robin. Morning comes, and Robin is led to the gallows with his hands tied behind his back. At the last moment, Robin's men arrive, shoot the guard and the hangman, Robin jumps onto a horse, and in the following action sequence Robin escapes with his life.

Viewpoint: A story needs to be told from some point of view.

Films, television shows, and plays are most frequently told from the viewpoint of an external observer. This is usually called the *objective* viewpoint, in which the audience is given no access to the inner thoughts or feelings of the characters. The audience must infer what the characters are thinking and feeling from what they say and do.

In written fiction a rich variety of other viewpoints have been explored over the years. Many of these are discussed by Hall [60].

There are three common points of view in modern fiction. In *first person subjective* the author is one of the characters and reveals his own thoughts and feelings explicitly.

The *objective* viewpoint is the one typically used for films; the narrator (or camera) describes what happens, but has no access to the insides of the characters.

This convention is sometimes broken, usually for comedic effect. In a running sketch on the television show *Saturday Night Live* called "The Continental," the action takes place in the apartment of a man who attempts to suavely seduce a female visitor. The camera plays the role of the woman, so that the character speaks to the camera, and reaches towards it when he wants to hold the woman's hand. The camera moves through the set as though it was her. In other words, we see the sketch through the woman's eyes.

In *The 39 Steps*, a shot in a train car is taken from the point of view of a man reading a paper, as he peeks over the top to look at the man sitting across from him.

The objective viewpoint is the one commonly used in stage plays. The audience watches the action unfold on a stage, which appears to them as a box with a back and sides, but no front. The invisible plane between the audience and the performers is called the fourth wall.

When actors speak directly to the audience, they are said to be breaking the *fourth wall*. In *Annie Hall*, the lead character Alvy Singer breaks the fourth wall when he tires of hearing a pompous professor hold forth about Marshall McLuhan's work, so Singer magically produces McLuhan in person to insult the man. Singer then directly addresses the audience and shares with us his dream of how wonderful it would be if we could actually do such a thing in real life.

The *omniscient* viewpoint is that of an all-knowing narrator, who knows everything about the story and is equally at home inside the minds of the characters as floating above the scene and simply describing the action.

There are many variations on these basic viewpoints. For example, some books use a *roving first person subjective* viewpoint, switching from one character's point of view to another's between chapters or even between scenes. A *roving single viewpoint* is a limited form of the omniscient narrator, where the storyteller has access to the inner thoughts of one person at a time. In the novel *The Amazing Adventures of Kavalier and Clay* the author tells the story of different characters by picking up their stories in different chapters, and describing events as that character sees them.

An unusual point of view called *first person assigned* appears in the novel *Half Asleep in Frog Pajamas*. The heroine of the story is Gwen Mati, a 29-year-old Filipino stockbroker in Seattle. The book places the reader in Gwen's shoes directly by saying things like "You feel hungry," and "The ringing telephone surprises you." This is a tricky stylistic technique, because readers know that in fact they are not Gwen and may find it difficult to adapt to being told what they are thinking and feeling.

Another interesting twist on the first-person subjective narrator is the *unreliable first-person subjective* viewpoint. This is a story told by a person from his own point of view, speaking in phrases like "I thought..." and "It seemed to me..." But we slowly learn that this narrator is untrustworthy. Either he is deliberately lying to his readers, for reasons of his own, or he is deceiving himself in some way. In either case, we feel that we cannot completely trust the report that he is giving us.

The novel *Lolita* is narrated by Humbert Humbert, and we quickly discover that his perceptions of the world, and his descriptions of it to us, are not to be trusted. For all his sophistication, Humbert Humbert is mentally and emotionally unbalanced, and he sees himself and his world through a lens that we learn is faulty and skewed. The narrator of *Remains of the Day* is Stevens, an English butler in post-World War II England. As the story unfolds, we come to realize that Stevens is not telling us what he really thinks either of his employer or of a female colleague that he is on his way to visit. We slowly learn that his feelings are deeper and more complex than he claims, because every now and then he lets slip some critical information that reveals to us his true thinking.

The novel *Ray* is narrated by the title character who is trying to make sense of the world around him. In this novel, written in a literary equivalent to jazz music, we learn that Ray's view of the world is idiosyncratic and often is at odds with the views of the people around him. The novel *The Fan Man* is narrated by the fascinating but bizarre Horse Badorties, whose distorted view of the world and the people in it are essential to the novel's quirky appeal.

An unreliable narrator strains the contract of trust between author and audience. The author must create a story and character so fascinating that the reader will stick with the story, even though he knows that the information he is receiving is deliberately or accidentally deceptive.

Maximum Capacity

Great characters remain in our memories for a long time. Alexis Zorbas (*Zorba the Greek*), Indiana Jones (*Raiders of the Lost Ark*), James Bond (*Dr. No*), Don Quixote (*The Adventures of Don Quixote*), Hannibal Lecter (*The Silence Of The Lambs*), and Rick Blaine (*Casablanca*) are just a few characters who have entered the popular consciousness and stuck. These fascinating people grab our imaginations in an enduring way.

Two qualities of all great characters are that they are *comprehensible* and that they *strive*, or try as hard as they can, at whatever they're doing. Zorba lives his life with vibrant gusto, Indiana Jones will brave any danger to find a precious artifact, James Bond will travel from outer space to deep underwater to stop megalomaniacal villains, Don Quixote is devoted to his ideals, Hannibal Lecter is committed to a refined and cultured life that embraces cannibalism, and Rick Blaine will work as hard as he can to cover his idealism with bitterness and idle distraction until he is free to be himself again.

When a character is comprehensible, that doesn't mean that he is entirely predictable. But it does mean that we understand the large outlines of what makes that person tick, what his values are, and how much he's willing to sacrifice for the people and things he believes in. He can constantly surprise us, and he often does, but these surprises are the result of pieces of his makeup that we didn't see before, or that have more or less importance than we realized. If a character acts entirely contrary to his personality, the audience will be confused. Carefully controlled, this confusion can be channelled into a desire to know more. But if the confusion is too extreme or goes on too long, the audience will lose interest. Once an audience decides that a character cannot be understood, they will stop trying to understand him and thus stop caring about him. At that point the audience has been lost.

A striving character is one who truly wants his goal. He won't hold back and he won't stop halfway. Frey calls this the principle of *maximum capacity*: a character will act to the limits of his abilities to get what he wants [51]. If a man is being chased by a tiger, then he will run as fast as he possibly can. If the man is fast, then perhaps he can outrun the tiger for a while. If he's not fast, he will still run as hard as he can, but he will also look for other options, such as a tree to climb, or a pit to lead the tiger into, or a weapon to fight with. He won't let the tiger simply catch him and eat him. Similarly, if a man wants something, he will use everything in his power to get it. If he wants to get a new job where his appearance will be important, he will shower before the interview and then wear his best suit, freshly pressed. If he doesn't have a nice suit, he'll borrow one, or rent one, or steal one. He will use all of his imagination, strength, intelligence, finances, and other resources to achieve his goal.

When a character acts below his maximum capacity, it results in what Frey calls the *idiot in the attic* syndrome. This refers to a classic scene in horror movies. The babysitter is on the downstairs couch when the lights go out, and then she suddenly hears the scary sound of chains dragging along the floor in the attic above her. She could yell for the neighbors, or phone the police, or collect the kids and get out, but she does none of those sensible things. Instead, she lights a candle and slowly creeps up to the attic, alone, to investigate. And when she gets there, the madman in the attic, of course, cuts her head off. Though we might feel some sympathy for the girl, we usually don't feel too bad, because after all, only an idiot would creep up to the attic alone with a flickering candle to investigate a spooky and dangerous sound.

A good character under stress will act to the limits of his abilities. In September 2003, the newspaper comic strip *Jane's World* [15] showed the lead character trying to work up the courage to invite her co-worker Dorothy out on a date. By coincidence, she is holding a comic strip that someone else drew that shows Dorothy in a bad light. Dorothy takes the page from Jane's hands, and as Jane simply stands there, Dorothy reads the strip, misinterprets it as Jane's work, and storms away in anger. This is just silly: Jane only had to say "I didn't draw that," and the situation would be defused. Any person in that situation would say that immediately. The only reason that Jane didn't was because the author wanted to create this subplot. This is a classic example of a character acting way below her maximum capacity in order to get the storyline going. It doesn't read true to the audience, and it makes the story feel forced.

This doesn't mean that characters are supermen. Fictional characters have their limits, just as real people do. A character can only run so fast, he is only so intelligent, so confident, literate, rich, and attractive. The point is that he will always act to the limits of his own abilities. A clever villain in a wheelchair won't put himself into a situation in which he has to outrun the hero in an empty parking lot. Rather, he'll use his intelligence to create a situation where the hero is at a disadvantage. The hero will do everything in his power to overcome that disadvantage and stop or catch the villain.

To see characters regularly acting below maximum capacity, watch some television soap operas. Eventually Alice will tell Bob that she knows of a terrible secret that will change Bob's life forever. The music will swell, and Alice and Bob will look at each other with deep meaning. It is extremely rare for Bob to immediately ask what the secret is. Instead, when we return to those characters the next day, Bob will deny that the secret exists, or insist that Alice hasn't the guts to use it, or that the person who told it to Alice is a liar. He still hasn't asked what the secret is, though, or if he has, Alice has declined to say. The producers are simply drawing out the suspense as long as possible. So the characters get embroiled in side issues and other debates until they are forced to part. The secret remains untold and hanging, the suspense building, for as many days or weeks as the producers can draw it out. The only thing tested to maximum capacity here is the patience of the audience.

Dialog

Dialog is what people say to one another.

In normal life, our dialog is filled with hesitations, false starts, awkward phrasing, and other linguistic speedbumps and potholes that get in the way of what we're trying to say. A lot of everyday dialog is also banal or trivial, simply acting as glue in our social relationships. Everyday dialog can be raised to the level of art, as in the novel *Ulysses*, but in general it's not too interesting.

The dialog in most fiction is neither so casual nor haphazard. Although fictional dialog may be "naturalistic" in the sense that it has the same rhythms of everyday language, it is in fact nothing of the kind.

Dialog is chosen and written to perform a job, such as to expose character, advance the plot, tell a joke, or provide breathing space for the audience. Even so-called "throw-away" lines are included for a reason. If they served no purpose at all, they would be cut, just as actions that serve no purpose are cut.

Great dialog works on multiple levels, satisfying several goals simultaneously. In many ways, great dialog is a form of action, because the character's speech is actually doing something in the world by affecting one or more other people in a direct or indirect way.

Stage plays and films do not provide the kind of inner dialog commonly found in novels. The audience has only two routes to learn about a character: what he says and what he does.

As I discussed earlier, a powerful way to reveal character is to show how the hero acts under pressure. When in a tense situation, what he says he will do is irrelevant, and only what he actually does matters.

This distinction between dialog and action is a fertile field for revealing complexities in a character, particularly when someone says one thing but does another. In the film *My Fair Lady*, Professor Henry Higgins repeatedly states how uninterested he is in his protegee Eliza Doolittle. His denials only become stronger and more frequent as he comes to care for her more and more.

In *All About Eve*, Eve Harrington inserts herself into the household of actress Margo Channing. Eve's every utterance is soaked in humility and devotion to her employer. But her actions slowly reveal that her intentions are hardly as gracious as her speech. As evidence of Eve's real intentions mounts, she still sticks to her role as the helpful and star-struck assistant.

People who don't know Eve very well are happy to take her at face value and believe what she says. But those who are closer to Eve see past her words and pick up the scent of her real intentions. The disparity between her words and her deeds helps fuel the plot by providing a source of conflict among Margo's friends and colleagues.

Great dialog is rarely direct. Dialog that says just what it appears to say is called *on the nose* and should generally be avoided. Suppose that two old friends, a man and a woman, are slowly falling in love with each other. It would be unusual for one of them to explicitly state, "Gee, I think I care for you a lot more than I used to." Instead, they would reveal it in indirect ways, through giving compliments and courtesies, paying increased attention to the other's desires, and spending more time together.

Just as scenes and actions have subtext, so too do most lines of dialog. In addition to imparting information, great dialog also reveals attitude and character. If a man is abrupt with a subordinate but loquacious and flattering with his boss, that tells us quite a bit about him.

In the film *Annie Hall*, the lead characters Alvy Singer and Annie Hall get to know each other standing on the terrace outside of Annie's New York apartment. Annie pours them each a glass of wine, and they make small talk. But as they speak, subtitles appear on the bottom of the screen that reveal their actual thoughts. Both are thinking along lines that are far removed from what they're saying. The huge distance between their dialog and their true intentions makes their conversation fascinating and funny, as both attempt to mask their worries and fears and fantasies with banal dialog that they hope the other will find attractive. The clash of text and subtext is very funny, and far more revealing than either one alone.

Great dialog is sometimes referred to as *parking-lot writing*, referring to that moment when you've left a conversation and are now on your way to your car, and halfway across the parking lot you suddenly think of a great comeback or line that eluded you at the moment. Because fictional dialog can be re-written, you can indeed go back and add that line. Dialog should be as carefully crafted as the plot and the action. This doesn't mean that the dialog should be over-worked or lifeless, but rather that it is a storytelling tool, and the author has the opportunity to sharpen it to a razor's edge. If the dialog is meant to be sloppy and vague, then it can be just exactly the right degree of sloppy and vague. If it's meant to be naturalistic, then the author can spend energy getting the rhythms and inflections exactly right so that the words appear to flow as naturally and easily as water in a stream. Whether the dialog is flirtatious, or witty repartee, or a cat-and-mouse interrogation, it can be written to be the best possible version of that exchange, down to the last nuance.

Characters can reveal a lot by what they don't say. In *Broadcast News*, Jane Craig needs to speak to her colleague Aaron Altman. She calls him on the phone, but Altman is already in bed. She says she needs to see him in person, tonight. He hesitates and finally agrees. Then they need to pick a place. Aaron says, "I'll meet you at the place near the thing where we went that time." Jane agrees, they hang up, and the scene is over. That line tells us a wealth of information about the shared history and present relationship between these two characters because of what's been left out, but understood.

Segmentation

Some stories are very short. Quick jokes, short-short stories, and 30-second commercials all strive for economy. Some stories are much longer. Soap operas can spin out the relationships between connected characters for years with no clean resolution in sight.

Stories can be serialized in popular publications for a long time. The serial *Tales of the City* first appeared in in the *San Francisco Chronicle* in May 1976, and that story (and its sequels) ran for over 10 years. Charles Dickens published many of his books in serial form: *Oliver Twist* started in 1837 and was published in monthly installments over a span of two years, and *A Tale of Two Cities* appeared in weekly installments starting in 1859. The authors of serialized works who publish as they write take a serious risk since they cannot go back and rewrite what has been published. This limitation requires them them to have an unusual degree of confidence.

Most films and stage plays are works of a few hours duration. Although movie sequels are nothing new, in recent years studios have begun planning on sequels when producing a film and even shooting more than one movie at a time. Principal photography for all three films of the *Lord of the Rings* trilogy was carried out at roughly the same time. Material for two sequels to the film *The Matrix* was shot at once as well.

Many television shows are history-free, in the sense that the characters begin each show in essentially the same situation. Classic situation comedies like *Leave It to Beaver* and *Gilligan's Island* could be watched in almost any order; except for the aging of the actors, the characters never changed, and with rare exception, nothing that happened to them in one show affected how they behaved in the next. Many television shows today follow the same model.

Some shows combine serialization with self-containment using a technique called the *arc*. Generally each installment of the show has its own plot and guest characters in addition to the regular cast. But some time is spent in each episode to develop the regular characters, and track their lives on a larger scale. Thus we have police dramas such as *NYPD Blue*, where every week there are new crimes to be solved, but we also see the detectives socialize, get married, raise children, and otherwise grow as characters. This formula can be applied to a wide range of shows, from children's entertainment to adult comedies and dramas.

Often the continuing stories are set aside from the particular story of the episode. Thus there might be a segment at the start and end of the show where the private lives of the characters are followed. These segments may pop up as well during the course of the show; but even though they appear in the midst of the show's plot, they are usually clearly personal and are set off separately. In this style, the continuing characters are said to be following an *arc*.

In contemporary television shows, it is not unusual for two or three separate plots to be woven together simultaneously. Sometimes one plot is dominant, in which case it's called the *main plot* and the others *subplots*. Often the subplots are designed to work with the main plot and illuminate aspects of it, or else they are designed to complement the main plot and bring to the episode ideas and emotions that the main plot tself doesn't contain. The different plots are typically presented in alternating scenes, and edited to create a sense of continuity in all the stories as well as a feeling for the overall show. The television show *Northern Exposure* often did a beautiful job of weaving together three or four stories thematically so that each one amplified and added depth to the others.

Layers of Cooperation and Conflict

A common source of tension arises from competition for resources. Those resources can range from the physical to the spiritual, and from the everyday to the obscure. People will work to get what they want but don't have, whether it's fame, money, love, attention, objects, security, sex, a better job, a bigger desk, or a richer mate. They accept the need to compete against others to get what they want.

On the other hand, we also need to cooperate in order to achieve goals larger than ourselves. We work together in companies and social organizations, and we form social partnerships and allegiances.

A rich source of tension arises in any situation that calls for cooperation but meets competition instead, and vice-versa. When we expect help but meet resistance, we are naturally upset. And when a competitor turns into an ally, it shifts the landscape for the others involved in the competition.

For the sake of dramatic tension, many social, business, political, and other professional relationships can be thought of as arranged within a framework of *alternating layers of competition and cooperation*.

For example, take a large company that manufactures a wide range of large and small office equipment. The company is arranged in a hierarchy many levels deep, with the CEO at the top and engineers on individual products at the bottom. Let's start with a team of engineers who are working together to develop a new photocopier. They are cooperating with each other because they want the product to be approved and marketed (an achievement that will bring them bonus pay and status in the company). The members of this team are in competition with the other photocopier teams, since only one of their products will be approved. So these teams compete with each other for limited resources like budget, space, material, administrative support, and headcount.

The company's photocopier group is made up of all of these teams and coexists in the company with other groups that make telephones, fax machines, and printers. Each of these groups is in competition for a bigger slice of the company's overall marketing and advertising resources, as well as intangibles like space in the best buildings and the best technical support. Since all of the teams in the photocopier group have a common interest in seeing photocopiers well supported, they cooperate with each other at the group level to defend their shared interests against the telephone, fax, and printer groups.

Rising in the hierarchy, the electronics division that contains all of these groups coexists with the furniture division that makes items like file cabinets, chairs, and desks. When the electronics division competes with the furniture division for resources and prestige, the groups in the electronics division work together for their common benefit.

If the company as a whole comes under attack, all the divisions that normally fight each other will work together to defend the company. The company is in competition with other companies that sell similar equipment, but if another nation starts dumping goods at a low price that cuts into their profits, the companies will cooperate as an industry to lobby for governmental intervention.

Thus we have a hierarchy of alternating layers of competition and cooperation.

In this sort of organization, people compete up and down levels of the hierarchy, and cooperate across.

This sort of model applies to many situations. In a family, often the kids compete with each other (for attention, money, or sneakers), but they will sometimes unite as a group against their parents on issues such as where to go for vacation. The parents find themselves in conflict on the normal range of issues that cause tension in a marriage, yet they will often present a unified front if the family is threatened.

We can draw similar parallels among groups of friends, social clubs, political parties, theatrical companies, and many other social organizations.

When we disrupt one of these relationships, we have a rich source of conflict. When people you're used to cooperating with suddenly become competitive, it can become disorienting and confusing. If they've planned their defection, they may be able to grab resources that you're now unable to recover, putting you at a disadvantage. When people you've traditionally competed with suddenly turn cooperative, it usually involves them betraying someone else. That betrayal can suddenly put you in the middle of a fight that you weren't ready for and didn't ask for, and you may discover your new friends bring along powerful enemies that now have you in their sights.

Unusual and unexpected allegiances and rivalries permeate many human relationships, and people compete and cooperate in webs of connections much denser than simple hierarchies.

But this simple model gives us a convenient way to create natural conflict: find two groups that are supposed to cooperate with another, and introduce a good reason for them to compete. Beyond the natural stresses of competition, this rivalry may reveal cracks and strains in the relationships between people that remained hidden when the pressure wasn't turned up. Alternatively, find two groups that have normally competed, and create a shared goal that forces them to cooperate. They may find that they have to navigate mutual distrust and a history of bad feelings in order to work together.

Baseball teams, commercial companies, rock bands, volunteer organizations, and other social groups that grow large enough inevitably develop internal fights for power and resources, and conflicting and cooperating goals.

When anticipated conflict is met with cooperation, and vice-versa, people are naturally suspicious, and that suspicion can be mined for drama.

Plot Sequence and View Sequence

I use the term *plot sequence* to refer to the chain of events that make up the plot of a story. As we've seen, stories always have a beginning, where the hero is confronted with a problem, a middle, where he tries to address it, and an end, where he makes a final attempt and then deals with the consequences. In contrast to this plot sequence, I use the term *view sequence* to refer to the order in which those events are presented to the audience.

Aristotle said, "A whole is what has a beginning and middle and end" [3]. A quote widely attributed to the French filmmaker Jean-Luc Goddard states, "I like my movies to have a beginning, a middle and an end, but not necessarily in that order." Obviously he wasn't referring to the literal presentation itself, which begins when the lights go down and ends when they come back up. Rather, he was talking about the potential difference between the order in which the events happen in the plot sequence, and the order in which they're communicated to the audience in the view sequence.

These two sequences are rarely the same, though they are usually close. The most common difference is that not every element in the plot sequence is in the view sequence. For example, it may be very important that the hero withdraws a lot of money from the bank. In the plot sequence, he enters the bank, makes the withdrawal, and leaves. In the view sequence, we may simply see him enter the bank and then walk out. From context, and from the tone of the story and the character's attitude, we can infer that he has the money, even though we haven't been shown every one of the story steps in which he filled out the withdrawal slip, stood in line, and spoke to the teller.

Flash-forwards, flashbacks, and other mechanisms can create view sequences that differ significantly from the plot sequence. For example, the film *Dolores Claiborne* relies on flashbacks as an integral part of the film. Rather than just providing details of earlier events, these flashbacks illuminate the characters and increase our understanding of the present situation.

Another example of distinct plot and view sequences appears in the film *Memento*. The lead character, Leonard Shelby, has a clear memory of his life up until the time his wife was murdered. But that incident traumatized him and left him with a mental condition in which he is unable to create new memories. Because Leonard lives with no knowledge of anything since that incident, except for the most recent couple of minutes at any time, he has adopted a variety of techniques that keep him oriented. To convey this feeling of no memory, the film is presented as a series of scenes that each flow forward, but precede one another in time. Thus Leonard will have a conversation with someone in one scene, meet him for the first time in the next scene, and never have heard of him yet in the scene that follows. Here the view sequence goes forward in small chunks, and then jumps backward to a much earlier time, flows forward for a little while, and jumps back again, until the film reaches the starting incident. The ending of the view sequence coincides with the beginning of the plot sequence, and vice-versa.

In the film *Midnight Cowboy*, the character Ratso sometimes enters a dream sequence where he imagines his future in Florida. These sequences aren't part of the narrative, as these things certainly haven't happened (and may never come to pass), but they help us see what kind of a world Ratso desires for himself one day in the future.

It's important to keep clear the distinction between plot sequence and view sequence. The plot sequence is determined by cause and effect and flows forward at a constant rate. The view sequence, on the other hand, can present that plot sequence in any order and at any speed.

The Story Contract

There are many different fictional forms, from plays and movies to novels and epic poems. Yet they all share a few characteristics. I characterize three of the most important common elements as terms of what I call *the story contract*. This is an implicit agreement between the author and the audience that makes meaningful traditional storytelling experiences possible.

Although rooted in traditional storytelling technique, the story contract is not a universal truth which must be honored in all forms of media to come. New ideas can change the rules. But when we step away from what has been historically successful, we should do so with an understanding of the principles that are being violated. This knowledge will help us catch bad ideas sooner, and help ensure that we don't spend time creating story forms that won't be able to mature. In later chapters I'll use the story contract to help us understand why some previous attempts at participatory fiction have failed to achieve mainstream success. For now, let's just look at the contract itself.

The story contract has only three simple clauses: two clauses for the author, and one for the audience. Like a stool with three simple legs, they are all necessary.

Main Character Psychology

Story Contract Clause 1: Psychology. The author is responsible for the psychological integrity of the main characters.

Interesting characters are those that we can understand and empathize with. Reaching that understanding requires us to be able to relate to them as people, which means that they need to have a satisfyingly consistent psychological core.

People are complex, filled with contradictions, and we all display unexpected behavior from time to time. But normal human behavior is broadly reliable; if we couldn't count on people's behavior, we wouldn't be able to create sustained, loving relationships.

When people we care about begin to behave erratically, we become concerned for them. We sometimes encourage them to find the physical or psychological cause for their behavior or suggest that they talk to a professional therapist to help them regain their stability. When people continue to act very unpredictably, we often avoid them and definitely avoid getting into new entanglements.

Although the hero of a story needn't be a potential friend (as we've seen, some stories feature anti-heroes that are decidedly unlikable), the most enduring heroes are always fascinating. Something about them grabs our attention and won't let go, and we get drawn into their heads because we see enough of ourselves that we can relate and care.

If we're not inside a hero's head as the piece progresses, then the story risks losing the audience's attention. If the audience simply stops caring, the story is over: without an audience, a story loses its reason for being. The audience might actually physically leave the venue to find something more interesting to do, or simply tune out (either literally or mentally), which is just as bad as leaving.

Whatever the cause, if the audience doesn't care about the hero, then the emotional pressure of the story will not build as it's supposed to, and the final climax will fall flat.

Storytellers create and develop their heroes very carefully so that audiences will empathize with them. Heroes often surprise us with their actions, but in a great character there is always an inherent consistency that harmonizes the character's personality.

This is also true of the villain, if there is one. In fact, in some stories the psychological integrity of the villain is even more important than that of the hero. If a villain is so incomprehensible that we can't predict his actions, then we lose the power of anticipatory tension. The more we know about the bad guy, the more we're afraid of him, and the more we feel the peril that our hero is in.

A villain who acts in truly erratic ways doesn't gain an audience's respect or understanding, and therefore never receives the kind of negative emotional involvement that gets released at the end of a great cathartic climax. An erratic villain is like a hurricane: it's certainly a problem, but you can't really hate a hurricane or wish it ill; you just want it to stop or go away. To really dislike a bad guy, we have to know him.

It's the author's job to create fascinating and coherent lead characters.

Plot Sequencing and Timing

Story Contract Clause 2: Plot. The author is responsible for the sequencing and timing of major plot events.

Since major plot events often serve the dual purpose of moving the plot forward and revealing character, this clause has implications for each of those applications.

Taken at face value, this clause of the story contract is just an encapsulation of common sense. In a kidnapping story, it's important that the victim be kidnapped before the police go searching for him.

The purpose of this clause is to make sure that the story actually develops as an integrated narrative, and not simply a string of events happening one after the other. Plot events are carefully chosen to cause the narrative to build in complexity and tension. The author trades off our hopes and fears by helping us see what can happen, or is likely to happen, and the risks that must be undertaken by the hero to prevent them from happening.

Thus the author must assume responsibility for the *plot sequence*, so that cause precedes effect.

The author also needs to control the *timing* of the events. Stories derive a lot of their emotional power from the rhythm in which events unfold. The audience needs a chance to catch its breath after a large revelation and absorb its implications. All art forms use some kind of rhythm to shape the overall experience, and stories are no exception.

As we've seen, many major plot events also serve to place characters in stressful situations, forcing them to act and thereby reveal their inner character. It's important that this character be revealed in a way that helps the audience understand how the person works and develop an emotional relationship with the person. The amount of tension in the story relates to the risks taken by the characters, and that risk comes from their responses to challenges. The tension needs controlled, sustained growth throughout the story.

The author needs to control the development of character and tension because he has "insider's knowledge" that enables him to anticipate what will be demanded of the character later. Suppose that the character's greatest challenge at the climax forces him to choose whether or not to overcome his essentially selfish nature and sacrifice some important object. If this climactic moment is to be powerful, we need to feel the character's pain at having to make this decision. We need to know just how selfish he is and just how much the precious item means to him. These sympathies need time to grow. Typically we'll see him act selfishly near the start of the story and perhaps see him pay an increasingly high price for both his repeated selfishness, and for coveting this precious object, as the story progresses. If, early in the story, our character makes a generous offering simply on impulse, it could undermine the tension that comes at the end. After all, what he did once he might do again, so his necessary sacrifice is not as inconceivable as it might otherwise be, and the tension would be reduced.

We need to learn about characters in stages, and the author needs to be careful not to play all of his cards too soon.

So the author needs to choose the elements of the plot sequence and their timing to cause the plot to develop in a way that is coherent, ensures that cause precedes effects, and serves the needs of a growing, interrelated story. He also needs to choose those plot points that reveal ever-deeper facets of his character's personalities.

Audience Involvement

Story Contract Clause 3: Audience Engagement. The audience must allow itself to be emotionally moved.

This third clause of the story contract is the only one that applies directly to the audience.

It may seem odd to say that the audience has a responsibility, but that's why this is a contract rather than just a set of rules: both storyteller and audience have obligations to each other.

The audience's job is basically to enjoy the story. But the audience has to be willing to allow that to happen. You can't enjoy a story if you're asleep, and you'll miss a lot if you're distracted or otherwise not paying attention.

This clause says that audience members have be willing to allow themselves to be moved. This willingness is required because in order for a piece of art to work, it needs to be able to speak to us on an emotional and personal level. If we remain at arm's length, or emotionally disconnected, then the piece cannot reach us.

For a piece of art to affect us, we have to allow it to have an effect. Sometimes an audience member will criticize a piece of art by saying that it didn't "move" him, implying that the work lacked emotional depth or resonance. A work can only move us if we open ourselves up and allow it to.

Allowing a story to have access to our emotions is an unusual act of deliberate vulnerability. Most of us spend the majority of our time with our emotional shields up, in order to protect us from the random people and events of the world. We experience all sorts of emotions through a day, but we typically only open up to people we know and trust. With those people we allow ourselves to be vulnerable. That is why we can shrug off a blunt insult hurled by a stranger on the street, but even an accidentally hurtful remark from a loved one can cause pain.

To allow a piece of art to have an emotional affect on us, we must deliberately offer at least some emotional access to the creator of the work.

A good piece of art can reach us on many levels, from emotional and spiritual to intellectual. To give it that opportunity, we must allow the work to affect us and perhaps even manipulate us.

This is why art can make us laugh, cry, get angry, and feel sympathy: we deliberately and consciously relax our defenses and allow our emotions to be engaged. In effect, we allow the total strangers who created the art to enter our trusted inner circle for a while.

The audience member who does this is still ultimately in control, because he can retract this permission and restore the emotional barriers at any time. If you're watching a horror film and find you're getting more scared than you want to be, you can easily distance yourself from this discomfort by leaving. Even if you stay in the theater, you can disconnect the emotional power of the film by getting very interested in the technology of the special effects or the saltiness of the popcorn. These are natural defense mechanisms that we use when we find that we have opened ourselves up beyond a comfortable point and don't find that the rewards of staying open exceed the discomfort.

Thus for a piece of art to have an emotional effect on the audience, the audience itself must open up emotionally and allow the opportunity for that emotional impact to occur.

Part III

Game Structure

Difficulties illuminate existence. But they must be fresh, and of high quality.

—Tom Robbins, from *Even Cowgirls Get The Blues*, 1976

The Nature of Games

People love to play games. We've played games in groups and as individuals, cooperating with teammates and competing with opponents, as far back as anyone can tell.

Games are important to us in this book because they are all about interaction. To play a game, we almost always deal in some way with objects in the physical world and often with other people as well.

We might see game development as a kind of natural selection: games have competed for people's attention, evolving a wide variety of enjoyable techniques for interacting with other people and the world around us. The games that people like have flourished and led to a wide range of sequels and variations, while the others have faded away. Learning what makes a great game will help us understand how to make interactive experiences that share the attractive and enjoyable qualities of the best games.

Like stories, games have internal and external structures. Knowing these structures will help us understand common features among those games that have endured. These structures will also help us build new entertainments that blend story elements and game elements without violating the foundations of either one.

Game Experience

E very culture has a legacy of games and game-playing. Some ancient games, like the African game Mancala (also known as Awari), are still played today. The game of Go originated in China, perhaps as long ago as 2000 B.C.E. It is still very popular today, and played by millions of people worldwide.

Not all ancient games have been so lucky. Archaeologists have unearthed Mayan ruins in Dainzu that are almost 3,000 years old, showing people wearing gloves and masks, and holding fist-sized balls [17]. Since the Mayans knew how to make rubber balls, it seems very likely that these carvings represent some kind of handball game. The rules of this particular game appear to have been lost to time, though handball games of many sorts are still popular.

Types of Games

There are many types of games. Some we play as individuals, others as groups. Some have time pressure enforced either by a clock or by the need to react to events. Other games move at more leisurely paces or with no time pressures at all. Games can be physical or mental, brief or lengthy, concrete or abstract, or any mix of these or many other attributes.

127

The enormous variety of games is part of their appeal, but it also makes them difficult to talk about in any general way. A number of authors have looked at the subject from different points of view. Crawford has looked at video games [31] [33], as have Rollings and Adams [116]. Salen and Zimmerman have looked at games in general [118].

There is one quality that is common to almost all games: winning. There is usually one person or team that is declared the winner of any given game. Some games allow ties or have other ways for a game to end with multiple winners.

Winning is the point of most games, but it's not the only reason most of us play [135]. After all, in every game there are at least as many losers as winners. In games with many players, most participants will not win. If our only purpose in playing were to win, we would be disappointed most of the time, and we'd probably stop playing. Winning is important, but it's not everything.

Rather, games provide us with opportunities to develop and exercise our abilities, and to spend time with other people. Often our teammates or competitors are friends and colleagues, and playing a game together is an enjoyable activity that allows us to spend time with one another.

Games, like stories, come in genres. Some abstract games have no preferred literal interpretation. For example, the card game 21 is simply a game of betting with cards. But many board games have specific flavors to them: *Risk* is a war game, *Monopoly* is based on finances and real estate, and *Space Invaders* is about shooting down aliens. You can take away some of these settings and create a similar but different game. For example, by changing nothing but the artwork and sounds, *Space Invaders* can become a game about popping helium balloons, or if we imagine that we're looking down at the ground, it can be a game about picking off predators that are trying to run into our garden. Take the game *Quake*, replace the monsters and environment with a different style of art direction, and with only a few other changes you get *American McGee's Alice*.

Although the world of games is vast, many of the best-known games can be divided up into a few general categories, depending on their primary activity. This classification gives us a nice overview of what people are trying to achieve in different games, which directly affects how they interact with the physical environment and with each other.

I've found it useful to think of most games in terms of five broad categories. These categories aren't exhaustive, as there are many games that don't fit into any of them, but they do capture a wide variety of important and popular games. For simplicity in the discussion below, I'll speak of competitive games as played by two "teams." The ideas are still the same for games with more than two teams or where the teams are single individuals.

Five Categories of Games

There are many ways to characterize the world of games. In *The Oxford History Of Board Games* [109] games are distinguished in several ways, such as those that are played with special equipment and those that are not, or those that are based on position and those that are based on themes. I've found the following categorization to be useful when thinking about designing different classes of games.

1. Accumulation of resources: In collection games, you win by accumulating more of something than your competitors. Often the resources being amassed are abstract *points*. The winning team is the one that gets more points than the other team.

   In many sports, a point can only be scored by the team in control of some object, such as a ball or puck. Thus an important related goal is to obtain that object and retain control over it as much as possible, using the simple logic that if the other team hasn't got the ball, they can't score.

   Many games have rules that force teams to relinquish control so that things can't get too one-sided. In baseball, only the team that is at-bat is able to score a run. The rules require the two teams to switch between offense and defense after every third out, so both teams get an opportunity to score. Basketball has a 24-second shot clock: the team with the ball must try to score a basket before it reaches zero or lose control of the ball.

   Sometimes points are somehow related to a limited physical resource. In straight pool, the goal is to sink as many balls as possible from the original 15-ball set. Each ball sunk by one player is thus made unavailable to the other. The physical pool balls are directly correlated to the points scored by the player who sinks them.

   Games that simulate military campaigns often focus on acquiring as much land as possible. These games are bounded because there is only so much land available on the board.

2. Conservation of resources: Sometimes the goal is to have less of something than the other team, rather than more. This goal often applies
   to games where you're penalized for all the resources you use in order
   to win.

   For example, a competitive sprinter wants to use up as little time as
   possible to get from the start to the finish of a race. Similarly, a golfer
   wants to complete the course with as few strokes as possible: each
   time he hits the ball, it counts one more stroke against his score.

   In some games, teams start with a quantity of something and try to
   get rid of as much of it as possible. In the solitaire computer game
   Nisqually, you're initially presented with a grid of colored blocks.
   To move, you choose two adjacent blocks and swap their positions.
   When you make clusters of three or more blocks of the same color,
   they disappear from the board, and the blocks above them fall down
   (as if pulled by gravity) to fill the hole. Your goal is to get rid of all
   the blocks, leaving nothing but an empty board.

3. Personal challenge: Players who want to win will perform at the limits
   of their abilities. Sometimes this participation hardly involves the
   other teams at all.

   In a swimming competition, each swimmer strives for his fastest time.
   Though there are psychological elements involved, each competitor
   is essentially independent of the others. In other sports, such as yacht
   racing, competitors actively jockey with with each other for position
   and get an advantage, or cause trouble for others, based on where
   they are in the group.

   Many sports competitions share this character of simultaneous but
   independent competition, in which each player is essentially striving
   for his own best performance. A javelin thrower seeks to simply throw
   the javelin as far and true as he can and doesn't need to spend a lot
   of energy dealing with the plans of the other athletes.

4. Survival: Sometimes the goal of a game is simple survival: the winner is
   the one who outlasts everyone else.

   In the word game Geography, each player needs to name a geographical location whose name begins with the last letter of the place named
   by the preceding player. If a player can't name a place before more

than a few seconds have elapsed, or if he repeats a place that has already been named, he is eliminated. The winner is simply the player who is able to keep going longer than anyone else. Many other children's games, such as spelling bees and dodgeball, share this quality of elimination.

There are also adult games that are won by the last one standing. Some versions of paintball are a free-for-all, where contestants eliminate one another until there's only one person left. Many computer games in the "gun and run" genre, such as *Quake III Arena* and *Unreal Tournament 2003*, offer the same gameplay in a virtual 3D environment. Some games in this genre, such as *Half-Life*, add puzzles to the need for survival.

5. Outwit: Some games are won by the team that is able to out-think the other. A superior plan may require superior physical abilities to execute, or it may be an almost entirely mental experience.

Intellectual games like chess and Go offer players a battle of wits. From puzzle games like *Clue* to memory games like *Trivial Pursuit*, the physical abilities of the players aren't as important as their mental powers.

Most physical games reward clever strategy and execution to some extent. But sometimes even a physical game is almost all mental. Although the children's game of hide-and-seek rewards the physical ability to get into small or unexpected places, the game is primarily a battle of wits between where people can think of hiding and where others will think of looking.

Puzzles

Puzzles are a special class of games. Puzzles are often played as solitaire, though they can be solved in cooperation with other people. A puzzle can usually be identified by a specific, predetermined *goal* which, when achieved, announces the *solution* of the puzzle and the end of the experience.

For example, take the game of *Hi-Q*. The game board consists of a collection of pegs arranged in a grid in the shape of a thick addition sign, with one hole left in the middle. The goal is to hop the pegs over one another, removing pieces as you go, until there's only one peg left, sitting in the center of the board. When that's been achieved, the puzzle is solved and there's nothing left to do short of starting a new puzzle.

The goal of a *Rubik's Cube* is to rotate the blocks so that all the little cubes on each face of the larger cube have the same color. Once that's done, the puzzle is solved. The only way to keep going is to scramble the cube up and start again.

In some puzzles, you can judge how far you've progressed towards the solution. In the classic puzzle Towers of Hanoi, you start with a stack of graduated rings, one atop the other, forming a cone. The rings are placed on a post, and there are two other posts available, each of which starts out empty. The goal is to move the rings one at a time, ultimately transferring the entire stack from one post to another, while never putting a larger ring on top of a smaller one. You can judge how far you've come by the sizes of the intermediate towers and how much of the new tower has been built.

Crossword puzzles let you judge your progress unambiguously. Your progress towards the solution is simply the number of remaining empty squares (assuming you're confident of the squares you've filled in).

Not all puzzles provide an obvious or reliable measure of how close you've come to the solution. Sometimes there's no way to tell how close you are until you finally solve it. And sometimes the solution is not as near at hand as it appears. For example, after some experience with the game *Hi-Q*, it's not too hard to get down to a small number of pegs, which might suggest that the solution is near. But if they're in the wrong positions, then it could be hard or even impossible to reach the final solution. Often this dead end leads to devising an entirely new strategy for solving the puzzle.

Some particularly fiendish puzzles are designed specifically so that following the "obvious" way of measuring progress will lead to a dead end, inspiring the solver to find a more subtle or clever approach. Many solitaire computer games are designed this way. For example, the game *Vexed* is made of many small puzzles. The board is a grid filled in with blocks, which are all pulled down by gravity. You move blocks horizontally, and each time you get two blocks of the same color next to one another, they disappear. Some of the initial configurations have been deliberately crafted so that it's not hard to make rapid progress in the beginning, but then the board quickly turns into a dead end. To get to the solution, you have to start over, and sometimes during the solution you must take some steps that seem to be going backwards, away from the answer.

In general, once you know how to solve a given puzzle, you can solve it again and again. In a puzzle like *Vexed* or The Towers of Hanoi, you need only repeat the identical sequence of moves again. Once you've mastered the strategy and basic moves of the *Rubik's Cube*, it's straightforward to complete the puzzle from any starting condition.

One thing that distinguishes puzzles from games is that most puzzles do not change over time, while many games have an element of unpredictability: victory today may not lead to victory tomorrow.

Toys

A third category of activity close to both games and puzzles is *toys*. Toys are typically pieces of equipment that have no specific purpose except to help us amuse ourselves and others. A yo-yo is a toy, since (unless you're a professional yo-yo demonstrator) the only reason for having one is to play with it. Toys have no goal state, and they can't be won: we just enjoy them for a while.

Many toys look like things that are not toys. A child's plastic tool set or light bulb oven are toys, while a carpenter's tool set or a baker's oven are both serious stuff. We often play with toys that approximate real things in the world: dolls are little people, and model trains are often very realistic small-scale versions of their real counterparts. Many toys are simply worlds unto themselves: a pogo stick or hula-hoop are oddball devices that are simply fun to play with.

Some objects can change their nature depending on how and why we're using them. A fishing boat may be a very serious tool by day to a working fisherman, but that same man may take his boat out for sheer pleasure with friends on the weekend. While on that trip the boat is now just a toy, albeit a precious and expensive one.

There are software toys as well. The simulators *The Sims* and *SimCity* have some game-like elements, but they're mostly free-form toys to be played with for the simple pleasure of playing.

Group Play

There are several basic ways that people organize themselves when playing games. Figure 5 shows a visual shorthand for these groupings. Let's summarize them briefly.

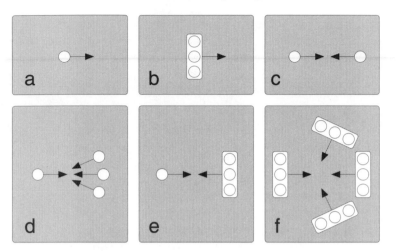

Figure 5. Types of group play. (a) Solitaire. (b) Team solitaire. (c) One-on-one. (d) One-on-many. (e) One-on-team. (f) Team-on-team.

Solitaire: One player plays alone. *Tetris* is a solitaire game, as are classic card solitaire games like Klondike (sometimes also known as Patience Solitaire).

Team solitaire: Two or more players work together to achieve a combined success against other players, but those players are not actively participating. *Pictionary* is a team solitaire game in which two players unite to deliver and guess a word strictly from drawings. Except for the All Play category, the other players simply watch the active team. In essence, that team is playing against the clock, which is why I see this game as a type of shared solitaire.

One-on-one: Two or more players face each other in competition. Singles tennis is a one-on-one game.

One-on-many: One player competes against other players who are acting independently of each other. The children's game of tag is a one-on-team game, where one player is singled out and labelled "it," and is effectively in competition against all the other players.

One-on-team: One player competes against other players acting as a coordinated group or team. Some games turn into one-on-team at certain points: in hockey or soccer, if an offensive group breaks through all the defenders, the game becomes one-on-team between that group of the players and the lone goalie. This category also includes those games where one player faces several teams.

Team-on-team: Two or more teams face each other at the same time. Baseball is a team-on-team game. This category also includes games such as road rallies where multiple teams are competing simultaneously.

Each of these styles can support a tournament, where multiple, independent games are all run at the same time.

In parallel competition, the players in one game do not interact with those in another, but the tournament can still determine overall victors by comparing the scores of the individual games. All the games in the tournament can be played at the same time, like a room full of crossword puzzle solvers competing for the most correct answers in the shortest time or tennis players playing on a dozen different courts at once. Parallel games can also be played sequentially, as when pole-vaulters follow each other in attempts to clear the bar at the same vaulting site.

The Game Experience

Before we look at the appeal of different types of games, let's take a moment to look at the varieties of experiences enjoyed by players.

There is something inherently satisfying about playing games, evidenced simply by their enduring popularity. After all, there are many ways to spend our leisure time: dancing, making love, playing music, watching movies, or even simply talking to friends. Games have been a popular activity across all peoples and cultures. Why is that so? What is it about game-playing that is so attractive to us?

Such a question can only be answered in very general terms, since different games appeal to different people at different times. But there are commonalities: almost all games involve competition, either against one or more other players or against one's self.

Structured competition seems to be a safe way for many people to exercise aggressive and dominating tendencies that they suppress in everyday life. Walker [135] discusses how competition provides an opportunity for us to selfishly perform at the limits of our abilities and compare the results against the best efforts of other people, in an environment that absolves us from any other considerations. When playing a game, we don't have to think about the feelings of our competitors, and we don't have to penalize ourselves in order to help them out. The sweetest victories are those that are won when all the other players are also doing their best, so the most respectful thing we can do for our competitors is to use our very best efforts to win and pay no attention to their own aspirations.

Games also give us a chance to exercise some aspects of our personalities that we normally keep in check. Within the boundaries of a game, two people can fight hard for domination and power without risking a personal confrontation. It is expected in most games between equally-matched competitors that they will employ traits like aggression, power, and courage in order to win. Friends often play games together, and because such inconsiderate behavior is limited to the game, it doesn't damage their friendship.

People can and often do take games seriously and can develop strong personal feelings about their opponents. But personal antagonism is not necessary to play a strong and winning game, and even those competitors who have those feelings don't need to retain them after the game is over.

So one appealing aspects of games is that they let us express behaviors and experience strong and aggressive feelings that we normally don't allow in daily life.

Challenges

Another part of the appeal of games is that they provide provide us with a rich, interactive environment in which to develop new skills. Some of these skills are particular to the game, but some of these abilities, and the processes of acquiring them, are generally useful in everyday life. We'll look at these skills in more detail later on, but they include skills like forming and testing hypotheses, exploring possibilities allowed and prohibited by sets of rules, and constructing strategies and tactics.

One of the pleasures of playing games is the sheer variety of skills we get to use. As we improve, we are rewarded with increased competence and mastery, which makes the game itself more enjoyable and opens the door to deeper and more sophisticated gameplay.

These skills are developed in response to the challenges presented by games. I've found it useful to distinguish several general classes of challenges that appear frequently in different games. Let's look at them.

Mental prowess: Games like Go and chess are exclusively about mental agility. Word games like Geography are also purely mental. All of these games can be, and sometimes are, played entirely in the minds of the participants, though the players also need some mechanism such as speech or writing to communicate their moves. Sometimes these mechanisms are outlawed, though: in some chess tournaments, speaking is forbidden.

Physical prowess: Few games are purely physical, because they all reward at least some degree of mental focus, as well as planning and strategy. But games with significant physical demands like football and *Ultimate Frisbee* are typically won by those with superior physical abilities.

Creativity: Games like Charades and *Pictionary* challenge players to be creative in both creating and responding to clues. Victory goes to those teams that are not only on each other's mental wavelength but are also open to exploring a wide variety of creative options in quick succession.

Bluffing: In some games, outwitting your opponent is a matter not just of thinking faster or better, but using your knowledge of his personality against him. When playing poker, players often bluff one another. Good bluffers are skilled at reading the other players at the table and noticing "tells" that reveal how they're feeling about the cards in their hands. In many games where players keep information secret from one another, bluffing and misdirection can lead to victory. For example, in the board game *Stratego* each player is trying to locate and capture the other's flag. Typically a player surrounds his flag with bombs as a last wall of defense, but knowing this, a player can deliberately plant bombs far away from his flag to misdirect his opponent.

Execution: Sometimes it's clear exactly what needs to be done, and the challenge is in doing it well. Although mental skills like concentration and focus may be important, the activity is primarily one of physical achievement. For example, in a game of bowling each new frame begins with ten pins, set up identically to the beginning of the frame before. Bowlers seek to simply execute their delivery of the ball as well as possible. Archers seek to send each arrow they shoot into the center of the bull's-eye.

Probability: In games that include an element of chance, players with a good sense of probabilities will do better than those without. In the card game 21, players who can count cards can improve their odds by estimating the likelihood of receiving different cards on their next draw.

Memory: Some games are all about memory. In the game show *Concentration*, each player is shown the same grid of images, which are then obscured. Players make a successful move by choosing a pair of grid elements that, when revealed again, have the same picture. They do this by remembering the original presentation and refreshing their memory when their chosen pairs are momentarily revealed. Trivia games like *Trivial Pursuit* reward a good memory for miscellaneous pieces of information.

Because many games provide a structured environment where focusing on the immediate task is rewarded, game-playing is an easy and attractive way for many people to enter into a *flow* experience [35]. As described by the psychologist Csikszentmihalyi, this is the sensation of being completely absorbed in a demanding but rewarding task, so that everything else seems to slip away.

The flow experience is the strongest form of *immersion* or the sense that the outer world has fallen away. To speak of an immersive experience is to invoke the idea of flow, which is difficult to achieve and maintain, as we saw in Chapter 3.

Flow, or immersion, is not necessary in order to have a great time. Many rewarding experiences are not based on flow. For example, working out at the gym while talking to a friend is stimulating to both the body and the mind but doesn't require getting lost in either activity.

Games that don't bring a player into a flow state can still keep that person engaged by a series of *offers and rewards*, also known as *teases and payoffs*. The game offers a glimpse of something very attractive that the player can obtain in the future and then places a series of obstacles in the way of getting it. This dangling carrot could be a new suit of clothes or a faster car, the ability to cast a more powerful spell, the combination to the lock on the secret vault, or anything else that the player desires. This goal gives the player a motivation to keep playing. As long as a player can think to himself, "Just *one more* ..." (whether it's one more enemy defeated, race won, or golden coin collected doesn't really matter), then he'll stay engaged, eager to collect the prize he's been tempted with.

Turns

Many multi-player games are set up so that the players take *turns*, offering only some of the players the option to act while the others must wait.

Board games like *Monopoly* or chess are turn-taking games. In some ways, tennis is also a turn-taking game, in that once one player has hit the ball, he must now wait to see what the other player does before he can commit to a response.

At the other extreme from these games are those where all players are acting simultaneously. In a soccer game the ball is often in continuous play for minutes at a time. No player knows when he will have have the opportunity or need to act, and so everyone remains constantly alert.

The Game Loop

In many games, players repeat a a series of actions over and over. I call this the *Game Loop*.

1. Observe the situation
2. Set goals
3. Prepare
4. Commit and execute
5. Compare result to the plan
6. Evaluate the result for self
7. Evaluate the result for others
8. Return to step 1

1. Observe the situation: The first step is to take in all the information you can gather and put it together. How are you feeling? What's the weather like? Who is your opponent, what is he thinking, what seems to be his strategy, what are his strengths and weaknesses? What are your own strengths and weaknesses? And how much time do you have to process this information?

Sometimes players receive help in this step from colleagues and coaches. For example, a baseball player who's running to first base will see and hear the first-base coach tell him either to stop at first or to keep running hard and try for second base.

This is the step where we observe any random or unpredictable information, such as the roll of a pair of dice or the dealing of a card. This is also when we also take in anything unusual about the world, as in a science-fiction or fantasy setting where the laws of physics might be unfamiliar.

2. Set goals: Determine what your next set of goals is. These goals include any mix of offense and defense, long-term strategy and near-term tactics. Your may want to run to a better spot on the field, improve the defensive positioning of your pieces, interfere with your opponent's opportunities, issue a challenge, or look for an opening in your opponent's play.

   If there's a time limit, you have to manage this process so you can do the best job possible in the time available. For example, a baseball batter only has a few moments to evaluate an incoming pitch and determine the best way to hit it. A *Pictionary* artist can only plan for so long, because he has to get his drawing down on paper and give his partner a chance to guess the word before the timer runs out. A poker player can only take his time until he exhausts the patience of his fellow players, but a patient Solitaire player can take years to make a move, since there's nobody waiting except himself.

3. Prepare: Now that you know what you want to do, you have to set yourself up so that you can accomplish it as successfully as possible. This step can involve preparations like getting into position or amassing necessary resources.

   A bowler knows at the start of a frame that his goal is to knock down all ten pins. He'll make sure his shoes are tied, the ball is clean and ready, and he's standing at the right distance that will allow him to make his best delivery. A soccer player who's determined to take a scoring shot with a header needs to line himself up, jump, bend, and thrust as well as possible to execute the move. He may also execute a few fakes along the way to take out or fool defensive players, in order to make his upcoming shot easier. A *Pictionary* player will makes sure that his pencil is sharp and he has a clean sheet of paper to draw on.

4. Commit and execute: Now that everything is in place as well as can be arranged, it's time to commit to an action and actually do it. This step can be daunting, because until this moment there's the chance of taking back the move and finding something better.

   In chess, commitment comes when you take your hand off the piece you're moving; it means that your turn is finished (in tournament chess, you're committed to moving a piece as soon as you touch it, even if you don't know what you want to do with it yet). A baseball batter commits when he starts his swing, anticipating where the pitch will go and how he can hit it best. A poker player commits when he bets or takes another card.

5. Compare the result to the plan: As soon as you've completed the action you planned, you can judge how well you carried it out. Notice that this step does not involve evaluating how well the move worked in the larger game: that comes next. Even before other players have a chance to respond, you can judge how well you managed to carry out the plan you intended.

   For example, a soccer player may have decided to pass the ball to another player, intending to strike the ball just so in order to make a clean pass. As soon as the ball leaves his foot, he can evaluate how well he hit the ball and whether it's headed where he intended.

   Although almost all physical games have this opportunity for comparison, some mostly intellectual games do not. For example, when playing checkers, you may decide to push a particular checker forward and to the right. Once you let go of the checker, the move is over, and all that's left is to evaluate the move strategically. Most players are unlikely to dwell upon, or even examine, their prowess in moving the physical checker from one square to the other.

   In purely mental games, like Geography, there's no comparison step at all. If you can name a real place (or bluff the name of an imaginary place) starting with the last letter of the previous place, you've executed a completely successful move.

   At the other extreme, beach volleyball offers constant opportunities for evaluation as you compensate for numerous changing factors as diverse as sand, wind, and sunlight.

6. Evaluate the result for self: Once the move has been made, it will have an effect on the environment.

In step 5 I discussed evaluating the quality of the execution of the move with respect to what you intended to do. Now you evaluate the move with respect to the effect you intended it to have.

There are two steps to this evaluation: evaluating the move based on your own expectations and criteria, and seeing how it was evaluated by the world. We'll take these in two separate steps, focusing here on the former, more personal consideration.

When we evaluate the quality of our move against an *internal* standard, we judge whether our strategy, tactics, and performance were as good as we were capable of, regardless of what the rest of the world thinks.

Let's suppose suppose you're playing tennis, and your opponent has just returned the ball badly, giving you an easy shot. There's enough time for you to hit the ball back almost any way you want to. If you see your opponent leaning to his forehand, you might decide to hit hard to his far backhand. That's even more attractive because you know that his backhand is weak. After creating that plan in step 2, you plant your feet in step 3, and you strike in step 4.

Let's say you execute beautifully and hit the ball exactly the way you imagined. We'll say that step 5 was perfectly satisfied, because you executed the shot precisely as you intended. Now you get to see what happens next.

Watching how your opponent reacts helps you evaluate everything that went into the move: your analysis of the situation and your opponent, your strategy for winning, the tactics of that particular shot, and the quality of its execution. All of these are judged against your own internal standards or expectations.

One benefit of a flawless execution is that you can see the effects of your plans. Because you hit the ball perfectly, it lands in your opponent's court exactly where you wanted. Suppose that you see your predictions come true: your opponent stumbles to get to his backhand but can't manage it and misses the ball completely. Your intuition and understanding are reinforced, and you are now slightly better against this player than you were a moment ago.

Remember that the opinions of the rest of the world are irrelevant at this step. So even if, despite your flawless execution, your opponent was still able to shift position, plant his feet, and wallop the ball back to you, it's still reasonable to feel that you achieved your own goals, since you read his balance and gameplay to best of your abilities.

Suppose that you didn't execute very well, and instead of going to your partner's far backhand, the ball went to his forehand. His reaction still tells you about how he plays in that situation, even though it wasn't the situation you intended to bring about. You get information, though it wasn't what you were after.

In all of these examples, you can learn from the experience and became a better player as a result.

The way to improve as a player is to act at the limits of your abilities and to learn from mistakes. Suppose that you're playing chess against someone more experienced, and you feel that your defenses need shoring up. You move a piece into position, but your opponent counters with a devastating attack through the hole you just left open. If that attack was subtle, you might reasonably feel that you couldn't have seen it at your present level of ability. So you still did as well as you could, and in that sense your move was a successful one.

So this step is about evaluating yourself honestly in terms of your current abilities. If you performed at maximum capacity for your present state of competence, then you can evaluate your move as successful.

If instead you look at the move and realize you could have done better, then this is the time to evaluate your own internal procedures for making plans. Perhaps you acted too hastily or went for the quick and greedy solution rather than a more elegant one. That information can be used to adjust how you plan for the next move.

When people urge us to draw pleasure from a game not from winning or losing but from "doing your best," they are trying to focus our attention on this step of the Game Loop. It doesn't matter what the world thinks, or what actually happens in the game, as long as you're performing at the upper limit of your own abilities.

7. Evaluate the result for others: Although it is rewarding to judge one's performance based on solely internal measures, there is indeed an outer world, which judges us according to its own standards.

At the broadest level, the outer world chooses the winner of the game based on the score or some other measure of achievement. That decision has nothing to do with the internal judgments that we talked about in the last step. So although one player may strive to perform at the limits of his abilities and feel proud of his achievements, and the other may coast through and feel somewhat embarrassed for not trying very hard, determining the winner has nothing to do with those internal feelings.

Since the outer world's judgments make such an important impact on the game and its outcome, we often give them a lot of weight. Thus we usually include those external decisions strongly in our final overall evaluation of any given move or action.

Returning to our tennis game, you may intend to hit a hard smash to your opponent's outer corner, but you don't execute well and instead hit it right down the middle of the court. If you felt that you should have been able to get the ball into the corner, you may judge that stroke internally in step 6 as only moderately successful. But your opponent, and the spectators, don't know what was inside your head, and they may assume that's what you meant to do all along. If the shot catches your opponent unaware, the fans may cheer your skill, assuming it was on purpose. So although the audience was very impressed with your abilities, inside you may feel disappointed.

On the other hand, suppose you place the shot exactly where you intended, but you find to your amazement that your opponent was able to respond after all, and struck back so strongly that you lost the point. This is the opposite of the last situation. Internally, you know you did your best in evaluating the situation and in executing the move you thought was appropriate, but the world sees a poor piece of strategy or a poor execution. Thus spectators are disappointed in your performance, while you may feel quite pleased with yourself.

Figure 6 shows a pictorial version of inner and outer judgments for our simple tennis example. The easy situations to deal with are where

Figure 6. Comparing internal results with external results. The vertical axis is the internal evaluation, with bad at the bottom to good at the top. The horizontal axis is the external evaluation, with bad at the left and good at the right.

they agree; keeping a clear head when they disagree is a tougher job emotionally.

8. **Return to Step 1:** When the move has been made, and we've had a chance to evaluate both how well we carried through our plans and what effect they had in the world, it's time to return to Step 1 and get ready for the next move.

The speed of the Game Loop depends on the game being played. When playing tennis, the speed is implicitly set by the rhythm of the volleys, since you have only a few seconds to assess the situation, come up with a plan, and respond. Players can start thinking about their next shot right away, but neither can commit to too much until he sees what his opponent chooses to do. When it's your turn to serve, you can take a little longer, but you can't stall indefinitely.

In tennis or backgammon, the Game Loop is *alternating*: each player makes his move, and then control passes to the other player.

In soccer, the Game Loop is *overlapping*: each player of each team is constantly running through the steps, each at his own pace. When the ball is stolen or there's a penalty, the rhythm of the game changes, and all the players need to reevaluate their decisions in light of the new situation.

In wrestling, the Game Loop is overlapping and very fast-paced: feeling your opponent twitch a tiny muscle can trigger a whole new set of plans.

The first few steps of the Game Loop address large-scale observations and strategies, and later steps move into specific choices and tactics. Once the move has been made, actions unroll in the opposite order. You can immediately evaluate the skill with which you executed your move and then judge its larger effect on the game.

Granularity of Choice

When we play games, we typically make decisions at many different levels. In the Game Loop, we must evaluate large-scale strategy and small-scale tactics constantly as we make plans and see how they turned out.

There are times when we are only able to make decisions at a certain level along the continuum of strategies and tactics, and times when we can move around much more freely.

For example, suppose you decide you'd like to go downhill skiing soon. Your first few decisions are at a very high level: where and when you'll go, and who (if anyone) you'll invite to come along with you. When you step onto the mountain, you need to decide which chair lift to get on, and then at the top, you need to pick which run you want to take. Finally, once you're skiing, you need to constantly make decisions about whether you want to turn left or right, and go faster or slower.

So your choices at different times are constrained by the situation itself. You can hardly think about avoiding a particular mogul weeks before leaving your house, and once you're flying down the slope, it's too late to consider if next weekend might have been a better time to go.

The granularity, or level, of choice in a game can remain constant once the game has started, or it can change frequently. For example, in the opening moves of *Go* your goal is to establish broad regions in which you have interest; in later moves you can find yourself maneuvering precisely for particular positions.

Participants and Spectators

Many people enjoy watching others play games: professional sports are a major entertainment form all over the world. In professional arenas, there are often thousands of live spectators for every player; when we add in television audiences, this number is much higher. The competition for these spectators is fierce. Because fans like to see their teams win, the best professional players are rewarded with fame, enormous salaries, and other benefits.

Even on an amateur level, people enjoy watching others play. High-school sports games are attended by more people than just the immediate friends and families of the players.

Many spectators identify closely with their "home team," which is typically a team that is based in or near their original or adopted home towns. The geography can be much more local: students cheer for their school teams, even when their only connection to the athletes is that they have a class or two in common.

People love to feel like a part of "their" team. Fans not only watch their team play games, but they also track the standings, read about their favorite players and teams in newspapers and magazines, listen and call in to radio sports shows, watch cable TV channels entirely devoted to sports, and talk about players, teams, referees, and everything else associated with the sport with other fans.

The depth of the connection between teams and their fans is apparent any time a professional team threatens to leave town, or there is a vote on allocating money to build a new sports stadium. Public funding for sports teams is a volatile issue that has polarized many cities, particularly when the teams ask for taxpayer money to help them build new stadiums and other facilities.

When professional teams win, their supporters celebrate, and when a team becomes champion, often their home town will reward them with a parade and other honors. People who have no actual relationship to the players or the team often feel part of the success, cheering "We're number one" during rallies (this traditional kind of team loyalty may be starting to erode with the evolution of contemporary professional sports, where players frequently leave one team for another, either voluntarily or because they were traded).

This level of enthusiasm from spectators is not common in other fields. People don't get so wrapped up in the dealings of other commercial businesses they're not associated with: there are no parades when one paint manufacturer sells more cans in a given year than a rival. Although sports teams are for-profit businesses, they hold a unique spot in the emotions of many people.

Clearly, sports enthusiasts and fans enjoy the social aspect of their shared allegiance, either by attending games in person or following them together on television or radio.

It's not clear if such a feeling of community can exist without the physical aspects of professional sports: the actual courts and fields, the influence of weather, the unpredictability of injury, and the opportunity to be physically present at the event itself (even if that opportunity is rarely taken advantage of).

Fans often get caught up in the personal dramas of the lives of famous players and pay as much attention to them as any soap-opera devotee. When these players get into legal trouble, their courtroom dramas become high-profile news stories.

Resources

Resources are the commodities, real or implicit, that players compete for in order to achieve victory.

Often more resources mean more points, which means a better chance of winning. But sometimes the resources are indirect and don't turn into points directly, but rather provide the opportunity for scoring points. In many games you need to control a ball or puck in order to score. Having that control doesn't guarantee that you'll accumulate points, but if you don't have control, it's almost certain that you won't.

Competition for Resources

In every game, there is competition for resources. Sometimes gathering resources is the entire point of the game. For example, scavenger hunts are won by the team that can locate the most items.

Resources may be tangible, like scavenger-hunt items or marbles won in a game of marbles. Resources may also be intangible, like the support of a crowd cheering for their home team.

Resources may be *unlimited* or *limited*. Although there are no truly unlimited resources in nature, in many games there are no explicit limits to what can be gathered. In baseball, you can score as many runs as you can manage during your turns at bat. Although a score of even 20 runs is very unusual, there's nothing in the rules that prohibits a team from scoring a thousand runs if it's able to.

Some games manage their resources with built-in limits. In checkers, for example, you start with twelve pieces, and though they can turn into kings, you can't increase the number of pieces you have in play. In *Risk*, each player's goal is to conquer all the territories on the world map. There number of territories is finite, so when you own them all, you win. In *Monopoly*, the most that you can acquire is ownership of every property, with a single hotel on each street.

Some games with limited resources are called *zero-sum* games. The idea here is that each advance by one player is marked by an equal decline by another, so the sum of their scores remains a constant (zero is just a special case in which the scores are positive and negative and add up to zero). For example, each time a *Risk* player seizes a territory, it is necessarily lost by another player, so the sum of the number of territories owned never changes. In other words, every time one player manages to improve his or her position in a zero-sum game, it is at the expense of the other players, who suffer exactly the same amount of damage to their own positions.

A nice example of a zero-sum game is Reversi (commercially marketed as *Othello*). Each playing piece is a flat disk colored white on one side and black on the other. Pieces are placed one at a time onto a square grid. When you place one of your pieces so that it flanks a straight line of the other player's pieces, they all flip over to your color. Thus each time a player flips a piece to his color, that piece is simultaneously lost to his opponent.

Obtaining Resources

There are many ways to go about obtaining the resources that are useful to winning a game.

Some resources are visible to some or all of the players, whose goal is simply to get them. In competitive games, this urge to acquire mutually available resources usually becomes a *race* to acquire the most number of resources or just the right collection of them.

The resources in Go are the intersections. There are only a finite number of intersections on the board, and once they're all controlled, the game is over. Players take turns placing stones in order to seize as much territory as they can. In *Monopoly*, the resources are the properties.

In the game of *Set*, cards are laid out on a table face up, where everyone can easily see them. Each card shows one or more instances of several different symbols, in one of several different colors. Players race to be the first to identify sets of three cards with similar characteristics.

There are many other types of races for resources. In some games, each time a resource is made available, everyone gets a copy of it. In Bingo, the resources are the letter-number pairs that are drawn and announced by the caller. Once that resource is made public, it's available to everyone. Each player marks his own card, or cards, and the first person to get the right pattern of marked squares wins the jackpot.

In contrast to Bingo, in which the resources are announced out loud, sometimes the resources are hidden and the point is to discover them. In the game of Bull-and-Cow (commercially marketed as *Mastermind*), one player (the decoder) tries to guess a pattern created by the other (the encoder). Often the pattern is a row of four or five symbols or colored dots. The decoder starts by making a guess at the pattern. The encoder then scores this guess by providing a report in the form of two numbers. The first number tells the decoder how many entries in his guess are of the right color and are in the right position, and the second number tells how many of the others are of the correct color but in the wrong position. The decoder combines that information with his previous guesses and reports to come up with a new guess and eventually determine the encoder's pattern. Each guess costs a point. Decoders seek to minimize their score by using up the smallest number of guesses to find the complete answer.

In Bingo, resources are freely granted. In some other games, resources must be taken by the other team, or by the structure of the rules themselves.

As an example of how the rules can allocate resources, consider the game of baseball. The team that is at bat is the only team that can score runs, so it's to their advantage to bat as long as possible. But when they've accumulated three outs, they move into the field and become the defense. On the other hand, resources can change hands forcibly. In soccer one can steal the ball by intercepting a pass or simply out-maneuvering an opponent, and then, once in possession of the ball, the team controlling the ball can try to score.

Growing and Shrinking Resources

Often an essential resource, such as time, is used up steadily over the course of the game. When that resource is gone, whoever is ahead is the winner. In timed games like basketball, or those with turn limits like bowling, the goal is to be ahead when the time or turn limits are reached. In games where the idea is to own resources, the game is over when they're depleted. For example, you want to have more points than the other person when all the *Scrabble* tiles have been played, or more disks of your color than the other player's when all the squares are occupied in Reversi.

Rules and Scoring

G ames have *rules*. The rules typically limit both the nature and duration of the game. In the great majority of games, the rules are determined and agreed to before play begins, and they don't change after that. The most common exception to this practice is in children's games, as they make up and change rules on a whim as they play.

Rules

There are also a very few games where the rules themselves change as the game goes on. For example, in the card game *Fluxx* you can play cards that change how the game is played or even the conditions for winning. The game *Nomic* also has rules that change over time. But these games still have rules for how they're played, so sometimes they're described as having *meta-rules*.

But *Fluxx* and children's games of "Let's pretend" are the exceptions to the rule of rules. Even though children enjoy playing with invented and malleable rules, they also enjoy traditional games like marbles and jacks, and board games like *Chutes and Ladders* with very traditional rule structures.

The rules that govern most games have a lot of similarities that we can identify.

Game Rules

Most traditional games have rules that are handed down as part of the oral or written traditions where the game is played. In some cases games have been taken up by professional organizations, who canonize the rules and enforce them in the competitions they sponsor. Because these rules are carefully thought out and generally well-balanced, many amateurs adopt these professional rules (or subsets of them) for their own informal play.

Rules can also be made up from the whole cloth by a game designer. Creators of commercial games sell the game equipment along with printed rules for how to play.

In some cases, the essence of the game is in the rules, and not in the equipment or explicit devices for implementing them. For example, one can play chess with seashells on a grid drawn in the sand or with a thousand-dollar hand-carved wooden set; it's the rules that make the game.

Some publishers sell nothing but rules, leaving it up to purchasers to create or assemble their own equipment. Or there may be only minimal equipment; games like *Set* and *Kill Dr. Lucky* are nothing but their rules and a deck of special cards.

In other cases, the equipment itself is inseparable from the game. The game of pool requires a flat and true surface, and well-machined balls that roll without surprises. Lacrosse is synonymous with its scoop-shaped nets on the end of long handles, and you can't play *Twister* without a colored grid of dots and a spinner. Players can save money by making their own versions of these items, but some, such as perfectly smooth pool balls, can be very difficult to manufacture at home.

Established rules, whether printed in a rule book or handed down from one person to another, have several characteristics in common. A few games deliberately defy these conventions to provide an unusual twist, but the great majority have the following traits.

Characteristics of Game Rules

Announced: The same rules are presented to all the players. Everyone receives a complete set of rules, and knows that everyone else has as well. They are publicly available, so any spectators following the game know what the players know.

Explained: The rules are intended to be as clear as possible. If a player has questions, the rules are explained and clarified. Often there are examples and demonstrations. If there's a rule-based dispute during gameplay, it's usually resolved by deriving a reasoned interpretation based on the rules.

External: The rules exist in a place that is outside of the player's minds. They may be printed on paper or reside in the collective memories of the people who have played that game and remember it. But in either case, they aren't dependent on the subjectivity or whimsy of any one person.

Fixed: The rules are set ahead of time, and they don't change over the course of the game. Some elements of the rules may pass in and out of effect, but those changes themselves are specified ahead of time. The rules aren't rewritten as the game goes on.

Objective: The rules are objective and are not tuned to the individual players, except as the rules themselves specify. For example, in some children's games the rules state that in the case of a tie, the youngest player wins. In games of skill, unequally-matched players may agree ahead of time to grant an advantage to the weaker player. A novice baseball player may be granted a fourth strike, or an experienced chess player facing a beginner might voluntarily give up one or more pieces before the game begins. Aside from these mutually negotiated exceptions, the rules apply equally and objectively to all players, regardless of their stature or previous accomplishments. Even if a newcomer faces the world champion, he always has an honest chance to win.

Refereed: When there is a dispute, the objective nature of the rules means that an impartial referee can step in to arbitrate and make a final decision. Baseball players abide by the calls of umpires who are employed exclusively to make such decisions by determining balls, strikes, and whether a runner is safe or out at a base. Tennis players live with the decisions of line judges who determine if a ball that lands near a line is in or out of play. Although players may argue with a referee over a call and attempt to sway him, the referee's final decision is usually the last word. In some extreme situations, a larger governing body may be brought into the situation, but it is still acting as a referee, albeit with more authority.

Learning the Rules

Novice players are often forgiven for not fully understanding the rules. More experienced players may guide or coach them during the game, or even offer guidance in developing an understanding of the game's basic strategies and tactics. It's not uncommon for someone learning chess to hear, after making a move, something like, "You don't want to make that move. Take it back, and look at what I'm doing over here on the left side of the board."

Many organizations run clinics to teach their games to players at different levels of skill from novice to advanced and also to help them refine their skills. And there are many books on how to excel at a wide variety of games.

Many popular games have very simple rules, yet allow for complex gameplay. For example, the rules of Go are short, and those of chess and Reversi are not much longer. Yet both of these games reward experience and knowledge, and advanced play can become extremely sophisticated.

In some games, players will take a "practice round" or two to familiarize themselves with the specific venue in which they are playing. This "warm-up" is particularly important for games based on physical skill and reflexes. The practice round gives players a chance to explore the physical possibilities of the space without risking points in actual games.

Many modern computer and console-based action games require players to be able to manipulate a character in a three-dimensional world. Much of the gameplay involves manipulating the character to run, jump, tumble, and perform other athletic acts. Frequently, games require careful aiming and timing, or else the character misses the move and may suffer consequences that range from inconvenience to loss of a "life." These demands are particularly prevalent in side-scrolling games for early consoles, but they survive in the platformer genre in games like *Super Mario Sunshine*. For players to enjoy the game, they must become comfortable controlling the character, so that they're not constantly struggling just to execute the moves they want to make.

Some games, such as *Tomb Raider* and *Max Payne*, begin with a training course before the game begins. The player cannot start the game proper until he passes the training course and thus demonstrates that he has the at least enough understanding and skill to have a good shot at succeeding in the game.

In both *Tomb Raider* and *Max Payne*, successfully completing the training course is a pre-requisite to moving on. When these training courses are well designed, you can experiment as long as you want with the controls and devices made available to you, but you can also make your way through the course quickly if you're already skilled. The penalty for failure in a well-designed training course is low: if you're learning to jump, for example, a failed jump requires only a moment's effort before you can try again. The goal is to master skills quickly and efficiently and not suffer punishment for being unskilled.

Sometimes the training courses are offered to the player as an option, rather than a requirement. In the console game *The Legend of Zelda: Ocarina of Time*, there is an area where you can practice fighting with your sword and shield, but you don't have to go in if you don't want to. In contrast to most of the required training courses, you can return to this one during the game, as frequently as you like.

Another way to learn new skills is to start out with low-pressure, low-skill tasks. The game *Jak and Daxter: The Precursor Legacy* plays like a traditional platformer game requiring carefully-timed acts of skill, but the first couple of levels double as skill-building practice environments. They also contain some higher-skill areas, so you can see the sorts of things you're ultimately aspiring to.

Rule-Guessing Games

Some games deliver fun and novelty value by violating convention and making the players figure out the rules.

A famous game that goes by many names was taught to me as *My Aunt Millie*. Without any warning or setup, someone in a group starts to make statements about "My Aunt Millie." He tells everyone what she likes and dislikes, and the other people in the group have to discover first what's going on, and then why Millie has these odd preferences.

For example, I might say, "My Aunt Millie likes apples, but dislikes oranges," or "My Aunt Millie loves puppies and kittens, but can't stand cats and dogs." When someone thinks he understands what's happening, he can try offering a few statements of his own. If those statements prove that he does know what's happening, he becomes part of the inner circle and is then able to contribute his own original statements to the rest of the group. The game typically continues until everyone figures out what's happening.

In this example, Millie likes words that have the same letter appearing twice in a row and dislikes words that don't. There are as many variations on *My Aunt Millie* as people care to invent, from the nature of the words involved to the concepts (e.g., Millie likes cleaning products that contain lemon scent, or songs that were on the pop charts in 1985).

I include *My Aunt Millie* in the guessing-the-rules variety of game because the first time you see it played, it's quite mysterious. Typically it begins when someone in a group, without fanfare, starts saying things about his Aunt Millie. Usually it's not preceded by a statement like "Let's play a game," but just begins as a non-sequitur. As some people begin to pick it up and get it, the whole situation becomes even more baffling to the others, until finally each person figures out first of all that there's a game being played and then that there's some pattern going on. Knowing the rules, people start trying to figure out the commonalities among the things Aunt Millie likes. Until then, it's not quite clear what's going on, and that's part of the game as well.

Another game where part of the fun is in guessing the rules is *Eleusis*. In this game a dealer lays out cards from an ordinary deck using a secret rule of his own device, and players try to guess that rule.

Computer-based simulator games have made a lot of use of this sort of rule discovery. In *SimCity* you are in charge of growing and maintaining a city, given only a small amount of information about how to manage people and what they want. On a more personal scale, in *The Sims*, you're charged with maintaining the existence of simulated people living and working in a simulated world. Your goal is to keep them happy, healthy, and materially successful. This means that you need to understand the simulator and how it works. Although there are books that detail much of how *The Sims* works, you can do well without them, as long as you pay close attention to the game and learn from each experience.

Much of the computer game *Black & White* is about discovering the rules of the game. The central thread of the game is that you are given the task of raising a young creature to adulthood by teaching it moral lessons as it grows. You reward the behavior you want to encourage and punish the creature when it misbehaves. But you must also take care of more mundane matters such as making sure your creature has food to eat. This demand naturally leads one to wonder, "What does my creature like to eat? What is good for it? How much of this type of food is too much, and how much of that type of food is too little?" The game doesn't tell you these things except indirectly, as you play. When you've fed your creature a certain amount of food and he won't eat any more, that's your cue that he's had enough of it. Through endless trial and error and extensive testing of different objects and situations, you can learn the rules and techniques for successfully playing the game.

Winning

As I said before, the *point* of every game, though not the only reason we play, is to win. Of all the ways that one can win a game, three are the most common: survival, racing, and scoring.

Survival

Some games are won by simply outlasting all the other players. In these *survival* games, the winner is the last person still playing. Free-for-all paintball is this way. The specific mechanics of how you get to the end don't matter, as long as you're the last person remaining. You can shoot everyone throughout the game, or hide until the very end and then shoot your one remaining enemy. You don't get any credit for style or elegance in a pure survival game: being the last one left is all that matters, without regard to how you got there.

Many two-player board games are won by survival. In chess, for example, the player who first loses his king is eliminated from the the game, leaving the other player the winner.

Many word games are based on survival. In Geography, each player must name a city or country whose name begins with the last letter of the previously-named city or country. Failure to come up with a name in a short period of time, or repeating a previously-used name, causes you to lose your turn and drop out of the game. Players thus fall aside one by one until there are only two, and then just one.

Survival games can appear even in unexpected circumstances:

> Bob and Dave are sharing a tent deep in the midst of Spooky National Forest. In the middle of the night they're jolted awake by the loud snapping of a branch. Staring at each other in fear, they hear the unmistakable snuffling sounds of a big, heavy bear as he discovers their food sack and starts eating his way through

it. After a couple of heart-pounding minutes, they hear the bear throw away the food bag and then the heart-stopping sound of the still-hungry bear approaching their tent.

Instinctively, both men scramble out of their sleeping bags in nothing but their underwear. Bob unzips the tent, and as he dives through the flap, he looks back to check on his friend. To his horror, he sees Dave sitting on the ground, lacing up his sneakers.

"You're wasting time!" Bob cries. "Those won't help you outrun the bear!" Quickly lacing up his shoes, Dave says, "I don't have to outrun the bear. I only have to outrun you."

In survival games, the last man standing is the victor, regardless of how he manages it.

Racing

Another common way to win is to come in first in a *race*. Here the essential resource is time, and each competitor gets his own supply. The goal is to reach the finish line having consumed as little of this resource as possible.

Foot races and sailboat races are two of the many common types of races. Many board games are a race from the starting position to the end. *Pictionary* is won by the first team to get their marker to the goal position, and Chinese Checkers is won by the first player to get all of his stones into the other player's home court.

Some solitaire games are races as well. The computer game *Space Invaders* is a race to shoot down the ever-descending space invaders before they reach the ground.

Not all race games have an explicit finish line. The board game *Clue* is won by the first player to correctly deduce the facts of the crime being solved. In this game, victory still goes to the swiftest, but it can come at any time.

Scoring

The third common way to win a game is by having a better *score* when the game ends. A larger score is not always better. The classic example of this is golf, a game in which the winner is the player with the lowest score. In most games, however, a higher score is better.

Sometimes there are limits on possible scores. Continuing with golf as our example, players must take at least one stroke per hole. So the best possible score on an 18-hole course is 18.

Some games combine elements of scoring and racing by playing until one player's score reaches a *threshold*.

For example, according to the official rules of racquetball from the United States Racquetball Association [108], a game is won by the first player to reach 15 points. Some amateur players amend this rule so that a win has to be by two points, but the official rules accept a 15-14 score as a victory. A *match* is won by the first player to win two games. If after the first two games of the match have been completed, each player has won one game, then there is a third, 11-point tiebreaker. Thus the maximum number of points that any player can score in a match results from losing one game by one point, and winning the other two, for a total of 14+15+11=40 points. The rules simply don't allow for any more than that.

In other games, the rules don't impose any upper limit to how many points can be scored. Let's look at three different regulated sports.

The rules published by Major League Baseball [105] spell out various ways to win a game. If the score is tied after nine innings, the game keeps going until the home team gets an advantage, or the visiting teams has an advantage at the end of an inning. There is no provision that ends the game after a specific amount of time has passed. The rules do allow the umpire to call the game and terminate it at any time (whether or not a called game counts in the league standings is also spelled out). In practice, the highest total number of runs ever scored by both teams combined in a professional baseball game is 49 (the game was played on August 25, 1922 between the Chicago Cubs, who scored 26 runs, and the Philadelphia Phillies, who scored 23) [117]. The longest that a game ever lasted was 26 innings, when the game was called because of darkness (played on May 1, 1920, the game between the Brooklyn Dodgers and the Boston Braves was called in a 1–1 tie) [117]. The reason that baseball can theoretically allow an infinite score is because there is no time limit on the game.

In the rules of American soccer, as published by Major League Soccer [47], a game is composed of two 45-minute halves, with a potential of two extra 5-minute periods if the score is tied after the two major halves have ended. If the score is still tied at the end of those extra periods, the game ends and is declared a tie. The speed with which the ball can be moved up and down the field, coupled with these time limits, puts an upper bound on how many points can be scored before the clock runs out. The highest-scoring game ever played in the international World Cup competition was only 12 goals (the 1954 game had a final score of Austria 7, Switzerland 5) [80].

A blend between these two styles of gameplay appears in the rules published by the National Basketball Association [106]. The game is played in four 12-minute periods, and possible overtime periods. Though the game quarters are limited, the overtime periods could theoretically continue in number forever. Again, the physical limits of the game put an upper bound on how quickly points can be accumulated during gameplay: the highest-scoring professional basketball game ever played had a final combined score of 370 points (played on December 13, 1983, the game went into three overtimes before it was won by the Detroit Pistons with 186 points, over the Denver Nuggest with 184) [112].

Time limits play an active role in many games, both casual and professional. The board game *Pictionary* is timed by an hourglass. If the sand runs out before the word is guessed, no points are scored. Party games like Charades are often timed so that the party keeps moving, and many board games place an upper limit on how long a player can spend before he must make a move. Some professional sports also impose short-term limits: basketball places a 24-second clock on how long a team can possess the ball before it attempts to score.

As we've seen, unlimited points are only possible if the game allows an unlimited amount of time in which to score them. More usually, the number of points is bound by time and physical constraints, so that the winner is whoever has the most points when time runs out. Other games place an upper limit on how long each move can take, or use the fact that eventually both players run out of moves to bound the score (e.g., a game of Go is over when there are no more free intersections available).

The Appeal of Scoring

As every student knows, numerical scoring is a brutal way to have your abilities evaluated. A numerical score strips away all subtlety and nuance and boils down the rich complexity of any intellectual or physical activity to a raw number. Even enormously subjective activities like figure skating competitions eventually come down to one or two numbers per judge. Scores seem terribly inhumane.

Why then do almost all of our games use numerical scoring?

The tyranny of numerical scores continues because it oppresses everyone equally. The numerical score, in theory, removes elements like favoritism, wealth, prestige, and nepotism from games, replacing them with an objective standard that applies to everyone alike. Numerical scores theoretically do what many social systems aspire to do: they create meritocracies. The winner is the person with the better skills (or better luck), not the person who won last time, or who enjoys better connections, or has more powerful friends or higher social standing. Numerical scores give people who are new to a game a feeling that they have a fair shot at winning and those who have won a sense that they won purely by virtue of their abilities. Numerical scores equalize across social and political borders, ethnicities, races, and genders.

That's the theory. In practice, scores can be abused in many ways. Referees are human, some people always seem to get the benefit of the doubt, and some people even cheat. There's no question that sometimes games are won in underhanded or unfair ways or that some players are given advantages over others. But numerical scores endure because, when fairly implemented, they reward the person with greater skill and abilities with victory.

An exception to this principle is when a winner comes out ahead by virtue of having better luck, rather than skill. I'll return to the ideas of luck and chance below, but for now we can treat them as just another part of the game that, over the long run, skillful players are better able to turn to their advantage than unskilled ones.

Scores are not only useful for determining the winner of a game, but they also help provide comparisons among different players and teams. Professional sports track the records and abilities of players and teams with league standings. These standings form the basis for many different forms of gambling (which is a numbers game of its own), as well deciding who advances into post-season playoff games.

Amateur and informal players often organize themselves into "ladders" based on relative standings within the group. A player can move up the ladder by defeating the person above him or can drop down if he loses or doesn't play often enough to defend his position. The ladder system lets people see hard evidence of their improving skills.

Scores also provide a convenient way for amateurs and casual players to find competitive partners. Most players seek to play with others whose skills are at roughly the same level, or slightly better, than their own. If we play someone far better than we are, we get trounced, which isn't much fun. If we play someone far less skilled, then we trounce them, and that also isn't much fun (it's easy to win a footrace against a toddler, but why bother?). The best opponent is someone who's just a little better than we are. During the course of the game, we are challenged to perform at the limits of our abilities, and we can learn from our competitor and improve our own skills along the way. If we win, it's a significant victory, and if we lose, we've still become a better player as a result. Scores help us determine other people's skills and thus find appropriate opponents.

A numerical score is an objective, external quantification of our skill, but only in a general way. Numerical scores in any activity that involves human judgment, or luck, inherently contain a certain amount of "noise," or ambiguity. In games without these elements, such as chess, a win demonstrates unquestioned superior ability. It is rare for such wins to be flukes, though excellent players sometimes have off days, and players still learning a game can exhibit flashes of unexpected insight or ability beyond their norm.

In games with luck or subjective elements, a low-ranked player can sometimes defeat a far better player because of factors outside of the control of either. A great tennis player can lose a game because of a glaring sun or unexpected winds, and a skilled figure skater can get a low score because of a personal grudge from one of the judges. In any given game of backgammon, a great player can get a run of absolutely awful rolls of the dice while his far less skilled opponent gets exactly the right role every time. In these types of games, a single win doesn't tell us a lot about the relative skills of the two players.

That's why many matches are determined by playing groups of games, or sets. Racquetball sets are made up of two or three games. Tennis matches are made of sets, each of which goes to the player who wins a majority of the games. The idea is that these contests are long enough so that random events will happen in roughly equal numbers to both players, allowing the one with greater skill to emerge as the victor.

Accumulating Points

In many games, you can accumulate points only when it's your turn. For example, in bowling, the only pins you get credit for are the ones you knock down yourself.

In some games you can accumulate points or resources during other people's turns. In *Monopoly*, you can only buy new title deeds from the bank when you control the dice, and land on an unpurchased property. But you can still collect money on other people's turns, when they pay rent as a result of landing on your properties.

Some games are run in segments that don't correspond to anyone's "turn." In Roulette, everyone has an equal opportunity to place bets during the first few moments of the wheel's spin, but after a certain point no new bets may be placed. Anyone can win or lose on any spin of the wheel.

In some games, particularly those that are played with teams, there are no explicit turns. Rather, the team on offense is the one with control of a contested object (e.g., a ball or puck). In soccer, for example, maximizing the time you're in control of the ball is key to success, because when you're in control of the ball you have the chance to score. Because soccer is a timed game, every minute you keep the ball under your team's control is a minute it's unavailable to your opponent.

Control of the ball gives a team two advantages. First, you get to create scoring opportunities for your team. Second, you deprive the other team of finding those opportunities for itself. These advantages are obviously closely related but they're not identical. Sometimes it makes sense to control the ball even when there's no hope of scoring, just to run out the clock and keep it away from the other team.

High Scores

In games where players compete sequentially, a local *high score* record lets players see how they stack up relative to each other.

Many arcade games maintain a list of the top few players since the machine was last reset. When a player beats one of those highest scores, he is offered the chance to enter his name (or initials), which will then take their place in the list, bumping off at least one of the previous high scores and its associated name. This is an electronic form of the racquetball ladder I mentioned earlier.

Even solitaire games maintain a list of high scores. The word-guessing game *TextTwist* for PDAs and pocket computers keeps a high-score table, even though those devices are almost always used by only one person. This score record provides a convenient way to measure your progress as your skills improve.

Sometimes these personal and public high-score tables are merged. The video game *Metal Gear Solid 2* is a solitaire game, played typically at home over several days or weeks. When you successfully complete the game, the system gives you a long code number to write down. This code number contains your name, final score, and some game data in an encrypted form. If you then go to the game's public website and enter your code number, the system validates it and then posts your name and score in the public area. By visiting the web site, you can compare your performance with that of other players, and they can compare theirs with yours.

Since people generally strive to earn ever-higher scores, it seems only natural that some game manufacturers would do their best to accommodate them. Pinball machines have seen steady score inflation over the last decade. Hitting a bumper with the pinball was once worth a point, then 10, then 100, and now it's not unusual for a bumper to be worth 1,000 points or more. The final effect is to basically tack on a bunch of zeroes to the end of every final score, so that scores in the tens of millions are not unusual on many pinball machines these days.

⇒ 7 ⇐

Gameplay

M ost games are based on competition, either with other people or with ourselves. In some games we play as individuals, in others as groups. We can identify a few different ways that people typically organize themselves into teams to help them compete.

Competition

Solitaire: Solitaire games are a special case of play, in which there are no other players.

In a skill-based solitaire game like *Hi-Q*, we play against our own best record. In a sense we're competing against ourselves, attempting to improve our prior best performance.

In a card game of Klondike or *Freecell*, we're competing against the random arrangement of the cards. Essentially, we're hoping that through skill we can take an unpredictable arrangement of cards and turn them into a winning hand.

In many games, we are playing against the limits set by the game designer. For example, we might find ourselves in a 3D computer environment where we have to jump over a chasm and grab a hanging rope. If we manage this act of skill, we pass that piece of the game. Completing all the tasks completes the game. The final score often reflects our skill level by factoring in numbers such as the number of attempts to accomplish some tasks, and how well we actually executed them when we finally achieved them.

In many video games, we can easily see ourselves actually playing against the game designer, who is present through his choice of challenges, artificial intelligence, and other embodiments of his design.

Individual free-for-all: Individual games that are not solitary can be played in a free-for-all.

This category includes many first-person shooter games such as *Doom* and *Unreal Tournament 2003* that feature a *deathmatch* mode, in which many players wander the environment, each man out for himself and free to attack anyone else he sees.

Not all free-for-all games require attacking other players; some can be played in peaceful simultaneity. There can even be more than one winner. The game of Bingo incorporates both of these ideas, since several people can simultaneously get a Bingo when a particular number is called. They may even get the same pattern of bingo (e.g., a diagonal), so that they both win the same prize.

An individual free-for-all game that combines chance with skill is *Take It Easy*. In this game, every player starts with an empty board of 19 hexagonal cells. Players fill up the board by placing hexagonal tiles in these cells. Each tile has three different colored lines painted on it, and the goal is to place tiles in the cells to create lines of constant color. Like a Bingo caller, someone dips one at a time into a pool of 27 different tiles and announces the selected tile to the group. Each player places a copy of the announced tile in one of the empty cells on their board; once a tile is placed, it's fixed in position. Players try to position their tiles to build lines and keep their options open for new lines, to get as high a score as possible.

Persistent teams: In team games we form cooperative relationships with other people, working together to defeat the other teams. There may be many teams playing at once, though right now I'll focus on the common case where there are only two teams.

The teams in most games are *persistent,* which means that the team relationships stay the same throughout the game. For example, in *Pictionary* each group of two players remains a team from the start of the game to the end. Not all team members are always active. Baseball teams have only nine players in the field at any given time, but there are typically several more sitting on the bench. Over the course of the game, the manager can remove some players from the game and put in others, so the subset of the group on the field changes over time. But the teams themselves don't change, since players do not quit one team and join another during the course of the game.

In persistent teams the players typically have different roles. In soccer, for example, one player is the goalie, and he is dedicated to a purely defensive role. Some other players are primarily defensive or offensive, and some move between these roles as the situation demands.

In a persistent team, players work both together and individually. Sometimes one or more players may dominate the team. This may happen for many reasons, from heightened aggression or ego to a simple desire to use superior skills to help the team win. For example, a basketball player who is much better than his teammates may decide to shoot almost every time he gets the ball, rather than pass it to another player.

People don't generally appreciate this kind of behavior, and his teammates will likely see him as a selfish player. After all, they want to enjoy their gameplay as well, and they want both to contribute and to be seen as contributors. Even if the dominant player is much better than the rest of the team, and the team as a whole wins because of his singular effort, many of the other players will still resent him.

Such dominance can cause the team to fragment. Rather than completely cooperating, each player starts to look out for himself and effectively becomes a one-man team, competing with his teammates for an opportunity to demonstrate his skills and be seen as a good player. Thus what began as a cooperative group changes into an internally competitive one, yet at the same time the team is competing externally against another team. Coaches work hard to keep teams from dissolving in this way.

169

Part of the pleasure of winning as a team is the group experience, which leads to feeling like you've accomplished something together with colleagues that none of you could have done alone. This sense of cooperation is a strong emotional incentive for people to put forth their best effort. So although the overall point of the game is to win, each member of the team wants to feel like he is important and useful as an individual as well as a member of the group.

Since a team is a social construct (and sometimes also a professional one), it's important that teammates feel a sense of mutual confidence and respect for each other. Developing and maintaining these relationships is an important part of creating a strong team. For these reasons and others, players who are much better than their teammates will often use their talents to create opportunities for their teammates to develop and contribute.

A common theme behind team play is that "when the team wins, everyone wins." For players to truly feel like they share in the victory, they need to feel like they shared in the effort. This doesn't require a high-visibility contribution. Even players who never play a minute can feel that they share in a victory because they helped with the training or other preparations or played some other important support role.

Dynamic teams: In contrast to the persistent teams in baseball or basketball, in some games the team composition can change over the course of the game.

The board game *Diplomacy* gives players the chance to simulate international political negotiations during war as they attempt to gain territory and hold control over it. Players spend much of their time between moves in huddles and confidential conversations, creating political alliances and treaties with other players. They commonly negotiate time-limited non-aggression pacts, and agree on plans to work together against common enemies. Those players are effectively forming a temporary team by virtue of their cooperation. Because the number and composition of such teams changes over the course of the game, I call them *dynamic* teams.

After a non-aggression pact has run its course, former allies may become sworn enemies. Each may then align himself with a former enemy, completely changing the allegiances in the game. And a player may betray the trust of his allies and reveal information about their plans to other players, or even openly attack when their teammate's defenses are vulnerable.

The "teams" in *Diplomacy* are temporary because players that worked together for a common goal at one point may find themselves rivals a little later.

Multiple teams: Some games allow for multiple teams to play at the same time.

For example, *Pictionary* allows several teams to compete at once. They don't all act at the same time, though, but take turns. Thus *Pictionary* is a sequential game. On the other hand, in a relay race, multiple teams compete simultaneously, with runners tearing down the track alongside seven or eight others.

Both of these examples are racing games: the first team to the goal wins. Multiple teams can also compete against one another in accumulation games. For example, in the game *Everquest* players move through a 3D world populated by a wide variety of fantasy creatures. Most players seek to rise in stature and power, which can be achieved by acquiring special goods and defeating powerful monsters. To bring down the largest beasts, groups of players often band together to pool their talents. By cooperating, they are able to defeat creatures that would be far too powerful for any one of them to beat alone, and together they share in the spoils of their victory.

Cooperation

When a team is running smoothly, the members cooperate with each other in order to bring about a shared victory.

In team solitaire games, people cooperate as a team, but they're not competing against any other people. Their opponent is the game itself, just as a player of Klondike solitaire is effectively competing against the random draw of the cards that make up his hand.

For example, consider the installation game *Pirates of the Caribbean: Battle for Buccaneer Gold*, at DisneyQuest in Orlando, Florida.

To start the game, several players enter a small room that is decorated to look like the prow of a pirate ship. A steering wheel and throttle are mounted near the rear center of the "ship." One player is selected by the group to be the "captain," and he takes control of the wheel and throttle. The rest of the players become the ship's crew and arrange themselves near two sets of cannons, one placed on each side of the ship. Each cannon has a rope attached to its rear. When a player pulls the rope, the cannon launches a cannonball. The cannons can swivel left, right, up, and down so that they can be easily aimed.

When the game begins, the floor starts to rock as though the ship were at sea and computer-generated graphics of other pirate ships appear on the walls. The captain's job is to steer the ship up close to these other pirates, so that the crew can then destroy them with cannon fire. Each time the crew sinks another ship, they capture the gold that ship was carrying. The game is time-limited: after the team has fought pirates for a while, the pirate captain emerges for a climactic confrontation. The final score of the group is determined by how many enemy ships the team managed to sink. Since there is only one team, and everyone works together, this is a completely cooperative game [122].

Another cooperative game at DisneyQuest is called the *Virtual Jungle Cruise*. In this experience, players board a rubber raft like that used to float down a river. Each player is given a paddle that has been instrumented so that a computer can read how it's used. The raft sits above a mesh of air-filled fabric balloons that can be inflated or deflated quickly to simulate the motion of water under the raft.

When the ride starts, the walls around the raft light up with computer-generated 3D graphics of a jungle river. The players see a cartoon character accidentally drop a precious gadget into the river; they are then given the job of chasing it. The raft starts floating down the river, and the fabric balloons underneath quickly fill and empty, causing the raft to roll and sway in a way that feels like a real raft on rushing water. By stroking their paddles against the balloons, players are able to guide the raft down the river. As they chase the gadget, they steer around creatures and other obstacles and navigate forks in the river.

The game is over when the players reach the end of the river, whether or not they've managed to retrieve the gadget along the way.

Both *Pirates of the Caribbean: Battle for Buccaneer Gold* and the *Virtual Jungle Cruise* are cooperative team games in which there are no losers. Although score is kept, it's clear from watching people play that the appeal of these attractions comes from the activity itself, not the final score. The journey is the purpose of these games, as is the chance to work cooperatively with friends, family, and even strangers in a situation in which competence is rewarded, but low competence is not punished. Players are carried along by the game, and their fun comes from sharing the experience with other people.

Parallel Competition

Most organized team sports, like football and tennis, involve *confrontational competition*: the two teams face each other and fight for resources. In *parallel competition* players are still competing with each other, but they're not directly confronting one another.

In a typical road rally, an arbitrary number of two-man teams competes against each other simultaneously. They're all trying to drive from the start of the course to the finish and perhaps to collect objects or evidence of their travels along the way. Some teams never see another team until they arrive at the final destination.

Swim meets also use parallel competition, because the swimmers are explicitly separated from each other by buoyed ropes. There are psychological elements involved in a swim meet, and many swimmers regulate their energies based on what they see the others doing. But in theory, each swimmer could simply swim his best race and then discover what the other people were doing only when he came up for air at the end. By contrast, you couldn't even be theoretically ignorant of the other players while playing basketball.

The county fair bake-off is also based on parallel competition. People come to the fair and bake their best cherry pie. Then the judges come around, taste the pies, and choose their favorite. The competing pie-makers may have strong personal feelings for their competitors, and they may try to tune their recipes to the tastes of the judges, but they typically don't deliberately interfere with each other's work. Winning isn't dependent on taking resources away from other players; everyone works simultaneously and separately.

Luck and Chance

Some games, such as Go and chess, are based entirely on the skill of the competitors. Some other games, such as flipping a fair coin, are about nothing except random chance. Many games are somewhere between these two extremes, combining chance and skill.

The term *chance* describes random happenings in the world. So when we roll a pair of fair dice, there are equal chances that they will come up as double threes as that they will come up as double sixes. There's no value judgment associated with chance.

By contrast, the term *luck* is our personal interpretation of chance. Suppose we're playing a dice game and really want to roll a five while also hoping we don't get a pair of ones. The pips that come up on the dice are the result of chance. If we get that five, that's good luck for us, but bad luck for our opponent. Similarly, if we get the snake eyes we feared, that's bad luck for us, but good luck for him. Luck is our subjective interpretation of chance, and the same chance outcome can be viewed as a different kind of luck by different players.

Because the two ideas are so similar, depending on the context it sometimes feels more appropriate to speak of luck rather than chance, and sometimes vice-versa.

Chance plays a role in almost any game played in a physical environment. In outdoor tennis, a player can miss a shot because he was blinded when the sun emerged from behind a cloud, or a shot heading into the net could actually clear it because of a sudden gust of wind. Or the ball can take an unpredictable bounce on the ground, hitting a soft spot of dirt or a small stone, and thus make an otherwise easy return much harder or even impossible. By their very nature these chance elements can be anticipated but not counted on. When they enter the game, the best a player can do is to try to recognize them and compensate for them.

Many games are made interesting by deliberately combining elements of chance and skill.

Types of Chance

Players can encounter different types of chance in their games. Some forms of chance add a little bit of unpredictable spice to what is largely a game of skill. On the other hand, some forms of chance so dominate the game that the outcome has little to do with the players.

There is no "best" amount or type of chance for any game. It's a matter of taste: different people enjoy having different amounts of randomness in their games at different times.

Built-in chance: Dependence on pure chance can be built into the very rules of a game.

Roulette follows no rules but those of probability: no "system" will ever beat the roulette table over the long run. No strategy can improve your long-term winnings, and no amount of experience can make you a better player. In the short term, you can bet on specific numbers and win on every spin of the wheel, but in a fair game eventually the odds will catch up with you and the house will take those gains away.

Any game with cards or dice has an element of chance built into it. A skilled poker player can reliably beat a beginner in the long run, but if they play only a few hands, the experienced player might get junk every time while the newcomer gets a full house on each hand. All other things being equal, over a period of time the chances will even out and favor (or disfavor) each player equally.

Consider the game of backgammon. Each turn begins with a roll of a pair of dice, dictating which moves are allowed. Skilled players try to distribute their pieces so they will be able to benefit from whatever rolls may come. But every now and then, every backgammon player finds himself in a game where he just can't catch a break: every roll he gets is the most useless possible roll, while his opponent gets exactly the most useful roll for himself every time. Nobody likes to be trounced like this, but it happens because of the chance element inherent in the dice. Over the long run, a better player will win more often than a lesser player, but chance can determine the winner in any particular game.

The game of *Scrabble* has a random component in the tiles you pick. If you happen to find yourself able to make the word QUIXOTIC and cover a triple-word-score bonus square in the bargain, that's good luck. If you have a rack full of As and Es and can't use them anywhere on the board, that's just bad luck.

Changing environment: Any game with a physical component can be affected by changes in the environment.

Suppose you're playing soccer on a rainy day. Advancing down the field, you find yourself alone, with nobody between you and the goal but the goalie. You fake to the right, and the goalie takes the bait, leaving the left side of the goal wide open. You straighten out, and as pull your foot back to smash the ball into the net and score, you feel your foot slide in the mud under you. Suddenly you're in the air, and then you land with a crash on your backside as you watch the goalie easily trot up to the untouched ball and send it back down to the other end of the field. Running into that spot of mud was just bad luck.

Environmental changes can affect any game with a physical component. Suppose you're playing checkers with a friend over at his house, and you're only a couple of moves from victory. Suddenly his kids come tearing into the room, chasing one another, and one of them bumps into the table, sending the checkers flying. By the time you get everything cleaned up, both you and your friend have forgotten the exact position of the game and decide you'll have to start over. That's bad luck for you, good luck for him.

The environment need not even be real. Many console and computer games take place in a simulated 3D environment. At one point in the game *Final Fantasy X*, players must pass through a region called the Thunder Plains, where lightning strikes are common. You can dodge a strike if you're fast enough, but sometimes your fingers aren't poised on the controller buttons just right, and you can't evade a lighting strike. If you get hit, you get hurt: that's just bad luck. In the game *SimCity*, occasionally disasters like earthquakes and tornadoes strike your growing, simulated city. If a disaster happens to take out all of your power-generating plants, you'll be in deep trouble. No matter how you try to plan for chance events, they can still be devastating precisely because they are so unpredictable.

Changes to the environment need not have an extreme effect on the game. Instead, they might simply make some activities easier or harder. In *Grand Theft Auto III*, you steal cars in order to drive around town and accomplish your missions. Sometimes you need a particular kind of car to accomplish a particular mission: for example, to win some of the races, you need a very fast car. You might have to spend a lot of time prowling the city looking for one of these to steal, or one might be driving by just when you need it. Although the game designers have tried to make it possible to conveniently get what you need most of the time, there's still an element of luck involved while searching for the right kind of car.

Calculated risk: Sometimes we can create opportunities for luck to help us, and take a calculated risk that it won't.

Suppose you're in a road rally and fear you've fallen far behind everyone else. Your map shows a road that would cut an hour off your driving time to the next checkpoint, but the road is marked as under construction. If you head for that road and it's open, it could help get your team back in the running. But if it's closed, you'll have to backtrack to where you turned off, putting you even further behind than you were before.

You can try to estimate the risk. Perhaps you notice that the map is two years old, and so you reason that's been long enough to finish construction. On the other hand, you're not driving in an affluent city, so perhaps there weren't enough funds to finish the road. You just have to make your best guess and then hope for good luck.

Calculated risks are at the heart of the board game *Risk*. Your goal is to take over other countries by defeating their armies. Battles are fought by rolls of the dice, and in general large armies will defeat smaller ones. But over the short term, the dice can deliver unusual results, and even a large invader can find himself decimated by a small foe. Players need to constantly assess how much they're willing to lose on the next roll of the dice.

Opponent error: Sometimes you get ahead when the other guy makes a mistake. Since you didn't cause his error, that's just good luck for you.

For example, suppose that you're batting in a game of baseball and you hit a line drive to the shortstop. The ball is coming right to him, so he should be able to just scoop it up, throw it to first base, and make an easy out.

But suppose the ball hits a rock and suddenly careens in another direction, evading the shortstop. Then you may have time to get to first base before the outfielders are able to get to the ball and throw it to second base. That's a piece of good environmental luck for you.

But let's suppose there's no rock, and the ball flies right into the shortstop's glove. He stands up, pulls the ball from his glove, and drops it. It rolls around a bit, and once again you have enough time to get to first base.

Your good luck here was that the shortshop simply fumbled the ball. His error is your gain. The scoring system for baseball tries to account for this situation so that you don't actually benefit statistically from his mistake. The shortstop gets a formal error assigned to him, and you don't get credit for a base hit. In fact, the three numbers that summarize most baseball games are "runs, hits, and errors," emphasizing that although the game is won by having more runs, the winning team might only have gotten those because the losing team essentially gave them up.

In shooting games like paintball, or its computer versions like *Unreal Tournament 2003*, you can also benefit from an opponent's mistakes. Your opponent may have a weapon at the ready when you encounter him, but he may have forgotten to reload it, making him a temporarily easy target. The result is that you get the drop on him and can shoot or not as you please, but it's not reflective of your better skill as much as his error.

Teammate error: A teammate's error is a frustrating form of bad luck.

Suppose you're playing doubles tennis and your partner moves to get out of the way of the ball, but accidentally steps right where you need to swing your racket. You check your swing at the last moment and the ball goes by you, winning the other team a point.

A teammate's error can be part of a larger pattern. You might go a games party one night and join up in a game of *Trivial Pursuit*, where the teams are picked at random. After the game has begun, you notice that your partner has missed every geography question so far, and you realize he doesn't know a thing about the subject. Even through you're a geography whiz, your teammate's inabilities will cost you both, since you're dependent on one another.

Self error: The most frustrating form of bad luck is when you cause it yourself. Technically, you can't cause bad luck to happen to yourself, but you can put yourself into a position where you are suddenly dependent on good luck to get through a tricky situation.

For example, in *Asteroids*, you fly a little spaceship around the screen and try to blow up all the rocks floating around you. Each time you blow up a big asteroid, it splits into smaller pieces. Blowing those smaller rocks and up splits them into yet smaller pieces. Eventually the pieces get so small that when you hit them, they just disappear. Your goal is to clear the screen of all the asteroids by repeatedly splitting them apart and then taking out the smallest ones.

Although the asteroids are initially flying around at random, when they're hit they break apart in predictable ways. A good player can assess the starting situation and then methodically fly around the asteroids, clearing screen after screen. But what if you find yourself in the middle of a circle of asteroids, all heading towards you? There's nowhere to run.

This would be an ideal time to use the *hyperspace* button: if you press it, you get teleported to another, random place on the screen. Upon arrival there, you are briefly protected by your shields so that you can get your bearings. Typically, you can only invoke the hyperspace jump once per "life." The trouble with hyperspace is that it can land you in a situation as bad as, or even worse than, the one you left. Most players treat hyperspace as an emergency escape of last recourse.

A similar teleportation technique is available in the game *Seven Seas*. The goal of this game is to navigate your sailing ship through a grid representing the ocean, while evading and destroying the pirates who are out to get you either by firing your cannons at them or by causing them to crash into each other and into islands. If you get into trouble, you can sail into a whirlpool, which will take you to another, random place in the ocean. But, as in *Asteroids*, you may find your new position no better than the last.

In both of these games it's certainly a stroke of bad luck if we teleport into worse trouble than we were in before. Such situations can upset us not just because of the bad luck, but because we've allowed ourselves to have to resort to that teleportation in the first place.

Amount of Chance

There are two aspects to how chance contributes to a game: the nature of the chance, and how much that chance matters.

War	Mastermind	Backgammon	Klondike	Chess
No Chance				All Chance
		Amount of Chance		

Figure 7.   The amount of chance in different games.

In the last section we looked at several different ways that chance can impact a game. Let's now look at a variety of games that use different amounts of chance, from a game that is nothing but chance to a game that is nothing but skill.

Figure 7 shows these games plotted according to the amount of chance they use.

The role of chance can be complex or subtle, and it can be hard to decide how big a role chance plays in a game. A simple test is to ask how much experience counts. In other words, can we expect that a more experienced player will regularly defeat another who's less experienced?

Suppose we play the simple coin-tossing game Heads or Tails: you'll throw a fair coin in the air, and I'll guess which way will land. No matter how much we play, I won't get any better at this game. At the other extreme, we could play Go, where the player with a lot of experience will defeat the player with less experience almost every time. We'd say that Heads or Tails is at the high end of the spectrum, and Go is at the low end.

The Degrees of Chance

Pure chance: The children's card game War is all chance.

> In War, a full deck of cards is shuffled, and half the cards are dealt face-down to each of the two players. The players then each turn over the top card on their stacks and lay them side by side. Whoever plays the card with a higher value takes them both (ties go to the winner of the next hand, or "battle"). When one player uses up his original allotment of cards, he shuffles the cards he has won and continues to play, dealing from them. The loser is the first person to run out of cards. There's no strategy to this game, and no way to improve one's performance based on skill. It's just pure luck from start to finish.

A lot of chance: Some games are mostly luck but reward some skill. These are the games at which you can expect to become better after you've

180

become familiar with the game, but your experience can only improve your average performance a little bit.

Take the classic patience solitaire card game of Klondike. Once the cards are dealt out into a hand, the rules are pretty simple. Although there are choices to make and one can try to use strategy, any given move that advances the game towards victory is about as good as any other.

But traditional, strict Klondike is not an easy game to win: only about 3 hands out of 100 can be won, even if you know all the cards and play perfectly. To make the game more fun, there are several common variations, such as turning the stock cards over only one at a time or allowing redeals from the stock once it's depleted. People who have played this game a lot are a little bit better (that is, they win a little more frequently) than those who haven't. But generally, practice at Klondike does not lead to significant improvement in the chances of winning.

Some chance: In backgammon, you can only move your pieces as directed by the roll of the dice. And yet, backgammon tournaments demonstrate that some players can routinely defeat most other players. Are they just very lucky?

Probably not. Over the course of many games, the odds should even out, and these winning players ought not to have any advantage just from luck. Advanced backgammon players are able to control their pieces so that they always have a good strategy available to them, whatever the next roll may bring. They also know which rolls are more likely on any throw of the dice.

A similar situation applies to the card game 21. Nobody knows what the next card will be, so any time you draw a card to a hand of twelve or more, you're taking a risk. Some people can reduce that risk by "counting cards," watching the cards as they're played and remembering them. This strategy allows them to determine what's likely to come next. Advanced counters can use quite sophisticated techniques to improve the odds in their favor [94].

Tetris is another game where the job of the player is largely to constantly evolve a strategy based on chance occurrences. In *Tetris*, you must create rows of squares by maneuvering randomly-generated pieces as they fall from the top of the screen.

Novice players often leave holes in their rows that are perfectly shaped for one of the Tetris pieces. They reason that when that piece arrives, they will clear a large number of rows at once. This strategy not only gets them a big bonus and clears up the board, but it's a fun sight to see. These players quickly learn, however, that all too often that essential piece doesn't arrive in a timely manner, and in order to deal with the other pieces as they drop, they are forced to cover up the carefully-crafted hole, so that by the time the desired piece does arrive, it can't be used as intended and is just another random shape to manage.

A good player knows how to build his rows so that he can deal with whatever comes and not fall too far behind. In some versions of *Tetris*, the pieces fall faster with each new level, until finally they're dropping like a rainstorm of anvils and the board fills up almost instantly. In other versions the pieces do not speed up, and experienced players can keep a single round going as long as they wish.

There are many computer games that present a randomized challenge like that of *Tetris* but remove the time pressure. For example, in *Alchemy*, the player's goal is to place randomly-generated tiles on a square grid. There are rules on where tiles can be placed depending on their markings and which tiles are already on the board. The tiles arrive in random order, but you can take as long as you like to consider where you want to make your next move.

Another game like this is *Battleship*. There are many ways to start a game of *Battleship*. The best way to get going is to have some lucky hits right away. Then you can apply any one of a variety of strategies to isolate and sink your opponent's ships [55]. If you're outrageously lucky, you could sink every one of your opponent's ships while never firing a miss; if you're incredibly unlucky, then your strategy reveals his ships at the slowest possible rate.

A little luck: In the game *Mastermind*, one player creates a hidden code and the other player tries to guess it. The game is largely one of logic and reasoning, but there is a little bit of luck involved. For example, it is possible (though very unlikely) for a player to guess the complete code correctly on his very first guess. If the two players know each other well, there may also be an element of psychology in the game, as players deliberately try to trick each other based on their shared history.

Adding a little bit of chance to a game can give it some spice and challenge.

The solitaire computer toy *SimCity* is largely about creating a thriving city. But every now and then unexpected disasters strike, and the player must scramble to get things back to normal again as quickly as possible.

No luck: Some games are so abstract and deep that they are largely unpredictable even without any chance elements.

In the West, the classic game of pure skill is chess. In the East, it's Go. Both of these games have relatively simple rules but quickly develop complex relationships among pieces. Although chess and Go masters often carry a wealth of opening, mid-game, and end-game positions and strategies in their heads, they still find themselves challenged when playing opponents of equal or greater skill. Many books have been written on the strategy and tactics of these games, and many more are sure to come.

In these games, a skilled player can reliably defeat one that is less skilled.

There's an interesting problem that arises from games with no element of chance: they run the risk of being completely mastered.

For example, children enjoy playing Tic-Tac-Toe (also known as Noughts and Crosses), but adults rarely play. That's because it's easy to master the game, thereby removing all the challenge. Played correctly, Tic-Tac-Toe always ends in a tie.

Some computer scientists are fascinated by the idea of solving games. The classic African game Mancala (or Awari) has recently been solved [62]. Played perfectly, this game always ends in a draw.

The game of Checkers recently matured to the point where there is no longer any challenge between skilled players. The best players are so good, and they understand the mechanics of the game so well and have studied so many positions, that actually playing the game seems like simply acting out a foregone conclusion. From the starting position, every move results in a familiar arrangement of pieces for which they already know the best response. Professional checker players and the tournaments in which they played were in danger of disappearing. To prevent the game from withering and to encourage new players to take up the game, the rules were changed [120]. Professional checkers games now begin with a position chosen at random from a large, carefully-crafted collection of partly-played games.

The idea is that these randomly-selected board positions are sufficiently complex and unfamiliar to the pros that they will be challenged, and newcomers won't suffer quite as much of a handicap because they lack an encyclopedic knowledge of openings.

In contrast to these developments, computer scientists have recently proven that there is no optimal way to play *Tetris*, even if you know in advance the entire sequence of blocks that are going to fall [38].

Game Theory

In the 1940s, the mathematician John von Neumann started studying the structure of games [95]. He looked at a variety of simple games and developed ways to characterize them in the precise and formal language of mathematics. In the process, he created a new branch of mathematics that is now called *game theory*.

The goal of game theory is to understand how people should act in situations in which they are in competition with others. Game theorists usually assume that everyone involved in the conflict will act purely out of reason, so psychological issues like friendship, loyalty, rivalry, spite, and revenge are considered irrelevant. Game theorists usually begin with a game with simple rules and clear-cut, numerical costs and benefits, and ask how people *ought* to behave in order to maximize their results.

The Prisoner's Dilemma

A classical example of game theory is an ingenious little problem called the *Prisoner's Dilemma* [6]. Here's one way to pose the problem.

> It's a beautiful day and Lou is walking to the park. As he crosses the street a police car suddenly appears, its lights flashing, and pulls up alongside him. The police jump out and

search Lou, place him under arrest for jaywalking, and take him back to the station house.

After sitting in a cell all afternoon, Lou gets a visit from the district attorney. Lou demands to know why he's been arrested simply for jaywalking. The DA takes a chair, looks Lou in the eye, and lays out the situation.

"The First Federal Bank was robbed this morning by two crooks. We got there too late to stop them, but witnesses described one of them as short and fat and the other as tall and thin. You fit the first description perfectly, which is why you're here now. Luckily, we also picked up another guy named Bud who fits the other description while he was cutting across a different street. Jaywalking is way out of control in this town."

"This is an election year," he continues, "and I need a high-profile conviction in this robbery. There were no guns involved, and only twenty dollars was stolen, so I don't feel I have to send anyone to jail for a long time for this. What's really important is that I get a conviction, and I can show the public I caught at least one of the perpetrators. So I'm going to make you a deal."

"Jaywalking is a serious crime. I could put you in jail for a week on that charge, and I will. I regret that's all I can do to you, but without some kind of confession, I'd have to let you go after a week. But if you confess to robbing the bank with Bud, and Bud says nothing, I'll let you go free right now as thanks for your cooperation, and I'll put him in jail for 20 years. Now it would be even better for me to get two convictions, so if you *both* confess, I'll send you both to jail, but I promise that I'll get you paroled after just one year."

"My assistant is right now offering exactly the same deal to Bud. Neither of you can talk to the other. We're going to leave you alone for five minutes to think over what you want to do."

Suppose that Lou feels that he can trust the DA, that the deal is legitimate, and that in fact Bud is facing the very same decision. What should he do?

The deal as presented is a lot of information to try to hold in our heads at once. The classic way to get a handle on this problem is draw a *payoff*

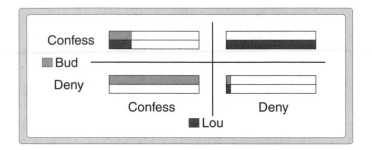

Figure 8.   A payoff table for the Prisoner's Dilemma.

table that shows what will happen to the two players in our drama based on their actions. Each player can either stay silent or confess, so there are four possible results in the payoff table. Figure 8 summarizes the situation.

Let's look at Lou's choices. If Bud confesses, Lou's best choice is to confess as well, and thus go to jail for only one year rather than 20. If Bud instead stays silent, Lou's best choice is again to confess, and thus go free rather than spend a year in jail. Remember that Lou is acting entirely rationally, so that any feelings he may or may not have for Bud are irrelevant. He's also unable to talk to Bud, so he has to make his choice based just on this information. Based on this analysis, no matter what Bud does, Lou's best bet is to confess.

Since Bud is looking at the very same deal, he would come to the same conclusion that his best option is also confession.

But if they both confess, they both end up going to jail for a year. If instead they both stayed silent, they would each spend only a week in jail.

This is the dilemma that the prisoners face. Unless they can get together and talk about the situation, they're in trouble. Each individual's best course of action is to confess. But if they both confess, they end up with a worse result for both of them than if they had both stayed silent.

The DA seems to have the game rigged in his favor, even though he appears to be offering the men a choice. Since nobody wants to go to jail for 20 years, they both confess and end up in jail for one year. Were they able to trust each other, they'd both stay silent and be free in a week.

There's no best solution to the Prisoner's Dilemma. It's tricky to analyze (you may have noticed that the Prisoner's Dilemma is not a zero-sum game). In a situation like this, each player has to look out for himself, even though that puts them both in jail for a year.

Game theorists have studied this problem and variations on it for years. A common variation is the *Iterated Prisoner's Dilemma*, where our two players play the game over and over again (using points to keep score, not years in jail!). Now issues like trustworthiness and selfishness start to appear, but again still in a completely rational way. Players can then adapt their strategies based on what they see the other person doing.

For example, they may play the game many times and realize that they can each trust the other to stay silent. Then one of the players will decide to betray the other, so that he can go free immediately. The next time they play, the other player will probably retaliate. Over time, different strategies will lead to different idiosyncratic patterns of trust, betrayal, retaliation, and sometimes even sacrifice to regain trust.

Following the Rules

Game theory is rooted in the idea that if you know the rules of a game, you can use those rules to help you decide what to do next. Sometimes you can even determine what's called a *dominant strategy*: a course of action that you know is your very best choice, no matter what the other guy does.

In other situations, two players can arrive at an *equilibrium*, where each player's move just balances that of the other.

Game theory is of limited value in real games for a few reasons. The biggest problem is that it's limited to games where each player can assign a numerical cost and reward to each action he might take and to each possible action of his competitors. Such costs are often hard to determine. Another problem is that you need to be very confident that you can make the move you plan. In a game like checkers, this isn't a problem, but in skill games like tennis, it's much harder to be certain that you can execute a move just the way you intend. It might be worthwhile sometimes to make a move that is less than optimal but that you're sure you can pull off, rather than attempt a better move that might fail.

What Am I Bid for a Hundred Dollars?

Game theory is based on the idea that we can expect everyone to behave in rational ways. This assumption can sometimes lead to surprising results, as illustrated in an odd kind of auction first studied by Martin Shubik [124]. The story below shows the basic idea:

Mack the Knife is on his way to the monthly meeting of the Opera Society when he finds a perfectly legitimate hundred-dollar bill lying on the sidewalk. Nobody else is anywhere around, so Mack decides that it's honorable to simply pocket the cash.

The only problem is that Mack's horoscope this morning told him not to accept any free gifts today. Regretfully, he decides that this found money would qualify as a free gift, and so he has to get rid of it. But Mack figures that if he can *sell* the bill, then the proceeds from the sale wouldn't be a gift, and he could keep those. By the time he reaches the Opera Society meeting, he has decided that he'll auction the money off.

Before the society meeting, Mack announces his auction but says that he's adding a little twist to the rules. Just as in a normal auction, the person who has made the highest bid when the auction closes will pay Mack the amount of his bid, and Mack will give him in exchange the hundred-dollar bill. But Mack will also collect the bid from the first runner-up. So even though the person who comes in second will get nothing at all in return, he still has to hand over to Mack the entire amount of his second-place bid. Nobody has to play, but anyone who makes a bid is agreeing to the rules of the auction and is promising to pay up if he comes in first or second. None of the other losing bidders need to pay Mack their bids.

Mack then asks the crowd if anyone wants to bid on his hundred-dollar bill. Someone raises his hand and bids a dime. Then the bids start to accumulate: twenty cents here, fifty cents there, and then a dollar or two. Eventually Bert raises his hand and bids twenty dollars. His friend Ernie raises that to twenty-one.

Now that there's some real money at play, Bert starts to think about how to respond to Ernie's bid. If he quits now and lets Ernie win, he will have to fork over his second-place 20-dollar bid to Mack, and he'll have nothing to show for it. But if he raises the bid, say to 22 dollars, then if he wins he'll get the hundred, so he'll still be 78 dollars ahead. He reasons that making 78 dollars is a lot better than losing 20, so he raises the bid to 22 dollars.

Ernie, reasoning the same way, raises again to 23 dollars. Locked in combat, these two keep raising each other until Ernie bids 99 dollars. Because Bert doesn't want to lose his 98 dollars, he bids a hundred. He figures that will be his last bid; after all, who would pay more than a hundred dollars for a hundred-dollar bill?

But then Ernie realizes that he's trapped. If he doesn't bid anything, Bert wins. Bert won't win much, because he'll be paying a hundred dollars to get a hundred dollars. But regardless of Bert's spoils, Ernie will now be out 99 dollars. On the other hand, if he raises the bid to 101 dollars, and wins, then he'll only be out one dollar. The choice between losing 99 dollars and losing one dollar is clear: he must bid.

And so it goes. The fact that the bidding for this hundred-dollar bill has passed beyond a hundred dollars has no relevance. Neither bidder can afford to lose what he's bid so far, and must continue to raise.

At the end of the evening Mack walks home with a few thousand dollars from the auction of his hundred-dollar bill.

Mack's strategy of taking the money from the second-place bidder completely transformed this auction. The sky's the limit in this game, with the bidding only stopping when either Bert or Ernie runs out of money.

What would have been a better strategy here? One approach would be collusion. All the members of the Society (except Mack) could have huddled before the auction started and agreed that one of them will bid a penny and the rest will refrain from bidding at all, and then they'll split up the hundred dollars among them.

If for any reason they don't make a deal like this before the bidding starts, the best course of action is to stop the auction after one bid. In our example, someone offered a dime as the opening bid, and rationally speaking, that should have been the end of it. As soon as a second person entered the bidding, it became a never-ending escalator ride.

The problem with not raising after the first bid of a dime is that it relies on entirely rational thinking. Most of us would be reluctant to let the guy next to us walk away with a hundred dollar bill for just ten cents, and we would be willing to give up a quarter or two to prevent such an easy and undeserved profit. People also get into bidding wars fuelled by human factors like ego and saving face.

Once the bidding starts to climb in this game, people could reasonably be expected to see what was happening and drop out, rather than chase the high bid all the way to the moon. Quitting partway and losing ten dollars could be reasonably seen to be a much smarter strategy than staying in the game and losing much more.

Threats and Promises

One player can attempt to influence another by making a statement about his future actions. In effect he creates a new rule for himself and promises to be bound by it. Suppose that Frank is attempting to get his son Sam to behave in specific ways. In game theory terms, we might say that Frank is trying to enlist Sam's cooperation.

Frank might decide to tell Sam that if he doesn't raise his grades, he'll punish him. In this case, Frank is issuing a *threat*. If he instead announces that good grades will be rewarded with an increased allowance, he's making a *promise*. Both threats and promises are designed try to get the other player to cooperate. Let's look at each of these more closely.

Threats try to force cooperation by invoking the fear of punishment. There are two types of threats, depending on whether the party issuing the threat is trying to make the other party take a particular action or refrain from taking an action.

A *compellent threat* is an inducement to cause someone to take an action he otherwise might not. For example, Frank could tell Sam that if he doesn't clean up his room, he'll be grounded for a week. Frank's compellent threat is designed to get Sam to take a specific action.

On the other hand, a *deterrent threat* is designed to prevent behavior from happening. To issue such a threat, Frank might tell Sam that if he comes home one more time after midnight, he will be grounded for a week. Frank's deterrent threat aims to prevent Sam from taking an undesired action.

Threats try to control behavior through the fear of punishment. Promises try to do the same thing by holding out the offer of reward. Again, there are two types of promises, depending on whether they're trying to encourage or prevent a specific behavior.

	Don't do X, get punished	Do X, get punished
Threat of Punishment		
Promise of Reward	Don't do X, get rewarded	Do X, get rewarded
	Deterrent	Compellent

Figure 9.   A summary of threats and promises.

A *compellent promise* offers a reward for an action. Frank might tell Sam that if he cleans up his room, he can use the car that weekend. Frank's intent is to get Sam to take a desired action.

Compellent promises are essentially bribes. Bribes have a bad reputation, but they're often helpful. In everyday life, an employer makes a compellent promise to his employees that if they do their jobs, they will get paid. We might also describe this as payment for service, a bribe, or even a *quid pro quo*, but the idea is the same: if you do what I want, I'll give you something.

A *deterrent promise* offers a reward for not taking action. Frank might tell Sam that if he avoids eating junk food for an entire week, then he can use the car on the weekend. Frank's intent is to get Sam to avoid a specific behavior.

These four methods for controlling behavior are summarized in Figure 9.

Threats and promises are transparently manipulative, and that is their entire purpose. The idea behind issuing one of these statements is that you're adding a new and explicit rule to the game and promising that you will be bound by the rule.

Eventually a rule can become so extreme that it turns into an *ultimatum*, which is basically a threat with extreme consequences.

Threats and promises must be *credible* in order to have any effect. If Frank makes a series of promises or threats to Sam and then doesn't follow through on them, Sam will quickly learn that his father's threats aren't credible, and they will thus lose their power to affect him.

On the other hand, credibility is enhanced when someone goes through with a threat or a promise even when he clearly doesn't want to. Suppose that Frank issued a threat to Sam that resulted in Sam being grounded for the next weekend. That Friday, Sam's best friend wins two tickets to see their favorite band in concert and invites Sam to join him. Though Frank understands how much Sam wants to go, he may stick to his guns and keep his son grounded. The result is that Frank's credibility goes up, and his threats will carry more weight in the future.

This last example points out one of the problems of any theory of behavior, such as game theory, that is based on strictly rational principles: we are not strictly rational beings. Frank may feel that enforcing this particular punishment and denying his son the trip to the concert would actually do more harm than good. Though his credibility would go up, his son might perceive him as cold and heartless, and it could damage their relationship. Such emotional and psychological factors are very difficult to quantify and thus are usually absent from strictly mathematical approaches.

Game theory is a relatively new field as mathematics goes, but it's already come a long way [139]. It's useful for working out strategies for strictly logical, rational games like Tic-Tac-Toe and for finding strategies during certain structured conflicts like politics, economics, and business [41]. But despite its name, game theory isn't of much direct use in the sorts of games we've talked about in this book. One thing that makes so many of these games fun is the unpredictability of other people, in all of their capriciousness, irrationality, and spontaneity. Contrary to the assumptions of game theory, we don't always do what's best: most people act not just out of logic but also generosity, spite, revenge, friendship, and other human impulses.

The Surprise Party

Let's look at another unexpected result of rational thinking in a human context.

Jeff is feeling excited as he drives in to work on Monday morning. His 40th birthday is coming up next Tuesday, and his wife Mary has been planning a big party with all his friends. But upon arriving at work, Jeff's boss calls him in and tells him that he needs Jeff to accompany him on a business trip this weekend and that they'll be leaving on Saturday. This is a very important trip, and there's no way Jeff can get out of it. When he tells Mary that night, she's disappointed but promises that they'll have the party anyway; only they'll have it before he leaves. But she adds that just to make up for the fact that the party will no longer be on his birthday, she'll make it a surprise dinner party.

As Jeff is driving home from work on Tuesday afternoon, he wonders about when the party could happen. Mary said it would be a dinner party, and since he's leaving on Saturday, the latest it could be held would be Friday night. But if Mary waited until Friday night, then by the time Friday rolled around, Jeff would know that evening was the last possible opportunity for the party, and that it would have to happen that night. Thus it wouldn't be a surprise any more. Since Mary promised it would be a surprise, she can't hold it on Friday night.

So he reasons that the last night it could be held must be Thursday night. But it can't be that night either, because then on Thursday afternoon Jeff would know that it would have to be that evening. After all, Friday has already been eliminated, so on Thursday afternoon the only choice left is Thursday night. But again, that would no longer be a surprise, so Thursday night is ruled out too.

In this manner Jeff works his way backwards from Friday night to Tuesday night, ruling out each evening. The inescapable conclusion is that there's no way that Mary can make good on holding a surprise party for him. Impressed with his logic, but disappointed with the result, Jeff walks in the house to tell Mary of his conclusion. Suddenly she shouts "Surprise!" and his friends and family leap out from behind the furniture. He's never been more surprised in his life.

How could this be? After all, Jeff eliminated each night from contention. Jeff's logic is sound, but his conclusion hinges on the sneaky nature of what it means to be surprised. If you have decided that surprise can't happen, that's precisely the moment when surprise is at its strongest.

Although Jeff's reasoning was just fine, he didn't get the right conclusion. Logical reasoning is often trickier than we suppose. So we should think of rational theories like game theory as useful tools for the specific types of games that permit us to assign numerical scores to different moves and the resulting consequences. There aren't too many of these.

Group Play

In team play, we usually cooperate with other players on our team in order to defeat one or more opposing teams of cooperating players.

Teams

Teams allow us a chance to combine our competitive instincts with our social and cooperative instincts.

In most games, both teams start out with the same number of players. Some games provide ways for players to be temporarily or permanently removed from the game. In basketball, a player who has committed more than a certain number of fouls may not play anymore but can be replaced by another player from the bench. In hockey, a player can be temporarily removed from the game as a penalty for fouling. This player is not replaced, giving the other team a temporary advantage in numbers.

Types of Teammate Cooperation

Independent: In some team sports each member performs independently of the others. So in a track and field team, each pole vaulter performs independently, but all the contestants from a single team may have their scores combined to create a team score.

Most games that use independent teams are not zero-sum. That is, as one player improves, other players aren't penalized. For example, in a swim meet, though only one player can win, it's possible that every participant in a given race could beat the previous world's record.

Sequential: Teammates can contribute to the overall effort one person at a time, yet still depend on each other. This is most common in timed events. For example, a running relay team is scored by the total time taken by each of its members, who (except for moments during the handoff of the baton) run only one at a time.

Simultaneous: This is the most common form of team play, in which everyone on the team is playing together at the same time. A basketball
or soccer team is playing simultaneously. Doubles players in tennis,
and actors and guessers in Charades, are also playing simultaneously.

These approaches can be mixed within a single game. For example, in
a baseball game the entire defending team is in the field acting in parallel,
but the attacking team puts up just one batter at a time, creating a serial,
or sequential, offense.

Sente

Before we close this discussion, I'd like to present a vocabulary of competition that is very useful when discussing the progress of many types of
competitive games, yet is not widely used.

The terms are drawn from the Go literature and name different strategic
situations. One idea in particular, *sente*, we saw earlier. This term has
applicability in almost every kind of game involving two or more competing
players.

The following list uses the Japanese names for these situations. You can
find much more extensive lists [5]. As you read these descriptions, you
may find it helpful to think of how each of these terms applies to your
favorite competitive games.

Go Terms for Strategy

Aji (ah'-jee): The state where a player has made a move that fails to address
important threats or possible threats. It can also refer to positive
opportunities left behind, as in a move that fails to exploit all the
potential in a situation.

Ate (ah'-tay), or Atari (ah-tar'-ee): The state where capture is imminent.
Often the player causing Ate or Atari will warn the other player
verbally. Saying "ate" or "atari" in Go is like saying "check" in
chess: it's a friendly warning to beware impending capture.

Fuseki (foo'-sek-ee): These are the opening moves of the game, where the
players develop and reveal their strategies. The opening steps of a
game are a delicate psychological moment, where players may make

bold moves to grab the advantage or play cautiously and guard their strategies.

Gote (go'-tay): A forced defensive move. This is a move you must make in order to protect yourself. Usually it's not the move you would choose for yourself, but it's the one you're forced to make in response to an opponent's attack. In chess you might be poised for a grand offensive, but if you're put in check, you must respond to move out of check, even if it means giving up on your offense and putting yourself in a worse position than you were in before. A player pushed into *gote* has no choice but to respond to an immediate threat. This move is often in response to a warning of *ate* (or *atari*) from the other player.

Sente (sen'-tay): The state of having the upper hand. This is a very powerful quality, because when you have *sente*, you not only have freedom, but more importantly, you have control. *Sente* is the opposite of *gote*. The player with *sente* is the one who is calling the shots. If both players are balanced and have freedom to play where they like, nobody has *sente*. But if one player is dominating the other and forcing a response, he possesses *sente*. The player in chess who says "check" has *sente* at that moment.

This idea of forcing the other player to answer you is key to holding *sente*. It means that you can attack, while he must defend. You can choose, while he must answer. You can even force your opponent to make self-destructive moves, because he must respond to your immediate threats.

Players often strive to obtain *sente* and then hold it as long as possible, using it to push their opponents around.

The player with *sente* may make a mistake, or simply run out of steam, and then the situation can go back to neutral. The player who's being pushed around in a state of *gote* may, by virtue of skill, find a move that both addresses the threat and creates a new threat, thereby capturing *sente* for himself and turning the tables on his opponent.

Part IV

Merging Stories
and Games

You've got to be able to assimilate what normally seem to be opposing
elements; that's the way reality is.

—Mose Allison, quoted in the liner notes to the album
Tell Me Something: The Songs of Mose Allison, Verve, 1996

Comparing Stories and Games

One of the basic arguments of this book is that we can unite storytelling principles from traditional fiction and participatory principles from traditional games to create something new and exciting.

Experience has shown that it's surprisingly difficult to combine these two fields into a single activity with mainstream appeal.

In this part we'll look at some of the reasons behind this difficulty. We'll see how and why stories and games are inherently different, and why the attempts to harmonize them in the past have not found a success comparable to other entertainment forms like movies, books, and television.

This chapter looks at a wide range of topics, from social interaction to story technique. I'll also discuss some design principles drawn from experience with video games. The subjects in this chapter are united by their common focus on the boundary that now exists between stories and games, and how we can start to eliminate that boundary.

Structures

This chapter looks at a wide range of topics, from social interaction to story technique. I'll also discuss some design principles drawn from experience with video games. The subjects in this chapter are united by their common focus on the boundary that now exists between stories and games, and how we can start to eliminate that boundary.

The Story of Games

If we take a sufficiently broad view of both stories and games, we might be tempted to say that every game tells a story.

For example, we might look at a game of *Monopoly* that we've just finished and describe the events in the form of a narrative. The elements of the plot would be simply the events themselves, and the characters would be the players: "And then John landed on Connecticut Avenue with a hotel on it and had to pay Jill a huge rent!"

If we simply described the events of the game, this story would have the same narrative punch as a baseball box score or a chess match history. Calling any of these lists of moves a "story" would stretch the term way beyond its breaking point.

We might add story elements by including things that happen outside of the game itself. For example, John might land on Connecticut Avenue but not have the money for rent and accuse Jill of putting the hotel on the property to force him out of the game because she doesn't like him. If they started to fight on a personal level, that conflict might contain the seeds of a story.

If there aren't any conflicts like this, we might be tempted to search for them or even invent them. Television sports announcers frequently try to imagine the psychology of the competitors they're covering in order to give the games a personal story. This approach probably reaches its extreme during the Olympic Games, when networks produce biographies of the athletes to try to inject human drama into the athletic events.

Because games usually contain confrontation, it's very tempting to develop that conflict into a story. But the game itself is not a story. To form a story from a typical game of *Monopoly* requires a storyteller to shape the raw material of the game's events and players into a narrative. The game itself does not translate into a good story.

Authoring

It's important for us to see the difference between the casual stories we all tell each other every day, and the stories that are told by professionals who use craft, technique, and experience to compose a really good narrative for general audiences. Anyone can cut wood, but really beautiful furniture is built by skilled craftsmen.

We create stories for ourselves all the time, and there are plenty of toys available that give us raw material for inventing such tales. Toys ranging from dolls to model train sets are catalysts from which we can weave our own narratives.

Many computer-based toys provide even more obviously story-like pieces that we can use to create personal stories. For example, *The Sims* is like an elaborate self-propelled dollhouse, where the people move around, eat lunch, buy things, and make friends.

A related toy is *SimCity*, where you're in control of a city, and it's your job to adjust growth and control development to make it thrive.

These simulation toys are actually partly toy and partly puzzle. Will Wright, the designer of both programs, describes it this way: "As a player, a lot of what you're trying to do is reverse engineer the simulation" [146]. Thus much of a player's time is spent trying to figure out how the program itself works, which is the puzzle aspect of it. Ultimately the puzzle is solved when the player has created a mental model of the program that can predict its behavior; that is, the player has managed to recreate essential aspects of the program in his own head. For players who don't find this puzzle aspect of the experience entertaining, there are a variety of books and articles available that give details of many objects available in the game and how they work. Once the puzzle aspect is solved, the program can be used simply as a toy.

Even a casual perusal of the web sites for these and similar toys and the sites that fans have made clearly reveals that many people entertain themselves with these programs by making up stories as they go. They invent a character and try to find her a job, or a date for Saturday night, or the perfect rug to go with her dining table.

Just as people have an innate ability to see faces in all sorts of objects, we also seem to easily create story-like structures for ourselves that are inherently interesting and rewarding.

We're all storytellers in everyday life. When a loved one sees us come by with a sad expression and asks what's wrong, we often respond with a narrative: "Well, this morning I decided to sleep in. So I got to work late and everyone was rushing around like mad. Apparently the new boss was upset, the one I told you about? And he wanted my report right away. Bill was covering for me but he was angry about it, so I..." and we're deep into a story, complete with characters and plot. We tell stories all the time, from how our day went to narrative jokes.

Sharing stories is a natural way for people to communicate with each other, as common as language itself. In fact, we're all pretty good at it.

In this book I'm distinguishing the casual stories that we tell one another in everyday life from the types of stories that are crafted for a wider audience. These latter stories are usually created by professionals who have studied the tools of the craft and who produce work that we as audiences are happy to pay money for. Those latter types of stories are different than the casual ones we create in everyday life: crafted stories use a wide variety of tools and principles, some of which we covered in Part I, to make a story as strong and interesting as it can be. These tools and principles are simply refinements of our everyday ability and can be learned by anyone with the interest. But they're a big part of what makes the difference between the stories that arise while playing a game or that we share with loved ones, and the stories that are meant to have a deeper, broader, and enduring appeal.

Let's illustrate this distinction with an analogy to architecture. We all have opinions on buildings of all sorts, from small houses to skyscrapers. Most of us have some ideas for our "dream house," where we'd love to live in a perfect world. We probably know whether we want big windows looking out on an ocean, or high ceilings, or a sunken living room. And most of us could sketch out a drawing of this house, or at least some of the rooms.

Many of us are good casual architects. Our dream houses are usually pretty reasonable places; they may be idiosyncratic, but people tend not to violate the laws of nature, nor the general ideas of what a house is about and roughly how it should look. We can communicate those ideas to others.

Now consider the change that occurs if you're an architect, designing a house that someone else will actually live in. The initial inspiration that we all share for our dream houses is an essential first step, but after that comes the craft of architecture.

Some of the issues an architect faces are obvious, yet require experience and knowledge to address. For example, does the building meet safety and fire codes? Is the indoor and outdoor lighting sufficient? Is there enough room to install and maintain the landscaping?

Some issues are more subtle. What are the traffic patterns going to be inside this building? Is there enough HVAC (heating, ventilation, and air-conditioning) for the planned number of occupants? What color and materials should be used inside and outside? Can the building be constructed on budget and on time?

The list goes on and on. To create a casual house for ourselves requires nothing more than imagination, and maybe a pen and a napkin. To create a house for ourselves or other people to really live in requires adding knowledge, or the expertise of the craft.

Architects also bring to their work an informed aesthetic. They know to look for issues that are important to people who live in a house but which might not be otherwise obvious. For example, it's often nice to be able to see from one room into another, so one has to make sure there are good sightlines. Homeowners go up and down their stairs frequently, so we need to make sure that the pitch of the stairs is neither too steep nor too shallow. If the house is being built in a rainy place, it may be important to have a covered path from the car to the house. These are issues that we could miss when we sat down to doodle on a napkin, but which we'd surely notice once we moved in.

We might feel that some great architects are born with vivid imaginations and a feel for buildings, but even they must study the crafts that keep their structures safe and make them pleasant.

Like most other arts, storytelling is a craft that can be learned. Inspiration is necessary, but once one has the skills to see it, inspiration is all around us.

Many courses and books teach story structure and the craft of storytelling. Most professional storytellers know these principles in their guts, if not in their heads.

Some writers are closer to jazz improvisers than to house builders and make stories up as they go. But jazz improvisation is not random playing: the best improvisers are masters of their instruments, and play within the melodic, harmonic, and rhythmic structure of the song they're improvising on. They're able to make up variations on these themes as they go because they have practiced so long that the tools are internalized and second nature. Thus they build a new musical composition as they go, and good improvisers make it work because they create good structures. Similarly, some writers may start with the opening sentence, having no idea how it will end. And those writers who have a very strong sense of character and plot will find a way to create those elements as they go, discovering the structure as they tell the tale.

As we think about developing participatory stories, we have to keep in mind that most players have neither the experience nor the skill (nor the desire) to write stories that will be interesting to lots of other people. Wirters with those skills will still be essential for creating great stories.

Survey

Let's begin with a quick overview of some different ways that stories and games have been combined. I'll also include two qualities that will be important to our discussion: whether or not they are social (as opposed to solitaire), and whether or not they use computer technology.

These are all fuzzy categories. A solitary game of Klondike can be social if someone is watching and helping. And some games have a bit of electronics in them, so we might be tempted to call them computer-based even though they're not very flexible or sophisticated. And we shouldn't forget that that just about anything can be turned into a game. As Mary Poppins sang to us in *Mary Poppins*:

Game	Story	Social	Computerized	
—	—	—	—	reading a car-repair manual
✓	—	—	—	Klondike
—	✓	—	—	*Lord of the Rings*
—	—	✓	—	a group hike
—	—	—	✓	*Hands-On Universe*
✓	✓	—	—	*Choose Your Own Adventure*
✓	—	✓	—	*Pictionary*
✓	—	—	✓	*Tetris*
—	✓	✓	—	a bedtime story
—	✓	—	✓	a *Flash* cartoon
—	—	✓	✓	a chat room
✓	✓	✓	—	a murder mystery train
✓	✓	—	✓	*Final Fantasy X*
✓	—	✓	✓	*You Don't Know Jack*
—	✓	✓	✓	*Degrassi TV website*
✓	✓	✓	✓	*The Beast*

Figure 10. The different combinations of the qualities of game, story, social engagement, and computerization. A — means the quality is not present, while a √ means that it is.

"In every job that must be done
There is an element of fun,
You find the fun and snap!
The job's a game."

But it's still useful to draw these broad categories, as they can help us see the big picture.

Figure 10 shows the sixteen combinations of these four criteria, and a representative example from each category. We can also show these relationships graphically. Figure 11 shows how to isolate four different regions inside a square to create sixteen different regions, using a technique invented by Lewis Carroll. Figure 12 shows the result of filling in the examples from Figure 10.

We'll begin with an activity that has none of our four qualities. A solo activity that has no game or story components, nor any computers, is studying a printed car-repair manual.

Now let's add in each of our four categories one at a time, giving us four examples. The solitaire card game Klondike is purely a game, and

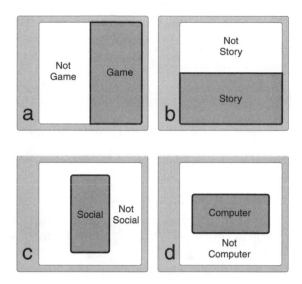

Figure 11. The sixteen categories of games resulting from our four criteria. (a) Activities that have game-like qualities are on the right hand side. (b) Activities that have story-like qualities are on the bottom. (c) Activities that have social qualities are in the vertical rectangle. (d) Activities that have computer-like qualities are in the horizontal rectangle.

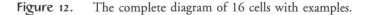

Figure 12. The complete diagram of 16 cells with examples.

the fantasy novel *Lord of the Rings* is pure story. A group hike is purely a social event with no story, game, or computer elements. The *Hands-on Universe* [57] program offers web browsers an opportunity to control remote telescopes and take pictures of the night sky. Anyone can enter a set of sky coordinates and exposure information, and when their request percolates to the top of the queue their digital picture will be taken and sent to them. This computer-based activity has no story or game elements, and typically you're not interacting with any other people (a person may actually carry out the request, but the two of you don't communicate directly).

When we add in a second category, we get six hybrids of two elements each.

A story-game hybrid is the *Choose Your Own Adventure Series* [26] series of books for children. In these books you're periodically asked to make choices and then flip to the appropriate page to see what happens. This type of construction is a part-story, part-game hybrid known as a *branching narrative* (I'll have more to say about these later on).

A community game with no elements of story or computer technology is *Pictionary*. A computer-based experience that is a game without story or community is the puzzle game *Tetris*. A common and enjoyable activity that combines story and community but excludes computers and gaming is the bedtime story. A computer-based story that has no social or game elements is a cartoon created in the *Flash* computer language. Such cartoons are similar to many television cartoons, but they require a computer to be viewed. And finally, a computer-based activity that takes place online among many people, but is neither a story nor a game, is the general-topic chat room.

Let's now consider those entertainments that combine three of our four qualities of story, game, social, and computers; there are four different combinations.

An activity that combines game, story, and social participation but has no computer element is a *murder mystery train* ride. You take part in this event by buying a round-trip ticket on a real train. You share the trip with other audience members and a collection of trained improvisational actors working from a general script. Over the course of the evening, one of the characters is "killed," and it's the job of the audience to figure out who did it, and why.

An activity that is part story, part game, and computerized, but has no social aspect, is the game *Final Fantasy X*. This is a solitaire game that combines fighting (which has a puzzle aspect), gameplay, and a sweeping story.

An activity that combines games, computers, and society is *You Don't Know Jack*. This is a computerized trivia gameshow for two or more players who compete to gain points by correctly answering questions.

Finally, an online experience that combines elements of computers, society and storytelling, but no gaming, is *Degrassi TV* [127]. This is largely a social site associated with the television show *Degrassi: The Next Generation*, directed at a high-school aged audience. Although there are some small, stand-alone games available, the site is primarily intended to foster communication among the show's audience, encouraging them to make friends with each other and discuss personal issues that are raised by the show.

The final example on our list combines all four elements of story, game, society, and computers. It's an online experience that was created to accompany the release of the movie *A.I.* The experience itself never had a formal name, but was referred to by its participants with several names, including *The AI Game*, *The Cloudmaker*, and *Who Killed Evan Chen?*, though perhaps it was most frequently called *The Beast*. *The Beast* was a collection of invented web sites with a huge wealth of information about an imaginary future. Players were invited to look through the sites and try to understand the how and why behind the suspected murder of a character. The puzzles were deliberately created to be too difficult for any one person, and properly interpreting many of them required a good knowledge of the story that was represented by the information scattered among the web pages. Ultimately a group of over 7000 people cooperated to crack the puzzles and solve the murder.

Some of the examples in Figures 10 and 12 are what I would describe as mainstream entertainments. By *mainstream* I mean something that has the same level of popular appeal as magazines, television, and movies. One way to test whether a type of entertainment has reached the mainstream is to see if it has spawned a large number of strong competitors who are serving a large or quickly-growing market.

One goal of this book is to help find ways to create mainstream entertainments that combine society, computers, gaming, and story. Our biggest challenge in creating these types entertainments is to find a harmonious balance of game elements and story elements. The fact that we have no mainstream successes in this domain is not for lack of trying: many companies have spent enormous resources of money and manpower trying to create such a hybrid.

Let's look at some of the challenges that arise when we try to create these kinds of entertainments.

Comparing the Structures

Games and stories are very different types of activities. Let's look at the differences explicitly. This will help us understand why they have traditionally been such uneasy bedpartners.

Structure

In previous chapters we've looked separately at the structures of stories and games. I'll now bring the ideas together and look at how games and stories approach different facets of their structures.

Units: The basic unit of gaming is the *turn*. This is when a player can take action. In some games, like baseball, the turns are distinct and easily recognized. In games like soccer, the turns are much more fluid. Some games group turns into larger entities: tennis has games and sets, baseball has innings, and poker has hands.

The basic unit of storytelling is the *plot point*. This is when something happens to change or advance the story. Plot points can happen in the physical world, as when the bank robber's getaway car refuses to start, or inside a character, as when someone decides to stand up for himself the next time he is bullied. Stories often group plot points into chapters and acts.

Time bounds: Most games are finite: they start at a particular time, and once they have run for a predetermined amount of time, or one player or team has accumulated enough points, the game is over. Games are self-contained: no part of the game exists before it starts or after it finishes. Players may continue to contest decisions made by judges and referees after the game is over, but those protestations aren't part of the game itself. The game may also figure into a larger picture such as league standings, but again, such factors are not part of the game itself as it's played.

When we're watching a game, much of the tension towards the end comes specifically because we know the end is coming. When a basketball team is ahead by one point with only one minute to go, the tension felt by players and spectators goes way up because suddenly the pressure has increased dramatically: a small change in position at this point can change the score at the moment the buzzer sounds, determining who wins the entire contest.

In the 2002 Winter Olympics, a controversy surfaced after the judges surprisingly awarded the gold medal in figure skating to the Russian team, who many people thought were surpassed by the Canadian team [101]. One judge in particular was accused of essentially selling her vote to the Russians. After a very public controversy, the International Skating Union asked the Olympic committee to grant a second gold medal to the Canadians, in addition to the one awarded to the Russians. Despite the very high stakes in this dispute, nobody seriously suggested that the two teams skate again When a competition is over, it's over, even if related legal wrangling continues.

In contrast, stories certainly have a beginning and an end, but the story is typically a slice from one or more lives that, except for births and deaths, are presumed to have an existence before and after the story.

There is no equivalent to gaming's time limit (or score limit) in stories. A story begins and ends based on an author's judgment, rather than in accordance with a predetermined, prescribed threshold. Some types of stories have a naturally built-in stopping point: mystery stories usually wrap up soon after the central puzzle has been unravelled and everyone knows who did the crime and why. But even then a story can continue for a while, following the characters in the aftermath of the resolution.

A serialized story may last only a few installments, or it may go on indefinitely. Armistead Maupin's newspaper serial *Tales of the City* first appeared in the *San Francisco Chronicle* in 1976. The serial continued to appear off and on over the next 24 years, ultimately resulting in six collections and two television mini-series. Radio and television soap operas also can continue their daily episodes as long as people want to watch. The BBC radio daily soap opera *The Archers* debuted on January 1, 1951, and new episodes continue to air today, over 50 years and more than 14,000 episodes later. In the U.S., the television soap opera *The Guiding Light* started broadcasting on TV on June 30, 1952, and also continues today, over 16,000 episodes later. To watch either of these serials from their start to the present would require a herculean effort.

Stories can continue to grow and develop as long as the audience and creators both remain interested.

Participants: In most games the participants don't change over time. In board games, such as *Monopoly* or *Trivial Pursuit*, individuals and teams almost always play all the way through without any change of personnel. An exception to this appears in team sports, when different members of the team can be swapped into and out of the game by the manager as the game progresses. Indeed, some players may never play at all in a given game. This is not universal in team sports; for example, there are no mid-game substitutions in a doubles tennis match.

Stories tend to have much more flexible casts. The lead character and the villain are usually present through much of the story, but others may come and go. Many large and sprawling books, such as classic Russian novels, contain a table of characters at the start to help readers keep track of their relationships and recall a character who re-appears long after he was last seen in the narrative.

At the other extreme, some stories have a very small cast. The film *Rosencrantz and Guidenstern are Dead* is dominated by the two title characters. Although other performers (drawn from Shakespeare's *Hamlet*) appear briefly, most of the time is spent with the two title characters.

Breadth and depth: Most games are not about much more than themselves. For example, intellectual games like chess and Go reward logical thinking and memory skills, but the purpose of the game is nothing more than simply playing as well as possible and trying to win. Physical games are similar: the point of soccer is simply to win. Though there are often beneficial side effects to mastering a game, they usually are not the point. We say that games are limited in *breadth*, because they are about little except themselves.

Note that games may or may not have much *depth*, in the sense that they have subtlety or complexity. Chess and Go certainly have depth, and many people spend a lot of energy thinking about the strategies involved in professional sports. By contrast, the children's game of Tic-Tac-Toe and the card game War have little depth, because applying time and energy to the study of these games does not improve one's performance.

Stories need not have depth or breadth. Many horror and adventure stories are simply enjoyable roller-coaster rides and aim for nothing more sophisticated. On the other hand, classic films like *Lawrence of Arabia* and *Citizen Kane* are both broad and deep, and continue to be watched today because they tell us something important about being human. Many great works of fiction in other media share these qualities. Shakespeare's *Hamlet* and Twain's *Adventures of Huckleberry Finn* continue to be popular because they have depth. Giving our attention to these stories is rewarding because we learn more about ourselves in the process.

Rules: The rules of games and stories are quite different. The next section is devoted to comparing these rules in some detail.

For the moment, I'll just note that the rules of games are usually *explicit*, or stated as clearly as possible before the game begins. The rules of a story are usually *implicit* and learned by the characters, and the audience, only by experience as the story unfolds.

Judges and referees: When two players in a game disagree, a judge or referee can step in to mediate the dispute and make a final determination. The ideal judge uses the rules and his knowledge of the situation to impartially arrive at a fair solution to the dispute. Such a judge can be formally hired for the purpose, like a line judge in a tennis match, or the referee may be informally or temporarily drafted, as when we call in a friend to arbitrate during a casual, friendly game.

In a story, there are no objective rules to go by. Who's right and who's wrong depends on the point of view of each person considering the situation, whether it's one of the characters in the story itself or the audience. A person who breaks the law is doing wrong in the eyes of a policeman, but if he's stealing bread to feed his starving family, he may be viewed less harshly by the audience, and may be considered a good man by his family.

Audience: In most games, the audience makes no direct contribution outside of sharing their general enthusiasm and support. Spectators cheer and boo to demonstrate how they feel. Sometimes the players pick up on these emotions and feel heartened or disappointed, while other competitors ignore the spectators as just a distraction and focus on their gameplay.

There are exceptions in which the spectators are directly involved in a game. The television game show *Family Feud* polls its audience for answers to questions put to the contestants. The game show *Who Wants To Be A Millionaire?* offers participants the chance to poll the audience for what they think is the right answer to a question. In some shows, the audience determines the winner of a contest based on the strength of their support for different contestants (often expressed via applause or votes cast by using a telephone or the internet).

Some games are specifically designed for audience involvement. For example, the *How to Host a Murder* series of games (and its competitors) provides each player a description of a character and information on his involvement in an ongoing story. Over the course of the evening, the players gradually reveal their confidential information to the other players, so that the mystery slowly deepens.

In popular durable media such as books and movies, the audience makes no impact at all on the development of the story. Films, books, and other persistent media don't change in any way in response to the audience.

Live story presentations can adapt in some way to the audience: stage actors subtly tune their performances from night to night in response to the mood they perceive from the audience. This give-and-take is particularly noticeable in comedies, where the audience is giving constant feedback in how much they laugh and when.

A live storyteller can change the style, rhythm, and pacing of a story to adapt to the audience. He can even delete characters and scenes, or invent new ones on the fly, to better respond to the audience.

Improvisational theater often turns to the audience for key pieces of information on which to base scenes. Skilled improvisors can even invite the audience onto stage with them and help guide these people on a journey from a role as spectator to one of performer [142].

Some activities are specifically designed to bring the audience into the story. Renaissance fairs often feature wandering storytellers who walk up to attendees and speak to them "in character," drawing them into some larger narrative. In plays like *Tony and Tina's Wedding*, the audience is actively invited into the ongoing story.

Purpose: As we saw in Part II, the point of a game is to win, but that's not the only reason we play. A player's purpose is to master a set of skills, perhaps both physical and mental, and then perform to the limit of his abilities.

A game player seeks *mastery*. He seeks to understand the rules as well as possible and to know his own abilities with honest objectivity. A player moves in accordance with the *Game Loop* discussed in Chapter 5, which involves assessing the situation and his own abilities, crafting a plan, executing it, and then measuring the result.

In many games some of these steps can be objectified. For example, a baseball player at bat might discern that the players on the other team have shifted to the right, since he usually hits in that direction. A coach or other outside observer could confirm or deny that perception. Or a player may try to hit a home run over the center-field fence; whether or not he achieves this is something that everyone can agree on.

There are games in which everything is internal. Intellectual games like Go can be difficult for others to qualify objectively, since one person's reading of the situation may reasonably differ from another's. Where one person sees an immediate threat that must be met with a head-on counterattack, another may see an overcommitted offense and a subtle opportunity to sneak up and take *sente*.

Whether evaluated internally or externally, we play to master skills, execute well, and win the contest.

On the other hand, the purpose of stories is to entertain and enrich the audience. The point of the story may in fact vary from one audience member to the next, and from one character to the next, as each draws his own premise from the events.

For example, in Shakespeare's *King Lear*, we see Lear betrayed by his daughters. Perhaps the premise for Lear is that one ought not trust other people too much, even if they're family. The daughters may conclude that honoring one's father is less important than acquiring and holding on to power and influence. Those who still care for Lear may decide that loyalty is the noblest of human qualities. And every audience member may come to his own own conclusions.

This flexibility of interpretation is one of the appeals of art: as with all enterprises that touch on the human spirit and emotions, there is more than one way to look at the elements of the work and what they ultimately mean.

The purpose of the story for the protagonist is to understand his problem and to solve it as well as possible. Stories can help us think through our own actions and attitudes by seeing how they are interpreted by other people and what happens to characters who put those actions and attitudes into practice in specific situations.

Another way to compare their purposes is to say that games are primarily about *results*, while stories are primarily about *process*. Speaking broadly, games give us a chance to develop and measure our abilities and ultimately win the challenge. Equally broadly, stories are descriptions of what happens to people in different situations and how they change as they try to solve a problem. In a game, as long as you play by the rules, a win is a win. In a story, a character can achieve his goal, but perhaps only by paying a terrible price. Alternatively, he can decide that what appeared to be his goal wasn't the real point at all and in apparent failure still perceive himself as a victor. Games focus on results: the final score is the final result. Stories focus on process: what characters do and think, and how they change as they pursue their goals, determines our interpretation of the outcome.

We can summarize the main points of this discussion for both games and stories by placing them side by side, as in Figure 13.

Rules

In the last section, I mentioned that we'd look more closely at the different ways that rules are used in games and stories.

	Gaming	Storytelling
units	turn	plot point
bounds	time or points	unbounded
participants	mostly stable	may change
referee	impartial judge	moral interpreter
purpose	develop and use skills	learn about the world

Figure 13.   Comparing the structures of games and stories.

In this sense, the "rules" are those basic constraints that determine the possible actions of the people involved in the activity.

In games, the rules are easy to identify. It can be a little tougher to find the rules in stories. Certainly the physical world plays a role: except in science fiction, people cannot fly very far unaided, nor can they read other people's minds or go without water for months on end. Other story rules are based not on possibility, but practicality. You can't hot-wire a car if you don't know how, and a character who wants to run a nuclear submarine won't be able to do it without help, even if he manages to get his hands on one. Other rules are simply enforced by consequences: usually you are effectively prohibited from killing someone, not because there's a physical force stopping you, but because the legal consequences are so great that in most situations that course of action is simply not even considered.

We've discussed most of the rules of games and stories in their respective chapters. Let's summarize them here, starting with games:

External: The rules are not dependent on the personal memories or interpretations of the players, but typically exist in an archived form, such as a rulebook.

Known: Before the game begins, all players are given a complete set of rules.

Explained: If a player doesn't understand a rule, he can ask for clarification. The game doesn't begin until everyone understands the rules.

Objective: The rules are the same for all players in all circumstances (the rules themselves may specify how they may be adjusted for different situations, but those adaptations are still part of the rules).

Refereed: An impartial party can be brought in to resolve disputes and produce a binding decision based on the rules and his best judgment.

Fixed: Players who are participating in the game do not have the power to change the rules.

Explicit: There is no mystery to how many rules there are or how they are to be applied.

The rules of games are usually easy to articulate because by their very nature, they are meant to be clear and obvious. They're often written down and for professional events they're even approved by an official governing organization.

Now let's look at how the rules of stories address the same issues:

Internal: What is permissible behavior is a personal decision made by each character using his own morality and ethics.

Unknown: Nobody knows what another person is going to do until he does it; sometimes our actions even surprise ourselves. The definitions of permissible and appropriate behavior vary tremendously depending on context.

Discovered: Characters can't always reliably predict what they will be allowed to do, what they can get away with, or what the repercussions of any course of action will be.

Subjective: An attractive course of action for one character may be repugnant to another. The courses of actions available to a character depend on his personal views.

Changing: Actions that are acceptable in one time and place, or in a particular set of social circumstances, may be unacceptable in another.

Implicit: The rules arise from a combination of the character's own moral code and the expected reactions of the world.

Figure 14 summarizes these elements in a single side-by-side table.

The most important feature of Figure 14 is evident at a glance: each row is a pair of opposites!

Games	Stories
external	internal
known	unknown
explained	discovered
objective	subjective
refereed	moral
fixed	changing
explicit	implicit

Figure 14.   Summarizing the rules for games and stories.

Figure 14 helps explain why it's been so difficult to bring stories and games together. Many such projects have been created as though ordered off the classical menu at a Chinese restaurant: some characteristics are taken from column A (for stories), and some from column B (for games). But each time we include a game-like rule in the hybrid, we are contradicting the rule that applies to stories, and vice-versa. Thus each game-like quality contradicts its story-like counterpart, damaging the story. And each story-like element we include violates some principle of good games.

The situation is not hopeless, but this comparison helps us see why it's been so hard to harmonize these two very different kinds of activities.

Alternating Hybrids

What happens if we simply try to mix stories and games by alternating between some of one and then some of the other? Mixing two unlike things by alternating between them works in some situations. For example, many cable television providers carry a channel that is all comedy all day, another channel that is all shopping all day, another that is all sports all day, and many others. A viewer can switch between these steady streams of monothematic material as his mood dictates.

But switching back and forth can be jarring and can harm both forms.

By analogy, suppose that someone decided to create a creature that was a hybrid of a frog and rabbit. It could hop like a frog to get over obstacles and run like a rabbit when it needed speed. A very crude solution would be to simply duct-tape a frog and a rabbit back to back. When you want it to move like a frog, you place its frog legs on the ground, and when you want it to be like a rabbit, you turn it over and put the rabbit's legs down. This alternating solution works, sort of, but it's inelegant and awkward.

This approach has actually been tried out in the marketplace of electronic games, with predictable results. For example, in games like *Myst*, the story goes on for a while, and then you're given a puzzle to solve. You solve the puzzle and get more story until the next puzzle, in alternating sequences. Although that game enjoyed tremendous positive press at the time of its release and became a runaway best-seller, much of this success was due to how the game set a new standard for 3D artwork at the time, and its offering of a slow-paced, contemplative, richly-designed world for people to lose themselves in.

The weakest part of *Myst* (and its successors in the same genre) is that although the puzzles are grounded in the environment, they are effectively independent of the story, and the story is independent of the puzzles. It wouldn't be hard to take the few story elements out of *Myst* and sell the product simply as a collection of miscellaneous puzzles. You could also take the puzzles away from the story, and in fact the book *Myst: The Book of Ti'Ana* expands the story of *Myst* into a novel. The computer game itself doesn't merge these two domains together in any way more sophisticated than simple alternation. Recent games like *Star Wars: Rogue Squadron II*, have precisely the same structure, except with different types of elements (that game alternatives between battle and story sequences, which are again essentially independent of each other).

Note that in most video games, it's the designer who decides when you need to confront a puzzle (or battle) and when you get to see more of the story. It's easy to see this as a system like a laboratory maze, where each success at a game or puzzle element rewards the player with another food pellet of story.

The essential problem with creating a hybrid by alternation is that the pieces don't really connect except by being near one another in time. Returning to our cable television example, we could flip back and forth between the shopping channel and the comedy channel. But this does not create a funny skit about shopping, or a chance to purchase funny products. There's shopping and then there's humor, but simple alternation doesn't merge them together in a way that creates something that combines elements of both.

Despite its beautiful art direction, the puzzle/adventure game *Syberia* continues in this vein and thus also fails to unite its backstory and its gaming elements. The story is advanced in the spaces between solving one logic puzzle and the next.

Arguments Against Participatory Fiction

The preceding sections were about some of the problems of creating a form of participatory fiction. It seems reasonable to wonder if those problems are insurmountable. In fact, one can advance some pretty good arguments that we're just never going to find a satisfying way to blend stories and games into a single form.

In this section I'll try to present those arguments as strongly as I can. Note that these aren't meant to be "straw-man" arguments, presented and shaped so that they can be easily dismissed later. Rather, I believe that these are important and valid issues, and that only by acknowledging and understanding them can we hope for success.

In the following discussion, I'll continue to use as a target the idea of mainstream acceptance, acknowledging that there have been many niche activities that have succeeded by other measures.

It's never worked before: Participatory fiction has been tried over and over again through the years by professionals and amateurs alike. Historically, travelling theatrical troupes would often tailor their performances to the desires of the audiences that came to their shows. Today, very skilled and experienced performers engage audiences at Renaissance fairs and other gatherings in ongoing and improvised stories. Skilled performers can turn audience members into performers [142]. Live entertainments like *Tony and Tina's Wedding* play in a number of cities, but there aren't many of them. And there have been any number of experimental theater pieces that involve the audience to different degrees. None of these are mainstream forms.

Amateur versions of participatory fiction haven't done much better. The game *Dungeons & Dragons* has been around for decades, but as we saw in Chapter 1 almost 80% of its players are under 18: it's mostly for high-school students, who stop playing when they graduate.

Surely if there was any mainstream potential to this idea of participatory fiction, by now at least one of these many forms would have resonated with the general public, and then a more sophisticated form would have grown from it.

Absence of evidence is not evidence of absence, so just because it hasn't happened yet doesn't mean it never will. But given the many professionals who have worked very hard in this field over many years, the lack of mainstream success for interactive fiction argues that it's just not out there to be found.

Adding computers doesn't help a thing: Many of the products sold today that advertise some form of "interactive storytelling" are just computerized versions of techniques that have been tried before and have three strikes against them even before they begin.

First, the previous forms of interactive story, as discussed above, have failed to attract a mainstream audience. Thus any games that are based on those ideas are likely to suffer the same fate.

Second, computers cannot come anywhere close to providing the kind of spontaneity, depth, and responsiveness we get from human beings. A game with computerized characters is doomed to providing pale shadows of real people. Artificial intelligence is still so primitive that even the most sophisticated programs that try to act like people are easily unmasked [83].

Third, it's not just the simulated people in the computer game that are less than real: *everything* is less than real. If someone throws water at you in a video game, you may see very interesting optical effects as the water catches the light, but you won't become actually wet. If someone threw water at you in a live performance, you *would* get wet. The computer experience today can only address sound and, to a more limited degree, graphics. Real-time computer graphics still don't look like real life, and even those that come close are only visible in two dimensions on a television screen.

The computer's presentation of the world experience is so shallow and constrained that it constantly dead-ends into its own limitations. It falls far short of the infinitely richer real world, with its real, trained performers, and where every one of our senses can be stimulated in real-time with complete realism and accuracy.

♦ 8. Structures ♦

Since interactive stories haven't worked very well so far in the real world, there's no reason to expect that they would work any better in the drastically constrained and limited simulations that are presented to us through any technology that exists today or seems likely in the near future.

Authors want control: Authors want to control their creations. When the character Neo in *The Matrix* takes the pill that lets him see the world beyond the world he's used to, that's not only an important decision used to drive the plot of the movie, but it tells us a lot about the character. The entire scene was hardly a random event: it was a meticulous and deliberate construction designed to give us a better understanding of a particular facet of Neo's personality and to tell us more about the world of the movie.

Authors want control over their work because they are trying to express a vision. They choose what to put in and what to exclude in order to communicate their ideas as well as possible.

In fact, we can argue that making choices is exactly what we pay creators to do. Painters select a color and a brush, writers select words, and actors select body posture and delivery. Making those choices, determining what to include and what to leave out, and the shaping of each detail are the results of intent shaped by skill, craft, and experience. A great creative work is the result of a carefully controlled environment.

When a creator loses control of his work, the result becomes inherently less focused and risks falling apart. No author would willingly take such a risk with any story he cared about.

Interaction doesn't improve stories: Let's suppose for the sake of argument that we've found an ideal way to give an audience member a chance to participate in a story. Just what does that do for anyone: the author, the story, or even the audience member himself?

To illustrate the problem, suppose that we've produced an interactive version of the movie *The Silence of the Lambs*. Near the start of the film, FBI agent Clarice Starling is being taken to meet Dr. Hannibal Lecter for the first time. As she approaches his cell, the audience gets to decide what happens next. Should she sit quietly and wait for

221

him to speak? Should she take on a very professional, no-nonsense attitude? Should she act more confident than she feels? Should she flatter him? Insult him?

If you've seen the movie, you know that this scene is beautifully written and executed. Just how is an audience's participation going to improve it? Those couple of minutes of film represent the best work of dozens of professionals and are probably the result of at least hundreds of man-hours all focused on delivering on those intentions as well as possible. The scene involved coordinated, expert attention not just to the writing, but to the set design, camera motion, acting, lighting, sound design, editing, costuming, and many other aspects of professional work. For example, the lights that illuminated that scene weren't simply sitting there: specific lights were chosen, they were given specific colors using gels, and they were placed in specific locations, with all of those choices designed to enhance the particular mood and events in that scene. All of these experienced professionals had the freedom to design their work in advance and go over it again and again to refine it before it was done, getting the pieces to work harmoniously with each other to deliver the best possible scene.

Do we really think that someone making spontaneous decisions in the heat of the moment is going to come anywhere near this level of sophistication and integration? Even if he focuses on just a single aspect, like the dialog, it's not reasonable to think that he's going to do better than a skilled writer who has both the experience and the freedom to plan, write, and rewrite.

Just consider how silly it would be for a movie theater owner to pause the movie as Clarice approaches Lecter's cell, and ask those of us in the audience what kind of lighting should illuminate the scene. First of all, it would completely break the mood: our feelings of tension and fear for Clarice would be lost in the mental shift required to answer that question. But even worse, we don't know what's to come. Lighting often helps set a scene and can foreshadow later action. Obviously, the lighting designer for the film knew what was coming and could choose to anticipate it or not. The audience member just doesn't have that option available. Suppose we choose creepy lighting, and it turns out that Lecter is a nice guy? Or we choose soothing lighting, and we turn the corner to see Lecter devouring a bloody human head? Either of these would ruin the emotional effect that the illumination was supposed to provide in the first place.

Audience members forced into such decisions will quickly learn to choose the blandest, most indistinct middle ground, so that in their ignorance they don't risk contradicting what is yet to come. The result would be mush.

Asking the audience to choose what a character ought to do or say only makes sense if they know the character inside and out. But in any piece of fiction, we don't know the characters until they are revealed to us by their actions. Authors put enormous effort into bringing characters to life and exposing their personalities in interesting and economical ways. Much of the fascination of a piece of fiction is getting to know the characters better as time goes on. If after talking to Lecter, Clarice pulled a flask of whiskey from her purse and started talking like a grizzled New York City homicide detective, our developing picture of her personality would be shattered.

Asking the audience to make production decisions puts them in a role that they simply cannot carry out well, because they don't have the necessary information, nor the opportunity to go back and re-examine their choices. They might produce something interesting, but it would instead probably be chaotic and disjoint. It certainly wouldn't be a story as meaningful, deep, or coherent as one written by a skilled and motivated writer.

Acting is hard: Performing as a character in a story requires acting. Acting is a specialized skill that can take many years of study and practice to learn. And in many ways it's not pleasant: acting out negative emotions can be difficult and uncomfortable. Most people don't know how to be actors and are not naturals at it. We've all seen bad actors perform, and it's not a pretty sight. Most people know this and shy away from situations where they are called upon to perform a role (I'll have to more say about this in Chapter 11).

These arguments seem to paint a pretty bleak picture for developing a form of interactive fiction. We can't ask the audience to write, to choose, or to act. It looks like nothing is left.

I have a lot of sympathy for these objections, and in many ways I agree with them. But I think that they arise in response to a vision of participatory fiction that results from adding game elements to a traditional story form. Unfortunately, we'll see in future chapters that that's just the approach taken by many contemporary products, so these arguments apply directly to those offerings and help explain why they have not achieved mainstream success.

Forms of participatory narrative that are going to work in the mainstream will need to avoid the problems identified by these objections.

Collaboration

We are social creatures, and though we engage in many activities alone, such as playing solitaire games and reading books, we also spend a lot of time with other people.

Computer games have started to appear which allow as many as thousands of people to play the same game at the same time. Games like *Everquest, Asheron's Call,* and *Star Wars Galaxies* are three examples of what are often called *massively multiplayer online roleplaying games.* This term is used to distinguish these games from those that bring together smaller groups of people, such as four to play bridge or even a small group at a party, which are simply called *multiplayer games.*

In many of these massively multiplayer games, people arrive with their friends, or they all meet online at a given time and in-game location, and then participate in the world together as a group. Other players that link up have never met, online or offline. Yet groups of people of different sizes spontaneously form, and the size of the group has a large effect on how its members relate to each other.

The Intimacy Matrix

When people gather together, sometimes everyone knows each other, and sometimes nobody knows anyone else. Usually it's somewhere in between.

We can distinguish gatherings by the *size* of the group of people involved and by the degree to which they *know* each other. Although we can count the number of people in a group, the degree to which they know each other varies for each pair of people.

If we plot size and familiarity against each other, we can identify where different gatherings land in that space. I call this diagram the *Intimacy*

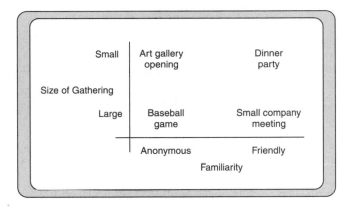

Figure 15. The Intimacy Matrix. The degree to which people know each other is along the horizontal axis, and the size of the gathering is along the vertical. The four examples represent extremes in this continuous space.

Matrix. Figure 15 shows the idea. A small dinner party of close friends is in the upper-right corner. Its opposite in the lower-left is a baseball game where there are tens of thousands of people who are mostly strangers to one another. Note that we often go to a big event (whether it's a game at a stadium, a live musical concert, or an online game like *Everquest*) with a group of friends. That way we're with people we know, even in the midst of a big crowd of strangers.

An opening in a new art gallery, in the upper-left, brings together a small group of people who may not know each other. Its opposite in the lower-right corner is the annual meeting of a company of a few hundred people: if the company culture is close-knit, many of the people may have already met one another several times.

If people are going to cooperate, it's important that they trust one another. If while playing a game of soccer I have a decent shot on the goal, but you're in a better position, I'll probably pass you the ball if I know your abilities and trust you to take a good shot. If we'd never met, I might be more inclined to rely on my own abilities and do my best. Getting people to meet one another and develop a sense of trust is essential to creating a team.

To develop trust, two people typically take a series of small steps. When promises are met and expectations are fulfilled, the level of trust in the relationship goes up.

You can force the creation of these trusting relationships by controlling people and their environment. Militaries create a sense of camaraderie among members of a unit by forcing them to rely on one another to endure basic training. Boot camp is both inescapable and deliberately overwhelming, and the challenges are designed so that no one person can complete them on his own. So members of the group are forced to rely upon and trust each other, and each time that trust is honored, their bond is reinforced and strengthened.

Some kind of enduring social relationship is necessary to create a stable and enjoyable experience among a group of otherwise anonymous people. As we'll discuss later, online anonymity is quite different from physical anonymity: when you're online and anonymous, you can act in ways that are essentially free of consequences. In person, anti-social behavior can be controlled through the dynamics of the group, up to and including physical exclusion. Once a person has acted in offensive ways, he'll be less welcome the next time. But online, someone can create havoc in many different ways without repercussion: if a troublemaker is somehow excluded from the group, he can rejoin easily under another name and start all over again. A variety of mechanisms have evolved to address this situation, but a feature common to many of them is the idea that people are held responsible for their past behavior. And as we saw above, when someone proves a history of reliability in his promises and abilities, we tend to grant him more of our trust.

In some online games, certain challenges are designed to be impossible to solve unless players team up and rely on one another. For example, really big monsters may be invulnerable to any attack but one coming simultaneously from many people in many directions.

When we play games as part of a team, our fate depends on our teammates, and their journey is critical to ours. We may find that we even sometimes defer our own goals and desires to help others, so that their stronger presence will later lead to a stronger overall team.

When to Participate

When we're in a game or story that invites our participation, when do we actually take action?

Many games alternate between periods of activity and relative passivity, when we get to either rest or simply catch up on what's going on elsewhere.

Many video games, particularly those that are played alone, can be paused even in the midst of intense action, giving us a chance to take a break.

There are several common types of situations in which a player can exert control. Generally these can be distinguished by whether or not the player can act at any time and if, when action is called for, the game will wait for the player or not.

Prompted with blocking: The term *blocking* comes from computer science and refers to a condition where everything comes to a halt until a necessary action is taken. In some electronic games, the player may be prompted to select one of several choices from an on-screen menu, and the game blocks (or waits indefinitely) until that choice is made.

Turn-taking games often use blocking: when it's one player's turn, everything stops until he makes his move. For example, in a board game like checkers, the game alternately blocks on one player's move and then the other's. In chess tournaments, a turn clock times how long each player spends thinking about his moves. Players may use up their individual allotments of time as they wish, but if one of them runs out of time, he loses.

Prompted without blocking: Sometimes a player is alerted to the need to act, but the game will proceed whether the player responds or not. In most games, a provocation is expected to be met with a response, but the provoked player may not be required to respond, and may instead choose for his own reasons to sit still and absorb the attack.

In video games, this style of interaction is most common in the platformer genre, where the player's job is to navigate a complex and moving 2D or 3D environment. Suppose you're on a ledge, trying to jump onto a moving horizontal platform. The platform moves back and forth whether you manage to jump onto it or not, and thus the game doesn't block on your action. But your character doesn't make any progress until you successfully make the jump.

This style of interaction is not based on strict turn-taking, but on windows of opportunity that come and go.

Continuous: In continuous interaction, the player can affect the game any time he wishes. In *Grand Theft Auto III*, you can hop into a car and drive around any time you want, for as long as you want.

In the first style of interaction, you're required to act when the need arises. In the others, you're free to act when you wish, but you need to pay attention and stay involved at all times, because you never know when your participation may be required. In games that block on your turn, or that provide some kind of pause or time-out opportunity, the pressure to respond is relaxed.

Time Control

While discussing stories in Chapter 4, I distinguished between the plot sequence and the potentially quite different view sequence.

In most media, the author determines both of these. In a traditional stage play, for example, the audience simply lets the performance flow over them.

But in some media, the flow of the presentation can be manipulated by the audience. Perhaps the lowest-tech example is the book. While reading a book, you can put it down whenever you want to, you can go back and reread chapters, and you can even skip around and read the chapters in any order you wish.

Watching a movie in a movie theater is like watching a play: you have no control. Watching that movie at home, though, on a VCR or DVD player, you regain all the control you have with books and then some. You can freeze-frame and even proceed forward and backward in slow motion.

Games can afford the same time flexibility.

In computer games, it's reasonable to think of providing all the same time controls to a player that he has on his DVD remote control. They may not all be useful (watching cut-scenes backwards may not do much for the game), but it's certain that some players would like to revisit their favorite moments and perhaps see them in slow-motion detail. Many games already scale time to some extent, usually by speeding it up: one second of player time may correspond to one hour of game time. Sometimes this time scale is even made explicit: in *The Legend of Zelda: Majora's Mask* there is a small clock on the bottom of the screen, marked in hours, and you can watch them go by as you play. Time is integral to this game, and understanding how to control it is important to winning. In other games, you can tell when a day has gone by because the sky changes color, or a new edition of the daily newspaper comes out. The two very different games *Pikmin* and *Grand Theft Auto: Vice City* both rely on a real-time clock, and their environments change as time goes by. Their worlds are synchronized to their clocks, so your plans have to be designed so that they can be carried out in harmony with what's happening in the world of the game. The game *Blinx: The Time Sweeper* explicitly provides VCR-like controls with which you can momentarily control the flow of time in the game.

In some games you can indeed rewind the whole thing and watch again. In the snowboarding game *SSX* you snowboard down a mountain, typically using a first-person or wingman's view. When the run is over, you can watch the whole thing again from a variety of other cinematic points of view. This type of feature is also offered by several real-time strategy games, such as *Age of Empires*.

In addition to rewind and replay, players in some types of games, particularly simulation games, can fast-forward: you can set up the environment and then quickly let a couple of years (or a couple of hundred years) go by without your intervention, to see how it all turns out.

When game time proceeds at the same rate as world time, we often say that the events in the game are happening in *real time*. Otherwise, events are happening *off the clock* (the awkward terms *fake time* or *false time* are also sometimes used).

One of the most useful buttons on a VCR or DVD remote control is the *pause* button. The beauty of pause is that it recognizes that the tape or disk you're watching may not be the number-one priority in your life, and that you shouldn't be forced to choose between watching your movie and whatever else might be demanding your attention (e.g., a ringing telephone, a pot of boiling pasta, or a crying baby).

Most video games also feature a pause button, but some games disable it at crucial moments. Sometimes, as in *Final Fantasy X*, it is disabled during the cinematic sequences. This constraint obviously makes no sense at all: those little movies are no more important than the movies you might go out and rent, and there's no reason to keep the player hostage while they play (or else force you to miss the information presented in the scene).

Although one can sympathize with game designers who want to make sure that players stay in the moment, it's arrogant to demand that a player chain himself to his controller for the duration of a sequence, no matter what else might come up in his life. It's simply a matter of acknowledging that a game is part of a larger social environment and that changing priorities are a normal part of the lives of its players. When a game becomes a lower priority, the lack of a pause button often can force a player to sacrifice all the progress he's made since the last save point.

Saving

How and when players are able to save video games varies significantly from one game to the next. When and how players can save is a topic of ongoing debate. Before discussing the issues, let's look at some of the common options.

Where: In some games you can save a game no matter where you are. Saving may be enabled all the time: you just pause the game and save your progress. *Golden Sun* has this style of saving. Alternatively, you may have a number of tokens (e.g., magic beans or spells to cast), each of which allows you to save once. You can invoke these items no matter where you are.

In other games, you can only save when you arrive at a "save point." Such points are typically scattered around in the game's world. Sometimes they're clearly artificial (e.g., a pillar of light that you enter), and sometimes they're integrated into the environment (e.g., a safehouse you own). *Final Fantasy X* places "save spheres" in the environment, and you can save whenever you reach one.

In most games, the save points are obvious. But some games hide one or more of them, to crank up the difficulty a bit.

When: In games that use save points, you can only save when you're actually there. A save point may disappear when you use it, or it may remain so you can return to it later and save again.

In games that let you save anywhere you want, this feature is frequently disabled at certain times, such as during battle. If you want to save, you need to remember to do so before getting into a fight.

How many: Some games allow you to have as many saved versions as you have the memory to store. Others, particularly console games, provide only a small number of "slots" into which you can save games. The game *The Legend of Zelda: Oracle of Seasons* gives you three save slots. *Advance Wars 2* has only a single slot for saving.

Restoration: In some adventure and fighting games, a side-effect of saving
is that you're brought back up to full health. In others, a saved game
is a faithful checkpoint of your current situation. If you're almost out
of health and weapons when you enter a save point, you'll emerge
the same way.

Many players and designers feel passionately about how saving is handled in a game.

Those who support unlimited, anytime saving argue that this respects
the player's time and lets the player take the game at his own speed and
in his own way. It promotes exploration and trying out new ideas. For
example, if you're about 10 minutes away from the nearest save point but
have an idea for something you'd like to try that just might backfire badly,
you'd probably be reluctant to give it a go since the cost of failure will be
that you'll have to repeat the last 10 minutes of play. If you can save just
before trying, and it's a total disaster, you could simply reload the saved
game and continue from there. Some people feel that flexibility strips
the game of its challenge. They're both right: it's a matter of taste and
preference.

Those who support limits on how and when you can save argue that
these restrictions promote challenge and tension in the game and reward
players for developing their skills. They point to those players who save
the game after almost every step and therefore virtually never take a risk
or face real challenges. If you can save after each micro-advance in the
game, then you can just reload over and over until you do well at the next
step, and then save that new situation. In adventure and fighting games
you could save after defeating each enemy, marching your way through the
game one opponent at a time (even when there are hordes to fight). In
card games, you could just reload and redeal each hand until you got a
great set of cards, basically building a record containing nothing but victories. Advocates of restricted saving also argue that saving is an unrealistic
and interruptive activity, so that each time a player saves he's yanked not
only out of any story experience, but the whole game experience as well.
Their opponents counter that people play games for their own pleasure,
and if they want to save after every tiny step of progress, they should
be able to, since they paid for the game and should be able to play it
as they want.

It seems likely that there is no "best" answer in this debate, but that saving mechanisms depend on the nature of the game and the tastes of its designers and players. Each particular saving scheme has its positives and negatives, and each is probably a good match for some particular type of game and playing style.

The saving scheme could even be made an option for the player. For example, if a player chooses to make saving harder (e.g., by specifying fewer save points), the game could respond by increasing that player's score by an appropriate amount to reward the increased challenge.

Identity and Reputation

One of the socially valuable functions of games is that they allow people to come together in situations where they can give free reign to aggressive and competitive impulses, yet not cause any lasting harm to other people, property, or personal relationships.

The freedom to wreak mayhem in a mob is largely due to a feeling that there will be no meaningful personal consequences. In Figure 15 I introduced the Intimacy Matrix, which characterizes social gatherings with respect to the size of the group and how well the members know each other. Typically, the better people know one another, the less likely they are to act anti-socially towards each other.

Online media seems to change things in a few ways, even among people who are introduced. *Flame mail*, or email written in anger, is a surprisingly frequent sight. People seem to be willing to hurl insults and derogatory epithets over email that they would never utter face to face. Like the mild man who becomes a terror behind the wheel of a car, the remoteness and isolation of sitting in front of a computer gives some people a feeling of insulation and license to act more impulsively and emotionally than when they're face to face.

Online games have contributed a new dimension to human interaction: true anonymity. This is different from being unknown: if you attend a party where you've never met any of the other guests, you're unknown, but you're not anonymous. You have *persistence*: after a conversation, people will remember your face, your clothing, and the sound of your voice.

In some online environments it's not hard to distinguish between people who are there because of a serious, shared interest, and those who are just visiting or simply curious. For example, in some specialized chat rooms, there is an expected fluency in the jargon of the subject, and someone who doesn't use the language correctly will stand out as an outsider.

Some online environments offer different forms of persistence, and we'll get to those in a moment. But many online environments have no persistence at all. Consider a typical non-persistent online gaming room. You arrive at the site, type in the name (or *handle*) you want to use, and as long as it's not already in use, it's yours. Now you're in the room, and you can start playing games.

Because players can log in using a different name every time they visit the site, or even appropriate the well-known name of another player, these sites offer no history or accountability. This is an invitation for trouble: there's no cost to those who want to create disruption for the sheer sake of doing so, and generally no lasting punishment to those clever enough to get around techniques designed to limit such behavior.

The web-based online game *Acrophobia* was a good example of this problem. The game offered a number of "rooms" for players to enter. When enough people entered a room, a web page opened for that room and the game began. The system announced a category and several letters chosen at random. It was the job of the players to invent a humorous acronym describing something in the category based on those letters. Players then voted on each other's answers, with the intent that players with the most clever or entertaining answer would get the most votes. For example, the category might be "Famous Animals", and the random letters "FWM." One player might enter "Flying Winged Monkeys," while another could submit "Foul-smelling Wombat Mascot."

With a good group, the game could be literate and entertaining fun. But some players would simply type in lists of obscenities that started with the given letters, without even trying to create a grammatical phrase. With even one or two people playing this way, the game degenerated quickly, and the other players soon left.

There was no cost to this disruptive behavior, since each time you visited the website, you were free to pick any name you pleased. There was no persistence, so there was no accountability. For some reason this particular behavior caught on, and before long, every time you joined a game, there was certain to be one or more of these disruptors. Eventually the creative players stopped coming, and the site folded.

Avoiding this problem means imposing some kind of control on the proceedings, for example by restricting access in the first place, or restricting options once the player has entered the environment. Another way to impose this control is to encourage participants to build up good reputations over time.

Anonymity

Pure anonymity destroys community.

People have tried a variety of techniques to deal with the problems created by anonymity on game servers. In a commercial context, the auction site eBay has created way of maintaining persistence by assigning its members numerical scores and written feedback. People are normally leery of buying from people with very little feedback, or significant negative feedback, and tend to patronize those sellers with very positive reputations. That patronage in turn further enhances those reputations, so the sellers with the best feedback tend to dominate when the same item is offered by multiple people simultaneously.

One can track people's contributions to a discussion based on how frequently they provide useful information, and other feedback solicited from the people who often read a site [125].

The people who frequent a given online site may also judge their own postings. The Slashdot online news site allows readers to provide feedback not only for every article but for every posting that follows up every article. Readers can set a threshold for the comments they want to see based on the average score those comments have received so far.

The idea of building and preserving reputations has started to take hold on many online entertainment sites. In multiplayer games like *Everquest*, players are naturally inclined to build up a positive reputation for their characters, because they will end up investing many hours in helping those characters grow their abilities.

Guided Interaction

Earlier I referred to times when an interactive system might prompt a player for participation. This is an example of *guided interaction*: the environment is not only telling the player that it's time to do something but is usually giving him some sense of what sorts of things he is expected to do. At the other extreme is *free interaction*, when the player is free to do anything the game allows.

In any environment, real or computerized, there are always limits on what we can do. In real life, we cannot jump over tall buildings. In a computerized baseball game, we're unlikely to be able to direct our players to go to the stationery store and purchase multicolored paper clips. The range between guided and free interactions is set by the environment itself. In a guided 3D environment, for example, you might be given the choice of walking down a street in one direction, or in the opposite direction. In a free environment, you might have free control over your character, with the ability to direct him to walk anywhere in the environment at whatever pace you like.

Physical games share these restrictions. A baseball batter must stand in a particular place when batting, but he can send the ball anywhere he wants to. If he does make a legal hit, he is constrained by the rules to run directly to first base and nowhere else.

Although constrained, many guided activities are fun. Square dancing is explicitly guided by a "caller" who tells the dancers which moves to execute. In the *Cinematrix* [27] system discussed in Chapter 1, a guide helps the audience through a variety of games and group experiences.

Another guided experience is the party game *Mad Libs*. This game begins with one person selecting a pre-written short story that is missing a few critical words. These missing words are labelled by their type of speech (e.g., adjective, noun, or verb), and the players are asked to supply the missing words without knowing anything about the underlying story. For example, the person filling out the form might ask the group for an adjective, and someone may volunteer "cross-eyed." Because people tend to choose silly or amusing words, and the stories themselves tend to be inherently absurd or risque, the resulting non-sequiturs and bizarre out-of-context juxtapositions of ideas can be very funny.

One variation to the basic *Mad Libs* format is to reuse the same volunteered words several times in the story. This repetition helps knit the story together, even in the face of odd choices in subject matter and new words. For example, suppose a story needs an adverb, and someone volunteers "suspiciously." It could then be used in several places, so all the characters in the story carry out some perfectly mundane tasks "suspiciously."

A computerized version of *Mad Libs* could take this idea even farther, by building on the player's words. For example, if a player describes a car as "old," it might later break down. If it's an "old junker," it might also get a flat tire with no spare in the trunk.

The degree to which an experience is guided might not be obvious to the participants: things can be much more or less controlled than they appear to be.

Many computer games guide interaction by controlling where you can go: if you need to leave a room that has only one unlocked door, then it's pretty clear what you're expected to do next. This kind of control can take place on a larger scale, such as requiring you to complete all the tasks in one area before you can move on to the next. In *Ratchet & Clank*, there are force fields in some rooms that prevent you from entering. You must deactivate these fields before you can get in and continue with the game.

This kind of controlled interaction can be used to gradually reveal a preconstructed story. As a character moves through a series of environments and has a variety of encounters, bit by bit an underlying story can be revealed in a carefully-sequenced way. The games *Deus Ex* and *Metal Gear Solid 2* gradually expose their stories this way.

Who Am I?

In many forms of interactive fiction, both current and speculative, the player is imagined to be "in" the experience as a "first-person" character. Perhaps the most common example of such games today are the so-called "first-person shooters," such as *Halo* and *Half-Life*. In these games you play a character who has some pretty powerful weapons at his disposal and moves through the environment destroying enemies.

The first-person point of view is a well-established narrative tool, as we discussed in Chapter 4, and it works very well in action-oriented genres such as shooters, where the decisions to be made typically don't have much to do with character development or personality, but rather with where to go and how best to blow up one's enemies. But in a game where a character must make personal decisions, and possibly change as a result, the situation is much more complicated.

Suppose that you're playing a mystery game, and your character discovers that he has unwittingly helped his best friend commit a murder. Your character may have freedom of action, or he may be given several choices to select from. Either way, your character faces a moral dilemma that forces him to choose between turning in his friend or risking his own freedom.

This dilemma raises a conceptual problem the size of a mountain.

The essence of the problem is that it isn't clear on what basis you, the player, should be making this decision. You, the player, are *not* the character. The character may be a young, rich adventuress in her mid 20's with a pony tail, exploring old ruins in her sunglasses and short-shorts, or he might be a 50-year old, hard-drinking, street-wise tough ex-cop with a short temper, a tendency to violence, and a chip on his shoulder. Whatever and whoever the character is, you might have little in common with him, yet it's up to you to direct how he should act.

Here are some perfectly reasonable questions you could ask yourself when faced with a character-guiding choice:

- Regardless of how the game has presented this character, what would *I* do? That is, what would *I*, the player, choose to do if I were the one in this situation?

- What do I think this character thinks *he* should do in this situation?

- What do I think this character, left to his own devices, actually *would* do in this situation?

- Given what I know of the game, which option would give me, the player, the sort of result that would be the most fun for me to play, regardless of this particular character's personality?

Each of these questions leads to an audience experience that's very different from the others.

A big part of the problem is that the games themselves are usually unclear whether you should be using the character's morality and personality, or your own. Acting as the character seems somehow true to the spirit of the game and story, but on the other hand, you're the one playing and you should be having fun.

The problem gets even worse, because if we care about this character, we will care about what happens to him. If we think about the future, we're led to consider another important set of mutually incompatible choices.

- Should I help this character achieve his present goals, even if it hurts him in the long run?

- Should I make choices for this character that will lead him towards personal growth, even if it's against his will?

- Should I ignore this character and use this opportunity to move the game's world in a direction that appeals to me?

A common thread here is deciding whether you're trying to live inside the character's head, or inside your own.

Living inside our own heads is easier, since that's where we spend most of our time. Getting inside the head of another person requires empathy. Performing from within their world is acting, and as we discussed earlier, that is a difficult and specialized skill. Even in the privacy of one's own home, getting into the mind of a character in a story sufficiently well so that we can perform as that character is difficult for many people.

It's essential that the player always know his role in an activity, and in what way and to what degree he should inhabit the character he's playing and take responsibility for him. The player needs to know if the character is meant to be himself, in the world of the game, or if the character is somone else that he is controlling. If it's the latter, the player needs to know the goal of this control, both inside the world of the game and in his own experience as a playing participant.

Games that don't explicitly guide the player toward establishing a particular relationship with his on-screen persona risk leaving the player in a quagmire of conflicting and confusing options.

⇥ 9 ⇤

Branching and Hypertext Narratives

L et's use the Story Contract to look at a couple of forms of interactive fiction that have appeared in several variations: *branching narratives* and *hypertext narratives*. These two techniques deserve close attention because they are by far the two most frequently used structures employed today for involving the audience actively in a story.

"Nonlinear Stories"

Despite a tremendous amount of effort and money, neither branching nor hypertext has found much enduring success in the commercial arena. There are several books devoted to building academic theories of narratives in each of these approaches, which look forward to a future when the technique has matured [13] [78]. That future has not yet come to pass, and I think it's not likely to.

The techniques of both branching and hypertext are certainly useful for many applications ranging from reference works to personal artistic expression; I'm certainly not suggesting that these forms are without value. But they are not good ways to tell the sorts of things we call stories.

Works in both of these forms are sometimes referred to as "non-linear stories." As I discussed in Chapter 1, this term is now so overloaded with alternative and contradictory meanings that it's no longer descriptive of anything in particular. Even worse, the term itself is an oxymoron, like "dry water." That's because, as we saw in Chapter 3, stories are inherently linear: a protagonist is confronted with a problem and takes a series of steps to solve it, leading up to a climactic conclusion. A story begins, develops, and ends. We also saw in Chapter 3 that the *view* order can differ from this plot order.

Telling a story out of sequence is a common technique used in many forms of storytelling. Some movies and books begin near the climactic end and then back up to the tell the story that brought that situation about. *A Prayer for Owen Meany* has a structure like this. The movie *All About Eve* starts with the presentation of an award to the title character and then backs up to show us how she got to this point. Other presentations hop about in time, as in the novel *Slaughterhouse Five*.

But regardless of whether the story is presented forwards, backwards, or randomly, the underlying plot itself is most certainly linear. The presentation itself is also linear, in the sense that it presents one piece of the story at a time. A creative mismatch can be created when the order in which the pieces are presented doesn't match the order in which they occur in the timeline of the story. Such techniques are based on *resequencing*, or changing the order of presentation, rather than on any non-linearity in the story itself.

A "non-linear story" is like a "non-reflective mirror"; take away the linearity and you don't have a story anymore. As we look to develop ways for audiences to enter into stories, we should retire the overloaded and self-contradictory term "non-linear story" and its relatives, and look for terms that are more precise and descriptive.

Branching Narratives

A typical *branching narrative* offers the audience a piece of a story and then asks them to make plot or character decisions. The effects of these decisions may be very small and short-lived, or they may make a huge difference to the story and change everything from that point on.

Writers have been trying out branching narratives for centuries. An early and widely-read example is *Tristram Shandy*, a very funny novel from the

1760s that still makes for great reading today. That book uses an astonishing number of literary devices and games throughout the text. In Chapter IV, the author introduces a digression this way: "To such, however, as do not choose to go so far back into these things, I can give no better advice, than that they skip over the remaining part of this Chapter...."

A common example of branching technique in today's games is the *multiple-choice dialog*. A computer character speaks to you, and then you are offered a series of responses that your character may say in return.

Branching narratives do not require a computer, or any technology beyond the printed page. The *Choose Your Own Adventure Series* [26] books for children present segments of stories, each followed by a multiple-choice question for the reader. Depending on which answer you choose, you're instructed to turn to a particular page and read on, until you reach the next decision point.

The simplest structure for such books looks like a tree, where each story segment corresponds to a branch, as in Figure 16.

Most branching narratives quite reasonably ask the audience to make decisions at points in the story where those choices matter. They rarely ask the audience just what temperature a character's bath water should be set to, or whether he should brush his upper teeth or lower teeth first in the morning. Rather, an audience's choices are solicited at moments when they make a difference. For example, our hero runs out of a burning building, but then hears someone upstairs cry for help. Should he run to a neighbor and call the fire department, or should he run back into the building and try to find the person he heard calling out?

It makes sense to ask the audience to contribute at such points, because that's where they feel their decisions make a difference. The most important of these moments are those times when the character is facing maximum stress and conflict. After all, if we ask the reader to choose a path when the choice isn't very important, what's the point of asking? So decisions are made when they matter.

But recall that such moments are when the writer's control is most essential! How characters behave under stress is precisely what reveals their real personality.

As time goes on, if the audience is not consciously constructing a coherent personality, they may end up making decisions that don't work together. For example, they might have a character take great offense to a perceived slight to his honor at one point, and then shoplift at another, and

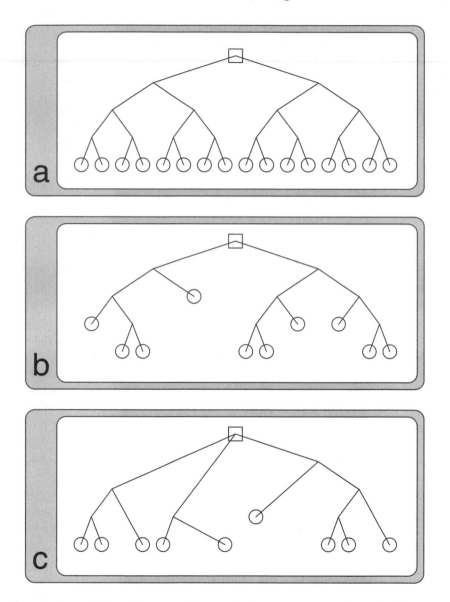

Figure 16. A branching narrative can be drawn as a tree, where decisions are at branching points, and pieces of story correspond to the branches themselves. In these examples, the story begins at the square node and ends at a circular node. (a) A fully populated tree. (b) A partially populated tree, also called an *unbalanced* tree. (c) An unbalanced tree where some of the decision nodes have been removed.

242

then betray a colleague later on. People are complex and harbor many contradictions, but those contradictions are able to coexist because they're part of a larger, integrated personality. Like a mosaic made of many differently-colored chips, close examination may show a random jumble of colors, while a larger view reveals a coherent image. That larger image is the personality that lives deeper within the character, and is not immediately obvious from just a few actions. Without that coherent core, we just have someone doing unrelated things.

As a character's personality becomes increasingly fragmented, it becomes harder for the audience to identify with the character, and thus harder to care about him.

Ultimately, a character who behaves completely unpredictably becomes uninteresting, because we have no idea what he's going to do, and no understanding of why he does it. He becomes like a force of nature: unpredictable and unthinking.

Allowing the audience to make crucial decisions for a character, and thus to implicitly determine his psychological makeup, is a violation of the first clause of the Story Contract, which places control of the main character's psychology in the hands of the author. The author has the large-scale view that allows him to develop a complete personality with many interesting facets, which can capture and hold our attention and sympathies.

When an author describes what a character thinks and does, he is working from knowledge and craft, shaping plot moments and actions designed to reveal particular aspects of the character for particular reasons. He often then returns to earlier material and edits it, going back and forth to make all the pieces work together. The audience doesn't have access to any of that information: they don't know what's going to come up later, so they can't anticipate it or design choices to create a rich conflict at the end. When the audience is making decisions for the character, they're working from ignorance.

It's interesting to note that these problems are not theoretically insurmountable. An author could work with the tree diagram of Figure 16, composing a good story for every possible path from the start to every ending. That way, no matter what option the audience chose at each step, the result would be a satisfying story.

This approach strikes me as an enormous endeavor with meager payoffs. Creating a single good story is hard enough; creating many good stories is much harder, and creating many stories that all work given a set of shared starting points and a wide variety of choices is daunting. If there are ten branching points over the course of the story, and three choices at each branch, that means the author must write a few more than 59,000 stories! They will have shared beginnings, but even if each ending is only a paragraph long, this is still an overwhelming amount of work, and most of it will be wasted on any given reader who is unlikely to see more than a tiny fraction of it.

Faced with this combinatorial explosion, authors of branching narratives often adopt a simpler structure, like that shown in Figure 17. Sometimes this structure is referred to as a branching narrative with *rejoined* branches, meaning that the different threads of the story line join up again after diverging. This is also called a *bulging tree*. This technique obviously can greatly reduce the workload on the story creators.

Other variations on the basic branching structure have also been tried out. Meadows has suggested the diagram of Figure 18 as a possible structure for an "open-structure" branching narrative [92].

The logical extreme of this approach is what mathematicians call a *complete graph*, in which every decision node is connected to every other node, as in Figure 19.

These structures are interesting from a theoretical point of view, but in the 240 years since *Tristram Shandy*, we're still waiting for a story told this way to become widely popular. The problem is that this kind of structure just doesn't work well for fiction.

Figures 18 and 19 are particularly troublesome because they limit the author's control over rhythm and pace, repetition, theme and variation, and even causality. If you can revisit the same piece of the narrative over and over, not only will it become boring, but it will eventually become annoying. With very rare exception, stories don't repeat without variation.

None of these branching structures, or their cousins, have achieved mainstream success. One reason is the simple fact that branching narratives are significantly harder to write than traditional forms.

Another reason is that their appeal to audiences is mostly based on novelty. What is it about the form that would attract an audience to a branching narrative, rather than an equally well-written story in a traditional structure? Is it simply that they can periodically make choices? That's certainly unusual, but it's hard to see why that in itself would make the story experience more attractive. In fact, it detracts from the experience,

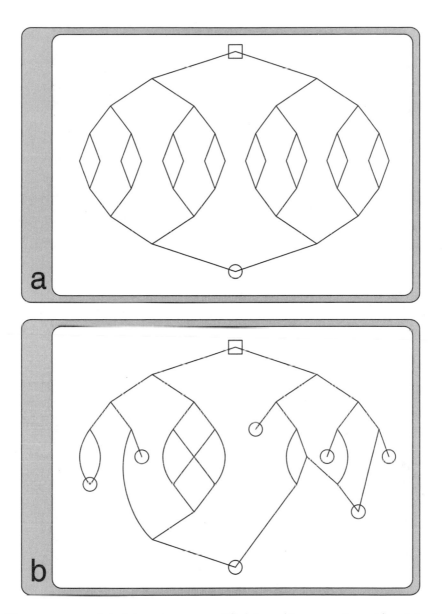

Figure 17.   A bulging tree: a modified branching narrative with rejoined branches. Diverging branches going down indicate a decision point. (a) A complete bulging tree. (b) A partial bulging tree with multiple endings.

Figure 18. A grid branching structure. Players may move from any intersection to any other.

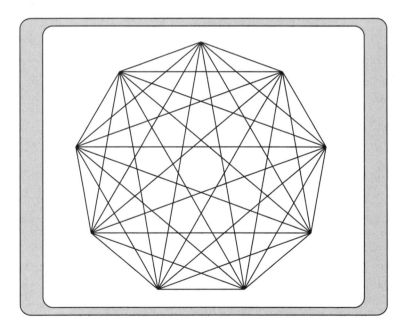

Figure 19. A complete graph with 9 nodes. Players may move from any node to any other.

since audiences are aware, implicitly or explicitly, that they know less about the characters and the storyline than the author. Why should they be deciding anything? If we choose a hard-boiled detective story set in 1940s Los Angeles, that's what we want, and we pick an author that we believe will deliver a rewarding story in that genre.

How is a story improved by our making decisions in ignorance of their implications? We want our stories to be rich and well-woven, and these stories come about when someone has broad skills and the opportunity to go back and revise and improve the work until it is all of a single piece. Forcing (or inviting) the audience to make decisions doesn't help the storyteller, the story, or the audience.

Branching structures are already widely used in other situations, with mixed results. Branching is great for creating a customized computer, for example. Using an online form, you can select a processor and then a disk drive. Your options at each step are generated in real time based on what you've selected so far, guaranteeing that you can only select individual parts that are guaranteed to work together.

On the other hand, if you call a large company these days, you're likely to have to deal with a choice-driven branching phone system taken straight out of a lower level of Dante's *Inferno*. After being told that "your call is important to us," and then being urged to "listen to all the options as our menu has recently changed," you need to listen to a litany of what each button-push will mean to the system. Once you choose the option that you hope is closest to what you desire, you often find it's not quite right, and you have to back up or even start over. It's hard to see just what part of this experience is so delightful that some people believe it's a good way to tell stories.

Another problem with branching narratives is that they destroy the delicate state of trance that people fall into when in the thrall of a great story. In such a state, we become lost in the world of the story, whether it's in a book or on a screen, and our intellects and emotions get wrapped up in the events.

Imagine that you're watching a drama unfold, and the hero is getting into terrible trouble at the hands of someone he loves but who is hurting him. The confrontation builds and builds until it seems clear that a major moment is at hand. At that moment he must make an important choice: does he fight back by telling a terrible secret, or does he turn and silently walk away?

In a traditional story, we'll hope for one choice and fear the other, and we are riveted to the scene until we learn the resolution. But when it's our choice, we are ripped out of our emotional engagement, the story comes to a crashing stop and all momentum is lost, and we now stand outside of the scene, outside of the characters, and start to think objectively about our choices. "Well, *if* I choose to insult her, she'll probably get upset, and the she'll probably ..." and the trance is utterly gone. Imposing a time limit on the choice doesn't prevent this violent detachment from the story, but simply adds a sense of urgency on top of the jarring return to our own thoughts and feelings. The worst thing that can happen in a story is to lose the audience; the last thing an author wants to do is create a situation like this that will actively push them away.

In the mystery game *Under a Killing Moon* you play the detective Tex Murphy. Frequently you find yourself questioning people that you bump into through the course of your investigation. You need to pump them for information using multiple-choice conversations, but you need to be careful not to annoy them so much that they don't want to talk to you any more. Since you don't know these characters, and you can't read their body language or look in their eyes, you end up thinking about the phrases you're offered to speak on each round, and try to guess what will be to your advantage and what will not. This process misses all the subtlety and intuition of a real conversation and destroys any emotional momentum in the story.

There's another side to this problem, which is that what we, the audience, are doing *for* a character is almost never what the character is doing. Unless the on-screen character in a video game is pressing a button on a controller or keyboard, then our actions don't correspond to his. In well-designed games we can become so intimately familiar with the controllers that we can transcend this indirection mechanism, and even though we're pushing buttons, we may feel like we're shifting gears in a race car, steering a plane, slashing a sword, spiking a volleyball, or spinning an opponent around and throwing him in the air. But when we only turn to the controller occasionally, it's harder to keep up this automatic correspondence. When driving a car in the real world, many of us accelerate and brake with hardly a thought to actually moving our foot to the proper pedal and pushing. But those learning to drive need to consciously make those actions: they learn how to work the pedals by discovering much pressure to use, and how quickly to press the brake to come to a halt at a red light. If we drove only infrequently, each trip would require a brief refresher period, during which we'd be very aware of the mechanics of what we're doing. Awareness of the mechanics is not a problem while driving, but suddenly having to think about the controller in your hands during a story causes you to leave the world of the story, and that's not something any storyteller wants to encourage.

So branching narratives, by virtue of suddenly making people move back into their own heads into order to make a decision, destroy the delicate thread that binds them to the story. Recovering that necessary connection is very hard, and after being jerked out of the story trace a few times, smart audiences will be unwilling to emotionally reconnect, knowing that they will just be disconnected again later. How much less emotionally stressful it is to remain detached, and then watch the story as an outside observer, rather than reenter and then lose again a delicate state of empathy.

Branching narratives have failed to find success in the mainstream because they offer no advantages to the author or the audience in terms of storytelling, and the sheer need for the audience to consciously make decisions destroys the vital empathetic connection between the audience and the characters they are identifying with and hoping and fearing for.

Note that branching narratives don't require computers. Putting branching narratives online lets audiences use new technologies for expressing their branching decisions, but it doesn't improve the basic form in any way.

Once you move to computers you can do other things, including extending branching narratives in a variety of ways. We'll return to that idea in later chapters.

But the basic idea of asking the audience to make story decisions, particularly at moments when those decisions are important, violates the first clause of the Story Contract, rips the audience out of the world of the story, disconnects them emotionally from the narrative and the characters, and, unsurprisingly, has failed to find acceptance as a popular storytelling form.

Hypertext

The idea of *hypertext* is to augment a document with *references* (or *hyperlinks*) that a reader can follow to other parts of the document, or to other documents altogether.

Easily the most widely-used form of hypertext today is the World-Wide Web, where the references are called *links*. By clicking on a link, readers can be taken to any other location on the web that the page's author thinks would be appropriate.

The idea of referencing one part of a document from another has probably been part of the written word since the transition from continuous papyrus scrolls to a set of individual pages. These collections of unbound pages were originally devoted exclusively to religious subjects, and together were called a *codex*. Today, the subject matter restriction has been lifted, and the pages are bound together, resulting in our now-familiar books.

Novels and non-fiction works are often treated like scrolls that have been segmented for easy handling: you start at the first word and read through to the end (though there's nothing to stop you from skipping around).

If the book is primarily meant for reference, like a dictionary or building code, then it's natural to go to an *index* which establishes a concordance between key words and the pages where they are defined and discussed.

Many books can be used both ways. We might read a book from start to finish once and then use the index at other times to revisit particular sections.

Many important religious texts have been organized in just this way. Because of the voluminous commentary that these works receive, the necessity of organizing everything led to the development of indexing systems that we would now call hypertext.

The Ramayana is an epic Indian poem about Indian life and culture, written about 1000 B.C.E. The stories often branch explicitly to other stories, so the reader finds himself moving through the book on a path determined by his interests at the moment, following the links between stories to get from one to the next.

A more explicit form of linking is visible in the central Jewish text called the Talmud, which was probably written somewhere in the third century. The Talmud contains not only the core text, but enormous quantities of commentary, and commentary on the commentary, and commentary on that commentary, many layers deep. Some of the commentators address each other in the form of direct rebuttal and references to other passages. Studying a section of the Talmud often means jumping around frequently, looking up how one definition affects another.

The Christian Bible was also augmented in this way. *The Eusebian Canons* is a multi-page document designed to allow a reader of the Bible to easily compare passages from different chapters (called books, or gospels). The pages of prepared Bibles were marked with numbers in the margins which took a reader to the right place in the Canons, where the reader could find a list of "links" to other related passages. Pages from the Eusebian Canons appear in the classic illuminated Celtic masterpiece *The Lindisfarne Gospels*, which may have been produced around A.D. 724.

Such hand-compiled and managed indexing systems were notoriously difficult to create, and daunting to change, augment, or update. Furthermore, they offered no memory of what searches you've made before or personalization to help you quickly find just the connections you want, rather than all the connections that are available.

The modern form of hypertext was first described in July 1945 by Vannevar Bush [20] and later elaborated by Ted Nelson [99].

As a reference tool, hypertext has proven itself useful beyond any doubt. The information revolution brought about by the rapid expansion of the Internet would probably have never happened without the ability of web pages to link to themselves and to each other.

It's clear that the hypertext idea, which has existed for centuries, has truly come into its own with the contributions of computers, thanks to their fast and easy access to enormous mass storage and programmable tools to discover related, up-to-the-minute information on demand.

But as a storytelling medium, hypertext has been unsuccessful. Despite many attempts at creating stories with a hypertext structure, a plethora of authoring tools (such as the well-known *Storyspace* [68]), and extensive bodies of hypertext narrative theory, there are not many mainstream successes.

There are a few famous examples of literary hypertext. The novel *If on A Winter's Night A Traveler* presents at least two different stories depending on how the book is read. In the introduction to the novel *Hopscotch*, the author encourages his audience to read the chapters in any order, though he does suggest two preferred sequences. One can argue that the 1939 novel *Finnegans Wake* offers an early version of hypertext. Published just a few years later, the short story "The Garden of Forking Paths" definitely offers linked pieces of text that we would recognize today as hypertext. About 20 years later, the poetry book *Cent mille milliards de poèmes* was published. The book contained 10 nontraditional sonnets, each of which was 10 lines long. The pages were cut into horizontal strips, so by flipping the strips over, you could "build" a new sonnet by choosing any of the 10 first lines, then any of the 10 second lines, and so on down through the poem. The 1991 work *afternoon, a story* is an example of literal hypertext, designed for reading on a computer.

These examples are not unknown; many are famous and are widely-taught and studied. Why then are we not all reading hypertext stories? *Finnegans Wake* was published over 60 years ago, and *afternoon, a story* was published over a decade ago. Yet there are very few popular works that have built upon these explorations and taken them to a wider audience.

There are several reasons why hypertext fiction hasn't caught on, but the central one is that hypertext destroys linearity. Although removing linearity can be an interesting idea to play with, and allows for a variety of artistic expressions that were previously difficult to create and share, we saw in the last section that it's not a good technique for storytelling.

After all, when an author selects an order in which to present the events of the story, he is choosing that order deliberately. Whether time flows smoothly forward or backward, or is interrupted by flashbacks and flashforwards, or advertises the future or links to the past, those are all decisions that the author has made in order to tell the story as well as possible. If the author felt there was a better order in which to present the story, he would have chosen it. The author is the right person to make this choice, since he is familiar with all the characters and all the events that are involved in the story. How is the reader supposed to make informed choices that are even nearly as good as those made by the author?

To make the situation even more difficult for the reader, hypertext connections are often unpredictable. As practiced in most online documents, certain words or phrases are highlighted (often they appear in a different color or are underlined) to indicate that they're a link. The reader doesn't really know what's going to happen when he follows a link.

For example, suppose we're reading a piece of hypertext fiction in which a character named Lucy appears, and at one or more points her name is identified as a link.

Clicking on her name may take us to Lucy's biography, a picture of her home, a piece of audio of her reciting the alphabet song as a first-grader, or a picture of her tombstone. These types of links aren't the worst of the lot, because even though they interrupt the narrative flow, they are supplemental information that can be viewed simply as a diversion.

Sometimes clicking on Lucy's name will take us to another piece of text that involves Lucy in some way. But which text? There's no way for the reader to know. Will it go to an action sequence? A quiet and contemplative reflection? A fight between Lucy and her son? A scene of her brushing her teeth? We just don't know. And since we don't know, our choice in following the link is essentially meaningless. If I'm given three choices, but I don't know what they represent, I'm essentially choosing at random. So why burden the reader with this at all? Just put a single button at the bottom of the page that unpredictably takes the reader to one of several other pages. If it's not random, then the reader needs to be given a lot more information in order to make an informed decision.

Reading most hypertext fiction is like looking at a restaurant menu that has just three words: "meat," "vegetables," and "drinks." You order one and hope that whatever the waiter brings you actually does belong in that category, and that you like it. You may be allergic to red wine, but if you choose "drinks" and you get red wine, too bad. Making readers click on links is one way to make them feel involved, but any sense of control or choice is largely illusory, and readers who are thirsty for a story experience quickly tire of the essentially random exploration.

Even if the reader were given enough information to make informed choices, we again need to ask what, if anything, is gained by this transfer of responsibility?

It's hard to see what practical benefits hypertext has for an author or a reader. Theorists enjoy thinking about issues like post-modern narratives, deconstructing texts, and hypothesizing what a successful form of hypertext might look like in a possible future. These ideas are fun to think about, but they're the wrong tools for the job of storytelling.

In no other field of art has this type of audience participation proved attractive. In the mainstream arts, dancers don't ask the audience to choreograph a ballet for them given a set of basic moves, painters don't give their buyers a set of painted tiles and invite them to assemble their own image, and composers don't ask the audience to take a series of short motifs and sequence them into a piece of music. Certainly all of these things have been tried as part of experimental works, but by their very nature those works were designed to test these ideas and see how well they were received. The fact that we don't see these sorts of things in the mainstream suggests that those experiments provided a consistent result: *audiences do not want to do the author's work.*

Nor should they.

The situation is made even more stark in storytelling, where sequentiality is critical. Reading a hypertext poem can be a satisfying experience: we can get a feeling for mood and imagery in a loosely-related series of vignettes. But reading a hypertext story is hard: it requires mentally piecing together the fragments of the narrative as they're encountered. Thus we might see an injured man in ripped clothes running down a street, then the same man eating breakfast in the same clothes except that they're in good repair, then an angry brawl between that man and a woman on an airplane, and then the same man looking through holiday photographs. What's going on? In a well-constructed story, the author will begin to tie these images together before the audience becomes hopelessly lost (the novel *Fierce Invalids Home from Hot Climates* begins with just such a series of disconnected vignettes, and then embarks on a traditional linear narrative that eventually unites them).

Because a story is inherently linear (no matter in what order it is presented), giving a reader too many of these disconnected pieces will force him to have to begin assembling them in his own head, like putting together a jigsaw puzzle. This is an interesting intellectual experience, but it's a huge distraction from the story itself. Rather than getting lost in the story, the reader is constantly pulled out of it, forced to step back and try to knit the pieces together before he forgets them.

This puzzle-solving experience is fun for some people, but frustrating for others. The television show *Twin Peaks* presented a linear (though loose) story amidst a dense set of images and what seemed to be relevant symbols. Many people got caught up in the puzzle aspect of figuring out the symbology until the whole thing got so complicated that, people gave up, viewership plummeted, and the show was cancelled.

Part of the author's job is to use rhythm, pace, control of detail, and many other techniques to help readers keep track of what is important and what is not. Hypertext eliminates that control over rhythm because you never know what piece of text the reader is going to encounter next. One person may never see a piece of text at all, while another will see it many times. If the author is willing to let this happen, then that means he has concluded that this piece of text is not essential to the story. If a piece isn't essential (that is, removing it doesn't damage the work), then it should be removed during the editing process. If on the other hand it is essential, then the reader should not be able to miss it.

With enough effort, an author can write the pieces of a hypertext story in such a way that he can control rhythm and pacing no matter what order the reader encounters the pieces, and he can make sure that everything important is discovered. This would be a prodigious amount of work, comparable to completely populating a branching narrative with good stories, but theoretically it's possible.

But again, we must ask who would benefit from this. Certainly not the reader, who is groping through the dark, choosing pieces of story to read next based on some combination of whimsy, intuition, experience, and randomness. Some hypertext stories don't even have an end; you simply stop reading them when you've had enough.

Take two readers who read the same hypertext story, and assume that it's a story that has one or more endings, so that each reader can say he's read it all the way through. Obviously, each reader had a different experience of the story. But that doesn't enhance either of their experiences. Suppose that you've just read the hypertext *Moby-Dick*, and so have I, but we read its chapters in different order. What has been gained? Until we compare notes, we don't know that we read it differently. But even then, beyond its value as an intellectual exercise, how has your experience of the story been improved over the sequence of presentation designed by the original author? If we both read the same pieces, we ended up reconstructing the same story in our heads eventually, but we got there by different routes.

Is your experience of the book somehow better than mine, or vice versa? Certainly it's different, but that doesn't make it a better story.

Traditional books weren't meant to be read as hypertext. But the problem is with the form, not with the underlying story. Suppose that we write a story that is designed explicitly to be read as hypertext. Perhaps there's a character that a reader can learn more about by clicking on her name, or there's a family home the reader can explore through photographs and sound files.

Again we come back to the central questions of why that material is there if it isn't necessary, and how the audience could be seen to be getting a better story from stumbling through the pieces.

Hypertext fiction violates the second clause of the Story Contract, because it puts the audience in control of the sequencing and timing of plot events.

Remembering Chapter 3, stories are carefully constructed to build an audience's involvement with one or more characters. Centuries of storytelling have shown us that great stories are created by an author who is in command of his material and shapes its presentation over time for maximum effect.

Hypertext is excellent for reference information, and for some forms of poetic expression, but the basic idea of giving the audience control over what piece of the story is delivered next is not useful for good storytelling.

Summary

We've looked at branching narratives and hypertext narratives in some detail in this section because today they are overwhelmingly the two most popular forms of giving audiences a say in the development of a story, whether used for fiction or as part of a game.

But neither of these forms has found mainstream success, in the sense that it has endured and grown to be popular in mainstream media such as television, films, and books.

Neither technique requires computer technology: they both work in book form, and writers have had hundreds of years to explore and refine them. Yet except for one line of branching narratives for children, and a few exemplars of experimental writing, there are very few stories told with either technique for sale in major bookstores.

There have certainly been computer games that use some of these ideas and have sold many copies. Looking over the field, we can see that those successes don't repeat well. There is always a market for novelty, and the first few people to try something new and interesting will find that their work attracts attention simply because the ideas are stimulating. But they're not proving to have much power to endure.

Beyond the appeal of their novelty, these forms don't benefit the audience. It's like selling a movie based on the technology behind the special effects. General audiences don't care about the mechanisms used to create or deliver a story, unless they improve the experience. In practical terms, branching narratives and hypertext don't make stories better. It's no surprise that audiences aren't clamoring for more.

I've been pretty hard on these two techniques because they reappear over and over in their basic forms. This proliferation means people are continuing to write stories and games based on branching narratives and hypertext, hoping that they will be the ones to make them finally work. This is like trying to build a house with a can opener and a staple remover: they're fine tools, just not the right ones for the job.

But there's a reason that these forms are so attractive, despite the lack of success: they're moving in the right direction. Both of these forms hold the seeds of an *adaptive* storytelling form, but they don't quite achieve it. The principle of *adaptation* will be an important part of the tools we need to create interactive stories that will be attractive to mainstream audiences. In Chapter 12 I'll expand on that idea.

✦ 10 ✦

Common Pitfalls

M any contemporary computer games that are designed to combine
stories and games use a variety of techniques to bring the fields
together. Some of these techniques, while they were fun as
novelties, didn't catch on in the long run. Often the problem is that they
violate one or more terms of the Story Contract, but sometimes the problem
comes from other directions.

It's useful to understand today's games, because they're our best source
of information on human-computer interaction for entertainment. Understanding some of the common pitfalls of today's games can help us
avoid repeating those mistakes in future forms that combine story and
gaming ideas.

The Myth of Interactivity

A common design flaw is a belief that interactivity itself is the key to
blending stories and games. Interactivity is essential, but it's not all there
is. Yet the trend is to heap on more and more interactivity, perhaps in hopes
that one will eventually reach some kind of "critical mass" of interaction
which will suddenly make things better. I call this the Myth of Interactivity:

> *The Myth of Interactivity:* More interactivity makes any experi-
> ence better.

259

Like all myths, it contains a kernel of truth, but it should not be swallowed whole.

The most compelling defense in its favor is that in our fast-paced and competitive world, a player must be constantly engaged or he will move on. If the experience becomes passive, goes the argument, engagement is lost, and the player will become bored and leave. But this is clearly not true: people spend a lot of time watching television and reading stories, and there is no interactivity in those experiences at all.

The worse effect of this myth is that it elevates interactivity to a special status above other elements of the experience. Interactivity itself is hardly novel or interesting: an ATM is interactive (you push buttons and out come pieces of paper), and the automatic doors in front of a supermarket are interactive. The whole world is filled with interactive experiences, from waving down a cab to sharpening a pencil. Simply providing opportunities for players to engage in interaction does not give them something that is special in and of itself.

Interactive entertainment is nothing new. We've had the occasional interactive story since the first campfire. Some interactivity is obviously desirable, but it's not the case that more is better, any more than we would say that more sounds are better.

Fun and Interesting

We saw in Part I that the idea of the premise gives us a test for deciding whether a given scene or plot development should be included in a story or edited out. Is there a similar test for deciding whether or not to include a contemplated kind of interaction?

There is indeed. We can start with our observation that sheer interaction for its own sake has little value (except possibly novelty). Simply barraging a player with demands for interaction (e.g., things to click, and choices to make) does not make an experience worthwhile. A maze-bound rat must always choose a direction at each intersection, but those choices don't make its life fun or even interesting.

And those are the key words: *fun* and *interesting*. Any interaction in a game must be fun or, at the very least, interesting. If it is simply a hoop through which the player must jump, the player will sense the subterfuge and resent it; the result is that the interactive moment will work against the game, rather than for it.

Interaction inclusion: An interactive experience should be included if it offers a chance for the player to have an enjoyable or illuminating insight, or an exchange with the game designer or other players. An interactive experience must be fun, interesting, or both.

There are endless examples of games available today, some of which are highly regarded, which are loaded with pointless interactive moments. For example, riding an elevator and waiting for it to reach another floor is neither fun nor interesting (often such elevator rides are inserted to cover the time it takes to load the next piece of the game into the computer's memory, but that's no excuse for boring the player). In the game *Grim Fandango*, you need to take not one elevator, but two of them, every time you want to travel between your office and the garage. That's a lot of downtime.

Needless Demands

A game can create interaction by forcing you to carry out mandatory actions. A very small amount of this forced interaction can be fruitful, because it helps you understand the game's world through direct cause-and-effect experience. But too much of this forced control gets boring at best.

For the most part, good designers in the real world create objects that automatically do everything possible. For example, a dishwasher may carry out a complex cycle of events to clean dishes, but the person who gets the machine started only needs to push a couple of buttons. When I start my car, it goes through an extensive battery of self-test diagnostics, but all I have to do to get going is turn the key. That's no accident: designers create intelligent products because that's what's most convenient for people. We like it when the objects in our world largely take care of themselves. This saves us both the time we'd have to spend checking up on them, and the time and effort we'd have to spend learning how to do our own maintenance. Most people want their VCR to clear tape jams by itself; we don't want to unscrew the chassis and disassemble the mechanism to clear every jam.

My DVD player came with a remote control. The remote has all the usual buttons, such as Power, Play, and Pause. It wasn't until one day that I accidentally hit the Play button when the unit was off that I found that it automatically turned itself on in response. This makes perfect sense: if you push the Play button on your remote, then you want the power to be on, because you want to play the DVD! So the designers of the remote made sure that if you hit Play when the power was off, the unit would first turn itself on. My VCR doesn't work that way: I can push Play a hundred times, and nothing happens if the unit is off: it's up to me to figure out that the problem is that the tape deck is powered off, and that it's my job to turn it on first. The DVD remote is a better design, because it's more considerate of the people who use it.

Game designers should be just as considerate of their players' time and needs. Unfortunately, many games require you to go through whole sequences of actions that are unnecessary. And sometimes you need to do them more than once, which is particularly infuriating.

For example, it's common in many adventure-style games to have to move back and forth between two or more locations several times. In some games, you must plod step by step through all the intervening locations, even though you've been to each one before and have no reason to revisit them. In such a game, you might leave your office and travel down to your car, only to receive a cell phone call that requires you to pop upstairs to your office to retrieve a piece of paper out of your office desk. It would not be unusual for a contemporary game to require you to explicitly get out of the car, close the car door, cross the street, open the building door, cross the lobby, call the elevator, wait, get into the elevator, push the button for your office floor, and so on, and on, carrying out the inverse of all the steps you just took to get to your car. Then, to return to your car, you must carry out this dreary process yet again in reverse order. This is interactive all right, but horrible.

The game *Syberia* looks beautiful, but it forces players to travel through endless screens to get from one place to another. At one point you find yourself in a train station next to a university, near a large field. If you're in the field but you want to get into the school to check something, you have to click to move your character to the edge of the screen, watch her run there and exit the screen, watch the next screen load, click to move your character to the edge, watch her run and exit again, over and over a dozen times or more as you plod through each screen on your way to your destination. You've already visited these intermediate locations and explored them, so there's nothing new here, yet there is no way to avoid this dull, mechanical process, which quickly degenerates into a numbing tedium.

The game *Myst* offered a nice solution to this problem by giving you the frequent option to jump from one location to another one at some distance away, as long as you'd traversed the path at least once already. When you saw the lighting bolt cursor, you knew you could zip to the other location in one hop if you wanted.

Another surprisingly common but useless mandatory action is opening doors. How many times in real life do you approach a closed door without the intention to open it? It does happen, for example when we want to lean against the door or examine a poster tacked up to it. And in an old castle, where the doors are huge and take great effort to move, we might only open them when we're really motivated to do so. But most of the time we approach a closed door with the intent to try to open it. Oddly, a great majority of contemporary games require you to expressly open a closed door when you reach it. The default should be to open the door and to require the player to do something special for the exceptional case when you don't want to open it.

Neither fun nor interesting, these types of pointless activities don't come close to belonging in a game. One reason they persist is because games sell better if they promise a certain number of hours of play; it helps the player feel he is making a reasonable financial investment since there's going to be a payback in a lot of play time, which he hopes will equal a lot of fun. But there's the rub: you don't get back fun, you get back tedium. Walking through the same rooms and corridors time after time doesn't make me feel like I'm really in the environment; rather, it makes me angry that my time is being wasted and thereby alienates me from the game's world.

After all, in real life many of us spend hours tied up in traffic. Should our games require hours of downtime spent behind the wheels of virtual cars in virtual traffic jams? Of course not.

Taken to an extreme, this argument might suggest that we should include a button on the start screen for any game labeled "Win Game." All a player would have to do is push that button, and he'd win!

Such a "solution" brings to mind the story of cake mixes introduced in the 1950s. All you had to do was add water, and the mix produced a perfectly fine cake. These mixes didn't sell very well until the manufacturers altered the mix so that you needed to add water *and* an egg [10]. Because bakers had to break an egg and mix it in, they felt more a part of the process and felt that the cakes they created this way also tasted better.

A "Win Game" button would do away with the need for driving, shooting, running, puzzle-solving, and all other activities. Obviously this would be going too far. We play games because they're fun; I'm only arguing for removing the parts that are not fun. So we should only include tasks that are fun, interesting, or both.

> *A player's time should be respected:* A game should offer the fastest and easiest possible way to do everything unless there is some entertaining or informative reason to prevent it.

Deception

Deception is a staple technique of fiction, where it can be coupled with emotional manipulation and other techniques to engage an audience. But this is very principled kind of deception. The audience is in a relationship with the storyteller and trusts the author to deceive them in a way that will ultimately prove to be worthwhile. This is why the audience is willing to be manipulated and controlled, and even deceived, without resentment.

Bad deceptions are objectionable to everyone. Imagine a child who calls a parent on the phone, crying in pain from a terrible injury. When the parent reacts in shock, the child laughs and reveals that it was just a prank. This trick may amuse the child, but nobody else finds it funny, particularly not the parent on the receiving end of the call. Few game players enjoy similar pranks, particularly since they've paid time and money for the experience.

For example, suppose that you've walked down a long hallway to enter the basement lair of a mob boss you've been chasing for some time. The room is empty, but there are three normal-looking doors leading off into the rest of the compound. Since they all look the same, and you need to leave the room, you open the left door at random. As soon as you open it up, a tiger springs out. You try to run, but you didn't get enough of a head start, and the nearest big crate to climb up on is at the other end of the hallway. The tiger catches up with you when you're only halfway there. Game over!

When this kind of unexpected danger appears in a book or film, it can be very exciting. In the best fiction, we identify with the character and feel his panic. We learn about the hero from how he responds to this threat to his life and are carried along by our fear and our trust. We trust the writer of the story to make it satisfying for us, and worth our time and concern. We can also feel justified anger with the villain who placed our hero in this predicament.

But in an interactive story, *we* are the hero of the story. Recall our discussion in Chapter 8 about our point of view when playing: are we the character, or the person controlling the character? In the best situations, this line is blurred, so in some sense we and the character are the same person. So the person who's been tricked is not the external, observed character, but rather we ourselves. It's not the evil villain who put the hungry tiger behind that door, but the game's author. We are in constant conversation with the game creator, more than we are with almost any author or screenwriter, because the very fact that we are actively involved brings us into constant contact with the game's designer through the agency of his creation. Bad things done to the hero in fact happen to us, personally.

Sometimes this kind of planned deception is defended with an appeal to verisimilitude, since we run across deceptive information all the time in the real world. True enough: in the real world, we get false promises from politicians and lies from the media. But such an appeal is weak: just because deception appears in the real world doesn't mean it belongs in our entertainments.

Being the victim of a deception isn't the same thing as making a mistake. We make mistakes for many reasons, ranging from poor judgment or execution to incomplete information. Mistakes aren't always bad. Part of the fun of learning about a new environment is learning its new set of rules. And part of that experience means making mistakes by misinterpreting instructions, or mistaking a new object for a familiar old one and using it incorrectly. That's a natural part of learning.

But a deliberate deception is an artificial roadblock, created solely to make life harder for the player. That's not fun, that's annoying.

A nice counter-example to this rule is the Mimic character in the hand-held game *Golden Sun*. This is a creature who looks just like the standard treasure chest that you encounter frequently in the game. You always want to open these chests, because they hold useful items. But every once in a while you discover that the chest is actually one of these monsters in disguise, and when you try to open the chest, you're plunged into battle with this strong and dangerous monster. This is fair because Mimics don't take the place of everything, just treasure chests. So you quickly learn to always get ready for a fight before opening a treasure chest.

Once again, we can use our test for fun or interest to determine if a deception is of value in a game. In this case, saying that something is interesting may mean that it provides insight. Such insight can take many forms, such as a better understanding of the environment, the characters, or one's own purpose in the world.

> *Players should not be deceived:* A game should not deliberately trick a player unless the deception is fun or interesting for the player.

Player Profiling

I've discussed how the distinction between a player and the player's character is often unstated by a game, and it's left up to the player to decide what his relationship to the character ought to be. That is, he may act as himself, as he believes the character would act, or as he believes the character should act.

Some games have tried to reduce this ambiguity by creating a character that mimics the player. By posing a series of moral choices to the player, the game builds up a psychological profile of the player and uses that to drive the character, in turn affecting the player's character's relationships with the other characters in the environment. So a selfish player may be met with rudeness and antagonism, while a generous one might be taken advantage of as a sucker. Most games try to hide this process, so that players are not explicitly aware that they are being profiled.

This approach has a basic problem: how do you characterize a player's psychology? It's hard enough for people to understand each other, much less to design a computerized analyst to handle the task. People have spent thousands of years trying to figure out how we work, and although today there are workable theories of psychology and psychiatry, we're still a very long way from being able to succinctly describe human personalities.

So games that take this approach are forced to use some tractable model of personality, which inevitably means some crude form of personality quantification. The typical method is to assign the player (or his character) personality values along several axes of opposites: e.g., peaceful and wrathful, generous and selfish, or timid and bold. To determine these quantities, the game presents the player with a series of choices, which in effect try to replicate, in miniature, standard multiple-choice diagnostic personality inventories, such as the Minnesota Multiphasic Personality Inventory–2 [104]. These in-game choices are usually disguised as game decisions rather than outright questions about morality.

For example, you might find that your character is one of just a few survivors of a shipwreck. You've discovered a small cache of food; it's not much, but you know everyone is as hungry as you are. The game asks you if you're going to tell everyone else (or even anyone else) about your discovered food, or if you're going to hold it for yourself. The obvious device here is that the game is going to use your decision to place you (or your character) somewhere on a scale of generosity.

This just doesn't work. Even children see right through the disguised choices. Rather than deciding what to do in a situation based on their own feelings of right and wrong, players make choices for the protagonist they are controlling because they want to "make him mean" or "see what happens if you make him really stupid." Players *game the game*. In other words, they attempt to infer and then influence the underlying mechanism of the game. So they are not playing the overt game itself, but rather the programming under the game. In some cases, such as explicit simulation games, these may be one and the same. But in games that are story- or character-driven, this change in level marks failure for a game designer. By analogy, when a filmgoer is watching a movie for the first time and finds his thoughts wandering to how the special effects were made or how the crew created the makeup, he's left the world of the story and the film has failed him at that point.

Adults see through these personality tests as easily as children, but because they are more aware of the fact that they are being labelled and pigeonholed, they are more likely to resent it. And having paid for the game and invested valuable time, they are apt to be offended by this attempt to describe the complexity of their personality by a trivial scoring system. In effect, the player is being told that he can be characterized by a few numerical scores on a few axes. And just like children, adults are clearly aware of the need to think about how the game will interpret their choices, which removes them from immersion in the game itself.

The game *Black & White* explicitly requires players to choose the morality of a creature they are given to raise to adulthood. Each time you reward or punish your creature, you nudge it along an axis from good to evil, which affects its later actions as well as how the people of the world view the creature (and, by extension, yourself). The game shows the result of your choices visually by evolving your maturing creature toward either a kindly, gentle-looking animal or a scary, vicious-looking beast.

A key problem of all models that try to guess or infer a player's psychology or mornality from his choices is that they have very little flexibility in how they interpret those choices. The games create both the context and the specifics of each moral choice, and then have a built-in meaning associated with each response. In one sense, they have the right idea: as we've discussed, character is revealed by action under pressure. But these particular situations present only a narrow range of responses and intepret each response as though they knew what motivated the player to act that way.

In the game *Knights of the Old Republic*, your character starts out midway between two extremes of the "light side" and the "dark side" of The Force; these roughly correspond to virtuous and malignant. You can always check where you stand by calling up a visual display of your current status. Specific actions taken in the game result in the system explicitly awarding you light-side points or dark-side points. For example, if you meet someone who needs money badly and you give him some of yours, the game rewards you with light-side points. You may have given him the money because you figured he would invest it, so you could come back to him later and steal everything from him and come out ahead. The game of course can't discern this unkind intent and simply assumes you're a nice guy with nice motives.

Another form of character tracking is used in *Eternal Darkness: Sanity's Requiem*. As you explore a spooky old mansion, you're transported to different places and times where you encounter monsters that you must fight. During these fights you can slowly lose your sanity, represented by a meter on the side of the screen. As you lose your sanity, you begin to hallucinate, and then the game itself begins to act in startlingly erratic ways. This is strong motivation to take actions that can refill your sanity meter.

In the game *Jak II*, you can collect dark energy that will allow you to explicitly transform your character from "Light Jak" into "Dark Jak," who looks considerably different, and picks up a host of special moves and attacks.

Returning to our example of finding food on a desert island, the game may interpret a player's willingness to share as indicative of a generous nature, when in fact he suspected the food was poison and really just wanted to see if anyone died from it before he ate. Keeping the food might be interpreted as selfish, but the player may believe that it's not yet ripe and that if the other characters ate it, they would get sick. Nuance is important.

Details matter. How and why someone acts is as important as what he does. Computer models have no way to guess a player's motivations. Until we have a breakthrough in psychological research, computerized inferences of personality are doomed to be trivial, superficial, and frequently wrong.

Some products and web sites try to profile their visitors so that they can find other products to offer them. The Amazon website suggests books that were ordered by people who bought the same sorts of things that you're buying. The TiVo personal video recorder analyzes what you've recently watched and compares that to what other people have watched to pick up patterns that describe your interests. It then looks for other programs that it thinks you would like and records them as suggested viewing. From these suggestions, it can seem that the TiVo is not only guessing the age and genders of its owners, but also their sexual orientations [147]. This mistake can be pretty amusing, and it's forgivable because it doesn't cause any inconvenience, nor does it affect how the device operrates. And the feature can be turned off.

> *Psychology is subtle:* Games shouldn't try to infer and characterize the psychology of players.

Multiple-Choice Conversations

Some games guide you through the action by asking you to make choices from lists.

Often these choices arise in conversations with computerized characters who inhabit the game. When you need to speak to one of these "non-player characters" (or NPCs), you're not free to say anything you please: the technology to understand free-form language and craft a reasonable reply simply doesn't exist yet. So instead, everything is pre-scripted.

In order to allow you to make some kind of conversation, you're presented with a list of utterances and then given the opportunity to pick one. In the terms we used earlier, this is typically a *prompted with blocking* type of interaction: you're given your choices, and everything stops while you ponder your decision.

Some games don't actually block, but rather wait a while and then move on. For example, in the trivia game *You Don't Know Jack*, the game's host verbally prompts you to enter your name. If you don't respond in a few seconds, he'll prompt you again. If you still don't respond, the game will pick a name for you and continue from there. The advantages of this approach and several others in the design of the game are discussed in *The Jack Principles of the Interactive Conversation Interface* [56].

In a multiple-choice conversation, eventually you make a decision, and your character utters your chosen line. In many modern games, you can see your character's body language as you hear the prerecorded voice of an actor deliver the line you chose, and then the character you're talking to responds. He doesn't respond simply to the words, but as in any normal human conversation, he also responds to its tone and style. Then when he's done speaking, he either terminates the conversation or waits for you to choose another thing to say. Your list now may depend on what you selected last time (for example, if you threatened the character, he may have become angry, so now you're offered choices that will either soothe him or incense him farther; but if you placated him in your last statement, you might now have only idle chit-chat available).

There are a few problems with this technique.

Most importantly, the choice you want may simply not be on the list. Suppose that you're stranded at the side of a road, and someone stops to offer you a lift. The choices that are offered to you are to politely thank him and get in, politely decline, ask his name, or ask how far he is going. If one of these fits your desires, great.

But this is a conversation, not the SATs. There's no right answer and no best answer. Your answer depends on your relationship to your character, as we discussed above, and your own personality, mood, and reading of this particular situation.

Suppose that you think you recognize the driver as a rude man you argued with about local politics in the coffee shop earlier. You want to make sure he's that guy by asking him his opinion on the upcoming election, but that option's not available. This is worse than unfortunate: it's a violation of any chance you have to feel like you're really inside the game, rather than an outside observer with some ability to control things. Simply put, you can't say what you want. Your best course of action is to game the game, or to step out of the game's world and try to figure out what the different courses of action will lead to and pick the one that's most attractive (or least unattractive).

The game *Golden Sun* is full of conversations that never let you ask the questions that you need the answers to. It's frustrating to face someone who has information that you need, yet have no way to ask him for it.

This lack of ability to act on your desires is a disaster for a story-based game: the player is ripped right out of the game's world, and all the production values in the world won't bring him back in, at least not for a while.

The apparent ways to save the multiple-choice scenario are either to provide an enormous number of choices, or to try to get the choices exactly right so every player can find just what he wants.

Both of these approaches just make a bad problem worse. Suppose that, through extensive testing, the game designer realizes the necessity of providing a question for our hitchhiker about some kind of local politics. Okay, now you have the question in the list, but it's still not enough. Human conversation is subtle and complex. Suppose you want to ask the question in an innocent way, or an insinuating way, or a deprecating way. There's no way to script for every possible nuance. So even a huge list of choices is too small.

And even if you are provided a huge list, you still must leave the game's world and try to guess what the right choice is. If you, as a player, are talking to a robot or a candy dispensing machine, choosing from a list is reasonable: we are used to having only a few buttons on the front of our candy machines, and we're willing to limit our interaction with such machines to one of those few predetermined choices. But not so with a person: the unpredictability and variety of human conversation are some of the things that make it so wonderful.

Another important issue is tone and body language. When you choose a selection, you often don't know how it will be delivered. A simple question like "How are you?" can be delivered in a million ways, from friendly to snide, from truly concerned to insinuating, and usually you can't tell what the tone will be until after you've made the selection. You could audition the responses first, but that would be time-consuming and even more distracting. And then, if the particular nuance you want still isn't available, once again you're stuck without the ability to say what you want.

The game *Under a Killing Moon* is full of multiple-choice conversations that are a constant surprise. You may choose what seems to be an innocent question, but when you hear it come out of your character's mouth, it has a sarcastic edge to it, which annoys the person you're talking to. I found myself frequently wishing I could take back the things that I had my character say, because although the words seemed to come close to my intent, the delivery changed their meaning.

Although current technology forces the computer characters to be pre-scripted, the shame of this approach is that it forces the player to be pre-scripted as well. In other words, the player's capabilities are reduced to those of the computerized characters, which are meager indeed. The computer characters have scripted, pre-authored questions and answers, and as the player, so do you. They are limited to what the game designer invented for them, and so are you. They have no autonomy, no individuality, no creativity, and no imagination, and in this situation, neither do you.

Multiple-choice systems sometimes have real value. One place where multiple-choice conversations are not just okay but are in fact appropriate is when the bandwidth for communication is very low. They're also useful when the designer feels the need to control what speech is uttered, or in situations where the conversation is naturally formulaic.

An example of the first instance are the "Q signals" used by amateur radio operators. When sending Morse Code to one another, every letter counts. Typical proficient operators can send about 100 characters a minute. Sending this paragraph, including this sentence, would thus take almost three minutes.

So amateurs have standardized a collection of three-letter sequences to stand for common phrases. Since they all begin with the letter Q, these are called "Q signals". For example, QRL means "Are you busy?" and QTH means "I'll now send my location." Because Q signals were designed by people for human communication, there are also some informal signals used just for fun. For example, experienced Morse Code senders usually develop a pleasing rhythm when they operate the telegraph key, which helps the person on the receiving end distinguish dots, dashes, and spaces. If you think someone's sending style is particularly sloppy, you can send the signal QLF. This means "Please switch to your left foot," implying that his technique is so bad that until now he must have been working the key with his right foot.

Q signals were not designed as an insider's jargon, but rather as a practical tool to save time.

Sometimes multiple-choice menus are useful if you need to control what's being said. For example, in some online gaming environments, such as the Internet Gaming Zone [128], anyone can anonymously enter and start playing a variety of board and card games. Many such sites welcome players of all ages, including children. It's certainly important to allow players to communicate with each other while the game is in progress so that they can feel that there really is someone at the other end. If you allow players to type anything they want to one another, that gives them a lot of freedom to express themselves, but it could expose children to coarse language or even abuse. So the IGZ instead provides a list of one or two dozen useful utterances, like "Good move," "Are you still there?" and "That was a lucky roll!" In general this pre-scripting is acceptable because the point of these game sites is not to have a conversation, but rather to play the games. The limited vocabulary of utterances works because the domain of what's to be discussed is very narrow and the comments are ancillary to the game itself. Unless someone wants to explicitly discuss a specific move, anything the players say to each other will not affect the game itself.

Formulaic conversations are a natural for multiple-choice. These arise in many formal, administrative, and bureaucratic situations. Suppose you're trying to gain admission to a secured building, and you walk up to a security guard. He might ask for your name or your ID, or for the name of the person you're visiting. You could try to strike up a conversation with the guard, but even in real life such officals remain focused exclusively on their job. If you're trying to get a refund at a store and you don't have the receipt, the store manager may simply say to you that without a receipt you'll get no refund. You can spin story after story, but the manager will just say the same thing over and over again until you give up. If you're talking to a maitre d', the conversation is usually short and formulaic, often beginning with his question, "Would you prefer a booth or a table?" You can answer any way you want, but the maitre d' is probably just going to listen for the key words "booth" or "table" and proceed on that. He might ask if you'd like to sit by the window, and again the list of reasonably responses is short and clear-cut. In these kinds of situations, multiple-choice conversations are just fine: they are an efficient way to communicate a specific response to a specific question, and it's normal to expect a very limited palette of questions and answers.

Multiple-choice questions are often associated with the player profiling I discussed in the last section: a model of the player's psychology based on what he chooses. This model shares all the problems of profiling which I discussed above.

In any social situation, what you say to other players, and how you say it, should be up to you. Multiple-choice is just too limiting a technique to allow the freedom of expression that we require in order to feel that we're inside the world of a game.

> *Multiple-choice conversations are dehumanizing:* Human players should not be reduced to the level of sophistication of the computer's own characters.

Don't Keep 'Em Guessing

Some games try to provide a sense of mystery or exploration on top of multiple-choice by offering poorly-labelled or unlabelled choices. As a player, you are presented with a series of options and asked to select one, without really understanding what they represent or what the ramifications of your choice will be.

In the game *Eternal Darkness: Sanity's Requiem*, very early on you find yourself in a room with three strange objects, each a different color, and you're instructed to select one. It turns out that the object you pick will have important effects on the rest of the game, but at the time of selection there's no way for you to know that this is the case, much less make an informed choice.

This is pointless interaction. If you're not acting intentionally, then why are you acting at all? If you don't understand the choice, your choice is essentially random and therefore not really a choice at all.

Even when used as a simple means of selection from a menu of options, such choices can sometimes run into trouble when they present metaphors rather than actualities. For example, the excellent game *Kingdom Hearts* begins by offering the player a choice of being a strong swordsman, a spell-casting magician, or a defensive protector. If you select the hero's sword, for example, the game tells you that this choice will lead you on a path of courage and physical bravery. This path may sound very appealing to someone who values those qualities, but in fact, choosing the sword is a metaphor for how the game will play. By choosing the sword, you're saying that your character's abilities will begin with a particular aptitude for hacking and slashing at your opponents. What that means in practice is that you're saying to the system, "I believe that I will be good at, and enjoy, fighting enemies by using this particular controller within this game's particular combat system." Just because you wish to play a brave and heroic character does not mean you're going to have the necessary twitch skills in your thumbs and fingers to be an effective swordsman with that hardware and that game's particular mix of joystick-pushing and button-pushing requirements for a successful battle. And just because you value courage and physical bravery doesn't mean that you want that to be your principal way of defeating opponents.

As with deception, one can claim that being presented with unclear choices is a reflection of the real world, where we often don't understand the nature of our choices. True enough. But as with deception, entertainment is not the same as real life. Players do not spend time, money, and energy to be faced with vague situations and feelings of lack of control in our entertainments. We get enough of that every day.

In art of all types, we are willing to tolerate and even enjoy a certain amount of deliberate ambiguity. Carefully controlled ambiguity allows an audience to enter into the work and interpret it personally. But too much ambiguity means the artist has been too lazy to properly shape the work. Players should have clear choices. Options that are poorly understood are false options.

> *Choices should be clear:* If a player needs to make a decision, he should have enough information to make an informed choice.

Repeat Painlessly

In many games a player must go through a process several times in order to achieve a goal, perhaps with variations. For example, you might have to drive your car around to a variety of destinations so that you can quickly pick up a particular small item at each one, requiring you to start the car each time you climb back in.

Many game designers create a little audio or video segment to accompany this repeated step, to liven things up. These pieces of production can be fun or illuminating the first time or two, but by the third time they are simply roadblocks to be endured before being allowed to continue playing.

In one of the games on *The Muppets CD-ROM*, you assemble some puzzle pieces in what you think is the right order, and then push a big button to submit your answer to an "inspection machine." Pushing the button initiates a sequence of visual and audio effects as the big machine "examines" your solution. Eventually it comes up with an answer: either that you got it right, or that you need to try again. The animation takes about 15 seconds, but it quickly begins to feel like a half-hour. By the third or fourth time I submitted an answer, I started to resent being forced to waste my time waiting for this now-boring effect to repeat. There was no way to hurry it up or skip over it. By the tenth time I went through the process, I was ready to climb the walls.

A more common example of forced repetition comes from action games in which you must defeat a variety of enemies before finally coming up against a really big enemy (often called a *boss*, because he seems to be the boss of all the smaller opponents you've been facing). Let's look at what often happens when you first meet the boss.

The boss is frequently introduced with a cut-scene (a pre-produced cinematic sequence) in which the boss crushes a town, awakens from his centuries-old slumber, or has a gloating conversation with his minions in which he reveals the extent of his anger and exposes his nefarious plans. Then there's a long zoom in to the boss, so we can see just how big and frightening he is, and a slow pan from our point of view on the ground up and up as we get to see just how tall he is, and then he spits some fire and taunts us for a bit before the battle actually gets underway. It's very exciting and a terrific addition to the game. Then you start to fight the boss, and in almost all games of this sort you must attempt this fight several times, if not many times, to figure out a strategy that will defeat him. That means that your character will usually "die" repeatedly in these boss battles.

And there lies the rub. When your character comes back to life, it's best that you re-appear at just the moment when you regained control of your character after the cut-scene finished playing. But this is rarely the case. More commonly, you're restarted back at the entrance of the area where the boss lives. You might actually have to fight your way all the way back to the boss again. Inexplicably, some game designers put their save points far away from the boss battles, so that each time you die, you then have to repeat the entire approach path, only so that you can try out one new twist on your boss strategy before being quickly killed again. Even if you're a master of all the fights along the way, it's going to take time, and by the fourth time through, it's both easy and boring but can't be bypassed. And even if all of the bad guys are gone, you still have to walk or run or jump your way from the starting point to the boss's lair. Again, this is just pointless and rude to the player.

Sometimes, to add insult to injury, you have to recollect weapons or other devices necessary to this battle, which may involve some additional running around. Again, after a few times you know just what to do and where to go, and this collecting process is just lost time and make-work.

Even worse, in almost every game produced today, the cut-scene introduction of the boss plays again when you meet him for the second time, and the third time, and the eighteenth time. Long before then, you're pushing every button on the controller hoping for some way to stop the cut-scene and jump right to the end, but far too often it's simply not there. You have to sit through this little movie, and what was once thrilling and exciting becomes boring and then very annoying. All of the pleasure you experienced on the first viewing of this movie gets slowly sapped away, until finally you've come to know and resent every frame.

Players who need a break should be able to choose to watch the cut-scene again or pause the gameplay. But players who have seen the cut-scene over and over and over again and are unable to bypass it will just get frustrated at the way the game wastes their time.

I suspect that designers make us sit through repeating cut-scenes and other performance pieces because they work hard on these entertaining segments and want to get a lot of mileage out of them. But too much mileage and their charm is lost, resulting in self-defeat. A far better approach provides the elaborate production pieces just the first time or two, and then switches to a highly abbreviated version that ends almost immediately ("*You again? Take this!*"). The player will remember the production piece but will not become angry or bored by being forced to sit through it endlessly. If a player *wants* to see it again, he should have the opportunity, but it shouldn't be unavoidable.

> *Endless repetition is maddening:* Players should not be forced to repeat lengthy sequences, whether they are active or passive.

Repetition is a great way to reuse expensive content and develop themes. But the player should never feel like he's being forced to travel the same road over and over. Sometimes a subtle change is all that's needed to make something seem original and different.

> *It should feel new:* A player's experiences through the game should each *feel* new.

Arbitrary Complexity and Magic Items

Many puzzle and adventure games embrace a technique that I call *arbitrary complexity*. This is the practice of making a game or puzzle artificially difficult by wrapping it in layers of capricious and difficult detail. Old text-style "adventure" games employed this technique when they required you to guess exactly the right word in a situation. For example, a troll might demand a banana as payment to cross his bridge. If you happened to have one, you might type in "Give banana to troll" or "Offer banana to troll," but only "Show banana to troll" would succeed. Players also had to guess and then do ridiculous things to get through a puzzle. For example, the player might have to show the banana to the troll three times and then throw it behind him. The solution is complex enough to be difficult, but arbitrary enough that there's no principled way you could have figured it out. Such solutions often required great leaps of imagination or credulity, or detailed analysis of very subtle or easily-missed clues. Arbitrary complexity makes things more difficult simply by making them complicated and obscure, not more fun.

Arbitrary complexity puzzles often depend on *magic items*. Magic items are objects that you find lying around the environment, often physically and temporally far from where they're needed. For example, near the start of a game you might find a sharp pencil on your office desk in San Francisco, and at the end of the game you find that you need that pencil to defuse a bomb while in a spaceship orbiting Mars. Nothing else will defuse the bomb: a hatpin that you found in Los Angeles will not work, nor will the pencil in your luggage.

Two conventions of these types of games are that you need to discover, pick up, and save all magic items when you run across them, and that their ultimate use is generally impossible to guess when you first encounter them.

There are two general approaches to helping the player locate and identify magic items. The first is to visually distinguish them from the environment. In the example above, a pulsing red spotlight might draw your attention to the pencil on your desk. This is the height of artificiality, even when the attractant is subtler, such as a thick black outline around the object. Drawing attention to mundane but ultimately necessary objects has no correlation to the real world, but is just an artifice used by game designers.

The other approach to locating these magic items is to make the player search every environment exhaustively, so that you just "accidentally" turn them up in the course of playing the game. For example, you might have to move your arrow-shaped cursor all over the screen, and when it moves on top of the pencil, your cursor turns into a hand, indicating that you can pick up the pencil. The testing might be more explicit: you might have to actually click on the pencil to discover if you can pick it up. Why, you might wonder to yourself, can't you pick up the scissors sitting next to the pencil? Or the paper under the scissors? Or the phone sitting on the desk? The answer is that they aren't magic items and aren't needed later in the game. If you could pick up everything, everywhere, you would quickly have an inventory far too large to manage. It would also make programming the game enormously more difficult, because the implementers would need to accommodate your using these items in all their reasonable ways. Returning our example of defusing a bomb in orbit around Mars, the designers would have to allow you to use any appropriately-shaped pointy thing, from a paper clip to a toothpick.

Whether magic items are indicated explicitly or are revealed when you roll over them or click on them, finding them requires you to perform an exhaustive search. Do you remember the last time you lost your keys? You looked high and low for several minutes in a tedious and frustrating search until you finally found them. This is the last thing you'd ever want to have to do for fun! There's nothing enjoyable in being forced to move slowly through each and every room of an environment, running your cursor over every visible surface and clicking on every visible object, just in hopes of finding one that's different from the rest and magical. Such *pixel-hunting* is an abuse of a player's time.

In *Under a Killing Moon* I found myself at one end of a long tunnel lined with bricks. There were thousands of bricks. A clue earlier on told me that there was an important, secret object hidden behind a brick in this tunnel. It was clearly essential to have this object in order to proceed in the game. I had to spend about an hour moving through each section of the tunnel, punctiliously clicking on every single brick around me, then moving forward one step and again clicking on every brick, again and again, for hundreds if not thousands of bricks, until I eventually clicked on one otherwise undistinguished brick, which then moved a little bit. Clicking on that brick a few more times worked it loose and eventually revealed a key behind it. I can't imagine that this boring, tedious, dreadful process could really be much fun for anybody, and finally finding the key did not make things all better.

One place where magic items are less offensive is when they are truly out of place. If you're a gem thief and walk into a museum to find a big, unprotected diamond on display, it's natural that you're going to want to try to pick it up. In first-person shooter games, ammunition and weapons are commonly found just lying around. There's generally little to no explanation for why these things are lying there, but if you're a soldier and you see ammunition or a weapon, it's natural for you to pick it up. It's still unnatural and contrived, but at least there's a sliver of contextual sense.

Some games, such as *Doom* or *Half-Life*, are set in military or quasi-military environments, so it's credible that ammunition could be lying around or stacked in crates. But in a game like *American McGee's Alice*, which is set in a distorted Wonderland, it makes no sense at all to find ammunition and weapons lying around for you to simply pick up and use.

In *Grim Fandango*, you need to unblock a pneumatic tube that's used to deliver messages. There is only one way to do this, and it involves going outside to a street fair and talking to a clown to convince him to give you some balloons, then taking those balloons into the shipping room in your building and filling them up with packing material, and then returning to your office and sending the balloons through the tube. You must discover and carry out this utterly improbable and unlikely chain of actions to make progress in the game. These balloons are very magical items: you'd never guess to obtain them in other circumstances, and there's nothing else you can do with them in the world of the game.

Magic items are those things, like an otherwise normal-looking pencil, that you must make sure you pick up at the right time in the right place because they will be later needed in some unpredictable way.

> *Arbitrary complexity and magic items create complexity without value:* Players should not be required to make highly improbable connections or embark on exhaustive searches to collect magic items.

Hidden Actions

Earlier I talked about how most games cannot be edited on the fly: when you take your hand off of a chess piece, that move is committed; and when you hit the tennis ball with your racquet, there's no taking the shot over a second time. This is fine because players know what their options are for a given move, and they choose and execute as best they can.

In some electronic games, this type of irreversibility can be frustrating if a player doesn't fully understand what he's doing, or if the action itself is hidden.

For example, a player may be walking down a forest path, unaware of the significance of a single beautiful yellow flower that's underfoot halfway down the trail. This flower may be essential to completing the game, or it may simply be useful, providing some magical protection or a medicine. Not expecting anything like this, the player is marching down the path and accidentally steps on the flower. This misstep can happen for a million reasons, from the game's camera being in the wrong place, or the player's choice to look up at the tree canopy to see a bird he just heard rather than at the ground, or the player simply wanting to get to the end of the path and on to the next section, to the real-world phone ringing.

When the player steps on the flower and crushes it, that eliminates forever his chance to pick it and use it later. The event may go unacknowledged. Or the game may indicate that this loss has happened in some way; perhaps the flower lets out a tiny cry when it dies.

This is a pretty unpleasant moment for a player. It could be avoided by taking painstaking care at every moment of the game, moving slowly and constantly scanning the entire environment after each step, but that's hardly a recipe for fun.

Stepping on the flower is an unpredictable and hard-to-see event, and it's irreversible. Once the flower's crushed, it's gone.

So what happens when a player hears the flower cry? He has two choices. The first is to march on and hope that nothing too bad has just happened. But the player probably doesn't know the significance of the flower, because he didn't have a chance to look at it before accidentally killing it. So more often than not, he'll restart the game from the last save point and repeat everything that he'd done since then up to the time when he approached the flower, and then slow down to look at it.

Obviously, repeating segments of the game that you've just cleared isn't a whole lot of fun. In the board games *Chutes and Ladders* and *Sorry* a player can occasionally be sent backwards. Those are competitive games in which being sent backwards is a penalty, giving the other players an advantage. In a solitaire game, the player is simply penalized for nobody's benefit.

The situation is made much worse if an event is invisible until it's encountered. Imagine a game version of the opening segment of *Raiders of the Lost Ark*. As Indiana Jones walks deeper into the hidden temple, he encounters a series of subtle and tricky traps. Because of his experience, Indy is able to avoid or disarm the traps that have killed his predecessors. Now if you're playing the role of Indy, and you're in a similar but different environment, you obviously don't have his expertise and knowledge: you're a player pretending to be an archaeologist-explorer. Perhaps one of the traps is triggered when you step on an otherwise undistinguished piece of paving stone on the ground. Though it looks like any other stone, when you step on it you hear a loud thunk sound, the stone moves a tiny bit, and a ten-ton weight drops from the ceiling, crushing you instantly and ending the game. There was no way to detect that this stone was a trap, and no time to avoid the ten-ton weight once it was triggered. This trap is simply a learning experience with a short message: don't step here.

This is even worse than stepping on the flower. The results of stepping on this stone are unpredictable, irreversible, and invisible. One you step there, you get crushed.

Once again, you need to restart the game from your last save point and try again, only this time remembering not to step on that stone.

In the game *Baldur's Gate II: Shadows of Amin*, you need to obtain a jewel called a Light Gem in order to visit a dragon who can cast a spell on you that lets you enter a place called the Drow city, where there are lots of things to do and collect, and a quest to complete. Once you're in the Drow city, you might decide to lighten your pack and get rid of some objects you don't need anymore, including the Light Gem. This is a reasonable thing to do, and the game offers no resistance or warning. But if you do put down the Light Gem, you're sunk, because later in the game you'll find that you need to return to the Drow city. But without the gem you can't get to see the dragon, and without the dragon's help you can't get back into the city. The result is that now that part of the game is now completely closed to you; you can never return there, and you'll never be able to complete the quest. Your only choice is to reload a saved game from long ago or, if you don't have one, start all the way over again from the beginning. This is a terrible thing to do to a player.

Another Baldur's Gate title, *Baldur's Gate: Tales of the Sword Coast*, is filled with traps that you can't see until they kill you. If you have just the right characters in your party, you can avoid the traps, but otherwise you simply have to find them one by one, by dying each time you step on one, and then committing to memory that you should never step there again.

Trying and dying is no fun.

Often "dying" costs you a life, health points, or depletion of some other resource. It always costs time. Often it means repeating some part of the game to make your way back to this point again, so that you can try a different strategy. This process may have to happen over and over again.

This is a particularly unpleasant violation of our maxim "don't repeat needlessly."

> *Invisible and irreversible events are not beneficial:* Players should not be forced to repeat sequences of the game in order to discover events that are invisible the first time through.

Difficulty Settings

Many games offer the player a choice of "difficulty setting" before the game begins. Typically these are chosen from a list, such as "easy," "medium," "hard," and "expert."

Such choices should be banned forever.

Several problems result from this kind of choice:

Too early: You can't reasonably predict how well you're going to play the game until you've played for a while, so at the start you can't choose a difficulty level that will be both fun and challenging. Besides, at this point you can't possibly quantify your abilities. Every game is different; even sequels often "feel" different from their predecessors. Some skills are easier to pick up than others. You can't sensibly predict your abilities before you start playing.

Too coarse: What if "medium" is too easy to be fun, but "hard" is too difficult to be fun? The categories are too widely spaced.

Too broad: Perhaps you're really good at some aspects of the game and so would like "hard" challenges when it comes to those activities, but you're not so good at other aspects and would prefer "easy" for them. For example, what if you're expert at car-driving, but no good at shooting? If this game involves both of those activities, what difficulty level should you pick?

Too persistent: If the level cannot be changed during the game, there's no accommodation for when you improve in skill. If you pick a level that's just hard enough to be fun at the start, it may well be too easy by the end. Many games increase in difficulty as they go. Perhaps you won't get better quite as fast as they expect, so the game will at one point become so hard it's unplayable. On the other hand, you might learn very quickly, and then the game becomes too easy.

Too general: Electronic games as a genre share an element that's missing from most other types of games: they introduce new skills. Traditional games usually don't introduce new elements as the game goes on: the skills you need at the start of a baseball game (e.g., run, hit, throw, and catch) are the same you need at the end. But in electronic games, it's typical that as a games goes on, the on-screen character learns new types of actions, such as a spinning triple-jump in *Super Mario Sunshine*, leaping from one vine to another in *Kingdom Hearts*, grappling onto moving targets in *Ratchet & Clank*, or steering a speedboat in *Grand Theft Auto: Vice City*. It's not unusual for some of these actions to be pretty easy to execute, and some of them quite tricky. And which is which varies from player to player. When confronted with a new action that's proving frustrating to master, you may regret choosing a difficult level.

For example, you may be an experienced hand at first-person shooting games. So you buy a new game recommended by a friend, expecting to spend most of your time running and firing a weapon, and you set the difficulty level to "hard" because you know your skills are very good at this kind of game. Then you discover halfway through that you need to skillfully pilot a helicopter to accomplish a mission. This may be very difficult for you on an easy setting, and just about impossible for you on "hard."

If a particular action, learned in the middle of the game and essential to completing it, proves to be really difficult for you, the game comes to a crashing stop.

As we'll see in Chapter 12, many of these problems can be addressed by an *adaptive* approach, which presents the player with the right amount of challenge for that player's skills.

Games should not ask players to select a difficulty level: Games should adapt themselves during gameplay to offer the player a consistent degree of challenge based on his changing abilities at different tasks.

Climactic Cut-Scenes

In many modern games, the gameplay is sometimes interrupted to accommodate the playback of a pre-recorded sequence. Sometimes it's actually a pre-rendered piece of video, and sometimes it's rendered in real time using the computer or console's hardware (a technique called *machinima* or *mechanimation*). During playback, the player's opportunity for interaction is suspended, and he becomes a passive audience member for the duration of the scene. Such short movie segments are often called *cut-scenes*.

Cut-scenes typically have three functions during a game: to show expository information, to provide transitions, or to show the results of a player's action.

Expository cut-scenes are often delivered when the player enters or leaves an environment. For example, when you arrive at a new part of the world, you are often shown a short movie that gives you an overview of the physical environment and perhaps some of the characters that inhabit the place, and what they're up to when you arrive. As we saw earlier, expository cut-scenes often precede confrontations with "boss" characters.

An interesting variation on the expository cut-scene is to use machinima to show events that happen around your player in real time, inside the game. For example, in the game *Half-Life* actions occur around you while you still have control of your character. If you choose, you can turn and look away from the action. This form of in-game cut-scene can provide game information while also letting you stay in control.

Cut-scenes presented during the course of normal gameplay can also show what is happening in a parallel storyline, often at a location that is far away in either space or time. For example, you might get to see what the mad scientist is cooking up in his laboratory far away, or you could see what's happening to a kidnapping victim you're trying to locate and rescue. The cut-scene connects you to the events that are going on elsewhere in the world, where your character is not present. *Ratchet & Clank* uses cut-scenes to fill you in on a villain's ongoing plot that you will ultimately need to foil.

Cut-scenes are also useful as transitions between places or episodes, like the markers between chapters in a book. They help us get back in the mood of the environment we're entering, like an establishing shot in short films, or the picture of someone's apartment building or office that many TV shows present when returning from a commercial break.

Such establishing shots could be briefly shown each time a game is restarted or turned back on, to help re-orient the player and bring him back into the game's world.

Cut-scenes also serve a more immediate expository purpose, by showing you the results of actions that your character has taken. For example, you might uncork a bottle you find on a sandy beach, triggering an elaborate cut-scene in which smoke emerges, slowly taking on the form of a genie.

For whatever reason they're initiated, many cut-scenes of this type include your own character, because your character is a major player, if not the critical one, in bringing the event about. The cut-scene shows you what happens as a result of your action (or lack of it), and perhaps some of the aftermath, or introduces a new plot twist that advances the story and gives you one or more new goals. Such cut-scenes appear in games like *Metal Gear Solid 2* and *Final Fantasy X*.

These overview and connective cut-scenes are often welcome and provide important information, a variation in pacing, or simply an interlude with high production values.

Another common class of cut-scenes is problematic. These are the ones that are delivered at or near a critical moment in the game, showing you the result of an important action. They often come after you've made a big decision, such as attacking the monster or running away from it.

This insertion may sound like a good idea, and these cut-scenes are often a pleasure to watch and listen to, but they create a serious disruption of the game experience.

The problem is that the game is sending you, the player, mixed messages.

When you are in control of your character, the game is telling you that your skill and imagination matter. Your understanding of the world and its characters through your personal insight is important. As you interact with the other computer-based, characters in the game, you build up a sense of who they are, and you form relationships with them. You might decide that one character is trustworthy, another is dangerous, and you find yourself romantically attracted to a third. These feelings affect how you act towards those characters.

In the best games, you can actually express this growing depth of insight in your gameplay. As you come to understand the psychology of the other characters in the story, your feelings affect how you treat them. This is a rewarding way to play and can help get a player out of his own head and into the world of the story.

But then the cut-scene takes over, and this illusion is utterly annihilated. As the player, you see your character acting in ways that you would never dream of. You cannot control what goes on, and you cannot stop things from going wrong. That is, you are irrelevant. Perhaps you perceive yourself (or your character) as a brave man, and you've taken many brave risks throughout the game. But then in the cut-scene your character sees a scary sight and hides behind a rock. Or you think he's a coward, and he leaps to attack the scary thing. Either way, most of the time the pre-produced cut-scene is not going to match the picture you've built up in your own head. Recall that modern games encourage us, by virtue of our free interaction, to enter the world and its characters. Thus the better the game, the more we internalize the characters and the environment and come to be attached to them, and thus the more unpleasant the jolt when that attachment is violated.

When cut-scenes appear, they play at their own speed, moving the story forward and carrying us along with it. Virtually always these cut-scenes are the cinematically interesting ones, which means that they have lots of physical or emotional action. Whether my character hides behind a rock or leaps to attack makes a world of difference.

But wait: when I'm playing the game, that character is me!

Well, not really. It's me during "interactive mode," when I am in control. I play at my speed, and make my choices. Then I am abruptly jerked into "cut-scene mode," where I am a passive spectator as the action plays out at its own speed, and my character does things I would never do. When the cut-scene ends, I am thrown back into interactive mode, and suddenly I am left with the problem of cleaning up the mess he left behind: a situation that is result of my character's actions, which should have been my actions, but which I never took!

And that's the mixed message that is destructive to the illusion of being in the game. During interactive play we're implicitly told that we need to exercise our imagination and involve ourselves in the world and its characters, only to be periodically shown during a cut-scene that we got it wrong. Even your own character acts in ways that disagree with your intentions! So every now and then control of "yourself" is ripped out of your hands, and you, the player, can only sit passively while the on-screen "you" acts totally out of character. This is frustrating to say the least and inevitably rips the player out of the world of the game.

The game *The Dig* places you on a remote asteroid with a group of computer-controlled characters. At one point one of the other characters starts to behave erratically. I spent a lot of effort to contain and control this character, and then a cut-scene appeared and my character behaved in a way that utterly contradicted everything I'd spent my time doing, treating this other character in a way that I never would. I never bothered to try to put myself into the game at all again after that.

The irony is that cut-scenes are usually produced at moments of the greatest tension in the game, because those are the places where the great production values pay off the best in terms of grand effects and large visual and audio events. But those are precisely the moments where the player's character must remain under the player's control.

> *Cut-scenes should never show the player's character acting in ways that can contradict the player's mental model of the character:* A game should never take over control of the player's character in a way that could conflict with the player's understanding of the character.

Random Behavior

Humans are difficult to understand. We are simultaneously reliable, unpredictable, and arbitrary. We are also quirky and self-contradictory. As I discussed earlier in the section on player profiling, the complexity of human character has been a subject of study by every culture, and though our sciences of sociology and psychology have given us some vocabulary, the human personality remains a mystery.

How then might a game designer today populate his world with computerized characters with whom the player may interact?

One popular model for creating synthetic characters is to adopt one of the more tractable models of human behavior and attempt to turn it into a quantifiable and programmable model. Then one can create characters by assigning them different numbers for key characteristics, such as aggressiveness and dominance. Careful design can create a character with both consistent traits and idiosyncrasies. This approach can work well for very simple or stereotypical characters, particularly those who are characteristically unresponsive.

Because of the complexity of human personalities, some game designers have taken advantage of the apparently self-contradictory nature of our personalities and modelled their characters using a layer of random behavior over the character's programmed behavior. Thus a character may be speaking to you calmly one day, but when you visit him the next day, due to some unseen roll of the dice, the character is unexpectedly hostile.

Remember from our discussion on story structure that the apparent contradictions in someone's behavior are in fact woven together with the rest of his personality. These contradictions arise from one or more causes, and the more we get to know someone we more we come to understand why he acts in different ways in different situations.

Sane people do not act randomly. They may act in ways that may appear mysterious, if we don't know them well enough, but their actions are integrated into their personalities. Even when a person holds simultaneous, opposing beliefs, the expression of those beliefs is a result of his history and personality. In short, in a sane person there is reason and justification behind the strangest acts.

Without those sometimes subtle and complex connections, we end up with random behavior. And this is a problem, because most people don't find random behavior appealing.

If there is no underlying connective thread behind someone's behavior, we call him crazy or psychotic, or at the very least unpredictable. And that's what behavioral control with too much randomness simulates. This may be a useful technique for simulating a psychotic character, or adding a little variation to a minor character, but is no good for people that are supposed to be reliable, dependable, or sane.

Highly randomized procedural behavior creates psychotic robots.

Random numbers should not control large aspects of characters behaviors: To avoid psychotic robots, character's personalities should be well integrated.

Moving On

In many cases, I looked at the techniques that are popular today and found them wanting. This assessment may seem to paint a bleak future, but there is reason for hope! Now that we've identified these problems, we have the chance to think about ways to address them and avoid their worst effects. We also have the understanding needed to create new techniques that eliminate these problems and help us create fun and interesting new ways to combine game playing and storytelling.

First Steps

In this chapter we'll start to cast our eyes forward and consider a few important topics that will help us understand the qualities of participatory stories. We'll consider the change in nature of the audience, from passive observers to active participants. Then we'll discuss how these participants interact with the underlying simulation; this is quite a different matter from a traditional user interface. Finally, we'll look at the issue of language.

Fun

Any style of storytelling that allows the audience opportunities to participate is implicitly asking the audience to be active: that is, to do something.

Most contemporary storytelling media entertain audiences who are passive, though their imaginations are engaged. Watching television requires no more physical effort than lying on the couch, and reading a book means only turning pages and scanning words with our eyes.

What then makes us think that people will want to engage in any new forms of storytelling that requires their active participation? After all, this is a leisure activity, so why would anyone want to work at it?

The answer is that people are willing to do all kinds of work as long as it's *fun*.

Why do people go to professional sports games when they can watch them on television? It's a lot more work to pack up and go to the stadium, park the car, buy tickets, and then get home again. Why do we play with our dogs, make love, take hikes, go canoeing, or make any other physical effort when we could instead be sitting motionless on the couch and watching television? Why do we *work* for our entertainment and pleasure?

The Most Fun Theory

We put in effort for many recreational activities because they're *fun*, and we're willing to put in work if we get back enough fun. I call this the *Most Fun Theory*.

> *The Most Fun Theory:* People are willing to put in as much work as required in any activity if they get back enough high-quality fun.

This is why we are willing to work so hard when we play tennis, go kayaking, play music with friends, or even participate in a physical party game like Charades. We're willing, and even quite eager, to work as long as we're getting back enough good fun. If the fun we get back isn't up to the effort we're required to invest, we'll back off or stop altogether. But if we're having enough fun, we'll keep doing it and even look for opportunities to do it again.

The Fun-to-Work Ratio

If we're willing to work for our fun, why then do people watch television? Much television programming is awful and, frankly, hardly any fun at all. Understanding why people watch TV leads us to the *Fun-to-Work Ratio*:

> *The Fun-to-Work Ratio:* People want to maximize the ratio of quality fun to invested work.

Let's find the Fun-to-Work Ratio for TV. The amount of fun in many TV shows is very small; often, it's tiny. The amount of effort required to watch television is effectively zero: we need do nothing but lie on the couch and keep our eyes open. The ratio of a tiny bit of fun to zero work is infinite! That's why television is so appealing: the Fun-to-Work Ratio is as high as it can be.

But there's a problem: it's generally not very high-quality fun. Determining the "quality" of fun is a very personal judgment, but we've all had the experience of watching television and, though we're not enjoying it, just being too lazy to turn it off. We're not expending much effort, and there's a good deal of some kind of fun coming our way, but the "fun" is pretty dreary.

The Fun-to-Work Ratio helps us see why we then get off of our couches and do any physical activity that brings us pleasure: it's not just the quantity of fun that matters, but the quality as well. The scale is very subjective and personal, but at some point we will choose to expend effort to get a smaller amount of good fun over a larger amount of lesser-quality fun.

This measure also explains the impressive sales figures and reviewer praise given to games that offer significant novelty. Many people find things that are new or different to be inherently interesting and fun to explore.

The Fun-to-Work ratio is the fundamental reason why people play with toys, which, after all, requires effort. It's because we get back enough fun, of a quality that we enjoy, that the effort is worth it to us. It's the same reason we go on hikes, ski, play with dogs, carve pumpkins, or go dancing.

Storytelling experiences that invite or even require the audience to actively participate, must make sure that they return enough fun of sufficiently high quality that the audience will find the Fun-to-Work Ratio both of high quantity and quality.

Home Drama

In Chapter 8 I presented a number of arguments against the very idea of interactive stories. One of those arguments I summarized as *acting is hard*, and I discussed it in only one paragraph, promising to return to it later. Let's now look at this issue more closely, starting with simply reading a great script.

Actors often first rehearse a play or movie by just reading out lines while sitting around a table; naturally enough, this is called a *table reading*, and it helps give everyone a rough idea of the general shape of the work.

Sometimes a playwright will test out a play with an acting company in a very informal presentation. After just one or two rehearsals, the actors walk through the play on stage in front of an audience. Usually there is no lighting or costuming, nor any sets or props, and the actors read their lines from the scripts in their hands as they walk around with only very rudimentary blocking. Such a *staged reading* gives the playwright and an audience a rough idea of how the characters come across, and a general feel for pacing and the overall feel of the play.

Table readings and staged readings aren't restricted to professional actors. Anyone can get together a group of friends to sit around a table and read a play out loud. This is very easy to do, yet it's rare for people to spend an evening this way.

This may seem something of a surprise, given our perspective from earlier chapters on the importance of stories in our lives. We read books and see movies, and we watch television and listen to the radio, so why don't we put on readings of plays at home?

After all, all the ingredients are there. We have a great story to work from. There are many popular plays, widely known and even beloved. The characters and plots are fascinating, and the words are already chosen and waiting on the page. We don't need props or other preparation: just show up, take a script, read along, and speak aloud when it's your turn.

It's certainly not necessary that everyone who takes place in a home drama reading group be a good actor. In most groups it's perfectly acceptable to read the lines with a minimum of inflection, simply so everyone can hear them out loud and enjoy the flow of the play. But most people naturally feel that the experience is better with at least a bit of emotion put into the process, and even this touch of emotion brings us to the world of acting and all the reasons people tend to avoid situations where they're called upon to perform as actors.

If people don't widely participate in home drama, it seems unlikely that they would want to take on the role of a fictional character in an interactive story. This reluctance returns us to the discussion in Chapter 8, where I talked about the difficulties inherent in controlling an on-screen character: are we acting as we would, as we think the character would, or as we think the character *should?* If we choose to forego games in which we act as ourselves, we're eliminating a huge element of what interactive fiction can do for us. If we include such identification, then we have a challenge. Active participation is the critical element that distinguishes any kind of interaction in a story from static media such as books, records, and movies.

The answer is to look more closely at the elements of home drama. By understanding just what features of this activity are appealing and unappealing, we can focus our energies on devising interactive experiences that keep the desirable elements while avoiding the ones people don't like.

The positives of the home drama experience are similar to those of any story, and we've covered those in detail in Part I: the pleasure of losing yourself in another time and place, of learning about other people's lives, of seeing how a fascinating character behaves in an interesting and challenging situation, and of discovering something about human nature. These are all reasons why we'd expect people to enjoy table readings at home. We can see why home dramatic readings are rare by applying the Most Fun Theory: the effort involved exceeds the amount of high-quality fun that people experience in return. So let's look at the nature of that effort, which takes the form of problems that must be surmounted.

We'll see that the main issues have to do with human nature and emotional risk-taking, rather than technology.

Social coordination is tough: Reading a play with several characters requires getting a group of people together. Although people can take multiple roles, it's best when each major character in a given scene is played by a different person, otherwise two characters have the same voice, which dilutes the pleasure of hearing them speak to each other. Some people use accents or otherwise try to distinguish their multiple roles, but that's hard. If the group can't get through the whole play in a single sitting, the coordination problem becomes harder, because then somehow roughly the same group needs to come together again to continue the play. This can become a scheduling nightmare for the person who volunteers to coordinate the activity.

There are no sets, props, or costumes: Some people draw inspiration from the physical objects that are associated with performance. Stories are legion about actors who "found" a character when they put on a particular shirt, pair of glasses, or a particularly outrageous wig. Though these physical objects aren't necessary, some home drama groups keep a small box of props and clothing accessories, from cigars to earrings, for people to go through and draw inspiration from. Sometimes just putting on a particular hat is enough to help us "feel" like a different person.

Performance is stressful: In any group reading a play together, it's inevitable that some people will get into it more than others. Some people are simply shy or insecure and reluctant to take part in what they perceive as a performance. Even though there's no formal audience, they may see the other readers as judging how well they read their lines. They may be nervous about not reading a line with the right inflection, stuttering, or committing some other *faux pas* in front of other people.

Creating a character is hard: When we accept a role in a staged reading, we can certainly read the lines right from the page, without inflection. But if we want to give them some feeling, we need to understand the meaning behind the words and the feelings of the person saying them.

In other words, we have to find the subtext. Subtext can be very subtle and difficult to discover, or it can be pretty close to the surface. It almost always depends on context and the shared history between the person speaking and the person he's speaking to.

For example, suppose Stan and Ollie work in an office, and they meet each other next to the coffee maker in the break room. Stan says to Ollie, "The coffee maker is empty." There might be no subtext at all; it could simply be that Stan is pointing out a fact to Ollie. But Stan probably has a *reason* for saying this, and that's the subtext. He might be petulant: "It's your turn to make coffee, since I did it the last three times," He could be complaining: "See? I told you that nobody in the office else would ever bother to refill the pot." Or he could be complimentary: "That new blend you brought in today was great! Everyone's already finished it off." Obviously these utterances mean three very different things and would come out in three different tones of voice.

Because the subtext in a conversation depends on the relationship between at least two characters, we need to know something about them to know *why* they're saying what they're saying. Creating a character, with a history and feelings and strengths and weaknesses and all the other attributes that go into making a personality, is hard work. Even for a simple character, you have to make up a lot of background and make sure it all fits together in some reasonable way. For each line, you have to discover an appropriate subtext. Actors call this "building a character," and it takes time and effort. If it's not a process that you enjoy, then it can feel more like work than play.

Good acting is hard: We're all good casual actors. As children, a natural part of development is pretending to feel one emotion while actually feeling another: pretending to be contrite for breaking a rule, for example, while not really feeling badly at all. Or a child might pretend to be brave in front of the school bully, when he's inwardly afraid. Such casual acting has the quality that we're trying to give the impression of having an emotion or attitude whether we actually feel it or not.

The modern style of acting builds on this natural tendency with a "naturalistic" technique (this hasn't always been the case). The "method" approach taught by Stanislavski is based on actors actually feeling the emotions they're called on to portray [131]. In other words, suppose that you're an actor in a play and you've walked into a surprise birthday party. Working from the script and the director's guidance, you know that your character is both surprised and very happy.

One way to play the scene is to *pretend* to be surprised and happy. That is, you try to remember the sorts of things people do when they're surprised and happy, and you do those things: perhaps you clap your hands to your cheeks and smile widely, take a gasp of air and hold it, and then speak in a rushed and loud voice. These are the sorts of things you've seen people do when they're happily surprised, so you emulate them. Such pantomime is a time-honored form of performance with a long history, but it's not in fashion today.

The naturalistic school takes a different approach. To greatly simplify a complex subject, you *actually feel* the emotions that your character is feeling, and then simply execute the lines and blocking that have been given you. So in our scene, you'd think back to a time in your life when you were happily surprised, and you'd bring back that emotional memory so vividly that you relive the moment. With such emotional recall, you're able to be now, on stage, as you were once before, truly happy and surprised. You don't have to think about specific gestures or how to make your voice sound: by virtue of feeling the emotions, you'll naturally do all of the things that you do when you feel that way, and the audience will clearly read your feelings. It's not quite that simple, and method actors study many other techniques as well [84]. But the basic idea is that you give priority to *feeling* the emotions you're portraying, rather than trying to pretend as though you were feeling them.

This is generally hard to do. As in any art, there are always a few people to whom method acting seems to come naturally. But most actors take classes, and like other artists they study, practice, and work at their craft to develop and increase their skills and range. For most people, becoming a good actor requires the same kind of substantial and sustained commitment required to become a good pianist or a good painter. Because we each have only so much time, we have as priorities the things that we most enjoy. Thus most adults have not put in the work necessary to become good violinists, sculptors, or actors.

Good acting can hurt: I described above how method actors train themselves to actually feel the emotions that their characters are experiencing, and then to perform while in the thrall of those emotions. I picked happy surprise for the example, and many of us would be willing to remember that feeling and let it inhabit us.

But rare is the story where everyone feels good all the time. Remember that the heart of drama is conflict, and conflict easily leads to uncomfortable and unpleasant emotions, such as frustration, anger, and fear.

Most people would naturally be reluctant to deliberately choose to feel these emotions unless there was a great need. Reading a play for pleasure with friends hardly seems to be such a need: why would anyone deliberately want to feel badly as part of his recreation? When we get together with friends, we want to enjoy our time with them. Getting angry or upset, or frustrated or hurtful or embarrassed or any of a million other negative emotions seems to be the last thing we'd want.

Yet that's today's acting style. People who see themselves as actors are willing to do this and even to eagerly compete for the opportunity, because it gives them a chance to develop and display the skills they work so hard to develop, and because they inherently enjoy acting. And professionals get paid for it, which doesn't hurt.

Because as amateurs we don't want to feel badly when we're relaxing with friends, many of us are reluctant to throw ourselves into parts that have a lot of conflict. But these are often the best and juiciest parts in modern plays.

We also don't like to see our friends hurt and in pain. It's hard to sit a table while a friend of yours is crying and sobbing. Even if he's wrenching out a confession that's written on the page, if he's feeling those emotions, he's still in pain. That's no fun to watch, particularly since you can't help him.

As a result of not wanting to feel badly, or to have to helplessly watch friends feel badly, many play-reading groups focus on light comedies, where negative emotions don't get too deep. But this self-censorship severely limits the range of stories that such groups consider for their get-togethers.

Bad acting is embarrassing: We've all seen bad actors perform, and we inwardly cringe for them in sympathetic embarrassment.

When it comes our turn to act, we remember that feeling so clearly that many of us shy away from taking the risk of being seen that way, even among friends. Even people with naturally outgoing natures can be reluctant to take on a role that they think may require them to do more than be themselves.

Acting is revealing: Whether we're reading our lines casually or with emotion flooding our veins, acting is personally revealing. Normally we don't cry in public, but if the role calls for sorrow that befits crying, then we cry to the degree our comfort and skill allow. Feeling an emotion like that and revealing it in public are difficult things for many people to do. In every culture there are norms for what sort of behavior is acceptable from men, women, adults, and children. If a grown man believes that grown men aren't supposed to cry, that can be a very scary thing for him to do in front of other people. Similarly, if grown women aren't supposed to be assertive, that can be scary for a woman who needs to perform that role.

Some emotions, like sorrow and fear, can leave us unusually vulnerable to others, so we often hide them in public. Even if we're simply taking on those feelings from some remembered moment in the past, once they're inside us, we're transported (again, to the degree our skill and desire allow) back to that state. So if we're truly in that open condition, even while reading lines off a page, our hearts are open and vulnerable. If someone in the room chooses to go off the page and ridicule or tease us, it's going to strike hard. Even if one of the other people in the room is just playing a character that attacks us this way, it can be just as bad or even worse. Each line read by that player was worked and edited by the playwright until it became a precise and deeply wounding weapon that can hurt us badly, even though it obviously wasn't written to attack us personally.

In some plays the writing is so intense that feeling pain is almost unavoidable. Sitting around a table and reading *Who's Afraid of Virginia Woolf?* is an emotionally wrenching experience, no matter how much distance everyone tries to keep from the material.

Some people try to avoid certain emotions not only because they're unpleasant, but because they are potentially dangerous or even toxic. A person prone to depression may spend years to learn how to handle feelings of depression and hopelessness and find ways to reduce their frequency and intensity in his life. If a play calls for him to feel such emotions, he's likely not going to be interested in participating, at least not in that role.

Letting people see the intensity of some of our emotions can be more revealing than we want. If a character is needy and clinging, we might be afraid of how it would look if we were too good at the role: it would imply that there is a needy and clinging part of ourselves that we're able to tap into. This is true of all sorts of emotions: someone may hide his anger, but if a role calls for rage and he is able to really sink into the role and erupt in fury, his carefully-cultivated peaceful image may be lost as the others in the room see what does indeed lurk inside of him. And the things we choose to hide are often precisely those things we don't want to show to others or possibly even reveal to our own selves.

Revealing and experiencing emotions, even if just while performing a part, can be personally risky.

So now we can see why most people don't get together to read plays out loud, even plays that they know well and love. Getting into the part at all means doing some acting. Not only is acting a learned skill, but it's emotionally risky in the way that picking up cars is physically risky: the activity may be enjoyable in some ways, but it also inherently opens you up to the possibility of injury.

We can now apply the Most Fun Theory and see why play-reading groups are rare: the combination of the logistics of getting people together and the risks of acting, real and perceived, simply exceed the fun that comes back. People need stories, but they can get them in a wide variety of passive media that don't carry the costs of actively performing a role.

Note that some, but not all, of these emotional risks depend on the presence of other people. Those that are based on exposing one's emotions to other people are closely related to those people being in the room. Those that don't depend on other people revolve around our feeling negative emotions that we wouldn't normally choose to feel, particularly when we're trying to relax or simply enjoy ourselves.

As we develop forms of stories that call on people to become active participants, we'll have to be careful not to require most people to take on the risky and unpleasant aspects of acting, even if it's within the context of a game or online story. There will always be people who will be attracted to acting opportunities and will thrive on them, but they are not the majority. As we seek to develop a form that will be popular to a wide spectrum of people, we need to make sure that we keep our eyes focused on the work and risks involved in participation, and always maximize the Fun-to-Work Ratio with high-quality fun.

System Interface and World Interface

Let's now consider a very different issue, coming not from the world of human emotions but from the world of technology. The focus is how we interact with the world of the story.

The term "user interface" has traditionally been applied to the hardware and software that is directly manipulated or perceived by someone using a piece of technology. Thus we see user-interface experts studying input hardware (keyboards and mice), output hardware (monitors and speakers), input software (scroll bars and context-sensitive menus), and output software (progress bars and smooth fonts). All of these elements have been extensively studied in the domain of user interface work, sometimes also called human-computer interaction, or HCI. I'll call these elements the *system interface*.

There is a second user interface, which I call the *world interface*, that will be increasingly important as we move forward in designing interactive

301

stories. Let's briefly review how to make good traditional user interfaces, so we can apply the relevant principles of the system interface to the world.

The System Interface

User-interface researchers have developed guidelines that they use to characterize a good user interface. Schneiderman's list of 8 principles is a good summary [121]:

1. Strive for consistency: There should be an overall pattern to the appearance of the interface. Layouts and shortcuts, for example, should be the same from one application to another.

2. Enable frequent users to use shortcuts: As people become more familiar with the system, they should be able to to accomplish their tasks more easily or quickly than a novice.

3. Offer informative feedback: People should know that their commands have been properly received and interpreted by the computer, and they should have some idea of how their instructions are progressing over time.

4. Design dialogues to yield closure: People need to know when they have given the computer enough information to carry out the intended process.

5. Offer simple error handling: The system should be designed to offer useful feedback for any possible problem, and the person should be able to undo any command that caused an error. The system should never crash or give an unintelligible error message.

6. Permit easy reversal of actions: Software should recognize that people make mistakes, and sometimes change their minds. The system should make it easy for a person to stop or undo any action, even if it didn't cause an error.

7. Support internal locus of control: The person should always feel that he is in control of the system.

8. Reduce short-term memory load: People shouldn't be forced to remember things. The system should provide a list of possible actions and

objects whenever something needs to be specified. It should be easy to find the command you want, or the object you want to apply it to, without having to remember it.

The traditional computer user interface is a tool. Its goals are to be as clear and simple as possible, while also being sufficiently powerful and robust to do complex work without undue effort from the user. These criteria require a careful balancing of many design tradeoffs. One can argue that successful user-interface design can benefit from many of the same techniques of artifice and directness that are used in theatrical design [81].

Most UI designers strive to create products that have a feeling of being *obvious.* They want a novice to be able to sit down and figure out how to get his tasks done without having to consult a manual, and they want experts to be able to work quickly and efficiently.

An automobile's dashboard and pedals are often used as an example of a very good interface. Running through the list above, we can see that just about everything is handled well, using just a small number of very simple input and output devices.

User-interface designers sometimes speak of the underlying data that a person is interacting with as the *model,* and any given presentation of it as a *view.* Thus one might have a model that is a text document, and it may have one view on a large screen at work and a different view on a tiny cell phone display. The interfaces associated with these two views would be very different, but they would both probably support some version of common text-processing operations like cutting and pasting, though by very different means. The game *Majestic* used a wide variety of devices and views (e.g., fax machines, cell phones, and email) to present a rich multi-media interface to the world of the game.

"Intuitive" Design

Before we move on, it will be useful to set aside a term that has been abused for years when it comes to human-computer interaction. Interface designers and marketers sometimes describe their products as "intuitive." This is at best a sloppy use of the word: intuitive means that something appeals to intuition, which the *American Heritage Dictionary* defines as "The act or faculty of knowing or sensing without the use of rational processes; immediate cognition" [107]. The term is slippery because the ability to immediately grasp something without thinking depends on one's experience and what one already knows.

> Professor Wilson's courses on theoretical physics were always standing room only. Though he wasn't the world's most lucid teacher, Wilson was a brilliant researcher, and students were eager to sit in his class and learn directly from the master.
>
> One day Professor Wilson was deriving a particularly tricky equation on the blackboard, speaking out loud to the class as he wrote. "So we can cancel this term, and the result simplifies to this expression. Now it's obvious that I can rewrite this equation in the following form." After writing the new formula, he suddenly stopped, stepped away from the blackboard, crossed his arms, and quietly contemplated what he had just written.
>
> After standing silently for almost a full minute, Professor Wilson walked out the door and down the hall to his office, where he pulled out a pad and a couple of heavy reference books. He spent a half-hour deep in study, flipping through his books and writing page after page of equations. Finally he stood up and strode back to the classroom. Smiling at the befuddled students still in their seats, he triumphantly announced, "I was right! It *is* obvious!" and then turned back to the board and happily continued where he'd left off.

To someone who's used today's graphical operating systems for many years, context-sensitive pop-up menus may seem obvious or even intuitive, as in free of "rational processes." To someone who hasn't seen either of these before, such gadgets are manifestly not intuitive.

Calling any contemporary computer interface "intuitive" without a complete description of someone's necessary prior experiences makes as much sense as calling it "familiar": without a clear description of who's going to use it, what they already know, and what they want to achieve, the adjective simply doesn't mean anything.

The World Interface

Most computer and console games have their own idiosyncratic user interfaces, which players must learn to control. For example, joysticks move a character or a camera, menus call up lists of objects in an inventory or magic spells at hand, buttons need to be pressed at the right moment to jump or tumble or crouch down, and there are the complex multi-button combinations that trigger sophisticated actions in real-time fighting games such as *Tekken Tag Tournament* and stunt games such as *Tony Hawk's Pro Skater 4* and *SSX Tricky*. These multi-button sequences are all part of the system interface.

In a *direct* user interface, a person's actions are turned into specific commands for the computer, which usually take effect immediately. For example, if you're using a word-processing program and select some text and then copy it, that text is immediately placed on the system clipboard. If you paste from that clipboard, you immediately see the text appear in your document at the location you selected. If you command a selection to be set in bold type, or double-spaced, you see those results right away.

Now let's think about controlling something that is dynamic and running on its own, like a simulator program.

To illustrate the following points, I'll use an imaginary game that I've invented just for this discussion. It's a boat-racing game that I'll call *Yacht Racer*. In this imaginary game you get to design and build your own yacht from a kit of parts, and then race it against other people's boats. The mechanics and physics of the boat itself, as well as the wind and water, will all be as accurate as possible, thanks to a sophisticated simulator.

The game has two basic locations: the workshop and the ocean. In the workshop, we try to build the best yacht we can. There's a limit to the total price of the parts we can use, and to the boat's maximum length, width, and height. Within these limits we can build whatever we desire from any of the parts that are available. Once we've built our yacht, we go out to the ocean, where we take to the water. We can test our design by taking as many practice runs as we want, through any or all of the courses. While sailing, we can adjust anything on our boat that's open to adjustment: we can trim the sails, move the crew around to redistribute weight, and steer with the rudder. We can also vary the environment, trying out our boat in choppy and calm seas, high storms and quiet, windless days. If we want, we can return to the workshop to adjust our design. We can then return to the ocean again and repeat the cycle as much as we like until we're happy with our boat.

When we're satisfied with our design, we can race our yacht against other boats that are created by the computer or against yachts designed by other people. The winner gets all the glory!

Let's consider what happens when we take our yacht out to sea. Suppose we've equipped our boat with a crew of seven able seamen, all of about the same age, weight, strength, and experience. We discover as we sail that a useful move in some situations involves pulling the sails in close and letting the boat lean over on one side. But we risk capsizing this way, so we'll send a couple of sailors off to the high side of the boat to lean over the railing and act as a counterweight.

We might use a traditional system UI to move these men, perhaps by clicking on each one in turn to collect them together as a group, and then clicking on the spot where we want them to go. By doing this, we'd be changing one element in the underlying, abstract state of our boat (the positions of our crewmen) to bring about our intent (establish a counterweight) to the system (the boat physics simulator). Programmers are used to this idea of communicating with abstract objects like a boat simulator through a programming interface, but I'd like to suggest that players can think of their system interface actions as affecting the underlying simulator through the *world interface*, as shown in Figure 20.

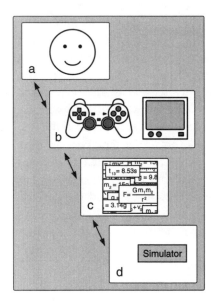

Figure 20.   The system interface and the world interface. The player (a) manipulates the system interface (b) that is made available to him. These actions change the information (c) stored in the computer that controls the simulator (d).

In this example, one of the inputs to the boat simulator is the distribution of weight. The boat simulator doesn't care about how the player selects crewmen or how he indicates where they should go, it just uses the locations of the men, however they got there. So when we move the sailors, we're using the system UI to issue a command to the boat, or world UI: move these sailors to this point in the computer's internal model of the ship.

The world interface is often invisible. In fact, the nature of this interface may or may not be accessible, in the sense that you can easily discover how to do whatever you want. You may not even know what all of your options are when you get started. As I mentioned in Chapter 5, many simulator games are played by people who enjoy solving the puzzle of figuring out what options they have for controlling the underlying simulator and how it works. This task is accomplished by exploring the world interface, which is accessed through the system interface.

For example, in a detective game you may come to a locked door. To open it, you might use the system interface to dig out your key and use it on the lock. The result would be a message to the world interface that this key is turning in this lock, and if they fit, the door would unlock. If on the other hand you decide to shoot the lock off with your gun, this single action in the system interface may trigger many changes in the world. The world interface may take the type of gun and where it's pointed, and calculate the trajectory of the bullet to find that it continues through the door and shatters a vase in the next room. So the vase breaks into many pieces, each of which crashes to the floor, and the resulting noise sets off a burglar alarm, which will alert the security guard to come running.

The reason for thinking of affecting the underlying world of the game through its own interface is that it lets us look at that the qualities of that interface. Considering the list of UI attributes in the previous section, we might say that a good interface is simultaneously *consistent*, *repeatable*, and *predictable*. The system interface is *direct*, while the world interface is *indirect*.

Returning to our imaginary yachting game, suppose we have all of our crewmen standing in the middle of the boat, and we select three of them to go stand by the railing to act as a counterweight. Since they're all of roughly the same weight, it shouldn't matter which three men we pick. So the interface is *predictable* and *consistent*: as long as we get the right distribution of weight around the boat, we'll get the proper effect. The underlying world is also *repeatable*, because if we make the same change to the weight distribution in a repeat of the very same situation, we would expect the boat to respond the same way.

The world interface to the simulator in many of today's games falls short in one or more of these properties. For example, in many fantasy games your primary weapon is a sword, usually used to hack monsters. But every now and then the sword is useful for something else, such as cutting a rope that holds a trap door closed. When we cut this rope, in effect we've learned one of the ways to manipulate the world through the user interface: ropes can be cut by our sword. The principle of consistency tells us that we should be able to cut any rope we can reach throughout the game. But that almost never happens: the only ropes we actually *can* cut are the ones that the game designers have explicitly enabled for this operation. Similarly, our sword can chop up a monster, but it can't slice the loaf of bread sitting on a table at an inn.

In terms of the system interface, this discrepancy is like a checkbox that we can sometimes click on to enable, but sometimes can't. System UI designers try to make these modes obvious by graying-out a disabled checkbox or hiding it altogether.

So now we can see why some game designers rely on the *magic items* I disparaged in Chapter 8: they're a way to distinguish the very limited opportunities to affect the world UI through the much richer system UI. If you can cut a couple of distinguished ropes in the world, but none of the others, then game designers will make those special ropes a different color, cause them to glow, give off a special sound, or otherwise give them a special attribute to tell that player that the checkbox has now become enabled: this rope is recognized by the world UI, and he may (or must) now affect it. The system UI is used to reveal an unpredictable inconsistency in the world UI, and the result is a clumsy mish-mash of unrelated concepts.

To see this problem in a familiar context, imagine a word processor that occasionally let you italicize text. Not all words can be set in italics, and it's hard to predict which ones can and can't be set that way. So as you type, some words appear in red to let you know that they can be set in italics. It would be a frustrating way to work.

In our rope-cutting adventure, once you've cut a rope and it lies in two pieces, in a repeatable system you'd be able to cut those pieces again into smaller pieces. Virtually no game produced today allows that action: once a magical rope has been cut once, it ceases to be magical, and thus cannot be cut any more. And other non-magical ropes in the world cannot be cut at all, so there's no predictability or consistency.

In another common situation, while adventuring through a dark chamber or cave, you sometimes need to light a fire. You may have a torch, a spell to create fire, or a flaming arrow in your quiver, and they can all serve as a flame and thus as a source of light. But you can't burn the wooden chair in the corner, or the old letter you carry in your inventory, or the bottle of cooking oil in the pantry. The system interface allows you to try most of these things: for example, you can move your torch onto the chair or shoot an arrow at it. But the world interface doesn't recognize this as an action it can handle, and thus the simulator ignores that action, and the chair does not catch on fire.

One reason for limiting the world UI so severely is that the world simulator is typically not very robust. If you're to be allowed to set fire to anything, then the system needs to "understand" how every object in the world responds to fire, and how fire itself behaves in an environment. If you set a chair on fire, could it burn down the house? If so, would critical clues to the story be lost forever, and the game effectively be made impossible to win at that point? How would the player know that? Could the hero accidentally set his own clothes on fire? Could a sudden wind blow out his flaming torch? If it started to rain, would it put out the fire? Writing a program that could handle all of these situations would be a monumental task.

Many recent game designs have opened up the world interface in a particular but useful way: your character in a 3D environment can walk or stand anywhere that he can get to. So if you can jump up to the top of a house, you can walk on the roof. If you can jump on top of a barrel, you can stand there and jump from that point, extending your vertical reach. If you can carry a barrel that you can stand on, then you can put it where you want and then stand on it. The game *Kingdom Hearts* uses this freedom of movement both to make the environments come alive and to give players more choices in how to manage real-time fights with the bad guys.

This flexibility has its limits: there are usually walls or cliffs or other barriers to the range available for you to explore. And lots of objects are too high or small for you to stand or climb on. But the beauty of this situation is that the 3D environment is not segmented into the places where you can stand or walk, and all the others that you slide off or can't even surmount. This part of the world interface is well-matched to the system interface: if you can reach a spot, you can stand there.

Many game designers naturally recoil in horror at the enormous demands implied by a robust simulator and its associated interface. Thus they place artificial boundaries in the system interface: if you walk into someone's office, you cannot pick up the telephone handset sitting on his desk, but you can pick up the pen that was engraved with the telephone number of the corrupt contractor. You can't walk into a well-stocked kitchen and make yourself any meal you'd like, but you can empty the box of baking soda to find the secret microfilm hidden inside. These are not limitations of the system UI, since you can move your character into place and *try* to do these things: they're limits of the world UI, because your actions don't have an effect on the underlying world of the simulator.

This mismatch is a source of endless confusion and frustration, as players try to discover which actions actually do something, and which look like they ought to do something but don't. The inconsistency between the system interface and the world interface is at the heart of the use of magical items, which I discussed in Chapter 8. Why must you get and use precisely one particular pencil, and no other, to defuse the bomb? Because the game isn't a general simulator, and it can't let you use objects any way you want, on the fly.

A better solution would be a system UI that greatly limited what you could do but was matched to the abilities of the world UI, and thus was consistent and predictable in how all of those actions affected the world. Perhaps you can do only three kinds of things as a player: walk and jump through a 3D environment, carry objects, and cut things with your sword. Then you should be able to walk or jump anywhere that you can reach, carry anything at all that isn't nailed down, and cut anything that your sword can get at. Then the world interface becomes a better user interface: it's consistent and predictable.

There have been a few systems that take this approach. *The Incredible Machine* offers players a deliberately goofy collection of parts with which to build gadgets. When you start the program, you're given a collection of fanciful mechanical parts and a 2D world in which to arrange them. During the design phase, you can put the parts anywhere you want in the 2D space. Then you turn on the simulator, and the world comes to life.

Gravity turns on and pulls everything downward, mice run away from cats and towards cheese, and helium balloons rise and bump into things.

You can use *The Incredible Machine* as a puzzle or a toy. As a puzzle, you're given a particular starting setup, a set of parts, and a goal (e.g., use a rope, two pulleys, and a toaster to catch the mouse). Your job is to add your parts to those that are already there to build a machine that, when you start it, will achieve the goal. You usually end up creating a Rube Goldberg-like device that accomplishes a simple goal using a ridiculously complex or unlikely arrangement of parts [143].

When using the game as a toy, you can simply build your own devices and then turn on the world and watch them run.

Although the world of *The Incredible Machine* is severely limited, it offers an excellent match between the system interface and the world interface. Because all of the objects work the way they ought to, it's great fun to experiment with the different pieces and create little machines to carry out creatively complex means to simple ends.

An action game that tries for the same level of match between the system UI and the world UI is the console game *Rocket: Robot on Wheels*. In this game you control a little unicycle-like robot named Sprocket as he wheels around an amusement park, trying to clean up the damage done by the park's disgruntled raccoon mascot. The game all takes place in 3D, and its distinguishing feature is a sophisticated physics simulator that applies to the whole world. So it's not just Sprocket that behaves in a physically realistic way; any time he affects the world, it responds in a realistic way as well.

This consistency is both a blessing and a curse. The uniformity between system interface and world interface is great, but managing to accomplish some of the skill tasks can be very hard. At one point you need to guide Sprocket across a lake by hopping over a series of pillars in a limited amount of time (or else they sink into the water, taking you with them). I found it very hard to get my little unicycle to move fast enough and precisely enough to cross the lake. Because everything was physically based, there was no way for me to choose an easier setting more suited to my ability (or lack of it) to accomplish this challenge.

A close fit between what you *seem* to be able to do in an environment and what you actually *can* do in the underlying world is the hallmark of a good match between the system UI and the world UI, and a sign of clarity and conceptual unity.

Language

Perhaps the most frustrating aspect of computer characters today, and one of the greatest challenges facing those who would develop better ones, is the question of language. We expect people to understand what we say, and what they say to us can reveal what they're thinking and feeling.

The ability to carry on an interesting conversation isn't sufficient to create a responsive, human-like character, but if we're to communicate with such a character, some kind of language is necessary. Creating and understanding any human language has been a central focus of research in artificial intelligence for decades, and still appears to be far away. It would be nice to have something that allows us to have meaningful exchanges with computer characters in the meantime.

If you've ever spent time in a country where you don't speak the language, then you've experienced first hand a frustrating mismatch between the system and world interfaces, but not in the way we've seen them so far. In most games, the system interface is more flexible than the world's. But when you don't speak the language, the problem is the other way around: you're surrounded by intelligent and helpful people, but you lack the tools you need to communicate with them.

The field of natural languages is enormous, and there's no way to even broadly describe the field here. Pinker's recent popular description of the field explores the subject, as well as reporting just how much we still don't understand [111]. The sheer difficulty of the task is beautifully illustrated by a well-known bit of wordplay: interpret the phrase "Time flies like an arrow, but fruit flies like a banana."

These kinds of ambiguous sentences also show up in real life. In December 2003, I saw this message on the outdoor marquee of a hotel in Vancouver, British Columbia: "Prime Dates Still Available for Christmas Parties." In addition to the meaning they probably intended, there are at least three more ways to interpret this message.

Writing a computer program that can figure out what these sentences "mean" is very hard.

Happily, our needs here are more modest. Since computer understanding of language is so limited, we need only look at some examples of languages that match that limited ability and are also easy to learn and use.

There are probably two principal uses of language in contemporary games and in the story environments not too far beyond the horizon: *information exchange* and *chatter*.

Information exchange is when two people are talking with the purpose of sharing information. It can be factual information, an emotional outpouring, or even just a casual conversation. A good two-way, natural conversation of this type is hard for computers to fake, since each participant needs to be paying attention and responding to what the other person is saying.

Casual chatter is just idle talk with no real purpose. Computers can fake this much more easily. Starting with the famous 1966 program *Eliza*, which simulated a Rogerian psychotherapist, computers have been able to carry on ever-better aimless conversations with people [138]. Such programs have come a long way; the *Alice* program today is able to respond in an engaging way on lots of different of topics [136]. Most of these *chatbots* aren't explicitly designed for the purpose of sharing information: the goal is that they can carry on a casual back and forth, like two people meeting at a cocktail party.

In recent years, people have begun to apply chatbot technology to commerce. So you might go to a website chat window and think you're speaking to a customer service representative about a problem you're having, but in reality you're talking to a chatbot who's designed to act as a first line of contact with customers. The chatbot is programmed to try to diagnose your problem and suggest a solution. If it can't figure out what you're saying, or doesn't know how to help, or "senses" you're getting frustrated, you may be switched to a real person. Sometimes that switch is announced, and sometimes the person simply picks up the conversation where the chatbot left off so that you, the customer, never know that such a handoff occurred. Chatbots are also used as salesmen, answering questions about products in a way meant to be more personal than a product description flyer.

Because children use language very flexibly themselves, they are often less critical of what comes back to them from a chatbot than an adult would be. Some marketing companies have used this observation to create chatbots that masquerade as real children and act as a child's "friend" on an instant-messaging platform. The purpose of speaking to the child and pretending to be his friend is to use that friendship to market products to the child [85].

Chatbots in general aren't going to be useful as central characters in storytelling for a while yet. The problem is that they can still be unmasked too easily: their knowledge of the world is so limited that as soon as you ask a question about something they don't know about, or about the implications of something they've said in a larger context, the illusion is shattered.

Chatbots are great for bit parts with very constrained interactions. A chatbot would make an excellent bureaucrat: if you ask it a specific question about its specialty, you'll get a specific answer. Anything else would be met with a polite shrug of the linguistic shoulders, or a suggestion that you speak to his supervisor. Chatbots also work well in very formal roles, like a waiter in a fancy restaurant, where there are distinct limits on the nature of the interaction they're supposed to have with clients.

Given these limitations, how then will we communicate with more interesting computer characters in a story? Perhaps the best way to go is to invent a new language.

In 1887, Dr. L.L. Zamenhof proposed a new language for international communication, which he called *Esperanto* [34]. This language is much too general and sophisticated to simplify our problem; writing computer programs to understand Esperanto would be on the same order of difficulty as writing programs that could understand English, and then there's the problem of teaching it to people!

The language *Loglan* [18] (a contraction of *log*ical *lan*guage) was invented by James Cooke Brown in the late 1950s. The language now has over 10,000 words and algorithms for making new ones. Loglan aficionados have written original essays and stories in the language and have translated poetry and novels into Loglan.

Because Loglan sentences are constructed with very specific rules, it seems initially to be a reasonable candidate for talking to computer characters. However, there are two immediate problems. The first is the learning problem: to use Loglan, you have to learn the rules of construction and amass a large enough vocabulary that you can express yourself and understand what others say to you. With 10,000 words in the lexicon, this is a lot of work, and much more than almost anyone would be willing to go through just to talk to computer characters. The second problem is that Loglan is simply *too* expressive: although a computer can break down the words of Loglan in a strict manner, the process of interpreting those words (that is, determining what it is that a person is actually trying to say) doesn't appear to be any easier than with any other human language. In other words, getting a computer to understand out what someone *means* when he speaks Loglan is still an overwhelming problem.

One way to get around this trouble is to greatly restrict the subject matter. If there isn't much to talk about, then the computer might have a fighting chance.

For example, the computer program *Shrdlu* [138] (prounouced shirred-loo) was able to carry on very limited conversations about a world of simple colored blocks. The blocks didn't originally exist in reality, but the computer was able to "move" them around in its memory to simulate what it would do in a real world. For example, you could ask it the question "Can a block be supported by a block?" and Shrdlu would correctly reply, "Yes." You could command it to "Put a small red pyramid onto the green box," and Shrdlu would do so. If you then asked, "Is the red pyramid on top of the green box?" the response would be "Yes." So in this very limited world, Shrdlu could carry on a simple conversation.

But there were all kinds of limits to what Shrdlu could understand. For example, you could completely confound Shrdlu by typing in a question like this: "If I were to take a red box and balance it on top of the green box but just a little bit off to one side, so that it was just barely balanced, and then I stacked up some other blocks and they fell down and shook the table, would the red box fall on the blue one?" Understanding a question like this, and all it implies about physics and blocks and the rest of the real world, is still far beyond the capabilities of even today's systems.

So narrowing down the domain of discussion isn't enough; we have to narrow down how we can talk about it as well. This suggests a language with a small vocabulary, and controls on how sentences can be built.

One of the easiest ways to do this is with a language that is *symbolic*.

By a "symbolic" language I mean that words are expressed by simple pictures or drawings. The simple drawings that distinguish men's and women's bathrooms are symbolic, as are the no-smoking sign and the image of an airplane taking off used to mark the departure gates at an airport. You can make little sentences with these signs. For example, putting a men's bathroom sign next to an arrow creates a two-word sentence (made of one verb and one noun), which we might verbalize as "men's bathrooms are in this direction."

There are other ways to create a symbolic language: Egyptian hiero-glyphics and Mandarin Chinese both use visual symbols for words rather than a collections of letters, as in English.

A different kind of visual approach is taken by American Sign Language, where many English words have a direct corollary. Though some ASL symbols represent composite concepts, I think ASL is closer to a translation of English into a different representation than a new language of its own.

I find new symbolic languages to be particularly appealing for today's interfaces for a variety of reasons. First, they can be designed to be very simple. As we'll see below, some languages can get by with just a couple of hundred words for limited domains. And if there's lots of context to help players understand the words, and the visual images of the words are well executed, then players can read and write sentences without the need to first memorize the entire vocabulary.

Second, symbolic languages normalize everyone's experience of the en-vironment. For any two players who are communicating, it doesn't matter if they are both people speaking the same natural language or people speak-ing different languages, or even if one is a computer: everyone's using the same words and the same construction rules. So native speakers of Japanese and Italian can converse in this new and limited, but common, language.

Third, symbolic languages let us communicate with less ambiguity. In many artistic expressions carefully-controlled ambiguity is essential, because it's in the undefined places that the audience can exercise their imagination and enter the work. But at this stage of computer language, just making ourselves understood when we're trying to be as direct as possible would be a step forward.

There are other benefits to these languages, including the simple fact that playing with a visual language is fun, and that there's something ap-pealing about communicating with pictures.

Written languages have a standard layout: for example, English is writ-ten left-to-right, top-to-bottom. Each visual language has its own rules as well. Generally each word must be adjacent to a previous word, so that a "sentence" is formed by a cluster of symbols. Often compound words are created from simpler words by overlapping them. For example, a single stick figure might mean a man, and a baseball could literally mean a base-ball, while a baseball in the man's hand would indicate a baseball player.

The pictures that are used for words in a visual language clearly make a world of difference both in how easy it is to use the language and in the aes-

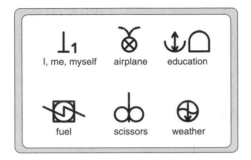

Figure 21.   Six words in Bliss. (Examples by George Sutton, and used by permission of George Sutton and symbols.net.)

thetics of the resulting sentences. An attractive-looking language is simply going to be more pleasant to use than one that isn't as nicely designed.

Another aspect of the pictures is that they need to be representational enough that they bring the right idea to mind, but not so specific that people assume they mean the very same thing as their closest natural-language counterpart.

Visual Languages

The visual language *Bliss* was created by Charles K. Bliss and described in his 1965 book [11]. The language has about 2000 symbols and is used by for communication by paraplegically disabled people. Figure 21 shows a few words in Bliss, and Figure 22 shows a couple of sample sentences.

Bliss is too rich for our purposes. With a 2000-word vocabulary, it's both too much for a player to learn for casual entertainment and too expressive. And since it's meant for human-to-human communication, Bliss allows people to express themselves in ways that would go right over the head of the computer we're talking to.

Another visual language with simple construction rules is *The Elephant's Memory* [70], designed by Timothy Ingen Housz. *The Elephant's Memory* has wonderful aesthetics, and it manages to get by with only 200 basic words in the vocabulary. Figure 23 shows a few words in this language, and Figure 24 shows two sample sentences. The way words go together isn't precisely defined: there is freedom in how the words are combined to construct sentences. This freedom provides some expressive nuance for people communicating with each other, but it makes it more difficult for

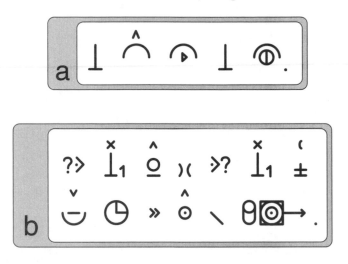

Figure 22. Two sentences in Bliss. (a) I think, therefore I am. (b) If we eat now, then we will have enough time to see a movie. (Examples by George Sutton, and used by permission of George Sutton and symbols.net.)

the computer to unambiguously determine what a player is trying to say. Compound words in this language are almost like poetry, rewarding and sometimes requiring sophisticated reasoning and interpretation.

A simple visual language was used in the computer game *Trust & Betrayal: The Legacy of Siboot*. In this game, the player communicates with the other players in the game (all computer-controlled) by creating short sentences in a graphical language called *Eeyal*. A very pleasing aspect of

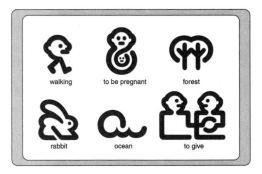

Figure 23. Six words in The Elephant's Memory. (Examples used by permission of Timothy Ingen Housz.)

Figure 24. Two sentences in The Elephant's Memory. (a) Running makes one tired, being tired makes one sleep, sleeping makes one happy, being happy makes one run. (b) The rabbit walks alone after running with the frog. (Examples used by permission of Timothy Ingen Housz).

this design is that this is exactly how the computer characters speak back to you. You also find that the type of information that the computer characters share among themselves follows the same lines, so it feels like everyone in the game is using this language. Since it's the only way characters can express themselves, using this language gives you the feeling you're on a level playing field with the other characters.

Figure 25 shows a couple of sample sentences from the game.

The language of *Trust & Betrayal* only allows you to construct legal sentences. When you start to write something, you're given a choice of all the symbols that can appear at the start of a sentence. When you've chosen one, the list is then replaced by all the symbols that are allowed to follow that word. In this way you build up a sentence by choosing the next symbol that expresses what you want to say. Since you don't transmit your

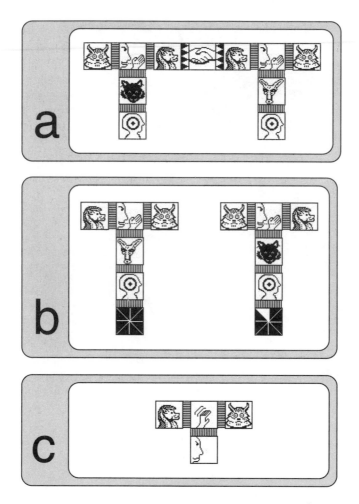

Figure 25. Three sample sentences in Eeyal, from *Trust & Betrayal*. The conversation is between two characters named Vetval (the horned mushroom) and Kendra (the seahorse). In the first sentence, they propose to trade secret numbers held by by Gardbore (the anteater) and Wiki (the black cat). In the second and third, they disclose those numbers and then say goodbye. (a) Vetvel will reveal to Kendra Wiki's shial-value if Kendra reveals to Vetvel Gardbore's shial-value. (b) Kendra reveals to Vetvel that Gardbore's shial-value is 8; Vetvel reveals to Kendra that Wiki's shial-value is 7. (c) Kendra says good-bye to Vetvel. (Examples used by permission of Chris Crawford)

sentence until you're done, you can always back up and rephrase yourself if it's not coming out the way you like.

The language has a vocabulary of only 80 words. Since words are only available when they can be legally used, it's easier to remember their meaning from context, and you don't have to memorize them all before you play the game.

This kind of language has been used more recently in the online browser-based exploration game *Banja*. The computer-controlled characters in the game speak to you (as you play the title character Banja) using an icon-based language. The Banja language is one-way: you can't create your own sentences. A nice touch in the design is that some of the Banja icons are animated. For example, a watch face that goes from night to day indicates the passage of one day. When a barman offers you a drink, the offer is represented by an animation of a glass travelling from his hand to yours.

Icon-based languages work for people who share the cultural ideas they represent, regardless of which human language they speak, and are able both to piggyback on, and be independent of, the written words they roughly correlate to. Someone looking at a representational icon can generally get a good rough idea of what it represents, but he's aware that it might be different from the natural-language term that it resembles.

Languages with strong construction rules make it easy to create sentences that are structurally sound, particularly when the system only allows words that are legal in the sentence that's been made so far.

These types of languages aren't the only techniques for communicating with computer characters. Semaphore, drumming rhythms, gestures, music, and any other form of structured interaction can form the basis of a language. The trick is to make sure that the language is so closely matched to the underlying character's abilities that both the player and the character are able to make themselves understood, and the player is able to say the sorts of things that he might reasonably want to say. Then the system interface's language matches the world interface's interpretation.

Procedural and Random Stories

As we've seen, writing good stories for general audiences requires skill and craft. If we could shift some or all of the work in this process onto the shoulders of a computer, it might free us up to attend to other interesting questions.

Many people have thought about this possibility, and they've produced a wide variety of theories, projects, and stories. A recent bibliography can be found in Lang [79].

Looking at the output of these prose-generating programs, we can see that they still have a long way to go. The structural pieces are present to different degrees, but the stories lack subtlety and nuance. They have the *form* of stories, but they don't seem to actually be *about* anything.

It's going to be a long time before computers produce any kind of story that we would actually want to read as a story, rather than as a novelty. For example, the book *The Policeman's Beard Is Half Constructed* [25] is a collection of poetry and prose created by a program called Racter, under the control of its developers. It's interesting from a computer-science point of view, but hardly a coherent piece of writing.

Some more modern systems are able to produce plausible fables and very short stories, but they still require a very generous reader to see these as anything more than proofs of concept.

There's nothing new about structural approaches to writing and story construction. Aristotle started it in the *Poetics* [3], and many people have picked up the ball since then. The book *Steal This Plot* [72] presents stories in terms of a few general categories and variations on them. The book (and related software) *Plots Unlimited* [119] presents over 1400 plot fragments and rules for stitching them together into a single story. These books, and others like them, can be useful tools for stimulating your imagination, but they don't actually write stories.

Whether or not computers will ever be able to write stories that will actually interest us as people is a difficult question. Because stories are such human creations, this challenge is similar to the problem commonly referred to as *hard artificial intelligence*, which in this case means creating a program that can converse like a person in all the ways that one chooses to care about. Debate rages on whether or not such a program is on the near horizon, the far horizon, or is in fact even possible.

The Frankenstein Effect

The main problem with computer-generated stories is that when it comes to people and art, analysis does not easily lead to synthesis.

This is what Dr. Frankenstein learned. He studied anatomy deeply enough to enumerate all of the pieces that go into a human being. He reasoned that this analysis meant that if he brought all the pieces together in the right arrangement, he'd have himself a human being.

This approach works just fine in the physical sciences, like chemistry: if you bring the right molecules together in the right proportion and mix them the right way, you'll get the same result every time. That's why we can have huge manufacturing plants cranking out vast quantities of synthetic chemicals.

But people certainly don't work like that, and neither does art.

If it did, we'd have very few flop movies, boring poems, or ugly paintings. And the world is filled with such things. People don't usually make unpopular art on purpose. Consider film studios: they would love to do everything in their power to make sure that every film they make is a smash hit. We know a lot about movies; as I mentioned before, *Citizen Kane* was made in 1941, and there have been tens of thousands of films since, resulting in runaway hits, flops, and everything in between. Everyone involved in making movies wants the work to be successful, are serious about the craft, and understand it as well as anyone. Why then do filmmakers sometimes make movies that are generally agreed to be awful?

It's because art doesn't get made by putting some of this next to some of that and heating it in a test tube. Art is just about impossible to predict.

The principles of storytelling and gaming are at their strongest when they tell us what we know does *not* work. People are turned off by lead characters that are boring, stories without internal conflict, and games that are based entirely on luck. If we think of artistic works as fishing boats in an ocean, the principles tell us something about the boundaries of the islands and continents. They tell us how to avoid getting beached on submerged reefs, but we have to hunt for the fish on our own.

This is why computer-generated art of all kinds is sterile. People who write programs to create stories, poems, paintings, music, or any other art are falling prey to what I call the *Frankenstein Effect*. They believe that because they have analyzed the pieces of something, they can create new variations of it by assembling the right pieces, and somehow, magically, art will emerge. It's easy enough to make works that are similar to art. You can get very close on all sorts of statistical measures, and sometimes you can even fool people into thinking that a computer-generated piece of art was made by a person.

But this is the artistic analog of junk food. Junk food is usually very tasty, and if you're hungry, it will fill your belly and make you feel well-fed. It might even give you a shot of energy. But it has little of the nutrition your body needs to survive, and eventually you need to eat food with real nutritional value. Junk art can fill your imagination and make you feel like you've had a good artistic experience, but it has none of the human qualities that artists put into their work to give it spiritual and emotional value.

Just as junk food lacks in nutrition, junk art lacks in meaning.

Some computer-generated art can have value. A person may look at the stories, poems, paintings, or other output of a self-guided program and select works that he thinks are interesting or beautiful. Like someone recording the sound of a thunderstorm, he may see beauty in these forms that was not consciously put there by any artist with something to say. Finding beauty is always something to celebrate, but if we're thinking of writing programs that require this interpretive step, we have to think about why we're doing so. There are many skilled and talented artists who have something important to say and the tools with which to say it. I believe that appreciating intentional works that have been created to communicate an idea is ultimately a more rewarding use of our time than searching for value in works that have no inherent meaning.

Research and analysis of the arts will continue, and slowly we will come to understand these very human activities better. But for now, the best art comes from people, and there's just no reason to pick computer-generated junk art when high-quality human art, and the artists to make it, are both so readily available.

In the meantime, we should recognize the magnitude of the gulf that exists today between the analysis of art (which gives us principles) and the creation of new art.

Audience Interpretation

I believe we're best served today by actually writing our own stories, rather than creating programs to make them for us.

We might alternatively try to create stories by using random events, in the way some modern composers use random sounds and events in their work. For example, the concert piece *Imaginary Landscape No. 4* [21] is scored for 12 radios tuned at random.

There are two levels of meaning in these accidental, or uncontrolled, works. One comes from the creator of the surrounding work (e.g., the instructions for when and where to play highway sounds, or how to tune the radios). The author may, for example, be saying something about the inherent artistic qualities in the natural or man-made world. But obviously, the person responsible for executing the work is not expressing anything specific in the random elements themselves, since that work is by definition uncontrolled and therefore without intentional meaning except when interpreted in context.

The other meaning comes from the audience, who may choose to create their own personal interpretations. As humans, we are remarkably good at detecting patterns, whether seeing the face of a friend in a crowd or hearing the sound of our name being called out in a busy airport. We often detect patterns where none exist, seeing shapes in the clouds and hearing songs in the wind. If we find structure in computer-generated poetry or in the sounds of traffic, it's because we as the audience are choosing and arranging what our senses are reporting to us. In other words, we extract meaning from these random presentations by imposing our own structure upon them. Without that structure, they remain meaningless in themselves and carry only whatever contextual meaning they have from their relationship to the other pieces of the work.

So we can piece together a series of events as a coherent narrative, but only if we do a lot of the work. In toys like *The Sims*, the events that happen to the simulated people in the world are not strictly random: they result from each person's state of "mind," what he's been up to recently, and his economic status. People without a penny don't build swimming pools, and those without friends don't throw wildly popular parties. When people tell stories about the lives of Sims, they're acting as creative storytellers, weaving a narrative out of the raw material of observed events. Shared toys like *The Sims Online* allow us to play together, but they still don't explicitly generate narratives.

As I discussed at the start of Chapter 8, authoring a story is very different from making one up for ourselves as we play with a toy. Similarly, making up a story from random events can be fun, but to make it entertaining for others, we need to use craft and the tools of authorship to arrange these events to shape a coherent story.

Random or unpredictable events can be fun, but great stories are still the work of great storytellers who have something to say.

Part V

Story Environments

Oh, no. No. No. I meant no scheme. I merely posed a little academic accounting theory. It's just a thought.

—Leo Bloom in *The Producers*, by Mel Brooks, 1967

Designing Participatory Stories

In the first three parts of this book, we looked at the structure of stories, the structure of games, and some of the issues that arise when we bring the two together.

In this part we'll look at putting stories and games together in ways that honor the fundamentals of both fields and are directed towards giving people opportunities to have fun with one another. My major goal is not to theorize about fiction or to try to develop something that challenges tradition. Rather, it's to develop a new combination of storytelling, gaming, and socializing that's just a lot of fun.

⋙ 12 ⋘

Story Environments

T he key to creating a new form of participatory fiction is the creation
of systems that are *programmable* and *adaptive*. These are qualities
that people have in abundance, which is why a dungeon master
can run a game of *Dungeons & Dragons*.

I see these new types of stories as taking place within *story environments*.
These are worlds where plot, character, physics, sound, visual appearance,
behavior, and everything that goes into a story are mediated by adaptive
software, which manages and maintains the environment.

What shall we call the people participating in these stories? I like *players*:
someone taking part in a game is called a player, as is a performer in a play
or film. Since a person participating in a story environment is doing a bit
of each activity, the term "player" seems both fitting and economical.

In this chapter I'll examine a number of different issues that are important to the development of story environments.

Programmability

Computers have had such a tremendous effect on our society partly due to
their ability to quickly and economically store, retrieve, and process large
amounts of information. Storing and retrieving data will both be important

329

to storytelling, but it's the processing, or programming, that's most relevant to our discussion here.

The value of programmability is that it allows us to create simulated systems that are extremely complex, yet consistent. Today we can create simulators for everything from the mechanical operation of an aircraft carrier to the evolution of a spy story, and someday perhaps even to human personalities.

Elaborate simulations themselves aren't all that novel. Perhaps the most common simulations we come into contact with every day are the worlds of television shows. Many TV urban dramas contain one or more exterior shots, where the lead characters perform in and around people hurrying up and down sidewalks, past stores selling all kinds of goods, steam hissing from vents, and traffic snarling in the streets. All of this ambience is fake, from the manufactured steam to the extras who are hired, costumed, made up, and told where and when to bustle past the camera. Films are the same way: science-fiction movies don't actually take place on spaceships or other planets, and 1800s costume dramas weren't shot in the 1800s.

Years of TV and film have helped us all become accustomed to imaginary, simulated systems, from the submarines in *Voyage to the Bottom of the Sea* and the spaceships in *Star Trek*, to the hospitals of *E.R.* and the political world of *The West Wing*. The difference between the imaginary worlds of television and movies and the ones that we can create in the computer is that we can actively participate in and change the computerized environments. This ability has two important consequences. First, rather than simply view those spaces, we can inhabit and move through them ourselves. Second, rather than passively watch other people take action, we can take action ourselves and see the effects of our actions in the world.

The first of these two qualities is simply a matter of technology: when we can create sensory stimuli that make the imaginary environment look and taste and feel like a real one, we've taken care of the presence part. This *holodeck* technology may be created in the world around us, or (by using direct cortical stimulation) it may be created quite literally within our own minds. Although nobody today knows how to create a perfectly realistic, simulated environment, it's doubtless that we will continue to move ever closer to that idea over time, however it's accomplished.

Believable environments don't have to be "realistic" to be believable. The world of the movie *Monsters, Inc.* certainly isn't realistic in any sense:

it doesn't look real, it doesn't behave realistically, and it's about imaginary monsters! Yet the movie is self-consistent and entirely believable.

The second feature of procedural environments is that we can act on them and see the results of our actions. This is the reason why today's technologies are attractive for our purposes: like the characters in a story, we can become participants in the environment.

The massively multiplayer game *Everquest* takes a straightforward approach to both of these ideas. The designers have created a large and complicated world using sound and 3D graphics. Players can see and hear that world and move their in-world character through it. Players "speak" to each other by typing text and can direct their on-screen character to physically attack monsters, cast magic, and otherwise affect the environment.

Computer-based environments will transport us to ever-more believable and responsive places and times, and that alone makes them very appealing.

But this technology by itself is not enough to create a viable form of story participation. After all, we already live in a perfectly believable, perfectly responsive environment: the real world. So if beautiful imagery and sound, and touch, taste, balance, hot, cold, and all the other senses were perfectly simulated, and all the physics of the simulated world matched this world perfectly, we'd still only be catching up with the real world. And that's where the signposts end, because as we've seen in previous chapters, we don't have a mainstream tradition of participatory storytelling already present in the real world to emulate.

The central question then is whether there is something that computer and communications technologies can add to the mix that goes beyond simulations of everyday reality (or fun but believable extensions of it, like magic spells and spaceships). There is, and those two extra ingredients are *adaptation* and *programmability*.

Adaptivity

Adaptivity is a very broad idea, so let's first creep up on it from the side to get a feeling for its scope.

Let's start with tools. Tools are, at their root, a means to reshape the environment to better fit our wants and needs.

The most basic tools address the first level of Maslow's hierarchy of needs (shown in Figure 3). We use physical tools to build shelter, obtain food, and satisfy our other bodily requirements.

Beyond that, our needs become more abstract, and so do our tools. We need love and affection, and part of growing up means learning what behaviors please our parents, other authority figures, and friends. We find, for example, that generosity is usually well received, so we tend to be generous when we're eager to make a good first impression (e.g., on a first date, or in a job interview). This is a behavioral tool.

As we mature and move up Maslow's hierarchy, we continue to find ways to shape the world and ourselves. Ultimately we may follow some spiritual practice, which often involves following a meditation regime or other traditional procedure for developing inner control and peace. Even though we can't see these psychological tools, they are still things we create to reshape the world to our preferences.

So we create and use both physical and abstract tools to fulfill our desires to change the world around us to make it more to our liking. In other words, we try to *adapt* the world and ourselves to create a more harmonious match. We customize the world every time we mow the lawn, add pepper to our salad, try to convince someone to vote for our candidate, or turn up the heat in the house.

Most media to date have not been adaptive. Books, CDs, movies, and radio shows do not change at all in response to what the audience is thinking or feeling. Live plays and dances change in only small ways based on audience feedback.

Branching narratives and hypertext provide very simple adaptivity, since readers have some control over which part of the work they see next. Indeed, in some hypertext works, the links themselves change over time, so the second time you visit a particular section, the links may point to different places than they did your first time through, depending on where you've been in the meantime. But the underlying work itself doesn't change: the media pieces that make up a hypertext or branching story don't change as a reader reads the work, and unless the links are changed at random, their only changes are those that have been programmed into the work.

The appeal of these forms comes largely from the fact that they offer any adaptivity at all. In the land of the blind, the one-eyed man is king; in the world of non-adaptive media, branching and hypertext structures are the best thing going today.

True adaptivity in a free environment, where the work itself changes in response to the player, will give us the chance to be part of our stories in a way that matches how we're part of the world: we can act as we wish, and the world will respond in ways that make sense.

Adaptive Forms

Adaptivity is a quality, so we can observe it along a continuum. Let's look at a number of different degrees of adaptivity, from the least adaptive to the most.

No adaptivity: This is the world of "one size fits all," which too often means "no size fits you." Whatever it is that you have, whether it's a book, a hat, or a time-limited test of skill in a video game, it is given to you just as it's given to everyone else, and you can take it or leave it.

A pair of scissors is not adaptive: you can open and close it to cut things, but the scissors don't change themselves in any way to conform to your hands or your task.

One-time customization: Some objects can be manufactured to order. For example, when you buy a new car, you can choose the interior and exterior colors, the type of sound system, and other features from a large list. Some options are mutually exclusive (e.g., stick shift or automatic transmission), and others can be combined (e.g., power windows and fog lights). Once you've made your choices, the object is created, and you can't change them again without significant effort.

Modern PC-type computers are often assembled this way: working with a salesman, you choose a sound board, a video board, a monitor, and a mouse, and the company then assembles the computer. You can later upgrade the machine by replacing parts, but that can be a significant undertaking.

When we order a meal in a restaurant and ask, for example, for a dish to be prepared "not too spicy," or "medium-well," this is also one-time customization (some dishes can be sent back to the kitchen and cooked more, but they can't be un-cooked if overdone).

Temporary customization: In some systems you can easily make a new choice at any time, but your choices aren't remembered from one use to the next.

333

For example, consider a typical bathroom shower with two water handles: hot and cold. You can adjust these as frequently as you like to control both the water flow and temperature. Once you're done and you turn the water off, your choices are forgotten. Unless you remember just how you set the knobs, you'll need to hunt for the settings you like the next time you need to use the shower.

I call this "temporary customization" because the customization lasts only as long as you're using the object.

Customization: Some systems remember your choices, and you can easily change them as frequently as you like. This is the kind of thing that most of us think of when we're told that something is "customizable."

Most office and business software falls in this category. If you open any modern word-processing or spreadsheet program, you'll find a wealth of options for controlling everything from colors and fonts to layout and printing. Most of these options are set by checking a box or selecting a choice from a list, and you can change your choices at any time by simply opening up the options menu again and making new selections. Many games are this way. For example, you can enable or disable the rumble feature on your console game's controller as often as you like.

Another example is a standard car radio. You can choose any station to listen to, and you can set buttons to remember a half-dozen of your favorite stations. If your tastes change, you can easily change the values assigned to the preset buttons to new stations.

One of the nice features of customization is that it is *reversible*: you can take back a choice. If you disabled the spell checker in your word-processing program yesterday, and then decide you want it back on again today, you need only check that box in the options page. If you don't like the stations to which you've set your car radio, you can just reset them.

The characteristics of customization are that your choices can be easily changed any number of times, and they remain in force until you change them again.

Tailoring: A special case of customization is when an expert helps you make choices or implements your choices for you.

Suppose that you walk into a men's clothing store and try on a suit. A tailor looks you over and starts to mark up the suit with chalk: he knows how it ought to look and uses his expertise to customize the suit for you. Naturally, I call this type of customization "tailoring."

The expert is usually happy to accommodate any requests you may have. If you go to get a haircut and you trust your stylist, you can simply say, "Please make me look good," and then take a nap. But you can also make any number of specific requests, such as "Let it hang over the ears," or even "Give me something trendy and hip."

One of the pleasures of working with experts is that they can handle the mechanisms of accommodating your requests, even if you have no idea how to do it yourself. For example, you might ask a piano tuner to make your piano "sound like an old honky-tonk piano." How this is done might be completely mysterious to you, yet you're perfectly competent to help the tuner by telling him how close he's getting to the sound you want.

Tailored systems are great for those times when you know how you want things to be customized, but you don't know how to do it yourself.

Tailored systems are a special case of *expert systems*, a term that encompasses software designed to help with everything from warehouse logistics to medical diagnosis. The more narrow term "tailoring" is useful here because it helps us keep the discussion focused on customization, rather than all the other things more generalized expert systems can do.

Interface customization: So far I've been using examples of systems that we customize ourselves: we set the car radio stations and we turn the shower handles. But some systems modify not their behavior, but the interface itself, in response to what we do.

A well-known example of interface customization is the "personalized menus" feature used in Microsoft Office XP [28]. For example, after you've used Word for a while to create text documents, the system looks at which pull-down menu items you've been using the most, and it moves them to the top of their corresponding menus. Unused items are all packed together behind a single menu choice that, when selected, reveals the others. The idea is that Word's large default menus will get replaced over time with smaller menus that contain just the commands that are useful to you. As your use of the program changes, the items in these customized menus also change so that your most frequent commands are always the ones closest at hand.

I personally find that this kind of thing drives me crazy: when I need to find a menu item that I use a lot, I can find it most quickly if it's always in the same place. Then I can just grab, say, the fourth entry from the top, without even reading it, because I know that's where it always is. If the menus are spontaneously adjusting themselves in unpredictable ways, then every time I need to use a menu, I'm forced to read through it until I find the entry I want. One of my first steps of customization with Word was to find the switch that turns this feature off.

Parametric adaptivity: Many software and hardware systems depend on a variety of numerical values to drive the simulation, such as the number of people living in a building, the water pressure in an underground pipe, or a person's degree of job satisfaction. These numbers, or *parameters*, drive the simulator. For example, if we increase the number of people riding on a city bus system, the busses will be fuller, and the city will make more money.

A common form of adaptivity occurs when a program automatically adjusts these values in response to what you do. I call this *parametric adaptivity*. Note that the simulator itself isn't changing: it's still running the same algorithms that were created by the designer and programmer. But the inputs to those programs are changing, and that affects what it does in ways that are perhaps very difficult to predict.

If a simulator's model is complex enough, and the parameters are at a sufficiently abstract level, it may be very hard for a person to understand the connection between what they do in the simulated world and what happens as a result. This means that the puzzle aspect of using the simulator becomes much harder (or even effectively impossible). If a game designer wants to make the puzzle aspect very difficult, or to encourage people to skip the puzzle altogether, then this is an effective way to do it. Designers must be careful when taking this approach that people know not to spend too much time trying to figure out how the obscure simulator works, lest they become frustrated because of the difficulty of the task.

We know from a variety of fields that some kinds of simple systems can result in very complex behavior. This kind of effect is best seen in *chaos theory*. This is the science that tries to understand how a butterfly flapping its wings in the Amazon can lead to a drought six months later in Chicago. The weather, like many other chaotic systems, is incredibly sensitive to the values of its parameters [53].

A rich and visually enchanting example of such complexity arising from simplicity is the *chaotic pendulum*, one version of which is shown in Figure 26. Although this is a very simple device, the placement of the weights and the length of the arms is enough to make the whole system *chaotic*. What this means is that if you give the whole thing a good push and set it spinning, after a while you won't be able to predict the motion of the circular weight. This unpredictability might be surprising, since we might think that the laws of physics would be sufficient to tell us how such a simple device is going to behave. And in theory, they certainly are. But in practice, to actually use those laws to determine the motion of the pendulum, we have to plug in actual numbers and compute with them. This sort of system is almost diabolically sensitive to tiny changes in those values. The rounding errors and other normal inaccuracies that are part of any computation accumulate each time we work with them, making the output of these equations increasingly "noisy," or unreliable, over time.

For example, just multiplying a number by the square root of 2 inevitably means we have to make an approximation somewhere. Since that number is *irrational*, it's essentially an infinite string of unpredictable digits. To actually calculate with that number, we have to chop it off at some point and use that approximate value. That creates an error due to the difference between the theoretically precise value and our numerical approximation. In practice, we can even make that error as small as we please simply by using more digits. We can make it small enough to enable us to send men to the moon and bring them back safely. But we can't eliminate it.

In many systems, regular errors can be understood and accounted for. In other systems, errors happen in such a way that they cancel each

Figure 26. Three snapshots of a chaotic pendulum. The center arm spins freely around its center, and has a weight on one end. At the other end is another arm that spins freely around its pivot. The motion of the circular weight is unpredictable.

other out over time. But in chaotic systems, the errors accumulate as time goes on. The errors eventually become so large that the values we're calculating don't match the system very well, and from that point on the match gets worse and worse until eventually what we're computing bears no resemblance at all to the physical system we're simulating.

If we want to extend our predictive range, we can use more digits, but we're always going to find at some point that the system has exceeded the precision of our calculations and we simply have no idea what it will do next.

Parametric adaptivity can be complex enough that people can't tell that the underlying system isn't changing. The chaos pendulum of Figure 26 doesn't change over time: the length and connectivity of its arms stay constant, as do the sizes of the weights. But if all we get to see as the audience is the motion of the circular weight, we might invent all sorts of reasons for its complex motion.

Structural adaptivity: The best kind of adaptive systems automatically attempt to improve in response to your use. Structurally adaptive systems are the most robust at this: they automatically reconfigure themselves to better fit your desires.

Living things often use structural adaptivity to help them survive in a new or changing environment.

A living tree in a forest relies on structural adaptation to live. As it grows, the tree seeks sunlight for its leaves. But those leaves are blocked by the leaves of other trees. So the tree grows upward, to rise above the other trees, while it also sends out new branches in different directions to seek out patches of illumination. A tree growing in a forest grows very differently than one growing in the middle of an empty field: the struggle for limited resources forces it to adapt and change its shape and form.

Let's consider a more lively example of a structurally adaptive system: a puppy.

When you and a new puppy meet for the first time, you don't know much about each other. As time goes on, the dog learns all sorts of things from you: house training, when and what it gets fed, and whether or not it's allowed on the sofa. As the puppy learns what's allowed and what's not, and which behaviors bring rewards and which bring punishment, it adapts. The puppy *learns* and *changes its behavior*. It actually becomes a different animal. This training has its limits: there's a point where nature will trump nurture. But in many important ways the puppy changes as it grows, and in ways that are much deeper than cosmetic. And certainly you'll find yourself adapting to the puppy as well.

A puppy is a very sophisticated creature whose behavior greatly exceeds the most advanced human-designed software and hardware on the planet. So although we'll certainly make progress and create ever-better simulators (such as the program *Dogz* and the robot dog *Aibo*), it's not likely that we're going to create anything that really comes close to being a puppy for a long time.

Not all structurally adaptive systems are living organisms, nor do they all try to satisfy just one individual's goals. Consider the organization of the mass transit system in a major city, which can involve busses, trains, streetcars, and other vehicles. As the population of the city changes, the demands on this system will change. If one neighborhood becomes popular for elderly people, it may need more frequent service to shopping and medical services. If another neighborhood becomes more industrial and less residential, it may be less important to have frequent service there during the day, though getting people to and from their jobs at rush hour and lunchtime would still be a

Level of Adaptivity	Characterisitic
no adaptivity	no change
one-time customization	the system is built to your specification
temporary customization	you can define temporary preferences
customization	your preferences are remembered and easily changed
tailoring	an expert helps set the system for you
auto-customization	the system changes the interface itself to accomodate you
parametric adaptivity	the system changes weights to accomodate you
structural adaptivity	the system changes structure to accomodate you

Figure 27.   Different levels of adaptation.

priority. The supervisors of the system watch the usage patterns and adapt the system as needed. They may make parametric changes by moving around the times of some of the busses or making some busses double-sized. They may also make structural changes by adding new bus lines and removing those with low ridership, and perhaps even by eliminating some old forms of technology and installing new ones, such as replacing cable cars with a monorail.

We've looked at eight levels of adaptivity, ranging from none at all to the ability of a system to change its structure. The range from no adaptation to structural adaptation is a continuous one, so there are an infinite number of intermediate points. But I've found these categories to be helpful for giving an overall shape to the range. I've summarized this discussion in Figure 27.

Suppose that we stand on top of an empty cardboard box, and it rips and crushes under our feet. The box has certainly changed, even in a structural way, but this isn't an example of adaptivity. A key feature of adaptive systems is that they strive to *improve*, not just change. A tree wants more sunlight, and a puppy wants to please you more. People adapt their environment in order to make themselves happier.

Not all change is voluntary: the crushed cardboard box, if asked, would probably not want to be crushed. A puppy who likes to sit on the couch will resist when you try to train it not to. So why do systems adapt? They change in response to some kind of impulse or stimulus.

Such an impulse can be internal or external. An internal impulse causes us to change because the result improves our life in some way. Someone who feels self-conscious about his accent when he arrives in a new city may choose to adjust his speech so that he doesn't sound so obviously out of place. An external impulse pushes us to change because something outside of ourselves is interfering with our happiness. If we live in a noisy city and find it hard to sleep at night, we might start closing all the windows every night, even though we would prefer fresh air.

I've found it useful to think of three different roads to adaptation.

Unconscious adaptation: Sometimes a system adapts without even being aware that it's doing so. While playing ping-pong, we may find that at the end of a game, we're standing not at the center of the table, where we started, but off to one side. That's because our opponent usually hits to that side, and bit by bit we moved in order to increase our ability to hit a good return. When we sit down in a new chair, it's not uncommon to have to squirm around a little bit to get comfortable; usually we're not even aware of doing so.

Voluntary adaptation: Sometimes we adapt as a result of a conscious, voluntary decision. For example, someone who's used to living alone can develop a lot of idiosyncratic housekeeping habits. When two such people start to cohabitate, they often need to work out their differences, and usually each compromises on different things. If someone who's used to throwing all the silverware into a drawer starts living with someone who likes to keep everything neatly sorted, there will usually be a negotiation, after which someone will probably change voluntarily as a result.

Forced adaptation: Sometimes we adapt because we must. If the environment changes around us, and we can't put it back the way it was, then we are the ones that have to accommodate. When winter comes, to stay warm we have to put on warmer clothing or turn up the heat: we are forced to adapt.

A tiger who's always lived in the jungle, but is then captured and placed in a zoo, must adapt to the zoo environment. He'll only get fed when the zoo personnel decide to feed him, and then they will be the ones that decide what food he gets and how much. His physical space is more limited, as are his opportunities for social interaction with other tigers. The tiger quickly learns to get as much value out of his environment as he can, but he also adapts over time so that his frustration is minimized.

When the world changes around us, and we're made unhappy by the change, we try to change the environment to make things better. If that's not possible, then we're forced to either suffer or change ourselves.

Creature Simulations

In recent years there has been significant progress in making synthetic creatures that appear to have some kind of intelligence.

For example, consider the Sony *Aibo* robotic dog. This toy is much more like a caricature or abstraction of a dog than an accurate simulation. It has a variety of behaviors, and as the owner of the robot, you teach it what you like and dislike. Over time the robot learns and adapts, reinforcing behaviors that bring it rewards, and suppressing behaviors that get punished.

A less ambitious type of robotic dog is the purely software simulation in the program *Dogz*. These on-screen dogs also learn based on how you treat them and slowly adapt their behavior to try to satisfy both your desires and their own programmed needs.

Unfamiliar creatures also have appeared. The software toy *Creatures* allows you to create and raise little software animals that appear to have intelligence and emotions. The popular electronic doll called a *Furby* operates in a similar way. As you play with a Furby, it changes its behavior to accommodate your style of play.

Some of the creators of these projects have discussed their approaches in print [132] [58], but in general the programming of most commercial products is a trade secret, so we can only speculate on their internal details. But all it takes is a short while of playing with these toys to get a strong feeling that there's some personality there.

This success suggests that we can get a long way toward making interesting and adaptive creatures without fully solving the problems of artificial intelligence and behavior.

Adaptation, Structure, and Presentation

In Chapter 3 I talked about the difference between plot sequence and view sequence. The plot sequence is the linear succession of events that make up the plot of the story, while the view sequence is the linear succession of descriptions of that plot as they're given to the audience. The view sequence can be very different from the underlying plot sequence.

Stories can adaptively change either or both of these sequences.

The underlying plot may change in response to a particular reader's desire. For example, a love story with a bit of action may change into an action story with a bit of a love interest.

On the other hand, the story might stay the same but the presentation adapts. A reader of a kidnapping story may want to see the events unfold from the hero's point of view, the villain's point of view, or even the victim's. The underlying story wouldn't change, but the way in which it's presented to the reader would accomodate his preference.

We see this accomodation frequently in games. In a friendly pick-up baseball game, players can adapt the structure of the game to novices by offering them four strikes rather than three. When a major league game is televised, a director may prefer to show a particular pitcher from the batter's point of view. Thus he'd make a presentation change by showing more shots from behind home plate than from the blimp flying overhead.

Contemporary Adaptation

To get a feeling for the relationship between adaptation and storytelling, let's briefly look at how contemporary stories have used the different levels of adaptivity we saw earlier.

No adaptivity: Traditional movies and books are not adaptive: nothing that the audience does changes the words on the page or the frames of the film.

One-time customization: Some writers take commissions: you tell them what you want in some detail, and they produce a story.

Some movies are available on videotape in two different aspect ratios: a wide "letterbox" format like a movie theater screen, and a "pan-and-scan" format that is shaped to match a typical television screen. You can customize your experience by purchasing one version of the tape or the other.

Temporary customization: Reading a book from the *Choose Your Own Adventure* series of branching narratives allows you to customize the story, as your choices send you in specific directions. Your customization doesn't have any memory in the medium itself: unless you damage the book, it's the same each time you pick it up.

Hypertext stories let you wander through their segments in any order that you want, but when you're done with them, they go back to their original form; the underlying story is unchanged.

Many movie DVDs now ship with both letterbox and pan-and-scan versions. You make your choice based on which way you load the disk into the machine. If you change your mind sometime during the film, you can stop the movie, eject the disk, put it back in the other way, and fast-forward to where you left off.

Customization: Some hypertext systems allow you to set a "level of detail" slider. As you go through the media that makes up the story, the slider determines how much additional information you're given. For example, when introduced to new characters you might be provided with a lot of information on their childhood and family of origin if you're set to high detail, or just a current photograph if you're set to low detail. The value of the slider stays put until you change it, and you can easily change the value of the slider at any time.

Tailoring: When a play is first mounted on stage, it typically goes through a "shakedown" period where the playwright and director watch both the performances and the audience reactions. They then go back and make changes, perhaps adding or deleting a song or a speech, or changing the pace of a sequence. These experts are working to improve the play for their audiences.

A more personal but general form of tailoring is offered by a sympathetic librarian, local bookstore clerk, or a video store clerk. Once these people come to know you and your tastes, they can make recommendations for you and help you along a personalized exploration of stories that you'll enjoy. The stories themselves are not changed in any way by this, but your overall experience is shaped by the suggestions of these helpful experts.

Interface customization: In some games you can change the makeup of your travelling party. For example, in *Final Fantasy X* you are almost always accompanied by a group of other characters, though only three of you at a time can fight any particular group of monsters. As you swap in different characters, the interface changes in response to their abilities. For example, if someone can't cast a particular magic spell, it doesn't appear in their list of abilities.

Parametric adaptivity: Sometimes profiling games make it obvious how they're changing the weights on the inputs to the simulator. In the game *Black & White*, the visual appearance of the creature you control changes explicitly over time to reflect the moral choices you've made while training it.

Structural adaptivity: A bedtime story can change in wildly unpredictable ways as a parent creates it on the fly to suit the child's desires. The story can change genre, gain or lose characters, change in location, rhythm, and length, and in almost every other way as it winds its way to some unpredictable conclusion.

Continuity of Experience

In Chapter 5 I talked about Csikszentmihalyi's idea of *flow*: the mental state that arises when you're completely focused on an experience and fully immersed in the moment, causing the outside world to slip away. Being in a state of flow can be extremely rewarding.

Although flow is a deep state, it's also a fragile one. If you're swimming laps and you're in a flow state of mind, you can lose it if someone else jumps into the pool and interferes with your rhythm. If you're reading a book or watching a film and you're in flow, a ringing doorbell or telephone can drop you right out of it.

Many computer games try to coax players into a state of flow, and there's at least preliminary evidence that video game players can find levels of flow as deep as those of athletes who are "in the zone" playing a demanding sport [126]. This result sounds reasonable, as biofeedback researchers have long used audio and video to help people learn to control their brain rhythms to help them relax, concentrate better, and sleep better [145].

One of the things that takes us out of flow is an unexpected change in the nature of the experience. We can sometimes stay in flow even when a situation changes: basketball players frequently switch from offense to defense, and find themselves dribbling, then rebounding, then shooting.

But despite this wide variety of activities, they can maintain a state of flow because these transitions are natural and expected part of the natural rhythm of the game, so they're all part of the same experience.

Participation Intensity

Many video games that try to present both action and story alternate between periods of action and cut-scenes. The cut-scenes in these games have a lot of positive attributes: they're often very well produced and provide story information to the player. But there is no smooth transition from gameplay to cut-scene and back again. In fact, many such scenes follow a period of very high interactivity: you defeat the monster, blow up the building, drive along a tricky course lined with bombs, fly through all the rings, or otherwise get through a lengthy, tense, and very interactive period of button-pushing and joystick-mashing. Your reward for this success is that your interactivity level plummets instantly from intensely absorbing to zero: once you deal the final blow or cross the finish line, the cut-scene takes over. You then watch passively as the monster dies, the crowd cheers, the castle gates open, or whatever else happens as a prize for finishing the task.

This is a classic flow-destroying event. The problem is that your level of involvement has gone from enormous to zero in no time. It's often good for pacing to have a time-out after such an intense period of activity, but the nature of this particular time-out is that the quality of the experience changes: as a player, you go from being an involved and critical participant to being an irrelevant bystander (the monster only dies if you actively defeat him, but the following cut-scene will play whether you stay in the room or not).

This change from interaction to cut-scene is an abrupt and dramatic change in the *continuity of experience*. If a player has reached a flow state during the interactive moment, this drastic switch will certainly throw him out of it. I call this a change in *participation intensity*.

A large change in participation intensity destroys flow.

Information Density

The sudden switch from interactive moment to cut-scene creates another important discontinuity: the *information density* changes. The idea of information density tells us how swiftly we're moving through the narrative.

This measure is just about impossible to quantify, but it's easy enough to get a qualitative feel for.

Suppose you have a job stocking shelves at a supermarket, and today your manager walks by as you're getting ready to put up cans of corn, and says, "Put them on the shelf with the top up and the label facing forward." That's a very specific order and easy enough to follow.

Now suppose he instead says, "Put them up like the other cans." This order is a little less specific, but it still tells us what he wants. The information density here is higher, because he's in effect telling you to do at least two things: look at how the other cans are shelved, and emulate that. Because he's expecting you to be able to figure that out, he doesn't need to say it all.

Now suppose he says, "Be sure to shelve those the way I like." Now he's relying on a lot of information that presumably you and he have already shared. In essence, this command incorporates all of the discussions you've had together in the past about how he likes to have things shelved, so the information density here is very high: just a few words stand for at least one whole conversation.

As a last example, suppose he says "Remember to shelve those the new way the company wants." This order includes not only conversations you and he have had, but the information that came from the company that presumably you and your manager have discussed. So the information density here is highest of all, since it implicitly contains (or refers to) your conversations and the company's new instructions.

When information density changes too fast, it disrupts flow. If you're used to processing just a small amount of incoming information and you're unexpectedly flooded, you need to snap to attention and deal with the new demand. If you're working hard at staying up to date with incoming information and it suddenly drops, or stops altogether, again you'll be caught short. Whether you accelerate your car from 0 miles per hour to 60 or decelerate from 60 to 0, you feel the change. Similarly, abrupt changes in information density require a shift of mental gears, which breaks the continuity of experience and spells the end of any flow state.

Maintaining Flow

Flow states can't last forever; sooner or later we need to eat lunch or walk the dog or go to sleep. But it's in the interest of the creator of a game or story to let their audience stay in flow as long as they want to be there. So designers never want to end flow themselves unless there's a very good reason for it; rather, the audience should only leave when *they* feel the need.

Some first-person sports games create and maintain a long-term flow experience. For example, the console snowboarding game *SSX* offers players runs of 5 or more minutes at a time. Even after falling or being shoved by another player, the nature of the experience doesn't change: you're still hurtling downhill. The controls remain the same throughout, and when racing to win, your job remains always to go as fast as possible, and to do as many new tricks as possible along the way. The participation intensity and information density both remain consistent throughout the lengthy run, so that you have enough time to find your flow zone and stay in it.

Compare this experience to, say, *Final Fantasy X*. In this game there are basically three modes: walking through the environment with your party (and solving puzzles), fighting monsters, and watching cut-scenes. The game doesn't give a player a chance to get into a flow state because the modes switch frequently and unexpectedly. In particular, monster battles occur at random as you move through the world, so you never know when one's going to happen. Thus you're yanked from one kind of experience into another, and then when it's done you're dropped back where you were until it happens again.

As bad as abrupt changes are, not all slow changes are better. Imagine a game where you're in control of a character, but then gradually the system creates a transition to a cut-scene. You might feel as if your control is slipping away like sand between your fingers, which would almost certainly be an unpleasant experience. Losing control of your character is never going to conducive to maintaining a flow experience, no matter how slowly it's done. Some people like to rip off a bandage quickly, and others prefer to pull it off slowly, but it hurts either way.

To summarize, when we tell a story, we typically want the audience to become lost in the imaginary world of the narrative and enter a state of flow. Maintaining the continuity of experience is critical to reaching and staying in that state. Books and movies and other static media are able to help readers find and stay in flow because they're able to control the quantity and quality of the participation and information. Abrupt changes in the participation intensity or information density destroy flow.

Story Environments

Computers provide us with an opportunity to create increasingly believable and complex worlds that can be inhabited by other people. These worlds allow players to interact with the environment and each other. Such worlds aren't entirely novel: Renaissance fairs are both believable (the physics of the real world are in place at a fair, and most performers stay in character), and they are both physically and socially complex.

An environment is a place where a story can happen, but it's not a story itself. We might be tempted to base interactive fiction on holodeck episodes of *Star Trek*, but that approach would not be very fruitful. Those shows were written and rewritten, rehearsed, edited, and performed by actors for the benefit of their audience. This process has little in common with real-time entertainments in which we ourselves participate for our own entertainment. What happened on the holodeck was one kind of participatory story experience, but even in the shows, it clearly required some pretty strong improv skills from the starship crew who entered the simulated world. A holodeck entertainment is a challenging place to be [98].

To have a story requires characters and, as we've seen, most people are not comfortable performing as actors, either scripted or improvisational. So we have two challenges in these simulated worlds: telling a story, and involving people actively in that story.

One way to tell a story in an environment is to put the player in the midst of interesting individuals and groups, each with their own abilities and agendas. Like most well-authored ensembles, this environment would be an artistically assembled microcosm of our own world, structured to create pleasing and interesting relationships and conflicts.

For the moment, let's not worry about whether these other characters and groups are computer-generated or are somehow controlled by other people.

As far as the player is able to tell, the other characters are intelligent and have their own lives and goals. They're willing to act when they deem it appropriate, taking both the initiative and any risks that come with it, to achieve their goals. So the environment contains multiple motivated and active characters acting simultaneously in a shared responsive world.

The technology with which we can create, simulate, and interact with such worlds will continue to improve in all directions, from the quality of the world simulation to the richness of the player's sensory input and output. So one day, we'll have something at least functionally similar to a holodeck available to us. How then would we go about putting together an interactive story?

Let's start by looking at the basics of the environment and the activities of the characters that inhabit it.

Two Characters

The simplest environment matches a player with a single other character whose goal is to win at a particular game. That's the model for a great many programs that pit a player against a computerized opponent, from chess to checkers to hangman. It's also the model for some single-player games, such as *Starfox Adventures* and *Super Mario Sunshine*. The "opponent" in these games is the programmer, who is present through the algorithms and behaviors he has written into the enemies the player encounters. This is most obvious during "boss battles," in games like *The Legend of Zelda: The Wind Waker* and *Final Fantasy X*. These can be thought of as special, one-time games with their own rules. The player's job is first to figure out the rules (e.g., where to stand, when and how to strike the boss, and what weapons or magic spells are most useful), and then execute them as skillfully as he can. In this sense the game is also partly a puzzle: the rules are predetermined and objective, but they're not made visible to the player. He must first discover them before he can perform well and win the game by defeating the boss.

If we apply this one-on-one model to stories rather than games, and the other character's goals conflict with those of the player, we get a two-character drama. Both characters in the drama marshal their resources to achieve their goal and to make life harder for the other along the way.

Bridging and Blocking

The participants in a story environment are story characters. That means that they should be well-rounded personalities with all the attributes of a good character that we discussed in Chapter 2. Whether they're the on-screen persona of another human player, a computer-controlled simulation, or something in between, they aren't standing by and waiting for someone else to tell them what to do or how to do it. They have their own needs, and they're busy acting in their own personal and unique ways, according to their natures. They're also living their lives, sleeping, eating, and otherwise carrying on like all people do.

If we're in a science-fiction story, the needs and habits of these characters may be very far from human, but they will still be true to their own natures. I'll stick to human characters here, with any required extensions to science-fiction and fantasy worlds taken as implicit.

So the other participants in the environment are frequently selfish, autonomous, initiative-taking, goal directed, and idiosyncratic, just like real people. They have their own abilities and limitations, both moral and physical.

Characters in such an environment do not take turns. They're not playing a game, but acting when and how they see fit. They're acting *asynchronously*, which means that they're not required to wait for anyone else before taking action. Someone can choose to wait for one another if he wants to. And sometimes it may be necessary to wait for another: if you want to Tango, you need two.

What we have then is a world filled with characters with their own personal agendas and personalities. Each character is the hero of his own story, and is trying to solve his own problems in his own way.

Think of these characters as cars driving in the desert. Most of the time most of the cars are speeding along on their own courses, independent of the others. There are some objects here and there on the desert, and sometimes more than one person wants a given object, so they're both racing towards it as fast as they can. Other cars are trying to get to their own destinations, which themselves may have parking room for only one car, or for many. You can see the problems: if more than one person wants the same object or to be in a given place, all but one will be frustrated.

Each driver is going as fast as he can. But if a car runs into quicksand, it's going to be stuck for a while. If a car needs to cross a river, that driver will have to find a bridge, build a bridge, or find another way around. And some cars will crash: they will play chicken with each other and one (or both) will lose, or they just won't see one another until it's too late.

In story terms, these are all good things! Even crashes are good. Crashes are the analogy for confrontation: in *Casablanca*, Ilse walks into Rick's bar late one night to try to reignite her relationship with Rick, but Rick just wants to feel sorry for himself and hurt her in the process. That's a great crash: each is going in his or her own direction, but they plow into one another, and the parts fly off in all directions.

So as characters hurtle towards their goals, they interact with each other. Following the metaphor of cars in the desert, I find it useful to think of characters taking action in four different ways; each of these types of actions can be taken with regard to another to character, or to one's own self.

When someone wants to cross a river, he needs a *bridge*. If there's a boulder in the road, he's facing a *block*. Players can create and remove bridges and blocks for themselves and each other. Here are the four basic bridging and blocking actions.

Create a bridge: Create a means for a character to get from one point to the next. A character might introduce someone who needs a job to an employer with a job to fill, tell someone a useful secret, or go to the gym every day for a month to train himself to run fast in high altitudes.

Remove a bridge: Remove something available from someone else, usually to slow him down, or send him on another course. The idea here is that you create a problem by preventing him from using something that he was counting on. A character might cause another to be fired from his job, steal his plane tickets, or let the air out of his car tires.

Create a block: Create an obstacle for other players. As opposed to disabling a bridge, where you remove something they were counting on, here one actually creates something to get in their way. A character might steal the identity of another and get them in trouble with the police, change the locks on their car and house, or write threatening letters signed with their name.

Remove a block: Remove something that is causing the player a problem. It might mean bailing someone out of jail, turning off the blinking billboard outside his house that's interfering with his sleep, or paying off his debts.

These aren't rigid categories, but just general ways to think about actions; the difference between a bridge and a block is often a matter of context and interpretation. These four actions are summarized in Figure 28.

Each character in a story environment is striving to fulfill his own goals and is using each of these types of actions, as well as their hybrids and variations, to achieve his desires. Note that for some people, being good to others, even strangers, may be one of their desires, so this intention will

	enable	disable
bridge	loan money to a friend	sabotage the car of a foe
block	spread lies about a foe	post bail for a friend

Figure 28.   Making progress in a story environment using the creation and removal of blocks and bridges.

limit how much harm they're willing to cause, directly or indirectly. Other people are not so concerned with those they don't know and are more inclined to let them look after themselves.

Although I've used mostly physical examples, the needs and goals of all the characters can be anything in the range of human desire, from emotional needs to spiritual longings, from romantic and sexual interests to intellectual development, and anything and everything else that moves us to action.

The activities that take place in this environment are similarly motivated not just by physical concerns (e.g., making money and killing monsters), but also personal concerns. In other words, characters are motivated by their individual personalities, rather than by externally-assigned mission objectives such as "infiltrate the base" or "collect all the gold coins." Interesting characters act for personal reasons that come from their personalities.

Another way to say this is that the characters are acting in a *contextual* way. Players in almost every first-person shooter are acting pretty much as they do in ever other first-person shooter: they collect ammunition and weapons and try to shoot the other guys before they get shot themselves. In a story environment, character motivations are more subtle and complex.

It's important to note that good characters are designed in such a way that their conflicts are built in. In other words, unless characters actively work to avoid conflict, confrontations will be inevitable simply because their goals have deliberately been designed to oppose each other.

Character Goals

We should strive to make characters in a simulated environment as interesting and believable as the characters in great traditional stories.

Every great character has his own goals and sees in the process of obtaining them his own payoffs, successes, failures, and revelations. Fictional characters, like most people, *learn* along the way as they seek their goals.

Great characters act at maximum capacity. They use every resource they can to accomplish their goals. A rich man will use his money to buy not only things, but also power and influence. A physically strong man may lift rocks or bully innocent shopkeepers. Everyone is doing everything in his power to meet his goals.

This is where the blocks and bridges come into account. When a character is marching along and finds himself stymied, what does he do? Characters that are truly driven to achieve their goals will find some way to handle the problems in their path. Some may even find a way to turn the problems into advantages.

Interesting characters find creative and unexpected solutions to adversity, just as people do in real life. You can divert a river by placing enough rocks in its path, and you can stop it altogether by building a dam. But that water has to go somewhere, and it will either find a new channel to flow down, or it will back up to create or fill a lake. A man who needs money desperately may decide to rob a bank. If someone else knows this man and wants to see him land in jail, he might offer him a gun. A friend would try to talk him out of it. Someone else might even feel that the best way to protect his friend would be to join him in the bank robbery, where together they may stand a better chance of getting out alive.

So the environment is populated by multiple, motivated characters, each on his own trajectory, limited by his own abilities and morality, but driven by his own needs, whether these are to steal the money, get the girl, or get elected.

Adaptive Environments

Today's online environments are not yet broadly or deeply adaptive. Structural adaptivity is one of the greatest opportunities in contemporary computer-assisted gaming.

Let's look first at social adaptivity. I discussed player profiling in Chapter 8, where I argued that most people don't enjoy being classified by a crude computer psychotherapist, and then being treated by the game in a way that is dependent on that analysis. One reason that game designers continue to do this sort of thing is that it allows them to provide at least some form of adaptivity.

But environments with responsive characters are naturally socially adaptive: if you interfere with someone else's plans, generally he will push back. The most rigid form of adaptivity is a simple preprogrammed expectation of action; for example, the ogre won't let you cross the bridge until you give him a chicken. You can't reason with the ogre or talk to him or offer him twenty gold pieces with which to buy a chicken himself or negotiate in any other way: you must satisfy this exact requirement to proceed.

Solving this kind of nonadaptive, preprogrammed requirement often means locating and using the "magic items" I discussed in Chapter 8. To get past the ogre, you need to have picked up the chicken in a house you visited two villages ago; if you didn't see the chicken or neglected to pick it up, you must now retrace your steps to locate what you're missing and obtain it. If you don't know what it is you're looking for, that makes this tedious search even harder.

You can live as a hunter-gatherer, but it's not a lot of fun.

Some games put you in the midst of computer-controlled characters with their own socially adaptive agenda. In the solitaire game *Trust &* *Betrayal*, you try to win a nightly contest by spending your days making allegiances with the computerized players. Your goal is to pump them for information on their strategies, and the strategies of other characters. Characters sometimes lie about what they know, form allegiances, and sometimes break those compacts and tell each other about who's been asking what about whom. Playing the game, you get the feeling that the other characters are frequently having conversations with each other that are very close to the conversations you're having with them, so that you feel like you're being treated no differently than any of the other characters.

The characters in *Trust & Betrayal* change their attitude towards you, and thus their behavior, as the game goes on, and they learn how much they can trust you and rely on the information you give them. Some characters can become helpful friends, while others turn antagonistic. If you work at it, you can sometimes change someone's opinion of you, but it takes time. And even if he likes you, he can still lie to you.

Physically adaptive environments are where most of today's simulation programs shine. The software toy *SimCity* allows you to control the growth and development of a city of increasing size and complexity. Your goal is to keep the citizens happy and the city working efficiently, which basically boils down to resource management. This is a big part of any real mayor's job, though real mayors must also deal with the human problems facing any civil manager, such as staff conflicts, out-of-control egos, empire building, and political strategy.

The game *Everquest* offers a social world made of other players, with whom one can strike up online friendships, rivalries, and other relationships. This social world is very adaptive because you're talking to other live people. But the game environment isn't socially adaptive: if you start out playing as a nice person and then become a total jerk, the game itself doesn't fundamentally change how it treats you. The physical changes in *Everquest* are a little more adaptive, because you can gain abilities over time that allow you to expand your impact on the world. But the rest of the physical world doesn't adapt to you as much as your increased prowess allows you to have more of an effect upon it (e.g., by killing bigger monsters).

Good and Bad Adaptivity

Adaptive systems modify themselves to serve us better.

But not all adaptivity is good. Clumsy or obvious adaptation is as unpleasant as bad prose in a book, or bad lighting in a stage play.

One way to look at adaptivity is to consider how it could be used in games today. Some computer games are already starting to incorporate adaptivity, and expanding the breadth and depth of their adaptation is a natural step for them. So let's consider some of the pros and cons of adaptation techniques in the familiar world of single-player video games, which will help illuminate their role in the less-familiar world of environmental stories.

Before we get into specific adaptation during game play, we should note that almost all games go through an early adaptation stage already: a quality-checking and debugging process called play testing. When a studio completes a rough version of a new game, it will often put it in the hands of a select number of players in order to get their reactions. This isn't the same as game testing, where players are usually looking for errors and technical problems with the game before it's shipped. Rather, this is testing to make sure that people enjoy the game, and that it's fun.

Most video games are comprised of mental and physical challenges, which we might describe as solving puzzles and defeating bad guys. Suppose that a player comes up to a battle with a particular bad guy and finds that he just can't push the right sequence of buttons fast enough to win the battle and as a consequence loses badly every time. Let's also assume that defeating this particular bad guy is required in order to continue making progress in the game. If the publisher finds that most of their early players are getting stuck at this point, he'll probably change the battle in some way in order to make it possible for the players to eventually win and continue playing.

Similarly, if other mental and physical challenges are too easy or too hard, they'll be adjusted to keep the players happy and engaged. So publishers adapt their game to the test players that represent their market.

When developers tune the game to be difficult enough to be fun, but still possible to win, they're making it a better experience, but the balance is delicate. Winning easily is no fun, but being trounced is also unplesant. We want to be able to win, but we also want to have to work for it.

Invisible Adaptation

Some games use the same skills from start to finish. The puzzle game *Tetris* is a great example of this: once you master the elements of play, the challenge is to get better and better at steering the incoming pieces so that you keep your options open.

The majority of the games that incorporate stories today are action and adventure games. As you travel through the game on your quest to defeat your enemies, collect all the secret spy microfilms, or solve the crime, you slowly come to learn the nature of the story. It's a staple of such games that you also learn new skills. Over the course of the game, you'll learn new magical spells, develop the ability to pick locks, make special attacks with your sword, jump extra high, or even fly. Sometimes these skills come along with their own objects (e.g., you can shoot grenades only after you find the grenade launcher).

Suppose that you've happily spent about 12 hours working your way through a non-adaptive game, and you're now about halfway through. You've struggled through a number of tests, and now it's time to beat a "boss" in a skill fight. To paraphrase a scenario from a recent adventure game, you might find yourself atop a flying bird, trying to shoot at the bad guy's head. Using a console controller, you're steering the bird with the left joystick, aiming with the right, and firing by pushing one of the buttons with your index finger. As we typically find in these games, you have to defeat this guy in order to move forward in the game.

Now this is an unusual task for most of us. It's not every day that you need to manipulate a joystick with each thumb while pushing a button as fast as you can. And even if you've done that before in a different game, this game is using its own particular physics and game dynamics. So maybe pushing the left joystick to the left causes the bird to bank and turn a little, or maybe it causes it to bank and turn a lot; you just have to experiment with it and learn. Your ability to hit the bad guy depends on the bird's speed, the accuracy and speed of your missiles, the size of the target, how quickly the bird responds to your control, and many other factors. In most games you don't get to take an endless series of potshots at the bad guy; he's shooting back at you, and so you also have to evade his fireballs and other attacks. If you take too many hits, you "die," and you have to try again from the start.

Suppose that in their play-testing, the developers found that most people enjoyed this challenge, and after two or three practice runs they managed to blow up the monster. Now let's say that you take to this control setup like a duck to water, and you manage to destroy the bad guy on your very first attempt. That's probably not going to disappoint you too much unless the whole game is too easy, in which case you might set it aside because it's no challenge. But if the rest of the game is fun, there's no great harm in occasionally just sailing through what ought to be a challenge.

Let's now suppose instead that you find this particular task very difficult. You try and try, but it's just too much: only a few of your shots hit the mark, and you have trouble evading the bad guy's fireballs and other attacks. The result is that after about a minute or two of battle, the monster is only slightly damaged when you run out of health and "die." So you try again. And again. And again. And maybe you're getting a tiny bit better, but not much, because you're also getting frustrated. So you turn the game off and do other things for a while. Maybe you even consult a cheat book or the web for help, but there's no shortcut here: you just have to improve your skills through practice until you can succeed.

So later you return to the game, sit through the introductory cut-scene yet again, and try again, only to "die" after a minute or two. So you try again. And again. And still you're not getting any better.

If this sounds frustrating, it is. I've been through this personally way too many times.

Now one choice at this point is simply to walk away from the game: just take the disk out of the machine and forget about it. But that's not a very attractive option, since you're already spent 12 hours playing and enjoying the game. This challenge is an anomaly: it's just harder than anything else, and you can't get past it. Note that it's harder for *you*, but perhaps not for anyone else. Maybe every play tester sailed through this after just two or three tries. But for some reason (and it doesn't matter why), you just can't get the hang of this one.

In almost every contemporary game, each time you enter the challenge, the world is just the same as before, from the layout of the arena you're flying in to the physics of the bird's handling. There's only one change from last time: you. And if for some reason your skill isn't improving, that's the end of this game for you forever. You put it away with disappointment and perhaps some anger and try not to think of it any more. Or if you *are* improving, perhaps you could eventually win this fight if you tried it another 70 or 80 times.

There's no way that game designers can anticipate how well *you* personally are going to adapt to the controls for this event. They have to make it just hard enough to challenge most people and hope that works for everyone. This is "one size fits all" design.

The best way to solve this problem is adaptivity. The game should recognize, over time, that you're getting nowhere. Before you get a chance to become frustrated and angry, it should make some kind of change to the event so that you can make some progress. Perhaps the bad guy's fireballs don't hurt you quite so much when they hit, or he doesn't fire quite so many, or your shots hurt him a little bit more than they did before. Bit by bit, modifying first this and then that aspect of the event, you get closer to winning. Eventually your rising skill will intersect with the declining difficulty and you'll pass the challenge, kill the bad guy, and move on.

This is good adaptivity.

Ideally, it's invisible and you don't even know it's happening. You can't really tell the difference between whether you're getting better or the game's getting easier. And that's just fine, because it doesn't matter. The goal is to create a game that's a challenge but can be won. A non-adaptive game is like a novice tennis player playing with a partner who has a great return shot and always plays it as hard as he can. Every time you serve, you get back a smash that you can't touch. It's going to be months or years before you're skilled enough to hit those returns. In the meantime, they're no fun. A real human opponent would see that you're having trouble with his returns and would slowly back them off until they're just hard enough for you to hit back that you have a decent chance.

Without adaptivity, the whole game can end. The game *Starfox Adventures* presents you with a skill test based on the game tug-of-war. This challenge is mandatory: if you don't pass it, you can't make any more progress in the game. The challenge appears about 2/3 of the way through the game, so you've put a lot of time into it so far and you're reluctant to walk away.

The idea is that you must prove your "strength" by besting a warrior at what is essentially a tug of war. The way you win this contest is this: hit the A button on the controller as hard and as fast as you can. That's it. That's all you do. And it's all but impossible. No matter how hard and fast I hit that button, I just couldn't manage to beat the computer-controlled enemy, and I lost the challenge every single time. I tried at least a couple of dozen times; I read the online bulletin boards; I talked to friends and looked in the hint book. There was no shortcut or trick to this challenge: you just had to find a way to bang that button like a bongo player trying for the world record. I just couldn't even come close. For me, the game was completely over at that point, after I'd invested many hours. This is a terrible design decision caused by a skill challenge that couldn't adapt to its players. I did eventually get past this point: I bought a special "turbo" controller that electronically simulates rapid-firing of the A button. This is obviously an absurd demand in an otherwise reasonable game, and I just can't imagine how it survived play testing.

By contrast, the console game *Jak and Daxter* adapts the degree of difficulty in many of its skill challenges for each player so that they're not so easy that you can breeze through them, but not so hard that you get frustrated.

As we design adaptations, we need to keep in mind the reason for adaptivity in the first place: to maximize the Fun-to-Work Ratio. If our computerized tennis opponent is so good that we're being shut out of every game, the computer might increase the size of our racquet or make the ball bigger. These wouldn't be good choices, since they wouldn't help us get better at playing the game itself. The skills we're trying to develop and the tools we use to exercise those skills should remain consistent. It's better to change the opponent: he could get a little slower, or less accurate. In other words, it's not our tools or abilities that get adapted, but the world around us.

Figure 29. A typical challenge in a contemporary game. The difficulty is fixed, and the player is expected to gradually build up the necessary skills to accomplish it.

Most contemporary game challenges are designed to prevent an experience outlined in Figure 29. The player starts out without enough skill to complete the challenge, but with repetition becomes better and better until his skill is equal to what's required, and he is successful and can move forward in the game.

But what if the player's skill is well below what the designer expected, as in Figure 30a? Then it's going to take a very long time for the player to get good enough to pass, which can easily become frustrating. Just as bad, the player's skill may advance more slowly than the designer anticipated, as in Figure 30b. Again, it's going to take forever to pass this challenge, and that's probably not going to be much fun. The problem of course is that the difficulty level is not changing to accomodate different players.

Something like Figure 31a would be an improvement. The specific shapes of these curves aren't the important part of this diagram, but rather that

Figure 30. When the player's skills don't match the designer's expectations, the result can be frustration for the player, as trying to pass the challenge can take a very long time. a) The player starts off much less skilled than anticipated. b) The player gets better much more slowly than anticipated.

Figure 31. The difficulty of a challenge should adapt to the player's demonstrated skill in achieving it. The specific shapes of these curves are not meaningful, except that the difficulty gradually adapts in response to the player's skill level. a) The difficulty adapts to the player. b) The adapatation should probably lag the player's performance by at least a short time.

in some way the difficulty is changing in response to the player's abilities. When the player is getting better quickly, the difficulty stays fixed. When the player is struggling, the challenge becomes gradually less difficult.

We'd probably want the adaptivity response to lag behind the player's activity by at least a small amount of time, as in Figure 31b. This would give the player a chance to figure out the challenge in the first place, and test out different strategies without necessarily causing the system to assume that he's having trouble and modifying the difficulty in response.

Good adaptivity lets us improve our skills while also having a better chance at success, and keeps things hard enough to pose a fun challenge.

Obvious Adaptation

The sort of adaptivity I've been discussing is an artificial technique and not a natural part of the world. After all, the world usually does not adapt to our wants and needs; we have to go out there and customize it ourselves with tools. If this artifice is handled in a clumsy way, it's going to look and feel bad.

Games (like movies and TV) are full of artifice. Camera control is a necessary artifice in 3D computer games. There's no third-person camera floating around in real life, but it's there in most 3D games. When the camera moves well and is positioned where it ought to be, we don't notice the non-reality, and we accept it as part of the experience. When the camera control is bad and we're constantly fighting to get it to point where we want it, then this clumsy implementation impedes our experience. Like a well-designed game camera, adaptivity should fly below our perceptual radar.

As an example of bad adaptivity, consider a chariot-racing game. You're taking six laps around the Coliseum against a half-dozen opponents, and you want to win. As you race, you control the reins on your horse, and your main concerns are to carefully manage his energy and steer him safely around the track and through the other racers.

Suppose you're in the middle of the race, and you notice that chariot number 3 is just ahead of you, and number 4 is just behind you. As you speed up and slow down, and as you take turns tight and loose, numbers 3 and 4 stay in these positions. Maybe the game designer felt that this would give you motivation: there's always someone breathing down your neck from behind, and someone just out of reach up ahead. But if they always stay in those positions, you'll quickly realize that you're not really racing them at all; even if they're based on elaborate physics models and are kicking up photorealistic dust, they're little more than props that move with you. Now there must be some way to win, and perhaps you can pass the guy in front if you pull off a near-perfect race. And if chariot number 3 was always an amazing performer, that would be okay, because you'd know he was the guy to beat. But when he slows down when you slow down, you know something's not right. Now it's possible that in some sophisticated way that rider is also trying to conserve his own energy by staying just ahead of you, but a little experimenting reveals that it's not the case: this chariot and the one behind you are indeed behaving in a very unnatural way for people trying to win a race.

That kind of obvious adaptation is like bad camera control or bad texturing: it's letting the game mechanics show through when they should be invisible. If the game designer wants to spur you on, you shouldn't be able to tell he's doing so.

Hustling

Bad adaptivity can be worse than none at all. Suppose that we notice that the chariot racers are gradually adapting to our speed. If we don't really want to run this race, we might go through it a few times with the brakes on, keeping our horse to the slowest walk we can manage. Bit by bit the other racers will slow down to accommodate us until finally they're all walking alongside us.

Then the next time we run the race, we kick into full gear and gallop as fast as possible, and we win the race in a landslide. This purposeful deception doesn't seem to be something we'd want to encourage.

I don't think most players would do this sort of thing. If you don't like chariot racing, then you wouldn't buy games with chariot racing in the first place. If you do enjoy it, this sort of gaming the system would take all the fun out of it.

This kind of trick is like hustling pool: you pretend to be worse than you so that you can later unleash your skill and collect the jackpot. Hustlers play that way to make money, not for the pleasure of the game.

When we buy a game and sit down to play it, it's because we want to have fun. Any adult who wants to easily crush a game need only buy one intended for small children: he could win every challenge overwhelmingly. Anyone who didn't want to engage in a particular game and work at it would probably have left it on the shelf. If we buy a game for ourselves, we're looking for fun.

Players should not be aware that the game is adapting. The game should be tweaking itself in small and invisible ways so that it always presents a challenge, not to set up a trivial win.

If a player does act in a way that makes every challenge so easy that it's no challenge at all, that's fine. The game ought not be designed to prevent that; it's your game and you should be able to play it any way you want. But I doubt most people would find this much fun on a regular basis.

In games that maintain a numerical score, that score could reflect the degree of difficulty the player faced. Winning a race against tough opponents would be worth a lot, while smoking sleepers would count for little.

One place where adaptation could be undesirable is in the competition for bragging rights. Maybe you've spent a lot of time and effort perfecting your battle skills, and you've managed to defeat the very powerful Yellow Ogre. When you tell your friends, it's not so impressive, because they've defeated the Yellow Ogre as well, since the game adapted until that victory was within everyone's grasp. If bragging rights are important to the players of a particular game, the game could compute scores based on each player's abilities. As the Yellow Ogre becomes slower and clumsier, the number of points you'll get when you finally defeat him slowly diminishes.

Other mechanisms could be invented to normalize abilities, so that you can still brag to your friends. For example, the local crime boss might always be surrounded by at least a few bodyguards, and you're going to need some pretty big weapons to get through to him and accomplish your mission of throwing a pie in his face. If you can get to him using just a flashlight and a false nose, that would be a much more impressive accomplishment than if you used grenades and a bazooka, and the records kept by the game could make it clear that you managed to pull this job off with elegance and skill, rather than brute force.

Adaptation

Creating effective and invisible adaptations can be hard, but it's important.

Finding and maintaining a level of reasonable challenge for each player requires first establishing a way to quantify his skills, and then a way to quantify the tasks that he has to execute in terms of those skills.

We can start easily with "twitch" games. The technique is to build a list of skills involved in each challenge, then a set of steps for that specific challenge to increase or decrease its difficulty for each skill type.

For example, suppose the player is running around inside a giant clockworks and needs to jump across a series of rotating horizontal gears to get to the far side. The challenge for the player is to jump at just the moment when the teeth of the gears line up, so that he can jump off of one gear and land on the next. If he misses, he plummets to his "death" and must start again.

We'd begin designing the adaptation of this challenge by asking what skills are involved. The player needs to aim his character in the right direction (character aiming), then jump at the right moment (jump timing) and with just the right amount of force (button pressure) to land on the next gear, but not overshoot it or fall into the hole in the middle. The gears are characterized by how fast they rotate (gear speed), how close they come to one another (tooth length), the size of the teeth (tooth width), and how big the center hole in each gear is (center size).

Let's say that this challenge is near the start of the game. The player would have some default values for each of his abilities: character aiming, jump timing, and button pressure. These values would then tell the system what values to choose for the gear speed, tooth length, tooth width, and center size.

If the player easily hops across all the gears on his first try, the system would bump up his skill levels on all of these tasks. But let's say that he just can't manage the first jump at all; though he is aiming in the right direction and has good distance, he's jumping at the wrong moment and falling between the teeth of the gears. We'd decrease his value for jump timing. This means that the next time he enters this room (say, when starting a new "life"), the values we assign to the speed and shape of the gears will be slightly different. If he still can't manage it after a few jumps, we'd decrease the value even more and continue doing so until he manages to get across the room.

The final values for his skills after this challenge become the starting values for the next one. The next challenge may be a water-skiing competition. If it depends on character aiming, this new challenge will use the player's most recent ability at that skill as a starting point for influencing the shapes and speeds of the objects involved in the task.

A regularly repeating event like a rotating gear is one of the hardest places to hide adaptive steps. It's much easier when the situation is at least slightly unpredictable. For example, suppose you're fighting an enemy who fights back by spitting poison at you. He's moving around, looking for openings in your defense, so you can never be sure just when he's going to spit. If you keep dying every time you fight this creature, there are lots of subtle ways the system can make the bad guy a little less bad without your even being aware of it. As time goes on, he could spit a little bit less frequently, his aim could get worse, each blob of poison could be a little smaller, and the poison itself could hurt you a little less. Eventually you'll be able to just barely defeat this enemy and move forward in the game.

Like a magician, a designer can use artful distraction to get a player to look in one place while making a change in another place. If an adaptive step just can't be hidden, we might have something very interesting occur elsewhere on the screen and quickly make the adjustment while the player's looking at this eye-catching distraction.

A well-designed adaptive game would help create a gaming experience that presents a roughly uniform level of difficulty, regardless of the skill level of the player: never so easy that it's a cakewalk, but never so hard that it's infuriating.

Playing

What happens when we step into an adaptive, responsive environment? What do we actually *do* there?

To Act or Not To Act?

If we're to emulate *Star Trek*, we'll dress in a costume appropriate to the story and participate in the world as a full-fledged character, talking to the other characters (some real, some computer-generated). We'll dodge bullets, dance at weddings, have a heart-to-heart with Julius Caesar, and join Robinson Crusoe and Friday on their island.

Although such adventures will doubtlessly appeal to some people, I don't think that this kind of participation is likely to ever become as popular as movies and TV are today. The problem is that it requires that the participants join in the story as improvisational actors, and as we've seen in the section on home drama in Chapter 11, that's not only a difficult and learned skill, but something that isn't even attractive to most people. The fact that very few people even read a play aloud around the table, much less join friends for a night of improv acting, suggests that a model of participation that requires people to become actors isn't likely to become a mainstream success. Add to this conclusion the fact that character role-playing games like *Dungeons & Dragons*, despite decades of development, still appeal to a relatively small niche, and it paints a pretty bleak picture for activities that depend on the audience turning themselves into actors.

These observations suggest that the holodeck model, like any model based on the participants becoming improv actors, isn't the way to go.

The next few subsections present some possible ways for people to be active participants in a storytelling environment, yet not have to become actors. They all require some new technology, but at any time we can always approximate the ultimate goal with the best technology we have at the time.

These designs are all based on the idea that there is an authored story happening in the environment and that players are participating in it, but that they are not responsible for creating or developing the story or the characters (in other words, the author is in control of the larger plot and the main character's psychology, in accordance with the Story Contract).

High-Level Direction

Players can take on the roles of directors, as in a stage play or film, but they control only their own character. Directors don't make up the character's lines, nor do they micro manage every little nuance of a live actor's performance. There's obviously a range in how specific any director gets with his actors, but generally directors provide high-level instruction to influence an actor's choices.

This direction is not unlike many contemporary games, where we might tell our on-screen character to go to a particular spot or walk in a given direction, and he does it. If he's in a sports car, he takes care of moving his feet to the right pedals to accelerate and brake; we just tell him when to do so. In neither case are we actually working the character's limbs, maintaining his balance, or exerting other low-level control. We give a general instruction, and our character carries it out in-character, using the tools that are available to him. Many combat systems in adventure games work this way, using a variant of the "Z-targeting" technique developed for *The Legend of Zelda: Ocarina of Time*. We identify the enemy and tell our character to "attack." A sword-wielder would then take an appropriate stab or slice with his sword, while a magic-caster would cast a spell.

Just as most people aren't interested in taking on the specialized skill of acting, they will want even less to spend much of their leisure time at the more demanding and specialized task of directing. But some of the high-level tools that could enable such direction will be useful for guiding characters in general. To get a feeling for these tools, let's look at how they could be used to direct a dialog-driven scene between two characters.

Suppose that Susan and Jean have been best friends for years, working together in the same store, but recently Susan accidentally discovered that Jean has been embezzling from the store in order to cover her husband's gambling debts.

One night after work, Susan invites Jean out for dinner. While at dinner, Susan will confront her friend with what she knows.

Now suppose that we're directing the character of Susan in this story. Since the story is set in the real world, the physical environment would probably be as realistic as our technology permits. We can hear the sounds of other people in the restaurant talking and eating, some faint music playing nearby, and maybe even some distant traffic noise outside. We can see the deep red of the wine, the flickering shadows from the small candle on the table, and the dressing on each tomato in the salad. Ultimately, we might feel and smell the scene as well, and even have our other senses stimulated. Visually, we might be seeing the scene in third person, like a movie camera standing to one side of the table, seeing both Susan and Jean at once. Or we might see it in first person, through Susan's eyes.

Because we're directing Susan, we know what she knows, and we know that she wants to talk to Jean about the money. But we don't know what her companion Jean is thinking, any more than we know what anyone else is thinking in the everyday world. We can see her face and her body language, and we can hear her speak and laugh, and from these outward signs we can try to gauge how she's feeling and how to approach this conversation.

As Susan's director, it's up to us to give her some general guidance. The mechanism for doing this can take almost any form the technology supports: we might type in our directions, or wave our hands using specific or vague gestures, or even speak to her directly.

In *Cyrano de Bergerac*, the title character whispered words into the ear of his friend Christian, who repeated them to his beloved. Our control is more abstract, like an opera prompter reminding the performers of their blocking during a performance. We help Susan through her conversation with general directions. But we don't tell her specifically what to say, or how to say it (we're directing, not acting).

Depending on the design of the environment, Susan may or may not follow our direction very well. The author might have it in mind that this conversation will lead to a big argument that will result in Jean storming out of the restaurant, angry with Susan and afraid her friend will report her to their boss.

So we can guide the way Susan behaves on a general level. But we don't control her low-level choices (e.g., which words she uses, and her gestures and body language), nor her high-level choices (e.g., where the conversation is going to go).

For example, let's suppose that Susan is a quiet and hesitant woman, uncomfortable with conflict. This conversation would be very hard for her, so she would try to bring the subject up obliquely, trying to hint at what she knows rather than saying it outright. This is the character of Susan created by the author of the story environment; it's who she is. We might find this approach frustrating. This annoyance isn't necessarily bad, since part of what hooks us into a fictive experience is wishing that characters we care about behaved one way rather than another. But since we're directing Susan, we might try to urge her forward. If we had a speech interface, we might be saying, "Get on with it! Tell her!" She would respond and move on a little faster, but she'd never just blurt out the evidence she stumbled upon, because that's not in her character.

Given the state of the art of computer simulations today, it's almost certain that if we're hoping to have a rewarding conversation, there will be another person whispering into Jean's ear as well (that is, she's not a computer character).

The author's desires are satisfied here: the characters he created are interacting in a way that is true to their personalities, and the necessary confrontation will occur, with the necessary result. But just how we reach that point, how long the conversation takes and where it meanders before it reaches the climax, is at least partly in our control. If we're feeling as nervous as Susan is, we might sympathize with her tendency to skirt the issue, and we might steer the conversation towards remembering the hike they took last week or how hard it's been to get her car repaired. By using our voice or hands, or typing in instructions, we'd urge Susan to go in the direction we want, and she'll do her best to follow, given her own desires, abilities, and limitations.

I said earlier that the scene would probably look and sound as realistic as possible. For story environments that simulate the everyday world, that's a natural choice. But it's not the only choice.

Because it's a computer simulation, we can set this world in many ways that are far from realistic. The scene could appear more like a film rather than real life, with lighting, camera angles, editing, even music. We might see a swirling colored cloud over Jean's head, revealing her general emotional mood (e.g., dark red for smoldering anger, or bright yellow for elation). All sorts of other non-realistic tools can be used to enhance the situation. If Jean receives a cell phone call, we might be able to listen in. Perhaps we can read her thoughts, or we have x-ray vision and can look into her handbag and see if she's carrying the stolen money. We might be able to speed up, slow down, pause, or even reverse the flow of time, or Jean might do these things to us. The look of the imagery may range from realistic to 2D cartoons. Instead of humans, Susan and Jean could be iguanas or big-eyed space aliens.

But however realistic or unrealistic the presentation, Susan and Jean remain recognizably as the author created them, eager to follow our direction.

This thought experiment in directing also gives us another insight into why multiple-choice discussions keep re-appearing in games: they are an attempt to provide this kind of directed, adaptive story environment. As I've discussed before, multiple-choice conversations are much too crude an instrument for this job; they're like painting your house by covering a cow in paint and then rubbing it against the side of house. It probably would get paint onto your house, but the result is going to be so unsatisfying that the next time you'll certainly get some brushes or rollers and do it right. But the motivation is sound: the author gets to control the general shape and flow of the conversation, as well as its main content, while the players influence how it unfolds. Although this form of directing is still too direct and demanding on the players, it's a step in a right direction.

Parametric Direction

In the previous section I talked about how we might direct Susan with voice and hand gestures or typed-in instructions. This form of direction would be very difficult given the current state of the art: computer programs that can understand what people say (even if they type it in), and then understand what they *mean* by what they say, are still a long way off.

A simpler and more direct technique uses the simple psychological models I denigrated in earlier sections but makes them appropriate by applying them in reverse. Rather than having the computer try to classify humans with a simple model, the computer can provide that model as an interface to the computer-controlled character. So we're using the simple model of psychology not to pigeonhole ourselves, but to control an automaton.

Suppose when you direct Susan, you're given a row of sliders (it doesn't matter whether they're contemporary-style user-interface sliders, or sliders in some other abstract form). The sliders are labelled with emotional characteristics for Susan; perhaps "anxiety," "warmth," and "curiosity" would be three of them. Similarly, the person directing Jean might see "fear," "anger," and "regret," among others. By moving these sliders, each player is able to influence the evolving conversation just as in the preceding section, but at a more direct level. Everyone could also have a set of standard personality descriptors (e.g., the four Myers-Briggs qualities) in addition to, or instead of, more specific controls.

A related display would show Susan's director where Susan currently is on each of these qualities. Except for occasional, sudden actions, generally

Susan's behavior will slowly catch up to changes in the sliders. If we crank up the anger slider to a huge value in one go, Susan might suddenly explode in rage. But it's more likely that she'll be authored to move to that emotion in a series of smaller beats. Each thing Jean says to her at that point makes Susan more and more annoyed until finally she reaches that point of anger that we pointed her towards.

Better software would allow a player to express a higher level of control. The sliders could be labelled with more conceptual names, such as "need to confront" and "reluctance to cause a scene" for Susan, and "honesty" and "tendency to cause a scene" for Jean. One director could try to push Susan towards the confrontation, while another could urge Jean to avoid the subject, answer it head-on, or become enraged.

A mix between these levels would be most useful: directors would probably want to express their desires at a very high level most of the time, but will occasionally feel the need to take very specific, direct action, such as instructing a character to draw a gun, jump into the pool, or storm out of someone's office.

Many psychologists today talk about "big five" personality models. A number of different personality models measure five different characteristics, and though they each use different names, they're starting to look like they measure similar ideas [82]. One such test is the NEO Personality Inventory [30]. Each of the five qualities measured by this test results in a normal distribution in the general public, so that most people get average scores, with increasingly unusual scores found in increasingly small numbers of people.

The test measures:

Neurotocism: This is a measure of emotional stability. High scorers are anxious, hostile, and impulsive, and have low self-esteem. Low scorers are calm, composed, and confident.

Extroversion: This measures happiness and the ability to connect to others. High scorers are warm, gregarious, and assertive. Low scorers are reserved, submissive, and independent.

Openness to experience: This measures creativity and the appeal of novelty. High scorers have an active imagination, artistic interests, an enjoyment of novelty, and intellectual curiosity. Low scorers have a desire for convention and order, conservative attitudes, and caution.

Agreeableness: This measures how one connects with other people. High scorers exhibit trust, altruism, compassion, warmth, and cooperation. Low scorers exhibit shyness, skepticism, self-centeredness, and dogmatism.

Conscientiousness: This measures how well organized one is. High scorers are motivated and disciplined, have a sense of duty, and are reliable. Low scorers are careless, spontaneous, absent-minded, and easily distracted.

We could provide a lot of satisfying and high-level control over a computerized character if we were able to influence these qualities over the course of a scene or story.

Living Masks

Let's look at another way that we might let a player participate in a story, while still respecting the Story Contract and not requiring players to become actors.

The presentation of the story environment appears in a way that's similar to Susan and Jean's conversation discussed above: you're participating in a consistent, believable world. It might be realistic or fanciful, but it's believable and understandable enough that you can lose yourself in it, and constructed well enough that you want to. And as before, you're "playing" a character.

Suppose that you've chosen an adventure story taking place on in the 1800s aboard the gambling riverboat *The Lucky Lady*, steaming up the Mississippi River. For this example, let's assume you've joined this story by yourself one evening as you're looking for a little casual diversion.

The description of the story you've chosen says that it's been written for six characters. You read over the character descriptions, and you're intrigued by the part of Sam Hobble: a professional poker player who's honest and friendly, but very serious about his card games. This character appeals to you, and you find that there are a couple of informal groups that have already gotten together, one of which still needs a Sam Hobble.

When you sign up to play Sam, you're given the chance to customize the character to your preferences. The author of the story (and perhaps his collaborators) have already created a Sam: what he wears, how he speaks, how he walks, how quick he is to anger, and how much he laughs at a good joke. All the things that go into creating a complete character for a movie today, from costuming to dialect coaching, have already been done: in many ways, Sam is ready to step into a story environment and be himself in all he says and does.

If realism is the goal, all of these aspects of Sam will be as good as our technology allows. If we're in an environment that doesn't strive for realism, then we can make our own rules and if they're conservative enough, Sam can be a very complete character indeed. I'll speak more about this later on, but for specificity right now let's just take Sam to be a good fit in a believably realistic 1800s riverboat social and physical world.

Before starting, you can modify Sam to suit your tastes. Perhaps you'd prefer he smoked thin cheroots rather than a cigar or that he didn't smoke at all. You might want to pick a different hat, maybe make him touchy about politics, or make his voice more growly and with a slight Eastern accent, and maybe he's getting over a cold or a love affair gone bad. While you're waiting for all the other characters to join up, you can tune Sam's looks, voice, and personality, look over what you have, and then tweak them again, customizing his appearance and behavior until you can recognize some of him in you, and you've put some of yourself into him as well. So you feel some affinity for Sam, and you feel comfortable in his shoes.

Let's pick things up at a scene around the card table. You're sitting in a smoke-filled room with three other professional poker players like yourself and two amateurs. The amateurs are struggling to look cool and collected and trying not to lose their entire stakes.

A long and tense hand has just finished, and everyone's agreed to take a break. As you step away from the table, you see one of the amateur players reach out and palm a couple of your chips. Sitting on your couch at home, you reflexively sit up in your chair and point at him and shout, "Hey! You're stealing my chips!" But that's not how Sam Hobble speaks, so that's not what comes out of his mouth.

With the camera and microphone in your room, the computer will automatically process your outburst and turn it into something appropriate for Sam. The camera not only picks up on the fact that you've sat up in your chair, but it can "see" your finger pointing at the other character, and it can work out who you're pointing at. The camera also picks up your facial expression, and it can detect the annoyance in your face. Similarly, the microphone is listening not just to your words, but to your inflection and tone of voice. It catches your irritation, shock, and surprise, and the fact that you're saying it loudly enough so that everyone else in the room will hear you and turn to see what's going on.

The computer takes all of this information and "translates" it into behavior appropriate for Sam. Your sudden straightening up in your seat and pointing finger might turn into something very subtle. All of the other players in the story environment see Sam freeze in mid-stretch and turn to glare into the eyes of the thief. In fact, if Sam was a very reserved kind of guy, that might be all that happens; with Sam's body language and reputation, and that icy look, it might be enough. But if this Sam was authored to be a little more active, perhaps his hand would drift to the butt of his gun. And he'd speak, slowly and distinctly, drawing out every syllable, loud and clear for everyone in the room to hear. "Open your hand," Sam might drawl, "If any of my chips are in there, I'm gonna shoot that hand off." And the scene would continue to play. The other players would never see or hear you directly; they only interact with Sam.

You didn't explicitly direct Sam to act this way, even at a very high level. And you didn't have to act like a riverboat gambler or learn a Southern drawl. And you didn't tell Sam what to do. You simply were yourself, though in Sam's shoes. The computer watched and listened, inferred your intentions, and transferred them to Sam.

I call this technique a *living mask*. Like a Halloween mask, you're there inside, though people can't see you directly. But a living mask goes further by becoming a performer. It's an expert actor who's been given a specific character to play, clothes to wear, an accent and a posture and a history, a twitching left knee, a fondness for whiskey, and a weak spot for playful redheads in tight dresses. He has an intent in this scene, and a sense of himself and his reputation. Everything you do comes out through the mask, in character.

A nice side effect of living masks is that they span language and social barriers. A young woman in Des Moines, an elderly man in China, and a teenager on the beach in Rio de Janeiro could inhabit a shared story environment together without any problem. Their languages and social customs would be interpreted by the computer and would come out appropriately shaped for the story environment. For example, a sideways shake of the head in many Western countries means "no," while that same gesture in some Arabic countries indicates assent. If it's right for the story, everyone's computer will interpret his worlds and gestures in an appropriate way, turning them into something fitting for the shared environment.

Outputs can be socially appropriate too. If someone in the West nods left and right, an Arabic player may see that player's character nodding up and down.

If we eventually reach a point where natural languages are supported, and we could translate languages, it wouldn't be a long way to go to also capture different idioms. If someone in London refers to "the tube," unless it was appropriate for local color, a person in New York might hear that character refer to "the subway."

As you participate in this environment, you're playing from your own understanding of your character's goals as well as your own. There may be many ways to bring your plans to fruition. It would be very rare for you to absolutely have to do anything, outside of something required for survival like putting on an oxygen mask. Rather, both you and your character have goals, resources, and abilities, and it will take the two of you together to achieve your combined desires.

How you choose to go about it will naturally affect the other people in the environment, and perhaps the environment itself as well, enabling and removing blocks and bridges. The changes that occur around you will help shape your next decision.

Stars and Supporting Cast

Some people like to be the center of attention, while others prefer to be on the sidelines. Most people are somewhere in between: we like to occasionally have the spotlight, but we don't need or want it all the time.

At a minimum, the demands on the "star" of a story, whether hero or villain, are typically twofold: he must be fascinating to the audience, and he must take action to achieve his goals. In a story environment, both of these qualities are built into the character by the author (and his collaborators).

This programming relieves the players of the burden of driving the story forward themselves, but doesn't relegate them to the dramatic backwater of the chorus. Players can inject themselves into their characters to whatever extent they wish, and though the general outlines of the story will inevitably go forward, the players can personalize the experience to the degree that they like.

In fact, if we're familiar with a particular story, then watching how a character behaves in that environment and responds to us may tell us a lot about the person who is playing that character. We may see some people who guide their characters elegantly and with a light touch, while others express more of their own personality through their characters and are more overtly in control.

Some story environments will work best as ensemble pieces, where there is no single star or villain that dominates the proceedings. Everyone has an important role to play and contributes to the group's evolution of the story.

Participation and Investment

In a story environment the characters that are pushing the story forward are acting according to the overall plot that's been written for them by the author. Like most simulators, the environment will run whether we're paying attention or not. For example, the game *SimCity* will continue to evolve the city even when we're off having dinner. If we leave the city in balance and there are no unexpected disasters, the city will probably hum along contently without us, at least for a while. In a story environment with well-created characters, the other players can continue to unfold the story and plot, even if we're not there.

This is a characteristic of most contemporary media: television shows and movies play whether we're there (or even paying attention) or not, and books don't change whether we're reading them or not.

If the story has been constructed in such a way that progress depends on our doing something (whether it's a specific action or not), then the characters will respond in their own way until this happens. If they're waiting for us (e.g., everyone's in the park waiting for us to push the button that starts the fireworks show), they may become curious, frustrated, or annoyed as they wait. If it's something they don't even know about (e.g., we're organizing a surprise visit to town by the circus), then they'll just go on about their lives without us. We can see some early examples of this idea in games like *Majora's Mask*, where characters go about their daily lives, delivering mail and visiting friends, until we do something to change their routine. Unattended characters in games like *The Sims* and *Animal Crossing* do the same thing, but they aren't being guided by an author's story.

A major difference between participating in a story and simply watching it unfold is the nature of the player's *investment* in the characters. We can become deeply attached to fictional characters in works from from soap operas to great literature. When we care about a character, we become attached to his story and we want to see what happens to him. This is different from when we care about a story because of what happens to *us*. Yet when we're playing a character in a story environment, is there a difference between the character's investment and our own?

There is, and it's important to distinguish the two. Suppose that a character, born and raised in the American midwest, has just spent five years studying Spanish so that he can achieve his dream of living in Spain. This is a significant investment for him, but if we're just meeting him now, then his sacrifice and study don't mean a lot to us personally except as general information about who he is.

So if we were to play or direct this character, we would have to be very conscious of his studies as he moves through the world. It wouldn't be second nature for us, because we weren't the ones who sacrificed.

At the other extreme of character investment is Mario in any of his games, such as *Super Mario Sunshine*. Except for a very sketchy overall mission, the character of Mario really isn't invested in what he's doing. Suppose that we've played the game for a dozen hours or more, and we've collected every last golden coin except for one. Mario doesn't seem to know this, and he certainly doesn't appear to care: for example, he doesn't look at us and urge us to find that last coin, nor does he kick a stone and mutter something about "just one more." Nope, in terms of his personality and mood, he's exactly the same as at the start of the game. But after all that time and effort on our part, building up our motor skills and control of the camera and Mario's acrobatics, we might care a great deal: getting that final golden coin is a testament to our mastery of the game and may give us a rewarding sense of having "beat" the game. Our investment is high, but Mario the character doesn't care.

So on the one hand we have a character with a lot of personal investment, directed by a player who doesn't care much one way or the other, and on the other hand we have a character who has no investment, directed by a player who cares a lot.

Both types of investment can draw us into an experience and keep us there. Good story environments will give us the chance to merge a character's involvement and our own, and create a new kind of rewarding investment. Suppose that we've spent a happy hour or two playing the living mask of a character named David as he spends a day working with his colleagues to design a new nightclub. The process involves creating both art and music, and it's a lot of fun both for David and for us. David loves his job as much as we do, and with a new baby on the way, and the economy in a recession, he's glad to have it and works hard. Then David's manager calls us into his office, sits us down, and starts a conversation that anyone would immediately recognize as a prelude to being fired. It's incredibly important to David that he keep his job. And it's important to us, too: we just spent an hour or two in his shoes, designing this nightclub to our tastes. We don't want him to be fired any more than he does. In fact, we may think that the boss is talking to *us*, as in both ourselves and David, rather than simply to David.

So David's investment in this meeting is high, as is ours. We don't just care out of empathy for David; we care because our own investment in him is at risk, too. We're both determined to keep his job. This is much different than watching a film actor in a similar situation, or getting Mario to climb to the top of the ladder. When we're in the story environment with David, we're in it together.

And that means that David's decisions along the way will matter to us. If at the story's end, David has to make a wrenching choice, sacrificing one thing to gain another, then by virtue of the time we've spent with him, there is the potential for our emotions to be influenced by what now is a meaningful, informed, and important choice.

Authoring

Creating a story environment is a huge undertaking. It will require new skills and a whole host of new technologies. Happily, some of those new technologies will help make the process easier and let authors create personal and expressive works.

The One-Man Band

Authoring a fully detailed story environment from scratch would be an enormous task for one person. In addition to creating the story part (the plot and characters), the author would have to create what developers call their assets: costumes and lighting schemes, music and sound and sets, interfaces and database schema, physics simulators, artificial intelligence systems, and a dozen other design specialties [9][97].

Consider the journey of a new piece of classical music from the composer to the listener. Typically things begin with the composer, usually working alone, notating his composition on paper. He might work quickly or take years to produce a work.

Then he often hands the work over to an arranger, who assigns parts to each instrument. The arranger then delivers the complete score to a copyist, who writes out an individual part for each performer.

Once the parts have been prepared, the piece is in a state to be performed. At this point two parallel groups get to work.

On the one hand, musicians work to turn these notes on paper into music. First, the conductor shapes the overall feel of the work by selecting tempo and dynamics and sometimes giving detailed instructions to the performers. Each of these performers also works on his own part, practicing his instrument and becoming familiar with the composer's work and the conductor's guidance.

The other group is the production team, led by the producer. The producer often chooses what music to record. The producer tells the recording engineer how he wants the music to sound, and together they choose and place microphones and other equipment, and select how they want to record the work.

Ideally, the conductor and producer work together to create the best recording they can, both musically and technically.

Because some parts of the work are typically recorded several times, the complete set of takes are given to an editor, who puts the pieces together into a seamless whole. When the producer and conductor finally sign off on the editor's work, the results go through a mastering process, where they're prepared for mass reproduction. The masters are then used to create CDs, or sold and distributed directly in digital form.

This is a lot of work for a lot of people, and it's a rare person who even contemplates doing it all himself, from composition to performance, recording, and mastering. It's sometimes done in popular music: musicians such as Prince and Todd Rundgren are known for creating some of their own albums from start to finish and doing a good job at each step of the way, but those exceptions prove the rule.

Consider now the more daunting task of making a movie by one's self, which is a little closer to creating a story environment. The task is huge, with many specialized jobs. If the work is going to have high production values throughout, then the division of labor, employing experts with specialized knowledge, will be a must. I don't mean to imply that people can't create wonderful hand-crafted films on their own; certainly many people do just that. But if someone wants to make a movie that has the same level of production values as a movie put together by teams of specialist professionals, the sheer quantity of necessary skills and time means that he will typically need to take that approach as well. The French film *Le Fabuleux Destin d'Amélie Poulain* (released in the U.S. as *Amelie*) names about 300 people in the credits. Larger films can enjoy the efforts of many more people, particularly when extensive special effects are involved. The film *Star Wars: Episode I–The Phantom Menace* lists over 1060 people by name in the final credits, in addition to many companies whose individual employees are not explicitly named. About 300 people is a common crew size for a contemporary, mainstream feature film.

By comparison, let's look at two examples of video games released in 2002. The console game *Kingdom Hearts* credits about 350 people, and *Grand Theft Auto: Vice City* lists about 300 people who contributed to the game. These numbers are comparable to today's feature films.

So the "one-man band" approach to creating a rich story environment seems daunting at best. But happily, new technologies will help give back what present technologies demand.

Five years ago, the task of creating even a simplistic 3D environment was monumental. It required teams of people, ranging from designers and modelers to lighting designers and texture painters. And then the software required to show these models had to be designed and built by computer scientists and programmers. All of this is changing rapidly. 3D modelling tools are becoming cheaper, faster, and easier to use every day. They're even appearing as parts of video games: in *Kingdom Hearts*, there's a little 3D modelling system called the *Gummi Garage* in which you can design and build your own spaceship out of geometric parts. This is a real 3D modelling system: you can install parts where you want them, rotate your ship to get a better view, remove parts, and paint them different colors.

You can't use the Gummi Garage to build a new level for the console game *Halo*; it's too simple and limited for that. But that's the point: 3D modelling is now so simple that it can be included as a little bonus feature in a traditional video game. Some specialized 3D modelers are even given away as free add-ons, like the level modeler for *Unreal Tournament 2003*.

Not only is it becoming easier to create a 3D world, but larger pieces of the process are now available in prepackaged form.

For example, game designers no longer need to write a new 3D rendering system for every product they design. Robust "rendering engines" can now be bought for computers and console systems, and customized or used right out of the box [103] [46].

Creating 3D models requires an artist's eye, an architect's sensibilities, and a miniaturist painter's attention to precision and detail. Because making great models is such a time-consuming and difficult process, several companies now offer catalogs of preconstructed 3D objects that are ready to be simply dropped into a world [29]. Designing a house with these catalogs is like interior decorating: select this couch, that mirror, and that end table, and simply put them where you want them. You can even get collections of textures so you can make your objects look like they're made out any material you wish, from wood to concrete [110].

People are notoriously hard to model and animate. The film *Final Fantasy*, for all its flaws, raised the bar on creating realistic-looking people, paving the way for characters like Gollum in *The Lord Of The Rings: The Two Towers*, a digital creature patterned after a real actor's performance [49]. Programs such as *Poser* [67] allow people to easily pose humans in anatomically proper ways, and programs like *Character Studio* [40] make it easier to animate them and get them to move where you want. These are programs that anyone can buy off the shelf and use for their own projects.

Making people move in interesting and believable ways has always required the skills of a trained animator. But you can now buy files of hand-tuned and parameterized movement for a wide variety of human activities, from walking to performing ballet [113]. By "stitching" these motions together, one can create complex composite movements on demand, though they usually lack some of the personality of custom-created motion.

You can also buy libraries of music and sound effects. These might not always be exactly what you want, but if you can get close enough, you can save time and money that would otherwise be spent with composers, Foley artists, and a recording studio and its personnel. Some sounds can also be synthesized in real time.

The largest missing pieces of technology in creating story environments are the characters that inhabit it, and the software required to create and control them. I'll return to that significant problem below, but for now we can see that if (and this is a big if) there could be a customizable "personality system" for creating characters, and a robust way to deal with language, it would be possible for a single motivated person to combine these programmable pieces to author a very personal vision of a 3D story environment, including characters, with high production values throughout.

Environment as Character

The environment in which a story takes place can serve simply as a generic backdrop or as an integral part of the narrative. For example, in the scary movie *Pitch Black*, the monsters only show up when it's dark, so the characters are very concerned with making sure that their surroundings are well-lit. When the sun goes down, the tension goes up.

Rich environments have a personality of their own. The two apartments that frame most of the action in the thriller *Bound* tell us a lot about their occupants: one spartan and direct, the other expressive and nuanced. The cartoon physics of the "toon" world in *Who Framed Roger Rabbit?* are a big influence on the action. And crucible movies owe a lot of their tension to the particular limits of their physically confining environments: the spaceship in *Alien*, the bus in *Speed*, and the boat in *Lifeboat*.

Each of these environments has a significant effect on the people in the story.

If we think of the environment as a potential character in its own right, we can look at it using the same sorts of tools that we used in Chapter 2 when discussing characters. For example, let's use Egri's three dimensions of character: physicality, psychology, and society [45]. But rather than considering how these qualities are internalized to the environment, we'll turn them around and look at how they're externalized, and thus affect the people in that world.

The physicality of an environment is its most obvious characteristic. An environment both offers and limits freedom of motion, and contains changing weather and its own kinds of sounds. Science-fiction environments may feature an unfamiliar cycle of the seasons or pattern of daylight, or alter gravity or other physical laws. The physicality of the environment is often its most important feature: things wouldn't have been so bad for the astronauts in *Apollo 13* if they could have just opened the door of their capsule and walked home, and the passengers aboard the sinking ship in *Titanic* wouldn't have been in such dire straits if the ship had gone down in balmy tropical waters within swimming distance of a hospitable coast.

The psychology of an environment is most visible in the effect it has on the characters that inhabit it. The feeling and mood of the world we move through can't help but have an effect on us. The effect of the war in *Saving Private Ryan* is visible on every character's face. A forest isn't an inherently creepy place, but in *The Blair Witch Project* the sights and sounds of the woods have a huge effect on the characters who can't get out.

An environment causes psychological, and sometimes even physical, effects on the people that inhabit it. The difficulty that a character has in adapting to a change from one environment to another can drive his story. In *Romancing the Stone*, the writer Joan Wilder is used to the big city, and much of the film is driven by her need to survive a South American political web she can't understand. In *Cool Hand Luke*, the story is driven by Luke's unwillingness to concede to the prison environment. The same is true of McMurphy's refusal to bend to Nurse Ratched's iron control of the psychiatric ward in *One Flew Over the Cuckoo's Nest*.

As we think of creating programmed and responsive environments, it may be helpful to consider them as important characters. In some situations, the environment may actually be personified as a helpful or malignant force. In the movie *Backdraft*, some of the fire fighters speak of fire as though it had a mind and purpose of its own.

Character Software

As I mentioned earlier, the biggest missing piece in the development of a story environment right now is some kind of autonomous characters that people will find sufficiently interesting and adaptive that they will be drawn to them.

Earlier in the chapter I mentioned the software toy *Dogz*, which lets you take care of a dog starting out as a puppy. The related toy *Babyz* does the same thing for babies. These creatures are a long way from their real counterparts, but their friendly adaptivity and behavior can make them very appealing.

Vehicles

There's a long history of people finding ways to get seemingly complex and almost life-like behavior from simple systems. For example, the simple robotic vehicles described by Valentino Braitenberg appear not only to have specific likes and dislikes, but even seem to have attitudes towards one another [16]. Because Braitenberg's vehicles are a great example of how simple behaviors can lead an observer to infer a complex personality, they're worth a closer look.

The simplest of Braitenberg's vehicles looks like a simple four-wheeled car, as in Figure 32. By analogy to how biological systems work on a cellular level, we'll say that all the components mounted on the car interact with *pulses*. A pulse is just a little burst of electrical current that flows down a wire. Every pulse is identical, so each one contains the same amount of energy and lasts for the same duration.

Each of the rear wheels is driven by its own motor. The speed of each motor is proportional to the number of pulses it receives per second. With no pulses, the motor just sits there. Each pulse causes it to turn a little, so more frequent pulses means faster rotation. The front wheels can be thought of as free-rolling casters: they can roll in any direction, but they're not connected to any power source. In each of the front corners, where we would expect a headlight, there's a light sensor. The light sensor is like a geiger counter: it emits a stream of pulses proportional to how much light is striking it. If the light is dim, the pulses are infrequent; if the sensor's picking up a lot of light, it fires off a rapid string of pulses.

The fun comes when we hook up the sensors to the motors and then put the car into an environment with one or more lights. For the following discussion, let's assume that there's a little bit of ambient light throughout the room, so that both sensors are always going to pick up at least a little illumination, resulting in a stream of infrequent pulses even when they're far away from a light source.

Let's first build a car in which we send the output of each sensor to the motor on the same side, as in Figure 33a. Braitenberg calls this a *Type 2* vehicle.

What happens when this car is in an environment? When it's nowhere near a light source, then the same amount of dim, ambient light is striking both sensors, and so they will send to each wheel roughly the same small number of infrequent pulses. The result is that the car will slowly cruise along straight ahead. Now suppose that the car begins to approach a light source off to the left side. The left sensor will fire more, which will drive the left wheel faster, and the car will turn away to the right. The same thing happens on the other side. The result is that this vehicle drives along slowly in the dark, but when it gets near a light source, it speeds up and turns away. Braitenberg characterized this as *cowardly* behavior.

This term isn't completely fanciful: when you watch one of these cars roll around, it does seem to be afraid of light.

Figure 32. A schematic Braitenberg vehicle. The two wheels in back are each driven by their own motor. The front wheels are casters with no power. In the front are two sensors. (a) A 3-D view. (b) The view from above.

Now let's cross the wires, as in Figure 33b. As before, this car will drift along going straight when it's far away from light sources. Now suppose it

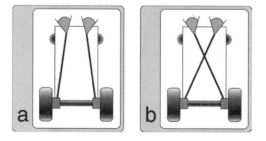

Figure 33. Braitenberg's Type 2 vehicles. (a) Cowardly: uncrossed and excitatory. (b) Aggressive: crossed and excitatory.

sees a light to its left: the left sensor fires more rapidly, so the right wheel gets more pulses and spins faster, and the car turns to the left and towards the light. It will turn far enough to overshoot, so that the right sensor will then be getting more light, causing the car to turn right a bit, continuing to pick up speed. In this way it will wobble back and forth until it zeros in on the light source and plunges directly into it, going faster and faster. If the light is inside a protective enclosure of some sort, the car will bash into the enclosure and stay there, grinding its wheels until something breaks. If the bulb is unprotected, the car will smash into the light and destroy it. So these cars slowly cruise around in the dark until they find a light, which they then zero in on, accelerate towards and destroy. Braitenberg called this *aggressive* behavior.

Now let's add another building block to our little circuits: an *inhibited clock*. This is a little self-powered unit that normally emits a steady stream of pulses. But the inhibited clock has an input. If a pulse arrives on the input line, it inhibits, or prevents, pulses from being sent to the output for a short while. So when there are no pulses coming into the input, the inhibited clock puts out a regular train of pulses on its output. If the input has a few pulses coming in, then a few of the outgoing pulses will be blocked. The more pulses that arrive on the input, the more pulses are prevented at the output. At the limit, a steady stream of input pulses causes the complete inhibition of outputs, and nothing comes out of the unit (Braitenberg called this a "threshold node" set to a value of zero).

Let's use one of these inhibited clocks on each side of Figure 33a, resulting in the *Type 3* car of Figure 34a. When the car is far from any lights, the sensors only put out a pulse every once in a while. That means that the streams of pulses made by the inhibited clocks are hardly ever blocked. So when it's far from a light source, both wheels get a lot of pulses, and the car zips along straight ahead.

Now suppose as before that the car sees a light off to the left side. The left sensor will fire more often, which means more of the inhibited clock's pulses will be blocked, so the left wheel will get fewer pulses and will start to turn more slowly. Thus the car will start to turn to the left, towards the light. If it turns too far, the right sensor will pick up the light and it too will start to fire, slowing down the right wheel, turning the car a bit to the right. So the car will travel more and more slowly until it gradually comes to rest, pointed directly at the light source, from what appears to be

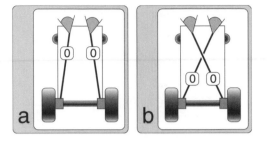

Figure 34. Braitenberg's Type 3 vehicles. The node with a zero inside it is an inhibited clock; it generates a string of pulses on its own, but only passes them along to the motor if there is no signal coming from its input sensor. (a) Loving and adoring: uncrossed and inhibitory. (b) Loving and exploring: crossed and inhibitory.

a respectful distance. Braitenberg characterized this as a *loving and adoring* behavior, as the car seems to find a light and then approach it slowly and reverently, coming to a standstill and then basking in its glow.

If we cross the wires of the circuit in Figure 34a, we get the circuit of Figure 34b. As before, this car zips along in a forward direction in the dark. If it happens to catch a light source directly ahead, then both sensors fire, both wheels slow down, and the car will come to a gentle stop before the light, just as if the wires weren't crossed. But if the car is even slightly at an angle to the light and senses a bit more light in its left sensor than the right, that will cause the right wheel to slow down, so the car will start to slowly turn to the right, away from the light, only picking up speed again when it gets away from the light's influence. Because it slows down in the presence of light sources, the car seems to be paying them some respect, like slowing down in a school zone. This is a light-loving behavior like the uncrossed-wire version, but the car then heads back out into the dark. Braitenberg described this as a *loving and exploring* type of behavior.

We can mix several these designs on one vehicle. Braitenberg imagined a *Type 4* car with four sets of sensors, each designed for a different kind of signal. We could wire up some light sensors using circuit type 2a, temperature sensors using circuit 2b, oxygen sensors using circuit 3a, and organic material sensors using circuit 3b.

If we set this car loose in a rich environment, it will demonstrate some very complex behavior. It avoids hot regions by turning away from them. It appears to dislike lights so much that when it finds a light, it charges and destroys it. The car likes regions with oxygen and organic material, but it isn't likely to stick around in a region with both of these resources if they aren't present in high enough density. Braitenberg suggests that after watching this machine for a while, we'll come to the conclusion that it is demonstrating *values* and *knowledge.*

We can continue to add new types of nodes and create ever more complex circuits. Braitenberg does so in his book, and so have other researchers who have carried on his work, but I'll stop at this point.

There are plenty of real-time simulators available on the web that will let you design and test out your own Braitenberg-style vehicles in a simulated environment. If you like to roll your own, designing and programming a simulator for these vehicles is a fun and rewarding afternoon project. If you prefer real-world experimentation, you can build these vehicles using any general computer-friendly construction kit, such as *Lego Mindstorms* [69].

Despite their simplicity, if you build a bunch of Braitenberg's cars and set them loose on a tabletop (either real or on the computer), it's hard not to feel sympathy for his characterizations of their behavior. These cars definitely seem to have something going on "inside" of them: it's easy to get a feeling of a lot of personality watching cowards creep along in the dark, speeding up only to turn away from the lights. The first time you see an aggressive car turn towards a light bulb and charge towards it, it's hard not to perceive this as some kind of intelligent action.

Braitenberg's vehicles are an example of what is sometimes called *emergent behavior.* It arises when a system acts in ways that are unexpectedly complex or interesting. Emergent behavior is usually a characteristic of a large or complex system, where the pieces interact in surprising ways so that the whole appears to behave in a way that you wouldn't have predicted based on just looking at the parts. As these vehicles show, emergent behavior can also come from very simple mechanisms.

Based on experiments with his vehicles, Braitenberg suggested that creating complex behaviors from scratch is easier than trying to understand how they come about. That is, it's easier to create something to simulate a behavior than to understand how that behavior arises in a particular system. In other words, analysis is harder than synthesis. Referring to the relative difficulties of these two processes, this idea is also known as *the law of uphill analysis and downhill invention.*

An important quality of Braitenberg's vehicles is that they have no randomness. They can be sensitive to input conditions, like chaotic systems (a coward will charge a light source only if it's dead ahead), but all the vehicles we've seen so far achieve their rich behavior without rolling any dice.

If we take things to the next level and put light bulbs on the vehicles themselves (on their backs, where their own sensors can't pick up the light), then the vehicles start to interact with one another. Cowards turn into loners, avoiding not just light bulbs but each other. Lovingly adoring types turn into stalkers, following the object of their affection wherever it goes. So Braitenberg's vehicles not only appear to display individual behaviors, but the vehicles can interact with each other in interesting ways.

The fascinating thing about Braitenberg's vehicles and other mechanistic approaches to behavior is that almost all of the interpretive work is being done by the observer, not the vehicle. With just a few simple parts and a few wires, we can make something that acts in such a way that human observers often think that they're watching intelligent behavior. It's like an optical illusion: all of the interesting things are happening inside the head of the observer. In other words, it's *interpretation* that creates the personality of Braitenberg's vehicles, since they clearly don't have any kind of built-in cognition or emotional state.

Some of the vehicles designed by Braitenberg, and by others after him, can learn behaviors such as how to recognize other vehicles. Others can reproduce sexually or asexually (and then natural selection will favor those that are best suited to the environment), and others are able to adapt to their environment and change their preferences in response to what appears to be available. These souped-up vehicles are fun to design and play with, but the illusion of consciousness doesn't get a lot stronger with each new addition. This isn't too surprising: in a limited environment, there's only so much you can do that's interesting.

Crowd behavior is another nice example of how simplicity can give rise to apparently complex behavior. Think of a typical crowd of people, gathered in the park on a sunny afternoon to listen to an outdoor musical concert. Some people are standing, others are sitting on blankets talking or eating: some are running around and playing with their children. From a distance, they stop being individuals and become just members of the crowd, engaging in "crowd behaviors." This observation has been of value to filmmakers, who are able to create crowd scenes with large numbers of digital actors, each of whom is behaving in a way that is based on a few preprogrammed motions and some general behavior rules [75] [49]. Characters in a simulated crowd "know" not to walk through one another (and try to keep some personal space around themselves and their fellows, even turning to the side when passing through a narrow corridor). These virtual crowd members also know and obey some general rules (e.g., at a musical concert they'd know to quiet down when the concert starts, applaud at the end of songs, or even hold up lighters to ask for one more encore after the sun has set). Because the individual members of a crowd may come and go from view, there's no need for each member of the crowd to display a unique and consistent personality; as long as everyone's behaving in a way that's appropriate for being in a crowd, nobody stands out.

This is the same conceptual approach that film studios take when animating special effects composed of large numbers of non-human elements, as diverse as the Orc army in *Lord of the Rings: The Two Towers*, the flood waters in *Atlantis*, the wall of fire in *Wrath of Khan*, or the horse stampede in *Mulan*.

The success of Braitenberg's vehicles is related to the success of these crowd-simulation systems. In both situations, we have some simple rules that cause a creature in an environment to behave in a way that can lead an observer to infer that it's aware of, and responsive to, what is around it. But in neither case is there much opportunity for the observer to become a participant. We can't carry on a conversation with Braitenberg's vehicles any more than we could with a random person in a simulated crowd. We can reach in and reposition a car or even reprogram it, but precisely because there's almost nothing inside, the cars don't have anything interesting to talk to us about (even if they had a way to talk). A coward would simply skulk around muttering, "I like the dark, I like the dark," and that would be about it.

These mechanistic approaches to behavior have been successfully used to model the behavior of simple creatures both alone and in crowds. Other models of behavior, drawn from the field of "artificial life" (or A-life) and the classical fields of psychology and sociology, are also providing tools to computer scientists for creating software versions of characters with personality with whom we can interact in a natural way. Over time, these techniques will improve, moving us slowly closer to believable, fully interactive autonomous characters.

Beating Expectations

The day we can write computer programs that approach the complexity and appeal of human beings is far away. So what do we do in the meantime?

The essential trick in any simulation is to at least meet the expectations of the people who are using it. If you can beat those expectations, so much the better.

Expectations are born of three elements: *experience from the past, interpretation of the present,* and *imagination for the future.*

Think about the last time you tried a new dish at a restaurant. You may have ordered at random, but it's more likely that you ordered it after reading the menu. Perhaps you saw that this dish features a salmon filet, and you know from experience that you love salmon.

As you look up at your dinner companion, you see the plates in front of other diners, you hear their conversations, and you smell the aromas filling the restaurant at this moment. By interpreting these stimuli, you get the feeling that although the salmon is expensive, this restaurant seems to do a really good job with it.

Then as you read its description from the menu again, you start to imagine how the different ingredients will taste when combined together. It's an appealing mix, and in your imagination you can see the plate being set before you, and you can almost feel your taste buds lighting up.

So your experience of the past, interpretation of the present, and imagination for the future all contribute to your decision to order this dish. At this point it's up to the chef to fulfill your expectations.

This buildup of expectations occurs in everyday life. Someone gambling on a horse race will choose which horse he thinks will win by considering each horse's past performance, the current conditions, and how he imagines this particular group of horses will run together. When we turn on the radio for some music to listen to while relaxing, we choose a station by considering what our favorite stations have played in the past and what we're in the mood for now, and by anticipating how nice it will be to listen to that particular kind of music.

Expectations are a notorious source of disappointment. When we build ourselves up for something and it fails to deliver, we're let down. On the other hand, something that beats our expectations generally leaves us with a good feeling. Some philosophies argue that we should learn to diminish the importance of our expectations or even stop making them altogether, but that's a difficult task. Since most people indeed do have expectations, then as designers of entertainment experiences we want to make sure that we don't fall short of our audience's expectations, and thus disappoint them.

When we think about creating realistic humans on the computer, most people typically bring pretty high expectations.

Our experience with people throughout our lives has given us a baseline feeling for people's abilities. Depending on their age and gender and a thousand other factors, we naturally anticipate that people we're meeting for the first time will be like others we've met. We generally think of most people as possessing a staggering array of standard competencies: they can express themselves verbally with a sufficient vocabulary, they can balance on two legs and walk, they know the difference between the truth and a lie, they know when we're angry at them, and they let us know when they're angry with us.

The trend in today's computer stories and games is to present human characters that are ever-more realistic. Artists create 3D models of people that have the proportions of plausibly real bodies (cartoon characters like Lara Croft being the obvious exception), and they create textures for them so they appear to have scars, eyeliner, five o'clock shadow, and even pimples. Their mouths lip-sync their dialog, and their facial and body expressions are created by expert animators. If they speak, the trend is to use skilled writers to create interesting dialog, and experienced actors to perform it. As hardware capabilities improve, the tendency will continue to be the creation of people that look and sound increasingly real. Given that these characters are meant to appear like real people, the first time we encounter such characters in a game or story, we naturally presume that they are like all of the other people we know. That is, they have the ability to use language, they understand the world and their role in it, they have the capacity to form and sustain social relationships, and they have an age-appropriate level of intellectual and emotional maturity.

Our imagination for the future then quite sensibly predicts that we'll be able to have the same level of interaction with these characters as we can with other people in real life.

We quickly learn that this isn't the case, and that despite the fact that these people kind of look and sound like people, and may act like them in some ways, they're missing most of the invisible qualities of personality and character that we associate with normal people. So our expectations are unmet, and we're disappointed. We certainly have learned over time not to expect too much from game characters, but game designers are constantly raising our expectations with each new title. Today's characters are, in some way, just a fraction more realistic than they were just six months ago, and six months from now they'll be even more so.

This clash of expectation and reality is another inconsistency between the system interface and the world interface. The system interface here is the presentation of the character: it looks, sounds, and sometimes acts recognizably like a real person, and so we try to use that representation as an interface to the person "inside." But the world interface isn't up to the task; the person "inside" the polygons and prerecorded bits of speech is far less realistic than the external appearance. The result is a classical mismatch between these two interfaces: although the presentation of the character tells us that we should be able to have a reasonable conversation with him, and treat him as an intellectually and emotionally aware person, in fact nothing of the sort can happen, and we're limited to very primitive forms of communication, on a very restricted range of topics.

As I've discussed, any time the system and world interfaces mismatch, players become frustrated by their inability to actually do in the world what the system seems to imply they should be able to do.

What then do we do? Simply remove all characters from games and story environments until the hard artificial intelligence problem has been solved? That's hardly an appealing answer.

A better solution is to change expectations, bringing the system interface and world interface into alignment. If a player is shown a character that looks, behaves, and talks like a person, he's going to expect it to be like a person in other ways, and thus he will be disappointed. So players should only interact with characters whose outsides match their insides.

Some contemporary games do this well by placing the game in an alien landscape, where you have few expectations. For example, the world of *Pikmin* is populated by the tiny Pikmin themselves, as well as a variety of insects and bugs. The Pikmin are very simple-minded, as are the bugs. This works out perfectly well. The bugs are not too bright, which matches what we'd expect. The little Pikmin are so foreign to our experience that we don't have any expectations of them. The system only allows us to communicate with them in very specific ways (such as calling them over, or setting them to work on a task like building a bridge), but that seems to be about all the Pikmin understand how to do. In other words, the system lets us communicate with the Pikmin in a way that fully embraces their capabilities, and we're never left feeling unsatisfied with their responsiveness.

Because the game provides everything we know about the past and the present, we don't come to the game with preexisting expectations about the future. Our imagined futures don't anticipate our being able to communicate with the Pikmin in great depth, or demanding the Pikmin to behave or respond in more ways than they are able. So the two interfaces are consistent, and our expectations are fulfilled.

Meeting or exceeding expectations is necessary but not sufficient: meeting them doesn't guarantee a good experience, but failing to meet them usually does mean that people will be disappointed.

It's to the advantage of a game designer to consider what tools, technologies, and tricks he has available to him, and then design a game that presents a system interface that never suggests the player can do more than what the world interface supports.

This is why it's often useful to have characters that are inanimate objects or even talking animals. We don't expect a toaster to have much to say to us. In the "Peedy the Parrot" project, visitors spoke to a parrot disk jockey, who could retrieve and play music from his library [7]. If we ask Peedy to bring us a record of preludes by Bach, but he instead brings the greatest hits by Burt Bacharach, it's not perplexing, because after all parrots aren't all that smart, and it's remarkable he could do as well as he did. We're willing to tolerate that error, and if it's infrequent enough, we might even find it amusing. If a person made that mistake, we'd wonder what the heck someone that dumb was doing working as a disk jockey in the first place.

If a talking parrot is consistent in what he gets right and what he misses, and he behaves in a way that makes sense to us, then he will be believable, even though a talking parrot disk jockey is not realistic.

When the characters in a game are space aliens, the problem is made a little simpler still, since we don't expect to have a lot of shared knowledge with them. For example, the simple word "day" may mean something very different to someone who lives on a planet with a day that takes 200 hours to pass. Concepts like "hot" and "cold" would be similarly suspect, and notions like "love" might be entirely mysterious. Every bit of communication we can squeeze out of a conversation with a space alien is a success, and we're not likely to take too much for granted or expect too much philosophical nuance.

It's always best to set player expectations slightly below what you can deliver. This way you never cause disappointment, and if you can occasionally manage to exceed expectations, players will be pleasantly surprised.

⤖ 13 ⤖

Designing for
Participation

S tory environments are social places. In this chapter I'll talk about
some social aspects of participating in a story environment. The technical hurdles to building a believable participatory world are formi-
dable, but they're already receiving a lot of intense attention. The social
issues are a little less obvious but no less important.

Theorizing about social environments is risky business: people are famously difficult to predict even in common situations we understand well.
But because the social part of these experiences is so important, it's useful
to at least consider the issues so that we'll understand how our decisions
can affect the human side of the situation.

I'll look at a number of different topics in this chapter, all united by
the theme of social engagement.

Imaginative Memory

Imagine a tasty salad. Now picture that salad drawn on a TV screen with
only eight colors in a square that's 16 pixels on a side. It probably isn't
too mouth-watering anymore.

In your mind's eye, picture a giant, eight-legged, hairy monster towering over you, gruesome saliva dripping from his razor-sharp teeth, his segmented legs reaching out to ensnare you in their decaying flesh. Now picture this monster drawn with 16 colors in a square that's 32 pixels on a side. He probably doesn't seem quite as menacing.

These are extreme examples, but the reality of today's technology is that it's not up to the task of creating interactive real-time sound and graphics that rival the real world. This is true even on high-end consoles and computers, where there are many thousands of polygons per character and dozens of shaders, animation files, textures maps, and lights. In a small handheld device, the problem is even worse.

How do we help people connect these abstracted and simplified images with the objects they stand for? How can we make that tiny, flat-colored salad seem appealing, and the little icon of a monster seem frightening? How do we make even a fully rendered 3D monster *really* scary?

If they're available technically, we can use all the techniques of cinema. We can first see the monster from a position low near the ground, so we see how much bigger it is than we are. Foreboding music and lighting can also help let us know that this guy is big, bad, and intent on doing us harm.

But if those techniques aren't available, the structure of the environment doesn't follow traditional cinematic conventions, or we still don't have visuals realistic enough to carry the day, what then? The common answer is a technique I call *imaginative memory*. The idea is to give players a great, high-quality visual early on. Then when we see the lower-resolution versions, the complete version comes to mind, and we "see" the beautiful version instead of its simpler representation.

In other words, the game elements remind us of how the richly rendered version looks and sounds, and we willingly transfer that memory and our emotional responses to it onto the little iconic version.

It's something like listening to a favorite song on our car radio tuned to a weak station. It doesn't sound like the CD on a nice stereo system, but it reminds us of that sound, and we fill whatever's missing in our own minds.

Games routinely provide high-quality art on the covers of their boxes. This art is primarily designed to attract buyers, but it has the secondary function of giving players a rich mental image that the in-game graphics can remind them of using imaginative memory. The instruction books, cheat books, and publisher's web pages often also contain "concept art," which again provides high-quality full-color presentations of characters and objects that will be encountered in the game with less fidelity.

Highly produced cut-scenes also provide this kind of information. Even if the graphics are produced in-game, high-quality animation can still give a feeling of motion and weight to characters that appear with much less sophistication during regular gameplay. For example, the pre-rendered cut-scenes in *Final Fantasy X* show the characters and world in great detail, which helps us see them that way the rest of the time. When we watch an in-game cut-scene, the motion and timing are such that we still get a feeling of the character's moods.

Sometimes video games can use each other as a reference. The hand-held games *Legend of Zelda: Oracle of Seasons* and *Legend of Zelda: Oracle of Ages* were designed to be played on the Gameboy Advance, which has a small handheld screen of 240 by 160 pixels. But they're related to the high-resolution console games *The Legend of Zelda: Ocarina of Time* and *Majora's Mask*, and share many of the same monsters. When you encounter a particular enemy in the handheld games, it may only be about 20 or so pixels on a side, which doesn't leave a lot of room for detail. But if you've played the console games, you can remember what the creature looks like in all of its full glory and complexity, including its scary way of moving and the sounds it makes. With that memory in your head, it's easy to imagine that you're fighting that creature, despite its tiny visual image in the game you're actually playing.

The video game *Grand Theft Auto III* uses an interesting variation of this technique by displaying high-quality cartoon drawings of the game's characters while the game loads. These simple drawings are loaded with personality and give you a great feeling for the people they represent. When you meet these characters in the game, they're rendered as richly-textured 3D models and are voiced by actors. But these polygonal models still don't look very much like real people, and their motion is jerky and crude. The voice acting helps them a lot. But so do the cartoons: when you meet someone, you remember the line drawing that told you so much about him or her, and it's easy to impress that memory on the clunky version being shown to you in 3D.

As always, designers must manage expectations: if someone buys a game expecting it to look like the elaborately rendered and designed front cover of the box, he will be disappointed when he sees what the game actually provides. It's important to make sure that players, and potential players just considering the product in a store, can distinguish between images given to them to flesh out the world from promises of what the actual playing experience will be like.

Groups and Gatherings

When we enter a game or story environment with other people, we're forming at least a temporary social group. I introduced the Intimacy Matrix in Chapter 8 to give us a handle on how the relationships among people in a group depends on the familiarity amongs its members and its size.

When we get together in the real world or online, we tend to form groups in three basic ways:

Team: This is a mostly stable group of people that enters the activity together as a unit. The team may be a family that plays together or a group of friends.

Pickup: This is a random gathering of people. Many online games today are this way: we join the website or enter the online world, and find ourselves playing with whoever happens to be around.

Mixup: This is somewhere between the previous two styles. We get together with a consistent pool of people, most of whom we know or have played with before. We may form spontaneous teams, play a free-for-all, or collect ourselves into a single team to play against another group.

The latter two types of games may happen on a fixed schedule, or they may just happen when enough people show up at the same place and want to play together with their friends. Team games benefit from some kind of schedule, so that everyone can get together.

Schedules describe when something starts, how long it lasts, and how frequently it repeats. People who enjoy first-person shooters will often get together over their business's local area network at the end of a work day for a half-hour's frag-fest. Some larger online worlds host events like marriages or other ceremonies, where everyone meets for an hour or two at an appointed time.

Story environments can share the same sorts of flexibilities. One-time events can happen for a half-hour (a "short story"), an afternoon, or even a few weeks or months. Stories that are like soap operas can meet on a regular schedule indefinitely. And some story environments can be like the massive multiplayer worlds of today, which are always on and always running. You can join in anytime and stay as long as you please.

In some environments players can communicate both in the world of the game (called IC, for *in-character* or *in-channel*) and outside the game (called OOC, for *out-of-character* or *out-of-channel*). An in-channel exchange in a fighting story might be "Attack the command post!" Out-of-channel exchanges can range from discussion about the game to other topics entirely, such as sports or the weather.

The game *Everquest* has a wide variety of message types, characterized by color. For example, normal chat is in white, while out-of-character chat is in violet-blue or brown. When systems don't provide explicit tools to distinguish between these two types of subject matter, players have created their own conventions. For example, out-of-channel exchanges often start with the letters OOC, e.g., "OOC: Nature calls–I'll be right back!"

No-Shows

Suppose that we have a scheduled event with other people, and someone doesn't show up. If he's not vital to the proceedings, we might decide to just roll on ahead anyway, but if the missing person is an important character, we have a decision to make.

Dealing with absent friends isn't novel to online experiences: absenteeism is a problem inherent in any group activity. But the online nature of the experience gives us a few options that are more convenient than in everyday physical situations.

Block: We simply wait for the missing person. If he never appears, then the activity will never get going again.

Muddle through: The group soldiers on despite the missing person. This approach might work in some situations, but isn't generally satisfactory.

Substitute: Someone comes in and takes the missing person's place. This could be someone from within the group who's willing to double up or an outsider brought in just for this purpose. Sufficiently powerful systems could prepare an auto-summary of what's happened so far to help get him up to speed.

Some substitutes could work almost like understudies in the theater. They would be familiar with the basic story and the characters and know roughly the shape of what's gone on so far because they know what the author has written. They would only need to catch up on the specific dynamics of that group and the particulars of their progress through the story so far.

Really exceptional substitutes might even charge for their services (I'll return to this idea later in the chapter).

AI proxy: The computer could fill in for the missing person with a computer-controlled character, who is at least able to keep the story moving.

Captain's control: Some groups may have a formal or informal "captain," with some power to delegate positions. The captain may choose one of the above options or might himself step in for the missing person.

Guides

Some people may hold a privileged position in the environment; I call these insiders *guides*. Just how privileged guides are can vary a great deal, but their common distinguishing factor is that they have access to information about the story that the other players do not.

A guide's inside knowledge can range from total omniscience to just a bit of experience the other players don't have. Let's look at a few stops along this continuum.

Guide is author: The guide may be the author himself. This is the *Dungeons & Dragons* model, where the dungeon master who created the world is actively involved in the player's exploration of it. In such situations this person usually stands outside the game and is not part of the exploring party.

Guide has overview: The guide may have access to the documentation that describes elements of the world such as the story, its characters, or its plot. The guide may use this knowledge to help shape the development of the story.

Guide knows secrets: The guide may have an inside line on a few secrets. These can range from big secrets (e.g., there will be a flood tomorrow that will cause havoc throughout the city) to small but important details (e.g., someone's car battery is on its last legs and the car probably won't start tomorrow).

Guide has done it before: The guide may simply be someone who has gone through the story before. Many of us have run into such guides inadvertently at the movies, when we sit in front of someone who has seen the movie before and is talking to a friend. When a new character appears on the screen, this person loudly whispers, "This guy's really a cop," ruining the suspense of the next half-hour of the movie. Such unwelcome guides are no more desirable in a story environment than a theater. But a subtle guide can help in desirable ways. He might urge us to check the mail or bring in bagels to work so we'll have eaten breakfast before the demands of some strenuous events that are to come.

In any of these situations, the guide may or may not choose to reveal himself as someone with inside knowledge, though if he is heavy-handed he may tip his hand accidentally. A subtle guide can exert influence in ways that he knows will be good for the story and its participants in the long run. Because guides are not tyrants, characters don't have to listen to them any more than they listen to anyone else. A guide may watch us win the lottery and try to convince us to save our prize money, knowing that we'll lose our job tomorrow, but if we're hell-bent on going to the race track and blowing it all on a long shot, short of tying us to a chair, he won't be able to stop us.

Clip Everything

Many contemporary storytelling media can be produced by a single person working alone. One person can create a novel, write a play or movie script, paint a mural, or write an epic poem. But large-scale pieces require a group of diverse specialists. Mounting a Broadway show, creating a commercial video game, or producing a feature film all require the combined and coordinated efforts of a lot of people with very different skills.

Most traditional media are not known for their reuse of materials. For example, movie sets are typically designed and built for a particular film, and then dismantled when it's done. Sometimes props are reused, and characters re-appear in sequels and prequels. For example, the filmmakers of the 1974 film *Young Frankenstein* discovered and reused much of the original equipment that was built for Dr. Frankenstein's lab in the 1931 film *Frankenstein* (there's an interesting description of this process in the documentary *Making Frankensense*). Films more commonly live in their own universe, separate from that of all other films.

On the other hand, community and local theaters will often reuse everything they can, from sets and props to costumes and lighting gels. They often modify these assets from one show to another, adapting them in style or form to fit changing needs. But modifying existing materials still requires skill: a costume alteration should be done by a tailor who knows how to do it, and if a stand-alone balcony is redesigned, an engineer should be on hand to make sure it's going to be safe to stand on.

Computer environments are perfect for reuse of everything from the simplest prop to the most complicated artificial intelligence system. Anyone who's had to arrange for space to store a stage for a community theater can immediately appreciate the luxury of saving an essentially unlimited number of virtual objects in perfect condition forever for almost no cost. It's easy to store a thousand varieties of chairs, for instance, in styles ranging from Elizabethan to post-modern. The same goes for cars, clothing, wallpaper, trees, Roman chariots, garlic bulbs, and any other physical object.

Finding an object again when you want it can become a problem when you have too many things to take care of, but that problem too is being addressed by database and graphics researchers.

Another nice advantage of the digital approach is that there are no inherent reproduction or distribution costs. If you have a chair you like, you can make six of them for a dinner party, or 500 of them for a convention, without paying a penny for materials. And you don't have to truck them in and then send them back when you're done with them, either.

Design-Time Models

Computer models can be much more than just bags of polygons and textures. If they're *parameterized*, then you can easily customize them to your needs. This is where the expert skill of a designer can be encoded in the things he makes. You don't need to hire a skilled gardener to plan your garden, for example, if there's a parameterized garden model available. The creator of the the model puts his knowledge and experience into the programs associated with the garden-making tool, providing an interface that allows you to express what you want. So our gardener might offer options for the shape of the garden, the degree of formality, the number of water features, where the paths should go, and whether or not there should be a hedge maze. Once we've made our choices (or left them at some default setting), the garden is created by the program by combining those parameters with the expert knowledge embedded into the system by the gardener and the programmer. The result is an expertly planned layout, whether it's a huge, formal flower garden or an small, informal vegetable garden.

These *design-time* parameterized models are a great step forward. The beauty of this type of design is that it can be *linked* to create a network of related and interdependent models. For example, you might want to set your story in a country estate. So you work with the estate-planning expert system to lay out the general plan for where the house should be, and the gardens, and the driveway. It then "sub-contracts" the work for each piece to other modules. For example, the job of building the house would go to the house program, which would in turn consult programs to design the architecture, plumbing, and wiring. The appearance of the rooms would be handled by programs expert in interior design and ergonomics for everything from the choice of floors to the types of paintings on the walls, which in turn would be produced by programs responsible for selecting (or creating) artwork appropriate for this time and place.

The flow of information is not strictly top-down, because you can step into any part of this system and express a desire: for example, you might want to put a fountain over *there*. That would necessitate a change in the garden's plan, which might move around some of the stairs leading to the garden from the house, which could have ripple effects throughout the house's floorplan. Then you might select a larger kitchen and more bathrooms in the house. The system adapts the entire design to create a consistent and expertly-informed world from your specific and general desires.

The system would also have access to contextual information, such as where and when the house is being built. A contemporary villa on a Greek island looks very different than an 1800s Alabama plantation house, but they could both come out of a planning session with the same estate designer system.

When we work with a real expert, such as an architect, he gradually learns our personal preferences and starts to make decisions that anticipate our desires. He includes or emphasizes features we like and leaves out those we don't care for. In a similar way, the computerized experts that are encoded into model-design systems can also learn from experience and adapt to our personal tastes.

So unlike community theaters which must make do with the closest approximation they can create or buy, in the computer environment we will be able to create exactly what we need, in a way that's as expertly designed as we wish. We won't have to take the expert's suggestions if we don't like them, but they're there if we do.

Run-Time Models

Things get even more interesting when models are *run-time* parameterized as well. Suppose we've created a model of a wooden chair, either by hand or with the help of an expert assistant. Once the chair is finished and in our environment, it's able to respond to what happens. If a very overweight person sits in the chair, it may snap under him. If the chair itself is old, it would probably break under less weight than a new chair. If the chair has been scraped across the floor a thousand times, it's probable that its joints would be loose and the chair itself is a bit wobbly. If the chair is pulled up near the fireplace and left there, the parts closest to the fire would probably start to discolor over time. If the chair caught a random spark and other conditions were right, it might catch on fire itself and start to burn.

If the chair is burning, that might start the rug and the curtains to burning, and before we know it the house is on fire. But if there's an automatic sprinkler system, it would trigger and put out the blaze, soaking everything in the process. That water sould then seep into the joints of the chair and dissolve what was left of the glue, so that we now have a rickety, charred chair that's weak and ready to crumble.

All of this happens in real time, and none of it is explicitly programmed. When we create the chair, it is naturally made out of some kind of wood, and that wood inherently has physical properties that include susceptibility to fire and the ability to float in water. None of this behavior is programmed into the chair itself; it's just a natural result of its being made out of wood. And it's not something that we, the designers of the chair, need to consider at all. The world just works naturally.

This web of interrelated effects goes both up and down in scale, with each element communicating with potentially all of the others. For example, the fire itself responds to the environment, burning up oxygen and pumping out black smoke. If its fuel gets covered up in water or the oxygen supply gets cut off, the fire will naturally go out.

World Models

The degree to which we model the physics of the world will be determined by what we want to say, the computational power available to us, and the sophistication of the software we're using. It may be that eventually we will include gravity and friction and even air resistance into every step of every calculation of a simulator, whether we're riding a roller coaster or watching a person walk across a room.

The more complete we make the world simulation, the closer the world interface will come to fulfilling the promises made by the increasingly realistic sights and sounds of the system interface.

One of the great pleasures of such systems is that we can move away from a literal implementation of ordinary physics, and create consistent and believable worlds that are unlike our own. Cause can follow effect, gravity can increase and decrease with the seasons, and the speed of light can slow down by easily perceived amounts on demand.

We could mix and match these models freely. So the world could use ordinary physics, with the exception that apples are intelligent and tell good jokes. Or the earth has three moons, but one of them is hollow. Things could be much more subtle: perhaps if a particular football stadium fills up by more than a certain amount, the probability of rain increases.

Some of these odd world effects are already visible in today's games. For example, in *Grand Theft Auto III*, when you're driving a particular kind of car, you come to realize that most of the other cars on the road are of that same kind. If you switch to another model of car, then the roads again are dominated by that model. This may be partly a joke on the "blue car syndrome," which is a psychological observation that says when you buy a blue car, there suddenly seem to be many more blue cars on the road. The explanation is that we're just more aware of the blue cars because of our purchase. In this game, that psychological effect is made real.

Stock Characters

Just as we can have libraries of physical models, so too can we look forward to one day having libraries of characters and personalities. We could start small with stereotypes and stock characters, such as the surly miser, the air-headed teenage girl, and the snooty waiter. When we need one of these characters, we'll just buy one off the shelf. They will come with a complete wardrobe, manner of speaking, way of walking, and a host of idiosyncracies.

The game *The Last Express* presents a variety of characters, most of which are easily-recognized types, on board the Orient Express just before World War I. They reveal themselves through how they dress and carry themselves, how they speak, and what they say and do. Such standard types are a very helpful shorthand for communicating someone's general personality quickly; we see them and think, "Aha, he's *that* kind of guy." As I discussed in Chapter 2, we can introduce one or more idiosyncracies to make the characters seem more rounded.

We can make our own characters from scratch or combine existing characters that have some qualities that we like. For example, we might create a miser that's 60% Harpagon (the title character from Moliere's *The Miser*), 30% Scrooge (from Dickens' *A Christmas Carol*), and just for fun, 10% British stuffed-shirt Professor Henry Higgins from Shaw's *Pygmalion* (or its film version, *My Fair Lady*).

We can adjust other parameters of this composite to make our miser just different enough from everyone else's, and then just drop him into his mansion.

The first few programmed personalities probably won't be very interesting or flexible, but as times goes on, they will begin to develop a wider repertoire of abilities. Perhaps our miser's first reaction to his world would be to sell his mansion and move into a small apartment in order to save on taxes. If we need him to stay in the big house, we'd have to give him a reason to keep living there.

Believable, interactive people are a long way off, but we can probably get a lot of value from simpler characters along the way. The trick is to make sure that they're created and used in such a way that they never need to step out of the boundaries inside which they're credible. In other words, they should always match or exceed the player's expectations.

Mods

So far I've been talking about creating a new world from scratch by assembling preconstructed pieces, much as a builder uses precut two-by-fours or an artist uses preformulated paints. By allowing someone to work at a high level, we give an individual the chance to express a complex personal vision.

But not everyone wants to build a whole world. Some people like to take an existing structure and build upon it, putting their own stamp on something that they and others already enjoy and love. For example, many web sites feature *fan fiction*: stories written by fans of specific television shows and movies that are based on the characters and environments of those shows. Some of these stories are very well-written, and it seems reasonable to presume that the authors had the ability to invent their own characters and worlds if they'd wanted to. But they prefer to take an existing world and build on it.

This is a common activity in the PC game community, where fans create *mods* (short for modifications) of their favorite games. They design and build the architecture of new levels, create new characters and modify existing ones, draw new textures, construct new weapons, and even change the rules of play. Some mods are tremendously popular, and there are many anecdotes about games that saw dramatic increases in sales after a particularly popular mod came out. Such mods are typically created as a labor of love by fans and distributed for free, but a few companies have already been formed by people who have written successful mods.

Creating new levels for games is nothing new; people have been hacking their favorite games since the beginning of electronic gaming. The game *Lode Runner*, which was written in 1983 and which soon appeared on Apple II computers, stimulated a widespread movement of players who created, played, and shared their own levels.

Specialized editors for creating new *Lode Runner* levels appeared not too much later, and the idea stuck. The game *Doom* was deliberately designed to allow easy editing of sounds and images, and a number of specialized level editors for *Doom* soon appeared for free downloading in the fan community.

The mod movement still embraces creating new architecture, puzzles, and sound sets, but it also has moved into larger territory. Mod creators can actually change the underlying game so much that it's fair to say they're creating a new variant of the game.

For example, the game *Half-Life* was released for the 1998 Christmas season, and mods for it started to appear within months. By June of 1999 a two-man team released a mod called *Counter-Strike*, which transformed the first-person shooter into a team experience requiring careful tactical planning and cooperation. Many people consider *Counter-Strike* to be a game unto itself, rather than just a mod of *Half-Life*.

Many of the mod communities for different games have produced large libraries that they freely share. As game publishers have come to recognize the power of the mod community to increase the sales and popularity of their products, some games, such as *Unreal Tournament 2003*, now ship with level-editing software included with the game itself.

Mods are at their most straightforward in first-person shooter games where each level is essentially independent of the others. Creating successful mods is harder in story-based environments where elements of the game interlock.

World Design

At some point the special-purpose editing tools for games will start to turn into more general-purpose environment-design systems, complete with expert assistance. We'll have libraries not just for environmentally-aware 3D models, but for weather patterns, forest growth, highway traffic, and orchestra performances. And we'll also have people.

It's useful to think about how cultural models influence the people that live in them. We can create several worlds that are identical in all ways except for their social norms. For example, we might have a society where individual expression is frowned upon, and another where it is the highest achievement. In two cultures guns might be freely available or forbidden. The presence of art and music, the way people behave sexually and think of sexuality both in private and public, and the support or repression of individual liberties are all part of the makeup of a culture. A sufficiently advanced simulation of cultures can offer adjustable parameters for all of these criteria and many more.

If they're well designed and implemented, all software components, from physics to sociology to artificial intelligence, will work with each other and be freely interchangeable. So if you don't like how fire is working in your world, or you'd like to be able to shape it into spooky glowing faces and your current system doesn't support that, you can just swap out one fire implementation for another that works in a way you like better.

Today we have "clip-art" that we can simply paste into documents, and "clip-photos" have been available for decades from stock photography houses. We're beginning to see the start of "clip-motion," or prerecorded bits of motion that can be used in different projects, some of which are even parameterized. Eventually we'll have "clip everything," and the expertise and talent of many different people with very specialized skills will be widely available through their interchangeable software implementations. Many of these products will be commercial and may come with a hefty price tag, but that doesn't diminish their utility. And competition will encourage a variety of affordable alternatives.

Eventually a single person will be able to create an entire story environment by customizing and orchestrating a wide variety of pre-built pieces. We'll also see coordinated groups, like today's movie crews, where different people focus on different aspects of the project.

Player Reputations

People organize themselves into groups aligned by shared interests. As we come to know each other and trade information about our interests, a community comes into being.

The Internet has fostered a seemingly endless number of online "communities," focused on a wide variety of both general and very narrow interests. Usually members communicate with each other using online technologies like bulletin boards, chat rooms, and file exchanges.

I spoke in Chapter 8 about the problem of anonymity in online environments. The new varieties of anonymity are appealing in some ways, but they also have a basic problem: there are no consequences for disruptive behavior. In an anonymous world, causing social disturbances is easy and has no cost.

Social scientists often speak of *reputations* as a way to counter this problem [125]. Reputations add history to an online presence, and even though a person may be completely anonymous, we have a record of how that person (or at least that identity) has behaved in the past. One of the curiosities of online presences is that a given identity might be shared among many

411

people, who may each behave very differently. A single reputation for that identity then represents their aggregate behavior.

This combined identity can serve as an additional social control: if several people share an online identity, there would be personal consequences for the player who damages that identity's reputation. Note that this doesn't mean everyone has to behave "nicely." The players controlling a gangster may have worked hard to have him be known as a selfish and crooked guy. If one of the people playing this identity starts to do spontaneous favors for people and give generously to charities, that could invoke some harsh feelings from the other people who have invested their time and energy building up this character's bad-guy reputation.

As I discussed earlier, probably the most widespread use of online reputations today is on eBay and other online auction houses. They need these mechanisms because there's real money changing hands. After all, when you win an auction and send in your payment, you're doing so without having ever actually seen the merchandise in person: it may not even exist. If it does, it might be far worse condition than described. Because of these problems and others, some measure of reliability is essential in these sites. Online auction sites usually have a simple but robust way for each person in a transaction to express his satisfaction with the other, so buyers give feedback on sellers and vice-versa.

People who have spent a lot of time and effort to develop a positive reputation usually work hard to keep that reputation. New online presences with no reputation at all, or just a very small amount of feedback, are unpredictable: they have such small investment in that online presence that there's little cost to them if they ruin it.

This is very different from real life. Stores that sell china or pottery can have a lot of their stock destroyed if someone walks into the shop and deliberately sets out to quickly decimate the place. This rarely happens, because we'd stop that person physically and then probably him them arrested. But in the online world, someone can come into a chat room or an ongoing game and be as disruptive as he likes, and then simply log off and come back under another name. In online games, some servers develop a reputation for very strict hosting rules, while others are considered very loose. The strict sites usually try to somehow hold their players accountable for their behavior. Some tools, such as Internet address tracking, can be applied to this problem, but it's still a long way from being solved.

One solution is to use good behavior as a reward for greater power. When you first enter an environment, you may not have the power to do much harm, so you're pretty defenseless against others. For example, if you enter an online public place and make a nuisance of yourself, more experienced other players could throw you out and ban your reentry for a day. As your character spends more time in the environment and develops a good reputation, then he gradually begins to pick up those abilities for himself. Much more sophisticated systems of social engineering have been experimented with in online worlds [36]. Some massively multiplayer systems are designed to encourage certain sorts of cooperative behavior; *The Sims Online* gets this flavor from offering rewards when people work together in group activities.

Pro and Semi-Pro Players

In any group some people are sure to stand out. In a story environment they may be the ones that are the most eloquent, that make the most attractive versions of their characters, or that are always reliable for steering the story in interesting directions.

Like really good *Pictionary* players, exceptional story environment players are likely to become well-known in their circle of friends, and perhaps even more widely as word of mouth spreads. It's natural that they would be welcomed by many groups and may eventually become sought out.

If demand for someone's participation becomes high enough, he will necessarily have to start scheduling his time carefully. He may even decide that he can charge for his services as a way of regulating his obligations and making money.

This expertise could lead to an entirely new occupation: the professional or semi-pro story environment player.

It wouldn't be the first time for this kind of commercial pinch-hitting in a game. Today, some professional golf and bridge players hire themselves out as partners for other players, helping to increase their partner's individual rating through their combined team play.

Word of mouth would be the way this ball gets rolling, but after a while things will get more formalized. Some people may advertise, while others may start offering their services for bid on auction sites, joining the winner's group for a specified length of time. Some people could follow a parallel path but work for free or donate their fees to charity.

Depending on their skills and flexibility, freelance players may specialize in one genre, or works by a given author, or even a specific story or a role within that story.

Eventually reviewers and critics will appear, and like critics from time immemorial, they will offer their judgments on every creative aspect of the work, from the quality of the story environment to the people participating. Critics and publicists may specialize in judging the high-profile, for-hire players, much as some people focus on movie stars today.

A group may choose to make its story environment private, visible only to people who are actively participating. But they may open it up to others to watch. Fans might follow around their favorite players, watching them in different roles and discussing their performances.

Spectators could be offered special opportunities to view the proceedings. For example, they might be able to jump immediately to particular confrontations that they're interested in (when they occur), or get to watch a particular player from another player's point of view [43]. One implementation of special provisions for today's spectators can be found in the PC game *MechWarrior 4*.

A group might get together and decide that they would like to have a freelancer join in and take on a particular role. Finding the right person for the right group might be a challenging task. Casting agents and editors, charging a flat amount or a percentage of the player's fee, would help groups finding their best matches. This system is something like the player-matching function offered today by some gaming sites, but more sophisticated and personalized.

The rise of a professional class of players will by no means end the pleasures of people playing with friends (and strangers) for the sheer pleasure of it. There are professional poker players, professional basketball players, and even professional players of video games like *Doom*. But the presence of such professionals doesn't diminish our own pleasure in enjoying these activities by ourselves and with friends.

Platforms

McLuhan famously summed up the relation between technology and the content it carries in the phrase, "The medium is the message" [91]. This is no less true in the world of story environments than in television, film, or any other means of communication.

The electronic, computerized medium of story environments is far more flexible than any medium that has preceded it. It can be as small and lightweight as a cell phone, or as large as a multi-person theme-park ride.

Activities that require specialized and expensive pieces of hardware will always happen outside the home. As that hardware becomes less expensive and moves into our homes, newer, and even more expensive, hardware will take its place. As long as the economics support it, there will always be something cool "out there" that relies on hardware that we can't reasonably own ourselves.

Movie theaters count on this limitation: their specialized hardware is the big screen, a large viewing space, projectors showing high-quality film, and powerful, high-fidelity surround-sound systems. We can recreate a version of this experience at home, with anything from a small black-and-white TV to an elaborate "home theater." But few people can afford a system with the size, power, and fidelity that are offered by movie theaters. Watching a movie at home has many advantages of its own, and the DVD industry is thriving. But the movie theater experience is different than the home experience, and some movies seem to demand that higher level of technology. For example, anyone who's seen the film *Lawrence of Arabia* in a well-equipped theater and also on a television set (even a large projection TV) knows that there's a world of difference in the impact of the piece in these two formats; the grand vistas that are so much a part of the story just have a stronger visceral impact when they're truly huge, and objects in the far distance are actually discernable. The same is true of the more recent *The Lord Of The Rings: The Two Towers*.

So location-based entertainments will continue to be appealing as long as they can offer an experience that is worth the trip. Such activities will continue to prosper as long as they stay on the good side of the Fun-to-Work Ratio. That is, people will continue to go out as long as the fun they receive is of high enough quality and quantity to balance the money, effort, and time required to pack up the family (or gather together a bunch of friends) and travel to the place where the entertainment is located.

Because of their inconvenience and expense, activities outside the home are likely to continue to be one-time, self-contained experiences. One can certainly imagine that these could be elaborate versions of home-based entertainments, but they would still have to work for people who were new to the story and its world. Again, this isn't unlike movies, where films are often made from television shows (e.g., *The X-Files–Fight the Future* or *Star*

Trek: Generations). These movies need to be appealing to the fans of the shows who already know everything about the characters and their history, but they also have to work for audience members who haven't ever seen a single episode.

I believe that the capabilities of specialized and advanced hardware can enhance the story environment experience as much as they enhance other media. We will enjoy going places where story environments can be experienced with enhanced vibrancy, responsiveness, clarity, and all the other qualities that make for great visceral experiences.

Specialized hardware at home will still have its place. For example, the game *Dance Dance Revolution* uses a floor mat to sense the motion of players as they dance to the visual and audio cues given them by the game. Car simulators use steering wheels, and flight simulators are made more realistic with yokes that behave like those in real cockpits.

Special hardware, the real world, and a participant's imagination can be tightly integrated to create exciting and memorable activities [130]. There will always be a range of available hardware at different times and places. We may not want to strap on our head-mounted display in a coffee shop, but we can bring out our cell phone or digital assistant without trouble. This convenience lets us casually drop in on story environments whenever we have the time or need. Today, some commuters play traditional games on their personal electronics while riding a bus or subway going to and from work.

The game *Samurai Romanesque* can be played in Japan on a mobile phone with a color display [59]. The game, which can be played by about a half-million people simultaneously, offers you the chance to visit over 1000 different villages, learning different physical and mental skills and having conversations with other players (all of whom remain anonymous). Your character only "lives" for 40 days, but in that time, you can fight wars, accumulate money, develop your Zen abilities, and engage strangers in conversation. There is no winning condition in the game, but you can accumulate skills and money. Different players may choose to seek fame (if you win many battles, you can become a famous samurai), or they may desire a high social standing or even romance. Although all player characters in the game are male, you can meet computer-controlled women, who may engage you in conversation. If a woman likes your style, and you like hers, you can get married and have children. When your character dies, you can then continue playing as your son, who inherits his father's status and many of his abilities as well.

With such a casual approach, we can "dip into" an ongoing story when it's convenient, for as long or short a time as we choose. Such a story environment is like a traffic flow: the particular cars that make it up come and go, and sometimes those that left return later, but the traffic itself is always moving along the road.

⇥ 14 ⇤

Experiments

T he opportunities for story environments are as broad as fiction: they can be set anywhere, at any time, and tell anyone's story. We can find ourselves in our own home town, on the far side of the moon, or in a parallel universe where elephants are the dominant species and commute to work on roller skates.

Participating in a story environment can be a one-time event of a few minutes or hours, or an ongoing, regular appointment spanning a few weeks, months, or even years. We can enter story environments with a group of known friends or family, or join up with strangers. We can take on the persona of someone else, retain our own identity, or blend the two.

The way to explore the world of participatory fiction is to actually go out and do it. So to wrap up the book, this chapter presents some experiments for us to try out.

Designing Experiments

Designing something as complex as a story environment means balancing a great many different demands. It's also critically dependent on the specific software and hardware that's available, both of which change rapidly.

As I mentioned in Chapter 12, it's always better to set expectations low and then meet (or exceed) them than to set them high and come in low. Just how much to promise, and how much can be delivered, changes with every new piece of hardware and software that contributes to the design.

Everything we do in a story environment must make sense and feel natural to the players. Anything that feels like an arbitrary restriction, imposed because of technology limitations or just incomplete design, will degrade the overall feeling of the experience. It's important that everything mesh smoothly and feel like it belongs.

This integration can be done with great subtlety, as practiced by the Old Masters of oil painting who chose how to compose, light, and render every object of every painting with great care.

It can also be done audaciously, by defying convention in the most obvious ways. The television show *Firefly* presented a world that is a totally incongruous mixture of science-fiction (with spaceships and phasers) and the Old West (with pistols and horses). But because every element of the show was carefully woven together with the others, this seemingly impossible mixture led to an idiosyncratic but coherent world. Such mixed-genre pieces are extremely difficult to create and can be hard to sell (as devotees of each genre may decide they don't care for the other, leaving the project with a very small audience), but they also provide a lot of opportunity for creative play between genres.

The following sections take some of the main themes and ideas in this book and boil them down to practical experiments which we can try out with today's software and hardware. Some versions of these experiments have been tried in the past, but I'm suggesting them (or variations on them) here because I think there's still something new to be learned.

Designs

In this section I'll present designs for games and story environments that I've created to explore the ideas in this book. But before we get going, it's important to explicitly note something that we all know: details matter. The greatest bridge in the world will fall if the rivets are poorly placed or the joints poorly welded.

My experience is that creating the general concept for a game is only the first step, not unlike writing a screenplay for a movie. A screenplay is like a blueprint: it provides a general structure and shape, but it doesn't really tell us what the resulting work is going to be like.

People are very sensitive to details in computer interfaces. If players are required to maneuver a 3D camera manually and find the task difficult or unpleasant, most will just walk away. If the camera moves itself automatically but ends up in the wrong place too often, again people will get frustrated and eventually simply give up. This is just one of a million implementation details that must be right, or the game will suffer. Like many movie special effects, the best implementations are the ones that are never noticed, because they just work so well.

Camera-control is an obvious mechanical issue, but more subtle issues can be just as important. For example, in a multiplayer game you might find that there's perceptible "lag" between your actions and when the environment responds. This time delay might be due to slow connection speeds, or loads on the server, or a dozen other causes. The problems associated with these issues are legendary. For example, suppose that there's a gold amulet sitting on a tree stump over there, and you and I are both in the environment, equal distances away from the stump, and we both want the amulet. So we both start running as fast as we can. I immediately see the world rushing past me as I run, but you're still standing still. Even if you started to run at the same moment I did, that information hasn't yet worked its way from your computer to the game server and then back to me. The result is that at the moment when I reach the tree stump, I see you just starting to move, and I easily claim the prize. But you have seen exactly the same situation in reverse: you've been running like the wind while I've been standing still and counting the flowers. From your point of view, you reached the stump long ahead of me. Only one of us can have the amulet: who gets it?

In this example, the arcane and complex implementation issue of network and server responsiveness has a dramatic effect on the gameplay. We can make this problem as complex as we choose: suppose we're wrestling. Moves and counter-moves are flying back and forth in real time, and it's absolutely essential that everything remain synchronized and immediately responsive if we're to have any hope of capturing the feeling of wrestling.

The work of designing a game, whether it's for a computer implementation or not, is constant balancing and rebalancing: a little more of something here needs to be compensated by a little less of something else over there. These are often subtle and intuitive choices, which is why design is best done by a single person with a vision, rather than committee.

Sometimes the design just "feels" wrong, and it can improved by nudging a few small things.

Once the design is complete, the implementation becomes a new balancing act, but it's made much more complicated because of all the other people involved. Like a film director, the person in charge needs to get everyone to see the work in the same way, and to produce media that contributes to the overall picture harmoniously. And as in films, that's essentially an impossible task: everyone necessarily sees the project through his own eyes.

In a computer implementation, where almost every detail has the potential to affect the player's experience, this balancing process becomes incredibly hard. And even when the production team sees eye to eye, realities like production schedules and budgets can force compromises and cut corners.

The story environments that I describe in this chapter will all be presented at a high level. Getting the details right is absolutely essential to making the whole thing work, but choosing them correctly is a moving target that depends on hardware, software, the intended audience, the designer's taste, the programmer's abilities, economics, and a dozen other factors. But at least these high-level descriptions will provide some feeling for how these story environments could work and how we'd participate within them.

In the next few sections I'll present designs for a few different interactive experiences.

Death by Video

The heart of this multiplayer online game is a social environment where people can meet and talk to one another. The driving goal is to solve a murder mystery.

In *Death by Video* you play a detective in the Media Crimes Squad. This is a special multi-state police agency that is dedicated to solving crimes that were caught on videotape. The unit was created because police in several states noticed the proliferation of video cameras, from surveillance cameras in stores and airports, to news teams roaming the city, to people with their own camcorders. With such a wealth of video constantly being shot, it's inevitable that some unlawful activity will occasionally be taped, either deliberately or accidentally. The police decided to pool their technical resources and create a centralized talent pool for investigating cases that depend substantially, or even entirely, on videotaped evidence. Each jurisdiction kicked in some money and some equipment. They each donated only the equipment that they didn't need themselves, which often meant that it was the oldest, slowest, and least-useful hardware in the place, ranging from a beat-up 128K Macintosh computer to an old Teletype with paper-tape input and output, and a desk chair missing one of its casters. But the members of the Media Crimes Squad have done their best to lash together this hodgepodge of mismatched equipment, and they've created a solid investigatory force with a good reputation for solving difficult crimes.

When you arrive at work on Monday morning, you find a video note from the dispatcher, who has assigned you a new case. Usually it's a murder. She tells you about the people involved, and then shows you the video footage that caught the death or the events immediately surrounding it. She then gives you the case file, which contains whatever forensic information the squad has put together on the case so far. It always includes videotaped interviews of the principals in the case, as well as whatever photographic, textual, and other evidence they've got. She then turns the case over to you and your fellow detectives to solve.

Much of the evidence that you receive is fragmentary, sometimes even contradictory. It's not unusual in the course of working on a case to find yourself going to the real-world public library, talking to a local expert, or reading up on a subject you previously didn't know much about.

The real heart of any investigation comes from talking to the suspects, witnesses, and other people involved. So the game makes these people available for you to question in real time, letting you watch and listen to them respond. Every night while the case is running, players can join either or both of two 45-minute interview sessions. Players ask questions by sending in text and then watch streaming video of the person answering that question live. The interviews are moderated and incorporate a variety of techniques for keeping it moving quickly, giving lots of people opportunities to ask questions, supporting follow-up questions, and providing side channels for groups to discuss and analyze the interview while it's happening.

Interview characters are played by trained improv actors who are briefed on the actual story of the case. Players can ask any questions they want. If the question is part of the character's backstory, he'll answer as best he can, and otherwise he'll make something up that is appropriate and fits into the bigger story.

At the end of the two interviews, detectives vote on who they want to talk to the next evening, drawn from anyone who's been mentioned so far. So if during the course of an interview one of the improv actors made up a younger sister, and people really want to talk to the sister, the production team will hire an actor, brief her, and make her available for questioning the next night.

Transcripts and video records of the interviews are available for anyone who missed the session or wants to go back over them.

Detectives can't be guaranteed that anyone is telling the unvarnished truth. People lie to police all the time because they have secrets that they don't want revealed, though these facts have nothing to do with the investigation. Most of our characters tell the truth most of the time, though. The only guaranteed lies come from the actual perpetrator (or perpetrators) of the crime.

The game provides chat rooms and bulletin boards where detectives can post information and theories, meet one another, compare notes, or just talk. The crimes are designed so that it is possible to solve them working alone, but it's more fun and productive to team up with other people.

At the end of a week, each player submits a one-paragraph statement that describes who committed the murder and why. Once we close submissions, a new piece of video is made available for anyone to watch that tells the true story of the murder from a traditional, omniscient camera's point of view. Players who got it right would have their names listed on the Wall of Fame, and a new crime appears the next Monday.

The player's goal in *Death by Video* is of course to solve the crime. My goals were different: I wanted to help people make friends and enjoy working with them. The crime is the common thread that helps people find one another, but it isn't a constraint on their conversation. If a couple of people hit on a similar theory for a crime, start emailing one another to compare notes, and discover they both have a son of the same age going to the same college, the conversation might to that and the crime left for another day's discussion. I'd consider that a total success.

I consciously balanced *Death by Video* to reward both logical thinking, based on forensic evidence and strict causality, and creative thinking, based on the character's personalities and behaviors. The video interviews are essential, because they let players get a feeling for a character's body language and speech patterns, and all the other behavior intangibles that are lost in text-only interviews.

Homeward Mars

Homeward Mars is another multiplayer online game.

Only weeks before asteroid Jakon-3 struck Earth and killed everyone, the politicians finally found a way for all the nations to cooperate long enough to build a small fleet of spaceships. It was a desperate, last-ditch idea: send representatives of the human race to Mars with everything we could give them, and hope they could find a way to keep mankind in existence.

Of course, the politicians agreed that the majority of those survivors should be politicians and government officials. But when the species is about to be wiped out, people tend to speak their minds, and the worldwide riots subsided only when that plan was changed. The few thousand people who would take the dangerous trip to Mars would be chosen by random lottery from volunteers among the planet's entire population. People on the ships would be grouped by language, and jobs on the ships would be assigned by aptitude tests.

The lottery was held, tears were shed, the ships were loaded, and the fleet of ten ships left orbit only hours before the asteroid struck. When the passengers looked out of their windows the next day, the familiar blue-and-white ball of the Earth was gone, replaced by a dusty, dark-brown orb. The Earth went silent: no television, no radio, not even Morse code on the amateur bands. The ships had no way to communicate directly with each other, since all traffic between ships was designed to go through satellites in Earth orbit. Freak ionization from the asteroid had knocked out all the satellites, leaving the ten spacecraft isolated from each other. Each ship was its own world, a survival pod of humanity hoping to find a new start on Mars.

You're on board the *Churchill*, the only English-language ship. The size of an oil tanker, the *Churchill* was lashed together in orbit mostly by cannibalizing space junk that was floating around. Nobody would call it comfortable or even appealing. The outer hull is covered with satellites that were snatched out of their orbits and hastily bolted on, their solar panels collecting what energy they can from the sun, their converted instruments relaying data about their surroundings only slightly better than what a person could see by just looking out the window.

Like everyone else aboard the *Churchill*, you're here because you won the lottery. And like everyone else, you're a stranger on a ship of strangers, with only a couple of days of training behind you. Everything about the ship is patchwork: there's enough water to drink but not enough to bathe or shower regularly, bunks have to be shared, and the equipment is anything but user friendly. There was just barely enough time to build the ships; helping the crew keep them running was a much lower priority. Some of the ship's essential equipment, like the water recirculators, the environmental controls, and even the engines, are barely documented. The ship reeks of sweat and cooked food, and every exposed surface is dirty and stained. Housekeeping was the lowest priority during construction.

You've been assigned to the navigation and piloting crew, where you and the six other people you've been thrown together with need to pool your incomplete training in order to keep the ship on course and safe. Your biggest challenge will be getting the ship into Mars orbit and then safely down to the ground, but that's a few months away. The auto-pilot seems to be functioning pretty well, so as long as you can avoid the big, slow-moving stuff, you can experiment with the controls and learn how to better guide and steer the ship. You'll also want to co-ordinate with some of the other crews. If the cargo folks move some heavy items around, they could throw off the balance of the ship. To prevent burning up fuel with unnecessary course corrections, you'll want to make sure that the cargo crew moves things when it's also good for your needs. There are about a dozen different stations on the ship, each staffed with a half-dozen people, and everyone's actions can potentially affect everyone else.

But navigating and saving fuel aren't your biggest problems. The people who have been given command are turning out to be the worst kind of petty despots. It's turning into a real *Lord of the Flies* type situation onboard, where a few jerks, with the support of a few bullies, are taking a tough situation and making it worse. The nominal breakroom has been turned into a jail, and there have even been rumors of beatings. Things are definitely not looking good for the next few months, trapped in this stuffy, hot, smelly ship with its human cargo.

You'll probably want to make some friends quickly and see who feels as you do. Then you can try to see what you can do to change things onboard and make life better for everyone.

Good luck, crewman!

I designed *Homeward Mars* to be attractive both to people who are attracted to puzzles and simulation games, and to people who like to socialize, network, and embroil themselves in political intrigue.

If you want to keep your head down and just do your job, there's plenty to keep you occupied. The simulator that controls the ship's functions is elaborate and sensitive to a wide variety of inputs, so to be able to work your station reliably, you need to understand not just what's happening in your part of the ship, but what other people are doing as well. As people discover more about how to control the ship, they will become better at their own jobs and can help increase the efficiency with which others do their jobs as well. In the first few weeks of the flight, the auto-pilot and other automatic systems work well. But inevitably they will start to fail, and then it's important that the crew will be ready to step in and run things manually. The ship's simulator can be figured out, but it will require a lot of coordinated experimentation to master.

If you're not into engineering and simulation, there's a political struggle going on worthy of your best social skills. The tyrants running the ship were selected because they had high leadership skills on the initial aptitude tests, but those tests didn't capture the fact that they were also narcissistic bullies. In the game, the ship's leaders and their enforcers are non-player characters run by the computer. You never interact with the officers directly, since they're isolated on the bridge. Your only contact with them is through their ship-wide video announcements, and the rare email reply that you receive if you choose to contact them; such email is usually terse and blunt. If you're unlucky enough to be visited by their self-appointed "security forces," you'll find that conversation is pointless; they have nothing to say except for an occasional grunt or insult.

The real social interaction comes from the other people running the ship. Some of your fellow crew members will doubtless be attracted to the promises of privileges and benefits offered by the officers in exchange for support. It's doubtful that everyone will ally themselves with the officers, because the rewards they're forced to offer diminish rapidly as more people join up. It's more likely that most people will resent this oppressive power structure and will want to find a way to bring it down. You'll need to be careful, because if a loyalist rats you out to the officers, you might find yourself punished with limited rations, restricted movement, or far worse. Working together, with careful planning and clockwork execution, enough rebels can work together to bring down the officers and take control of the ship, but that's not the end of the problem. Someone's going to need to take over after that, and there's no precedent or manual. If you do oust the officers, you'll need to establish and enforce a new social order.

The goals of *Homeward Mars* were to create a single shared space for these two very different types of players, in a world where it's in their self-interest to work together. The game provided plenty of channels for in-game communication among players, but I expected that there would be a lot of out-of-game communication as well. I could see small groups of people phoning each other on a conference call and coordinating their actions. Folks interested in the simulator could run complex experiments to figure out just how to control the ship, and those into the social side of things could hold a negotiation online with another group, while simultaneously discussing what's happening on the phone with each other.

Although one might expect from popular stereotypes that men would gravitate towards the puzzle and simulation aspects of the game, and women to the social intrigue, I think we'd see significant crossover since everyone would be starting out with roughly the same goals and abilities. The idea of the game was to run lots of ships in parallel. If the experience worked out well, players could move on to *Mars Colony*, which extended the experiment to larger groups of players and eliminated the computer-controlled characters in favor of different groups who had preassigned but fundamentally conflicting goals for the development of the colony.

Flight 437 Down

I designed the story environment *Flight 437 Down* for a live network of connected consoles. The game was targeted at players in North America.

You've been saving for years for your month of wildlife sightseeing in Africa, and in the two weeks you've been here so far, it's been everything you and your traveling companion have ever wanted. You've been taking more photos than you'll ever be able to look at, but you know that they'll never capture the smell of the wild grass, the feel of the baking sun as you watch a lion stalking a zebra, the sound of small animals running around and under your hammock as you try to fall asleep, and the taste of trail food cooked over an open fire.

Yesterday morning your guide said that a friend of his was organizing a five-day trip into a remote region of the jungle backcountry. Though your companion wanted to take a few of days of rest, you jumped at the chance, so you parted amicably and you rode the Jeep to a small airstrip 50 miles away. There you met the ten other travelers that you'd be traveling with, all of which had arrived from different tour groups, and your leader for this side-trip, an experienced guide and pilot named Mbewe. By mid-morning your gear was all aboard the small plane, everyone was in their seats, and Mbewe had slipped into the pilot's seat and fired up the single propeller. After clearing the airport, Mbewe turned to the cabin, smiled broadly, and announced, "You're going to have a great time. Flight 437 is airborne!"

For three or four hours you chatted with the other passengers as the little plane flew over a seemingly endless Jackson Pollack canopy of dark and bright greens. Vibrant blue rivers slashed through the trees, extending to the horizon in both directions. Then something felt different, a vibration that wasn't there before. And suddenly it was more than a vibration: the whole plane was shaking, and then the passengers were jerked back in their seats as the plane nosed down. Mbewe was at the controls, but unconscious, his limp body draped over the yoke, pushing it forward. The passengers in the front row rushed into the cockpit, trying to pull Mbewe out of his seat, but he was strapped in by two sets of seatbelts that wouldn't give. People were screaming, the plane shook madly as it plunged downward, and you knew you were about to die.

With only seconds to spare, one of the men in the cockpit pulled Mbewe, still strapped in, away from the controls, and the other man pulled the yoke back as hard as he could. The plane fought back, but the nose came up a little bit, and then a little bit more, and then everything exploded as the plane entered the canopy and ripsawed its way through the trees, the roar of the engines almost lost in the thunder of giant trunks shredding the hull, the plane twisting as it hurtled deeper into the forest.

When you regained consciousness, you were, miraculously, unharmed except for minor scratches. Most of the rest of the passengers were the same; somehow the fuselage had survived. One person was badly hurt and hobbled out of the plane to lie down in the forest. The two men who were in the cockpit alongside Mbewe were all clearly dead, crushed by a thick trunk of a tree that had impaled the cockpit somewhere along the way.

As you rise from your seat, a fire starts in the cockpit. Quickly, you and your fellow passengers grab everything you can: luggage, food, toilet paper, whatever isn't bolted down. You throw it outside, as far from the plane as possible. The fire lurches into a blaze and you know you're out of time;

everyone dives out of the plane and runs. A few seconds later the plane erupts in a black and orange fireball, and even from a safe distance it feels like a blast furnace at your back. Surprisingly soon the flames die down, and you and your fellow passengers look at each other. You're utterly lost in the African forest, with only the meager, random supplies you salvaged from the plane before it exploded. It's possible that Mbewe radioed for help before the plane went down, but it's equally possible that he didn't. Perhaps nobody has any idea that anything has happened, and nobody is expecting you for almost a week. You're on your own.

Welcome to *Flight 437 Down*.

The game takes place in 3D environments that are run by rich simulators. If you make a loud noise in the jungle, you'll startle the birds, and they'll fly away, making noise of their own, which might alert other animals. Each player controls his own character, a 3D living mask that was authored by the production team, but which each player can modify and personalize. Players communicate with real-time voice chat. Using their handheld controllers, players can do the standard things available in most action-adventure games, from picking up and throwing things to climbing trees.

There are no magical objects in the game: you can pick up anything that's not nailed down, and you can go anywhere you can reach. You can only carry as much stuff as you can fit in your backpack and in your hands. This load limit isn't mediated through a menu screen and an inventory list, but literally through opening up your backpack (if you have one) and trying to put the object inside. The world is responsive in natural ways: if you have a match or a lighter, you can burn anything that can catch on fire, and that fire can spread in the normal way if you're not careful. Objects aren't limited to their obvious use. If you've salvaged a ballpoint pen from the plane, you can use it to puncture a plastic bag, hold up a box trap, or act as a paperweight, but it's not strong enough to puncture a tin can.

The game is played episodically, typically for an hour at a time, once a week. Players who really get into the game may elect to meet more frequently or for longer periods of time.

Each one-hour episode has a specific plot point embedded within it. To keep the game on track, and to make sure that the plot points are revealed, the game is guided. Each episode includes someone who joins the group and provides information or helps them make progress. In this game, the guide isn't disguised as a player, but is easy to spot. Providing a dedicated guide is a very expensive way to run a game, but I felt that it was the best way to understand directly how people liked to behave in this world, how they naturally acted and reacted, how they developed socially with each other, and what they would think of doing and trying. It also would give us a chance to experiment with different ways of introducing guides and their interactions with the players, to find approaches that fit both the nature of the experience and also serve the author's intentions.

The guides fit into the game because the players soon begin to realize that they've landed in the midst of something that's already going on, but that they don't understand. In fact, they've landed in a part of the forest that is being actively fought over by several indigenous tribes. The larger picture revolves around a plant that grows in this region and is held sacred by the local tribes. They honor this plant because it can be processed and then brewed into a tea with two very interesting properties. First, it's a non-addictive sleep aid. The second property is that during that sleep, the drinker experiences very enjoyable hallucinogenic dreams. Normally these dreams are as unpredictable as any others, but the natives have found that by brewing the tea along with one of two other specific local plants, those dreams can be channeled towards fighting or sex. A multinational pharmaceutical company has found out about this plant and is trying to reshape local politics so that it can have exclusive control over the region where the plant grows. Specifically, they're encouraging war among the local tribes, with the idea that when one group ends up on top, they can pay off that leader and use the tribe to harvest and process the plants cheaply, which will then be shipped off to a packaging plant and sold at huge profit as a recreational sleep aid. Although the drug company wants to create a single monopoly to solidify their control over the area, they are concerned with the welfare of the natives and provide them with free anti-malarial drugs, contraceptives, antibiotics, water filtration pumps, and other technology to improve the quality of their lives.

Episode 1 starts with the introduction up to the explosion of the plane. Then the story environment is in the hands of the players. Their goal is simply to survive: find a place to sleep, gather some food to eat, come up with a plan, and try not to squabble too much among themselves in the process. The guide is the one fellow who crawled out of the plane. He dies of his wounds near the end of the first episode, but he's able to help people understand the situation and nudge them toward developing a plan.

Episode 2 introduces the fringes of the surrounding story. The group is discovered by a local tribesman who speaks no English, of course, but is able to communicate with gestures, body language, and non-verbal sounds. He helps the group learn basic survival skills in this forest, such as what is safe to eat, and how to recognize the tracks and other signs of dangerous animals and avoid them. He also points them towards what they understand will be a village, where perhaps they can find a way to start their journey home.

In Episode 3, the group arrives at the village only to find that it's recently been burned to the ground, and nobody is left. As they search for clues, they meet up with Reginald Scott, an Englishman who's working in the area as a representative of the drug company. Reginald is friendly, chatty, and truly sympathetic with their situation. He doesn't reveal the whole surrounding story, but he tells them who he works for and says just enough to let them realize that something important is going on around them. He explains that he doesn't have a radio with which to get them help, and that he's heading deeper into the forest (later they'll learn that both statements were lies), but he tells them to head west to find another village. As night approaches and he prepares to leave, he offers them some of the local sleeping aid tea, which he carries in a thermos. If anyone in the group accepts, he will have a vivid experience waiting for him between this episode and the next.

In addition to the simulator that controls the environment, there are simulators for each tribe. Since communication with tribe members is inherently limited, and their behavior is expected to be unusual and strange, this is a fine place to use computer-controlled characters. The very best AI available will probably be just barely enough to make a tribesman that seems somewhat inscrutable and unpredictable, yet plausibly human. The tribes in general can respond to how their representatives are treated, under the idea that those characters eventually make their way back to their villages and tell everyone else about the group they met. Their experiences with the group will thus set the emotional tone for the next encounter with someone from the tribe. But the tribes are in conflict, so helping one tribe may be interpreted as antagonistic by another, or interfering with one tribe may be interpreted as a friendly act by one of their enemies.

The story environment proceeds episodically until the group manages to find their way to rescue. Along the way, they can choose to befriend and help one or more tribes, the representatives of the drug company, both, or neither. They can try to make peace among some or all of the warring tribes or to inflame the tensions. And of course they need to find ways to get along with each other, since probably no two people will agree on just what they should be doing at any moment, yet they all need each other in order to survive.

This structure was also designed to let us try out different ways for groups to proceed when someone needs to miss an episode.

My goal was a story environment that let us experiment with the use of guides, highly responsive natural environments, and a very free, self-directed group that is moving through a highly structured story taking place around them and responding to their choices with both simple computer characters and a natural environment.

Complete Experiences

The designs above are sketches for complete experiences that test a number of ideas simultaneously. Creating a new entertainment has a lot of appeal, and it can be a lot of fun and potentially a financial success. But it also carries a lot of risk, since there are so many new things introduced at once that it can be hard to interpret from the results which ideas worked well and which didn't.

In the next few sections, I'll separate out the components of these experiments, and discuss individual experiments that we can use to explore each component idea.

Language

Language is essential to the social environments we're talking about in this book.

Text: Many of today's games use text to allow players to talk together.

Even the most casual form of text, such as that used in instant messaging systems, has a few distinct advantages over voice. First, you can take your time when composing a message and make sure you phrase it just right. Second, you can edit it after you've written it (but before you hit the send button), so if you didn't express yourself well, you can improve your words. Third, text allows a convenient record of the conversation, offering each participant the chance to scroll back to recall who said what.

There are other situations where text is more convenient than voice. For example, simultaneous but distinct conversations with different people can be indicated with different colors, or placed in different locations on the screen (e.g., in a separate window for each conversation, or near the person who said each phrase in a graphical environment).

Pure text, even in an electronic setting, can lead to romance and love. Although stories of relationships and even weddings on the Internet are well known, they are nothing new. The 1879 novel *Wired Love* tells the story of Clem and Nattie, two telegraph operators in far-separated and remote towns who exchange messages over the telegraph and fall in love. Theirs is not a private correspondance, because the other telegraph operators in their system are able to listen in on their exchanges, and sometimes offer their own comments and unsolicited advice.

Text also has some disadvantages. Slow typists may feel penalized because it takes them a long time to compose a message, and people with arthritis and other disabilities may find typing to be difficult or even painful. Putting text all over the screen can be unattractive and distracting. Many people find it challenging to express themselves clearly in text. And people who like to carry on many conversations at once can find that it takes them a long time to type all of their thoughts. These issues partly explain why we've seen the sudden rise of the now-ubiquitous emoticons (e.g., :-) to indicate humor), new acronyms and abbreviations (e.g., YMMV for "Your Mileage May Vary"), and shortcut spelling (e.g., "cya" and "u2" for "see you later" and "you, too").

During thousands of years of letter-writing, people have gotten by without these textual shortcuts, but the reality today is that people have embraced these conventions as a speedy and convenient way to communicate. Emoticons, acronyms, and other shortcuts are everywhere now because people like them and find them useful, not just on computers but also on pagers, text-enabled cell phones, and other electronics, where small screens make every character precious.

Voice: The positive qualities of voice are easy to see: virtually every household in the U.S. has one or more telephones. Voice has some wonderful qualities: it lets you express emotions without thinking about them, punctuate your speech with rhythm and dynamics, and use your tone of voice to communicate nuance.

But voice has drawbacks that are complementary to text's advantages. Voice is fleeting; once said, the words are gone (unless they're recorded or transcribed). Sometimes people don't pick their words carefully, give a wrong impression, or just blurt out something that they immediately regret. There's no editing with voice: once you've said it, it's gone (an exception to this is provided by some voicemail answering machines, which let you listen to a message that you've just left, and delete and rerecord it if you're not happy with what you've said).

Pure voice also has led to many romances. The novel *Vox* tells the story of a sudden emotional and sexual relationship between a man and a woman who meet randomly on a telephone chat line.

Both voice and text have their place. Right now, it doesn't seem reasonable to ask which is "better," but rather to see them as different styles of communication. Sometimes you want to wear a blue shirt, and sometimes you want to wear a red one. They're both fine as long as they fit the rest of your choices and are appropriate for the context.

Non-verbal language: There are all sorts of other ways that people communicate, such as body language, drawn symbols, and behavior. In Chapter 11, I talked about some visual language systems, but not all visual languages are designed to parallel spoken languages as closely as those examples.

For example, in the 1800s flowers were used to send covert and not-so-covert messages across great distances. The language of flowers was extensive, covering over 1000 different ideas and phrases [19]. Flowers were most often used to express matters of the heart, and by arranging a bouquet with just the right proportions of the right flowers, one could express very subtle shades of meaning and intensity of feelings. Although the recipient had to connect the pieces, generally the message carried by a well-executed floral arrangement was unambiguous. For example, "Your sweet voice (Tuberose) casts a spell upon me (Witch Hazel). It calms my anxiety (Christmas Rose) and allows me to sleep (White Poppy)." But flowers could also be used to communicate much more serious messages. Rather than send a diplomatic message over formal govenrmental channels, one could express an informal warning through a carefully-crafted arrangement. For example, "I am made uneasy (Garden Marigold) by your deceptive words (American Laurel). You have no claims (Pasque Flower), and further confrontation may lead to war (Milfoil)."

Preconstructed phrases: We can take a cue from the party game *Mad Libs* and offer people prewritten dialogs that are just missing key words. So we might select a phrase, such as "When you visit me, please bring a (blank) and be prepared for (blank)," and then put any word or phrase into the blanks. Then the translation problem into other languages is much easier: the overall message can be hand-translated ahead of time by a native speaker and saved, and the words entered by the person are translated automatically and inserted. There might be some slips in grammar, but this system could offer a reasonably powerful and convenient way to communicate with people who speak a different language.

Keeping it short: Sometimes less is more. Particularly in environments where the length of a message is an issue, it's a good idea to encourage people to keep their communications as short as possible.

This is often the case when we're talking to computers, rather than other people. The more limited and constrained we can make our utterances, the better chance we have of writing a computer program that will be able to make sense of them.

When every word is dear, people can pack a lot of meaning into short, well-chosen phrases. In a granite headstone set at a gravesite, every letter must be chiselled by hand, so people compose messages to get their money's worth.

This brevity is a step in the right direction for some applications, but it's unlikely that we would design a story environment where people communicated only via headstones.

There are other ways to encourage players keep their messages short. For example, if the only communication channel is bugged (or just suspected of being bugged), then it's in everyone's interest to keep messages as short as possible so that they give the eavesdroppers as little to work with as possible. When using electrical equipment that is running low on batteries, again they'll naturally keep their messages short out of self-interest. We can also force the issue economically: telegrams charge by the word, so there's a strong financial incentive to keep things as brief as possible.

People can also communicate with larger chunks. We organize letters into words, then sentences, paragraphs, and so on. Some games provide players with prewritten phrases which they can string together to make sentences. In the game *Battlefield 1942*, different keyboard keys are mapped to different orders and commands. Pressing one key changes the meanings of the others, so you can send complex messages to your teammates by just pressing a few buttons.

New languages: Some players will enjoy creating their own special-purpose language, driven by the needs of the story environment. Designers could accelerate this process by providing language tools, such as snippets of grammar or syntax rules, and dictionaries of words or symbols.

Players may also enjoy inventing their own languages together as a group. Cooperating to make a language, players could build bonds across cultural and other barriers, since the people involved in the design must build on those things that they already have in common.

Language Experiments

1. Offer transcriptions of voice conversations automatically so they can be read as text.

2. Support chunking using prewritten phrases.

3. Provide prewritten messages with missing words and phrases to be filled in.

4. Offer ways to communicate using short but carefully-chosen phrases.

5. Give players a variety of visual languages.

6. Help players to communicate with non-verbal languages, such as the language of flowers.

437

7. Offer players a chance to develop their own languages.

8. Provide tools for groups of people to create their own collectively-invented languages.

Conflict

Allies, rivals, and enemies: Any time we come together with other people in a social setting, we'll usually find allies: friends and colleagues who are sympathetic to our goals. We also find rivals, who want to claim our goal for themselves instead. And we can find enemies, who are determined to stop us from achieving our goals for reasons of their own.

As we've seen, drama is fundamentally about conflict, and we get conflict when faced with rivals and enemies. Not everyone enjoys such conflict with other people, though.

Certainly some people are more than happy to stand up for themselves, in real or simulated situations, and enjoy the give-and-take of a personal tug-of-war. For these people, facing off against another person may be welcome.

But some people are put off by person-to-person confrontation. They shy away from games where you need to bargain or make political deals where everyone suspects each other as a matter of sensible paranoia.

For people who don't enjoy personal confrontations, the conflict necessary for drama can be found by facing some impersonal feature of the world: a runaway train that must be stopped, a hopelessly tangled bureaucracy to be overcome in some sneaky or clever fashion, or a hurricane heading right for downtown. Players can still rally together, and even split into different factions or groups with different agendas or approaches, while never directly coming into personal conflict with the people or forces causing the trouble. Alternatively, those antagonists can be so far over the top that they seem more like cartoon characters than real people, so confronting them doesn't feel quite so real.

I think of an environment as possessing a different amount of *weight* depending on how personal the conflict appears to the player. The environment is *light* if the conflict seems impersonal or far away, and *heavy* if the conflict is personal or direct and immediate. Environments can present the same amount of weight to all players, change it on a per-player basis, or even change the weight over time for a single player.

Conflict Experiments

9. Create story environment that lead to natural allies and rivalries.

10. Offer different environments different amounts of weight.

11. Change the weights over time.

12. Assign different weights to different people, perhaps according to their preferences.

Identity

Anonymity: Online environments let us be someone we're not. We can be younger, older, a different gender or race, or even a different species. As we've seen, this is a two-edged sword.

Total anonymity implies total freedom from responsibility. That lets people try out all sorts of personal and social experimentation, but easily leads to anarchy and allows some people to freely indulge their desires to see how much trouble they can make.

Total identity, on the other hand, can be too restricting. When we meet someone for the first time in everyday life, we may be fairly free with our names, but we're often more reluctant to give out personal contact information such as a private email address or a telephone number.

People who feel that they have an established or high-visibility reputation in the real world may feel that they need to uphold it in fantasy worlds as well. A steely-eyed corporate raider may read tear-jerking romance books when he's in the privacy of his home, so he might enjoy being part of romantic story environments based on those themes. But just as he wouldn't want people to see his bookshelves, he wouldn't want them to know that in fact he personally was the young maiden in a flowing red skirt picking flowers for her beloved.

439

Reputations: In between the two extremes of total anonymity and total identity is the *persistent online identity*, in which people invest time and energy to build up a reputation. That reputation can be used not just as a social tool, but also as a key to control which players get access to different elements of the environment, ranging from specific abilities to physical locations. That access can be controlled by the designer or by other players.

Note that this control is subtly different from the way some of today's games use experience levels to accomplish the same ends. The difference is that experience systems usually only track *what* you've done. If you kill a particular monster, the system grants you a certain number of experience points. In a reputation-based system, not only what you've done, but *how* you did it, is permanently associated with your character. This information may come from the system, or it may be granted by other players.

Personal reputations are a result of how people treat one another. Story environments can support a more professional form of reputation, where people can become known as being particularly good at some aspect of the activity. This reputation extends both to creators and players.

For example, some creators might be considered extremely clever at using the world's physics to drive their stories, and others may be valued for their visual touch and humor. By the same token, some players may be very good at creating memorable dialog, comic riffs, or at moving the story in a direction that's rewarding for everyone involved.

Reputation systems: A system can allow players to evalutate creators, particular story environments, and other players, based on whatever criteria they like. Most online commercial auction services use a numerical scale for reputations, with the option of short written comments to expand on the score. We can certainly support a system like that for story environment creators and participants.

When there are enough story environments, creators, and players around that it becomes hard to know them all from personal experience, then we open the door to editors, critics, and other reviewers who make it their job to provide detailed and thoughtful analyses and discussions.

Suppose that a group gets together to play a particular story environment, but finds that they're short one person. Alternatively, they may know that one position in the story is key, and they want to fill that with someone who's done it before and can bring that experience to their group. Matchmakers can offer a service to connect individuals with groups.

People can also expand this service to assemble entire groups from individual players. A casting agent can take a large collection of people and, considering their preferences and reputations, assemble compatible groups.

Collectives: Groups of friends can develop a *collective identity*. Each time anyone from this group joins up with a story environment, he presents himself as this person (he may or may not wish to reveal that the identity is a collective). That identity is treated like anyone else's, developing a reputation and working with other players, matchmakers, and casting agents.

A related idea is a group that shares a single character in a particular story environment, creating a *collective character*. This is a more limited form of the collective identity, since it only extends to that one character in that one environment. Again, the group may or may not choose to reveal that different people are playing that character at different times. This collaboration would require a lot of trust and cooperation among the members of the group, so that their shared character has a consistent personality and behavior in the environment.

Identity Experiments

13. Offer the opportunity to trade increased amounts of identity for increased powers and freedom.

14. Reward good reputations, regardless of identity, with increased powers and freedom.

15. Give people the chance to determine other people's developing reputations.

16. Create tools to manage reputations in a way that's fair to everyone.

17. Build story environments where people can coexist at different levels of anonymity.

18. Provide a forum for editors and reviewers.

19. Offer support and tools for matchmakers and casting agents with which they can bring together players and groups.

20. Let a group of friends play together as a collective identity, with a shared long-term reputation.

21. Let a group of friends play together as a collective character, working together over the course of a story.

Structure

Stars and ensembles: Taking on a starring role in a play mounted by a local theatrical society is a major commitment of time and energy. Some people find this activity attractive, others find it appealing once in a while, and some people prefer to stay on the sidelines. It will be the same way in most story environments.

Although we're fascinated by great characters, both heroes and villains, not everyone aspires to be one of them. Most people feel like the star of their own life story, and many children naturally think that the world revolves around them. But being the star takes a lot of work, and sometimes it's more pleasurable to let someone else carry the ball, if only for a while.

Some story environments will doubtless have traditional structures with a hero and villain and lots of supporting roles. Others will feature ensemble casts, where everyone matters but nobody has to feel like he has too much of the burden of keeping the story on track, or is too much of a spectator.

Participation intensity: We can provide players with an opportunity to control their experience by adjusting their desired participation intensity over time. If when you enter a story environment, you feel like jumping in with both feet, you can crank up this level of intensity; if you're in a quieter mood and just want to be part of the story without exerting a lot of effort, you might choose to lower it. This control would give you a dynamic handle on adjusting your own Fun-to-Work Ratio. You can select how much work you want to put in, and the story environment adapts to require only that much work. This adaptation would occur smoothly: if you're in the middle of a discussion and you dial your participation intensity to near-zero, you wouldn't want to appear to your conversation partner as though you'd suddenly frozen into a statue.

Information density: By adjusting the information density over time, players can control how much of their attention the story demands. If you're expecting someone to come over for dinner soon, you might turn the information density down a bit while you're chopping vegetables, so that you can focus on your knife and hands without being too distracted. Once everything's in the oven, you'd turn the information density back up again and get enmeshed in the goings-on in the story environment. As with the participation intensity, you'd want changes to the information density to ease out of their old values and ease into new ones gracefully.

Maslow hierarchy: We can structure a story environment so that players find themselves trying to satisfy different levels of the Maslow hierarchy. A player who gets off the bus in a new city without much money in his pocket has some very basic needs to attend to: where to sleep, where to find food to eat, and how to earn money. These needs will bring him into contact with other people in similar circumstances, and they may choose to work together to solve their common problems.

Then as time goes by, his needs change. With a stable income, a place to live and sleep safely, and access to food, he will start to put more emphasis on social relationships. He might find himself eventually working at a large company, agitating for social change, or working for himself and trying to make a living as a freelancer. As a character changes in social status, he'll work to maintain old friendships and develop new ones.

The levels of self-knowledge at the top of Maslow's pyramid can refer to either self-knowledge by the character in the story environment, or self-knowledge of the player himself. In the best case, playing the game can become a personally transformative experience.

Create and remove bridges and blocks: Story environments need characters and plots. I've argued that it's not a good idea to require players to write their own plotlines.

When characters have a clear-cut goal, their players can use their creativity to take concrete action in their world of the story, within the limitations of the character's abilities and resources.

By banding together with other players, people can create complicated plans and then carry them out together. Some of these plans involve building bridges to create opportunities to move forward, or removing blocks to take care of problems in their way. They may also damage some of their opponent's capabilities by removing bridges or put obstacles in their way by building blocks.

Bridges and blocks can be literal, physical objects like a pair of shoes or a strong horse, intangibles like a good job or social standing, or personal abstractions like a sense of pride.

Alternating cooperation and conflict: Another source of conflict is finding opposition where it is unexpected. When two or more people agree to cooperate with each other on a common goal, and one person turns out to be not quite as advertised, that's a sure way to get tension.

One source of problems emerges when a player tells others that he's capable of something he's not. Whether it's running a 4-minute mile, carrying on a fluent conversation in Swedish, or defusing a bomb, a player might overestimate his abilities. Everyone else who was counting on him is sure to be disappointed at least. If the job was a critical one, this person's failure could have widespread repercussions. If the misrepresentation was a deliberate lie, tensions can rise even higher.

Another type of unexpected conflict is when someone discovers something at the last second, or perhaps even while he's in mid-act, that changes his abilities or intentions. A bunch of people may be holding up a bank together, but when the one man who knows how to open the vault looks around and realizes that this is where his mother keeps her money, he may have second thoughts about the job and no longer want to pick the lock. This change in plans will not endear him to his masked, gun-wielding colleagues, adrenaline racing in their veins.

On the other hand, unexpected conflict can arise quite on purpose. When someone betrays his friends or colleagues, they usually have a strong and immediate emotional response.

The flip side of the coin is when people expect there to be conflict, but there isn't. When an enemy suddenly acts like a friend, most of us usually suspect there's something more going on than meets the eye.

It's certainly possible for people to have a change of heart, regret their past actions, and want to make amends. Many people reject such an abrupt reversal as too implausible to be believed, doubting the overtures of friendship. Although others will take the person's new attitude at face value, most of us will be cautious.

This sense of distrust will cause tension when our new colleague realizes that he's not fully trusted. Regardless of his true intentions, he may find that being treated suspiciously is insulting, and once again we've got conflict.

So we can find tension either from facing conflict when we expected cooperation, or vice-versa.

System and world interface match: In Chapter 11, I talked about the importance of matching the system interface and the world interface.

The system interface is the part of the program that touches the player. It's the graphics, sounds, hardware, on-screen sliders and menus, things to point at and click on, places to go and conversations to enter, and other elements that make up the communication between the virtual environment inside the computer and the player's mental image of the environment inside his head.

The world interface is how the system interface communicates with the program in the computer. No matter what the player tries to accomplish with the tools available to him, if the program doesn't know how to respond to those actions, there will be no effect.

World interfaces are typically far less powerful than system interfaces. That's because the system interface only has to make it *appear* that you can do something, while the world interface needs to actually handle that action.

If you crash your car into a building in *Grand Theft Auto III*, the car will get dented and scratched. If you crash it repeatedly, you'll see the windows pop out, the hood fly off, and other damage accumulate until the car catches on fire. That much makes sense: the system interface says you're driving a car into a building, and the world interface knows what happens to cars in that situation and changes the internal representation of the car accordingly, which makes the graphical image of the car change as well.

But how about the building the car crashes into? It should suffer damage too, ranging from a scraped finish to structural failure, depending on the impact. With enough run-ins, the building ought to fall down, which might lead to a fire, which could spread to other buildings. None of these things happen in *Grand Theft Auto III*, because the hardware and software that are responsible for simulating the world simply aren't powerful enough to do everything necessary to simulate a complete world. Because the buildings are forever unscathed, the system interface promises more than the world interface can deliver, and the player sees rough edges in the game.

Games can be frustrating to play when the system interface and world interface don't match up. As a player, you have to learn the arbitrary rules about what you can and can't do. And if the game is large or takes you to new environments and new situations, you may be constantly banging into unexpected and unpredictable limitations. Some game designers turn this problem into a feature by incorporating the limitations of the world interface into puzzles that you need to solve, but that's not a general solution to this inconsistency.

Ultimately, computer hardware and software will become powerful enough to simulate everything we might care about. But that's many years away.

In the meantime, we have a couple of choices for our story environments. One is to make players relearn with each new experience the nature of the particular mismatch between what he seems to be able to do, and what he really can do. This forced matching leads to an experience that feels arbitrary and conceptually disjointed.

Another alternative is to make the system interface weaker. Since there's an upper limit on how powerful we can make the world interface, we can reduce the power of the system interface so that the two are matched. That means that the system only allows you to do the things that you actually *can* do. In a well-designed, suitably restricted environment, a player will *feel* powerful, because he can predict and plan: if he can use the system interface to do something, then it will actually happen in the environment.

There's a middle ground between these two approaches. We can make an environment with a very powerful system interface and a much weaker world interface, but create the world interface so that it is completely consistent. For example, if you can pick up and put down an object, then you can pick up and put down *every* object that's of a size and weight that you can grasp. If you can use your in-game tape recorder to record a voice conversation at some point, then you can use that recorder anytime, anywhere (as long as you have tape and battery power available). There would be no cases where, for example, you'd come to a bookshelf and find that you can remove only one or two specific books. If you can take down a book, you can take down any of them, or even all of them.

Although in this midground the differences are still arbitrary between what you seem to be able to do as a player and what you can actually accomplish, they don't change over the duration of the experience. Once you figure out what effects you can have in the world, then you can make plans with confidence, because you know what actions will be available to you.

Structure Experiments

22. Provide opportunities for people to be stars or supporting members of the story.

23. Give people the chance to join a story environment as part of an ensemble.

24. Provide a way for a player to conveniently adjust the participation intensity required of him over time.

25. Provide players with a convenient way to control the information density of their experience.

447

26. Let players work their way up the Maslow hierarchy of needs over the course of a story.

27. Shape a story so that players can make visible progress by creating and removing bridges and blocks for themselves and each other.

28. Introduce conflict where cooperation was expected.

29. Introduce cooperation where conflict was expected.

30. Design an environment where the system interface is no more powerful than the world interface.

31. Create a world interface that is entirely consistent and predictable.

Finding Friends

Group sizes: Different story environments can support different group sizes and mutual familiarity. As we saw during the discussion of the Intimacy Matrix in Chapter 8, people in groups of different sizes tend to relate to one another in different ways.

With the rise of massively multiplayer online role-playing games, it's not unusual to share a virtual space with hundreds or even thousands of other players. As the population grows, the percentage of people we know personally gets smaller and smaller.

Different games probably will have different ideal group sizes. There's some evidence that when groups are fewer than about 250 people, generally people can feel like they know one another (at least in passing) [52]. Past that point, people begin to form separate, smaller groups, and their feelings of shared purpose can turn into feelings of fragmentation and even competition.

Shared experiences: One way to build a relationship is to go through a trying experience together. Armies use basic training to deliberately force people to rely on one another and develop feelings of trust, friendship, and mutual obligation.

Entertainment experiences can't force people to do anything, but people who have a common experience often are able to use it as a jumping-off point for a friendship. People who went to the same school, or even just enjoy the same books or movies, can talk about their shared interests and then branch off into other discussions.

Sometimes a shared experience is so unusual or remarkable that nothing further is needed. Theme park rides are an example: when you get off of a particularly exciting or unusual ride, it's not unusual to trade smiles or comments with other people getting off at the same time. The intensity and unusual nature of the experience brings people together at that moment.

Story environments can provide experiences where people meet one another and slowly forge bonds.

Implicit bonding: Bonding experiences don't have to advertise their intention. People form relationships during these experiences because it just feels like the natural thing to do. We can make an analogy here to exposition in stories. As I discussed in Chapter 4, the best exposition happens when it can't be seen, often hidden in the midst of action or dialog that doesn't seem to be obviously about providing background information. Skilled writers can tell an audience a lot about the characters and the world of their story without lecturing to them. In the same way, players may be offered an opportunity to do something that's fun or interesting for its own sake, without realizing that it's also been designed to encourage them to get to know one another, and build personal friendships.

Reasons for gathering: Modern cities have lots of different places where people can socialize, from small, quiet nightclubs for couples on dates and big square dances for singles looking to meet one another or just have fun, to bowling alleys for small groups who want to relax and compete together casually. Your destination on any given outing depends on whom you're with, what you're in the mood for, and whether or not you're looking to meet new people.

Large online story environments can involve hundreds or thousands of people, some acting as individuals, others as members of different companies, groups, or tribes. They can enjoy the same kind of diversity of recreation and socializing opportunities in the online world as we enjoy in the real world. So the story environment provides not just a focus during the activity itself, but places for people to enjoy one another's company if they want to just relax and socialize.

Friendship Experiments

32. Find ways to help people form small, tight groups within large environments.

33. Provide ways for people to get to know one another.

34. Offer ways to help people develop networks of mutual respect and obligation while doing some other activity that's attractive in itself.

35. Develop environments where people can meet others like themselves, or people who are very different, depending on their preferences.

36. Explore the Intimacy Matrix and look for the ranges of group sizes that work best for different types of stories and activities.

37. Provide different types of places for people to gather within a single story environment, depending on how well they know each other.

38. Give people the tools to create their own entertainment destinations for themselves, friends, and strangers.

Duration and Frequency

Length of time: Sometimes people are looking for a momentary diversion, and sometimes they're willing to put in the time and energy for something with more scope and depth.

Short experiences are easy to find. Half-hour television shows and short stories let us get into a story, enjoy it for a while, and then wrap it up. If we thirst for more, we can indulge in another of the same or turn to something longer, perhaps an hour-long TV show, movie, or novella. And for larger experiences we can take in a TV mini-series, movie trilogy, or a novel.

One of the qualities shared by these different media is that the duration is fixed and known at the start: without this information, we could get more or less than we wanted. If we were reading a short story and reached the end and found that we wanted more, we'd be out of luck. If we started a novel and then wished it was only half as long, we'd have to try to selectively edit as we read and hope we get the gist of it.

In computer-controlled environments, we can provide stories of any length that participants desire. We can also imagine expanding and contracting those stories, or pieces of them, as players wish. At one extreme, story environments can focus on a narrowly-defined conflict that is presented and then quickly solved. At the other extreme, stories and characters can be woven into soap-opera structures that can be continued for decades.

Obviously the shortest stories can be taken in at a single setting. Like a 30-second television commercial, they can economically set up the situation and then come to a swift conclusion. Longer stories lasting hours, days, or more will need to absorbed in pieces.

One advantage of online media is that it can adapt. People can slow down the pace of their story or speed it up, or even expand the world to make it last longer. We've all had the experience of reading a book and wishing it wouldn't end; in procedural story environments that's possible.

Scheduling: For a solo experience like reading a novel, we can control our own schedules. If we put a book down and then don't find the chance to get back to it for a week, nobody else will mind. But if we're in a story environment with other people and our participation is required, then we have a responsibility to them to show up.

If we are in a situation where we meet other people on a regular basis, scheduling can become very difficult. It may be hard to get everyone together at the the same time, even for just an hour or two. Some story environments can let people join in when they have some free time, so players don't have to promise to honor a recurring commitment weeks or even months in advance of some of the meetings.

One approach would be set things up so that players need only contribute for some period of time during a given interval; for example, we might ask everyone to join in for an hour a week every week, though it needn't be the same hour as everyone else (or even anyone else). This way everyone contributes to the evolution of the story and knows what's happening, but if something comes up in his life he doesn't have to feel that he's letting down his friends. Obviously we would want people to be present with their friends as much as possible, and we'd design the activity to support and encourage that. If someone's having a busy week and can't make the regular time, but is able to squeeze in a half-hour somewhere during the week, this flexible scheduling would allow them to stay involved in the developing story.

Duration and Frequency Experiments

39. Allow people to skip a session and not ruin the story.

40. Offer storytelling structures that allow other people to fill in for missing participants.

41. Create stories that can continue in a sensible way that's fun for everyone even when some people must be absent.

42. Offer stories that can progress whenever enough players are able to assemble, whether it's for only a few minutes or a longer period of time.

43. Provide ways to allow the story to move forward when only small groups, or even individuals, are able to participate at a time, yet allow everyone to contribute for a total of some amount of time during a given period.

Boundaries

Traditional boundaries: Where and when does a story environment begin and end? The answer is hard to know. Consider the modern movie.

Contemporary movie ad campaigns begin months before the movie is released, with trailers in the theaters, ads on television, and articles in media outlets (using a technique called cross-promotion, articles frequently appear in magazines owned by the same parent company that owns the studio). Usually the basic plot, the lead characters, and the world of the movie are all communicated to prospective audiences in order to whet their appetites. In some ways the movie has already "begun" by this point. A movie that makes an impact on us can linger in our minds long after the lights come up and we leave the theater.

Movie companies have also found ways to move the film outside of the theater and into the larger world. There are the videotape and DVD versions that people can take into their own homes, often with additional features that weren't present in the theatrical release. There are also endless opportunities for purchasing products that are based on the characters or stories of children's films, from bedsheets and lunchboxes to key rings and plush toys. And movie-based video games typically come out with each new big summer action film.

These extensions of the movie can be just reminders, or they can actually provide original material. Some successful children's movies such as *Toy Story* have turned into weekly television series. And television is happy to play the same game: some TV shows such as *Star Trek* have generated novels and movies based on their characters and settings. The game *Enter The Matrix* builds on and expands the story of the film *The Matrix Reloaded*.

So it's not clear where these entertainments begin and end, either in space or time. Story environments will blend into the larger world in much the same way.

Treasure hunts: Some games have been produced that reach outside of the limits of a computer or console. They create pretend web sites or give clues hidden in other media. The game *Majestic* could offer you clues by calling your cell phone.

Bringing the worlds of games and the real world together is not a new phenomenon. The 1984 book *Masquerade* appeared to be an illustrated fairy tale told through a series of elaborately detailed paintings. But as the text of the book itself announced, there was more to it than that. Several years before the book's publication, the author created a statue of a golden rabbit with a ruby eye, had it appraised at about one million British pounds, and buried it somewhere in England. The paintings in the book contained a wealth of clues through visual puns, references to historical figures, buried systems of sequences based on colors and numbers, and other encoded messages. Each painting, when properly decoded, added another piece to a master riddle that revealed the location of the statue. If you could figure out the puzzles, interpret the riddle, and thereby determine the location of the rabbit, you could simply go out and dig it up. The book was a sensation on both sides of the Atlantic for over two years until it the rabbit was finally discovered.

A follow-on book by the same author explained the puzzle by revealing the clues in each painting and explaining how they went together to form the master riddle [140]. Looking at this book today, and its many successors, it's easy to see it as the model for the complex visual puzzles in *Myst* and the genre of visually rich adventure games that followed it.

One of the lessons of *Masquerade* is that it's probably not a good idea to give people a strong incentive to run around public and private places with metal detectors and shovels, stomping around and digging holes.

Nevertheless, the way that this book extended into the real world made such a big impact that it created a new genre called the "armchair treasure hunt," which resulted in a variety of other books and even CD-ROM games and jigsaw puzzles based on the same premise.

When story environments reach into the physical world, they can build on the *Masquerade* model, or try some new variations. One nice alternative not available to print media is to run the process the other way, bringing the real world into the story environment.

One way to have a real-world treasure hunt with non-destructive results is to participate in the sport of *geocaching*. The activity begins with someone placing a small and usually inexpensive object inside in a tight or waterproof box, and then hiding the box. The hider might place it in a hole in the ground, deep in a cave, at the bottom of a lake, or on a remote mountaintop. Then the hider announces the geographical coordinates of the object, often by simply posting them on a website. Seekers look for the box using a portable Global Positioning System (GPS) receiver, which gives them a constant readout of their latitude, longitude, and altitude. They use this information, their knowledge of the terrain, and their wits to find the prize. In geocaching the journey is usually the reward, since the prizes themselves are typically of moderate or little value. When geocachers claim their prize, they often put something new back in the box, and put the box back where they found it so it's there for the next party.

Incorporating the real: Some games are deliberately designed to incorporate parts of the real world. Fantasy sports leagues let players build up imaginary teams that are made up of real players. As the season goes on, the statistics of each player's team are updated constantly to track the actual real-world performance of the professional athletes, and thus determine standings in the fantasy league.

In stock-trading games, investors get some sum of money to spend at the start of each period, and strive to buy and sell stocks to get the highest return of all the players. The value of a player's portfolio rises and falls in real time with respect to the actual stocks, as though he really owned them. The player who has the most valuable portfolio at the end of the game wins a prize, typically a large fraction of the money that players ante up to enter the game. This game is just like buying and selling real stocks, except the downside risk is limited to the entry fee, and the upside reward is limited to the winner's purse.

The card game *Magic: The Gathering* is usually played face-to-face with decks of real cards. Unlike ordinary playing cards, there are many different cards in *Magic*, and players sometimes must purchase or trade many cards to collect the ones they want. Players can also compete online if they wish, by purchasing electronic cards and then playing with them over the Internet. The electronic cards have no physical existence and are not valid in face-to-face games. Similarly, ownership of a physical card is irrelevant online. The company that produces the game does offer a redemption feature: you can trade complete sets of electronic cards for physical ones, which are mailed to you, and the electronic cards are then deleted. You can't trade the other way.

The *Pokémon* card-playing game also has an electronic counterpart, this time on the handheld GameBoy Advance. This device can be outfitted with an optional card reader, which can read encoded information on specially-printed *Pokémon* cards. These cards can download new games into the unit, add an extra creature to the game, or unlock a game feature that is already present in the cartridge. To get access to these extras in the electronic game, one must own (or borrow) the corresponding physical card.

When elements of the game world appear in different parts of the real world, people naturally work together. For example, at one

455

point players might need to know the color of a specific house in Philadelphia or the total number of windows facing the street along a particular block in rural Scotland. It's unlikely that any one person has easy access to both of those places, so people will have to find one another and cooperate. We can make this information much harder to find, more geographically diverse, and require many more pieces in order to make progress on a particular puzzle.

We can also use elements of the real world that change. Players might need to know how long a specific traffic light stays red in the eastbound direction at 3 A.M. at a particular intersection.

Producers can recruit volunteers or even pay people to perform duties for players. For example, we might give information to a waitress in a specific diner. To learn what she knows, people would have to identify her, enter her diner when she's on shift, buy a cup of coffee, and ask her the right questions.

People can also work in a non-personal way, for example by putting out a sign on their lawn (perhaps only on Tuesday afternoons), or doing something subtle like leaving one of their car windows slightly rolled down. If a game can afford to pay people to participate, there are more possibilities. For example, consider benches that have advertising painted on them. It's easy to rent a bench and paint a normal-looking ad on it. But on Thursday between 12 and 1, someone recognizable (e.g., "a woman in a red hat with a leopard-skin bag") could sit at just the right spot to obscure some key letters, revealing a secret message to those who know to look for it.

Reaching out to the real: Extending the story environment into the real world needn't be limited to puzzle-like clues. In a particular story, a character might be sad to see that his favorite tree in his front yard is slowly dying. If we decide to help him out and keep the tree alive, we could get advice from a real-world arborist, or we might look up the symptoms of his tree's illness ourselves at the library or on the web.

There are many online mechanisms for helping people find one another, from the highly-structured websites of electronic dating and matchmaking services to the free-form world of chat rooms. But people also enjoy meeting one another in the real world, based on their online interests.

The Lovegety is an almond-shaped electronic pendant that was introduced in Japan in 1998 [71]. The Lovegety has three settings to indicate what you're looking for; these translate into English roughly as chat, friendship, and sex. You set your Lovegety to one of these modes and indicate your gender. Then as you go about your day, your pendant is always searching for other units in a 5 meter radius, seeking out a match. If your Lovegety finds another that's set to the same preference and belongs to a person of the opposite sex, it starts to blink green. If it finds a Lovegety but it's not a match, it shows a red light. If two people have blinking green lights, they look for each other, make eye contact, and then take it from there.

Obviously, the Lovegety is just the tip of the iceberg, and other devices of more sophistication have appeared since, such as Thinking Tags [14]. These little devices could broadcast and receive all sorts of information, can search out a broad radius, and have less immediate or personally challenging ways of making contact than simply walking up and saying hello. When such devices are able to connect to your story environment, very rich kinds of real-world communications become possible. It would be fun to develop systems that used Lovegety-like devices along with story environments to help people make contacts in the real world.

We could couple this real-world contact with changes in the story characteristics: people who know one another in real life may be able to team up and accomplish things together that others cannot. This collaboration would have to be very carefully implemented, so that actions are not biased toward people who are already friends, or against those who simply live far away from other players.

Real abilities: A very different way to bring the real world into a story environment is to tie someone's abilities in the computer world to the abilities he has in the real world. Today, players describe themselves in most role-playing games by providing scores on a list of characteristics. For example, on a scale of 0 to 10, a brutish character might have a strength of 9 but an intelligence of 2, while a thief might have a physical dexterity of 9 but wisdom of 3.

When people build their own characters this way, they can explore a role that's unavailable to them in real life. A short person can play as a strong giant, a shy person can play as a gregarious tavern keeper, and men can play as women and vice-versa. This is an important part of the appeal for many people.

But in some circumstances it may be useful to tie people's abilities in a story environment to their abilities in real life. For example, if you want to be rated as an expert carpenter in the world of the story, you would need to demonstrate that you're an expert carpenter in the real world. This desire would create a need for some way to substantiate or display your abilities in front of a tester or governing body (this demonstration might be unacceptably risky in situations where the ability is dangerous, like high-speed car driving or parachuting). If you want your character to be a great baseball catcher, then you can practice in real life until you are indeed a great catcher. Once you've proven your skills, your in-game character reflects your abilities.

This skill could be enhanced with specialized input devices. Right now, most people steer their on-screen cars using their mice, keyboards, or console controllers. Specialized steering-wheel controllers are available, but they're not widespread. Some arcade machines offer very specialized simulation hardware, from guns and snowboards to motorcycles and airplane cockpits.

But perfectly natural activities like walking and running have no corresponding natural input devices. We may be able to do something about this lack with enough technology development, but in the meantime, for us to carry out these everyday physical skills in the computer world, we have to learn how to translate them into the available input hardware and then become proficient at operating the device. This problem isn't so bad for walking, but imagine how frustrating it would feel if you were an expert archer and a friend invited you to play an online archery game with him. Your skills with a real bow could win almost any contest, but in this game you'd only be as good as your skill with the controller, and your friend could defeat you easily.

If we can demonstrate competence at complex abilities in the real world, then our online characters could inherit them from us, saving us the need to master the arbitrary mechanics of keyboards, mice, and controllers to simulate that ability.

Boundary Experiments

44. Bring the real world into the story experience.

45. Encourage people to collaborate and work together for mutual benefit.

46. Incorporate natural or staged events into the story environment.

47. Build real-world rewards into story environments, and vice-versa.

48. Encourage the use of unusual objects to help players communicate with the computer in the most natural way possible.

49. Provide opportunities for people to express themselves using their bodies, voices, and faces.

50. Help people hook up with others in the real world who share their online interests.

51. Tie people's abilities in a story environment to their abilities in real life.

External World Environments

Tracking the real: One interesting feature of online media is that it can be reproduced and distributed almost instantly. While this reproducibility has important economic implications, it also opens up the door to story environments that can track current events.

Let's begin with politics. Suppose that a story environment takes place in a mid-level governmental office, such as a state's department of transportation. For the most part, that environment will serve as a backdrop and source of story ideas. But now suppose that the real governor of the state in which the story is set presents a new, real budget to the legislature, and that this new budget cuts funding for that department. If the budget is passed, the author of the story environment can write changes into the ongoing events to reflect this cut in funding, perhaps even throwing some people's jobs into jeopardy.

If we move the story into a situation that's even more fluid, then the connection to events as they happen in the real world can be that much tighter. We could set the story in a place where political tensions already run high. As events unfold in the real world, the environment constantly reflects the latest changes. It may prove advantageous to players to closely track local or world news reports to stay on top of what's happening in the real world and why, which will help them understand the short- and long-term implications of the changing story environment.

We're not limited to politics: any section of the daily newspaper could serve as the real-world source for a tracking story environment. We could be caught up in a professional sports team over the course of a season. In the story environment we play the scouts, publicists, travel coordinators, and other back-room people whose fortunes rise and fall as the team wins and loses its games out on the field. The story could take place in a physics or biology lab as scientists race other groups to be the first to discover or confirm some important new development, or in a stockbroker's office whose fortunes rise and fall with the Nasdaq index.

Online environments can incorporate the external world in much simpler ways that still have a lot of impact. The cell-phone game *Samurai Romanesque* tracks the real-time weather of its participants and reflects that in the game (even though the game is set during Japan's warlords era, from roughly 1467 to 1600) [123]. For example, if you're in a place where it's actually raining outdoors today, the on-screen dirt paths become muddy and slower to traverse, and you can't fire your musket because the gunpowder it depends on is too damp to ignite.

Imaginative memory: We can use imaginative memory to enhance games with very little cost. Famous places are a natural: if we set a story in a well-known environment, then people will bring to the story all of their knowledge and associations with that place without requiring us to explicitly create them all. In some ways, the place itself can handle some of the exposition. Even for people who have never visited the location personally, a place that's well-known throughout the culture can still evoke strong feelings. A story in the U.S. could start at Mount Rushmore, and a story in Japan could begin near Mount Fuji. We could place the events at Uluru (or Ayer's Rock) in Australia, or under the Eiffel Tower in Paris.

Enhanced real world: Another opportunity for bringing the external world into the computer world is to use it as source material. Some broadcasters already use real-world events to enhance their programs. For example, many televised football games include a yellow line on the field that the ball must pass for the team to gain a first down. Although the line looks real, and is obscured by players and other objects on the field, it is added electronically in real time [48].

If information on the positions of the players and the ball could also be gathered in real time and broadcast, then people at home could watch the game not from the live broadcast feed, but using game consoles running a football game program. This technique would allow them to view plays from any angle, including that of the quarterback, a player who just made a great interception, or even from the point of the view of the ball itself. The graphics could include some imagery from the live event, or they might be created entirely on the fly from a relatively small data broadcast. With such a technique, people with intelligent cell phones can "watch" a game being played as though their small screen were a television set, when it's actually rendering everything synthetically from a steady stream of real-time data.

We could use such techniques in story environments. For example, a story might be set in a baseball or soccer stadium, with players in the stands. As the story develops, they can watch the real-time game and talk about it when they want (just as people do while at a game), but also participate in the unfolding story.

External World Experiments

52. Bring the outside world into the story environment.

53. Build a story environment that directly parallels the rises and falls of a specific, real-world organization or field.

54. Include current events in the story environment, directly and indirectly.

55. Step into the shoes of public individuals in real-time present situations.

56. Set the story in a well-known place, leveraging imaginative memory for the particulars.

57. Incorporate real-time sporting events into story environments.

Artificial Intelligence

Libraries: Story environment designers will be able to use artificial intelligence (or AI) to create interesting environments and characters to populate them.

One of the major goals of AI is a computer program that can carry on a text chat that is indistinguishable from that of a living person. Despite the serious attention of a lot of very thoughtful people, progress towards this goal has been agonizingly slow.

Some people argue that the very idea of AI is a moving target, because once a computer is able to do something well, we cease calling that activity "intelligent." The logical result of this argument is computers will never manage to step over the magical (though invisible and blurry) line from mechanical device to sentient being, because no matter what advances we manage to achieve with software, human pride will cause us to keep moving the finish line. I have some sympathy for this point of view, but we're so far from the goal right now that it's premature to draw any conclusions.

Despite some impressive achievements in some areas, it would be hard to make a case that contemporary computer software is intelligent in a general sense. Computers have been programmed to excel at a wide variety of games from Go to chess, and expert systems are available for a staggering variety of traditional tasks, from medical diagnosis to air traffic scheduling. Computer systems let us do things that we just wouldn't be able to manage without their computational power, from safe spaceflight to the design of massive skyscrapers.

Yet computers are still pretty lousy at emulating human beings. They lack reasonable emotional behavior, common sense, a knowledge of the world, and many other large and small elements of human personality that let us know when we're talking to a real person, even if we're doing nothing but simply typing back and forth. This will gradually change as computer scientists, psychologists, and others continue to work on the problem. Slowly, computer-generated characters will seem increasingly human and robust. But for the time being, they're not even close.

In the meantime, AI can offer us general-purpose tools and also special-purpose tools for particular applications.

There's a lot of power to be found in building up libraries of general-purpose routines. For those times when a general approach is sufficient, we can just grab one, plug it into the story environment, and move on. This adaptibility can lead to designs that are much more complex and rich than would be possible if designers had to create and implement everything from scratch.

The range of what's possible to provide in this way is huge, from the physics of how the world works to the style of the camera that's used to create the graphics for players. Library modules can help environment designers enhance their work with elements like music, realistic motion, weather, ambience, and secondary action. AI can also provide generic human behaviors, as long as the people aren't expected to have individual, sustained personalities.

We can do all sorts of unexpected things with such libraries. For example, with a good weather system we could let in-story composers create symphonies of weather. Just as composers today create parts for different instruments, so too could a weather composer write parts for clouds and rain, sun and wind. Crowd-control systems let us choreograph dances for thousands of people, and with the ability to control gravity, we could invent all kinds of new games.

Designers can apply these general-purpose solutions to unexpected types of problems. For example, we might develop a rich model of predator and prey mechanics on an island, and then use it to model the flow of goods in a chain store.

People: A really good simulation of a person is far away. We can create an interesting character if we are able to script everything he says and does, but if the player has the chance for a natural free-form conversation, he's going to see through the illusion quickly. We may be able to get some traction on narrow simulations of specific types of people. Such stock characters will need to provide some form of customization so that they don't all look the same, and they will have to be used in limited domanis.

If we're going to use the "bored teenaged girl" stock character, we need to put her in a place where she will never be expected to exceed her very narrow performance abilities. Even better, we should make sure she's always in a position where those limited abilities make sense.

So if we use this stock character as a coat checker in a busy nightclub, then we're in good shape: players' interactions with her will typically be short, and if anyone does try to initiate a conversation, he won't be surprised when he's rebuffed with ennui and condescension.

High-level control: We can use simple personalities in another way, by putting the player in control. Players can specify how a character is to behave by using general-purpose tools for specifying the character's mood.

Players can move emotion sliders to explicitly control the mood and personality of their on-screen characters, which will affect how they move, talk, and react. As AI techniques improve, the computer simulation can take on more and more qualities in itself. Eventually we'll be able to do away with the sliders and deduce player intentions from their tone of voice and body language. Ultimately we could reach the level of living masks, where players are simply themselves, yet appear to the world as the fully-realized character designed by the author for that environment.

Plots: Computer-generated plots and story structures are barely off the ground today. Just as AI characters will need to be in the background for a long time to come, so too will computer-generated plots. We may find it useful to let the computer develop and maintain little sub-plots or secondary stories. Like computer characters, the nature of such computer plots would need to be narrowly defined by the author of the environment, and used mostly as decoration or enhancement, rather than the main focus.

Such side plots could derive from what players do in the game. Wirth uses the term *reincorporation* to describe the act of bringing up something that happened earlier and including it in new material [142]. Reincorporation is a powerful tool; even the original *Eliza* program would save some of your responses and then bring them back up again later, implying that it had been paying attention to you and was curious about you. This reincorporation may prove to be fertile ground for experimenting with computer-generated plots: an author can create a system that will occasionally reincorporate our previous actions and use them to drive some small sub-plot that feels interesting because it's a direct result of what we've done before.

Genre: When we choose entertainment, we often make our selection based on several criteria, including genre. When we're in the mood for adventure, we probably won't curl up with a quiet romantic story, and if we're looking for a historical drama, we probably won't select a slapstick comedy. For the same reasons, players should be able to control the genre of a piece. Just as a set of sliders can specify the mood of an on-screen character, so too could we provide the ability to set the mood of the side stories that are generated on the fly. The plots could be created by using a little of this genre, and a little of that one, so the player could cook up what he's in the mood for. It may even be possible to have those side stories shared among many players, yet viewed by each one differently. So the same events could be presented to one player as though they were a coming-of-age story, while another player might see them as part of a teenage horror film.

Auto summaries: AI can also be used to help people come up to speed on stories that are already in progress, review what's already happened, or just catch up on something they've missed or forgotten. Rather than replay the entire histories, we can develop tools to provide automatic summaries. These might be as simple as a string of extracted bits of media (like the short "Our story so far" segments at the start of some television shows), or as complex as a computer-generated narrative description of what's gone on, with newly-created sound and graphics to make the events appear to belong together.

AI Experiments

58. Create general-purpose AI libraries for physics, motion, weather, music, sound, camera control, and other problems.

59. Give general-purpose AI to players for their own use in story environments.

60. Give players the chance to control largely autonomous characters through high-level mood and personality controls.

61. Approximate living masks as well as possible, so that players can control their characters without explicitly referring to those controls.

62. Create stock characters and put them in supporting positions that are sufficiently constrained that they can be mistaken for real people.

63. Use computer plotting to create small sub-plots to provide ornamentation for the main story, and give players the pleasure of seeing their choices reincorporated into the story.

64. Provide controls for players to select the genre of dynamically-created subplots.

65. Present stories using the type of genre selected by the player.

66. Provide auto-summaries of an evolving story.

Creatures

The animal point of view: Who among us hasn't watched a bird soaring gracefully through the sky and wondered what it would be like to be inside the bird's head, seeing with its eyes, feeling an innate conviction that sailing through skies is as safe as walking down a street, and that every tree is a potential home?

Many of us feel an affinity with animals. We wonder what goes on inside the minds of dogs and cats, we try to imagine what fish think about all day, and we dream of what whales might be singing to one another over long, deep miles of cold ocean.

Telling stories through the eyes of animals is a staple of fiction. Sometimes the animals are thinly-disguised human beings, cast into their roles to make satirical or oblique points, as in the novel *Animal Farm*. And sometimes the animals are simply animals, their story providing us a possible glimpse into how they might see the world, as in the novel *Watership Down*. Stories told from an animal's point of view can be appealing and interesting for children, adults, or both.

Animals probably have different priorities than we do, and they certainly have very different resources and abilities. Outside of science fiction, animals provide us with what are probably the most foreign points of view that are still comprehensible to us.

Animals give us a different perspective on the world we share with them. Entire populations can be wiped out by natural phenomena like hurricanes and forest fires, man-made events like giant oil slicks and hunting, and environmental changes like dam construction and oil pipelines. They can also provide a perspective, albeit imaginary, on our everyday lives: a dog may not understand why we think we need a new car when the old one is working fine.

Story environments can help us see the world from the point of view of animals by putting us in their position. Computers can help us do this even more literally than a book, providing us with 3D graphics that show us what a dog or cat sees. These synthetic images can go beyond just picking an unusual point of view, and actually show us what an animal could be seeing, based on what we know of its visual systems. A dog's view would be restricted to black and white, and a cat's view would fuzz out things that are standing still but see exaggerated effects of motion. We could fly like a hawk, sharing its amazing razor-sharp vision for small animals running on the ground. As a bat, we could learn to navigate with sound rather than sight.

Animals can give us access to parts of the world that our senses aren't able to pick up. For example, sharks detect their prey from the tiny variations in the Earth's magnetic field that are created by swimming fish. We could find a way to turn that knowledge into something that we could sense, helping us get an idea of how a shark finds its way.

It would be interesting to enter a story environment where we were animals, able to do anything they can do, but at the same time subject to the same limitations. I expect we would take some liberties with reality, though, and provide some way for players to communicate with each other using human language. Dogs may be able to figure out what's going on with barks and yelps, but we'd probably have a hard time with that vocabulary.

The animal point of view can also be much simpler than our own, which can make the artificial intelligence problem easier for computer-controlled characters. As we saw in the discussion of Peedy the Parrot in Chapter 12, we're willing to tolerate unintelligent behavior from animals, because our expectations for their intelligence are very low in the first place.

Society and conflict: Though some animals are loners, many animals travel in groups. We could join a herd of buffalo as they march from one plain to another, or become part of a flock of geese heading south for the winter. Story conflicts would come from the natural tensions between individuals in a group, perhaps including issues like leadership and direction, as well as dealing with the rest of the natural and human-made world along the way.

Any genre of fiction could be adapted into an animal world. We could see conflicts between animals of the same species fighting over resources, as one pack of leopards protects its hunting grounds from another pack. Or the conflicts can be between traditional predators and prey: one group of players could be a herd of zebra trying to get home, and another a group of lions that are hungry and out for food. The many predator-prey relations in the world, from eagle and mouse to bear and salmon, offer a wide variety of ready-made conflicts rich with dramatic opportunities.

Animals are able to take our imaginations to places that are inaccessible to us. Birds can fly, mice can squeeze through tiny holes, and urban cats can explore nooks and crannies of cities that have become inaccessible to people. By taking on the roles of these animals, we can see our own world in new and revealing ways.

Creature Experiments

67. Offer players the chance to enter the mind of an animal.

68. Give players a chance to experience the sensory world as animals do.

69. Provide players with the chance to communicate as animals do, by using sounds, body gestures, and other natural languages.

70. Create stories around conflicts between members of the same group, or between competitive groups, within the same species.

71. Create stories that pit one group of animals against another, perhaps those in classic predator-prey relationships to each other.

72. Give players tools to see their own world through an animal's eyes.

Looking Forward

One of the pleasures of thinking about story environments is that everything is still wide open: we haven't even begun to scratch the surface of what's possible.

This chapter presents only a few starting points for creating story environments that people can visit and spend time in.

Any one of these experiments can be the seed for a great new kind of participatory experience that gives people a chance to explore their own worlds, and those of their neighbors next door and around the world, living today or a thousand years ago. Story environments can captivate our imaginations, challenge our minds, and expand our hearts, while we spend time in the company of other people that we know and enjoy, and others we've not yet met.

I think that there's every reason to be optimistic about developing this new form of story, participation, and expression, and that it will eventually be capable of carrying significant human meaning.

This is a very exciting time for storytellers who want to embrace the potential of inviting their audiences to actively engage in their stories. There are challenges everywhere we look, and fascinating new questions are popping up faster than we can answer them.

With imagination and hard work, we will be able to create story environments that are full of people, stories, and fun.

Bibliography

General References

[1] Espen J. Aarseth. *Cybertext: Perspectives on Ergodic Literature.* Baltimore, MD: Johns Hopkins University Press, 1997.

[2] Stephen E. Ambrose. *Undaunted Courage: Meriwether Lewis, Thomas Jefferson, and the Opening of the American West.* New York: Simon & Schuster, 1996.

[3] Aristotle. *The Poetics of Aristotle, Translated by Preston H. Epps.* University of North Carolina Press, 1967.

[4] Mark Armstrong. "NBC Puts Competition on Ice". February 22, 2002. See http://www.eonline.com/News/Items/0,1,9563,00.html.

[5] The British Go Association. "The British Go Journal Glossary". See http://www.britgo.org/bgj/glossary.html.

[6] Robert Axelrod. *The Evolution of Cooperation.* New York: Basic Books, 1985.

[7] Gene Ball, Dan Ling, David Kurlander, John Miller, David Pugh, Tim Skelly, Andy Stankosky, David Thiel, Maarten Van Dantzich,

and Trace Wax. "Lifelike Computer Characters: the Persona project at Microsoft Research". In Jeffrey M. Bradshaw, editor, *Software Agents.* AAAI Press, 1997.

[8] Matt Berger. "Video Game Executives Predict Shakeout". *IDG News Service,* October 2002. See http://www.idg.com.sg/ idgwww.nsf/unidlookup/ 2806917A6C6219AD48256C60000909D8 ?OpenDocument.

[9] Erik Bethke. *Game Development and Production.* Plano, TX: Wordware Publishing, 2003.

[10] Kathy Biro. "Delivering Customer Value Through the World Wide Web". In Stephen P. Bradley and Richard L. Nolan, editors, *Sense and Respond: Capturing Value in the Network Era.* Harvard Business School, 1998.

[11] Charles Kasiel Bliss. *Semantography (Blissymbolics).* Sydney, Australia: Semantography Publications, 1965.

[12] Theobald Boehm. *The Flute and Flute Playing.* New York: Dover Publications, 1964.

[13] Jay David Bolter. *Writing Space: Computers, Hypertext, and the Remediation of Print, 2nd Edition.* Mahwah, NJ: Lawrence Erlbaum Associates, 2001.

[14] Richard Borovoy, Fred Martin, Mitchel Resnick, and Brian Silverman. "Groupware: Name Tags That Tell About Relationships". *Proceedings of ACM 1998 Conference on Human Factors in Computing Systems,* 1998.

[15] Paige Braddock. *Jane's World.* United Media, 1999–present. See http://www.unitedmedia.com/comics/janesworld/.

[16] Valentino Braitenberg. *Vehicles: Experiments in Synthetic Psychology.* Cambridge, MA: MIT Press, 1986.

[17] Tom O'Connor Bray. One-Wall Handball in Mexico, 2000.

[18] James Brown and Bob McIvor. "Loglan". See http://www.loglan.org.

[19] Katherine Bryant. "The Language of Flowers".
See http://www.cybercom.net/~klb/flowers.html.

[20] Vannevar Bush. "As We May Think". *The Atlantic Monthly*,
176(1):101–108, July 1945. See http://www.press.umich.edu
/jep/works/vbush/.

[21] John Cage. "Imaginary Landscape No. 4", 1951. John Cage Volume
4, Music for Merce Cunningham, New York: Mode Records.

[22] John Cage. *Music Walk: For One or More Pianists, at a Single Piano,
Using Also Radio and/or Recordings*, 1990. John Cage: Complete Piano Music, Vol. 4 (Pieces 1950-1960), New York: MD&G Records.

[23] Joseph Campbell. *The Hero With A Thousand Faces*. Princeton,
NJ: Princeton University Press, 1972.

[24] Lewis Carroll. *Pillow Problems and a Tangled Tale*. New York:
Dover Publications, 1976.

[25] William Chamberlain. *The Policeman's Beard is Half Constructed:
Computer Prose and Poetry by Racter*. New York: Warner Books,
1984.

[26] *Choose Your Own Adventure Series*, 1960–present. New York: Bantam Books.

[27] Cinematrix. *The Cinematrix Interactive Entertainment System*, 2000.
See http://www.cinematrix.com.

[28] Microsoft Corporation. *Microsoft Office XP*, 2002.
See http://www.microsoft.com.

[29] Viewpoint Corporation. Viewpoint Catalog.
See http://www.viewpoint.com/vp/index.jsp.

[30] Paul Costa and Robert McCrae. *NEO Personality Inventory*, 1991.
published by the US National Institutes of Health.

[31] Chris Crawford. *The Art of Computer Game Design*. Los Angeles: MindSim, 1982. See http://www.mindsim.com/MindSim
/Corporate/artCGD.pdf.

[32] Chris Crawford. *The Art of Interactive Design: A Euphonious and Illuminating Guide to Building Successful Software*. San Francisco, CA: No Starch Press, 2002.

[33] Chris Crawford. *Chris Crawford on Game Design*. Indianapolis, IN: New Riders, 2003.

[34] John Cresswell and John Hartley. *Teach Yourself Esperanto*. Columbus, OH: McGraw-Hill, 1992.

[35] Mihaly Csikszentmihalyi. *Flow: The Psychology of Optimal Experience*. New York: HarperCollins, 1991.

[36] Pavel Curtis. "Mudding: Social Phenomena in Text-Based Virtual Realities". *Proceedings of the 1992 Conference on the Directions and Implications of Advanced Computing*, May 1992.

[37] Ryan S. Dancey. "Adventure Game Industry Market Research Summary (RPGs) V1.0", 2000. See http://www.thegpa.org /wotc_demo.shtml.

[38] Erik D. Demaine, Susan Hohenberger, and David Liben-Nowell. "Tetris is Hard, Even to Approximate". Technical report, Massachusetts Institute of Technology, 2002. See http://xxx.lanl.gov/abs/cs.CC/0210020.

[39] Rusel DeMaria and Johnny L. Wilson. *High Score! The Illustrated History of Electronic Games*. New York: McGraw-Hill/Osborne, 2002.

[40] Discreet. *Character Studio 3*, 2002. See http://www.discreet.com.

[41] Avinash K. Dixit and Barry J. Nalebuff. *Thinking Strategically*. New York: W.W. Norton, 1991.

[42] Clark Dodsworth, editor. *Digital Illusion: Entertaining the Future With High Technology*. Boston: Addison-Wesley, 1997.

[43] Steven M. Drucker, Li wei He, Michael Cohen, Curtis Wong, and Anoop Gupta. "Spectator Games: A New Entertainment For Modality Networked Multiplayer Games". August, 2000. See http://research.microsoft.com/~sdrucker/papers/spectator.pdf.

[44] Jody Duncan. "Star Wars Episode II: Attack of the Clones: Love & War". *Cinefex*, 90, July 2002.

[45] Lajos Egri. *The Art of Dramatic Writing*. New York: Simon & Schuster, 1977.

[46] Epic Megagames, Inc. *Unreal Engine*, 2002. See http://www.unreal.com.

[47] U.S. Soccer Federation. *The Official Rules of Soccer*. Chicago: Triumph Books, 2002. See http://www.mlsnet.com/about/rules /overview.html.

[48] Joe Flint. "TV Football's MVP–Yellow First-Down Line". *The Wall Street Journal Online*, January 26 2000.

[49] Joe Fordham. "The Lord of the Rings: The Two Towers: Middle-Earth Strikes Back". *Cinefex*, 92, January 2003.

[50] Jon Franklin. *Writing for Story: Craft Secrets of Dramatic Nonfiction by a Two-Time Pulitzer Prize Winner*. London: Plume Books, 1986.

[51] James N. Frey. *How to Write A Damn Good Novel*. New York: St. Martin's Press, 1987.

[52] Malcolm Gladwell. *The Tipping Point: How Little Things Can Make a Big Difference*. New York: Little, Brown, and Company, 2000.

[53] James Gleick. *Chaos: Making a New Science*. New York: Penguin USA, 1998.

[54] David Goetzl and Wayne Friedman. "Highest-Priced TV Show: Friends". October 3, 2002. See http://www.adage.com /news.cms?newsId=36204.

[55] Peter Gordon and Mike Shenk. *Solitaire Battleships : 108 Challenging Logic Puzzles*. London: Sterling Publications, 1998.

[56] Harry Gottlieb. "The Jack Principles of the Interactive Conversation Interface". Technical report, Jellyvision, Inc., 1997–2002.

475

[57] Alan Gould and Carl Pennypacker. "The Hands-On Universe Program". See http://handsonuniverse.org.

[58] S. Grand, D. Cliff, and A. Malhotra. "Creatures: Artificial Life Autonomous Software Agents for Home Entertainment". *Proceedings of the First International Conference on Autonomous Agents*, pages 22–29, 1997.

[59] Justin Hall. "Be an iMode Mifune?". *Wireless Gaming Review*, February 2002. See http://www.wirelessgamingreview.com/reviews /samurai021402.php.

[60] Oakley Hall. *The Art & Craft of Novel Writing*. Cincinnati, OH: Writer's Digest Books, 1989.

[61] Charles Hampden-Turner. *Maps of the Mind: Charts and Concepts of the Mind and its Labyrinths*. New York: Collier Books, 1982.

[62] Dap Hartmann. "Amsterdamse Supercomputer Lost Bordspel Awari Op". *Het NRC Handelsblad*, September 2002. See http://awari.cs.vu.nl/newspapers/nrc.jpg.

[63] David Howard and Edward Mabley. *The Tools of Screenwriting*. New York: St. Martin's Press, 1995.

[64] Interactive Digitial Software Association (IDSA). "Essential Facts About the Computer and Video Game Industry". See http://www.idsa.com/2002SalesData.html.

[65] Interactive Digitial Software Association (IDSA). "Game Sales and Graphs, 2001". See http://www.idsa.com/2001SalesData.html.

[66] Interactive Digitial Software Association (IDSA). IDSA Web homepage. See http://www.idsa.com.

[67] Curious Labs Inc. *Poser 5*, 2002. See http://www.curiouslabs.com.

[68] Eastgate Systems Inc. *Storyspace 2: A Hypertext Tool for Writers and Readers*, 2000.

[69] Lego Inc. *Lego MindStorms*, 1998. (See www.lego.com).

[70] Timothy Ingen-Housz. "The Elephant's Memory: In Search of a Pictorial Language". *Learning Technology Review*, Spring/Summer 1999. See http://www.apple.com/education/LTReview/spring99/elephant.

[71] Yukari Iwatani. "Love: Japanese Style". *Wired*, June 11 1998. See http://www.wired.com/news/culture/0,1284,12899,00.html.

[72] June and William Noble. *Steal this Plot: A Writer's Guide to Story Structure and Plagiarism*. Middlebury, VT: Paul S. Eriksson, 1985.

[73] Geoff Keighley. "Could This Be The Next Disney?". *Business 2.0*, December 2002.

[74] Steven L. Kent. "Making an MMOG for the Masses". October 10, 2003. See http://www.gamespy.com/amdmmog/week3/.

[75] Dan Koeppel. "Massive Attack". *Popular Science*, 261(6), 2002.

[76] Elisabeth Kubler-Ross. *On Death and Dying*. Hampshire, UK: Macmillan Publishers, 1969.

[77] Ray Kurzweil. *The Age of Spiritual Machines: When Computers Exceed Human Intelligence*. New York: Penguin USA, 2000.

[78] George P. Landow. *Hypertext 2.0: The Convergence of Contemporary Critical Theory and Technology, 2nd Edition*. Baltimore, MD: Johns Hopkins University Press, 1997.

[79] R. Raymond Lang. *A Formal Model for Simple Narratives*. PhD thesis, Tulane University, Department of Electrical Engineering and Computer Science, 1997.

[80] Duncan Lau. "Hungary's Hot Streak", 2000. See http://www.worldcup101.com/history/1954.html.

[81] Brenda Laurel. *Computers As Theatre*. Boston: Addison-Wesley, 1993.

[82] Graham Lawton. "Let's Get Personal". *New Scientist*, 179, September 2003.

[83] "The Loebner Prize". See http://www.loebner.net/Prizef/loebner-prize.html.

[84] Mary Luckhurst and Chloe Veltman, editors. *On Acting: Interviews with Actors*. London: Faber and Faber, 1988.

[85] Dianne Lynch. "Companions or Commercials? IM Bot Buddies Offer Kids a Computer Companion, But Also Push Products". *ABC News*, April 2002. See http://abcnews.go.com/sections/scitech /WiredWomen/wiredwomen020411.html.

[86] Donald Marinelli. "Entertaining the Future". October 24, 1999. See http://cbi.gsia.cmu.edu/Conferences/1999SFconference/Marinelli/marinellipresentation.htm.

[87] Abraham H. Maslow and Richard Lowry. *Towards a Psychology of Being, 3rd Edition*. Hoboken, NJ: John Wiley & Sons, 1998.

[88] Scott McCloud. *Understanding Comics*. San Francisco: Kitchen Sink Press, 1994.

[89] Pamela McCorduck. *Aaron's Code*. New York: W.H. Freeman, 1991.

[90] Robert McKee. *Story*. New York: HarperCollins, 1997.

[91] Marshall McLuhan. *Understanding Media: The Extensions of Man*. Cambridge, MA: MIT Press, 1964.

[92] Mark Stephen Meadows. *Pause & Effect*. Indianapolis, IN: New Riders, 2002.

[93] H.L. Mencken. *The American Language*. New York: Knopf, 1921.

[94] Ben Mezrich. "Hacking Las Vegas: The Inside Story of the MIT Blackjack Team's Conquest of the Casinos". *Wired Magazine*, September 2002.

[95] Oskar Morgenstern and John Von Neumann. *Theory of Games and Economic Behavior*. Princeton, NJ: Princeton University Press, 1947.

[96] Mark Mowrey. "Street Talk: The Five-Year Game Plan". *Red Herring*, September 2001. See http://www.redherring.com /investor/2002/09/gameplan091102.html.

[97] Jessica Mulligan and Bridgette Patrovsky. *Developing Online Games: An Insider's Guide.* Indianapolis, IN: New Riders, 2003.

[98] Janet Murray. *Hamlet on the Holodeck: The Future of Narrative in Cyberspace.* Detroit, MI: Free Press, 1997.

[99] Ted Nelson. *Literary Machines.* Sausalito, CA: Mindful Press, 1987.

[100] CNN News. "3D Movies Still Jump Out Of the Screen". November 29, 2002. See http://www.cnn.com/2002/SHOWBIZ /Movies/11/29/3d.movies.ap/index.html.

[101] CNN News. "Canadian Skaters Get Gold". *CNN Online*, February 2002. (www.cnn.com/2002/US/02/15/oly.skate.row).

[102] PR Newswire. "Xbox Live Starter Kits Virtually Sell Out in First Week of Sales". November 22, 2002. See http://www.microsoft.com/presspass/press/2002/Nov02/11-22Xbox LiveStarterPR.asp.

[103] Numerical Designs, Ltd. *NetImmerse*, 1998. (See www.ndl.com).

[104] University of Information. *Minnesota Multiphasic Personality Inventory-2.* See http://www1.umn.edu/mmpi/.

[105] Editors of Sporting News. *Official Major League Baseball Rules Book, 2003 Edition.* New York: Sporting News/McGraw-Hill, 2003.

[106] Editors of Sporting News. *Official NBA Rules Book, 2003 Edition.* New York: Sporting News/McGraw-Hill, 2003. See http://www.nba.com/analysis/rules_index.html.

[107] Editors of The American Heritage Dictionaries, editor. *The American Heritage Dictionary of the English Language, 3rd Edition.* Boston: Houghton Mifflin Company, 1992.

[108] "Official Rules of the United States Racquetball Association". See http://www.usra.org/usra/pub&ref/01rules.htm.

[109] David Parlett. *Oxford History of Board Games*. Oxford, UK: Oxford University Press, 1999.

[110] Canz Photographers. Texture CDs. See http://www.canz.biz /index.html.

[111] Steven Pinker. *The Language Instinct: How the Mind Creates Language*. New York: HarperCollins, 2000.

[112] Detroit Pistons. Detroit Pistons History. Official Website of the Detroit Pistons See http://www.nba.com/pistons/history /team_history.html.

[113] Mantis Motion Productions. Clip Motion. See http://www.mantismotion.com.

[114] Cindi Rice. "The Business of RPGs: The Role of Market Research". Technical report, Wizards of the Coast, 2000. See http://www.wizards.com/dnd/article.asp?x=dnd/br/br20010323a.

[115] The Adrian & Blissfield Rail Road. *Murder Mystery Dinner Train*, 2001.

[116] Andrew Rollings and Ernest Adams. *Andrew Rollings and Ernest Adams on Game Design*. Indianapolis, IN: New Riders, 2003.

[117] Emil H. Rothe. *Baseball's Most Historic Games 1876–1993*. Boulder, CO: Rothe, 1993.

[118] Katie Salen and Eric Zimmerman. *Rules of Play: Game Design Fundamentals*. Cambridge, MA: MIT Press, 2003.

[119] Tom Sawyer and Arthur David Weingarten. *Plots Unlimited*. Malibu, CA: Ashleywilde, Ltd., 1994.

[120] Jonathan Schaeffer. *One Jump Ahead: Challenging Human Supremacy in Checkers*. New York: Springer-Verlag, 1997.

[121] Ben Scheiderman. *Designing the User Interface, 3rd Edition*. Boston: Addison-Wesley, 1997.

[122] Jesse Schell and Joe Shochet. "Designing Interactive Theme Park Rides: Lessons From Disney's Battle for the Buccaneer Gold". *Gamasutra.com*, July 2001. (www.gamasutra.com/features /20010706/schell_01.htm).

[123] Daniel Scuka. "A Weather-Affected, Massively Multiplayer, Java-Based i-Mode Game". *Japan, Inc.*, July 2001. See http://www .japaninc.net/mag/comp/2001/07/jul01_filter_game.html.

[124] Martin Shubik. "The Dollar Auction Game: A Paradox in Non-cooperative Behavior and Escalation". *Journal of Conflict Resolution*, 15:109–111, 1971.

[125] Marc Smith and Peter Kollock, editors. *Communities in Cyberspace*. London: Routledge Press, 1999.

[126] BBC Staff. "Gamers Get Into The Zone". *BBC News*, July 2002. See http://news.bbc.co.uk/2/hi/technology/2154092.htm.

[127] CBC Staff. "Degrassi TV Website". See http://www.degrassi.tv.

[128] Microsoft Staff. "The Internet Gaming Zone". See http://www.igz.com.

[129] NPD Staff. "NPD Funworld Essential Market Information". See http://www.npdfunworld.com.

[130] Christopher Stapleton, Charlie Hughes, and Michael Moshell. Mixed Reality and the Interactive Imagination. *Proceedings of The First Swedish-American Workshop on Modeling and Simulation (SAWMAS-2002)*, 2002.

[131] Constantine Stanislavski. *An Actor Prepares*. New York: Theatre Arts Books, 2002.

[132] A. Stern, A. Frank, and B. Resner. "Virtual Petz: A Hybrid Approach to Creating Autonomous, Lifelike Dogz and Catz". *Proceedings of the Second International Conference on Autonomous Agents*, pages 334–335, 1998.

[133] Dean Takahashi. "The Games Industry Still Has Much To Prove". *Red Herring*, May 2002. See http://www.redherring.com /insider/2002/0529/tech-games052902.html.

[134] Christopher Vogler. *The Writer's Journey: Mythic Structure for Writers, 2nd Edition.* Studio City, CA: Michael Wiese Productions, 1998.

[135] Stuart H. Walker. *Winning: The Psychology of Competition.* New York: W.W. Norton, 1980.

[136] Richard S. Wallace. "Alice Chatbot". See http://www.alicebot.org.

[137] Noah Wardrip-Fruin and Nick Montfort. *The New Media Reader.* Cambridge, MA: MIT Press, 2003.

[138] Joseph Weizenbaum. *Computer Power and Human Reason: From Judgment To Calculation.* New York: W.H. Freeman, 1977.

[139] J. D. Williams. *The Compleat Strategyst: Being a Primer on the Theory of Games of Strategy.* New York: Dover Publications, 1986.

[140] Kit Williams. *Masquerade: The Complete Book With the Answer Explained.* New York: Workman Publishing, 1983.

[141] Terry Winograd. *Understanding Natural Language.* San Francisco: Academic Press, 1972.

[142] Jeff Wirth. *Interactive Acting: Acting, Improvisation, and Interacting for Audience Participatory Theatre.* Fall Creek, OR: Fall Creek Press, 1994.

[143] Maynard Frank Wolfe and Rube Goldberg. *Rube Goldberg: Inventions.* New York, Simon & Schuster, 2000.

[144] Curtis Wong. *A Passion For Art: Renoir, Cezanne, Matisse, and Dr. Barnes,* 1995.

[145] Karen Wright. "Winning Brain Waves". *Discover,* 22(3), March 2001.

[146] Will Wright and Celia Pearce. "Sims, BattleBots, Cellular Automata God and Go". *Game Studies,* 2(1), July 2002. See http://gamestudies.org/0102/pearce/.

[147] Jeffrey Zaslow. "If TiVo Thinks You Are Gay, Here's How to Set It Straight". *The Wall Street Journal Online*, 2002. November 26, 2002, See http://online.wsj.com/article_email/0,,SB1038261 936872356908,00.html.

Films and Plays

[148] *The 39 Steps*. Written by Charles Bennett, Alma Reville, and Ian Hay (from a novel by John Buchan), directed by Alfred Hitchcock, 1935.

[149] *A Bug's Life*. Written by Andrew Stanton, Donald McEnery, and Bob Shaw (from a story by John Lasseter, Andrew Stanton, Joe Ranft, Geefwee Boedoe, Jason Katz, Jorgen Klubien, Robert Lence, and David Reynolds), directed by John Lasseter and Andrew Stanton, 1998.

[150] *The Adventures of Robin Hood*. Written by Norman Reilly Raine and Seton I. Miller, directed by Michael Curtiz and William Keighley, 1938.

[151] *The African Queen*. Written by James Agee and John Huston (from a novel by C.S. Forester), directed by John Huston, 1951.

[152] *Artificial Intelligence: AI*. Written by Ian Watson and Steven Speilberg (from a short story by Brian Aldiss), directed by Steven Spielberg, 2001.

[153] *Aïda*. Libretto by Antonio Ghislanzoni, music by Giuseppe Verdi, 1871.

[154] *Alien*. Written by Dan O'Bannon (from a story by Dan O'Bannon and Ronald Shusett), directed by Ridley Scott, 1979.

[155] *All About Eve*. Written and directed by Joseph L. Mankiewicz, 1950.

[156] *Le Fabuleux Destin d'Amélie Poulain (Amelie)*. Written by Guillaume Laurant and Jean-Pierre Jeunet, directed by Jean-Pierre Jeunet, 2001.

[157] *American Beauty*. Written by Alan Ball, directed by Sam Mendes, 1999.

[158] *An Enemy of the People.* Written by Henrik Ibsen, 1923.

[159] *Annie Hall.* Written by Woody Allen and Marshall Brickman, directed by Woody Allen, 1977.

[160] *Antz.* Written by Todd Alcott, Chris Weitz, and Paul Weitz, directed by Eric Darnell and Tim Johnson, 1998.

[161] *Apollo 13.* Written by William Broyles Jr. and Al Reinert (from a book by Jim Lovell and Jeffrey Kluger), directed by Ron Howard, 1995.

[162] *Atlantis: The Lost Empire.* Written by Tab Murphy and David Reynolds (from a story by Tab Murphy, Gary Trousdale, Kirk Wise, Bryce Zabel, and Jackie Zabel), directed by Gary Trousdale and Kirk Wise, 2001.

[163] *Backdraft.* Written by Gregory Widen, directed by Ron Howard, 1991.

[164] *Beauty and the Beast.* Written by Linda Woolverton (from a story by Roger Allers), directed by Gary Trousdale and Kirk Wise, 1991.

[165] *Being There.* Written by Jerzy Kosinki, directed by Hal Ashby, 1979.

[166] *Best In Show.* Written by Christopher Guest and Eugene Levy, directed by Christopher Guest, 2000.

[167] *The Birth of a Nation.* Written by Thomas F. Dixon Jr, D.W. Griffith, and Frank E. Woods (from a book and play by Thomas F. Dixon Jr.), directed by D.W. Griffith, 1915.

[168] *Blade Runner.* Written by Hampton Fancher and David Peoples (from a novel by Philip K. Dick), directed by Ridley Scott, 1982.

[169] *The Blair Witch Project.* Written and directed by Daniel Myrick and Eduardo Sánchez, 1999.

[170] *Body Heat.* Written and directed by Lawrence Kasdan, 1981.

[171] *Bound.* Written and directed by Andy Wachowski and Larry Wachowski, 1996.

[172] *Brazil*. Written by Terry Gilliam, Charles McKeown, and Tom Stoppard, directed by Terry Gilliam, 1985.

[173] *Broadcast News*. Written and directed by James L. Brooks, 1987.

[174] *Bullets Over Broadway*. Written by Woody Allen and Douglas McGrath, directed by Woody Allen, 1994.

[175] *Bwana Devil*. Written and directed by Arch Oboler (based on the book "The Man-Eaters of Tsavo and Other African Adventures" by J.H. Patterson), 1952.

[176] *Casablanca*. Written by Julius J. Epstein, Philip G. Epstein, and Howard Koch (from a play by Murray Burnett and Joan Allison), directed by Michael Curtiz, 1942.

[177] *Cast Away*. Written by William Broyles Jr., directed by Robert Zemeckis, 2000.

[178] *Chinatown*. Written by Robert Towne, directed by Roman Polanski, 1974.

[179] *Citizen Kane*. Written by Herman J. Mankiewicz and Orson Welles, directed by Orson Welles, 1941.

[180] *Contact*. Written by James V. Hart and Michael Goldenberg (from a novel by Carl Sagan), directed by Robert Zemeckis, 1997.

[181] *Cool Hand Luke*. Written by Donn Pearce and Frank Pierson, directed by Stuart Rosenberg, 1967.

[182] *Cyrano de Bergerac*. Written by Edmond Rostand, 1897.

[183] *Dave*. Written by Gary Ross, directed by Ivan Reitman, 1993.

[184] *Dead Man Walking*. Written by Tim Robbins (from a book by Helen Prejean), directed by Tim Robbins, 1995.

[185] *Die Hard*. Written by Jeb Stuart and Steven E. de Souza (from a novel by Roderick Thorp), directed by John McTiernan, 1988.

[186] *Dog Day Afternoon*. Written by Frank Pierson (from an article by P.F. Kluge and Thomas Moore), directed by Sidney Lumet, 1975.

[187] *Dolores Claiborne.* Written by Tony Gilroy (from a novel by Stephen King), directed by Taylor Hackford, 1995.

[188] *Dr. No.* Written by Richard Maibaum, Johanna Harwood, and Berkely Mather (from a novel by Ian Fleming), directed by Terence Young, 1962.

[189] *Dr. Strangelove.* Written by Stanley Kubrick, Terry Southern, and Peter George (from a novel by Peter George), directed by Stanley Kubrick, 1964.

[190] *E.T. the Extra-Terrestrial.* Written by Melissa Mathison, directed by Steven Spielberg, 1982.

[191] *Fatal Attraction.* Written by James Dearden and Nicholas Meyer, directed by Adrian Lyne, 1987.

[192] *Final Fantasy: The Spirits Within.* Written by Hironobu Sakaguchi, Al Reinert, Jeff Vintar, and Jack Fletcher, directed by Hironobu Sakaguchi and Moto Sakakibara, 2000.

[193] *Forrest Gump.* Written by Eric Roth (from a novel by Winston Groom), directed by Robert Zemeckis, 1994.

[194] *Frankenstein.* Written by Francis Edward Faragoh and Garrett Fort, adapted by John L. Balderston (from a play by Peggy Webling based on the novel by Mary Shelley), directed by James Whale, 1931.

[195] *Galaxy Quest.* Written by David Howard and Robert Gordon, directed by Dean Parisot, 1999.

[196] *Geri's Game.* Written and directed by Jan Pinkava, 1997.

[197] *Ghostbusters.* Written by Dan Aykroyd and Harold Ramis, directed by Ivan Reitman, 1984.

[198] *The Godfather.* Written by Francis Ford Coppola and Mario Puzo (from a novel by Mario Puzo), directed by Francis Ford Coppola, 1972.

[199] *Goodfellas.* Written by Nicholas Pileggi and Martin Scorsese, directed by Martin Scorsese, 1990.

[200] *The Graduate*. Written by Calder Willingham and Buck Henry (from a novel by Charles Webb), directed by Mike Nichols, 1967.

[201] *The Great Escape*. Written by James Clavell and W.R. Burnett (from a book by Paul Brickhill), directed by John Sturges, 1963.

[202] *Groundhog Day*. Written by Danny Rubin and Harold Ramis, directed by Harold Ramis, 1993.

[203] *Hamlet*. Written by William Shakespeare, c. 1609.

[204] *The Insider*. Written by Eric Roth and Michael Mann (from an article by Marie Brenner), directed by Michael Mann, 1999.

[205] *Jaws*. Written by Carl Gottlieb (from a novel by Peter Benchley), directed by Steven Spielberg, 1975.

[206] *Jurassic Park*. Written by Michael Crichton and David Koepp (from a novel by Michael Crichton), directed by Steven Spielberg, 1993.

[207] *Key Largo*. Written by Richard Brooks (from a play by Maxwell Anderson), directed by John Huston, 1948.

[208] *King Lear*. Written by William Shakespeare, c. 1608.

[209] *Lawrence of Arabia*. Written by Robert Bolt and Michael Wilson (from writings by T.E. Lawrence), directed by David Lean, 1962.

[210] *Lifeboat*. Written by Ben Hecht (from a story by John Steinbeck and Jo Swerling), directed by Alfred Hitchcock, 1944.

[211] *The Lion King*. Written by Irene Mecchi, Jonathan Roberts, Linda Woolverton, and Jorgen Klubien, directed by Roger Allers and Rob Minkoff 1994.

[212] *The Lord of the Rings: The Fellowship of the Ring*. Written by Frances Walsh, Philippa Boyens and Peter Jackson (from a book by J.R.R. Tolkien), directed by Peter Jackson, 2001.

[213] *The Lord of the Rings: The Two Towers*. Written by Frances Walsh, Philippa Boyens, Stephen Sinclair and Peter Jackson (from a book by J.R.R. Tolkien), directed by Peter Jackson, 2002.

[214] *The Lumière Brothers' First Films.* Written and directed by the Lumiere Brothers, compiled by Bertrand Tavernier, 1996.

[215] *Making FrankenSense of Young Frankenstein.* Written and directed by Patrick Cousans, 1996 (available on the *Young Frankenstein* DVD).

[216] *The Maltese Falcon.* Written by John Huston (from a novel by Dashiell Hammett), directed by John Huston, 1941.

[217] *Mary Poppins.* Written by Bill Walsh and Don DaGradi (based on books by P.L. Travers), music and lyrics by Richard M. Sherman and Robert B. Sherman, directed by Robert Stevenson, 1964.

[218] *The Matrix.* Written and directed by Andy Wachowski and Larry Wachowski, 1999.

[219] *The Matrix Reloaded.* Written and directed by Andy Wachowski and Larry Wachowski, 2003.

[220] *Memento.* Written by Christopher Nolan (from a story by Jonathan Nolan), directed by Christopher Nolan, 2000.

[221] *Midnight Cowboy.* Written by Waldo Salt (from a novel by James Leo Herlihy), directed by John Schlesinger.

[222] *The Miser.* Written by Moliere (Jean-Baptise Paquelin), c. 1668.

[223] *Monsters, Inc.* Written by Robert L. Baird, Jill Culton, Peter Docter, Ralph Eggleston, Dan Gerson, Jeff Pidgeon, Rhett Reese, Jonathan Roberts, and Andrew Stanton, directed by Peter Docter, David Silverman, and Lee Unkrich, 2001.

[224] *Mulan.* Written by Eugenia Bostwick-Singer and Dean DeBlois (from a story by Robert D. San Souci, Rita Hsiao, Chris Sanders, Philip LaZebnik, and Raymond Singer), directed by Tony Bancroft and Barry Cook, 1998.

[225] *Mutiny On the Bounty.* Written by Charles Lederer (from a novel by Charles Nordhoff and James Norman Hall), directed by Lewis Milestone, 1962.

[226] *My Fair Lady.* Written by Alan Jay Lerner (from a play by George Bernard Shaw), directed by George Cukor, 1964.

[227] *North By Northwest.* Written by Ernest Lehman, directed by Alfred Hitchcock, 1959.

[228] *On Golden Pond.* Written by Ernest Thompson, directed by Mark Rydell, 1981.

[229] *One Flew Over the Cuckoo's Nest.* Written by Bo Goldman and Lawrence Hauben (from a novel by Ken Kesey), directed by Milos Forman, 1975.

[230] *Othello.* Written by William Shakespeare, c. 1604.

[231] *The Perfect Storm.* Written by William D. Wittliff (from a book by Sebastian Junger), directed by Wolfgang Petersen 2000.

[232] *Pitch Black.* Written by Jim Wheat, Ken Wheat, and David Twohy, directed by David Twohy, 2000.

[233] *Pygmalion.* Written by George Bernard Shaw, 1916.

[234] *Raging Bull.* Written by Paul Schrader and Mardik Martin (from on a book by Jake LaMotta, Joseph Carter and Peter Savage), directed by Martin Scorsese, 1980.

[235] *Raiders of the Lost Ark.* Written by Lawrence Kasdan, directed by Steven Spielberg, 1981.

[236] *Rain Man.* Written by Ronald Bass and Barry Morrow (from a story by Barry Morrow), directed by Barry Levinson, 1988.

[237] *Rashomon.* Written by Akira Kurosawa and Shinobu Hashimoto (from stories by Ryunosuke Akutagawa), directed by Akira Kurosawa, 1950.

[238] *Romancing the Stone.* Written by Diane Thomas, directed by Robert Zemeckis, 1984.

[239] *Rosencrantz and Guidenstern are Dead.* Written and directed by Tom Stoppard, 1990.

[240] *Run Lola Run.* Written and directed by Tom Tykwer, 1998.

[241] *Same Time, Next Year.* Written by Bernard Slade, premiered 1975, Brooks Atkinson Theatre.

[242] *Saving Private Ryan*. Written by Robert Rodat, directed by Steven Spielberg, 1998.

[243] *The Shining*. Written by Stanley Kubrick and Diane Johnson (from a novel by Stephen King), directed by Stanley Kubrick, 1980.

[244] *The Silence Of The Lambs*. Written by Ted Tally (from a novel by Thomas Harris), directed by Jonathan Demme, 1991.

[245] *Sling Blade*. Written and directed by Billy Bob Thornton, 1996.

[246] *Snow White and the Seven Dwarfs*. Written by Dorothy Ann Blank, Richard Creedon, Merrill De Maris, Otto Englander, Earl Hurd, Dick Rickard, Ted Sears, and Webb Smith (from a story by Jacob Ludwig Carl Grimm and Wilhelm Carl Grimm), directed by David Hand, 1937.

[247] *Speed*. Written by Graham Yost, directed by Jan de Bont, 1994.

[248] *Star Trek: Generations*. Written by Ronald D. Moore and Brannon Braga (from a story by Rick Berman, Ronald D. Moore and Brannon Braga), directed by David Carson 1994.

[249] *Star Wars: Episode I–The Phantom Menace*. Written and directed by George Lucas, 1999.

[250] *Star Wars: Episode II–Attack of the Clones*. Written by George Lucas and Jonathan Hales, directed by George Lucas, 2002.

[251] *Star Wars: Episode IV–A New Hope*. Written and directed by George Lucas, 1977.

[252] *Sweet and Lowdown*. Written and directed by Woody Allen, 1999.

[253] *Taxi Driver*. Written by Paul Schrader, directed by Martin Scorsese, 1976.

[254] *Terminator 2: Judgment Day*. Written by James Cameron and William Wisher Jr., directed by James Cameron, 1991.

[255] *The Threepenny Opera*. Libretto by Bertolt Brecht, music by Kurt Weill, 1928, translated by Marc Blitzstein, 1954.

[256] *Timecode*. Written and directed by Mike Figgis, 2000.

[257] *Titanic*. Written and directed by James Cameron, 1997.

[258] *Tony and Tina's Wedding*. Conceived by Nancy Cassaro, 1988.

[259] *Toy Story*. Written by Joss Whedon, Andrew Standton, Joel Coen, and Alec Sokolow (from a story by John Lasseter, Andrew Stanton, Peter Docter, and Joe Ranft), directed by John Lasseter, 1995.

[260] *Toy Story 2*. Written by Ash Brannon, Andrew Stanton, Rita Hsiao, Doug Chamberlain, and Chris Webb (from a story by John Lasseter, Peter Docter, Ash Brannon, and Andrew Stanton), directed by Ash Brannon, John Lasseter, and Lee Unkrich, 1999.

[261] *Twelve Angry Men*. Written by Reginald Rose, directed by Sidney Lumet, 1957.

[262] *Urbania*. Written by Daniel Reitz and Jon Shear, directed by Jon Shear, 2001.

[263] *The Usual Suspects*. Written by Christopher McQuarrie, directed by Bryan Singer, 1995.

[264] *La Vita è Bella (Life is Beautiful)*. Written by Vincenzo Cerami and Roberto Benigni, directed by Roberto Benigni, 1997.

[265] *When Harry Met Sally*. Written by Nora Ephron, directed by Rob Reiner, 1989.

[266] *Who Framed Roger Rabbit?* Written by Jeffrey Price and Peter S. Seaman (from a novel by Gary K. Wolf), directed by Robert Zemeckis, 1988.

[267] *Who's Afraid of Virginia Woolf?* Written by Edward Albee, 1962.

[268] *The Wizard of Oz*. Written by Noel Langley, Florence Ryerson, and Edgr Allan Woolf (from a book by L. Frank Baum), directed by Victor Fleming, 1939.

[269] *Star Trek: The Wrath of Khan*. Written by Jack B. Sowards (from a story by Harve Bennett and Jack B. Sowards), directed by Nicholas Meyer, 1982.

[270] *The X Files: Fight the Future.* Written by Chris Carter (from a story by Chris Carter and Frank Spotnitz), directed by Rob Bowman, 1998.

[271] *Young Frankenstein.* Written by Gene Wilder and Mel Brooks (from a novel by Mary Shelley), directed by Mel Brooks, 1974.

Radio and TV Shows

[272] *The Archers.* Created by Godfrey Baseley. BBC Radio serial. January 1, 1951–present.

[273] *Degrassi: The Next Generation.* Created by Linda Schuyler and Kit Hood. Produced by Stephen Stohn and Linda Schuyler, October 1991–present.

[274] *E.R.* Created by Michael Crichton. Produced by John Wells, Michael Crichton, and Jack Ormon, 1994–present.

[275] *Family Feud.* Created by Mark Goodson. Produced by Goodson-Todman Productions, originally aired 1977–1985.

[276] *Firefly.* Created by Joss Whedon. Produced by Gail Berman, Sandy Gallin, Fran Rubel Kuzui, Kaz Kuzui, Tim Minear, Brian Wankum, and Joss Whedon, 2002.

[277] *Friends.* Created by David Crane and Marta Kauffmann. Produced by Kevin S. Bright, Marta Kauffman, Michael Curtis, Adam Chase, David Crane, Greg Malins, and Michael Borkow, 1994–present.

[278] *Gilligan's Island.* Created and produced by Sherwood Schwartz. 1964–1967.

[279] *The Guiding Light.* Created by Irna Phillips. Radio version: January 25, 1937–present, Television version: June 30, 1952–present.

[280] *Leave it to Beaver.* Created by Joe Connelly and Bob Mosher. Produced by Harry Ackerman, Joe Connelly, and Bob Mosher, 1957–1963.

[281] *Lexx*. Created by Paul Donovan, Lex Gigeroff, and Jeffrey Hirschfield. Produced by Paul Donovan and Wolfram Tichy, 1996–2001.

[282] *M*A*S*H*. Adapted by Gene Reynolds. Produced by Larry Gelbart, Gene Reynolds, Burt Metcalf, John Rappaport, Allan Katz, Don Reo, Jim Mulligan, Thad Mumford, Dan Wilcox, Dennis Koenig, 1972–1983.

[283] *Northern Exposure*. Created by Joshua Brand and John Falsey. Produced by Joshua Brand, John Falsey, Charles Rosin, and Robert T. Skodis, 1990–1995.

[284] *NYPD Blue*. Created by Steven Bochco. Produced by Steven Bochco, Mark Tinker, and David Milch, 1993–present.

[285] *The Continental*. Sketch on *Saturday Night Live*, Directed by Dave Wilson, January 20, 1990.

[286] *Seinfeld*. Created by Larry David and Jerry Seinfeld. Produced by Howard West, Jerry Seinfeld, Larry David, Fred Barron, George Shapiro, Alec Berg, and Jeff Schaffer, 1990–1998.

[287] *The Simpsons: Trilogy of Error*. Written by Matt Selman. Directed by Mike B. Anderson. April 29, 2001.

[288] *The Sopranos*. Created by David Chase. Produced by David Chase, Robin Green, Mitchell Burgess, Ilene S. Landress, and Brad Grey, 1999–present.

[289] *Star Trek*. Created by Gene Roddenberry. Produced by Gene Roddenberry, John Meredyth Lucas, Gene L. Coon, and Fred Freiberger, 1966–1969.

[290] *Star Trek: The Next Generation: A Matter of Perspective*. Written by Ed Zuckerman. Directed by Cliff Bole, February 12, 1990.

[291] *Star Trek: The Next Generation*. Created by Gene Roddenberry. Produced by Gene Roddenberry, Rick Berman, Michael Piller, and Jeri Taylor, 1987–1994.

[292] *Teletubbies*. Created and produced by Ragdoll Productions for the BBC, 1997–present.

493

[293] *The Twilight Zone*. Created by Rod Serling. Produced by Rod Serling, Buck Houghton, William Froug, Herbert Hirschman, 1959–1965.

[294] *Twin Peaks*. Created by Mark Frost and David Lynch. Produced by David Lynch, Mark Frost, Gregg Fienberg, David J. Latt, and Harley Peyton, 1990–1991.

[295] *Survivor*. Created and produced by Mark Burnett, 2000–present.

[296] *Voyage to the Bottom of the Sea*. Created and produced by Irwin Allen, 1964–1968.

[297] *West Wing*. Created by Aaron Sorkin. Produced by Aaron Sorkin, Tommy Schlamme, and John Wells, 1999–present.

[298] *Who Wants To Be A Millionaire?* Created for the BBC by Celador Productions. Produced in the US by Paul Smith and Michael Davies, September 1999–present.

Novels and Stories

[299] Richard Adams. *Watership Down*. New York: Avon, 1999 reissue.

[300] Dante Alighieri. *The Divine Comedy: Inferno, Purgatorio, Paradiso*. New York: Knopf Everyman's Library, 1995. (originally published c. 1472).

[301] Nicholson Baker. *Room Temperature: A Novel*. New York: Vintage Books, 1995.

[302] Nicholson Baker. *Vox: A Novel*. New York: Vintage Books, 1995 reissue.

[303] Joge Luis Borges. *Collected Fictions*. New York: Grove Press, 1985. Translated by Andrew Hurley.

[304] T. Coraghessan Boyle. *Riven Rock*. New York: Penguin Books, 1999.

[305] Ray Bradbury. *The Illustrated Man*. New York: Bantam Books, 1990. Contains the short story *The Veldt*.

[306] Italo Calvino. *If On a Winter's Night a Traveler*. Fort Washington, PA: Harvest Books, 1982. Translated by William Weaver.

[307] Miguel De Cervantes. *The Adventures of Don Quixote*. New York: Penguin USA, 1605.

[308] Michael Chabon. *The Amazing Adventures of Kavalier & Clay*. New York: Picador USA, 2001.

[309] James Clavell. *Shogun*. New York: Dell Books, 1986.

[310] Robert Coover. *Pricksongs & Descants: Fictions*. New York: Grove Press, 2000. Includes the short story *The Babysitter*.

[311] Julio Cortazar. *Hopscotch*. New York: Pantheon Books, 1987. Translated by Gregory Rabassa.

[312] Daniel Defoe. *Robinson Crusoe*. Princeton, NJ: Princeton Review, 1999. (originally published 1719).

[313] Charles Dickens. *A Tale Of Two Cities*. Toronto: Signet Classic, 1997. (originally published 1859).

[314] Charles Dickens. *The Adventures of Oliver Twist*. New York: Tor Books, 1998. (originally published 1838).

[315] Charles Dickens. *A Christmas Carol*. New York: Bantam Classics, 1999. (originally published 1843).

[316] Christopher Golden. *A New Hope (Choose Your Own Star Wars Adventures)*. Hoboken, NJ: Skylark, 1998. Illustrated by Eric Cherry.

[317] Barray Hannah. *Ray*. New York: Grove Press, 1993.

[318] Homer. *The Odyssey*. New York: Puffin Classics, 1998. (originally written about 720 B.C.E.).

[319] John Irving. *A Prayer for Owen Meany*. New York: Ballantine Books, 1990.

[320] Kazuo Ishiguro. *The Remains of the Day*. New York: Vintage Books, 1993.

[321] James Joyce. *Ulysses*. New York: Vintage Books, 1990. (originally published 1922).

[322] James Joyce. *Finnegans Wake*. New York: Penguin Classics, 1999. (originally published 1922).

[323] Michael Joyce. *afternoon, a story*. Watertown, MA: Eastgate Press, 1991.

[324] Nikos Kazantzakis. *Zorba the Greek*. New York: Scribner and Sons, 1986. Translated by Carl Wildman.

[325] William Kotzwinkle. *The Fan Man*. New York: Vintage Books, 1994.

[326] Armistead Maupin. *Tales of the City*. New York: Harper Perennial, 1994.

[327] Herman Melville. *Moby-Dick, or, The Whale*. New York: Bantam Classics, 1994. (originally published 1851).

[328] Rand Miller and David Wingrove. *Myst: The Book of Ti'Ana*. New York: Warner Books, 1997.

[329] Vladimir Vladimirovich Nabokov. *Lolita*. New York: Vintage Books, 1989.

[330] George Orwell. *Animal Farm*. Toronto: Signet Classic, 1996. (originally published 1945).

[331] Raymond Queneau. *Cent mille milliards de pomes*. Paris: Gallimard, 1961.

[332] Tom Robbins. *Half Asleep In Frog Pajamas*. New York: Bantam Books, 1995.

[333] Tom Robbins. *Fierce Invalids Home from Hot Climates*. New York: Bantam Books, 2001.

[334] Shel Silverstein. *The Missing Piece*. New York: HarperCollins, 1976.

[335] Laurence Sterne. *The Life and Opinions of Tristram Shandy, Gentleman.* New York: Penguin USA, 1998. (originally published 1759–1767).

[336] William Styron. *Sophie's Choice.* New York: Bantam Books, 1994.

[337] Jonathan Swift. *Gulliver's Travels.* Toronto: Signet Classic, 1997. (originally published 1726).

[338] Ella Cheever Thayer. *Wired Love.* London: W. J. Johnston, 1879.

[339] J.R.R. Tolkien. *The Lord of the Rings.* New York: Houghton Mifflin Co, 1974. (originally published 1954).

[340] Mark Twain. *The Adventures of Tom Sawyer.* New York: Puffin Classics, 1998. (originally published 1876).

[341] Mark Twain. *Huckleberry Finn.* Princeton, NJ: Princeton Review, 2001. (originally published 1885).

[342] Kurt Vonnegut. *Slaughterhouse Five or the Children's Crusade.* New York: Dell Books, 1991.

[343] Kit Williams. *Masquerade.* New York: Schocken Books, 1984.

Games and Toys

[344] *Acrophobia.* Designed and produced for the Internet by Berkley Systems, 1997.

[345] *Advance Wars 2: Black Hole Rising.* Produced for the Nintendo GameBoy Advance by Intelligent Systems and Nintendo, 2003.

[346] *Age of Empires.* Designed by Bruce Shelley, produced for the PC by Ensemble Studios, 1997.

[347] *Aibo Entertainment Robot.* Designed and manufactured by Sony Corporation, 2002.

[348] *Alchemy.* Designed and produced for the PC and PDAs by Popcap Games, 2001.

[349] *American McGee's Alice.* Designed by American McGee, produced for the PC by Electronic Arts, 2000 .

[350] *Animal Crossing.* Designed by Takashi Tezuka, produced for the Nintendo GameCube by Nintendo, 2002.

[351] *Asheron's Call.* Designed and produced for the PC by Turbine Entertainment Software, 1999.

[352] *Asteroids.* Designed by Ed Logg, produced for standalone kiosks by Atari, 1969.

[353] *Babyz.* Designed by Adam Frank, Rob Fulop, Ben Resner, and Andrew Stern, produced for the PC by P.F. Magic, 1999.

[354] *Baldur's Gate II: Shadows of Amin.* Produced for the PC by Black Isle Studios, 1999.

[355] *Baldur's Gate: Tales of the Sword Coast.* Produced for the PC by Black Isle Studios, 1999.

[356] *Banja.* Designed by Sebastien Kochman and Olivier Janin, produced for the Internet by Team cHmAn, 2001.

[357] *Battlefield 1942.* Designed by Electronic Arts, produced for the PC and Internet by Electronic Arts, 2001.

[358] *Battleship.* Designed and produced as a board game by Milton Bradley Company, 1967.

[359] *The Beast.* Also known as *The AI Game*, *The Cloudmaker*, and *Who Killed Evan Chen?*, Designed by Elan Lee and Sean Stewart. Produced for the Internet, 2001.

[360] *Black & White.* Designed by Lionhead Studios, Ltd., produced for the PC by Electronic Arts, 2001.

[361] *Blinx the Time Sweeper.* Designed and produced for the Xbox by Artoon, 2002.

[362] *Chutes and Ladders.* Designed and produced as a board game by Milton Bradley Company, 1943.

[363] *Clue*. Designed and produced as a board game by Parker Brothers, 1949.

[364] *Concentration*. Designed and produced as a board game by Endless Games, 1958.

[365] *Counter-Strike*. Designed and produced for the PC by the CS Team as a mod of *Half-Life*, 1999.

[366] *Creatures*. Designed by Steve Grand, produced for the PC by Mindscape Inc, 1997.

[367] *Dance Dance Revolution*. Designed by KCE Tokyo, produced for the PlayStation by Konami, 2001.

[368] *Dark Age of Camelot*. Produced for the PC by Mythic Entertainment, 2001.

[369] *Deus Ex*. Designed by Harvey Smith, produced for the PC by Ion Storm LP, 2000.

[370] *The Dig*. Produced for the PC by LucasArts Entertainment, 1995.

[371] *Diplomacy*. Designed by Allan B. Calhamer, produced as a board game by Games Research (later Avalon Hill Games), 1971.

[372] *Dogz 5*. Designed by Adam Frank, Rob Fulop, Ben Resner, and Andrew Stern, produced for the PC by P.F. Magic, 2002.

[373] *Doom*. Designed by John Carmack, produced for the PC by id Software, 1993.

[374] *Dungeons & Dragons*. Designed by Gary Gygax and Dave Arneson, produced as a standalone game by TSR, 1973.

[375] *Eleusis*. Designed by Robert Abbott. See http://www.logicmazes.com/games/eleusis.html.

[376] *Enter The Matrix*. Produced for multiple platforms by Shiny Entertainment, 2003.

[377] *Eternal Darkness: Sanity's Requiem*. Designed and produced for the Nintendo GameCube by Silicon Knights, 2002.

[378] *Everquest*. Designed by Brad McQuaid and Jeff Butler, produced for the PC by 989 Studios, 1999.

[379] *Final Fantasy X*. Designed and produced for the PlayStation 2 by Squaresoft, 2001.

[380] *Fluxx*. Designed by Andrew Looney, produced as a standalone card game by Looney Laboratories, Inc. 1997.

[381] *Freecell*. Written for the PC by Jim Horne 1981.

[382] *Furby*. Designed by Dave Hampton and Caleb Chung, toy manufactured by Tiger Electronics, 1998.

[383] *Golden Sun*. Produced for the Nintendo GameBoy Advance by Camelot and Nintendo, 2002.

[384] *Grand Theft Auto III*. Designed and produced for the PlayStation 2 by Rockstar Games, 2001.

[385] *Grand Theft Auto: Vice City*. Designed and produced for the PlayStation 2 by Rockstar Games, 2002.

[386] *Grim Fandango*. Produced for the PC by LucasArts Entertainment, 1998.

[387] *Half-Life*. Designed and produced for the PC by Valve Software, 1998.

[388] *Halo: Combat Evolved*. Designed and produced for the Xbox by Bungie Studios, 2001.

[389] *Hi-Q*. Traditional board game dating back to 1697 or earlier See http://www.ahs.uwaterloo.ca/~museum/puzzles/solitare/, produced by Pressman Toys, 1989.

[390] *How to Host A Murder Series*. Series of games designed and produced for standalone play by Decipher, Inc. 1985.

[391] *The Incredible Machine*. Designed and produced for the PC by Dynamix, 1993.

[392] *Jak and Daxter: The Precursor Legacy*. Designed and produced for the PlayStation 2 by Naughty Dog, 2001.

[393] *Jak II*. Designed and produced for the PlayStation 2 by Naughty Dog, 2003.

[394] *Kill Dr. Lucky*. Designed and produced as a card game by Cheapass Games, 2001.

[395] *Kingdom Hearts*. Designed and produced for the PlayStation 2 by SquareSoft, 2002.

[396] *Knights of the Old Republic*. Produced for the Xbox by LucasArts, 2003.

[397] *The Last Express*. Designed by Jordan Mechner, produced for the PC by Smoking Car Productions, 1997.

[398] *The Legend of Zelda: Ocarina of Time*. Designed by Shigeru Miyamoto, produced for the Nintendo 64 by Nintendo, 1998.

[399] *The Legend of Zelda: Majora's Mask*. Designed by Shigeru Miyamoto, produced for the Nintendo 64 by Nintendo, 2000.

[400] *Legend of Zelda: Oracle of Ages*. Designed and produced for the Game Boy Color by Capcom Entertainment, 2001.

[401] *Legend of Zelda: Oracle of Seasons*. Designed and produced for the Game Boy Color by Capcom Entertainment, 2001.

[402] *The Legend of Zelda: The Wind Waker*. Designed by Shigeru Miyamoto, Takashi Tezuka, and Eiji Aonuma, produced for the Nintendo GameCube by Nintendo, 2003.

[403] *Lode Runner*. Designed by Doug Smith, produced for the PC by Broderbund, 1983.

[404] *Mad Libs*. Written by Roger Price and Leonard Stern, published by Price Stern Sloan, 1958.

[405] *Madden NFL 2003*. Designed by Tiburon, produced for multiple platforms by Electronic Arts, 2003.

[406] *Magic: The Gathering*. Designed by Richard Garfield, produced for tabletop and online play by Wizards of the Coast, 1993.

[407] *Majestic.* Designed by Anim-X, produced for the PC and other media by Electronic Arts, 2001.

[408] *Mario Party 4.* Designed by Hudson Soft, produced for the Nintendo GameCube by Nintendo, 2002.

[409] *Mastermind.* Traditional board game, produced by Pressman Toy Corporation, 1971.

[410] *Max Payne.* Designed by Gathering of Developers, produced for multiple platforms by Rockstar Games, 2001.

[411] *MechWarrior 4: Vengeance.* Designed by FASA Interactive, produced for the PC by Microsoft, 2000.

[412] *Metal Gear Solid 2: Sons of Liberty.* Designed and produced for the PlayStation 2 by Konami, 2001.

[413] *Monopoly.* Designed by Charles B. Darrow, produced as a standalone board game by Parker Brothers, 1933.

[414] *The Muppets CD-ROM.* Produced for the PC by Starwave, 1997.

[415] *Myst.* Designed by Rand Miller and Robyn C. Miller, produced for the PC by Cyan, 1994.

[416] *Nisqually.* Designed and produced for the PC and PDAs by Popcap Games, 2001.

[417] *Nomic: A Game of Self-Amendment.* Designed by Peter Suber, 1982. See http://www.earlham.edu/ peters/nomic.htm.

[418] *Othello.* Traditional board game, produced by Pressman Toy Corporation, 1975.

[419] *Pictionary.* Designed by Rob Angel, produced by Hasbro, Inc., 1987.

[420] *Pikmin.* Designed by Shigeru Miyamoto, produced for the Nintendo GameCube by Nintendo, 2001.

[421] *Pirates of the Caribbean.* Designed and produced for live-action play by Walt Disney Imagineering, 2001.

[422] *Pokémon*. Designed and produced for tabletop play by Nintendo, 1995.

[423] *Quake*. Designed and produced for the PC by id Software, 1996.

[424] *Quake III: Arena*. Designed and produced for the PC by id Software, 1999.

[425] *Ratchet & Clank*. Designed and produced for the PlayStation 2 by Insomniac Games, 2003.

[426] *Ratchet & Clank 2: Going Commando*. Designed and produced for the PlayStation 2 by Insomniac Games, 2003.

[427] *Risk*. Traditional board game, produced by Parker Brothers, 1959, See "Risk: The Evolution of a Game," by Dave Shapiro, in *The Games Journal* December, 2002.

[428] *Rocket: Robot on Wheels*. Designed and produced for the Nintendo 64 by Sucker Punch Productions, 1999.

[429] *Rubik's Cube*. Designed by Erno Rubik, produced by OddzOn, 1979.

[430] *Samurai Romanesque*. Designed and produced for the NTT Do-CoMo I-Mode service (available in Japan only) by Dwango, January 2001.

[431] *Scrabble*. Designed by Alfred Butts, produced by the Milton Bradley Company, 1948.

[432] *Set*. Designed by Marsha Falco, produced by Set Enterprises, Inc., 1995.

[433] *Seven Seas*. Designed and produced for the PC and PDAs by Popcap Games, 2001.

[434] *Sim City*. Designed by Will Wright, produced for the PC by Maxis, 1989.

[435] *The Sims*. Designed by Will Wright, produced for the PC by Maxis, 2000.

[436] *The Sims Online*. Designed and produced for the PC and Internet by Maxis, 2002.

[437] *Sorry*. Designed and produced by Milton Bradley Company, 1934.

[438] *Space Invaders*. Designed by Toshihiro Nishikado, manufactured as a stand-alone kiosk by Taito, 1978.

[439] *SSX*. Designed by EA Sports, produced for the PlayStation 2 by Electronic Arts, 2000.

[440] *SSX Tricky*. Designed by EA Canada, produced for multiple platforms by Electronic Arts, 2001.

[441] *Star Wars Galaxies*. Designed and produced for PCs and the Internet by Sony Online Entertainment, 2003.

[442] *Star Wars: Rogue Leader–Rogue Squadron II*. Designed and produced for the Nintendo GameCube by Lucas Arts Entertainment, 2001.

[443] *Star Wars: The Clone Wars*. Designed and produced for the Nintendo GameCube by Lucas Arts Entertainment, 2002.

[444] *Starfox Adventures*. Designed and produced for the Nintendo Game-Cube by Rare, Ltd., 2002.

[445] *Stratego*. Designed and produced by Milton Bradley Company, 1961.

[446] *Super Mario Sunshine*. Designed and produced for the Nintendo GameCube by Nintendo, 2002.

[447] *Syberia*. Designed by Benoit Sokal, produced for the PC by Microids, 2002.

[448] *Take It Easy*. Designed by Peter Burley with artwork by Peter Zafris, produced by FX Schmid USA, 1997.

[449] *Tekken Tag Tournament*. Designed and produced for the PlayStation 2 by Namco, 2000.

[450] *Tetris*. Designed by Alexey Pazhitnov, produced for the PC by Spectrum Holobyte and Mirrorsoft, 1985.

[451] *TextTwist*. Designed and produced for the PC and PDAs by Popcap Games, 2001.

[452] *Tomb Raider*. Designed by Core Design, Ltd., produced for the PC by Eidos Interactive, 1996.

[453] *Tony Hawk's Pro Skater 4*. Designed by Vicarious Visions, produced for multiple platforms by Activision O2, 2002.

[454] *Trivial Pursuit*. Designed by Chris Haney and Scott Abbott, produced by Hasbro, Inc., 1983.

[455] *Trust & Betrayal: The Legacy of Siboot*. Designed and produced for the Macintosh by Chris Crawford, 1991. Out of print, but available free online at http://www.erasmatazz.com/free.html.

[456] *Twister*. Designed and produced by Milton Bradley Company, 1966.

[457] *Ultimate Frisbee*. Designed by Joel Silver, Buzzy Hellring, and Jon Hines, 1968. See http://www.upa.org/ultimate/rules/10thFinl.pdf.

[458] *Under A Killing Moon*. Produced for the PC by Access Software, 1995.

[459] *Unreal Tournament 2003*. Designed and produced for the PC by Digital Extremes and Epic MegaGames, Inc., 2002.

[460] *Vexed*. Designed by James McCombe, produced for PDAs by Team Vexed, 2001.

[461] *Virtual Jungle Cruise*. Designed and produced for live-action play by Walt Disney Imagineering, 2001.

[462] *You Don't Know Jack*. Designed and produced for the PC and Internet by Jellyvision and Berkeley Systems, 1995.

Index

About the Author

Andrew Glassner is a writer-director, and a consultant in story structure, interactive fiction, and computer graphics. He is currently developing a feature film for Coyote Wind Studios. *The New York Times* wrote, "Andrew Glassner [is one] of the most respected talents in the world of computer graphics research." Dr. Glassner is the author or co-author of a number of books, among them *Andrew Glassner's Notebook, Andrew Glassner's Other Notebook, Graphics Gems*, and *An Introduction to Ray Tracing*.

Photograph by Becky Brendlin

More praise for *Interactive Storytelling*

The intersection of story and games will be one of the most influential creative impacts in the future of media. Andrew Glassner's book is the most comprehensive and in-depth reference I have seen that examines how both story and games can work in concert to create the future of storytelling.

— Chistopher Stapleton, Director of Entertainment Research,
Institute for Simulation and Training

I found this book both enlightening and a good tool to test and temper my own beliefs on the subject. It combines solid foundational material with clear insights into current problems along with possible solutions, all in a readable style.

— Eric Haines, co-author of *Real-Time Rendering, 2nd Edition*

Glassner provides an incredibly insightful look at modern media and entertainment today. This book is a huge resource to anybody in the field of interactive entertainment because it addresses some of the fundamental structural issues in movies and games that are often not covered in existing game design literature. Some of the new concepts, like the idea of a "fun to work ratio" struck me as so profoundly true and simple that I wondered why this hadn't occurred to me. This is exactly the kind of experience that I want to get out of a book like this.

— Steven Drucker, *Microsoft*